MAHANAYAK

Vishwas Patil is one of the most acclaimed Marathi writers today. He has written iconic novels like *Ranangan, Chandramukhi, Pangira, Zadazadati, Panipat* and *Sambhaji*. He received the Nath Madhav Award and the Bhartiya Bhasha Parishad Award for *Panipat;* the Priyadarshini National Award, the Vikhe Patil Award and the Sahitya Akademi Award for *Zadazadati*; and the Gadkari Award for *Mahanayak*.

Keerti Ramachandra is an editor and translator. She is conversant with seven Indian languages, and translating works from Marathi and Kannada into English is more than a serious hobby for her. She has edited and translated many important books, including *Home and Away*, a collection of Kannada short stories by Ramachandra Sharma and *Sleepwalkers*, a novella by Joginder Paul. She was awarded the prestigious A. K. Ramanujan Award for translation in 1995.

TRANSLATED FROM THE MARATHI BY
KEERTI RAMACHANDRA

VISHWAS PATIL

MAHA NAYAK

SUBHAS CHANDRA BOSE

A NOVEL

ekadā

ekadā

First published in Marathi as *Mahanayak* in 1998 by Mehta Publishing House

First published in English as *Mahanayak* in 2004 by Mehta Publishing House

Published in 2019 by Eka, an imprint of Westland Publications Private Limited, by arrangement with Mehta Publishing House

Published in 2022 by Eka, an imprint of Westland Books, a division of Nasadiya Technologies Private Limited

No. 269/2B, First Floor, 'Irai Arul', Vimalraj Street, Nethaji Nagar, Alapakkam Main Road, Maduravoyal, Chennai 600095

ISBN: 9789395767330

10 9 8 7 6 5 4 3

Typeset by Jojy Philip, New Delhi 110015

Printed at Gopsons Papers Pvt. Ltd

One

Geography is created by the Almighty, but the contours of history are designed by man. The embers of the 1857 rebellion, eighty-eight years ago, have turned to ashes. The Red Fort, pride of Delhi, is under the control of British rulers, and is now reduced to a mere arsenal of old weapons and ammunition. Today, Lal Qila has assumed the role of destiny and become the eye of a storm that has swept the entire country.

It has witnessed many events in its three-hundred-and-fifty-year existence. From splendorous coronations, bejewelled zenanas of indescribable beauty, caparisoned elephants swaying proudly, golden bells tinkling around their necks, foreign emissaries bent under the weight of their tributes of salvers piled with emeralds to flashing knives and murderous intrigues, bloodshed and treachery. Sometimes the walls have echoed the groans of a beleaguered emperor trapped in debt; at others they have resounded with the wails of his starving harem. So many victories and defeats. So much pride and humiliation. Delhi, the heart of Hindustan, and Lal Qila, its heartbeat. Yes, it is the golden-winged bird which soars with the dreams and aspirations of the people, but it also seats the bloody wounds of unfortunate rebels and adventurers. Only one other time had Lal Qila's heart skipped a beat.

In 1857, for the first time, a wave of protest washed over the country, breaking barriers of caste and religion, language and culture. It was the first united uprising against British arrogance. It was from Lal Qila that the rebels had proclaimed Bahadur Shah emperor of India.

The flag of revolt was soon soaked in blood. Tragically, this symbol, still in its infancy, snagged on the thorns of treachery and deception and was torn to shreds. The same palace, from where the imperial proclamations of independence were issued, now became a prison. In front of his age-dimmed eyes, Bahadur Shah saw his beloved consorts being shot dead. Lal Qila looked on as the frail emperor's handcuffed hands feebly covered the coffins of his kin with fistfuls of soil.

What remained was a drama of deceit. A case was lodged to reiterate that all British actions were legally sanctioned. Bahadur Shah, who had fought for his motherland, now stood in the dock, charged with treason. False statements, corrupt witnesses and heartless yellow papers stained with lies snatched away his sovereignty. He was forever banished from his homeland. The Badshah was denied even two bighas of land for his grave.

Will Lal Qila ever forget that evening? Proclaimed guilty of treason, the emperor walked out of Lahori Gate. Overcome with grief, he glanced around at his remaining subjects. Helpless peasants stood in tears, their fists clenched in vengeful fury. His impoverished soldiers wandered around the country, feeling lost. Coins stamped with his image were no longer a valid currency. Strangers made off with his throne. As the broken Badshah took his leave, a gust of wind blew across the land. Suddenly his bowed head lifted and his bent back snapped erect. Fire blazed from his eyes. He turned towards Lal Qila. His arm rose in the air like a flag, and the poet broke into a cry:

Gazhiyon mein bu rahegi jab tak iman ki
Takht-e-London tak chalegi teg Hindustan ki

Time: Eighty-eight years later, November 1945.
Place: Lal Qila, Delhi.

Once again, the Lal Qila was to witness another drama, infinitely more sensational. The noose this time was not around one neck. Three senior officers of the British Indian Army were in the dock. They had been carefully chosen, to ensure that no religion felt any neglect. Shah Nawaz Khan was a Muslim, Gurbaksh Singh Dhillon a Sikh and Prem Sehgal a Hindu. They had been accused of declaring war on the British Sovereign and betraying those whose salt they had eaten.

Shadows spread across the Yamuna and an eerie silence descended on the fort. Winter crept into Delhi, but the British troops barred entry of everything else. Soldiers patrolled the streets while sentries manned the gates. In the mohallas and chawls, behind closed doors, people discussed the impending trial in hushed whispers. The stillness of the night was shattered by the cries of gurkhas, the clattering of boots, the harsh crackling of wireless sets and the screech of speeding vehicles. The whole city seemed to be one big military encampment. The walls of Lal Qila became formidable monsters in the dark, as if the devil himself had captured it and was reigning there. Soldiers ran zigzag along the ramparts throwing long, ghostly shadows.

Over the previous years, all sorts of stories had echoed off Lal Qila. But when truckloads of ammunition finally left its gates, ready for the Second World War, the fort shuddered. News arrived, filling some hearts with joy and making others miss a beat. All India Radio announced that Japan had attacked India. The country would be enslaved again. A few days later, the Azad Hind broadcasts began. People heard Netaji Subhas Chandra Bose's exhortations, 'Chalo Dilli! Onward to Delhi!' The words were sweet to Lal Qila's ears. Until then, in the past two centuries, no man had dared to openly defy the British. Netaji's call set Lal Qila on fire. 'My brave warriors of the Azad Hind Army, I know you are impatient to see the sun rising, free and independent over the horizon. Come! Let us go to Delhi. Break the noose of slavery that is strangling thirty-eight crore lives. Tear down the Union Jack that flutters over the Viceroy's mansion and hoist our beloved tricolour. Then we will conduct the drill of our victorious army at the Lal Qila itself. There's no rest until then. No peace until then.'

The brave soldiers of the Azad Hind Fauj had reached the eastern gates of the country. The British stations at Imphal and Kohima were rattled. The road to Dimapur was cut off. Bishenpur fell. Subhas's commandos landed in Gujarat, Bombay and Madras by submarine. Some said that the British papers of surrender were typed and ready. In a day or two, a week at most, Subhas would storm Delhi with his forty thousand soldiers. Their victorious cries would rend the skies. The Lal Qila was eagerly waiting to honour Subhas. However, the stars played a cruel game. Unseasonal rains lashed Imphal and Kohima. The INA met the tragic fate that Napoleon's prize mare had on the slush-covered road to Moscow in the Russian campaign. Hiroshima and Nagasaki were bombed. The arena of war changed. Delhi was also caught in the onslaught of the monsoons. No news came from the eastern borders. Thousands of jubilant soldiers who were to join in the final victory parade became easy prey for the British Army. They were arrested on the eastern borders and crammed into barracks within the fort. The British were now in a quandary. What would they do with these traitors? Congressmen like Rajagopalachari declared, 'Hang them all, every rogue and ruffian among them.' Until then, not one soldier had dared slip out from the British Indian Army. But now forty-five thousand soldiers heeded their consciences and revolted. From Churchill to Viceroy Wavell, indeed the entire bureaucracy was nonplussed. Who was this upstart who was threatening to blow the empire up?

An uneasy calm enveloped the fort. Only the night-patrol and the sharp wind rising from the Yamuna dared move. As midnight struck, a police van screeched to a halt inside the building. Boots clicked to attention, weapons slapped in salute. Perhaps a witness had come to give a statement – a common occurrence. As the footsteps turned in the direction of the cells where the three rebels were confined, the guards became alert. What was this? Was there going to be a trial or were they to be hanged before the court heard their case? All the prisoners began to shout in unison, 'Azad Hind, zindabad, zindabad!' and 'Victory to Netaji, our great leader.' Or, 'Netaji ki jai!'

Two bats suddenly flew out of the darkness. The cell door was thrown open. A pool of light spread across the floor. A thirty-year-old convict was crouching in the corner. The barbed wire outside cast jagged shadows on his defiant face. The convict remained seated as one of the senior officers stared at him. Another officer whispered to his colleague, '*This* is Shah Nawaz Khan.' Shah Nawaz's face reflected his aristocratic lineage – an aquiline nose and a neatly trimmed, finger-thick moustache. But the stress of war had taken its toll on his handsome face and he looked haggard. On his sleeve, next to the proudly displayed 'Best Cadet of the Dehra Dun Military Academy' badge, were the grimy letters, INA. His clothes were dirty and hung loose on his frame. The officer who stared at Shah Nawaz was overcome. Putting his hand on the young man's shoulder, he said, 'Son, will anyone looking at you and your borrowed uniform believe that today at least sixty men from your family are obediently serving in the British Army?'

Shah Nawaz was startled. Whose voice was that, so familiar? A voice that had been imprinted in some deep recess of his mind. Whose was it?

Peering at the strapping man in uniform, Shah Nawaz suddenly exclaimed, 'Sir! Sir Collins, sir?', and rushed forward, chains and all.

They embraced warmly, their eyes damp. Collins lamented, 'You would have become the commander-in-chief of the Indian Army, my son.' Shah Nawaz could not hold back his sobs. The Military Academy at Dehra Dun could not have had another commandant like Collins. His reputation as the man responsible for moulding Indian cadets into soldiers superior to British soldiers had reached the army headquarters. Suddenly, Collins, the Britisher surfaced. He contemptuously pushed Shah Nawaz away.

'I hate you, Shanno, I hate you!'

'Sir ...!'

'Shall I hold you to my breast as my beloved student, or kick you for being a traitor?'

'Sir, what wrong have we done?'

'Shanno, you fool, you didn't respect the salt you ate.'

Shah Nawaz calmed down. 'Whose salt?' he asked.

'The army's, the King Emperor's.'

'I'm sorry, sir. Why would I come to British shores to eat your Emperor's salt? What I have tasted is the salt of my own land.'

'Totally misguided by the enemy,' the agitated Collins spat. 'If only you had stuck to your goal, you would have definitely become commander-in-chief. You have destroyed your future with your own hands, my boy.'

'Sir, I consider it a boon from Allah, peace be upon Him, for letting me be an ordinary guard at Netaji's doors rather than a commander of the treacherous British Army.'

'Stop it, you bastard!' roared Collins. 'By Netaji you mean that Bose ... driven by ambition, that power-hungry fellow, willing to join hands with the Japs – that Bengali traitor.'

'Collins, sir, mind what you say!' shot Shah Nawaz. 'Had it been anyone else, I would have ripped his tongue out. How can you understand what Netaji stands for, what Gandhiji means?'

'Bose must be a magician!'

'Yes, indeed he is a wizard.' Admiration dripped from Shah Nawaz's words. 'What were we, sir? Soldiers, simpletons who had sworn undying loyalty only to fill our stomachs. Our dreams, what were they? A career, promotion, pay, more pay, a wife, a couple of chubby children, the army club and mindless parties. We sold our consciences cheap, sir, for the medals on our chests. Did my country figure anywhere on the world map? Once we met Netaji, we saw the real contours of our country. Association with him stripped the veil away from our eyes, and we began to identify with our land, our soil, the very air we breathe.'

Collins, filled with pity for Shah Nawaz, once again laid a warm hand on his pupil's back. 'Reconsider your decision, son. You are young.'

'Why? Is my youth a disqualification for the noose?'

'Don't be a fool, listen to me. The generosity of the British is boundless like the ocean.'

'What are you trying to say?'

'You can still retrieve your career.'

'How?' Shah Nawaz asked sharply.

'I discussed the matter with the command headquarters before I came here. You will get back the same job, the same seniority. On your own merit, you can still become the commander-in-chief of the Indian Army. That avenue is still open for you.'

Shah Nawaz sighed deeply and looked at Collins. There was something more to this ... Collins' trembling voice, his rapid breathing ... what did it all mean?

Shah Nawaz could not hold back any longer. 'Sir,' he asked pointedly, 'why this concern?'

'Shanno, just agree to become a defence witness. That way, Bose and his mercenaries and the Japs will be discredited.'

The words pierced Shah Nawaz's heart like an arrow. He cried out, 'Sir, don't even utter such words. It is only once in a while that we encounter a noble soul in our life. Even if his fading shadow falls on us, we feel enlightened. Perhaps I will become commander-in-chief. But what after that? Six feet of earth over me, isn't it? All the medals and honours from a lifetime of sycophancy will laugh at my corpse. How can your promise of promotion be compared to that great glory one gets from being Netaji's soldier?'

Collins was speechless. He sighed. 'Son, either I failed as a tutor, or I was unable to understand you fully.' He made to bid Shah Nawaz goodbye. Kissing his favourite pupil on the forehead, he whispered, 'God bless you, my son,' and strode out.

The sound of Collins' footsteps grew faint. Shah Nawaz's gaze flew over the vast length and breadth of the jail. The prison walls dripped dark, black shadows. This symbol of imperial power had grabbed this ancient land by its scruff and was licking the fat off its head. Shah Nawaz choked. He was stifled by the walls of his cell. Death on the open battlefield would have been infinitely better. An anguished cry escaped him, 'Arre Gurbaksh, my Bakshi, why did you save me? I should have died and met my Allah!'

'Be patient, Shanno, be patient. Why should we demean ourselves to save our lives? Suppose we had died quietly in the jungles of Burma? Who would have told Netaji's story to the world? The enemy is trying hard to prove that the Azad Hind Fauj is only a gathering of renegade soldiers and mutineers. They have set out these allegations in a military court. We will present our defence in the same court and enumerate the triumphs of the Azad Hind Fauj. Only Time will show who the traitors are and who the patriots, who are the mercenaries and who the revolutionaries.'

Gurbaksh, a sturdy Sikh youth, was barely thirty-one. He had flat, slightly hollow cheeks, glinting black eyes, a broad chest which of late swelled with pride, and a complexion tanned from all the recent exploits. His muddy Azad Hind Fauj uniform was bloodstained. On his threadbare shirt, Netaji had pinned the badge of honour. The past was still fresh in their minds. Japan was shattered by the atom bomb. Dissent had flared up in Burma. In this violent storm, Netaji was trying desperately to keep the flickering lamp of the Azad Hind Fauj burning. It was then that Shah Nawaz, Gurbaksh and Prem Sehgal, intoxicated with the spirit of rebellion, found themselves caught in the fire in the jungles of Burma. Gurbaksh could still see the torrential rain along the banks of the Pegu River and the desolate landscape. The abandoned villages. The starvation. The impoverished boatmen, running for their lives, their forlorn boats bobbing helplessly on the water ...

The three of them were fleeing from the death traps. British and American aircraft, blinded by vengeance, buzzed overhead, like a swarm of bees, seeking out the Azad Hind soldiers. Mountbatten's troops were moving quickly to lay siege to Rangoon and capture Netaji. These three and the breakaway group of the Azad Hind Fauj had been creating all sorts of obstacles for them. But how far could they run? The Irrawaddy in spate, the formidable Popa Mountain ahead, the forests of Moulmein.... This terrible game of 'catch-me-if-you-can' and 'I spy' was being played over five hundred miles. At last, they received secret information that Netaji had escaped to Thailand via Moulmein. The three continued to run. Their lungs felt like they would burst. Their legs creaked at the knees.

The British were closing in on them. They were just five hundred yards away. In the sky, lightning danced to the drumbeats of thunder. Keeping time with it was the continuous clatter of machine-gun fire. In a deserted hut on the banks of the Pegu, as bullets licked the walls of the hut, the three held a discussion. What would be the next course of action? Death? But that was a coward's option.

Gurbaksh tried to calm his companions. 'Let's surrender and become prisoners of war.'

Prem and Shah Nawaz were aghast. 'You're joking!' they exclaimed.

'No, Shanno, Prem Pyare! Look, if we are tried, then we will get an opportunity to tell the world Netaji's immortal tale. Anyway, death is inevitable. Once we have made known Netaji's story, we will be free to go under the earth.'

When the troops surrounded their hut, Shah Nawaz took all eight bullets from his pistol and flung them out as if he were skimming stones over water. At the time of surrender, the commander of the British regiment and his troops stared open-mouthed at the remnants of the Azad Hind Fauj – their shoes were ragged, it is true, but their hearts were firm. They were weather-beaten, but their medals glowed proudly on their chests. Shah Nawaz gave the order, 'Azad Hind Fauj, from the right, take guard.' Even in this moment of adversity, a note of pride rang out in his voice. The British commander watched in amazement. Neither were these a group of deserters nor did they look like Japanese agents. On the contrary, they were the rebel army, who in the face of great misfortune retained the courage of their convictions. They had their own commands, their rules, their objective to free India and a leader like Netaji.

A stricken cry escaped from Shah Nawaz's lips. 'Bakshi, Khuda should have done me just one favour. If only we could have seen Netaji hoist and salute the tricolour from the ramparts of this Lal Qila, death would have been welcome. It would have all been worthwhile. Bakshi, the morsel reached the lips, but didn't get to the stomach, that's what hurts the most.'

'Never mind, Shanno, it wasn't an auspicious moment even for God. He is also like us humans – a first-grade politician!'

Netaji's image floated before their eyes. It was his magic that had made a foreign country like Japan alter its appointed course and inspired thirty-five thousand Japanese soldiers to sacrifice their lives for the freedom of India, causing the Irrawaddy, Chindwin and Salwin rivers to bloat and blacken with corpses. Swayed by his exhortations, thirty thousand Asians had offered up their money and jewellery, their hearths and homes, even their sons and daughters. Netaji's eastern sojourn was barely twenty-two months long, but what miracles he had wrought during that brief period.

Sometime later, Gurbaksh dozed off only to be woken up by a white guard posted outside his cell. What is this new problem, at this time of the night? he wondered. Gurbaksh's old father and wife were waiting outside the barracks, requesting a meeting.

Gurbaksh came out. When he saw his father's wrinkled face, sparse white beard, sunken eyes and dirty turban, his eyes moistened. He rushed to his father, who held him close to his chest. He looked up through his tears and caught sight of Basant Kaur standing there, like a graceful sonechafa flower, the early morning breeze ruffling her hair and dupatta. She had not changed one bit. The salwar-kameez covering her firm, curvaceous figure and the sparkle in her dark eyes were just the same. She gazed at him.

Bakshi's father began, 'Arre Bakshi, your elder brother is counting his last days. Your old mother keeps vigil by his bedside night and day. If you are sent to the gallows, what will we do, losing both our sons? Where should we drown ourselves?'

'Bauji, thousands of our companions starved to death in the Kaladan Valley. Hundreds were washed away by the Sittang River. To gain victory over Bishenpur, so many were sacrificed. Had they no mothers? No sisters?'

Bauji wiped his eyes. He looked around. The guards had moved some distance away. He whispered to his son, 'An officer from the Lahore Commissioner had come a couple of nights back. My son, even now something can be done.'

'Like what?'

'You can become a major once more.'

'That's all?'

'Your family will even get a small jagir in Punjab.'

'And what do I have to do for that?' Bakshi asked warily.

'No going to the Congress for help. Surrender to the government. Listen to me, son. Heed these white hairs.' Bauji wept as he placed his turban at Bakshi's feet.

'Bauji, a rock never bleeds. Because I can steel myself when required, Netaji entrusted the reins of the Nehru Brigade in my hands. Why are you hankering after a jagir? Even if ten such jagirs were offered for free, they would not equal one Netaji. No, Bauji, I can never betray Netaji – it is tantamount to betraying myself.'

Bauji stopped pleading. He knew his son. Bakshi would not be swayed. 'Beta, don't obey the British, fine. But will you at least follow our sacred religion? The Akal Takht is prepared to plead your case in court.'

'Bauji, Shah Nawaz received a similar message. Barrister Jinnah and the Muslim League are willing to represent him. If Shah Nawaz fights for the Muslims and I fight for the Sikhs, then who will fight for Netaji's dream of a mighty, united India? Who will weep for it?'

Bauji could say nothing. Bakshi turned towards Basant. He took her warm, mehndi-decorated hand and placed it on his heart. He spoke to her with his eyes. What else could he say? Although she was fluent in Hindi, Gurmukhi and English, how could he tell her all that had happened? He had neither words nor time to explain to her what he had faced.

Basant looked at Gurbaksh in his tattered clothing. Then she spoke. 'In the 1942 movement, I led a women's morcha in Lahore's Anarkali Bazaar. I was arrested. Bauji suggested that I apologize to the British government.'

Holding his breath, Bakshi asked, 'And?'

'I refused. So he shut the door on me.'

'Bauji, what's this?'

'Beta, I didn't want it to jeopardize your career, that's why I asked her to do it. But she turned out to be even tougher than you.'

Bakshi broke into a smile. 'Waah, Basant, you are the perfect companion for me.' Just then the British officer told them their visiting time was up. Bauji stood up. 'What shall I tell your mother, son?' he asked.

'Tell her to forgive me in this life. I will fulfil my remaining duties in my next birth.'

Bauji turned away, wiping his eyes. Basant continued to stand in front of him, like a creeper that stands erect even as it is tossed about by the wind. Once again Bakshi raised her hand to his chest. 'Basant, as soon as this game is over, I will go to heaven. I will meet our Guru before you do. Tell me, what shall I ask for you?'

'I don't need anything. Only don't agree to anything that will make us lower our heads in shame.'

Bakshi felt a sharp surge of sparks through his body. He recalled his meeting with Netaji in the jungles of Meiktila. In the thick of battle, four officers had betrayed Netaji and the nation when they crossed over to the enemy camp. Netaji had, with utmost confidence, handed over the yoke of a fractured Nehru Brigade to him. Saluting Netaji, Bakshi had pledged, 'Netaji, this Gurbaksh will do nothing that will make you hang your head in shame.' Netaji had replied, 'Bakshi, I am sure of that.' The same words. Total commitment to sacrifice. Why were these same words echoing around him? Bakshi gently wiped a teardrop from Basant's eye. 'I am going to ask the military court to grant me one last wish ...'

'What is it?'

'That I be hanged in front of your eyes.'

'I don't mind,' Basant replied bravely. 'Go to the gallows wearing the same kangan of courage with which you fought for your beloved Netaji. If you are hanged ten times over for your ideals, I will witness it unflinchingly.'

Two lives parted. Perhaps forever. Dawn was breaking. Their tears were like a heavy rain on the face of the earth. Bauji and Basant left. In the distance, Gurbaksh could hear Ram Singh's thin reedy voice singing to the breeze:

Netaji hamaare, hanste hanste jeena.

The third accused was Prem Sehgal. He was also in his cell, unperturbed and unconcerned. The youngest of the three, at twenty-eight years he looked like a prince in some fairy tale, with his oval face, fair cheeks, shapely lips and eyes dark as the ocean's depth. He had also been accused of rebelling against the British crown.

Prem held a magazine with a picture of a striking young woman of about thirty in army uniform. She was wearing the regulation salwar-kameez, which was decorated with service medals. Her hair was knotted at the back of her head and her army beret was smartly angled. Even in this attire, she looked stunning with her fair complexion, sharp features and sparkling eyes. There could not have been a more beautiful woman in Malaya. She was Captain Lakshmi.

The thought of Lakshmi still brought a lump to Prem's throat. He had last met her in the military hospital at Maymyo. Where are you now, Lakshmi? Where is our beloved Netaji? The court-martial stands before me with its jaws wide open. Will I see you once more, Lakshmi, before the noose tightens around my neck and the plank is snatched from beneath my feet?

A meeting with someone important was destined that day. Two cars skidded to a halt outside the barracks. Prem watched curiously as his father Achcharuram emerged from the first one. The sentry and guards snapped to attention and saluted smartly. Quite rightly too. He was after all a judge at the Lahore High Court. Prem was seeing him after five long years. Those around them stared as the father and son embraced. The father was a High Court judge and his son was an unrepentant criminal, being tried for high treason. The judge introduced his son to his companion, a large, saggy gentleman. 'This is Barrister Bhulabhai Desai.'

Prem bent to touch his feet. He was an eminent lawyer and for many years, a member of the Congress Working Committee. Bhulabhai Desai exclaimed, 'Achcharuram, I am proud of your son.'

Soon two senior officials arrived. Whistles were heard and the tramping of boots grew louder. Prem was elated to know that Pandit Nehru was due to arrive soon. He was going to see Chachaji after so long. As a child, he had gone with his father to attend the Congress conference at Lahore where he had stared in awe as Nehru came on a black horse. He also recalled the impressive Subhas Chandra Bose in starched white khadi. Nehru and Bose were usually together, surrounded by young Congress workers.

Judge saheb was familiar with his son's firm and uncompromising nature. So he did not waste time asking how all this had happened or why. He and Bhulabhai had deliberated over how this court case was to be handled. Prem could see that although Bhulabhai was quite animated, he did not seem to be in very good health. His weight appeared to give him much discomfort. Even his feet were badly swollen.

Bhulabhai said, 'Look, Judge saheb, had Prem not joined the army, he wouldn't have been drawn to Subhas.'

'Papaji, Netaji's exhortations come straight from his heart. They were so powerful that even the dead would have been roused.'

A car drove in through the main gates of Lal Qila. As he stepped out of the car, Nehru's bemused gaze swept over the fort. Yes, it was the same Lal Qila – ornate with Shah Jahan's fine filigree work, resounding with Bahadur Shah Zafar's immortal ghazals. Slogans of 'Chalo Dilli! Chalo Dilli!' and 'Netaji zindabad!' echoed off the fort walls. In the last few days, the whole nation had been caught up in the Azad Hind Fauj wave. It wasn't a wave, more like a typhoon. Not since the Non-cooperation Movement of 1930 had the masses come to the streets in such large numbers in support of a cause.

Nehru had just emerged after four years in prison. The oppressive British regime had completely crushed the 1942 movement, leaving the Congress crippled. When Nehru visited the Congress offices, he found dusty rooms, tattered receipt books, termite-infested files and ledgers, dry stamp pads, caked inkwells and dull, dispirited office bearers. Campaigning for the constituent assembly elections had begun, but it was listless. Congressmen deliberately refrained from any mention of Subhas Chandra Bose or the Azad Hind Fauj. But Subhas's supporters were well aware of the activities of the Azad Hind Fauj thanks to the national press. They came to the Congress rallies and cried out 'Jai Hind!' and 'Chalo Dilli!' When the Congress and the Muslim League realised that the people's response to the Azad Hind Fauj was genuine, they hastened to support it.

Nehru's Patna rally was particularly notable. After Rajendra Prasad's welcome address, the audience began shouting slogans. Two veterans of the Azad Hind Fauj were pushed on to the dais. 'They sing well. Let them sing,' demanded the office bearers and the audience. Nehru looked skeptically at the two scrawny jawans standing in front of the mike in their tattered khaki uniforms. But the manner in which they stood in their tunics, the way the sinews in their throats stood out as they roared, 'Jai Hind!', the fierce pride in their voices as they uttered 'Subhas', 'Azadi' and 'Watan', left Nehru speechless. The two men sang,

Hindu ho ya Mussalman, Sikh ya Isai saare,
Maati ke nain sukh hain, Mata ke hum dulare.
Sabse ooncha hai jhanda hamara
Netaji zindabad, azad karenge …

The audience was left spellbound by these Azad Hind songs. Nehru too was deeply moved. Like a young scout making his debut jump on the field, Nehru moved forward. Waving the tricolour, he joined the two men, and sang and danced to their songs.

In his heart of hearts, he was worried. Subhas couldn't possibly be obsessed with power and authority. He had given up his appointment to the prestigious Indian Civil Service as easily as throwing something into the dustbin. He had suffered prison eleven times and had been battered by lathis. Nehru had read his recently published war speeches very carefully. 'In this mortal world, everything perishes and will perish, but goals and aspirations are immortal. An individual may die so that the nation can survive. Let me die but let my motherland, Bharat, live on.' Was it possible to achieve this spirit, this supreme self-sacrifice and total dedication without a baptism by fire.

In the national press, ballads were sung in praise of Subhas. As Nehru became aware of each of Subhas's achievements, the poet in him took possession of the politician in him. The picture was not as distorted as the foreign government made it out to be. Under those ashes would smoulder the embers of some magical, resplendent reality. Hence, Nehru personally tabled a resolution to save the Azad Hind Fauj, at the Bombay conference.

Nehru entered the visitors' room. He greeted Bhulabhai with a namaskar. If Bhulabhai was an expert on International Law, Nehru had acquired a mastery over world history. The two of them debated on what aspects of the case to focus on when arguing the Azad Hind case. But one thing was apparent: Subhas and his associates appeared to have met several times in different corners of the world. Who was Lafayette? An ordinary French soldier? What had provoked him into fighting for the American War of Independence? Which nation could lay claim to patriots such as Garibaldi, Mazzini and Cavour? The aspiration for freedom was not limited by geographical boundaries or time. From time immemorial, men had been clamouring for the liberation of human beings from the heinous chains of slavery.

An emotional Nehru addressed Bhulabhai, 'For the defence of the Azad Hind, I will don the barrister's robe myself and take the stand.'

'Don't you think it will be a little difficult for you to defend Subhas at this late stage?' Bhulabhai asked, eyeing Jawaharlal quizzically.

'It's true,' Jawaharlal mumbled.

'All of us, not just Gandhiji, even you and I, did not lose a single opportunity to humiliate Subhas after the Tripuri Congress,' Bhulabhai said. 'Whether we like it or not, Subhas went to the East and shone like a star.'

Nehru asked that the three prisoners be brought to the visitors' room. No sooner were they brought in than it seemed as if all the prisoners in the fort had sung in unison, 'Netaji ki jai!' 'Nehru zindabad!' 'Lal Qile se aayi aawaz/Dhillon, Sehgal, Shah Nawaz!'

The prisoners raised the three fingers of their right hands in salute and cried out, 'Jai Hind!' Joyously they paid their respect to Nehru and stared unblinkingly at that matchless figure seated before them. His face had dark, deep-set eyes which stood out against a camphor-fair complexion, an aquiline nose and deep laughter lines. He was clad in a woollen ash-grey knee-long achkan, churidar pyjamas, a sharply-creased white khadi cap and pathani sandals. He was indeed an imposing figure. One could not help but be charmed by such an outstanding example of Kashmiri male pulchritude.

For a long while, Nehru sat with his chin cupped on his left palm. His discussions with Achcharuram and Bhulabhai ended. He heard the brief statements of the Azad Hind trinity. In a soft but firm voice, he gave his reassurance, 'We will not abandon you at this critical juncture, when the nation is on the path to freedom. Isn't it, Bhulabhai?'

'Exactly. My young friends, it is our national duty to defend you. Legal luminaries like Kailashnath Katju, Tej Bahadur Sapru and I are always with you,' Bhulabhai said.

Prem had been silent all this while, but he was unable to contain himself any longer. 'Chachaji,' he said, his voice rising sharply, 'all of you are advocates of non-violence. We are Netaji's warriors. If the Congress party's ahimsa image is going to be blackened as a result of our swords, why do you want to enter the fray? Leave us to our fates.'

Prem's outburst affected Nehru's expression somewhat, but he responded instantly, 'Don't get emotional. We will consider you Maquis.'

This comment had a remarkable effect. For a moment, the three men did not know who had spoken to them. Netaji or Nehru? So many times they had heard the story of the Maquis from Netaji. The time-honoured tradition of supreme self-sacrifice, offering one's blood at the altar of the goddess of freedom. That was the story of the noble Maquis. Every time they were lost or their path was obscured by darkness, Netaji had reminded his compatriots of the guiding lights of the revolutionaries Garibaldi, Cavour and the Maquis. Prem calmed down.

Their discussions came to an end. Nehru stood up to leave. He threw one last look at the trinity. Then swallowing the lump in his throat, he said to Bhulabhai, 'I want to use every one of Subhas's colleagues in the task of nation building. I don't want to lose them among the millions thronging towards freedom.' Nehru left but his warm, reassuring words remained behind. Bhulabhai struggled out of his chair. He had to prepare his argument. He said to Achcharuram, 'Judge saheb, may God grant that Nehru's sentiments endure.'

'What?'

'When Jawahar is smitten by an idea, it completely overwhelms him,' Bhulabhai explained. 'That doesn't always mean that those optimistic emotions last very long.'

The epicentre of the cyclone was Lal Qila. The trial proceedings were to begin on 13 November 1945. But in view of the tense atmosphere, the proceedings were postponed by three weeks. There was, however, not much change in the situation. In fact, tension spread like wildfire. Thousands of people rushed to Lal Qila every day.

'What will happen to the Azad Hind bravehearts?' This question was uppermost in all minds. The British government had repeatedly declared that they would punish only those who had committed heinous and dreadful crimes. But the people were not prepared to believe this.

Lord Wavell, the governor general, was extremely uneasy. An emergency meeting of several high-ranking officials was in progress at his residence. It was a crisis situation.

The officials fell silent when they saw the governor general so disturbed. The stenographer darted in and out with telegrams and news bulletins. It was important to know what the reactions to this court case were going to be in every corner of the country. On the day of the hearing, a total strike had been observed not only in cities like Bombay,

Calcutta, Madras and Delhi, but even as far as the remote town of Lido in Assam. Workers, students and government clerks had all boycotted work. Besides, the Gurdwara Prabandhak Committee in Amritsar had donated Rs 7,000 to the Azad Hind Bachao fund. The municipalities of Pune, Kanpur and Madras had also liberally contributed to it. The tongawalas of Amravati went around with tins collecting contributions for Azad Hind. Punjab was a simmering cauldron. Dhillon and Shah Nawaz belonged to that region. For their defence, the Muslim League, the Congress and the Communist Party had all joined hands. The law enforcement authorities in Rawalpindi and Karachi had informed them that even in the smaller towns, at least fifty thousand people had gathered together.

One of Wavell's commanders remarked snidely, 'Your Excellency, you summoned Nehru to discuss this matter, did you not? What came of that meeting?'

'Just discussion, nothing else. In fact, even Nehru has been collecting funds to save the traitors. Mahatma Gandhi, who proclaims his faith in ahimsa at every opportunity, is the same. We've sent countless emissaries to him, requesting that he make a statement to the press against this violence, but he conveniently observes his vow of silence.'

'Sir, the situation in Bengal is not good either. There are at least ten thousand students milling around Wellington Square at any given time. Hindu and Muslim students mingle, singing songs and shouting slogans together.'

'I am aware of that,' Wavell replied. 'In many cities, there are more Muslims who support Subhas than Barrister Jinnah. But all this must stop at once. We are sitting on a volcano that is about to erupt.'

The turrets of Lal Qila coiled around the fort like a cobra. Inside the fort, the trial was in progress. Crowds, demonstrating vociferously, surged around the fort like an ocean at high tide in spite of the prohibitory orders that were in force beyond the ramparts. Their frenzied cries were growing louder by the minute and could soon be heard inside the cells.

Bhulabhai addressed the three of them in the reception room. 'My young friends, it does not matter if, for some reason, you cannot be saved. Be prepared to sacrifice your lives for the honour of your leader and for the nation, for the principles he stands for and for whom you have fought this bitter war.'

'We will never accept an India that is crippled by casteist, sectarian, factional divides,' Shah Nawaz responded.

Prem added, 'Netaji used to tell us, if the reins of the nation are going to rest with the authoritative rule of one particular caste, we are better off being slaves of a foreign power.'

Bhulabhai could see the glimmer of hope in the three faces. He had spent the last few days in his study working tirelessly. His failing health had deteriorated further under this new stress. As the wheelchair was lowered from the ambulance for him, onlookers were shocked by how unwell he looked. He was a large man, with a fair, highly expressive face, a big bald head, fringed by grey hair above his ears and a booming voice. Bhulabhai sat motionless, his gaze travelling from one face to the other. Justice Achcharuram sat beside him. His face reflected all the pain and confusion of the situation. In a quavering voice he exclaimed, 'You are all so young!' Then he fell silent.

The case proceedings continued. Among the fifteen eminent jurists lined up for the defence of the nation, stood Pandit Jawaharlal Nehru. He had donned his barrister's gown after thirty years, as if it was a grand ceremonial attire. Rajaji and Acharya Kripalani smiled to themselves when they saw him. Barrister Tej Bahadur Sapru, Kailashnath Katju and other luminaries were present before the court of military justice. But every pore of Bhulabhai's body told him that this was his turf. Which was why, even in his condition, he was determined to argue this historic case. All eyes were on the Japanese emissaries of the Azad Hind Fauj – Hachiya, Major Fujiwara, Takaki and other Japanese witnesses. When the Japanese military officers sang India's nationalist songs, 'Jana Gana Mana,' 'Vande Mataram' and 'Kadam Kadam Badhaye Jaa' with a fervour that could be described as 'religious', most people, including Bhulabhai, were moved to tears. Bhulabhai said, 'I consider myself supremely blessed to have the opportunity to argue this case. But I am sad that I was unfortunate enough not to have been in East Asia to see the exceptional Netaji in person.'

Every day the crowd gathered for the hearings grew larger. The rising passion in both Punjab and Bengal caused the British great concern. A rally of over seven lakh people was held in Calcutta's Deshapriya Park to save the Azad Hind Fauj. About two lakh students and civilians held demonstrations at the Maidan in Calcutta for three days. The main speakers were Sardar Patel, Pandit Nehru and Netaji's elder brother, Sarat Chandra Bose. The millworkers of Bombay took to the streets with slogans of 'Netaji zindabad'. Many were killed during the unabated firing in Madras.

The trial for treason was no longer limited to the Azad Hind Fauj and the Government of India. It was a bitter battle between England and India, with the historic Lal Qila as witness. Several officers of the British Indian Army openly attended Congress meetings in their uniforms. There was pressure on them from the soldiers to support the cause. This shook up the British administration.

As the days went by, the case became more and more intriguing. At every corner, in each paan shop and eatery, Netaji's photos were hung and pictures of Shah Nawaz, Sehgal and Dhillon were prominently displayed. When Basant rode her bicycle through the crowds to attend the hearing, people cleared the path for her. Whether it was Prem's sisters or Shah Nawaz's brothers, or any of their friends and relatives, people gathered around them with pride. When the students started their protest march from Chandni Chowk with cries of 'Liberate the valiant soldiers of the Azad Hind Fauj', the crowds became uncontrollable. A volley of shots was fired. The streets of Delhi were littered with bodies. Inside the fort, Bhulabhai's voice boomed. Outside, the guns boomed. The police chief of Delhi had no choice but to seek Pandit Nehru's help to bring the crowds under control.

The government emphatically told the court that the Azad Hind Fauj was a band of rebels. The soldiers had not honoured their oath of loyalty to the British monarch. Articles of the International Code of Law would not be applicable to these common prisoners of war. At this remark, Bhulabhai started out of his chair. Wagging his finger at the judge, he stated, 'Milord, it was not a band of rebels. It was a cry for freedom erupting from thirty-eight crore throats. The Azad Hind had its own government ...'

'What government? Did it have even a square inch of land under its control?' taunted the government lawyer, Naushirwan Engineer.

Bhulabhai summoned Hachiya, who was the Japanese Ambassador in Netaji Subhas Bose's parallel government. Looking the judge in the eye, Hachiya said, 'Milord, the Japanese Parliament, the Diet, has accorded recognition to the Azad Hind Fauj. Our government has handed over the Andaman and Nicobar Islands to Netaji. Not only that, we have even granted them fifty square miles of fertile lands in Zeyawaddy, in Burma. Besides, when the Japanese Army marched into Manipur along with the Indian National Army, all the territory we conquered was handed over to Netaji. Prime Minister Tojo made this categorical announcement in front of the parliament.'

After Hachiya's deposition, Bhulabhai once again reminded the court how eight nations including Japan, Germany, Indo-China and Burma had accorded recognition to the Azad Hind government. The director of the Azad Hind Bank, Dina Nath, also testified. He informed the court how in the past six months, sweetmeat vendors and milkmen, barristers and laypeople had made available more than twenty crore to Netaji's cause.

As the moment for the defence's final argument drew near, Bhulabhai's gaze swept across the hall, like a general casting a last look over his troops. It was as though every brick of Lal Qila whispered encouraging words, and the breeze felt heavy with Bahadur Shah Zafar's sighs. Barrister Bhulabhai Desai had fought and won innumerable cases from Lahore to Madras. He had, on many occasions, literally shaken the Goddess of Justice's throne with his arguments. But this occasion was unique. On the one hand his health was failing him; on the other, the historic moment waited, with bated breath, for his defence.

Bhulabhai clenched his fists. His voice was thick as he addressed the Judge. 'Before I begin my defence, I would like to ask Major General Katakura Tadashi a question.' Katakura stood up. 'You had drawn up the first plan for the Imphal campaign, had you not? Answer just one question. What did you give Netaji Subhas Chandra Bose then?'

'What didn't we give! Vast sums of money for the army, recognition of his policy. But more than that, fifty thousand Japanese soldiers gave their lives in the Imphal campaign for his sake.'

'Major General Katakura, what do you mean by "for his sake"?' Bhulabhai asked.

'We had planned the Imphal campaign before Netaji arrived in Japan. But the military officials abandoned it, as it would have been impractical and expensive.'

'Then why did you revive the plan and march into Imphal?'

'There is only one answer to this complicated question – Subhas Chandra Bose,' declared Katakura. 'Netaji's personality is like that. His fervour, his willingness to undergo any suffering inspired us. When he met our prime minister for the first time at the Imperial Hotel, his impassioned plea for India's freedom moved us all. It seemed as if he were standing at the gates of heaven and arguing his case before the Almighty himself.'

Major Fujiwara stood up and spoke. 'Netaji's charisma was his greatest weapon. So, although Tojo was compelled to resign as Prime Minister, assistance to Netaji did not stop.'

At these words, Savda, the Japanese deputy minister, Ohata, Hachiya, Katakura and the other delegates rose from their seats. Together they said, 'Netaji taught us what love for one's motherland is and what one must be prepared to do for that love. That is his legacy.'

'When any civilized human being declares patriotism, love for one's country, is it a crime?' asked Bhulabhai, loudly enunciating each word. 'No court of law in the world can classify working for the glory and the pride of one's motherland an offence. When revolutionaries spill their blood for the liberation of their country, they automatically acquire the label of terrorists. What happened when the Macquis waved the flag of revolt to prevent their beloved France from being swallowed up by Germany? While the secret rebel army laid its life on the line, the French emperor became a German collaborator. The Maquis rebelled against the emperor. Do we then say that they were not loyal? How can we, when the same Maquis were feted by England and America as nationalist? For you they were nationalists. So what about these three men? You incarcerate them like petty criminals because under Netaji's leadership, they are willing to die for the liberation of thirty-eight crore slaves? On the one hand, you pretend to dispense justice; on the other, you erect gallows to strangulate it. What kind of justice is this, Milord?'

Bhulabhai cited innumerable articles from International Law as well as commentaries on them by people such as Lawrence, Eden, Pitt, Churchill and Oppenheim. Pointing at the judge, Bhulabhai questioned, 'When Garibaldi battled against the Italian monarch, who acknowledged his nationalist status? England and America, of course! Milord, if the appropriate declaration is made about the birth of a nation and disciplined planning of a war is chalked out, then where is the question of betrayal or treason? When a bitter battle is waged against a corrupt ruler, you cannot expect loyalty to rule. The bonds of loyalty cannot be binding when the issue is the freedom of one's country.

When Colonel Hunt handed over forty-five thousand prisoners of war to the Japanese at the Ferrer Park in Singapore, on whose behalf was he acting? The British emperor, was he not? It means that in a time of crisis, the emperor himself did not honour his responsibility. He handed them over to strangers like lambs. What kind of moral right has he to expect allegiance from the same men whom he threw to the dogs?'

Bhulabhai spoke for four hours without a break. At the end, the strain began to show. His throat was parched. His experience as a history teacher in a college in Ahmedabad had stood him in good stead. History and law were together picking holes in British culture and beliefs. Every now and then, Kailashnath Katju picked up Bhulabhai's hand to check his pulse and glanced nervously at his colleagues. The clock struck five and court was adjourned. As he sat down, Bhulabhai looked at the judge and said, 'Even I can see how much damage has been caused to the British Army and the empire by the establishment of the Indian National Army government. If you can cast aside your prejudice and disdain for a moment, you will admit the hollowness of this case.'

Around the same time, an emergency meeting was in progress at the Viceroy's residence. The governor general and senior military officers were following the court proceedings and discussing the fallout. A messenger arrived with a confidential dispatch from the governor of the Frontier Province. The message read: 'Situation in Frontier deteriorating. Stall case at once. Province could be lost.'

The wireless message from Bombay had already declared that there was dissatisfaction in the navy and it could trigger a riot at any moment. Lakhs of people would not budge from the streets of Calcutta; Punjab was smouldering. In many small towns near Madras, protest fires were burning. Lord Wavell was desperate. In the past, he had tasted defeat at the hands of the Japanese in Burma. He had been disgraced as a commander. To avenge that humiliation, he had planned this malicious court case. He pounded the table and thundered, 'We set up this courtroom drama to expose that traitor Subhas Chandra Bose and his Indian National Army. And now the swords have turned against us. The man whom we wanted to discredit as a traitor, has, in absentia, become a great hero to his followers. What is the difference between the anarchy that followed the death of Caesar and this? If only we hadn't chosen Lal Qila as the venue.'

It was dusk. Bhulabhai looked at the three prisoners with great affection. It was time to leave the barracks. The sentries and guards were getting impatient. Just then, Kailashnath Katju thrust a piece of paper into Bhulabhai's hands. 'What is this, Kailash?'

'Sir, please sign. We will appeal to the judge for a four-day break.'

'Why?'

'Sir, your health ...?'

'Kailash, you worry too much about my health!' Bhulabhai wiped his eyes. 'I want to wager my life for the defence of these young patriots in the temple of justice. Tomorrow, my defence will conclude. You keep watch. If despite all this, Death's messengers still turn up at this gloomy courtroom, make a special request for them to wait until I finish my deposition. Don't let them enter until I have fulfilled my duty.'

Two

A class was in progress.

'Tell me, who was responsible for dragging Hindustan, this great country of ours, into slavery?' Principal Beni Madhav Das asked his students.

'The Bengalis,' replied a fair, round-faced youngster in the front row.

'Hurr!' the boys shouted. When the class settled down, the boy, still standing, asked Beni Madhav, 'Sir, do you think my answer was wrong?'

Everyone burst out laughing. Rapping the desk with his cane to silence the class, Beni Madhav said, 'This boy is absolutely right. Had we reined in the topi-wearing British in time, they would not be ruling over us today.'

Walking up to the slender, bespectacled boy, Beni Madhav placed a hand on his shoulder and asked, 'What is your name, young man?'

'Subhas.'

'Whose son are you?'

'Jankinath Bose.'

Just then the bell rang and school ended for the day. Subhas got into the waiting carriage and the horse set off at a trot towards Oriya Bazaar. It was getting dark. The municipal lamplighters were atop their ladders lighting the street lamps. The houses in the neighbourhood were a challenge to the Empire's middle-class dwellings; some even had palm leaf thatches. Subhas could see his double-storeyed house in the distance. Another buggy was standing by the door. His was the only family with three horse carriages – a reflection of his father's status. Jankinath Bose seemed to have returned from court earlier than usual.

When Subhas reached home, he learnt from the servant that his father was not going to the Union Club that day. Normally as soon as Jankinath Bose came home, he would put on his tennis shoes, adjust his dhoti, wear a coat and then, accompanied by his wife, set off for the club. This routine had never changed as far as Subhas could remember. Later when he went up to the terrace to get a panoramic view of Cuttack, he noticed that the servants' quarters were unusually quiet. The all-pervasive silence suggested that his father was upset about something.

After dinner, Subhas went up to the children's room. From the adjoining room, his mother's voice floated up to him. 'Is being appointed a district government pleader a small thing? That too for an Indian?'

'And for that one honour, should one suffer humiliation time and again?

'What about the status and power that comes with the position … herd of servants, so many subordinates … socialising with commissioners and governors …'

'Prabha, even if what you say is correct, my disagreement is on principle. If the honourable judge is mistaken, should he not admit it? Our fault is that we are Indians – born to be slaves. They are British, the masters.'

'But what will you gain by resigning?'

'There is no point remaining in a position where you have to compromise your values. I have decided to hand in my resignation first thing tomorrow morning.'

Nobody slept that night. When Subhas's mother picked up little Sailesh and strolled towards the terrace, Subhas followed her. The night was bathed in moonlight.

'Ma …'

'Yes, raja?'

'Can I ask you something?'

'What is it?'

'How and where did you first meet Baba?'

She was taken aback, but soon her face softened. 'Once upon a time, there was a town called Calcutta, a place full of palatial houses. Of them all, Ganganarayan Dutt's mansion stood out with its beautiful objects, a huge front garden and a host of servants. One day, a bold young man was walking past the mansion gate when he saw an enchanting sight. A little princess. Immediately, he entered the garden.'

'He was our Baba, na, Ma?'

'Shhh ... do you know why the young man did that? To ask Ganganarayan for his daughter's hand. He was only an impoverished village school teacher, but he wanted to pluck a star out of the sky. Ganganarayan's other sons-in-law were barristers and judges. A teacher's salary was less than what Ganganarayan's gardener earned. Ganganarayan was outraged at the boy's temerity. With utter contempt he said, "You do not have a measly inch of your own to stand on, yet you dare to step into a palace. If you have the courage and your resolve is as strong as your ambition, go and achieve something that will bring you on par with us. Then come back and ask for my daughter's hand."'

Sailesh piped in, 'Baba must have felt bad, Ma?'

'Terrible. Like a fish thrown on the sand. The little princess too was very unhappy. She would go around in the buggy but not look out of the window. Soon the young man who had so often been seen hovering around the Dutt mansion vanished from the streets of Calcutta. Three or four years went by. Then one day, he appeared like a hero at their gates again, stylishly riding on a black and white horse. The young man had toiled night and day and established a name for himself in the Cuttack bar as a lawyer.'

Prabhabati's story ended. The children clapped their hands with joy. But Prabhabati was lost in her own world. Her tears had shown her devotion to Jankinath. When she stepped into the Bose household, good fortune entered with her and they flourished. Jankinath and Prabhabati were blessed with six girls and eight boys. For Janki Babu, there was no turning back. He went from success to greater success – from a lawyer to a district government pleader, to the president of the Cuttack municipality and a member of the Bengal assembly. Though Prabhabati had protested at first, she soon accepted his decision to resign from his post as government pleader because she had full faith in his abilities.

That night Subhas told his mother all about Beni Madhav, his idol, in whom he felt he had found a fount of inspiration. No one besides his accomplished father had influenced him so much until then. Although he was middle-aged, dignified and composed, Beni Madhav's vitality was like the rustle of peepul leaves. Subhas felt compelled to listen to everything that he had to say. Once, he had approached him with a question: 'Sir, what is the meaning of ghulam, slave?'

'One who mortgages his mind and soul to another and silently suffers repeated humiliation and injustice is a ghulam.'

'How many such ghulams do we have in our country?'

'Thirty crore,' replied Beni Madhav, his face hardening. The memory of some deep humiliation sent a tremor through him. He joined his hands together as if invoking the vayu devta, the wind god, and then clenching his fists, murmured to himself, 'Our most revered Swamiji declared that our motto for the next fifty years should be, "I will not live as a slave. Unless India gets political freedom, there is no future for us, no progress, no hope". He didn't say that without any reason.' Who was this Swamiji that Beni Madhav spoke of with such awe? Subhas discovered that the Swamiji was Vivekananda. A few years ago, he had done Hinduism proud at the Congress of World Religions in the USA.

One of Subhas's relatives, a man named Ghosh, lived in Oriya Bazaar. In Ghosh's house, Subhas came across a treasure trove of Vivekananda's works. Every sentence that Subhas read sent a thrill through his body. 'This is no nation where there is no compassion for the poor, this is hell. What religion is this that denies workers their rights? It is no religion; it is the devil's dominion. We have lost our identity as a nation. Raise your voices for the upliftment of the poor, the deprived, the backward of this earth. Arouse the common people. Give shape once again to our motherland.' Vivekananda's ideas reverberated in Subhas's head.

Soon, the buggy no longer plied from the Bose home to Ravenshaw Collegiate School. Like all the other children, Subhas too walked to school. Vivekananda's words, 'As long as hunger and ignorance afflict our countless brethren, I will look upon every privileged person as a traitor,' became supremely important to young Subhas. His compassion for the weak and deprived became so strong that many beggars and mendicants, sadhus and fakirs began to wait for him outside the school gate.

Prabhabati shouldered the responsibility of a large family. Yet, like a mother eagle, her eyes were always on her brood. How could this radical change in her son escape her. Under the influence of Sarat and Satish, Subhas blossomed. His command over English was so strong, many of his teachers in middle school felt intimidated.

Once his Sanskrit teacher, Acharya Bagchi, came to his house. He told Prabhabati and Jankinath, 'I gave your son only 100 out of 100 in Sanskrit.'

'What do you mean, only a hundred?' Prabhabati laughed.

'I wanted to give him 110, but you know we cannot do that.'

Subhas's parents did not need to worry about his studies. He would begin to prepare for an exam only four days before it and yet he always stood first in his class. But they were concerned about his strange behaviour of late. He would go around looking sombre and preoccupied. That was not how boys his age should behave. One day as he was leaving for school, Prabhabati stopped him. 'Why have you become so quiet, my son? You no longer laugh and joke. You look rebellious these days.'

'Ma, the first cry of an infant is the mark of a rebel,' Subhas replied calmly.

'And who says so?'

'Swami Vivekananda.'

'Oh, I see. As if Swamiji meets you every day and discusses profound matters with you ...'

Jankinath Bose had given up his government job and was once again working hard to get his private practice together. Recently, he had suffered a heat stroke and Prabhabati had to supervise his diet and medication. Satish and Sarat were studying law in Calcutta, while Sunil had joined the medical college. Their expenses had to be taken care of. And now there was this anxiety about Subhas. No one could fathom his thoughts and the turbulence therein. He belonged to everybody and yet was nobody's.

One night his mother found Subhas tossing and turning in bed, muttering in sleep. 'Really, where are those towering personalities? Where is that land of gods and holy men, seers, sages and wise men? Where are the secret banks of the jnana-Ganga, the river of knowledge and our ancestors who discovered it?'

'Wake up, raja, wake up! What is the matter?' she asked gently.

Subhas was sweating. She held out a glass of water. He drank it in one gulp. His father, standing at his bedside, asked anxiously, 'Was it a bad dream?'

'No, Baba, not a frightening dream – a beautiful one,' Subhas said.

'About what?'

'I saw a bright golden ray break out of a thick bank of black clouds.'

Subhas's parents exchanged worried glances. Something was wrong with their child. Jankinath advised his wife to take him to Calcutta to spend a few days with Sarat.

Subhas agreed to go to Calcutta. He got on well with Sarat whom he addressed as Mej-da. But Calcutta being the capital city of the British,

Subhas was uncomfortable there. Whether in a restaurant or on a tram, he saw British oppression everywhere. On the streets of Calcutta, people were dying of cholera, pneumonia and malnourishment; their bodies were carried away like pariah dogs on municipality carts. For the last ten years, money had been squandered on the construction of the Victoria Memorial monument. Marble and granite were brought all the way from Rajasthan, and labourers from various parts of the world, underpaid and exploited, toiled night and day. Subhas found the very idea revolting.

There was so much ignorance and darkness. Women considered train travel a sin. They were shocked to see Prabhabati in a train compartment, while their men raised eyebrows. The devastating effect of the famine was visible all along, from Orissa to Hooghly. Skulls, both human and animal, were scattered across the land. Cattle were reduced to dirt. People fenced off their dwellings for fear of disease and abandoned their villages in search of food. Subhas thought, this is not right, the king is not behaving like a king.

The people they met on the train were fleshless, bloodless corpses. The third-class compartment was a hellhole. So why should one pay obeisance to the king. Why sing hymns to the British queen in school every morning, and praise George V.

He returned from Calcutta and rejoined school. And one morning when the bell clanged harshly, all the students of Ravenshaw Collegiate School assembled. One student began the prayer and the rest joined in the chorus. Once every year a student would get a chance to lead the prayer. Today, the prayer had not started. The sports teacher, Mr Srivastava, shouted, 'Whose turn is it today? Why has the prayer not started?'

'It is Subhas's turn,' several students called out. Srivastava glared. 'Hurry up, begin the prayer!' Subhas was taken aback. He had not known that it was his turn. His back stiffened. 'No. I will not sing the Queen's prayer,' he retorted.

'Why? Why not?'

The cane descended swiftly, stroke upon stroke on Subhas's hands. Like an animal Subhas bore his pain, but he repeated vehemently, 'No, I will not say the Queen's prayer.'

'Why?' demanded the cane.

'Who is the Queen of England to us?'

'I will flay you alive,' screamed the livid Srivastava.

The school was speechless with shock and horror. Just then a stern voice called out, 'Stop it. Stop at once. Are you a man or a demon?'

It was Beni Madhav Das. He took Subhas's swollen, red hands gently in his own.

That night Subhas came down with fever. A worried Jankinath Bose sat in the terrace with Beni Madhav, who asked him, 'Suppose someone complains to a higher authority? Even a schoolboy's refusal to sing the Queen's prayer can be termed an act of rebellion, can't it?'

Jankinath had no answer to the question. He just stared into the darkness.

'I am worried about Subhas; he is constantly in the company of the revolutionaries,' Jankinath told Prabhabati.

'He is the most intelligent student in his class, earnest and good-looking. That's why some boys are jealous and make up such stories about him.'

'Don't be blinded to the truth out of love for your son – you could lose him that way,' Jankinath warned. 'Have you asked him recently what he reads, what he writes, in whose company he spends his time? The police inspector from the Cuttack thana has made a similar complaint to me.'

Later that day, just as Subhas was leaving the house, Janki Babu accosted him. 'Let me see that notebook,' he said, snatching it away. Janki Babu's forehead creased into a frown. 'Have you seen this, Prabha – our son's talent?' he asked his wife.

'Show me,' she said. Looking at the book, she said, 'What's wrong with it? Look at the lovely garden he has painted – and all the colours ...'

'Look at those Britishers in the garden – every one of them looks so villainous.'

She smiled and asked, 'Why, son, have you given them such misshapen noses? And those bushy, sloping eyebrows, the elongated ears – all your foreigners resemble a bad-tempered ox. Why don't you draw more pleasant pictures?'

Four years ago, a young man, Khudiram Bose, had thrown a bomb at Kingsford, the magistrate of Muzaffarpur and a known anti-Indian. Later, Khudiram was sent to the gallows. When Subhas saw his photograph in the newspapers, it had upset him. For a long time, he had kept Khudiram's picture on his desk. Of late, he spent much time with bold young men like Khudiram.

Janki Babu demanded an explanation. 'Tell me, when you were in Calcutta, whom did you meet with? Do you know anyone called Suresh Banerji?'

'Yes.'

'Where did you go with him?'

'I met him only three or four times and that too in a top floor flat of a dark old house on Chowringhee.'

Janki Babu glared at Subhas, then turned to Prabhabati. 'This is the Suresh Banerji of the Anushilan Samiti, a secret revolutionary organisation of Calcutta. He is a history-sheeter – with a police record. Why does Subhas need to hobnob with such men? Is this what a middle school student should be doing?'

'Subhas, tell us the truth,' she said.

'Prabhabati, you stay out of this,' Janki Babu admonished her and addressed Subhas once more. 'You must have visited Girish Banerji as well?'

'Yes,' Subhas admitted calmly.

'Why?'

'Because I get to read rare books by Vivekananda at his place.'

'Girish is one of the leaders of the Cuttack Anushilan Samiti and the Cuttack police are keeping a close watch on him. Bidhu Roy and Shashanka Mukherji are his accomplices.'

'But all these people have been to our house several times,' Prabhabati interjected in a small voice. 'I never imagined they would be embroiled in such activities!' she exclaimed. Now, when she thought about it, some things had been suspicious. Young men like Hemanta Sarkar or the rough-looking Romendra Ghosh and Mahadev Ghosh would come from Calcutta to stay, claiming to be friends. Prabhabati recalled their furtive movements, their all-night vigils, their serious discussions despite their young age. Her brow creased.

'Go now and focus only on your studies in the future,' Janki Babu dismissed Subhas sternly.

That afternoon Jankinath did not attend the court. His fears about Subhas had left him uneasy. He told Prabhabati, 'Do you know, Beni Madhav has also been transferred?'

'Oh! Who will guide Subhas now?' Prabhabati's anxiety intensified.

Although he had resigned from a senior government post, Janki Babu was still considered a socially responsible citizen and was highly respected by the British. His Cuttack home was a haven for several indigent relatives and poor students. He had never sent a deserving student away empty-handed. Whether it was the temple in his birthplace, Kodaliya, or the charitable hospital, the cattle shelter or any other cause, he had supported all of them. That is why he was the only man in Cuttack on whom the British had conferred the title of Rai Bahadur.

The British emperor, George V and his consort were on a visit to India. As the capital was to be shifted from Calcutta to Delhi, a grand reception, the Coronation Durbar, was to be held there and a great number of guests were expected to travel to Delhi for the occasion. To provide for all of them, the British had created a beautifully laid out township called New Delhi, a little away from the old city. The Durbar was to be held in the Viceregal Lodge in New Delhi. When Jankinath Bose received an invitation to attend the Durbar, the Bose household was delighted.

Prabhabati thought that if Subhas accompanied his father, he would get to travel a bit and perhaps his obsession with Vivekananda and his anti-British feelings would gradually disappear. When she suggested this to Janki Babu, he readily agreed.

New Delhi was as resplendent as a new bride in the first week of December of 1911. The native maharajas were ecstatic, as if their saviour had descended from the heavens. The Ranas of Rajasthan, the proud Marathas, the Pants and so-called learned lords from the South, the zamindars of United Province and Bihar were all present. Richly caparisoned elephants and horses formed part of George V's ceremonial parade that marched through the streets of Delhi. Receptions and felicitation ceremonies were held. Some native rajas were so obsequious, they barely stopped short of laying their heads at the feet of the British emperor. To Subhas, their grovelling and fawning seemed very theatrical, like actors in a jatra performance.

He stared unblinkingly at the emperor as he moved forward, shaking hands with the guests. Finally, George V approached Janki Babu. Janki

Babu was introduced to him, but George's attention was immediately drawn to Subhas. He patted Subhas's cheek, but Subhas did not react. Someone from behind called out, 'Son, don't just stand there, staring. This is God himself. Bow down and touch his feet.' But Subhas stood still, silent. A ripple of fear passed through the gathering. King George looked at him for a moment, then moved on.

Later, in Calcutta, Hemanta Sarkar asked Subhas, 'So how was the Delhi Durbar?"

'What Durbar! It was a procession of costumed corpses!'

Subhas's engagement with the revolutionary youth group had decreased somewhat, but the Vivekananda Mandal was quite active. As soon as the holidays started, Subhas and his group rushed off to the villages around Cuttack, providing medicines and taking care of patients suffering from smallpox and cholera. They collected rice from the neighbouring villages, or occasionally from their own homes for the poor students staying in the rent-free hostel in Cuttack. Subhas developed a taste for books and soon he was seen carrying tomes like Bankim Chandra's *Anandamath*, Mazzini's *Man's Duty*, Gibbon's *Decline and Fall* and the Ramayana and the Mahabharata.

One evening, a lawyer friend of Jankinath's came up to him as he and Prabhabati sat at the City Club, and informed him that some revolutionary youth had thrown a bomb at the viceroy in Delhi.

'Really, if something like this had happened during King George V's procession last year, the world would have known at once what ails our country,' Janki Babu overheard Subhas talking to his brother.

'So your animosity has raised its head again, Subhas?' Janki Babu said.

'This is not hatred or animosity, Baba. Thousands of our people are dying like flies from hunger and disease. In our region alone, thirty thousand have succumbed to cholera. Shouldn't our emperor know what his primary concerns ought to be?'

For several days, the discussion in Ravenshaw Collegiate School revolved around this incident. Who was the young man who had dared to throw a bomb at the viceroy? The day the police were able to identify him, Subhas ran home with the newspaper. With absolute delight and pride, he told his mother, 'See, Ma, the man who threw the bomb was a Bengali!'

'What's his name?'

'Rash Behari Bose of Chandernagore.'

Prabhabati also seemed pleased, but she scolded Subhas, 'There's no need for a schoolboy like you to be interested in all this. Just study, that's enough.'

As for Subhas, until his father's buggy pulled up at the door, he went about dancing with glee.

Another day, while Janki Babu was looking for something, he happened to go into Subhas's room. He noticed a few posters hidden among some sheets of paper. He pulled them out. Printed by Gadar, the revolutionary party of Lala Hardiyal Singh of America, they read:

Wanted: Young soldiers to bring about a rebellion in the Indian Army.

Salary: Death

Reward: Martyrdom

Pension: Freedom

Battleground: Hindustan

He was shocked to find such provocative literature in his own home. He warned his wife, 'You better control Subhas right now or else this bird will fly away and leave us heartbroken.'

A few days later, a news sent shock waves through Cuttack. Apparently, Rash Behari Bose had recently spent two days in Cuttack. The police commissioner was completely demoralised. He had to give an explanation to the Governor House. He set in motion the usual police enquiries. Girish Banerji and his colleagues went underground.

During the investigations, another piece of startling information came to light. A secret fund for Rash Behari had been collected to which prominent businessmen and respected citizens had made generous contributions. The police began a surveillance of eminent homes.

In court, the public prosecutor stated that one of the accused had declared in his confessional statement that Subhas himself had contributed Rs 200 towards this fund. Hearing this, Janki Babu's heart sank. 'What now?' he asked, sweating profusely as he thought of Subhas's future.

'We'll find a way out,' the public prosecutor reassured him.

Janki Babu rushed home that afternoon. Seeing his anxiety-ridden face, Prabhabati became frightened. When he confronted his son that evening, Subhas immediately admitted the truth. 'Was that all, or is there anything else?' Janki Babu asked him.

'Nothing else.'

'Did you ever meet that ... that Rash Behari?'

'No, Baba, I was not fortunate enough,' Subhas replied.

Tears filled Jankinath's eyes. His voice trembled as he said, 'When will you understand your duty as a student, Subhas? Prove your worth first, before ...'

'Subhas, son, you must change your ways,' his mother interrupted.

'Such great hopes I had for this boy. The matric exam is barely a fortnight away. The other day, Bhattacharya, a lawyer from Calcutta, came in connection with a case ... he was talking about a young boy named Khitish Chattopadhyay who he said was so brilliant that he was going to top the matric exam. His father has helped him with his studies. He has prepared over a hundred essays in English. And do you know what my colleagues at the Bar told him, Prabha?'

'What?'

'Write it down. This year's topper at the matric exam is going to be our own Subhas Bose.' Jankinath could not hold back his tears as he spoke. 'Forget about the merit list, if you clear all your subjects, I will consider myself fortunate,' he added.

Just then a police inspector from the Cuttack police station appeared at Janki Babu's residence with a message from the deputy commissioner.

'Saheb says the boy is a student, moreover he is your son. That's why we have chosen to ignore this incident. But the thought of a Rai Bahadur's son in the company of terrorists pains us deeply!'

Jankinath Basu and Prabhabati were going back to Cuttack. The tonga waited for them outside, but the thought of leaving Subhas behind was holding Prabhabati back. She turned to her daughter-in-law Bibhabati and said, 'Bibha, I am leaving Subhas in your care. Do look after him. Every moment away from him will seem like an age to me.'

They departed. Subhas's favourite older brother Sarat Bose, Mej-da, had gone to England to become a barrister. But the other two brothers, Satish and Sunil and their families lived at home. Janki Babu was at the pinnacle of his career. He had recently acquired a grand three-storeyed mansion in Calcutta's Bhowanipur area where elite doctors, lawyers and industrialists lived. One had to be a person of considerable means to own such a large property in that affluent locality.

Subhas was to study at the Presidency College, the most reputed college in Bengal, from where his brothers had graduated. Before stepping onto its grounds, Subhas said to Hemanta Sarkar, 'This time I will not let the opportunity slip.'

'What opportunity?'

'I missed the first rank in the matric exam by a couple of marks. But I will graduate from Presidency College in philosophy with a first class degree.'

Hemanta replied, 'You can do anything once you make up your mind. You could even uproot a tree with one blow.'

Subhas's classmates were Dilip Kumar, his favourite poet Dwijendralal Ray's son and Khitish Chattopadhyay, who had competed with him in the matric exam. Subhas was delighted to be in the company of such bright young men. Besides, Suresh Banerji's secret office on the second floor of a dilapidated old building on Chowringhee Lane nearby provided him a mental haven. That is where he had access to an assortment of rare books and to news of the anti-British activities of the underground revolutionaries.

Even before Subhas entered college, an aura had formed around him. He was always surrounded by a group of students, because of his second rank in the matric exam and more because of his magnetic personality. Once they decided to visit the site of the Battle of Plassey and Murshidabad. Subhas saddled two horses from his stable and galloped towards Plassey. Upon arrival, Subhas was moved. This is where Hindustan had succumbed to Robert Clive's treachery and the noose of slavery had been thrown around their motherland's neck forever.

Soon the Nava Vivekananda Mandal was revived. Subhas and his friends devoured books on meditation, yoga and hatha yoga. They drew a black circle on a white cloth and stared at it for hours to improve their concentration. They woke up very early, poured buckets of cold water over themselves in mid-winter and trudged, barefoot, for miles in the scorching heat of summer.

Once again, Subhas began dreaming that Mother India was calling out to him in the middle of the night. He could hear the shackles clanging around her feet, and woke up with a start. His thirst for spiritual knowledge intensified. How could he find the 'ananta', the ultimate, in the soulless walls of his classroom or in the sheltered environs of his parents' home?

One day when a meeting of the Vivekananda Mandal was in progress at Kalighat, Subhas suddenly exclaimed, 'No, friends, the lifeless wooden benches of our classroom are not the tiger-skin seats of the sages and saints. We must look for Truth in the outside world. Let us seek a guru first, for without him, life will be meaningless.'

'I agree,' Hemanta declared.

They decided to set off in search of a guru immediately. Hemanta undertook to gather the preliminary information. In a fortnight, he sent a coded message. That was all very well, but where would the money for the journey come from? Khitish, they knew, was a scholarship-holder. He was prevailed upon to fund them. And then the fledglings quietly flew out of their cosy nests.

There was no limit to their speed or their aspirations. Tirelessly they roamed. Through Lakshman Jhoola and Haridwar, Mathura and Vrindavan. They traversed all of North India. They came across holy places and ashrams, gardens and riverbanks, dancing peacocks and frolicking deer's. There were temples and shrines, but not one living god. They encountered ancient sages and seers, sadhus and fakirs, sanyasins and saints, but not a single guru. They found a mauni baba who had not uttered a word for years. But they did not find a guide. No direction. Where was the beginning? Where the end?

One night, they were sleeping in the ruins of a temple, stiff from the bitter cold, when Subhas was startled awake by dry leaves falling down on him. A strong wind rattled the branches as the trees swayed wildly. To Subhas, those branches appeared as if they were Bharatmata's arms, flailing about in grief. He began to weep inconsolably.

For two months, Subhas and his friends wandered around. The exquisite mirrors of their hopes and dreams were now chipped and dusty.

The rampant, blind practice of casteism all around had further disillusioned them. Finally, in the Ramakrishna Math at Banaras, they met Swami Brahmananda. He recognised Subhas at once. Subhas was surprised. 'How do you know me?' he asked.

'I have just returned from Calcutta. Have you any idea of the panic you have created there? Your mother hasn't eaten anything nor drunk water for days. She just lies in front of the puja room, with only one refrain on her lips, 'Where is my little prince?' Your relatives are looking all over for you, from Badrinath to Belur.'

Subhas was overcome at the thought of his mother's sorrow. Also, Bibha boudi. He had betrayed her. Ma had left him in her charge. What must she have gone through.

All of them were exhausted from their two-month journey. Enough of travelling now, they thought.

'Let us go back tomorrow,' Hemanta announced.

'I am not coming,' retorted Subhas. 'What use was all this effort if we have to return empty-handed like this? No, Hemanta, I will not go back until I find something worthwhile.'

'Haven't we looked everywhere? Where do you think you are going to find a guru?'

'I learnt this afternoon that beyond the three mountains behind Badrinath, in a cave, under a wild fig tree, lives a great sage.'

'And how long will it take to cross those three mountains?'

'Two days.'

'Baap-re! We don't have the energy left to climb three mountains,' exclaimed his companions.

Subhas found a guide. He was to set off early in the morning. When Subhas was ready to go, he found Hemanta waiting for him. 'Subhas, my friend, would I ever let you go alone?'

The two-day climb was completed. In a hollow on the banks of a stream sat the venerable swami. There was a distinct aura about him. But Hemanta was exhausted. He collapsed as soon as they reached there.

Swamiji quickly realised that Subhas had studied Vivekananda's writings. He was pleased. After speaking to him for a while, Swamiji advised Subhas to return home instead of wandering about. This made Subhas's resolve stronger. 'No, Swamiji, I am prepared to don the bark of a tree and remain in the forest. I will torture my body into a state of samadhi; unless I find something that will become the guiding principle of my life, I will not turn back.'

'No, son, God does not dwell in these mountains and caverns. He is there among those toiling poor, the suffering masses. Go and awaken the sleeping masses of this country. Dispel the darkness of their ignorance, free them from exploitation, says Swamiji.'

'Which Swamiji?'

'Vivekananda.'

'You know him?'

The sage laughed out loud. 'Know him? My entire youth was spent with him. I heard him, I read his work. But I was not able to assimilate his thoughts. I did not have his ability to take situations head on. That is why I smeared my body with ash and slunk away into the depths of these mountains.

'This land has given us many sages and saints. But Swami Vivekananda is the only modern, progressive sage. He was the first to realise how insignificant India's place was on the world map. It had neither shape nor identity. I was present at his Dacca meeting where he first declared, in categorical terms, that this country needs political freedom first and foremost. He dared to speak bluntly against British oppression and injustice, which is why police spies were always hovering around him.'

'But then why didn't the British arrest him?'

'After the Chicago Parliament of World Religions, Swamiji became a global figure. If he had been arrested, the whole country would have risen against the British.'

Reading Subhas's mind, the Swami Brahmananda said, 'You seem to be a very motivated and courageous young man. Swami Vivekananda placed all his faith in the youth of this country. Son, your fighting spirit shows on your face. Preserve this attitude, cherish this love for your motherland always. Only when water flowing down a mountain is dammed and channelised, do fields get irrigated and crops grow. What use is lightning if it strikes randomly? Go, turn homewards.'

Subhas was puzzled.

'Go, use your zeal for the service of your country. This splintered society needs you.'

Dawn was breaking. Subhas shook Hemanta awake. 'Come on, Hemanta, let's go.'

'Where?'

'To Calcutta. My battle is not here in the forest; it is in the ripples of life,' said Subhas.

Early one morning, like a whirlwind, Subhas appeared at the door of the Elgin Road house. As soon as they saw him, Satyen-mama, his uncle, and the servants ran about calling out, 'Subhas, Subhas.' Prabhabati, who had lain listlessly for days, leapt out of bed. She ran into the puja room and lay her head at the feet of the Durga idol. Jankinath Bose, who had become weak, remained seated in his chair in the room. His eyes were blank. He looked like King Dasarath during Rama's exile. He wept uncontrollably seeing Subhas.

'Baba, forgive me, punish me in any way you like, but don't cry like this,' pleaded Subhas.

'You stupid child! Children like you should not endear themselves to their parents and if they do, they must never abandon them. It is too painful, son.'

Subhas went into Bibhabati's room. Tears flowed down her cheeks. Subhas took her hands in his. 'Forgive me, Boudi, please, I am really sorry.'

'It's all right, Chhor-da, you are back now. That's what matters most.'

Subhas's elder brother Sarat Bose, whom he addressed as Mej-da was extremely worried. Not so long ago when he and Satish sat on the banks of the Mahanadi and read aloud Shakespeare's plays, little Subhas would listen to them with rapt attention. Who would have thought that the same Subhas would one day provoke his friends to go on a strike. And that too at Presidency College, the pride of British Calcutta, an institution with a predominantly British staff, running on government grants. What was to be gained by treading on an elephant's tail. Pacing up and down, Sarat Bose told his wife, 'Bibha, I tell you, you have spoilt him. That's why he has become so defiant. The students' strike has created a stir in the city. The telephones from Governor House have not stopped ringing.'

'Then you must admonish him today.'

It was dusk and the shadows lengthened in the back garden. The tiny leaves of the tamarind tree stirred gently. An uneasy quiet prevailed over the whole house. Even Sarat babu's office downstairs was unusually silent. It was like the calm before a storm.

When Subhas said goodbye to his friends at the gate, it was nine o'clock. As he climbed up the steps, he could sense the tension in the house. He sat down at the table. Without a word, Bibha boudi placed dinner before him. She waited awhile for Sarat babu, but when he didn't turn up, she went into her bedroom to find him buried in a book.

'Why are you sitting here? You were going to scold Subhas, weren't you?' Bibha asked mischievously.

Sarat babu was embarrassed. 'What can I say, Bibha? He is such a lovable boy, a mere smile from him melts my heart.'

'I haven't seen brothers like this before,' Bibha laughed.

But what had happened was certainly worrying. Should the outcome of the strike be serious, what explanation would they give to their parents? Bibha went and sat down at the table and asked Subhas, 'Chhor-da, what exactly happened in the college?'

'Boudi, we have a history teacher called Oaten. He always criticizes our leaders. He says, Rani Laxmibai and Tatya Tope were traitors. He says, we Indians are barbarians. Tell me, how can we tolerate such remarks day in and day out? Surely it is offensive to our self-respect, isn't it?'

'But why don't you complain to the principal?' asked Bibha, sympathetically.

'We did, but he says we must first apologise to Oaten.'

'So do it. You are students, after all, Chhor-da.'

Subhas's face turned red as he retorted, 'Waah! Apologise, she says! Are we students or animals?'

The events at Presidency College the following day were unprecedented. Instead of the bustle of eighty-odd classrooms, there was a deathly silence. Seeing the empty classrooms and the deserted corridors, Principal James's anger knew no bounds. The crowd outside was growing bigger by the minute. The reputation Presidency College had built over the years was about to turn to dust.

That afternoon, Principal James summoned Maulvi Saab to the college. 'At least try and persuade the Muslim students not to be influenced by these neckless Hindu boys,' he requested. But Maulvi Saab's efforts were in vain. Not one Muslim student went back to class. They felt Subhas was one of them.

So a meeting between the student leaders, Professor Oaten and the principal was held, and a solution was reached. However, Professor Oaten continued to bully the students. He imposed a fine of five rupees on every student who had participated in the strike.

One day, Oaten was taking a class when he saw several students wandering up and down the corridor outside. That was provocation enough for him. He marched out, grabbed a couple of students by their collars and began abusing them. Though many complaints were made to the principal, no action was taken. Professor Oaten's vilification of Indian culture and Indian leaders continued unchecked. The students seethed in silence.

Professor Oaten declared that the Indian National Congress was a movement of Indian eunuchs with no future. The class was outraged. 'Sir, take back your words,' one group of students shouted angrily.

Quivering with rage, Oaten flung the chalk and duster down and declared, 'Why should I? My observation is based on research and study. I have no time for such troublesome students.' He was about to leave the room when the class stormed out in protest. Since Oaten's tirades against India and Indians showed no signs of abating, Khitish, Subhas and Hemanta decided it was time to teach him a lesson.

One morning Oaten hit yet another student. In no time, word spread through the college. During the break, Oaten was pinning a notice on the board, when, like a swarm of bees, he was surrounded by a group of students and assaulted. Before he knew what was happening, Oaten was on the floor, his spectacles broken, his clothes torn. Subhas watched this pathetic sight from some distance.

Though it had all happened within minutes, it had very far-reaching consequences. Oaten was an Englishman, and a member of the Indian Education Service. Presidency College was a symbol of prestige for the British government. So when news of the attack reached the administration in Writers' Building, the government decided to take punitive measures at once. The college was closed.

The next day, as if *The Statesman* headline screamed at Janki Babu. 'Indian students attack British Professor.' He was shaken and decided to return to Calcutta at once. For three nights, neither he nor Prabhabati could sleep.

Janki Babu was aware of Subhas's rebellious nature. How was one to dissuade him from such activities. Janki Babu's life was now like the setting sun. What could he say to his rising son.

Bansilal, a peon in the college, testified that Subhas was present when Oaten was assaulted. Everyone was convinced of Subhas's role in the incident. The governing body of Presidency College came under tremendous pressure from the government. Sarat Bose, an expert in criminal law, doubted that Subhas would come out of this enquiry unscathed. It looked as if his future would be blighted before it bloomed.

'Subhas, tell me the truth. Did you attack Oaten?'

'No. It just happened in my presence.'

'Wasn't it your duty to prevent a student from hitting a teacher? You failed there, didn't you?'

'Yes, I admit I failed. But then as a teacher, shouldn't he have respect for us? He shows no sign of that.'

'Does it mean, then, that you did not attack him?'

'Yes. Besides if I had to hit him, I would have done so from the front, not from behind,' Subhas said defiantly.

'You have injured the pride of the British. Oaten will avenge this insult,' Jankinath Bose warned Subhas.

Principal James summoned Subhas to his office. Through clenched teeth, he said, 'My dear Bose, you are the most troublesome student in the college. I hereby suspend you.' The doors of the college were shut on Subhas. A sword precariously dangled over the Bose household, filling all its inhabitants with fear. Jankinath seemed to have lost interest in life. Prabhabati's fasts and visits to the Kali temple increased.

The British had been keeping a strict watch on Presidency College since the movement against the partition of Bengal. Several students belonging to the secret revolutionary organisations, Anushilan and Yugantar, were studying there. In addition, English newspapers like *The Statesman* added fuel to the fire. The police conducted several raids on Eden Hostel. The Presidency College incident came to be viewed as an Indian versus British conflict.

Subhas's future rested with the enquiry committee. The entire Bose family spent a sleepless night before the day of the committee meeting. Janki Babu was overwhelmed by Subhas's patriotism and fervour. But what about his future? Fortunately, the chairman of the enquiry committee was Ashutosh Mukherji, a colleague of Sarat Babu's. But it was against his principles to seek personal favours. A common friend intervened. 'Does one mistake by such a young student merit so harsh a sentence?' he appealed. Chairman Ashutosh Mukherji replied, 'Ask Subhas to express regret.' Beni Madhav too had advised similarly.

Prabhabati could not contain herself. She told Subhas, 'One word of apology and the calamity will be averted. Son, just say you're sorry.'

'But why, Ma? For what should I apologise?' Subhas retorted. 'What wrong have I done? I did not beat Oaten. That was the students' anger bursting forth. It was not unjustified. I cannot bring myself to apologise for something I did not do.'

The next morning, Subhas presented himself before the enquiry committee. Around a long oblong table, three square faces gazed directly at him. The triumvirate of Bengal's education system were present on this committee. In the centre sat Chairman Ashutosh Mukherji, stroking his thick moustache. The education department had already transferred Principal James. The matter was not simple. Everybody viewed this enquiry from the perspective of the growing influence of politics on education and the surge of terrorist activity in Bengal. In the preliminary conversation, Ashutosh Mukherji directed everyone's attention to Subhas's marksheet at the matriculation examination.

Then the questions began.

'Who beat Oaten?'

'Not me.'

'Then who was it?'

'I don't know.'

'You don't know or you won't say?'

Subhas said nothing.

'Look here, Bose, if you don't wish to tell us who was responsible for the attack, don't. But at least do you regret it?'

'Certainly not.'

'And why not?'

'Students are human, not animals. They too have self-respect. Why do people like you not remember that?'

The committee was taken aback. Not only did he not condemn the act, he wasn't even sorry about it. How could a student, no matter how bright he was, or how illustrious his family background might be, defy the entire education system like this? As soon as Subhas left the room, the committee turned to Ashutosh Mukherji. He lowered his eyes and said, 'Please give your individual verdicts in writing.'

The inevitable happened. Eden Hostel was permanently closed. Subhas would not be allowed admission to any other institution of Calcutta University.

He sat by the window, staring wide-eyed into the darkness. His condition was like that of a sapling uprooted prematurely. He wasn't feeling helpless, merely confused. When he was leaving, many students had come to bid him goodbye. After many stressful days, his parents fell asleep from sheer exhaustion. Much later, Prabhabati awoke. She drew Subhas into her arms and gently ran her hands over his back. She asked, 'What are you thinking about, raja? Why aren't you sleeping?'

'Ma, who knows what my destiny will be,' said Subhas. 'But I know a day will come when I will sit down in style and have the British polish my shoes!'

'A first class at the degree exam, second rank in Calcutta University, who are you? What's your name?'

'Subhas Bose.'

'Jankinath's son?'

Ashutosh Mukherji was astonished. His white whiskers relaxed and a twinkle came to his eyes. He examined the marksheet once more. He called out to his family and narrated Subhas's story – how he had dismissed the boy from college and sent him on a two-year exile of sorts, then his readmission in Scottish College and now, a second rank in the university.

Subhas and Hemanta left Ashutosh Mukherji's house, delighted. Hemanta owned a bookshop in Calcutta called the Book Club. In that summer of 1919, Calcutta was exceptionally hot. Around that time, a repressive bill, the Rowlatt Act, was introduced in the Legislative Council. It would give the British unlimited power to arrest people without warrants and to imprison suspects without evidence. Gandhiji had called for a nationwide strike to protest against it. Subhas saw how the bustling city of Calcutta had gone absolutely quiet within moments of receiving Gandhiji's call. There were no tongas on the streets, no trams ran, bazaars, courts, factories and shops were all shut. Howrah Station dozed during the day. Not a single boat or ship left Kidderpore docks nor entered the port that day.

Jankinath Bose had just arrived from Cuttack on work. He expressed satisfaction with Subhas's performance. But Subhas felt that neither Mej-da nor his father had celebrated his grand success as he had hoped they would. They seemed to be labouring under some great burden. Their discussions went on till midnight. That night when Subhas returned home unusually late, Sarat and Jankinath Bose were talking. Their voices carried out of the room.

'So what if the corpse is covered ... the stench is bound to spread,' Sarat Bose said.

'The newspapers are heavily censored, otherwise news from the Punjab would have reached here by now,' Jankinath Bose replied.

'Satish was saying that martial law has been declared there. Gandhiji has been arrested. In Calcutta, too, people are being detained,' his brother said.

'Sarat, when the war drums are beaten in the Punjab, the echoes will be heard in Bengal. If Bengal even whispers, Maharashtra is bound to erupt. If these three provinces are provoked, all of India will turn into a blazing furnace. Lal, Bal and Pal have proved this earlier.'

'Keeping Subhas here under these circumstances is like throwing a match on an ammunition dump,' Sarat Bose said.

The next evening, Subhas was summoned by his parents and brother. 'Baba, have I done something wrong?' Subhas asked.

Jankinath Bose averted his eyes, not sure what to say. Dabbing at his eyes with the end of his dhoti, he said, 'No, no, Subhas, what wrong can you do. You proved us wrong. Despite the big blow to your education, you worked so hard. We are all very proud of you.'

Sarat Bose took his hand. 'You ought not to stay here any longer. You should go to England at once.'

Subhas was shocked. 'Why?'

'To prepare for the Indian Civil Service.'

Subhas fell silent. Affectionately thumping him on the back, Sarat Bose said, 'That's it, Subhas. Let those three words – ICS – be stamped on your forehead and you will have reached the pinnacle of your life overnight. Those magic words will see a queue of kings offering their daughters' hands in marriage and it wouldn't even matter if the prospective groom was actually a pauper from the streets!'

'Subhas, except Sarat and you, no one is capable of bringing such an honour to our family. Sarat cannot do this because of his age. That leaves you. You alone can grab this prestigious bouquet and bring it to us,' Jankinath told him. 'You have twenty-four hours to make up your mind.'

Just then Prabhabati spoke. 'I haven't asked you for anything until now, son, and it is my desire that you grant me this one wish today.'

Subhas did not know how to react. His mind was in a whirl. To be an ICS would be marvellous. The honour, the power, the glory! A life of endless comfort and absolute security.

He returned to his room. Sarat Bose followed. He did not want Subhas to lose this golden opportunity. Students worked themselves to the bone for four years, sometimes five, before taking the exam, but he had only seven months left. He should begin his preparations immediately.

After a night spent tossing and turning, Subhas got out of bed at dawn to run to Hemanta's house. But Hemanta was neither there nor at his bookshop. Where could he be. Subhas dragged his feet across the Maidan. Where was Hemanta. He had to pour out all his confusion to him. As he walked along, despairing, he suddenly heard a voice. A tonga drew up in front of him. Hemanta and his family were heading for the bazaar. Hemanta leaped out of the tonga. Quickly Subhas told him of the previous night's discussion. Hemanta did not say a word.

'What is the matter, Hemanta? Why don't you say something? Who, besides you, can I turn to for advice?'

'Subhas, the ICS, no doubt, is an honourable service. But, my friend, so what if it is a golden knife ... will you stab yourself with it?' He couldn't keep the anger out of his voice. He continued, 'Aren't you the same disciple of Vivekananda who was prepared to spurn all the comforts and luxuries of life in the service of society? What makes you ask me this question today? Subhas, if Lord Krishna walked away from Gokul, who would hold up the Govardhan Parbat?'

'Look, this is an extremely difficult exam. I can always reject the service after qualifying. I will resign,' Subhas said confidently.

'Such things don't happen, Subhas. Once a man begins to wallows in the lap of luxury, he is blinded by its golden smoke. His sensitivity dulls. He changes.'

'Well, it will not happen in my case.'

Subhas returned home. The battle continued to rage in his mind. Should he give in to his father's wishes and become another pillar of British Imperialism? There were only two options and they ran in opposite directions. One path was strewn with rose petals, the other covered with prickly thorns. On the one were the delights of power, wealth and comfort; and on the other, the dry fodder of sacrifice and deprivation.

What was really going on in Punjab? Why had Gandhiji been arrested? His companions' quest for answers to these questions at the Vivekananda Mandal made them all very restless. Finally, Subhas, Bholanath and Hemanta went to the secret house on Chowringhee. The same dilapidated, three-storeyed building with the winding staircase. The bell on the ground floor mysteriously opened the window on the top floor. Someone peeped out of that to make sure they were friends, before letting them in. There was no electricity, only earthen kerosene lamps. Two young men recently arrived from Punjab sat there, narrating their experiences.

Jallianwala Bagh was a meeting ground in the heart of Amritsar. Punjab Province erupted violently in response to Gandhi's call to protest the Rowlatt Act. On 9 April 1919, people of three major religions, Hindu, Muslim and Sikh, participated in a procession through the city. Invoking the Defence of India Act, the government arrested the popular leaders Dr Kichlu and Dr Satya Pal. An enraged public took a morcha to the deputy collector's residence. Incidents of heated verbal exchanges and stone throwing were reported. On 11 April, General Dyer imposed a ban on public gatherings in Amritsar city, but people were ignorant of the order. On 13 April, at 4.30 p.m. a huge public meeting was held in Jallianwala Bagh to demand the release of their leaders. The meeting had barely begun when General Dyer's troops surrounded it. Without a thought to the women and children in the crowd, or to the fact that the crowd was completely unarmed, Dyer ordered his troops to open fire. The only exit was blocked. People panicked. There was a stampede. Bullets struck unsuspecting targets. Terrified screams mingled with agonised groans. Bodies of the dead and wounded began to pile up. In ten minutes, 1,650 rounds were fired.

'The government says that four hundred people have died. But in reality, more than two thousand fell to their bullets,' one of the young men was saying.

'Aerial bombs are being dropped on farmers working in the fields. Indians are made to crawl through the streets of Amritsar. Such oppression and injustice, from a so-called civilised nation?'

'Revenge! Revenge! Down with the oppressors! Inquilab zindabad!' all the members cried out in unison. The blood in their veins was boiling. Holding their palms over burning lamps, they shouted 'Inquilab zindabad!' as the room was filled with the smell of burning flesh.

Just then the sound of loud moaning was heard.

'It's our Dr Bhattacharya inside. He looks after the bomb production unit. Two days ago, he was testing a bomb on the banks of Hooghly when it exploded in his hands,' Suresh Bannerji told Subhas and his friends.

They went into the darkened room. In the flickering light of a lamp, they saw a strong, well-built youth lying on a cot, suffering excruciating pain. A young lady was looking after him. Everyone addressed her as Mai. Dr Bhattacharya pleaded with her, 'Anjali, give me some opium, let me die in peace, I cannot bear it any longer!'

'You will get better, just be brave. You have so much more to do for our beloved country, so many more battles to fight,' Mai said, reassuring gently.

A few minutes later, Subhas, Hemanta and Bholanath headed towards Victoria Memorial. Suddenly Hemanta burst out, 'Do you realise, Subhas, that you are going to the land of monsters like Dyer?'

'Really, Hemanta, now I understand why Gandhiji has been referring to British rule as a "diabolical government". Men like Dyer should be squeezed out like lemons.'

That night, Subhas made up his mind. 'I don't wish to have even a glimpse of that cruel country.' The Calcutta police were aware of Subhas's past record. He was fairly confident they would never issue him a passport. And on that one hope, he rested.

The following evening, Sarat Bose came up to Subhas and said, 'Raja, forgive me, I am going to disappoint you.'

'How, Mej-da?'

'Your passport has come. You will have to leave for England. Along with the ICS, try for a degree from Cambridge as well. Our Satish-da is also studying to be a barrister there. You will gain much from his guidance.'

Subhas just about managed to hold himself back. 'Okay, Mej-da,' he muttered. 'It will give me an opportunity to find out what it is about that tiny island that has allowed it to hold sway over a huge subcontinent like ours for two centuries. Let me beard the lion in its lair.'

The day of departure dawned. *S.S. Calcutta* was set to sail from the Kidderpore docks at 6 a.m. The city was still asleep. As they sped past Kalighat, Subhas asked Amin, the driver, to stop. Some devotees, shivering in their wet clothes, were offering baskets of flowers to Goddess Kali. His sister-in-law Bibhabati bought some flowers and kumkum. Subhas stared intently at the goddess's fearsome face – her large, bloodshot eyes, her outstretched tongue dripping blood, and the garland of serpents and skulls round her neck.

He resolved, 'Ma, I apply the sacred ash on my forehead and swear that like the great Shiva, I will bear the burden of my beloved, suffering, enslaved motherland on my shoulders. I will also perform the cosmic dance of tandava across the world for the liberation of my motherland. For that, I need your help, Ma. Bless me, and let that drum resound incessantly to remind me of the need to release my motherland from the alien yoke.'

When Subhas reached the harbour, Hemanta and a dozen others from the Vivekananda Mandal were waiting for him. Hemanta looked quite forlorn. Subhas took his parents' blessings. That morning the newspaper carried a brief report about a raid on their building in Chowringhee. The police had found some explosives. No one knew what had happened to Dr Bhattacharya and Mai. Jankinath Bose was relieved that even under these circumstances, Subhas had not turned back, and was ready to leave the shores of Calcutta. But Hemanta, standing amidst his friends, was a picture of abject despair.

The ship sounded its horn. Subhas hastened towards the gangway and climbed aboard. Hemanta watched as the ship slowly moved away. No one knew what lay buried in the dark depths of the ocean's belly.

So far, his stay in England had been worthwhile. The student community there was not under the shadow of threat as in Calcutta. The police did not view every individual as a potential revolutionary. Here Subhas had access to fascinating books. The youth of Europe had plenty of time to enjoy life. But for Subhas, preparing for the exam was a priority. If, in addition, he could quench his insatiable thirst for knowledge in as short a time as possible, so much the better. There was a dogged determination in him. His companions, Khitish Chattopadhyay, Dilip Kumar Roy and C.C. Desai continued to be amazed by his efforts.

One day during the holidays, a friend had called Subhas and said, 'Read the *Morning Post* tomorrow.' As he lay in bed that night, he wondered what the newspaper would carry. Certainly not the ICS result. He had not had enough time to prepare to expect success.

The early morning breeze stirred Subhas awake. The newspaper boy was calling out at the top of his voice. Subhas hurried downstairs and picked up the *Post*. The ICS results had been announced. His eyes ran down the column. He was ranked fourth in the merit list. He set off for Cambridge immediately. When he reached home, he found the room filled with bouquets. Satish Bose's joy was indescribable. Dilip yelled 'bravo' and hugging him, twirled around the room.

Satish had already sent their father a telegram. Khitish, C.C. Desai, Sukhtankar and others arrived soon after to congratulate him. Though he had scored the highest marks in English Composition, Subhas had lost marks in Sanskrit due to his own carelessness. But this was compensated by his performance in all the other subjects. Subhas's friends began to excitedly discuss the bright future that awaited him. From district collector to commissioner to secretary, he would easily go up the bureaucratic hierarchy and even become the chief secretary of a province one day. There was no turning back now. The telegram must have reached Elgin Road and celebrations must have begun. All of Bhowanipore must have gathered to congratulate his Mej-da.

When Subhas went to bed that night, he felt a great satisfaction. But soon a knot began forming in his stomach. All day he had ignored the little voice that had been whispering to him. Now he had to acknowledge it. Was it his conscience reminding him that he had lost himself in a world of success? Was passing the ICS exam such a great achievement? Was it his ultimate goal? Was all this enough for his soul? Hemanta's depressed face floated in front of his eyes again and again. The voice seemed to say, 'You have lost your way, traveller!'

Subhas sat up and gulped down several glasses of water. He was drenched in sweat. In the shadowy darkness, he looked down at his feet. These feet that had wandered around tirelessly in search of a guru, bled and blistered in the service of the starving, cholera-stricken poor – where were they dragging him now? His feet seemed to weigh him down, as if they were shackled by some strange burden. Suddenly he wondered, what had happened to the idealism that had kept him awake night after night. The anguished cry of his beloved motherland. She was silent now, her head bowed in shame, clutching the chains at her feet. Subhas shot out of bed. 'No! I can never ever do this. It is impossible! I will not sacrifice my life's purpose and ideals at the altar of the British government,' he said aloud.

His loud voice woke Dilip up. 'What's the matter, Subhas? Are you ill?' he asked anxiously.

'I don't wish to serve the British,' Subhas declared.

Dilip was taken aback. 'Are you all right? Why are you bent on kicking aside the ladder to heaven and treading the path of a pauper?'

'Your heaven is my hell!' Subhas said, his voice hard with a new resolve.

Satish Bose overheard this exchange. He walked in. Subhas's face sent a chill down his spine. He said, 'It is my duty to break the fetters around my motherland's ankles. I don't want to be trapped in the service of the same government that put the chains on her feet.'

Every day, letters from friends in Calcutta arrived in the post. Many were from fathers of prospective brides. They were all proud of his success. But Subhas's mind was in turmoil. A part of him said, 'You might be happy if you reject a government job, but what about your family?' Subhas, though, felt prepared for a life of deprivation and insecurity in the service of his people. The practical, materialistic world would think his decision foolish, but what of that.

'Subhas, you must get a hold on yourself,' Khitish told him.

'Why should I? To be a part of this system is a living death. This is an administration that sides with the devil. It has sown poison seeds among Hindus and Muslims who have lived amicably since the times of Sher Shah and Akbar; it has gorged on our golden land,' Subhas roared. 'The real problem is how to convince my parents. My brother showers love on me and Boudi indulges me like a younger brother. How can I hack the silken ties of their emotions with the cruel axe of duty? I must respect their feelings, I need their consent. After all, they have really stretched their resources for my education and this trip to England.'

Oh, the burden of obligation to his family! The weight of their affection! He started writing a letter to his father, but Dilip stopped him.

'How are you going to face your family, Subhas? All your brothers are well-placed engineers, judges, doctors, lawyers. Will any of them take kindly to your decision?'

'I can't help it. But I am sure of one thing. Even if everyone turns against me, my Mej-da will stand by me. And Boudi too,' Subhas replied confidently.

'What about your marriage?'

'I will remain unmarried. The freedom of my country is more important than that.'

Subhas returned to his letter. He wrote another letter to Chittaranjan Das about his decision to resign from the ICS, and that he was eager to offer himself for national service under his guidance. Chittaranjan Das, the stellar lawyer, by now called 'Deshbandhu', was actively involved in the freedom struggle.

Subhas's decision stunned all the Indian students. Khitish and Dilip were grim-faced. They were preparing for the ICS exam in earnest. Khitish was already engaged to be married to the granddaughter of the first ICS in the British administration, Satyendranath Tagore.

Soon, Subhas received a telegram from Janki Babu. 'Think a thousand times before throwing it all away,' it admonished. A letter from Sarat babu followed. Dilip was proved right. No one in the Bose family was in favour of his decision. Sarat Bose too was furious. Subhas's news had added to their anxiety about their younger daughter, Salulbala, who was in hospital, fighting for her life. It was too much for them to bear.

In a sense, Subhas was trapped. No one, not even Sarat Bose, had backed him. There was no response from Chittaranjan Babu either. If he had to continue studying he would have to sign the contract for the civil service. Finally, his dilemma was resolved. He heard back from Chittaranjan Das. 'Our country urgently needs self-sacrificing patriots, willing to serve the people, like you. There is plenty to be done. I need strong arms to take on all this work. Come, Subhas! Come soon.'

'Why don't you do as Baba says,' suggested Satish Bose. 'Take up the service, try it for a while and then quit if you still wish to.'

'No, Dada, slavery is slavery, be it for two days or two years. Swamiji exhorted us to pledge that we would not remain enslaved. Das Babu threw a flourishing legal practice to the winds. I am single. I have no responsibility. So why should I worry about the consequences?'

Dilip pitched in. 'So, none of your family understands anything. You are the only wise one, is it? This won't do, Subhas, I'm telling you.'

It was the night of reckoning. The contract had to be signed the following day. What kind of future did he want? A lifetime of 'Yes, sir,' and trotting obediently after the annual promotion like a cart-horse led forward by a fistful of grass? Wearing blinkers and earplugs, to keep on course? Acknowledge some nincompoop as a boss, just because he happened to be one rung above? Or one who merely warmed the chair after having carried around a spittoon for his superiors for years? No, you don't need that kind of security. Kick it away. Insecurity is the true security. Your country beckons you. Do you want to ignore that and become a rusty cog in a corroded British system?

Thoughts of his mother jostled in Subhas's mind. Baba might, on the off-chance, reconcile with his decision. But Ma, daughter of the renowned Dutt family of Hatola, would never be able to accept it. She had made so many plans and was all set to get herself a daughter-in-law.

A restless night of tossing and turning finally ended. While at Subhas breakfast, he received his mother's letter. Reluctantly, he opened it. As he quickly ran his eyes over it, tremors coursed through his body. 'My child, the lamps of my eyes have burnt for nights worrying about your welfare. My dreams for you were those of an ordinary mother's. But the mother you are setting out to serve today is a far greater one. Don't worry about what others will say. Go forward on your chosen path. You are entering Gandhiji's arena. I am not sad about it; in fact, I feel proud. My son, my beloved golden boy is facing the challenge of his life. My blessings are with you.'

Subhas read and reread that letter, and each time, he exulted. Suddenly, it was a clear day – no storm clouds, no haze.

He wrote out his resignation. He was free – no more yokes or harnesses.

The ship was to dock in a few minutes. Subhas, Dilip and Khitish stood gazing at the vast ocean. He wondered who would lend him some money for the return journey. Before he could ask, Dilip came forward and made all the arrangements. Thumping him on the back, Subhas said to him, 'Dilip, I stood fourth in the ICS. Study hard. Next year you must come first.'

Dilip laughed. 'Why should I sell my soul. Music is my passion, and I am off to Germany to study it. But never mind about me. Ask what happened to Khitish. He has also decided not to take the exam.'

Subhas was astonished.

'I have no desire to disembowel myself with a golden sword. I will study anthropology. No civil service for me.'

It was time to board. Dilip smiled and bid farewell. 'Subhas,' he said, 'will you please try and curb your natural instinct to drag people towards yourself? That way at least some families will remain safe.'

All three friends burst out laughing.

Subhas watched his friends on the shore. His ship was on course now.

Three

'Subhas, Gandhiji is in Bombay. Do meet him before you go to Calcutta,' Rabindranath Tagore had advised Subhas, and Subhas had not forgotten. Through coconut groves and sandbars, his tonga clip-clopped to Mani Bhavan.

He was informed that Gandhiji was busy spinning cotton with his disciples in the first-floor hall of the school next to Mani Bhavan. Mahadev Desai, Gandhiji's secretary, sent a message to him, and in a short while, Subhas was summoned upstairs.

When he reached the first floor, he noticed Gandhiji seated in the middle of the room, on a rough, hand-woven mat. On either side of him, were approximately fifteen disciples and as many charkhas turning in unison. Subhas's tall figure, in stylish western garb, caught Gandhiji's eye. 'Come in, come in!' Gandhiji welcomed him. Subhas was a little flustered as he took off his shoes and left them by the door. He crossed over to where Gandhiji was and sat down. Quickly he glanced around; all the occupants of the room were clad in coarse khadi or in pathaan-pyjamas and pagdis. Subhas, in his fancy western clothes, felt out of place.

He stared at Gandhiji. The man in the photographs and the one in real life – what a contrast! He had crossed fifty a long while ago, but his brown eyes gleamed as they indulgently observed Subhas from behind steel-rimmed spectacles. Gandhiji was aware that a young Bengali had given up a coveted ICS post, and was returning to India to serve his motherland. Hence, he felt pride and affection for the young man in front of him. Subhas had met many eminent intellectuals in Europe, but he was struck by Gandhiji's personality.

Gandhiji's appearance was that of a simple peasant. He wore only a dhoti and his bare upper body revealed a sharp ribcage. His face was gaunt, with its sharp cheekbones and hollow cheeks, and eyes that were remarkably calm. A large nose with its fleshy wide nostrils folded over the upper lip, while the lower lip jutted forward. Several teeth were missing, having fallen out one by one. And from either side of his unevenly shaved head – it seemed as if he had done it himself – stood out two enormous ears. Years of hardship, his journey from South Africa to India, his frequent incarceration in different prisons, hard labour and confinement had taken their toll on Gandhiji.

Gandhiji smiled fondly. 'Such a tough exam and you passed it with distinction. I congratulate you for it.'

'I got out of that bondage long ago.'

Once again Gandhiji smiled. A hundred questions milled around in Subhas's mind. He wanted to discuss them all at length with Gandhiji. Outside, a delegation of workers from the Northern Frontier Province were waiting impatiently to see him. 'Have you had anything to drink since coming here?' Gandhiji asked.

'No, nothing.'

One of his disciples brought a glass of lime juice and after one sip, Subhas learnt the difference between lemon and neem, or bitter lemon as it is often called. Noticing the grimace on Subhas's face, Gandhiji looked at Kasturba. She quickly went downstairs and a moment later was back with a glass of buttermilk. The buttermilk too was typical ashram fare.

Gandhiji looked at Subhas. 'You seem to be full of questions. I also want to get to know you. You aren't leaving for Calcutta today, are you?'

'No.'

'Then stay for a couple of days. Either here or in a hotel, it's up to you.'

Subhas was given a room – a bare ashram room. Hungry for a meeting with Gandhiji, he had forgotten all about lunch. Now half the day was gone. When Gandhiji was there, Mani Bhavan followed a strict regimen. Mealtimes were fixed, and everyone was expected to eat together. Tobacco, tea, coffee or other addictions were not allowed. Subhas was ravenous. He dumped his cases in the room and went out.

In the next lane was an Irani restaurant. Subhas attacked the strong tea and biscuits. Just then, he saw two of Gandhiji's followers, clad only in flimsy dhotis, staring at him with big eyes. How could he go to an Irani restaurant when he was here to see Gandhiji!

There was a continuous stream of visitors at Mani Bhavan – people of different faiths and from different regions – Parsis, Pathans, Muslims, Madrasis and Bengalis were among them. Barely two decades ago, Gandhiji was referred to contemptuously as 'the barrister without a brief'. Today, the entire nation's political activity was centred around this same man! Later that evening, a very important person came to Mani Bhavan accompanied by a dozen others. He was about the same age as Gandhiji, with a flowing white beard, aquiline nose and piercing eyes.

Subhas felt he had seen this patrician face somewhere. When he learnt that it was Vithalbhai Patel, Subhas was overjoyed. Vithalbhai had played the lion's role in the Kheda peasants' agitation in Gujarat and led Gandhiji through all the remote villages in 1918.

The goats tethered outside were making a huge racket. Gandhiji loved to drink goat's fresh milk. Mahadev Desai took great pleasure in personally looking after the goats. As the evening wore on, the crowds at Mani Bhavan increased. There was always a community prayer in the evening when Gandhiji was in residence, and large numbers of his followers, men and women, freedom fighters, came all the way from Byculla, Dadar, Worli to participate in it.

Dinner was still a long time away. Should he slip out and go to the Irani restaurant, wondered Subhas. But just as he was going into the lane, one of the ashramites stopped him. 'Ba has sent for you,' he said.

Kasturba was in the kitchen. Subhas greeted her. She replied, 'You will not go to the Irani hotel again.'

Subhas was taken aback. 'I have made some tea for you,' she continued. 'Your poor stomach is not used to this. But what could I do? We observe strict discipline here.' Subhas was amused by her words. Sipping the hot tea, he said, 'Excuse me, everyone including Gandhiji calls you Ba. But can I call you Ma?'

'Of course!' Kasturba smiled. 'Isn't Ma so much better than Ba?'

As soon as Gandhiji sent for her, Kasturba ran to the prayer hall. He managed very well without her, yet he could not do without her by his side. Gandhiji was married at thirteen, and the virtually illiterate Kasturba had become an indispensable part of his life.

After 'Raghupati Raghava' and two other bhajans, Gandhiji read out a chapter from the Ramayana about Ram's truthfulness. When the prayer meeting ended, Gandhiji introduced Subhas to Vithalbhai.

As he lay in bed that night, Subhas's mind went over Gandhiji's whole life. Again and again, his strong, smiling face floated before his eyes. The British government considered him a Bolshevik agent. Subhas had encountered young men in Cambridge and London, at restaurants and musical soirees, cracking jokes about his precariously tied loincloth. But Rabindranath had defended him, dispelled his prejudice by telling Subhas, 'He has identified with his country so completely that every Indian has become a part of his own flesh and bones.'

Subhas woke up early the next morning. He wanted to join Gandhiji on his morning perambulations. Gandhiji was already walking, no, running, amidst the coconut groves along the seashore. Young Subhas found it difficult to keep pace with his long, even strides. His admiration for Gandhiji crystallised into a kind of reverence. Vithalbhai had also joined them.

When Subhas asked Gandhiji what the next step would be, he said, 'What the common people of India want, what they can afford and what they can digest, will decide the next step,' Gandhiji replied. 'That is why we have kept the membership fee to the Congress only four annas. Even the sand from the humble squirrel's fur was used to build the bridge for Sri Ram. So our oppressed and downtrodden poor, too, must be gathered under the Congress flag.'

'But how can the British government be brought to submission through mere non-payment of taxes, non-cooperation and boycott?' asked Subhas.

Vithalbhai was surprised at this question, but then he smiled and turned to Gandhiji. Gandhiji too was impressed by the young man's intrepidity. 'Our permanent agenda is to boycott all foreign goods and opt for swadeshi. We are confident that our plans will succeed. The next step aims at civil disobedience and then we will court arrest.'

'But what will that achieve? How will it put pressure on the merchants of Lancashire and consequently on the British Parliament?'

'What do you mean by "pressure"?' Gandhiji asked sharply.

'Unless you show them the power of the fist, will the British fall in line?'

Gandhiji looked at Subhas, puzzled. 'Bringing any kind of pressure on anyone does not fall into my plan of action.'

'Then how do you propose to get swaraj in one year as you have declared?'

Both Gandhiji and Vithalbhai burst out laughing. Gandhiji raised the watch tied to his waistband and glanced at it. It was a little later than usual.

In the ashram or wherever he stayed, Gandhiji forbade the use of hot water. Subhas could not bathe unless the water was steaming hot. He asked one of the disciples for hot water. All present looked horrified at the request. They denied the demand considering it unethical. Finally, the matter was taken up with Ba, and she immediately provided Subhas with two buckets of hot water. All the inmates of the ashram were most intrigued by this burly, overbearing fellow who had dared to break the code of conduct. After a satisfying bath and a hot cup of tea, Subhas felt much better. Kasturba hastily picked up the empty cup and hid it in the next room. Just then Gandhiji appeared. 'Ba, have you given Subhas tea?' he asked.

'Umm, yes ...'

'If you've done it once, you can do it again. A habit acquired abroad. Besides, young Bengali blood has a natural taste for sweets!'

All three of them laughed. In the afternoon, Gandhiji sat down at his spinning wheel. Though he was prepared to leave for Calcutta, Subhas still needed some of his doubts to be cleared by Gandhiji. At the end of two days' discussion, he was not convinced that Gandhiji's strategy was revolutionary. His own mind was filled with ideas of Mazzini, Garibaldi, Cavour and the Irish Revolution. Compared to them, Gandhiji's plans appeared limp and weak. Gandhiji told the dissatisfied Subhas, 'Meet Deshbandhu Chittaranjan Das in Calcutta. When you have such a towering personality in your city, why do you need my guidance?'

Gandhiji, accompanied by Kasturba, walked down the stairs to see Subhas off. Everyone was surprised to see this. Subhas bent down and touched the feet of both Gandhiji and Kasturba. Then he said to Gandhiji, 'You have of late referred to the British government as diabolical. What do the Jallianwala Bagh tragedy and the subsequent glorification of Dyer by the British people tell you? Unless it is given one violent blow, this old giant of British Imperialism will not stir.'

Gandhiji only smiled. Subhas felt terribly restless. He'd met the Mahatma, but somehow their chords had not matched. As a person, he could imagine Gandhiji's stature as monumental. But the strategy he had adopted against the British was tenuous to Subhas's mind.

When his tonga had gone quite a distance, Gandhiji told Kasturba, 'Ba, I found that boy very promising. But why is he so impatient?'

'Your honour, days will pass, the wheels of time will turn, this momentary debate will lapse into history, but the ordinary criminal standing in the dock today will be lauded as the bard of freedom, the voice of nationhood, and a friend of humanity by future generations.'

The person being referred to was Aurobindo Ghosh, who had been accused of treason. Practically every household in Bengal had contributed towards the fee to save him. The lawyer making this impassioned argument had spent ten whole months preparing his defence. Even after the people's donations ran out, he continued defending the case. His personal resources had diminished. He sold his beautiful horse carriage, then the horse. He had staked his life on this case and for nine whole days he continued his argument. At one point, the judge, the jury and the accused were worried that he might collapse in the courtroom.

At last, Aurobindo was acquitted. And that one case earned Chittaranjan Das the reputation of being one of the greatest lawyers in the country. Today, the same Chittaranjan Das was the true voice of freedom and nationalism in Bengal. Having heard all this, Subhas could not wait to meet him.

The train steamed into Howrah station. Subhas looked out of the window and smiled as he heard loud yells of 'Ranga kaka babu ...' It was his young nieces and nephews calling their favourite uncle by his pet name. The entire Bose family was there. It was not an ICS officer in a smart suit that stepped out of the train, but a simple young man in Indian attire. Bibha boudi was the first to greet him with a spoonful of misti. Subhas was surrounded by a happy gathering of family, friends and well-wishers. His eyes fell on his mother. Subhas bent down to take her blessings. Behind them all stood Jankinath. Gone was his strong, muscular body. In its place was an emaciated, tired-looking figure. Still, he was smiling, and looked serene, even if a little lost. 'Baba!' exclaimed Subhas, as he embraced him. It was too public a place to display deep emotion. Yet, there was no stopping their tears.

Two cars headed towards Bhowanipore. Subhas was seated between his mother and father in the back, while Sarat Bose, his Mej-da, sat beside the driver. Janki Babu clasped Subhas's hand tightly. As they crossed the bridge over the Hooghly, Subhas asked Sarat Bose, 'What is Chittaranjan Das doing these days?'

'A few months ago, a Congress session was held at Nagpur. There, in Gandhiji's presence, Chittaranjan renounced his lucrative practice of fifty thousand a month, and donated all his personal wealth to the nation. On hearing this announcement, someone from the audience shouted, "Waah, Deshbandhu, friend of the nation!" Ever since, he has been addressed as Deshbandhu.'

Subhas instructed the driver to turn the car towards Moosa Street. At the next intersection, he got down. 'Where are you going?' asked Sarat Babu, puzzled.

'To Deshbandhu's house.'

'Son, you've just arrived, you can go later,' his mother said.

'I'll be back in a minute, Ma,' replied Subhas.

The two cars drove off with their dejected occupants. The little ones were distinctly annoyed with their Ranga kaka. Subhas faltered momentarily, but then he followed his feet to the guru he had been seeking for so long. He paused outside Deshbandhu's stately mansion, and stared at its grand arches and elegant marble pillars. Hesitantly, he asked a worker, 'Is Deshbandhu at home?'

'No. He is away on tour.'

Subhas's shoulders drooped. Just then someone called out from inside, 'Who's that? Is it Subhas?' The voice was familiar. Subhas saw a wiry, khadi-clad youth rush down from the floor above. 'Hemanta!'

Hemanta stopped Subhas right there and went into the kitchen. An honourable young woman came down the stairs. She greeted Subhas with a polite namaskar. Hemanta introduced her as Shrimati Basanti Das. Immediately Subhas bowed down in a respect. On her face, he saw a mixture of surprise and affection. 'When did you arrive?' she asked.

'Today, from Bombay. I came straight here from Howrah.'

'You write very interesting letters. My husband often reads them out to me. He talks of you very often,' she said and then went back into the kitchen.

Hemanta cried, 'Did you see that, Subhas? Deshbandhu has had no peace of mind for the last three years. The Congress appointed a committee to inquire into the Jallianwala Bagh massacre. He has had to travel so much for that. He has borne all the committee's expenses of nearly fifty thousand rupees. This lady who just greeted you, do you know which family she comes from?'

Subhas shook his head. 'She is the daughter of the fabulously wealthy Diwan Badrinath, owner of the famed Abhaypuri Estate of Assam. They have acres of tea gardens and splendid mansions in Calcutta that would put royal palaces to shame. But now that her husband has decided to live in penury, she has stood beside him like a rock. The blisters and scars on her hands tell the tale – they have no cook!'

Hemanta, now a permanent fixture in Deshbandhu's home, took Subhas up to his little room and told him all about Deshbandhu. Chittaranjan Das came from a small village in East Bengal called Vikrampur. His father, Bhuvan Mohan, was a successful lawyer at the Calcutta High Court. The principled Bhuvan Babu, brought up in the Brahmo Samaj tradition, had stood surety for some good man who eventually disappeared without paying back the thirty thousand he had borrowed. As a result, a year before his marriage, Chittaranjan Babu and his father had to declare bankruptcy. With his father's retirement, the burden of the large family fell on Chittaranjan Babu's shoulders. But he toiled with dogged determination day and night. He staked his name, fame and fortune to defend Aurobindo Ghosh, accused in the Alipore conspiracy case. And that case brought him nationwide recognition as an expert criminal lawyer.

When the infamous Rowlatt Act was passed in the Legislative Assembly, Das became a fiery new entrant on the political horizon. He joined the fray as a rebel. Though he was past fifty now, his friends were all in their thirties. Very soon he developed a knack for identifying potential political workers. There were hordes of young men in Assam waiting to respond to his call.

Before they knew it, the street lamps were lit. A car horn was heard, someone entered the house. It was Deshbandhu. After a whole day's journey, he was exhausted. Subhas took one look at him and a shiver ran through him. How frail he was! What must have gripped him but patriotism, he thought.

Slowly, Das climbed the stairs. Taking his shawl from him, Basanti Devi smiled and said, 'Your disciple has arrived from England.' Chittaranjan Babu's eyes lit up. He looked at Subhas with surprise and pleasure. Subhas rushed forward and touched his feet. Das looked at Subhas long and hard. He was a sturdy young man of twenty-four, with a fair, flat, round face, high forehead and darkish brown eyes that glinted from behind gold-rimmed glasses. They had an enigmatic expression in them. For a moment he wondered, is this Subhas or the mysterious Sabyasachi from Sarat Chandra Chatterjee's novel *Pather Dabi*.

'I have come to you with whatever little experience one can accumulate in one's youth,' Subhas confessed.

'Now, what is all this, Subhas?' Deshbandhu laughed, and turning to Basanti Devi, he said, 'He also gets emotional like me, see!'

Basanti Devi served food. Sitting down to the meal were her husband, their children, Subhas and Hemanta. Chittaranjan Babu picked up the sandesh from his own plate and put it on Subhas's. Then he asked rather sharply, 'Do you really believe our Congress is so ineffectual, Subhas?'

'What?' Subhas was confused.

'What was all that you had written in your letter? "The Congress has no well-defined plan for the upliftment of adivasis, tribals and other poor. Nor is there a policy regarding laws for factory workers. Keeping the mantra of freedom as its basis, the Congress must immediately set about preparing a constitution."'

Subhas was embarrassed. Deshbandhu continued, 'Subhas, you haven't even set foot in the Congress and you already want to measure its height. But I am proud of you. The organisation needs fresh new streams feeding into it, only then will its waters remain clear. One should be prepared to rebel in the cause of truth, if necessary. One must not allow great people to intimidate oneself.'

'Why are you saying all this to me?' Subhas asked, somewhat perplexed.

'Study the history of any struggle in the world, Subhas, and you will find that those leaders who were the most progressive in the beginning will become the most conservative in the last days of their life.'

'And why is that?'

'Because time has slipped out of their grasp.'

On the way home, Subhas felt elated. At last, he had found the guru he had been looking for. It was past midnight when he entered home. When he saw Subhas, Jankinath Bose said, 'Your mother and I feel blessed to have a son like you – a son with the courage and conviction to give up a life of comfort and ease, and plunge into the service of the nation. Forget whatever I said to you before this – it was the concern of any father for the welfare of his son. From now on, we shall nurture you as an ascetic guru-bandhu.'

As he boarded the third-class compartment of the train at Howrah Station, Gandhiji said to Chittaranjan Das, 'I am entrusting the responsibility of the struggle to you, Deshbandhu, so I have no reason to worry about Bengal at all.' The people of Bengal too had accorded Gandhiji the respect due to him. Chittaranjan Babu had spared no pains to make sure that the work of the Congress and Gandhiji continued without any impediment. And an evidence of his hard work was the huge bonfire of foreign textiles at the Hazari Park Maidan. Even Gandhiji had not seen anything like it before.

That day, a very important meeting of the youth leaders of Bengal was being held in his house. Barrister Kiran Shankar Roy, Hemanta Kumar Sarkar, Savitri Prasanna Chattopadhyay and the leader of the railway employees from East Bengal, Barrister Jatindra Mohan Sengupta, were some of the prominent people attending. Also present were young revolutionaries like Gopinath Saha and Jatin Das.

The Prince of Wales had come on a visit to India, supposedly to thank the people for the assistance they had rendered to England during the World War. On 17 November 1921, he was received with much fanfare at the specially constructed Gateway of India in Bombay. Gandhiji called for a nationwide strike.

Clashes between those who had gone to attend the reception for the Prince and the protesters led to widespread violence. But in Calcutta, the strike had met with stupendous success. Das's two disciples, Subhas and Barrister Sengupta, ensured a total Calcutta bandh.

Deshbandhu's health had suffered due to continuous travelling. But his willpower kept him going. The Prince was due to visit Calcutta on 24 December. He wanted to muster a huge aggressive mass movement before that. So he sent groups of swayamsevaks out into the streets. Boycott and picketing began. But they had little impact. Finally, he selected his son, Bhongal, to lead the first group of protesters. The British administration arrested Bhongal. Deshbandhu was desperately looking for some method by which the struggle would enter every household and cause a stir in every field of human life. His eyes flashed as he spoke, his hand on his heart. 'Compatriots, in this struggle not just my son but even my wife, Basanti Devi, will participate. She too will break the law.'

Kiran Shankar and Subhas were speechless at this announcement. Women in the struggle? Chittaranjan Das's family taking to the streets? Such a sight had never been seen in all of Bengal. The atmosphere at the meeting became grim. Gopinath and Jatin Das spontaneously declared, 'No! We will not allow such a thing to happen.' Subhas had never raised his voice in front of his revered leader. But now, angrily he turned to Basanti Devi, 'Ma, how do you feel about this?'

'Subhas, I may perhaps go against my husband's wishes, but how can I defy my beloved leader's command?' Basanti Devi's reply left everyone dumbstruck. In a patriarchal society, where a woman did not cross the threshold of her home and was rarely seen inside a school, whose world revolved around hearth and children, who considered travelling by train a sin, and like a helpless creeper entwined herself around the man – that woman was now to participate in the struggle ...?

'Deshbandhu, as long as there is one man alive in this city, our women will not be allowed on the street,' Kiran Shankar said firmly.

'It makes not a whit of difference to my decision,' Deshbandhu replied equally firmly. He felt a sudden rush of strength in his veins. Dismissing the protests of his followers, he continued, 'I believe that not only my wife, but my two daughters should also sacrifice themselves for the nation. Since the older one is married, I have no control over her. What is my younger one, Prajakta, going to do?'

The slender young girl with bright eloquent eyes seemed to be inspired by her father's question. 'Baba, you have given me every comfort till now. I will accompany you in your banishment. I will shout anti-British slogans and call for a strike in front of Writers' Building.'

'Well done, my girl! You are indeed a very brave girl.'

Subhas said to Deshbandhu, 'It seems you have gone completely mad. Have you forgotten that Prajakta is engaged to be married? Why should she choose a locked room over a new home? Patriotism has made you blind, Deshbandhu!'

'How can you forget the sword-wielding Jhansiwali? Women must become a part of the national movement. Only then will our struggle gather force.' Deshbandhu's voice rose as he spoke.

'Yes, Deshbandhu, women will join the struggle, but from our families, not yours,' all the workers said in unison.

'Don't be foolish. My family will have the prerogative of being the first to sacrifice themselves in a people's movement. They will lead the march. We will tread the path of fire, like the family of a naked hermit striding towards holy Kashi.'

The next day Basanti Devi and Deshbandhu's sister, Urmila Devi, took part in the protest rally. Someone saw Basanti Devi and Urmila Devi being driven away in a police van. The news spread quickly. People rushed forth to join the demonstrations. Hordes marched towards the police station. As the two women alighted from the van, the policeman saluted them, as if a superior officer had arrived. The constables began to murmur among themselves, 'We will also be a part of the freedom movement; we will work for the Congress!' As the local policemen revolted, the officers were in a quandary. The crowds outside the police station swelled as the sun began to set. 'Basanti Devi ko chhod do!' they yelled. Writers' Building feared some untoward incident might occur. The same night, several prominent businessmen and other elite of Calcutta had been invited to a banquet at Governor House. But when they heard of Basanti Devi's arrest, they boycotted the function.

The whole city was in uproar over the arrest. Deshbandhu was pleased. The doorbell rang. It was 1.30 a.m. He shivered as he went down to open the door. Basanti Devi and Urmila stood there. 'Why did you come back so soon?' he asked angrily.

'They let us go.'

'But why? You should have stayed there. I wanted complete humiliation of the government today,' Deshbandhu said irritably.

'Well, where do you expect us to go, then? They will not keep us in jail and you will not take us into the house,' retorted Basanti Devi, in feigned anger.

When the flames that engulfed Bengal showed no signs of dying down, Deshbandhu was arrested. It was almost impossible for the authorities to wade through the milling throngs outside Presidency Jail. Despite his failing health, the intrepid lion bid farewell to the public gathered outside with the words, 'Let me enter the Swaraj Ashram.'

The constable who opened the massive gates of the prison was moved. Seeing Deshbandhu's sway over the people, the deputy commissioner of police was bewildered too.

As the day of the Prince's arrival drew near, the wheels of oppression began to grind fast and furious. One by one Hemanta, Savitri Prasanna, Virendra Sasmal, Kiran Shankar and Subhas were put behind bars. It seemed the government was bent on systematically chopping off the branches of Deshbandhu's influence.

Finally, 24 December 1921 arrived. The Prince of Wales was greeted by a deafening silence. The streets were deserted; not a bird stirred. The strike was total. The news of its success was conveyed to the jail inmates by the police constable. According to Deshbandhu, this was a victory for all Bengal, and they spent the day rejoicing. That evening, Deshbandhu had an unexpected visitor – the jailor himself. Saying he had some urgent business to discuss, he took Deshbandhu away to his office.

Deshbandhu was astonished to find himself before the infamous Charles Tegart, police commissioner of Calcutta. His six-foot-six-inch frame and handlebar moustache on a ruddy, stern face made most hardened criminals break out in a sweat. Some even confessed to crimes they hadn't committed to escape his wrath.

Tegart spoke, 'Mr Das, you must accompany me to the Governor House. The Prince and his cousin Dickie Mountbatten wish to discuss something with you.'

'I am not well. Can my colleagues go instead?'

'The Prince would prefer to meet with you. Many of Calcutta's distinguished citizens will be there.'

Deshbandhu sent for Subhas and Kiran Shankar. The three held a discussion in the jailor's office. He asked Subhas, 'Did you ever hear the name Mountbatten in England?'

'Yes. Dickie Mountbatten. He was at Cambridge before us, to study military administration. He's a cousin of the Prince of Wales and accompanied him as his ADC. But what of him?'

'They want to hold urgent discussions with the Congress. Both of you go and see what they have to say.'

The viceroy, Lord Reading, had made his personal luxury railway coach available to the Prince. The sparkling white and gold coach looked like a piece of divine architecture as it sped across the tracks. People said that more money was spent on equipping it with all the amenities than on building a plane. After winning the First World War, British Imperialism was at its zenith. Therefore India, the jewel in the imperial crown, had put on this extravagant show for the Prince. Polo matches, tiger hunts, elephant rides on moonlit nights, lavish receptions and sumptuous dinners had been arranged in his honour.

There was a message that the Prince of Wales had come down with a bad cough, and so would not come down to meet the guests. The native princes were extremely worried. A royal cough amounted to a state calamity. The viceroy and the governor were busy attending to the Prince's needs. Mountbatten also appeared to be peeved that Chittaranjan Das had not heeded their summons. From what he said, it seemed that they were trying to put pressure on Gandhiji through Das Babu. Dickie felt if they could bring about a temporary halt to the demonstrations, it would be a feather in his and the Prince's cap. Gulping down his drink, Dickie said, 'Come on, let us enjoy ourselves. The king is occupied elsewhere, but his subjects are all here.'

'Mr Mountbatten, there are only subjects in India. We have no king,' Subhas made a rejoinder.

Mountbatten was surprised by Subhas's remark. 'And what did you say your name was?' he asked, although the young man had been introduced to him.

'Subhas Chandra Bose, one of Chittaranjan Das's pupils.'

Tegart intervened hastily. 'Sir, he is a very intelligent and highly qualified young man. He stood fourth in the ICS exam. But he resigned from government service.'

'Resigned? For what?' Dickie Mountbatten asked in disbelief.

'For my unfortunate country.'

'Consider yourselves fortunate to have England as your ruler. In England, we have an enlightened democracy, a legal system and an opposition party.'

'Only for the British people, isn't it?' asked Subhas.

'What do you mean?'

'As soon as he crosses the Suez Canal, the justice-loving Englishman becomes a despot. For us, there is a biased judicial system. When an

English judge sees an Indian accused, he views him with prejudiced eyes. The interpretation of the law, provisions for education, all the articles are locked up in files. Our country also wants a parliament like England's – free and independent thinking.'

'What are you saying, Mr Bose? We do have Indians on the viceroy's council, don't we?'

'Well, some of them may be competent. The rest of them are kittens at the viceroy's table. Can indigent nawabs and petty rajas of impoverished kingdoms ever be true representatives of our country?'

Mountbatten felt the heat in Subhas's words. He became wary. 'That Gandhi of yours! His strikes, fasts, the drama of demonstrations in the streets – can these ever get you freedom?'

'We will try these means for a while and bide our time. At the opportune moment, we will pinch the nose so that the mouth automatically opens.'

'This is not a threat, is it?' asked Mountbatten.

'No, it is deeply felt anguish expressing itself.'

'Anguish about what?' said Mountbatten, fixing his gaze on Subhas.

'Those who are used to trampling others cannot understand the pain of those under their boots. The moment an opportunity presents itself, we will uproot the oppressive foot and throw it away.'

Mountbatten was on full alert by now. He remembered that terrorist activity was high in Bengal. And in Subhas's words, he could smell the violence.

As Police Commissioner Tegart escorted Mountbatten to the ballroom, Mountbatten said to him, 'Mr Tegart, keep an eye on that fiery young man. He has all the makings of a hardcore terrorist. I could see the fire of rebellion flashing in his eyes.'

'Sir, we have been trailing him ever since he returned to Calcutta after resigning from the ICS. He can flap his wings, but we have our cage ready for him,' Tegart replied with pride.

Gopinath Saha came to the prison with the tiffin that Bibha boudi had given him. When he saw Subhas, he demanded, 'So what if it is Mahatmaji's doing? How can he stop a moving train? We will set Bengal on fire.'

'Calm down. I will speak to Deshbandhu.'

'We turned our backs on college only after we had been assured that Gandhiji's war against British Imperialism would end when we got freedom, but what have we got? No, Subhas babu, I am neither on your side nor on Gandhiji's.'

Subhas could say nothing to appease Gopinath. He himself was so agitated, he found nothing to say. Gopinath walked off in a rage.

Subhas went back into his cell with a grim expression. Deshbandhu was alarmed to see him like that.

'A terrible incident has taken place at Chauri Chaura in Gorakhpur district of the United Provinces,' he told Deshbandhu.

'What happened?'

'A procession consisting of some Congress and Khilafat workers was harassed by the police. The group attacked the police, who opened fire on them. The infuriated mob chased the police, set fire to the police station, and as a result, twenty-two policemen were killed.'

Deshbandhu buried his face in his hands. 'It is most unfortunate.'

'I agree. But for Gandhiji to call off the entire movement on account of one little incident that happened in a corner of the country ...!' exclaimed Subhas.

'What? A crime is committed at the North Pole and the South Pole faces the punishment? This is not right at all,' Deshbandhu said, shaking his head.

'"Freedom in one year" – he has promised. How will it be possible now? I just cannot understand Gandhiji. First, he creates huge waves. Then just when the destination is in sight, he drops anchor or changes course.' Subhas's voice was tinged with disappointment.

'Why should it happen?'

'I think a mahatma and a politician, both, dwell in Gandhiji's heart. It could be the result of the conflict within himself, don't you think?'

Deshbandhu laughed. 'Even great people have feet of clay. Don't make the mistake of forgetting that.'

The Non-cooperation Movement was withdrawn. Gopinath and Jatin Das, along with other workers, felt they had been betrayed by Gandhiji. Gandhiji's popularity took a beating. The police filed a case against him, and he was awarded a six-year jail sentence for treason.

The mantle of the Congress fell on the shoulders of Deshbandhu and Motilal Nehru. A Congress party session had been held in Gaya in December 1922, presided over by Deshbandhu. On the last day, Deshbandhu himself put forth a resolution to join the council and create problems for the British from within and without. Gandhiji's followers opposed it strongly. The issue was put to vote. It was rejected by 1948 votes to 890 votes. Deshbandhu immediately resigned from his post as president, as did Motilal Nehru from the post of secretary. Lala Lajpat Rai joined them, and it was here in Gaya that the Swaraj Party was born. Both Das and Motilal Nehru spared no efforts to popularise their party. Subhas was learning valuable lessons in politics from his guru.

Presidency Jail did not sleep. A young man was to be hanged at dawn, and even the prison walls mourned for him. The young man had already created a stir in the jailhouse. Ever since the Non-cooperation Movement had been withdrawn, Gopinath Saha had been wandering around as if unhinged. He had stopped going to the Congress office, and it was believed that he was often seen in the company of terrorists. When he was arrested, Gopinath had admitted to killing an innocent employee of Kilburn and Company in broad daylight. 'I wanted to empty my gun into Police Commissioner Tegart's chest. But his good fortune was my misfortune. My eyes deceived me. That foolish man, Day, his whiskers were just like Tegart's. He was as tall. The poor fellow paid the price.'

Subhas's car stopped outside the prison gate. As soon as he and Puran Das got out, a group of young men gathered around them. Subhas's face was creased with worry. He asked for an urgent meeting with the jailor.

'Yes, Bose Babu?'

'We must be given Gopinath's body. We must cremate him on the banks of the Ganga with our customary rituals.'

'Sorry, that will not be possible,' the jailor replied. 'We have received instructions from the police. The last rites of prisoners will be performed behind the prison walls.'

Just then the wail of a siren was heard. The jailor quickly moved towards the door. As Subhas put out his arm to stop him, he cried, 'Don't you see, Commissioner Tegart is coming here himself. Ask him whatever you want,' and hastened inside. Tegart's vehicle stopped. Heels clicked, arms shot up in salute. As he was getting out of the car, Charles Tegart spotted Subhas. Subhas saw a faint smile curl his lips and felt annoyed. He rushed up to him and said, 'Mr Tegart, let us be present at the last rites.'

'Why? Haven't you lit enough fires already?' Tegart said. 'We have already given the prisoner's brother permission. No one else will be allowed inside.'

'But ...'

'It's all over now. You can go.'

'We will not. Gopinath means something to us.'

Tegart was in no mood to listen. The prison doors creaked shut. A constable offered Subhas a chair, but he pushed it away and sat on the ground with his companions. Was it all truly over? Or was it just the beginning? Subhas was overcome. From his trembling lips came out a heartfelt cry, 'Vande ... Vande ... Vande ... Mataram!' No one could hold back their tears. The words 'Vande Mataram' had acquired a new significance.

Inside, there was hectic activity near the gallows gate. Outside, songs and poems of Bankim Chandra, Rabindranath and Nazrul Islam echoed off the prison walls and wafted away on the morning air.

Preparations for the hanging were over. Charles Tegart could not have been happier. How dare a seventeen-year-old brat taunt him that every day of his life was a bonus! He had to see the rascal hang. No one could recall a senior police officer ever attending a hanging.

Gopinath had bathed and applied sandal paste to his forehead. He looked just like a pilgrim setting out on a long journey. His eyes fell on Tegart a little distance away and he smiled. In a voice just loud enough for Tegart to hear, he said, 'You are a lucky man indeed, saheb, your fate saved you.' Then raising his voice, he declared, 'I tell you again before stepping on to the gallows, what I said in the court, saheb. Every drop of my blood will give birth to a new revolutionary, believe me!'

The sub-jailor rushed in. 'A crowd has gathered outside, sir. Members of the Swaraj Party and from the corporation. Subhas Bose is shouting, "Let us in, allow us to go in!"'

Hearing Subhas's name, Gopinath's face lit up.

Tegart's annoyance reached its peak. He growled at Gopinath, 'Tell me, who else belongs to that secret group operating in Bengal? Will you speak or shall I slough the skin off your back?'

'I am on my way, saheb, what good will it do, skinning me? All I will tell you is that as long as our wizard Subhas Chandra Bose is alive, take care of your own skins!'

As dawn broke, smoke from the pyre climbed over the high prison walls and rose into the sky. Cries of 'Vande Mataram' rent the air. It was seven o'clock. Madan Mohan, Gopinath's brother, came out carrying his brother's clothes. A lump rose in his throat when he saw Subhas. Hugging Subhas tightly, he wept. 'My brother did not get the Ganga ghat, dada!' Subhas took Gopinath's *chador* and pyjamas. He raised the mute garments to his eyes and his lips, and wept. Tegart watched the scene from the jailor's office window. 'Did you see that drama?' he asked the jailor. 'It seems the source of Calcutta's violence is that terrible man.'

As he came out and got into his car, he said to Subhas, 'I know you have instigated several terrorists to kill me. I have enough proof of it.'

'If you do, then present them in court,' Subhas replied.

'I will see what I have to do,' said Tegart, not so confidently.

'Deshbandhu, having just rid myself of one pair of chains, I have absolutely no desire to stick my neck in another noose,' declared Subhas.

A grave atmosphere enveloped Chittaranjan Bhavan. Deshbandhu's Swaraj Party had contested the elections and won. The brothers Subhas and Sarat had also been victorious. Deshbandhu had been elected unopposed from the Bhowanipore ward. He was voted the first mayor of Calcutta. He wanted to make the administration clean, transparent and people-friendly. That's why he had requested that Subhas be appointed the chief executive officer. Subhas refused him outright. 'I don't want any kind of bondage.'

Actually, Deshbandhu had several gems in his treasury. There were Birendra Nath Sasmal, Barrister Kiran Shankar, Barrister Jatindra Mohan Sengupta, novelist Sarat Chandra Chatterjee, Hemanta Kumar and Savitri Prasanna. But he was keen on Subhas. And Subhas would not relent. Basanti Devi too was worried. Explaining the importance of the task of municipal administration, Deshbandhu told Subhas, 'This will be a sort of dress rehearsal for the job we will have to do when we get independence. These municipalities should become centres for the service of the people. I need your help to accomplish that. If I have your support I will be able to keep British officials in check.'

A smile came to Subhas's lips, and Basanti Devi heaved a sigh of relief. Deshbandhu felt a load lift off his mind.

14 April 1924. Subhas stood on Chowringhee Road, gazing at the elegant, brick-red building of the Calcutta Corporation. He held so many dreams in his heart. At the same time, so many pairs of English eyes were watching him with disdain. At the entrance to the building stood a number of men – employees, cleaning staff and native clerks, waiting to welcome Subhas. Soon a new spirit pervaded the office. Work gathered momentum. Files that had lain on tables forever, suddenly sprouted feet and began moving quickly. There were many complaints regarding the roads in the city. Subhas Chandra Bose instructed the peon to fetch the chief engineer. The peon returned saying, 'He said he was busy.'

Later in the evening, he was sent for again. Then too J.C. Coates was 'busy.' One day Coates entered Subhas's room without permission, made himself comfortable on a chair and lit a cigarette. Subhas looked up from the file he was reading, and said with a smile, 'It is quite in order for you to smoke in the presence of your superiors, isn't it, Mr Coates?'

Coates was taken aback. Stubbing out the cigarette, he muttered, 'I'm sorry, sir!'

'And remember, this is an office, not the club. Kindly don't loll in your chair.'

'I am very sorry, sir,' replied Coates, shamefacedly.

The Calcutta Corporation was implementing the Swaraj Party's agenda effectively. Cottage industries got loans. Workers were given locally made khaki uniforms. Primary education was made free. A new water supply scheme was put in place for the city. Long-cherished dreams began to be realised. All this began to sting British eyes.

Writers' Building began to view the copper-red corporation building with trepidation. The bastion of the Swaraj Party became stronger day by day. One young man looked on the city with an artist's vision. People watched him grow in stature, with amazement and awe. As did the eyes that had followed him from the day he had stepped on to Howrah Station after having resigned from the ICS. Now their gaze was fixed on the municipal building night and day. They kept track of all visitors. They would retire for the night only after making sure that Subhas Chandra had actually gone to bed. Very often, Subhas stayed behind in the company of Basanti Devi till late, chatting away. He would have his meals there. If it were raining, Basanti Devi would admonish him and refer jokingly to people who stalked him: 'Go now, it's very late. How long do you want to keep those poor fellows awake?'

One day, an emaciated-looking woman came to Subhas's room.

'Do you recognise me, Subhas?' The voice of a tall thin woman in a widow's white saree trembled as she spoke.

Her voice was so familiar. He kept looking at her.

'Remember, that building on Chowringhee, Dr Bhattacharya, a bomb ...' Recognition flashed. 'Mai!' he exclaimed. 'Mai, what happened? Doctor saheb ...?'

'Shhh ...!' Mai whispered.

Subhas ordered the peon to shut the door. Mai drank some water and quietly narrated her story. 'He is alive ... sometimes in Andhra, sometimes in Delhi. He has the magic of bomb-making in his hands. That passion caused him grievous burns, but he has survived. He continues to make them.'

'Then why are you dressed like this?'

'There are young schoolchildren in the house and old parents. There's daily harassment by the police, searches, statements ... To put them off, he suggested this. He is happily making bombs, while we suffer. You are at a high post. Can't you find me some small job?'

'What will you do here, Mai?'

'I am willing to work as a sweeper.'

'You can be the mukadam and supervise the sweepers,' said Subhas, glad to be of help. He summoned the municipal officer Ramaiyya and instructed him to put Mai on the payroll.

As she was leaving the room, she said, 'Subhas, I am not the only one. Just look at all those political prisoners languishing in Andamans and Shinai. Their families also need help.'

Soon, numerous people came to meet Subhas. They were impoverished, crippled in mind and body, with frightened eyes. They were given jobs immediately. Ramaiyya could not figure out why Subhas was taken in by these sob stories and why his heart melted.

One day, the police commissioner's car pulled up outside the corporation office. As the imposing figure of Charles Tegart got out, the office went into a flap. Seeing him trespass on his territory, Subhas raised his eyebrows in surprise and said, 'Come in, Commissioner.'

'I have come for the list.'

'What list?'

'Of new employees.'

'If you had called, I would have sent it across.'

Charles Tegart looked at Subhas and recalled the words of Dickie Mountbatten: 'He is dangerous, very dangerous.'

He had just returned from a meeting with the home secretary at Delhi. The home secretary had said to him, 'Your Calcutta is a state within a state, it appears?'

'Sir?'

'You didn't understand? The state of Bengal is ruled by the Swaraj Party, and our British government functions within the state. Right?'

'Sir ...!' he stuttered.

The home secretary's voice rose sharply. 'Control Calcutta, Mr Tegart. Or else the governor will have to go to the municipal office and salute those brash native youngsters. That day doesn't seem far off either.'

Tegart had never been castigated like this. A hundred questions jostled in his mind. Why would a young man give up the ICS? Maybe it was part of an international plot. No doubt he is Das's prized pupil, but why did the mantle of chief executive officer fall on his shoulders? Perhaps the spy reports are true. The revolutionaries of the Yugantar Samiti must have compelled Das to appoint him to this post. So, to repay his debt to them, this man is on a spree handing out jobs, providing unauthorised employment to the kin of revolutionists. It is definitely a conspiracy hatched by the terrorists. There could be an uprising in Calcutta any time.

Tegart went around the office building escorted by Subhas.

'What do you think of it? It has been our endeavour to make it accessible to even the poorest of the poor,' Subhas declared.

'Forget the poor. At least the revolutionaries must feel at home here. That should serve your purpose well.'

'Subhas, you better get married now. So many young women are mad about you, and even more fathers are pining for you to say yes.'

Basanti Devi smiled in agreement with her husband. Subhas addressed her, 'No, Ma, I cannot afford to even think of marriage right now. Let's talk about something else.'

He did change the topic, but Basanti Devi's thoughts were still on the subject of his wedding. Having to deal with the parents of prospective brides was bad enough, but dealing with pressure from Subhas's mother was worse. 'Look, Basanti,' she would say, 'there are proposals from so many lovely young girls. Convince him to get married. He listens to you more than to me.' Deshbandhu interrupted her reverie. 'What are you thinking about?'

'Subhas, what else? Shyamakant Dutta's wife has sent so many messages. What a match that would be! They have an export–import business in three countries. Their girl Mohini is not only very beautiful, she is also a very talented artist.'

'So, then what happened?'

'I told them the boy is not ready yet, but the lady is adamant. She is coming here in a couple of days with her daughter.'

They finished breakfast. The guru and his pupil had to leave early on some work. Just then a car horn was heard downstairs and soon after, Hemanta came rushing up the stairs. 'Deshbandhu, a lady from a wealthy house has come in a big car; there is a young girl with her.'

Basanti Devi and Deshbandhu exchanged amused glances at Subhas's discomfiture. 'Subhas, what are you going to do now?' Deshbandhu teased.

'I'm leaving,' said Subhas hastily.

'How will you go out? That dream-girl is standing in the doorway.'

'Now that they are here, let us at least introduce the two of you,' Basanti Devi said with a smile.

'No, Ma. Don't do that. Give me your word. I will sit here very quietly, if you like.'

Before they knew it, the two women had entered the drawing room downstairs. Deshbandhu and Basanti Devi went to receive them. From where he sat, Subhas could see the mother–daughter duo clearly, but they could not see him.

Like her name, Mohini was extremely attractive. With doe-eyes, rose-petal lips, a delicately rounded chin in an oval face, and luxuriant hair hanging down her back – she was enchanting. Even her voice was musical; one would want to hear it on and on. Basanti Devi was instantly charmed.

'Our Mohini has graduated from Presidency College. She got a first class.'

'Ma, tell them I did philosophy,' Mohini prompted her mother.

Mrs Dutta suddenly became solemn. 'In addition to our export business, we also have factories in Kharagpur. Mohini is our only child. She is heir to a huge fortune. All of us think highly of Subhas.'

'I know, but he has attached wheels to his feet, literally. He's constantly on the move and has no time to settle down,' said Basanti Devi.

'My Mohini will handle all that. If you take an active interest, there will be no hurdles to this auspicious alliance.'

Making an excuse about attending to some task, Basanti Devi went upstairs. She whispered to Subhas, 'How is she?'

'Very nice.'

'I'll go down and tell them, then!'

Subhas shook his head, frowning. 'Ma, don't say anything,' he admonished her gently.

Mrs Dutta proudly opened up the portfolio of her daughter's paintings. They were as beautiful as the painter. Vast oceans, mysterious riverbanks, clouds reflected on moonlit waters, the fine Shravan drizzle – they were captivating landscapes indeed. After that, Mrs Dutta presented two framed portraits her daughter had drawn – one was of herself, the other was of Subhas's. Subhas stared at his picture.

'He has such a majestic personality and such good looks, had my portrait not captured his essence totally, I would never have forgiven my brush,' Mohini said.

Deshbandhu turned to Mohini. 'However capable Subhas may be, people like him don't make good family men. He is an enemy of the British. His life is fraught with danger, he could even face capital punishment. What is the point in wanting to nurture a burning ember in your life?'

'I will consider it a great honour to be the widow of such a fearless man, if I can have him as a husband for even a short while,' Mohini said, her eyes filling with tears.

After some moments, Mrs Dutta broached the topic. 'It will not be a problem donating a lakh or two to the Tilak fund,' she announced condescendingly. Without waiting for a response, mother and daughter stood up to leave. Mohini told Basanti Devi, 'Please give these two paintings to him. They are a gift. Let me meet him, at least through the medium of paint and canvas.'

The car drove off. Subhas, who had been sitting still all this while, stood up and stretched. Deshbandhu marched up the stairs and said in mock anger, 'Mr Subhas Chandra, your one decision has deprived the Congress party of a couple of lakhs.'

Everyone burst out laughing. Subhas had liked the portraits. Basanti Devi reminded him to take them with him. She was upset that such a good match had slipped out of their hands. She told Subhas, 'A housewife like me believes that love has as important part to play in one's life.'

'But, Ma, there is love in my life – the love of my ideals.'

'What is the point of walking ahead while leaving your destiny behind?'

'But, Ma ...'

Basanti Devi cut him short. 'I will not listen to another word, understand?' she said angrily and went off.

'You don't want to impose martial law in all of Bengal, do you? Unless you act at once and get things under control, it might be too late,' said Lord Victor-Bulmer Lytton, Governor of Bengal. Behind him, two uniformed ADCs stood at attention, more tense than usual. As soon as the law and order situation was mentioned, the chief secretary's eyes turned to Police Commissioner Tegart. 'Sir, much before Bose was appointed chief executive officer, I had filed a detailed confidential report. My recommendation was that his appointment be prevented at all costs,' Tegart submitted humbly.

'There was no way I could have possibly turned down the mayor's request under the law,' said Lord Lytton, polishing his glasses.

The meeting of a few select officers at the governor's residence went on for a long time. Lord Lytton confessed to his colleagues, 'The growing acts of terrorism in Bengal are like anthills harbouring deadly cobras. Which hole do we put our hands into first? And yet if we do nothing, we will be stung. Some solution must be found.'

'All we are asking for is permission to put handcuffs on that chief executive,' said Tegart.

'Mr Tegart, you are the police commissioner, go ahead, file a suit, lodge a complaint.'

'He leaves no evidence behind. He has given jobs to relatives of several revolutionaries. He instigated Gopinath Saha to kill me. Not only that, he and his other friends, Jatin Das and Satyaranjan Bakshi, are in constant touch with the revolutionists. The Bengal volunteers have made many senior bureaucrats their targets. The fire continues to rage.'

A sudden hush fell over the meeting. The governor looked grim. Clearing his throat, he said, 'All this while, the Muslims of India have been loyal to us. Now Chittaranjan Das has appointed Huseyn Shaheed Suhrawardy as the deputy mayor. All the Muslim youth of Calcutta are with Subhas Bose now. If this alliance grows stronger, how are we going to rule the country?' Lord Lytton took a couple of sips of water, then said in confidence, 'These days, whenever I participate in a Governor's Council meeting in Delhi, I feel a sense of panic. I am telling you today how sarcastically Viceroy Reading referred to us. He said that the gazetted officers of Bengal should surrender their posts in favour of the Swarajists and go home. And all because of one or two people.'

No one had anything to say. Lytton continued his tirade. 'Now the governors of other states are also picking on us. The governor of Bombay complained that Subhas Bose went to Pune for a students' convention. He learnt that there was a fort there from Shivaji's time, called Sinhagad. Also, that the nationalist Tilak had a house there. So he went and sat there for two hours, shedding copious tears remembering Shivaji and Tilak. Imagine the effect it must have had on those around him. The Punjab governor has sleepless nights when he hears that Subhas is visiting the Punjab.'

Again, the issue of not having enough evidence against Subhas came up. Lord Lytton was really annoyed by this. 'Oh sure, he is not guilty of anything. And yet he makes it all happen. Now take note. We make the law. We also implement it. And we interpret it too.'

'The government has to go beyond customary law.'

'Where is the viceroy these days?'

'In Shimla.'

'Get all the documents organised. We leave for Shimla in a couple of days.'

From Howrah Station, the car drove straight to the police headquarters. It was after a long time that the citizens of Calcutta were seeing the dusky figure of Deshbandhu clad in crisp white khadi.

It was Tegart's practice to make any visitor who sent in his card sit outside and sweat for a couple of hours before letting him come in. But when he saw the mayor, Chittaranjan Das's car, he did not dare put it aside. As soon as he entered the room, Das Babu asked, 'I heard you were in Shimla on vacation?'

'If you allow us to take a vacation,' Tegart replied. Ignoring that remark, Deshbandhu continued, 'Under what law did you arrest the chief executive officer of Calcutta Corporation, Subhas Chandra Bose?'

When Tegart merely rolled his eyes skywards, Barrister Sarat Bose thundered, 'Will you at least tell me what he has been accused of?'

'I don't know.'

'Have you given Subhas a chance to explain?' asked Sarat Bose.

Silence.

'Mr Commissioner, we have not come here to listen to tales from the Panchatantra,' Deshbandhu roared. 'You consider yourself protectors of the law. I hope you are aware that the two people who have come to speak to you are both barristers. Please answer our questions.'

Deshbandhu's direct attack made Tegart sit up in his chair. He had no option but to answer their questions. Calmly he proceeded to explain. 'The night before Mr Bose was arrested, an ordinance was passed.'

'An ordinance? In such haste?' Deshbandhu's mouth went dry.

'Lord Lytton took the proposal personally to the viceroy in Shimla, and issued the ordinance telegraphically from there.'

'Whatever it is, you will have to present Subhas before court.'

'That will no longer be necessary.'

'Why?'

'The ordinance was to amend that law,' said Tegart with a smile. 'The government can, at any time, arrest any individual and keep him in jail for an indefinite period. There is no need to bring him to court.'

Neither of the two barristers could speak. They just exchanged nervous glances. Twirling his moustache and narrowing his eyes, Tegart said, 'Mr Das, I feel extremely sorry. I can understand Subhas's behaviour, perhaps, but I did not expect a cultured person like you to react in this uncivil manner.'

Deshbandhu pinned Tegart with a sharp stare. 'Mr Tegart, can you place your hand on your heart and say that you have the moral right to arrest Subhas Chandra Bose? At least he is fighting for his country. People who barge into others' homes uninvited and ransack the place are usually called thieves. Mr Tegart, all of you, including the Queen of England, you are all thieves. You have absolutely no right to talk about democracy or a civilised society.'

Deshbandhu stood up. He got into the car with Sarat babu and drove to the corporation office. Referring to the latest ordinance, he advised Sarat, 'Find out the exact words of the ordinance and the evil intentions behind it. They have played a very dangerous game. I don't think Subhas will come out from behind bars very soon.'

'Deshbandhu, if you get emotional, I will lose courage too. I cannot live without my dear brother very long,' said Sarat babu.

'Old age too troubles me at such a crucial moment, Sarat!' said Das Babu ruefully.

Tension gripped the city. Seventy Swarajist workers including Subhas, Satyendra and Anil Baran had been taken into custody. News spread that Deshbandhu had returned from Shimla and was in his office. Councillors from all thirty-three wards rushed to see him. The corporation office resembled a public meeting of the Roman Forum, the shawl-draped Bengali babus looking like Roman statesmen in their togas.

Cries of 'Vande Mataram' rent the sky as large crowds waited outside Deshbandhu's office. Bengal had seen the many faces of Chittaranjan Das since the famous defence of Aurobindo Ghosh. His novels had been read. They had attended huge rallies in which he was present alongside Gandhiji. But there was something different about his demeanour that day. He was an ageing lion, tossing his mane tiredly, and attempting a roar at British Imperialism.

'Subhas Chandra's arrest is an unjust, reprehensible act. No charges, no evidence, no courage to face a trial in court. You reject an appeal for defence, you deny us an opportunity to defend him. If you consider Subhas Bose a revolutionary, I am his guru, his teacher. If he is an offender, I am ten times guiltier. Lay your hands on me if you dare. Come on, brothers, let us begin a public campaign. Fight until Subhas is released.'

Deshbandhu complained openly to Gandhiji, 'Bapuji, call for a fight. They have taken my beloved son from me!' Gandhiji issued a statement: 'Because they could not bear to witness the success of the Swaraj Party in the legislative council, the British have struck at its very roots. They have incarcerated an extremely capable young man like Subhas Chandra, completely unlawfully.'

Deshbandhu's grief was as deep as Janki Babu's. He could not sleep. He could not concentrate on anything. He said to his wife one day, 'Basanti, why did he cast his spell on us? My heart has not bled like this even for our own son.'

For some time, Subhas continued to perform his executive functions out of Presidency Jail, so he could keep in touch with the public. To prevent this the British administration decided to move him to the distant Behrampore prison. Subhas went far away and Chittaranjan Das lost heart. Finally, Basanti Devi said to him, 'Since you cannot stop thinking of him, go and meet him.' She put together a hamper of Subhas's favourite sweets – sandesh, rabdi, gulab jamun, rasgullas – and sent her husband on his way.

Behrampore Jail was located in one of the filthier, congested parts of an out-of-the-way town. Seeing Subhas in those unhygienic conditions, Deshbandhu was furious. Subhas told him, 'Baba, I had a dream.'

'About independence?'

'No, didn't you impress upon us that unless you pay the price of supreme sacrifice, you cannot hope for freedom?'

'So, what was the dream about?'

'That you were annoyed with me and were going away, far away.'

'No, son, that will never happen. Have no fear. I will scour the heavens, give up my life if necessary, but I will not let you remain behind bars for long,' Deshbandhu said, wiping his eyes. 'You know, Subhas, the shadow of age has reached my threshold. But battle drums are just beginning to be heard. I am going to leave all my weapons for you. Don't worry, son, this darkness will end. You will light up a bright new day. The russet colours of sunset are dissolving in the darkness of night. It is time for the tired birds to take their last dip in the water.'

'Don't allow a man like Subhas Chandra Bose to walk free down any street, not just of Calcutta, but anywhere in the country. In the interest of the security of the empire, it's best that he is kept locked behind bars forever. That is the only way you can guarantee the safety of the empire,' warned Lord Lytton.

Deshbandhu had toiled night and day to obtain the release of Subhas and all the political prisoners of Bengal. The administration could not understand why this old man was jeopardising his already delicate health, striving so hard. He had held innumerable meetings to demand Subhas's release. But neither the citizens nor the police would forget the rally of 31 October 1924, which was attended by over two lakh people. The fiery speeches of Gandhiji, Motilal Nehru and Chittaranjan Das still echoed in people's ears.

At a meeting of senior government officials, Charles Tegart reported that they were keeping a watch on all of Subhas's correspondence. 'But we have not come across any incriminating papers yet. However, Chittaranjan Das and Sarat Bose seem to be on very good terms with diplomats from Japan, Germany and other countries. They are often seen socialising with embassy officials at clubs and hotels. Something seems to be brewing behind the scenes.'

'He must not get out at any cost,' said Lord Lytton.

Standing instructions were given. Keep Subhas in confinement for as long as necessary. If you cannot do it under the law, change the law. Wherever he is held, ensure that the surroundings sap his very life. His arrogance, spirit and confidence should be sucked out by scorching zinc-sheeted roofs and cold, damp walls.

Deshbandhu smelt something cooking in the law department of Bengal. The new Bengal Criminal Law Amendment Act was to come up soon for discussion in the legislative assembly. On the day the ordinance was presented, Deshbandhu was down with high fever. Many people tried to dissuade him from going to the assembly. They feared for his life. 'Why are you so worried about me? I am an old and sear leaf,' Chittaranjan Das growled. 'I owe it to all those young men like Subhas who are going to create the history of this country. They are languishing in jail. I must fight this unfair law that strikes at the roots of individual liberty and freedom.'

Despite his raging fever, Das Babu entered the hall. Everyone was astonished to see his frail but resolute personality in a wheelchair. He took the platform and once more, with his profound knowledge, was able to rattle the assembly. The Swaraj Party had a number of members in the legislative assembly. But other party members, too, upheld his objections. The government bill was defeated.

Das Babu went to bed early that night. Basanti Devi heaved a sigh of relief. But the next day, newspapers told a different story. Lord Lytton had exercised his special powers and converted the inhuman ordinance into a law. Deshbandhu's fever shot up again in the afternoon.

One morning, outside the main door of 148 Russa Road, stood a mendicant-like, khadi-clad, Chittaranjan Das with Basanti Devi beside him. They each carried a small tin trunk and a bedroll. Overnight the prince had become a pauper. There was a time when even the governor's residence could not match the luxuries found in his house. Giving up all that, Chittaranjan Das had sold his imposing mansion and all its exquisite and rare articles for three lakh rupees. Then he collected some more money and set up the Chittaranjan Trust for eight lakh rupees. Dr B.C. Roy was to handle the functioning of the trust.

Crowds gathered to witness the sight. Many eyes were moist. Das Babu's students and well-wishers came forward. Someone took Basanti Devi's trunk from her hand. Dr Mukherji asked, 'Deshbandhu, where will you live now?'

'What use does a mendicant have for a house. If the Congress builds us a hut on the banks of the Ganga, that's enough. We don't need anything else.'

Das Babu was very restless in Calcutta after his return from the Faridpur conference of the Congress party. He decided to go to Darjeeling for a short break. But from his preparations, it seemed as if he was setting out on a very long journey. He had no servants, no helpers and hardly any luggage. Like an ascetic, he arrived in Darjeeling. Basanti Devi, too, was seeing her husband in a new avatar. He was so weak that walking for even a furlong was too much of an effort. And yet his laughter still echoed youthfulness, and his eyes were still soft.

'Basanti, I feel like meeting Gandhiji,' he said to his wife one day. 'The Faridpur meeting was too brief. I have so much more to discuss with him.'

'But you are not fit enough to travel, are you?'

'Write to him. See if he can come here.'

Gandhiji received Das's letter. Cutting short his tour of Bengal, Gandhiji agreed to come to Darjeeling. Das Babu was preparing to welcome Gandhiji. He had ordered five goats since Gandhiji preferred goat's milk. Accommodation was arranged for those who were accompanying him. When Gandhiji and his entourage arrived in Darjeeling, Das Babu seemed to be rejuvenated. A new enthusiasm coursed through his weary veins; strength returned to tired legs. Both would rise early and walk along the mountain paths. They talked about charkha, khadi and rural development. Together they spun cotton yarn.

In the course of their conversation, Gandhiji said to Chittaranjan Das one day, 'I truly appreciate your generosity towards the Muslims.'

'The partition of Bengal in 1905 has taught me that we must strive for Hindu–Muslim unity together. Bengal had organised a massive campaign under Bipin Chandra Pal,' Das replied.

'I am willing to spill my blood for Hindu–Muslim unity. But will the religious leaders become any wiser?' Gandhiji sounded discouraged. 'If any god or any religion in the world advocates violence and falsehood, to me, it can't be a god, it is just a stone; it is not a religion, it is anti-religion.'

One night the discussion was quite animated. Both wondered regretfully why they had not met earlier and more often. As he spoke, Deshbandhu's voice quivered. 'Gandhiji, I cannot say anything about myself now. My health betrays me. There are only two concerns I have – one is communal unity, which is equally dear to you; the other is Subhas.'

'I too admire his courage and incomparable passion for his motherland. But he has a long way to go before he attains your kind of maturity. He has much to learn, much to experience.'

'No, Gandhiji, don't make the mistake of underestimating Subhas. Over the past six years, I have seen his energy, his organisational skill, his unparalleled patriotism, from very close quarters. He is a diamond. That is why he is sometimes hard, impatient and impulsive. Putting restrictions on him is like trying to confine a cyclone inside one room. For the good of the country, he can raise any number of storms. Utilise his resources to the maximum, in the best way you can. Don't abandon him when I am gone.'

Deshbandhu was drenched in sweat. He took Gandhiji's hand in his own and asked, 'Will you promise to take care of my Subhas, Gandhiji?'

'Asking for a promise is a sign of formality, isn't it?' Gandhiji said evasively.

'I had to tell you this, Gandhiji. Tomorrow's generation may ask you what I did for my country. If you feel I have done nothing, so be it. But don't ever forget that I gave Subhas to our nation.'

After Gandhiji departed, Deshbandhu once again fell very ill. One evening, before a panel of doctors from Calcutta reached Darjeeling, a cool breeze extinguished his flickering flame.

When Deshbandhu's body was taken to Calcutta by train, huge crowds gathered; they had come from everywhere. Bengal had sunk in gloom.

Gandhiji received the news when he was on the way to Assam. For a few minutes, he sat in silence. He decided to return to Calcutta immediately. From Sealdah station, he saw the two-and-a-half-mile-long funeral procession moving towards the burning ghat. There must have been at least five lakh people. But one person was missing. Subhas was behind bars. The pyre was built with the setting sun as witness. As it was lit, a collective sob broke out. Gandhiji wept with all the mourners. Sarat Bose and Maulana Azad tried to console him. Swallowing his tears, Gandhiji spoke, 'The whole country is bereft. But Bengal has become an orphan. Years ago, when time swept away Tilak, I felt helpless just as I am today. But at that time, Hindus and Muslims lived together amicably. Today, protectors of religion wander about with hidden daggers, ready to pounce on each other. At such a time, the bridge between the two communities, our Deshbandhu, has collapsed. Who will hold our country together now?'

Four

From his prison cell, Subhas Chandra had been staring at the hills on the outskirts of Mandalay town and the pagoda that stood above them. He had been brought to Burma along with seven of his close associates and imprisoned in Mandalay Jail.

'Subhas, what are the exact charges against us?' asked Bipin Ganguly.

'It seems we plotted to kill the governor of Bengal, and for that we imported weapons into Calcutta.'

'How stupid!'

'Bipin, with the devilish power it has, the government can colour any incident as it pleases. Their intentions are to cut off Deshbandhu's hands by imprisoning young workers like us, thereby putting an end to his movement for national awakening, and in turn hacking at the roots of the Congress. And that they have achieved.'

Mandalay Jail was like a fortress. It was surrounded by a moat. Once upon a time, it had been the seat of Burmese kings. Political prisoners were kept in wooden cages like circus animals, out in the open. In biting cold, searing heat and torrential rain. The climate of Burma did not allow even a few hours of comfort. Subhas Chandra often looked at Lokmanya Tilak's yard. How could the great man have written the profound *Gita Rahasya* in these hostile conditions?

Sarat Bose's concern and affection for Subhas was almost maternal. His letters were full of questions: what was his cell like, did he have something to cover himself with, was he getting enough to eat, etc. He had sent Subhas a woollen coat, an overcoat and a blanket. Side by side, he continued to knock on the doors of the police authorities. He demanded a copy of the chargesheet and appealed that a case be filed against him.

Mandalay was full of hardships. During the dry spell, dust swept up in gusts throughout the night. Many fell prey to smallpox every year. Those who escaped the pox became victims of plague-carrying rodents. From the time he came to Mandalay, Subhas was afflicted with acute stomach pain. In two months, he lost eleven kilos and became very weak. How many years of one's life were going to be spent like a caged animal? The political prisoners tried to keep themselves entertained in the company of cats, parrots, mynahs and pigeons. Sometimes, their hearts too would echo the cooing of the birds. Often his bustling home, his family, brothers, sisters-in-law, nephews, would appear before Subhas's eyes. The man who invented the prison must have been a heartless creature.

One day one of the clerks in the jailor's office came rushing in, carrying a radio. The newsreader was announcing the news of the sudden demise of Deshbandhu Chittaranjan Das. Subhas and his seven companions crumpled to the ground as if struck by lightning. They sobbed inconsolably, their loud lamentation rattling the entire jail.

Subhas wept all night. Between sobs, he said to Surendra Ghosh in the next cell, 'How will I survive this unexpected bolt from the heavens!'

'Bengal is orphaned today, Subhas.'

'Yes, Surendra. How could he do this to us, leave us to manage on our own. Who will carry our cries of grief to Basanti Ma.'

After Deshbandhu's death, the dark shadows of the prison began to seem more ominous. Days went by. All the political prisoners yearned for a glimpse of their motherland. The struggle continued. In the midst of all this, elections to the Bengal Legislative Council were due. This was the first election in Subhas's life. The candidate was behind bars, the canvassers outside. Subhas's younger brother, Sailesh, had come to Mandalay with the nomination papers to get them signed. The idea of fighting an election from prison was unusual to say the least. Subhas Chandra's friends and supporters worked tirelessly round the clock. Basanti Devi got posters printed. Subhas's mother and Bibha boudi led a spirited campaign. Calcutta walls were plastered with posters of the candidate looking out from behind bars.

'Surendra, what do you think? What will happen in the elections?'

'It will be a landslide victory for you, what else.' All his friends assured him confidently.

Their words came true. Subhas won by a huge margin. Once more 'Vande Mataram' resounded through the prison.

But the euphoria of victory did not last long. Subhas was ill. His condition was causing concern. Even the jailor was worried. The government sent a team of doctors to examine him. His brother Dr Sunil Bose and Dr Kelsall diagnosed him with tuberculosis. The question of his health was brought up in the Bengal Assembly. It was imperative to shift him from Mandalay as soon as possible.

One day, the jailor himself told Subhas the truth behind the delay in his treatment. No prison in all of India was willing to accept such a 'dangerous' inmate. Madras, Bombay, Karachi had all sent their refusals. Sunil Bose made a couple of visits even though it was very difficult for him to enter Burma. During his second visit, he was deeply upset to see Subhas's condition. He thought the only way to save Subhas was to take him to Switzerland.

The prison authorities in Burma were getting increasingly anxious over Subhas's deteriorating health. They did not want the blame if something untoward were to happen. Telegrams went back and forth between Calcutta and Rangoon.

Early one morning, Subhas Chandra awoke from his stupor and found himself on board a boat, bobbing on the waters of the Hooghly. The sky was overcast. A couple of seagulls were riding the waves. On the pier, jail officials waited to receive their guest. But when they saw Subhas Chandra's emaciated, near-lifeless form, they were most reluctant to accept the responsibility. Sarat Bose came aboard. He could not hold back his tears when he saw Subhas.

'Sunil,' he said in panic, 'how is this bag of bones ever going to reach Switzerland in time?'

Tegart too was at the pier. He saw Subhas's condition and rushed to the Governor House with his medical papers. Governor Stanley Jackson glanced through them. 'From these reports it seems the prisoner is more dead than alive. How will he get to Switzerland?'

'Well, sir, if he recovers from this illness, fires will erupt once again.'

'But if he dies on our hands, the entire blame will be on the administration. Why invite trouble. Hand him over to the family.'

Several hours later, Subhas Chandra opened his eyes and looked into the gentle eyes of Basanti Ma. He was lying with his head in her lap, and she was stroking his gaunt face. He noticed her bare forehead and immediately he felt a wrench. Like a small child, he buried his face in her lap and cried. Basanti Ma too was overcome.

'Control yourself, Subhas,' she told him.

'How can I, Ma? To see you like this ... Where is my guru, Ma?'

'Subhas, the real homage to your guru will be for you to rise again. You must get well. You must wage a war on the barbaric British Imperialism.'

Barrister Sengupta and Subhas Chandra were guests of the Nehrus in their home, Anand Bhavan, in Allahabad. They had come specifically to persuade Motilal Nehru to accept the post of party president at the Congress convention in Calcutta later that year, in December 1928.

At the time of Deshbandhu's death, Subhas Chandra was in prison. So Gandhiji had handed over the reins of the party to Barrister Sengupta. Now there were two separate groups within the Bengal Congress party – Subhas Chandra's and Barrister Sengupta's. But both agreed that Motilal Nehru should be the next president.

Subhas Chandra and Jawaharlal Nehru spent all their time together. They had much to catch up on. Barrister Sengupta and Motilal Nehru too seemed to have hit it off. Motilal Nehru's bearing, his demeanour, his manner of speaking were all quite aristocratic.

Popping a cashew nut into his mouth, Motilal Nehru asked Barrister Sengupta, 'So what have you all decided? Who will be the president?'

'You alone are worthy of that position. Subhas Chandra and I have come here to request you to take it up.'

For a long while Motilal Nehru was silent. Then taking a sip of wine, he said, 'Sengupta, why don't you propose our Jawahar's name for the post?'

'No, he is still young. Right now, we are in dire need of the guidance of an experienced leader like you.

Instead, changing the subject Motilal Nehru asked, 'Sengupta, why doesn't this Subhas Chandra of yours get married?'

'No one really knows. But he is remarkably focused.'

'How much influence does he have on the youth?' asked Motilal Nehru, pointedly.

'Well, he is from the opposite camp, but so what, I can tell you the truth. There isn't another youth leader who can motivate the young people of Bihar and Bengal as much as he can. Besides, because of youth forums and student unions, Jawahar and Subhas have become familiar figures across the country.'

'That's why I say, instead of me, make Jawahar the president for the coming year.'

Barrister Sengupta was perplexed. What exactly was Motilal Nehru trying to say?

Motilal stared out of his window overlooking the fresh green lawns. At sixty-eight, he was on the last lap of his life's journey. Yet his broad forehead and fair, chiselled face were striking to this day. He seemed preoccupied today. Intimations of the final journey seemed to have cast their shadow on his subconscious. Again and again, his gaze turned to Jawaharlal and Subhas chatting endlessly like long-lost friends.

After tremendous hardship and effort, Motilal had brought the Nehru family to this position of glory and recognition. The Nehrus were simple Kashmiri brahmins, known for their educated, refined and handsome men and their beautiful fair-skinned, clear-eyed women. One of their ancestors, Raj Kaul, had been in the service of the royal court of the Mughals in Delhi. He used to live next to the Shah Nehar, which in Hindi meant 'canal'. And so, they came to be known as Nehrus.

When the rebellion of 1857 broke out, the Nehrus had to relocate to Agra. Motilal was born there. His elder brother Nandalal acquired name and fame as a lawyer in Allahabad. But fate dealt him a cruel blow. Motilal was only twenty-six at the time of his brother's death, yet he shouldered his responsibilities with fortitude and courage. His fluency in English and command over the law quickly took him to the top of his profession. Jawaharlal was now thirty-nine. Perhaps it was because he was the first surviving child in the family, Jawaharlal always held a very special place in the hearts of Motilal and his wife Swaruparani. When Jawaharlal was ten, Motilal had built, Anand Bhavan. On all four sides were wide verandas and in front, a velvety green lawn. At the back were the orchards. Two swimming pools, a tennis court and for the summer, two small, fully furnished, independent cottages. The main house had three kitchens – Mughlai, continental and Indian – an equal number of cooks and several servants, a well-stocked cellar and a stable of excellent horses. It was as if Motilal Nehru had tried to create a heaven on earth for his dear son.

After a while, Motilal spoke. 'Six–seven years ago, Jawahar had raised a storm in Anand Bhavan. The name Mohandas Karamchand Gandhi and his reputation entered this house, and Jawahar got swept away into the Non-cooperation Movement.'

'You had objected to his involvement, hadn't you?' Barrister Sengupta said.

'Not just objected, in a fit of rage, I even ordered him to get out of the house. Jawahar went to jail and to understand what hardships he was facing, I slept on bare chilly tiles and shivered through the winter night. When I think of those days – those angry words, those fights, I feel like laughing.'

'But how did the conflict end?'

'Gandhiji paid a visit to Anand Bhavan and everything changed. The inhuman massacre at Jallianwala opened my eyes to the barbaric face of British regime. And my illusions were dispelled.'

It was quite late. A message came from Swaruparani that dinner had been served.

A large table was laid by the swimming pool. Subhas and Jawaharlal were already seated. Eleven-year-old Indira was in the chair beside her grandmother Swaruparani. Jawaharlal's wife Kamala was herself supervising the table. As soon as Motilal Nehru and Barrister Sengupta sat down, Jawaharlal asked his father, 'Dadu, shall we start?'

'Yes, of course. I hope you have had some Bengali mithai prepared for Subhas and Sengupta?'

Swaruparani replied, 'Everything is taken care of. Bengali food has been made, but knowing these boys' tastes, continental dishes too are ready.'

There was a lavish spread, but everyone ate moderately. Subhas noticed that the Nehru family did not eat to their hearts' content, as his own family was known to do. Throughout dinner his eyes kept straying to Kamala Nehru. She looked so calm and forbearing. Just like Kasturba. So it was true, then, that small creepers get stunted in the shade of large trees.

At crack of dawn the next day, the stables of Anand Bhavan stirred with activity. Father and son went out riding every morning. Today, Subhas joined them. Barrister Sengupta refused to climb on to a horse, so a special buggy was arranged for him. The ever-enthusiastic Indira accompanied him. They left Allahabad behind and approached the river. Subhas and Jawaharlal trotted ahead, talking all the while.

'British rule is a national calamity,' said Subhas.

'Slavery is a curse,' was Nehru's rejoinder.

'Gandhiji is not yet ready to demand complete independence. Nor is Motilalji,' Subhas said.

'If the senior leaders are not prepared, then, Subhas, we the younger generation have to set the horses at a gallop,' Jawaharlal stated firmly.

Their horses actually galloped far and away. The sun was almost overhead when they turned back. Motilal had reined in his steed under a mango tree and was waiting for them, anxiously. Soon Barrister Sengupta's buggy too drew up beside him. Finally, they appeared, and Motilal let out a huge sigh. Turning to Barrister Sengupta, he said with a smile, 'They have come back together. Had my Jawahar lagged behind, I would not have liked it at all.'

'Why?'

'Because he is the brightest star in all Hindustan and he must always stay ahead.'

Barrister Sengupta and Motilal had another round of talks later that afternoon. Motilal Nehru was reminded of Jawaharlal's visit to Russia much against his wishes and the Madras Congress where, disregarding opposition from Gandhiji, he had ensured that the Purna Swaraj resolution was passed. He was perturbed by the rapid spread of communist and socialist ideas among the youth of the country. Also, Jawaharlal's growing proximity with Subhas, Nariman, Lala Shankar and other such resolute and daring young men was causing him concern. He told Barrister Sengupta quite candidly, 'If Gandhiji is not willing to take over the reins himself, Jawahar must become the president.'

'But, Babuji, our Provincial Committee is determined to hand over the post to you.'

'Reverse your decision, then.'

'That is not possible.' Having said that, Barrister Sengupta was in a quandary. To be the Congress president was the highest honour in the country. Why was he refusing it? Were the rumours doing the rounds for the last two years, that Motilal was determined to see his son offered this highly prestigious post, true, then?

To meet the challenges of the new age, the Congress had to take revolutionary steps. It had to present India's problems before the rest of the world and bring the international opinion to its side. The two friends were in agreement on this. In this context, Jawaharlal informed Subhas that he had asked Krishna Menon to handle the work of the Congress in London. Having recently returned from Europe, he said, 'Subhas, we had been invited to participate in the tenth anniversary celebrations of the Russian Revolution. What a vast and amazing country it is! I was shocked to see the president's house – just a three-room place.'

'And when I see our viceroy sprawled out in three hundred rooms, my head tingles with anger,' Subhas replied.

'Our first goal is political independence, no doubt. But a socialist system is imperative for the development of our country.'

'Of course, merely getting freedom will not do. We must start preparing the blueprint for a reconstruction programme.'

Subhas was very pleased to hear Jawaharlal's opinion on socialism, slavery, and his fierce opposition to feudalism. But then, recalling the Madras Congress, he became a shade cautious. 'Jawahar, the Congress is forty-three years old, but still the senior leaders falter while demanding complete independence. In that case, how can we take the ideals of socialism further? We must be prepared to go against the senior leaders including Gandhiji, if required.'

'That is why I sowed the seeds of protest at Madras. Dadu did not at all approve of my defiance of Gandhiji.'

'He is not going to appreciate it in future either.'

'Let us affirm that complete independence is the aim and objective of the Congress. And let us pledge our lives to attain that goal,' declared Jawaharlal.

'So what are we waiting for? We will make a beginning at the Calcutta Congress,' responded Subhas enthusiastically.

Both were pleased with this new resolution, but the thought of the responsibility weighed them down. A restless Subhas said, 'Look, Jawahar, neither of us should back out at the last moment.'

'No reason why the step we have taken should be reversed,' assured Jawaharlal confidently.

'Well, Motilalji is one of our weightiest national leaders and your father too.'

'But, Subhas, even our goal is lofty,' said Jawaharlal, somewhat uneasily. 'If the situation is such that I have to defy my own father, I will not hesitate to do it. I will not commit the sin of letting even one spark of revolution that has been ignited among our youth because of you and me get extinguished. That is my promise to you.'

It was resolved that four days before the Calcutta Congress, a Youth Congress convention would be held and the bugle call of revolution sounded.

Motilal Nehru was worried after the recent visit of the Simon Commission. It had been greeted by protests and demonstrations. Congress workers had raised slogans of 'Simon go back!' across the country. The police had resorted to a lathi charge on the demonstrators at Lahore and grievously injured Punjab Kesari, Lala Lajpat Rai. The elderly statesman had succumbed to his injuries. Punjab was seething, vengeance was on every mind.

Consequent to the Simon Commission, Lord Birkenhead had thrown a challenge to the Indians to formulate a policy that would be acceptable to all religious groups. It was accepted by Indian leaders and under Motilal Nehru's presidentship, it was worked on for a year. Subhas Chandra too had been actively involved in drafting the report alongside Barrister Sapru and Motilal Nehru. But it was clear that now both he and Jawaharlal were thinking beyond this policy.

In the meantime, the Youth League had been started in Delhi with Srinivasa Iyengar as the president and Subhas and Jawaharlal as secretaries. Gathered around them were Nariman from Bombay, Kedarnath Sehgal of Punjab, Jamnadas Mehta, Kiran Shankar Roy, Lala Shankarlal and other inspired young men. Also, Vivekananda's brother Bhupendranath Dutta had joined them. Motilal Nehru was concerned about this.

On the way back from the station, no words were spoken. As they approached Anand Bhavan, Motilal Nehru began, 'Jawahar, you must devote some time to other matters as well now.'

'Dadu?' Jawaharlal noticed the sharp note in his father's voice.

'For the last three days, I have heard only one word from you – Subhas this, Subhas that ...'

'Have I done something wrong, Dadu?'

'Friendship is all very well, but is it necessary to sink one's identity and one's purpose in life in the dark waters of friendship? I had personally sent your name up to Gandhiji for the post of Congress president. Why did you withdraw?'

'Whether it is the father or the son, the honour will come to Anand Bhavan, won't it?

'Jawahar, I am now looking to the future. My time is up. But before I depart, I would like to put everything in order. I want to see you wear the Congress president's crown – it is meant for your brow only.'

Jawaharlal was taken aback. 'That I will, but why this insistence, this urgency?'

'Because I can see a number of luminous stars on the horizon who can be a potential challenge to you.'

'Well, the stars can only illuminate the sky, make the country's future brighter.'

'I am not concerned with the whole firmament. My sun is setting, and all I can think of is the kind of steed the rising sun will ride.'

'Why are you speaking in riddles like this, Dadu? Tell me what you have in mind,' a puzzled Jawaharlal said.

'Yes, yes, I will tell you exactly. Several young men like Subhas are being groomed to be your rivals in the future.'

'You are mistaken, Dadu. Subhas is my compatriot, dear to me as a brother.'

'Son, what lessons have you learnt from the great epics, the Ramayana and the Mahabharata? From the beginning of time, it has been proved that two swords can never occupy the same scabbard.'

'Why do you have such high aspirations?'

'Has any religious text stated that it is a sin to be ambitious? If one has to compare the two of you, right now both of you are general secretaries of an organisation as important as the Congress. You are a barrister, he is an ICS. If you are as handsome as the brilliant Kohinoor, Subhas has the radiance of a crystal. If the youth of this country are crazy about you, there are an equal number eager to give their lives for his cause. At a time of crisis, you get slightly unsettled, but he is steadfast, like a flaming torch …,' Motilal explained. Then placing a fond paternal hand on Jawaharlal's back, he continued, 'Jawahar, it would be better if you dissociate yourself from Subhas and the left-leaning youngsters right now. All of them appear to be anti-Gandhi to me.'

'Bapuji goes by his own instinct. It is not through rural upliftment, cleanliness, cottage industry and constructive work, but through

Socialism and infrastructural development and heavy industries that the country can progress. That's what all of us believe. And we are preparing ourselves to oppose Gandhiji to prove our point, if necessary.'

'Jawahar, who are you talking revolution to?' Motilal Nehru's voice rose. 'Today Gandhiji and his greatness have such a strong hold over the minds of the public that your revolt will die down in no time at all.'

'But, Dadu, displaying courage is a mark of the youth, isn't it?'

'Courage? That too against Gandhiji? My dear son, what your own father, with the support of noble souls like Deshbandhu Chittaranjan Das and Lajpat Rai could not accomplish, you and your leftist brat-party expect to achieve ...'

Motilal could not sleep till late that night. Finally, well past midnight, he got out of bed and wrote a letter.

> *Bapuji,*
>
> *Please do not fail to attend the Calcutta session. The youth are in full strength and bursting with enthusiasm. There is no telling what they might do.*
>
> *I cannot vouch for my own son, let alone the others. You have to be present.*
>
> *Yours respectfully,*
> *Motilal*

The vast Maidan was still covered in early morning darkness. A police van stood in one corner. Commissioner Tegart had come there with his junior officers. Across from them, at the other end, the parade of Congress swayamsevaks slowly emerged. Subhas Chandra had been training about two thousand young men and women for the past one month. He marched alongside them, in full military uniform, his head held high, his bearing like that of a French or Japanese general leading his men to the battlefront.

Tegart was furious. Not about their early morning training sessions, but because his informers had told him that this parade was planned by the leaders of Yugantar and Anushilan. They had persuaded Subhas to participate. There was reason to believe that several terrorists had sneaked into the city under the pretext of attending the Congress session. Naturally, Tegart was a worried man. 'This has got to stop,' he fumed.

Right behind Subhas Chandra marched his lieutenant. As soon as Tegart recognised him as Jatin Das, his eyebrows shot up. According to his spies, Jatin Das had been making frequent trips to Punjab and was in constant touch with the militant members of the Naujawan Bharat Sabha. Also, a third radical activist group, the Bengal Volunteers was in the process of being formed. Trembling with rage, Tegart left the Maidan.

After the parade, Subhas returned to Woodburn Park. Preparations for the Congress session were in full swing in the house as well. Bibhabati saw him, all sweaty and grimy after the parade, and began to tease him, 'Chhor-da, be careful, don't break the young girls' legs with such rigorous practice!'

Basanti Devi asked, 'Are you planning to build a women's army or what?'

'If God wills it, sure, I will. Both of you will have to be captains,' he said.

The women laughed and promised to be his first recruits. Then Bibhabati asked, 'Why this sudden enthusiasm for women volunteers?'

'I am a pupil of Vivekananda and Deshbandhu, after all, boudi!'

'Even so ...'

'It's plain calculation, boudi. Suppose, of the thirty crore Indians, fifteen crore are earning members. Fifty per cent of human power, which all of us, from Swamiji downwards, looked upon as Adishakti is confined within the courtyard. Which means that what we earn you spend.'

'What nonsense! You think we women are lazy?'

'Jokes aside, boudi, if thirty crore pairs of hands come together, how wonderful it will be! If this resource is properly used, we can become one of the most progressive and developed nations in the world.'

Sarat Bose had recently constructed a three-storeyed building in Woodburn Park, a short distance away from the Elgin Road house. With their growing families, the brothers had felt the need for a larger house, so Sarat babu, Bibhabati and Subhas Chandra had shifted there.

A big bedroom on the ground floor was prepared for Jawaharlal Nehru's visit. He arrived a few days before the Youth Congress session. The charismatic and magnetic personalities of both Subhas and Jawaharlal had drawn youth leaders from all provinces. All night long, they held discussions on how to press the demand for 'complete independence' or 'Sampurna Swaraj' in the forthcoming session.

That morning Subhas Chandra rose early and got ready. The previous night he had told Jawaharlal Nehru not to shave but to wait for him in the morning. Subhas went to his room, followed by a tall, well-built man wearing a fluffy fur cap and a long pathani coat, looking like a Congress leader from the Frontier Province. Running his hand over the stubble on his chin, Jawaharlal asked, 'Arre Subhas, where is your royal barber?'

'I am the royal barber, Panditji!'

Nehru stared at him in amazement. With a smile Haricharandas fished out his instruments from the many pockets in his coat, like a magician. As he lathered Jawaharlal's face, Haricharandas began to talk. 'No one else in Calcutta dares touch the beards of the rich and the famous except myself,' he boasted.

Subhas interrupted him with a question to Jawaharlal. 'Do you know why, during the Non-cooperation Movement, the hair and beards of lawyers and judges had grown longer than those of the prisoners?'

'Simple. Your royal barber must have been ill.'

'No, he was not ill, but in jail for two months, in the service of his country!'

'But talent cannot be concealed. If the judges suffered outside, the jailor had a field day in the prison,' said Haricharan. 'He was so pleased with my touch that he used to say, "Haricharan, I hope your sentence never ends."'

Jawaharlal and Subhas burst out laughing. Jawaharlal was pleased at the smooth shave he had been given. But Haricharan seemed reluctant to pack up.

'Panditji,' he said, 'so far I have held many important heads in my hands, even the governors'. If I can shave Gandhiji's head just once, my instruments and I will consider ourselves blessed.'

Only after getting an assurance from Panditji that it would be done did Haricharandas depart.

Subhas and Jawaharlal had begun to find the weak and dilatory attitude of the senior leaders annoying. There was great similarity in the approach of the Irish patriots who were ever prepared to give up their lives for their country and the revolutionary youth of Bengal. Jawaharlal was deeply affected by the establishment of a classless society in Russia, workers' rule and other such new ideas. Twenty thousand workers of the Tata Steel factory in Jamshedpur had called for a strike, and Subhas was to lead it. If these new ideas had to be implemented, the youth leaders had no option but to demand complete independence. Freedom meant total, complete freedom and the thirty-nine-year-old Jawaharlal and the thirty-two-year-old Subhas had been instigating the whole country to accept nothing less than that.

Sarat Bose informed them that Gandhiji had arrived at the Sodepur Ashram early that morning. Subhas and Jawaharlal looked at each other, surprised. Then Subhas said to Jawaharlal, 'We had requested, begged, pleaded with Gandhiji to be present at the session, but all our invitations met with a lukewarm response. What do you think has happened that has brought him to Calcutta so unexpectedly?'

The tenor of the session would be changed now with Gandhiji's presence. Subhas and Jawaharlal were deep in thought. Then, unable to restrain himself, Jawaharlal spoke. 'The youth will still demand complete freedom. What will happen to our proposal, Subhas?'

'The old guard will make Motilalji's 'Nehru Report' a prestige issue. If that is rejected, Motilalji and Gandhiji will be annoyed. If it is accepted, the younger members will turn against us for veering away from our objective of complete independence. Brother, you had better think over this very carefully,' Subhas suggested to Jawaharlal.

He threw a question back at Subhas. 'With your principles in one pan of the scales and your father in the other, which one would you choose, Subhas?'

Subhas laughed. 'Easy,' he said.

'I will do the same. My decision will not change. Why bend one's life-sustaining idealism?'

With firm steps, Jawaharlal climbed down the stairs. When he and Subhas reached the courtyard, hundreds of spirited citizens had gathered by the gate. From the balcony, Sarat babu and Bibhabati gazed fondly at the pair below. They were greeted with cries of 'Mahatma Gandhi ki jai! Vande Mataram, Hindustan ke pyare lal, Subhas aur Jawaharlal!' The clamour followed them as they sped away in their car. Bibha boudi continued to stare after them till Sarat Bose jokingly asked her what she had been looking at so intently. 'I was trying to figure out which one was the sun and which the moon,' she replied.

'So did you find the answer?' he asked teasingly.

'Actually, it's very difficult to say. May God protect the two of them from all evil.'

Sarat Bose muttered, 'One mountain range can have many peaks, but two mountains always have a deep chasm between them. It is a curse.'

Subhas Chandra and Jawaharlal entered the beautifully decorated shamiana at the Park Maidan to resounding applause from thousands of youth workers who had come from all over the country. The seniors felt that by holding the session of the Youth Congress at the same venue where a major party meeting was scheduled a few days later, some kind of a challenge was being thrown at them. The Nehru Report had cast its dark shadow on this meeting as well. It had been rejected at the Muslim League convention in Calcutta recently. If the young people decided to tear it to shreds here too, there would be big trouble. That is why Gandhiji's special emissaries were looking into all arrangements very carefully.

The meeting was chaired by Barrister K.F. Nariman. After welcoming him, Subhas began his speech. First, he paid tribute to the late Lala Lajpat Rai and condemned the brutality of the British soldiers who had attacked him. His remark provoked cries of 'Shame! Shame!' from the crowds. The young men from Punjab stood up and started screaming, 'Inquilab zindabad! Lalaji amar rahein!' The members of the Naujawan Bharat Sabha were a sizeable number. They were now fully roused by memories of Lalaji.

When the clamour died down, Subhas addressed the gathering. 'Brothers, a youth organisation is not a body of idle, unemployed, unmotivated young people. Nor is it a social service body. Or a drought relief committee. It is an association of people in whose hearts the fires of idealism burn bright and who, dissatisfied with the present state of affairs, raise their voices in protest and are prepared to sacrifice everything for their principles.' Keeping the examples of Russia, China, Germany in mind, he continued, 'Wherever the old leaders have been found incapacitated, weak or infirm, the younger generation has come forward and taken over the responsibility of reconstruction. The British have trapped us economically and socially. Only if we can get out of their stranglehold completely, will the path of progress be open to us. Let us all commit ourselves to this freedom and take the challenge head on.'

Subhas Chandra's voice had reached a high pitch. He glanced at Jawaharlal seated on the dais, and then his gaze swept over the galvanised audience in front of him. The unease which had been gathering in a corner of his mind over the past so many days made him very restless. In a razor-sharp voice, he declared, 'Today there are two streams of philosophical thought in India where it seems our minds are held captive. One is Sabarmati Ashram, Gandhiji's hermitage, and the other is Pondicherry, Aurobindo's seat. When I view both these schools of thought, objectively and as a pragmatist, I find that Pondicherry advocates nothing more than meditation and introspection. Yoga and metaphysics are given undue importance.'

Subhas's words caused consternation among some of the senior members of the Aurobindo group. Then Subhas shifted his attention to Sabarmati. Making highly critical comments about Gandhiji's philosophy, he said, 'Modernity as a concept is anathema to Sabarmati. Mass production of goods is a sin. Increasing one's needs and improving one's standard of living is a sin. Should we then regress into the age of the bullock cart? Excessive importance is given to the soul while physical culture and military training are neglected.' After a pause he went on, 'Mathas and ashrams are not new to this ancient land. Ascetics and saints have always been accorded the highest respect. They will continue to receive it. But I am only suggesting to my young friends here that if we wish to create a free, independent India, prosperous and happy, we cannot follow these outdated ideals. Discard old and worn turbans, pick up the weapons of the younger generation.'

Some of Gandhiji's followers stood up. 'Babuji, then what should this country follow: the path of violence or of non-violence?'

Subhas replied with an example. 'When India becomes independent, it will have to fight against modern enemies with modern armaments. That's all I have to say.'

Subhas Chandra had managed to capture the imagination of the entire gathering. With a smile, he asked them, 'Tell me, how do you want to get freedom?'

'By whatever means possible,' they shouted in unison.

Elated, he turned to Jawaharlal and said, 'Note these precious words, "by whatever means possible", in the proposal.'

Soon after the proposal was put to vote, Jatin Das and some Punjabi youths in their twenties and thirties, all members of the Naujawan Bharat Sabha, came on to the stage from behind. Jatin had worked with Subhas shoulder to shoulder during the Bengal floods. One of them, an extremely impressive personality, was attracting a lot of attention. Jatin introduced the young man with eloquent eyes and neatly trimmed beard. 'This is Bhagat Singh,' he said.

Subhas Chandra smiled in recognition. 'I know him,' he said. 'You are Ajit Singh's nephew, aren't you? So how is Punjab?'

Bhagat Singh's face darkened. Angrily he replied, 'Lalaji's murder still rankles in the heart of every Punjabi youth.' But now, hope bloomed once again in Bhagat Singh's heart under the leadership of Jawaharlal and Subhas. He asked Subhas, 'Really, Babuji, will the British give up this land purely on principles of non-violence?'

'What do you think?' Subhas countered.

'I say it is impossible. At least one telling blow will have to be struck.'

'Absolutely right,' cried Subhas, delighted.

The Youth Congress had received an unprecedented response. 'We will most certainly honour our gurus and thinkers. But how far will they be useful in the modern world?' Gandhiji's conservative supporters were greatly offended by these remarks. 'This is the first time we have heard such a blatant call for revolt and that too from the general secretary of the Congress,' they whispered among themselves.

Sodepur Ashram was barely six or seven miles away from Calcutta. A graphic account of the inciteful words and the bold proposal, with much exaggeration, reached there soon after. 'Come and see me at once,' came the summons from Gandhiji to Jawaharlal. But it was quite late in the evening and Nehru was tired. Sarat Bose went into Subhas's room. Subhas was about to go to bed. But when he saw Sarat Bose's worried face, he asked, 'What's the matter, Mej-da?'

'Gandhiji has received complaints against us for having indulged in underhand dealings in the sale of the session tickets.'

'Who has complained?'

'Our own Bengali brethren.'

'Should we worry about such frivolous and unsubstantiated allegations, Mej-da?'

'Subhas, there will be an enquiry.' Sarat Bose sighed. 'Whether it is a genuine charge or a trumped-up one, how one views a criminal is very subjective. Besides, you have a lust for living life dangerously. The future is fraught with more such hazards.'

The Calcutta Congress assumed a rather unusual colour. Never before had a Congress party convention seen such a large turnout of young people. The procession drew near. In front were about two thousand young men and women, marching in step like army personnel. Behind them was a young man, riding a brown and white horse. He looked like the commander of some western cavalry brigade. They were followed by thirty-four milk-white horses drawing the presidential carriage. Seated inside it were Motilal Nehru, his wife Swaruparani and their daughter Krishna. It reminded one of a victory march of some Roman potentate.

As soon as Motilal Nehru saw Gandhiji at the entrance, he quickly alighted. They embraced each other warmly. Gandhiji caught sight of the young soldier as he jumped down from his horse. He marched up to Gandhiji, clicked his heels and saluted smartly. Gandhiji kept staring at him. A round peaked cap, khaki shirt with several pockets and flaps and brown military boots. Kasturba looked at him with affection. Seeing her, Subhas exclaimed 'Ma' with such tenderness and bent down to touch her feet, Kasturba involuntarily placed her hand on his head in benediction. Just then she glimpsed Gandhiji's stern face and quickly withdrew her hand.

'Subhas, why are you masquerading as a military man?' Gandhiji asked, barely able to control his laughter. Nor could his companions Ghanshyamdas Birla, Rajendra Prasad, Satish Dasgupta, Acharya Kripalani and others.

'Because it will generate a sense of discipline and self-esteem in the youth.'

'Where's the need for such drama?' asked Gandhiji, obviously very amused. 'To me it appears like Burtman Circus.'

Motilal Nehru and Gandhiji rushed off ahead. The Subject Committee meeting that day was going to be a tense one. The Nehru Report had to be accepted at any cost. Speaking every word with utmost gravity, Gandhiji said, 'Please remember that it is very important for the Congress to accept the Nehru Report which has been drawn up after months of hard work and careful thought.'

'But now it is impossible for us to survive without Sampurna Swaraj,' declared Jawaharlal.

'We are not willing to agree to anything but complete independence,' reiterated Subhas Chandra.

The youth rebellion showed no signs of abating. Tension was mounting. Vallabhbhai Patel and Rajendra Prasad felt that Subhas and Jawaharlal were putting Gandhiji in a spot. Motilal Nehru was extremely worried. If his plan was rejected here, it would be ripped apart in the open session. Exasperated, he said, 'If the president's report, prepared with so much effort, is going to be dismissed like this, why should I remain here? Instead of being humiliated further, I will return to Allahabad at once.'

Gandhiji realised how troubled Motilal Nehru was. He pleaded with him to remain calm and took the reins of the meeting in his authoritative hands.

It seemed that Subhas, by openly attacking Sabarmati Ashram in his speech the previous day, had crossed all limits of decorum. Not only that, in the parade of the Congress swayamsevaks, he had included several radical nationalists with a definite bent towards violence, from the Anushilan and Yugantar groups. Gandhiji was already irked by the tiresome swayamsevak parade, the command of 'Slow March', the heels coming down, then Subhas appearing in full military regalia. They were an affront to his pet principle of ahimsa. It looked as if the Congress ship was heading for the rocks. However, Gandhiji turned to the young people and told them, almost like a warning, 'You of the next generation, remember one thing – the temple of freedom, of swaraj, cannot be built in a day. Much sweat, toil and tears go into its construction. Plain defiance will not get you freedom.' Gandhiji suddenly began to look distressed and fatigued. He continued, 'Look, I am moving the resolution before the Subject Committee that we adopt the Nehru Report. Well, Subhas and you, Jawaharlal, if you believe that I have done a little bit in the service of this country, support my resolution. Otherwise, like Motilalji, I too will go away, then you and your Congress – do whatever you like.'

A hush fell over the meeting. Everyone knew what Gandhiji's tone meant. If he was hurt, he would not hesitate to give up the party and go into retirement once again. But if Gandhiji was firm about his resolve, the youth leaders too would stick to their stand. The idea of complete independence had intoxicated them. They were not willing to wait indefinitely for freedom. And then a new suggestion was thrown up to give the British government a fixed period of time. The moderates among the Congressmen persuaded Gandhiji to agree to give the British time till 31 December 1931, and if they did not grant dominion status by then, the agitation would be renewed.

Gandhiji's words had affected Jawaharlal profoundly. He said, 'Friends, I must confess, I do not have the strength to oppose Gandhiji's resolution. How can I, when it is at that great man's feet that I learnt my lessons in politics? Instead of daring to defy him, I will consider it an honour to be his flag bearer.' Determination floundered. Jawaharlal had surrendered.

Motilal dabbed at his eyes. The youth members felt betrayed by Jawaharlal's sudden turnaround. Restlessness spread among the workers of the Youth League. Subhas Chandra was stunned. How could he change like this at the mere sight of Gandhiji. As for Gandhiji, the smile returned to his face when he saw the youngsters retreat. The tension had eased. He folded his knees, assumed his characteristic position and spoke, 'I am going to alter my previous statement. We will give the British not two but one year only. If they don't respond by then, I will myself call for action.'

His words were greeted by enthusiastic applause. For a while, Gandhiji remained silent. His face, his thin bare body seemed transformed. When he started to speak, his words sounded like the clear chants in a temple, but accompanied by the fearsome warning of temple bells. 'Young men and women with the blood stirring in your veins ... by the time all of us reach our goal, my end too will be nigh. At that time, none of you will stop by my crippled, emaciated body. You will not remember me. Nor will you listen to me. At that time, you can throw me off the platform.'

'If you always wanted to drink out of Gandhiji's cup, why did you deceive us in the first place?' the angry youth demanded.

Subhas and Jawaharlal were surrounded by students and youth workers, furious that the two leaders had given up their goal of complete independence and agreed to dominion status in a compromise with Gandhiji. 'How did *both* of you succumb to pressure from him? Why did you agree to this partial freedom?' an irate Jatin Das wanted to know.

'Jatin, we have given Gandhiji our word. Now we will have to keep it,' Subhas tried to explain.

'Well, you will have to break it,' four voices shouted in unison.

'Otherwise the youth of the country will have to chart a separate course,' declared Satyaranjan Bakshi.

Subhas requested them to leave him alone with Jawaharlal for a few minutes. For a long moment, both of them just stared at each other. Break their promise to Gandhiji? The repercussions were unimaginable. A thoughtful Subhas said, 'Jawahar, I am repeating what you said at Lucknow ... These young people are also harping on the same matter. To settle for dominion status will prove suicidal for the country. Besides that, brother, I had not proposed the complete independence resolution at Madras. It came from you.'

'That is true, Subhas. Personally, I too don't believe we should go for dominion status.'

'I had reminded you right at the beginning that to oppose the report would be to oppose your own father.'

Jawaharlal had nothing to say to that. After a long silence, he seemed to have come to a decision. Gruffly he said, 'Subhas, freedom is our very breath. We cannot live without it.'

In the Subject Committee, there was a sense of relief. There would be no confrontation, now that Jawaharlal and Subhas had retracted. Gandhiji was most pleased. Every time he thought of these two young radical leaders, he was reminded of the Porbandar story. When he was a little boy, he had gone with his father Karamchand to see a circus show. There were several wild animals there and a ringmaster who was able to make them do whatever he wanted. At the sound of his voice and the crack of a whip, the fiercest animal would tremble. There were also two lion cubs in the circus. When they were together, they would create a huge uproar. If they were tied apart, they protested so loudly that no one could sleep all night. Sometimes they wrestled playfully with each other, sometimes they ganged up and defied the ringmaster himself.

That would make him fret and fume, thwarted as he was in front of the other animals and spectators. The ringmaster was very fond of the cubs, no doubt, but their pranks often became an embarrassment. Besides, he had to run the circus, he had to keep all animals under control. One day he decided to end the daily stress. When the circus caravans were crossing a forest, he set the more aggressive of the cubs free in the deep jungle. After that the other cub never raised its voice. Every animal had been shown its place.

Subhas and Jawaharlal's proclamations, their defiant postures reminded Gandhiji of this story. Thankfully, with their recent withdrawal, the crisis seemed to have blown over.

The open session of the Congress began in the customary fashion. Gandhiji took the stage, the yellow paper of the resolution recommending that the Nehru Report be adopted in his hands. He was about to start reading when suddenly Subhas Chandra rose, walked up to Gandhiji, and held out another sheet of paper in front of him. 'What's this?' said Gandhiji, taken aback.

'An amendment to your resolution.'

Anger, disbelief, sadness, regret – several emotions played on Gandhiji's face. He looked at Subhas and Jawaharlal reprovingly. Without even reading it, he handed the paper to Motilal Nehru. The audience began to fidget. What new hurdles had these young Turks introduced, wondered the Gandhi loyalists. A wave of excitement swept over the youth.

Subhas Chandra stood there. All eyes were fixed on him. 'Most of the points in the resolution are commendable. But can any one of you place your hands on your hearts and say that the British government will keep its word? Within a year, can we get dominion status? Tell me?'

'No!' roared the delegates.

Having made his point, Subhas Chandra continued, 'We youngsters had hoped that this Congress would take some bold steps in the future. But sadly, we are today putting under wraps the demand for complete independence raised aloft at Madras.'

Resounding applause greeted his words. Slogans echoed through the air, 'Zindabad, zindabad, inquilab zindabad! Hindustan ke do lal, Subhas aur Jawaharlal!'

'The demand for complete independence has been put forth by the radical youth. My dear friend Jawaharlal and I may seem to you to be a part of this radical activist group. But we are the moderates among them. Ahimsa as a principle is fine. But it is not enough. All nations of the world are arming themselves and preparing for self-protection and self-defence. In this environment, to follow a policy of non-violence and disarmament will prove disastrous in the long run. When our country is free, we will have to fight modern enemies with modern weapons, don't forget.' Subhas spoke straight from the heart. This open advocacy for arms and weapons made Gandhiji very uneasy.

Subhas Chandra continued, turning towards Motilal Nehru and Gandhiji, 'Forgive me. Please don't think we have no respect for our seniors. Personal respect and loyalty is one thing, accepting principles without debate is another. If my amendment is accepted it does not mean that I am deliberately disrespecting my elders. We have the utmost regard for all our senior leaders. But if they refuse to understand the fire burning in our hearts, they may be forced to walk along with us. We want them to keep abreast of the times.'

Subhas's frank and fearless criticism had surprised and infuriated Motilal Nehru and Gandhiji. Subhas was being acknowledged with thunderous applause. Once more shouts of 'Inquilab zindabad' echoed all around. It was as if the Congress party had been taken over by young people. Subhas Chandra went on, persuasively, 'Many poets have sung hymns to complete independence till today. Martyrs have spilt their blood. I promise you, the flag of freedom we have held aloft will not be put down, not even for a second. Vande Mataram!' The deafening applause continued for a long time. For a brief while, everyone felt that independence was just a moment away.

If Satyamurti spoke in support of Subhas Chandra, Hari Sarvottam put forth Gandhiji's point of view persuasively. Both sides had their own advocates and they took turns in making their presentations. The delegates and audience kept getting tossed about – sometimes to this side, sometimes to that. For a full five hours, the discussions went on. It was 7 p.m. How long more would this debate go on? Who would decide? Motilal Nehru talked to Gandhiji and then whispered something to Jawaharlal. He took the mike into his hands and announced, 'Subhas's amendment may be put to vote. Let us take an hour's break before that. The president feels that it will be difficult to conduct the vote since the audience and the delegates are all merged together.'

The crowd dispersed. Gandhiji's acolytes gathered around him. They knew how deeply hurt Gandhiji was. The meeting reconvened at 8.15 p.m. When Jawaharlal stood up to speak on the amendment, the twenty-five-thousand throng listened in pin-drop silence. Motilal Nehru and Gandhiji's eyes were on him, hoping that like the previous day, good sense would prevail and he would support the Nehru Report. Everyone wondered what was going to happen. Here was a father holding the highest position in the party and there, his son openly challenging him. Jawaharlal spoke in his mellifluous Lucknowi Hindi. 'Hindustan was never a dominion of England. That is why I feel that if we have to leave the path of slavery and walk with self-respect, we cannot waver even slightly on our demand for complete independence. That is why I tender my unequivocal support for Subhas's amendment.'

Motilal Nehru's face grew dark, while Gandhiji looked frighteningly composed. It was 10.15 p.m. when Gandhiji stood up to speak against the amendment. Everyone held their breath. Gandhiji started off solemnly, 'If the youth of Bengal feel that a Gujarati bania, a merchant, is playing with their emotions, do be kind enough to dispel this misunderstanding.' Then throwing a bitter glance at the youth leaders, he continued, 'Jawahar, Subhas, last night both of you gave me your word that you would support the Nehru Report. The entire Subject Committee is witness to that. If you cannot keep your word for even twelve hours, how dare you talk about freedom!' Subhas and Jawaharlal's faces fell. Again, Gandhiji took the Congress members into confidence. He began to explain, 'You think if you are prepared to take bullets on your naked chests, you will be able to achieve your goals. But that time has not come yet. Don't raise your voices for nothing. Don't be afraid of shadows. Build up your courage. You are prepared to die for freedom, aren't you? Then wait for the appropriate time. I want you to die an honourable death.'

At midnight, the amendment was put to the vote. Subhas and Jawaharlal had a huge band of enthusiastic supporters on their side, but very few delegates. It was 1 a.m. The old year faded into the past. The new year dawned. President Motilal Nehru announced the result. 1550 votes were cast in favour of Gandhiji's resolution. Subhas Chandra's amendment got 973. Now it was only 'Gandhiji ki jai'. The Rightist group was extremely angry that Gandhiji had been challenged so strongly. The revolutionaries, radicals and the youngsters were unhappy that freedom had moved further away.

Jawaharlal and Subhas returned to Woodburn Park. Future conflicts seemed imminent and promised to be severe.

Letting out a long sigh, Jawaharlal said, 'I think though his resolution was adopted, the protests by the youth have made Gandhiji very unhappy.'

'You know, Panditji, it's better to be cursed by ordinary people – for in their curse is an element of forgiveness. But the wrath of sages and saints is deadlier than the sharpest blade. Their piercing gaze can turn rocks into dust. Imagine what the fate of mere mortals will be.'

Gandhiji reached Sodepur Ashram at 1.45 a.m. The ashram was a replica of Sabarmati and in its serene atmosphere, Gandhiji always found peace. Acharya Dasgupta was still awake. He escorted Gandhiji to his cottage. But Gandhiji could not sleep.

About forty-five minutes later, Motilal Nehru's car drove into Sodepur Ashram. Expressing his gratitude, he told Gandhiji, 'Bapuji, because you came to Calcutta, my prestige survived. If the boys had had their way, the Nehru Report would have been consigned to the Hooghly.'

'Yes, I realised that just in time.'

'Bapuji, you must be aware that the majority of the public of this country are with you.'

'What kind of majority are you talking about, Motilalji?' Gandhiji asked despondently. 'If our resolution got 1,550 votes, the opposition got 973, that is not an insignificant number, I'm sure you would agree.'

Gandhiji again recalled the circus at Porbandar and the two lion cubs that could terrorise the whole jungle. He said to Motilal, 'One cannot tell with these Bengali babus. Aggression and extremism are in their blood. Have you heard of Subhas's association with the revolutionists?'

'Is there any concrete evidence of that?'

'One cannot get attested proofs for everything. Subhas may not be a revolutionary himself. He may not even be an active member of their group. Yet, he is one of them. I admired Deshbandhu,' he said.

'Why?'

'How did he manage to remain Subhas's guru for so long. To hold that position with Subhas is not an easy task, I assure you.'

Gandhiji wanted to steer the Congress according to his vision. It was not going to be possible to keep the ship on course for long unless it had the winds of the new generation in its sails. To prevent the wind from turning into a gale was going to be difficult. It was possible that the waves caused by the winds would wreck the ship.

'I speak as an individual now, not as Jawahar's father, Bapuji, but I am convinced that your profound wisdom and Jawahar's voice are the need of the hour.'

Gandhiji looked at Motilal Nehru, surprised. The ringmaster's hand was itching. Almost exactly ten years ago, a cheetah named Jinnah had dared to snarl at him. At that time, the politician had overpowered him and using all the means at his disposal, fair and foul, he had cast Jinnah aside like a pebble. Now that cheetah was again growling out of his tiny cage, the Muslim League, all by himself. And so the circus show was on.

Again, Motilal said, 'I have been trying to persuade you for the last two years to make Jawahar the Congress president. Bapu, the two of you just come together.'

Gandhiji kept seeing the aggressive little lion cub who defied the ringmaster during the show, saying to him, 'We will make you keep abreast of the times.'

Then he smiled to himself. The master statesman, emerged from behind the saint. The Mahatma, who accused the British of adopting the 'divide and rule' policy, would resort to the same tactics. The ringmaster decided it was time to abandon the mischievous cub.

The early morning breeze had set in. Soon, the ashram bell announced the morning prayer. Gandhiji had made up his mind. He held Motilal's hand in a reassuring clasp, and the two of them set off for the prayers.

Five

Subhas Chandra had just returned from a trip to Delhi and he was exhausted. Basanti Ma served him his meal without asking any questions. Though he ate the sweet dish she had prepared for him, the usual pleasure was missing from his face.

'Subhas, what is weighing on your mind? Are you unwell?'

'Ma, what is more painful than separation from a dear friend?'

'Who are you talking about?'

'Jawaharlal.'

'Why, at the recent Calcutta session, the two of you shone like the sun and the moon. What has come between you?'

'The evil eye.'

'Whose?'

'A mahatma's,' Subhas Chandra smiled wanly. 'Succumbing to Gandhiji's influence, Jawahar seems to have given up his support of complete independence and with that of our left wing.'

'Oh, come on! It's all in your head. You are imagining it,' Basanti Devi replied.

As Kiran Shankar Roy and Subhas Chandra reached Howrah Station on their way to attend the Lahore Congress, someone thrust the latest newspaper into Kiran Shankar's hand. Glancing at the front page, he said, 'Gandhiji made a last-ditch attempt at talks with the viceroy. Unfortunately, it was an inauspicious meeting. The viceroy had just returned from a tour of south India that day. Earlier that morning, an attempt had been made by the revolutionists to blow up his train as it neared Delhi.'

Subhas Chandra quickly went over the news report. Lord Irwin had managed to escape unhurt, but his orderly was injured. Subhas Chandra said, 'According to the viceroy's statement, our leaders did not even raise the issue of dominion status, so then where's the question of the British doing a turnaround? Tell me what the British government is saying. Tell me, Kiran, where do such hollow negotiations leave the reputation of our leaders?'

'What are you implying?'

'Aggression. Confrontation,' Subhas Chandra roared. 'Gandhiji should forget his faith in discussions with the British and give a call for action.'

'According to him, the time is not yet right for attack. The situation in the country does not merit action yet. That's why he is not ready for a revolution.'

'That is the tragedy! The people are all set to fight. It is the leaders who are vacillating.'

'You have heaped praise on revolutionists like Bhagat Singh and Jatin Das,' Kiran Shankar told Subhas Chandra. 'That's why the British government considers you the most dangerous of all their enemies.'

'I know they do. But because of my open criticism of Gandhiji's policies, his followers do not look upon me as a friend. It is a very odd situation indeed.'

The Naujawan Bharat Sabha had been established by Sardar Bhagat Singh. On 8 April 1929, Bhagat Singh and Batukeshwar Dutt had hurled a bomb in the Central Legislative Assembly. The two revolutionists declared that their motive was to open the ears of the deaf British administration. They did not flee the scene of the bombing, but courted arrest. John Simon was present in the assembly when the bomb was thrown. Soon after, news came of Jatin Das's arrest in the Lahore Conspiracy Case. That shook entire Bengal.

Commissioner Tegart now cast his net around Subhas Chandra. The police kept a close watch on him. Surveillance was maintained through the night. Everyone knew that Subhas Chandra and Jatin Das were very close. The police found out that Das had taught Bhagat Singh's associates the art of bomb-making.

Lala Lajpat Rai had paid with his life for protesting against the Simon Commission. In that incident, an officer named Sandhurst had played a major role. To avenge Lalaji's death, Bhagat Singh and his friends had shot Sandhurst. Bhagat Singh had become the symbol of courage throughout the country. The political prisoners arrested in the Lahore Conspiracy Case undertook a fast to protest against the treatment meted out to them in the jail. Leading this was Jatin Das. The British attempted everything to disrupt his fast, even force-feeding. But Jatin Das was a hard nut to crack. Finally, on 13 September 1929, the sixty-first day of his fast, he achieved martyrdom.

When the body of this young, twenty-five-year-old was brought to Calcutta, Subhas Chandra and Barrister Sengupta were by his side through the night. They took part in the funeral procession barefoot. It was the biggest funeral Calcutta had ever seen – second only to Deshbandhu's.

In these intensely stressful times, Subhas Chandra undertook a tour of Punjab. He was welcomed by enthusiastic young people shouting slogans of 'Inquilab zindabad' and 'Long live the revolution'. Subhas Chandra tried very hard to meet Bhagat Singh in Lahore Jail, but he was refused permission. The fact that both Subhas and Jawaharlal had held the post of president of the All India Trade Union, and their increasing involvement in the rapidly growing peasants' and workers' movement, filled the British with trepidation.

On a 200-acre plot on the banks of the Ravi was built the beautiful Lala Lajpat Rai township. The youth had been incited by the propaganda of the Naujawan Bharat Sabha. They came to pay floral tributes to Lala Lajpat Rai who had been cremated near the venue of the session, their hearts filled with his memories and burning with thoughts of avenging his tragic death. Gandhiji and Jawaharlal had also arrived. Gandhiji had taken on the full responsibility of conducting the proceedings during the session, but the atmosphere was tinged with the extremist nationalism of Bhagat Singh and the Naujawan Bharat Sabha.

Alongside Jawaharlal's camp was Gandhiji's cottage, while the tents of Subhas Chandra and others were some distance away. Twenty-four hours had passed since the youth leaders of the country had arrived at Congress Nagar, but not a word was mentioned about the Youth

Congress nor a meeting of its leaders held. The disappointed brigade gathered in Subhas Chandra's tent and later that night, they landed at Jawaharlal's camp.

Nehru was looking unusually pleased. He welcomed all of them warmly. Subhas Chandra came straight to the point. 'We had talked about holding a session of the Youth Congress here too as we had done in Calcutta ...'

'I know, I agree. But Bapuji said, "Jawahar, when I am handing over the reins of the whole country to you, why have a separate Youth Congress?" Besides, he is going to propose a resolution for complete independence himself. What more do you want?'

'What are we going to achieve with mere resolutions? When is Gandhiji going to initiate active protest? The Congress is forty-four years old. What has it actually achieved?' asked Subhas, almost petulantly.

'Subhas, don't think that because I have accepted Gandhiji's tutelage, I have distanced myself from the Leftist ideology.'

'Panditji, don't ever forget that together we had vowed to introduce progressive, radical and rational thought into the Congress.'

Subhas paused for a while, calmed himself down, and then asked Jawaharlal again, 'Who started the Youth League? Who made the demand for complete independence at Madras? It was you, wasn't it?'

'There is no doubt about that. Tell me, Subhas, what are you afraid of?'

'That Gandhiji will cause a rift among the leftists."

'That is a very serious allegation, Subhas.'

'There is proof.'

'What kind?'

'Why did he turn up at the Calcutta Congress when he had vowed not to attend? Why did he postpone his previously planned trip to Italy and Turkestan?'

'That's all?'

'No. Why did he appoint you Congress president? The position rightfully belongs to Sardar Vallabhbhai Patel, even if you go by totally democratic practices.'

Jawaharlal was annoyed by Subhas's rapidly rising pitch. He flared up, 'Subhas, do you think I wanted this thankless post? I had in fact gone to meet Bapuji at Sabarmati to prevail upon him to become the president himself. Trust me, Subhas, I have been pitchforked into the chair.'

The discussion went on late into the night. Jawaharlal gave the young associates his word. 'I will definitely show due respect to a noble soul like Mahatmaji and my dear father. But my heart will always be with the Left and their progressive ideology. I am also young. A young forty-year-old.'

When the session got underway, Gandhiji stood up to table a resolution condemning the attack on Lord Irwin. He wanted it to be adopted unanimously. But it was opposed and the dissent grew louder. People started talking among themselves. Subhas Chandra's disapproval was heard. Kavishwar said, 'Subhasji, do we give Gandhiji unanimous support?'

'For what? Why is Gandhiji concerned only about the viceroy's life? Did he utter a single word about our Jatin Das's death? Normally he writes umpteen articles about health and nutrition in his *Young India* magazine. Did he have any words of condolence on Jatin Das's passing away?'

There was no unanimity on the resolution, so it had to be put to the vote. It received 942 votes in favour and 794 against. Those figures again sent Gandhiji's temper soaring. He was also hurt by the fact that such a large number did not believe in non-violence.

When he rose again to propose the resolution for complete independence, the entire gathering was staring at him with hawk eyes. Nehru, Subhas and the Left groups were all rejoicing, but Gandhiji seemed very troubled. He was truly convinced that the country was not yet ready for complete independence. Ironically, time had forced him to put forth the same proposal introduced by Nehru and Subhas a year ago at Calcutta, which he had then opposed tooth and nail. He had come to this decision after conceding defeat at the hands of the youth brigade. The resolution was received with thunderous applause. Suddenly, Subhas stood up on the dais. The clapping stopped abruptly. Now what more does he want, was the question everyone was asking. Calmly Subhas babu walked to the mike. First, he congratulated Gandhiji on the Sampurna Swaraj resolution. What next, wondered the delegates, recalling the events of the previous session. Subhas Chandra said, 'Gandhiji's resolution had also mentioned civil disobedience as a means towards achieving complete independence. But, as long as we are unable to bring the peasants, workers and deprived classes into the mainstream movement and make it a mass, national movement, as long as we do not sever all existing ties with the British and establish a parallel government to the white regime, we will not be able to get complete independence.'

Gandhiji was surprized by the idea of a parallel government. His resolution about the viceroy had met with such violent opposition. If opposition to him continued and Subhas's amendment was approved, it would mean a personal defeat for him and all that he stood for. Therefore, in order to maintain his grip over the proceedings, Gandhiji stood up to reply to Subhas's amendment. Using all the tools at his disposal – humour, wordplay, paternal authority – he said, 'I have the greatest regard for Subhas Chandra Bose. But he views me only as an old man past sixty years. Age has made me so frail that he can easily pick me up and hold me aloft.' Those seated on the dais laughed. Gandhiji too found it amusing. Still laughing, he continued, 'But I assure you, I am still a young man at heart. Although my bones are sixty-plus, I can vanquish any youth. I can ride a horse too. Tell me, gentlemen, can I ride a horse?'

Delegates, spectators, everyone shouted in one voice, 'Gandhiji, you can do anything!'

'I may not mount the horse myself, but I will certainly make it gallop. You know how?'

'How, Bapuji?'

'I have handed the horse's reins to Jawahar. Subhas's steps towards a parallel government will prove slippery. The country will be safe in Jawahar's hands.'

At that instant, the clock struck twelve. And complete independence became the Congress Party's declared objective. Lakhs of people had gathered on the banks of the Ravi that cold winter night. The national flag was unfurled. Saluted. Jawaharlal was ecstatic. At least on paper, the demand of the youth for Sampurna Swaraj had been accepted and hailed.

The following day, a meeting was held to elect the new Congress Working Committee. One list had been prepared by Motilal Nehru, another by Jamnalal Bajaj. Both had studiously excluded Subhas Chandra and his associates. The decision not to include the president of the vast east-west Bengal province in the working committee was as controversial as it was bold. But Motilal Nehru had staked his prestige on the inclusion of Barrister Sengupta in the working committee. Gandhiji agreed to it.

Even the ordinary party workers returning to their respective homes from Lahore, were conscious of the fact that Gandhiji had clamped the bit on Subhas. Several felt injustice had been done to him, and they were angry. But the British spies were thrilled at the growing divide between Gandhiji and Subhas. The same realisation left Subhas very unhappy. Jawaharlal had found a protective armour in Gandhiji.

The police headquarters on 14, Elysian Row Road was quiet. The next day was 26 January. Subhas Chandra and his brave comrades had resolved to take the pledge for freedom at the historic Maidan. As decided at the Lahore Congress, 26 January was to be celebrated every year as Independence Day. Police Commissioner Tegart had been informed that Subhas had gone all out to conduct the oath-taking ceremony on a scale that was unparalleled in the country. His angry gaze swept over the room, then jerking his head to one side, he announced, 'The increasing activities of the revolutionaries in Bengal are proving to be a great nuisance to us.'

'Sir, the attack on you the other day was both cowardly and shameful.'

Seeing that the discussion returned to him, Tegart winced. Once earlier, Gopinath Saha had killed an innocent Englishman mistaking him for Tegart. But recently, the revolutionaries had openly threatened him. His car had stopped for a few minutes in Dalhousie Square. Two young men, Amiyo Sen and Dinesh Chandra Majumdar, had hurled a bomb from behind the car. The alert driver had seen some commotion in the rear-view mirror and sped away. And then there was a deafening explosion. Tegart still shuddered at the thought of what might have happened.

The incident had proved once more that Bengal was the hotbed of terrorist activity. He was also convinced that the patron of the terrorists was none other than the mayor of the Calcutta Corporation. Barely two years ago, he had let Subhas Chandra go at the Kidderpore docks. How wrong he had been! Tegart rued the decision.

Discussions were on about what steps could be taken to prevent the next day's celebrations. Tegart said to his officers, 'Keep your cavalry ready. If a couple of satyagrahis break their ribs under the horses' hooves, it doesn't matter.'

'Yes, sir.'

'And if one of the beasts is fortunate enough to leave its imprint on the mayor's forehead, so much the better. We'll be rid of the irritant once and for all.'

As the officers were leaving the room, Tegart stopped them. 'Four hundred men died at Jallianwala Bagh. Was Dyer hanged for it? As long as you take whatever action is necessary in the service of His Majesty, no harm will come to you. Remember that.'

He spewed out the poison that was choking him. 'Let the world know that the Calcutta police are not eunuchs. Just as the Lahore police finished off Lajpat Rai, you too accomplish this task honourably. The panchnama, the whitewashing and all that, our benevolent government will take care of.'

The Bose households in Woodburn Park and Elgin Road were wide awake. Subhas Chandra was in the drawing room of the Elgin Road house, surrounded by workers and swayamsevaks. The clock on the wall struck two, and his mother peeped into the room. She was worried about Subhas and his imprisonments. Eight days ago, he had been arrested on Malda Station for making inflammatory speeches. Yesterday, he had been released on bail. And now he was preparing for another.

Sarat Chandra Bose and Bibha boudi too had stayed over at Elgin Road. They had heard that the British were trying very hard to nail Subhas on some charges and put him away for good. They were all seated at the dining table. Today, Subhas would eat a proper meal. Who knows, tomorrow onwards, it could be the tasteless jail fare again, Bibhabati thought.

Suddenly, Subhas exclaimed, 'I cannot understand what game fate is playing with my relationship with Gandhiji. Sometimes when I keep insisting that he call for action, for a fight, he doesn't respond. And every time his faith in the British is shaken, he is disillusioned by their not keeping their word and he calls for action, I am invariably in jail. Even during the Dandi March, that's what happened.'

'Subhas, don't forget, Gandhiji is my favourite leader,' Bibhabati warned him.

'Boudi, I too love and respect Gandhiji as much as you do. We have arguments, but we argue about principles. Unfortunately, whatever happens is exaggerated so much in reports.'

It was a cold night. Present at their house that night were all the senior colleagues of Subhas's: Narendra Narayan Chakravarty, Khitish Chattopadhyay, the convener of the women's wing, Jyotirmoyee Ganguly, the experienced and elderly Lalit Dasgupta, Satyaranjan Bakshi, and others. Subhas Chandra was explaining to them, 'If this country, bent under the burden of slavery for so long, is to stand upright and free, it is absolutely necessary to awaken its people. A mass movement has to be launched. Nothing significant has happened in one year's time. Nothing is likely to, either. Even if several generations are lost, this flame has to be kept alive.'

The still of the night was broken by the shrill siren of the police van and the clacking of boots. The meeting ended, and as Subhas Chandra said goodbye to his friends, he told them, 'Now that you are awake, don't go back to sleep.' While he was going down with some select members of the group, footsteps were heard on the outside staircase. It was Pulin Chatterji, with a message from the police. 'Subhas babu, the police commissioner says that in your own interest, call off tomorrow's parade. This is a final warning to you.'

'Go tell your boss, I will break the law. I am ready.' His voice was firm as he spoke.

Immediately, the Elgin Road house was surrounded by the police. All of Bhowanipore was awakened by hectic activity. Before daybreak, Narendra Narayan somehow broke through the police cordon and reached Subhas's house. On the stairs, he encountered his mother and told her breathlessly, 'I must meet him at once!'

The morning papers carried the news that Kiran Shankar and Purna Babu were in jail. Many others were being rounded up. And word spread like fire, that Subhas Chandra was missing. Calcutta's very heart quaked.

The cool night gave way to a warm day. The whole country was going to take the oath of freedom that day. The vast Maidan of Calcutta wore a new look. Along the boundaries of the Maidan were deployed bayonet-toting soldiers and other armed personnel. Tegart himself had inspected the arrangements. 'This time I will not let the city be taken over by Congress swayamsevaks,' he shouted at his officers.

The sun was climbing steadily. At Howrah Bridge, Alipore, Fort William and other places, crowds had begun to assemble for the oath-taking ceremony. But an uneasy calm prevailed over the area around Chowringhee Lane and the Octerlony Monument. Shopkeepers had partially downed their shutters. Trams were running empty. No one had any idea where Subhas Chandra was. Was he behind bars or was he sitting in some secret corner, plotting the overthrow, once and for all, of foreign rule?

Around two o'clock that afternoon, one side of the Maidan suddenly exploded with slogans, rallying cries, shouting and commotion. Everyone rushed to find out what was going on. In the blazing afternoon sun, Subhas had appeared in the middle of the road, boldly waving the tricolour in his right hand. About fifteen hundred young men and women stood around him in an orderly manner. Dressed in stark white khadi, they looked like a flock of swans descended from the skies. Countless tricolour flags fluttered in innumerable hands. Suddenly like the guerrilla armies of Shivaji or Rana Pratap, hordes of swayamsevaks poured out of the surrounding lanes, by-lanes and buildings and joined the parade, which swelled like a river in flood. Beside Subhas Chandra was Jyotirmoyee Ganguly, leading her four-to-five-hundred-strong women's battalion. They too wore white khadi saris, but the tricoloured bangles on their wrists attracted the most attention. And then suddenly, the heavens reverberated with 'Vande Mataram! Vande Mataram!' As the strains were picked up around the grounds, they were mixed with cries of 'Inquilab zindabad! Inquilab zindabad!' The swayamsevaks had formed a wall around Subhas Chandra and to the command of 'One, two! One two!', the columns marched forward. Soon, freedom songs and patriotic verses were sung in chorus, interrupted by slogans and swayamsevaks shouting, 'Aage badho! March on!' Subhas walked on, barefoot. His feet were invariably unshod whenever something untoward or unusual happened. Just after the parade crossed Chowringhee Road, Robertson and Banerji halted them with instructions from Tegart. 'Don't take one more step forward,' they threatened.

'We are going to take a pledge for the freedom of our country. Who are you to stop us?'

'These are the police commissioner's orders.'

'The call for freedom is more sacred than the mantras of the Vedas. God Himself cannot stop us. Who are you?' said Subhas, brushing past them.

The cries of 'Vande Mataram' grew louder. Defying the law, the procession moved forward. Suddenly, a series of gunshots rent the air. A wave of horsemen came at the marchers. Baton-wielding soldiers swung their weapons left and right. Hooves slashed foreheads, broke open skulls. Hapless young swayamsevaks fell bleeding, their limbs broken, skin lacerated. Blows rained on Subhas Chandra's body as the horses approached him from all sides and began to circle him. Though soaked in blood, he continued to cry out, 'Vande Mataram! Inquilab zindabad!' Volunteers ran helter-skelter. Indiscriminate firing and baton attacks continued. One soldier on horseback tried to wrench the flag out of Subhas's hands, but did not succeed. More soldiers gathered around him. When Subhas saw them, he pulled the flagpole back and yelled, 'I may fall, I may break, but I will never let the tricolour go.'

The soldiers were frustrated. Two of them signalled each other, mouthing 'Crush him', then dug their spurs into their horses' flanks. The horses reared. As they confronted Subhas Chandra, one of the men heaved his baton and hit Subhas on the head. Blood spouted like a fountain. Jyotirmoyee, standing right next to him, was splattered with it. Like a tigress, she rushed forward. Holding Subhas's bleeding head close to her body, she screamed, 'You sons of Satan! Don't you dare lay a finger on our beloved leader again!'

The batons kept coming down hard. Subhas was flitting in and out of consciousness. Someone shouted, 'They are killing Subhas babu!' In a split second, a crowd gathered around him. They turned the flagpoles they were carrying on the soldiers. Their white tunics too were soon patched with red. Once again, the spirited defence put up by the swayamsevaks shattered Tegart's dream of teaching the Congress volunteers a lesson they would not forget.

A police van picked up a grievously wounded Subhas Chandra and headed towards the dark cells of Lal Bazaar police station. Subhas's right hand was broken. His khadi shirt was in tatters. Every inch of him was aching from numerous bruises and gashes. The darkness in front of his eyes was getting deeper, thicker. But he kept muttering, 'Inquilab zindabad!'

He had been sentenced to six months' imprisonment. Sarat Bose had come to Presidency Jail with some sweets for him. But Subhas was preoccupied. For the last several days, negotiations had been going on between Viceroy Lord Irwin and Gandhiji, and everyone was anxiously waiting to see what the outcome would be.

The First Round Table Conference was ineffective. It was attended by a few zamindars, rulers of some small states and several industrialists. Prime Minister MacDonald had realised how futile it was to discuss India without including Gandhi and Congress party. Taking advantage of this, the viceroy had initiated discussions with Gandhiji. To contain anti-government feelings, front-ranking leaders had been immediately released from prisons.

This was the first time the British had held discussions with the representatives of a colonised country on equal terms. Hosts of reporters and press photographers had gathered at Governor House and Ansari Mansion where Gandhiji was staying. Column after column was filled with news of these talks.

The night brought with it a whole host of questions. This second nationwide movement of Gandhiji's had left the British incensed. The no-tax movement had spread to Gujarat, Uttar Pradesh and most of Bengal. The boycott of foreign goods had been successful. Sixty to seventy thousand Congress workers were in jail. All the prisons were overflowing. At several places, temporary shelters were erected for the detenues. Abdul Ghaffar Khan's Red Shirts Brigade in the North-West Frontier Province was openly defiant of the government.

Gandhiji's fight had left not just India but the whole world stunned. But the supporters of British Imperialism found his success intolerable. The leader of the Conservative Party, Winston Churchill felt the government ought not to have entered into any discussions at all. And he expressed his displeasure forthwith. 'What a shameful and contemptible scene we are forced to witness. Once a common lawyer of the Inner Temple, this naked fakir now sits at the viceroy's table and bargains as an equal with His Majesty's representatives – what could be more humiliating!'

The following day, all the papers carried the news of the Delhi agreement. Kiran Shankar, Sasmal, Bagchi, Khitish and others crowded around Subhas Chandra. All the terms of the agreement had not been announced in the news. Just then the jailor informed them that they might all be released in a day or two. Instructions to that effect had been received from Delhi.

It did not take long for supporters of the Bose faction to reach their homes from Alipore Jail. Party workers were celebrating their release. But no one was interested in them. They all assembled at Woodburn Park in a couple of hours. Somebody had picked up a copy of the *Gazette of India Extraordinary* from one of the newspaper offices. The terms of the agreement had been spelt out in detail in the gazette. Subhas Chandra read through it several times. Finally, he folded it in half and threw it down. 'What's the matter, Subhas?' asked Sarat Bose.

'See it yourself. After a month-long discussion, what have we got? In this entire agreement, the words Sampurna Swaraj have not even been mentioned! Of what use are such agreements!'

'So what has been achieved, Subhas?' asked Bagchi.

'A royal invitation to the Second Round Table Conference and an enquiry into the police atrocities on satyagrahis. That's all. Take this pumpkin and be quiet.'

All faces fell. Sarat Bose exclaimed, 'Gandhiji won the battle but lost the war. Such an astute politician should not have been vanquished thus.'

Subhas stayed in bed all day like a convalescent. The agony of defeat made him very restless. After a while, Sarat Bose came into the room with the gazette. 'Have you read the clause about political prisoners carefully?' he asked.

'Did you find anything new in it?'

'Those activists who have charges of violence against them will not be released. The pity is that the government will decide what the definition of violence is.'

Subhas became extremely agitated to hear this.

Both the brothers knew how heartless and inhuman the attitude of the authorities towards political prisoners was. Just a few days ago, four patriots, Mallappa Dhanshetti, Jagannath Shinde, Sarda and Qurban Hussain, had been sent to the gallows at Sholapur. The Delhi pact had taken all the steam out of the movement. How many more families of political prisoners were going to be ruined, no one could tell.

Prabhabati, Bibhabati and the rest had hoped that after coming out of jail, Subhas would spend a few days at home. But this pact between Gandhiji and Irwin had left him distraught. He did not want to remain in Calcutta any longer. He wanted to meet the signatory to the pact, Gandhiji himself, and ask him to explain the terms.

The Karachi Congress was round the corner. What kind of reactions would the pact evoke there? What would the Congress's future course of action be? His mind was beset with questions, doubts, arguments. Saying, 'Ma, forgive me,' Subhas Chandra took leave of her and boarded the train to Bombay to see Gandhiji.

He went to Mani Bhavan accompanied by Barrister Kiran Shankar. Seeing the frown lines on his face, Gandhiji laughed and said, 'Subhas, I was certain that you would be unhappy with the pact.'

'Tell me, Mahatmaji, which clauses of the agreement should I be pleased about?'

Gandhiji became uneasy. Subhas Chandra could not hold himself back. Involuntarily, his voice began to rise. 'Gandhiji, if in your demands, you had at least made a passing reference to the words Sampurna Swaraj, I would have been thrilled.'

'Hmm, must have been left out ... oversight...'

'Such important words?'

'All right, they were not mentioned. Does that mean we have given up our demand for freedom? Is that what you think, Subhas?' said Gandhiji, more than a little annoyed. In a disappointed tone, he continued, 'You are a very big leader, such peevishness and irritability does not suit you.'

'It's not a matter of my being peevish or angry. The framing of the agreement was important, Gandhiji.'

'It hasn't made much of a difference.'

'How can you say that? The British government does not run according to the mantras in a temple.'

'What exactly are you trying to say, Subhas?'

'The workers are playing with their lives, the wise men in British administration with words!'

Scenes from Lahore Jail flashed before Subhas Chandra's eyes as he spoke. Lowering his voice, he asked Gandhiji, 'What will happen to Bhagat Singh, Rajguru and Sukhdev?'

'What about them?'

'In this agreement, it says, "Immediate release of political prisoners who participated in non-violent demonstrations". So where does Bhagat Singh stand?'

Now Gandhiji looked distinctly uncomfortable.

'The government is making preparations at Lahore Jail to hang him and his associates. That's why I am asking you this question. They can do it at any time. Very soon. Perhaps even before the Congress session.'

Gandhiji was silent. Kasturba and Kiran Shankar remained still, holding their breath. Gandhiji found Subhas's high-pitched voice jarring on his nerves. Intolerable. Thousands used to come to the ashram for an audience with him, for guidance. They would write down their questions. None of them had ever been impertinent like Subhas Chandra Bose to demand an answer. Swallowing his pain, Gandhiji muttered, 'Subhas, there is a huge chasm between your way of thinking and mine.'

'So let it be. After all, both roads lead to the same goal – freedom.'

'However, I do not approve of your path. Remember, Subhas, I am prepared to wait for years and years for freedom, if need be. But even in my dreams, I cannot imagine taking the path of violence to attain it.'

Kiran Shankar and Subhas Chandra stood on the platform at Bombay Central, watching the huge crowd of young men and old women, coolies and party workers gathered around a third-class compartment of the Frontier Mail in which Gandhiji was travelling to Delhi. With them were Senapati Bapat and other colleagues. Finally, the train steamed out, followed by cries of 'Gandhi Maharaj ki jai!' Subhas Chandra and Kiran Shankar Roy were in the first-class compartment, some bogies away from Gandhiji.

'Subhas, come to think of it, Sardar Patel should have been given the presidentship much earlier.'

'You're right. All credit for the Bardoli Satyagraha goes solely to him. Gandhiji has revealed his duplicity in favouring Jawahar.'

'But why so?'

'Primarily to win over one important leader from the Left group and strengthen his own position and authority. Before the Lahore session, he kept singing Jawaharlal's praises all the time. He said that the nation is safe in his hands ... but he should first let this country take birth as a nation.'

'Another thing, Subhas. What will become of Bhagat Singh?' asked Kiran Shankar worriedly.

'One of the inhuman clauses of this agreement dangles the hangman's noose before all revolutionists,' replied Subhas.

The discussion ended abruptly when Kiran Shankar fell asleep.

Subhas went to Gandhiji's compartment. It was very crowded, with several workers and other passengers, coarsely clad farmers and labourers – who stared at Gandhiji's brown, half-naked figure with oration. Gandhiji quickly made space for Subhas opposite himself. Travelling like this was difficult for someone getting on in years, but it gave him a tremendous sense of satisfaction too.

Only the other day, a furious Subhas had met Gandhiji in Mani Bhavan and strong words had been exchanged. But now, the talks had taken a frank and cordial turn. Subhas began, 'Gandhiji, your principle of non-violence is universal. It can only benefit mankind.'

'But, will be detrimental to Hindustan. Is that what you want to say?' Gandhiji asked with a hearty laugh.

'Not quite that, Gandhiji,' Subhas clarified. 'It only sets our political goals back somewhat.'

'How?'

'Suppose I had been in the talks with Irwin in your place ...'

'What would you have done?'

'I would have insisted on something substantial in our favour.'

For a while, Gandhiji was silent. Then the conversation turned to inconsequential matters. Subhas continued chatting with Gandhiji, Kasturba and Mahadev bhai, and before they knew it, it was past midnight. Subhas found that his head was throbbing, probably because of the constant travelling and running around. He stuck his fingers into his ears to minimise the noise. 'Subhas, aren't you feeling well?' Kasturba asked.

'I keep getting these severe headaches every now and then,' he replied.

Immediately, Gandhiji placed his hand on Subhas's forehead. Then he took out a batuwa and a small pestle and mortar. In the cloth bag were various kinds of herbs and roots. Subhas Chandra knew about Gandhiji's faith in naturopathy and herbal medicine. He had read several of Gandhiji's articles on the subject. He ground some herbs into a paste and applied it on Subhas's forehead. Subhas was touched. A cool breeze blew in through the window, and Subhas fell into a deep slumber in the crowded compartment.

When the train reached Agra, Gandhiji got a sense of the public sentiment in the north. Crowds began to gather around his compartment. They were clamouring, 'Gandhiji! Gandhiji! Save Bhagat Singh's life!' 'Do something! Save the three of them!'

The death sentence of Bhagat Singh, Rajguru and Sukhdev had become a burning issue. Gandhiji sensed an aura of fear around Ansari's bungalow. Subhas Chandra and Jawaharlal too met there. Jawaharlal looked perturbed. But even in that undecided state, he upheld Gandhiji's stand.

'We have achieved so much because of this Delhi Pact,' he said.

'Is that so? But in informal talks with foreign journalists, you declared that Gandhiji had surrendered before Irwin.'

'Never mind, Subhas. You know what the truth is, don't you?'

The upcoming events were going to take a serious turn. The pressure of public opinion was increasing. Gandhiji rushed off for an urgent meeting with the viceroy. Patel, Prasad and other followers of his stood around his car. Closing the door, Jawaharlal said, 'Bapu, do something. Get a pardon for Bhagat Singh.'

'It is important to respect the agreement,' Gandhiji replied.

'Why be cowed down by it? It is not the sacred word of Brahma,' Subhas interjected. 'Gandhiji, you can break the pact. The leaders of the Sinn Fein party in Ireland have done it many times.'

Gandhiji went off without replying. But when he returned from the viceroy's meeting, all hearts sank. His grim expression sent out the clear message, Bhagat Singh could not be saved.

'So the death sentence will not be commuted?' asked Sardar Patel.

'Nothing like that. An appeal signed by ten thousand people, saying "Do not take any hasty action" has been handed over to the viceroy today. He will have to take note of it.'

All Congressmen were heading to Karachi for the annual Congress session. Before leaving Delhi, Gandhiji had written a letter to the viceroy, telling him that the Bhagat Singh matter was a delicate one and advising him not to act in haste. Even Jawaharlal and other senior leaders had requested patience and care in dealing with the issue. On 23 March 1931, they were all crossing into Karachi.

The 24th day of March dawned. It was as if a bomb had been dropped on the train. An eerie silence descended on the compartment and spread through the train. The British government had played a dirty trick. On the night of the 23rd, the three noble young patriots had been sent to the gallows in Lahore Jail. Their families were not allowed to see their mortal remains. They were cremated within the jail premises, and the ashes were thrown into the Sutlej. It was the only thing people talked about in all of Punjab – its marketplaces, its neighbourhoods, its homes.

Soon, crowds began to gather at the railway stations along the way. The red-shirted Naujawan Bharat Sabha members dominated the scene. The enraged public tried to stop the train and shouted angry slogans, 'Gandhiji, go back!'

'What did Gandhi baba do?' 'Our dear Bhagat Singh was sent to the gallows!' 'Mahatma Gandhi murdabad!' 'Bhagat Singh zindabad!'

The number of demonstrators at Maleer Station near Karachi was unbelievable. The young men offered Gandhiji black flags. The whole of Punjab was asking the same question. Gandhiji had no answer.

At one spot in Congress Nagar, Gandhiji was making a speech. The atmosphere was extremely volatile. The youth leaders were trying their best to disrupt the meeting. Finally, Gandhiji also lost his temper. 'You are all angry with me. Fine. It will not take much effort for you to crush these fragile bones of mine. But you will never be able to destroy the principles for which I am fighting, for which I stand.'

At the Karachi session, Vallabhbhai was the president. In his precise and to-the-point presidential address, he emphasised the issues related to the farmers. Gandhiji began by denouncing violence. Then he condoled the death of Bhagat Singh and his comrades. 'It is true I neglected Bhagat Singh,' he admitted. 'But while signing the agreement, I did not believe I had made a mistake.' The Congress Right had learnt well how to get out of sticky situations. With profound respect, they escorted Bhagat Singh's old father, Kishan Singh, to the stage and tried to appease the fury of the youth.

A short distance away from the Congress tent, a different kind of preparation was on. Overnight, another tent had been erected by the Naujawan Bharat Sabha and another session of the youth force was being held there. They unanimously elected Subhas Chandra as the leader of all the youth bodies in the country. Subhas was intoxicated with a sense of power and glory. In his speech, he emphasised the importance of discipline and love, along with justice, equality and freedom.

While explaining the system of governance that would be good for the country, he said, 'For Hindustan, we need a socialist democracy. And our freedom shall be total and complete, a pure and unadulterated revolutionary system. Unless extremist and revolutionary means are adopted, freedom will not be attained. In the policies of the Congress, I see a terrible languor and shameful compromise.'

A young man asked, 'Subhas babu, what is your plan of action?'

'First let us stick to the basic principles of socialism, let us form peasants' and workers' organisations. Youth leagues shall be established under stringent disciplinary measures. Let us get rid of the cruel caste system. Let us free the common people from blind faith in rituals and superstitions. By creating awareness groups, let us work for the all-round emancipation of women. Boycott British goods. The spark of inspiration that has ignited the flame in our hearts, we will never let it be extinguished.'

Acharya Kripalani could not bear the excited sounds coming from the nearby tent. To find out what aspersions were being cast on Gandhiji, he quietly went in and sat down. After decrying the agreement that Gandhiji had signed as being loose, meaningless and unsatisfactory, Subhas went on to say, 'I have no reason whatsoever to doubt the patriotic sentiments of the signatories to this offensive pact. We will no longer allow the kind of politics which, should a tricky situation arise, will keep the public dispirited while intentionally strengthening the hands of the wicked British government. Come on, rise, get ready! Ignite such a fire of revolution in this land that imperialist powers throughout the world are scorched by its heat.'

A two-lakh strong crowd had gathered at Azad Maidan to receive Gandhiji when he returned from the Round Table Conference in London. Tight security arrangements were made all round the venue. The commissioner of police himself was seated there. The political scenario in the country was changing rapidly. In the United Provinces, the 'no-tax, no-revenue' campaign had been revived. Angered by this, Nehru was on his way to meet Gandhiji, but the police arrested him on the way. Abdul Ghaffar Khan's Khudai Khidmatgars (the Red Shirt Army) were gaining strength in the North-west Frontier Province and causing the British government considerable annoyance. So they arrested Ghaffar Khan. From these two incidents, it was clear that the government was going to adopt a more aggressive and repressive approach.

The following day, a closed-door meeting of the working committee was held. When Gandhiji announced that the Civil Disobedience Movement would be launched very soon, Subhas Chandra was happy. Although the working committee seemed enthused by this on the face of it, a nagging feeling of guilt, of being cheated, troubled them all.

The new viceroy showed signs of being more hostile, and he had no sympathy for the Congress. He wanted to strip it of all its revolutionary tendencies. Terrorist activity was on the rise in Bengal. Surya Sen and his associates looted the Chittagong armoury. Eleven officials had been killed in various shooting incidents. Bombs and live cartridges were recovered in large quantities from different places. One thought plagued everyone – was India turning into another Ireland? Informers, native British collaborators and Tegart's officers were clueless. When Sarat Bose himself took up Surya Sen's case, confidential directions had come from Delhi to take action against the Bose brothers. The only question was – on what grounds? Trying to arrest them in Bengal was worse than playing with fire.

Subhas was staying with Nariman in Bombay. Khurshid Nariman, who had risen to the highest post in the Bombay Congress, was born into a middle-class Parsi family of Thane. His father was the diwan of the erstwhile state of Janjira. Then he joined the British Police Service and became an inspector at Belgaum. Nariman did his law from Bombay. For the last fifteen years, he had been voted the mayor of Bombay by a thumping majority. Several times he had been the Congress president. He had supported Gandhiji's call for boycott of the legislative council. He had participated in the Non-cooperation Movement too. And he was the first satyagrahi from Bombay to violate the salt tax.

Many workers had come to Nariman's house to meet Subhas.

'Subhas babu, be careful,' one of them warned.

'Why do you say that?'

'The news is that the Calcutta police are looking for you.'

Just then the phone rang. It was for Subhas. Nariman handed the receiver to him. 'Hello ... hello ...!' There was no reply from the other side.

Subhas put the receiver down. Again, the phone rang. The same thing happened.

'What is going on?' wondered Subhas.

Nariman asked him, 'Subhas, do you have any special friends in Bombay?'

'Well, some relatives, a few friends.'

'A young lady?'

Subhas Chandra was taken aback. 'So it's even reached you,' he exclaimed.

'Oh yes! I hear of your visit to Bombay from her, long before you inform me. She calls very often. Her name is Mugdha.'

'Yes, I know. Her letters have created quite a furore in Calcutta. Several people including the police believe that I am secretly married to her.'

Subhas Chandra set out early the next morning with Nariman. About fifteen yards away from the house stood a young woman, staring in his direction. She was tall, fair, slim, her hair was tied in a beautiful knot, she wore mojris on her feet, and had a purse in hand. She had the proud bearing of a typical Maharashtrian. As soon as she saw him, her whole body broke into a smile, then bashfully she covered her face with her long slender fingers and giggling, ran into the nearby lane. Nariman exclaimed, 'That's her!'

'Why did she run away like that?' asked Subhas.

'That's what being coy means among the Maharashtrians. You are supposed to be that way when you see a dear one.' Subhas shook his head in embarrassment.

After a hectic day of meetings, Subhas finally boarded the Calcutta Mail at Dadar station. So many thoughts were crowding his mind. He had to show Gandhiji Bengal's capability in national work. They had been travelling for an hour and a half when the train pulled in at Kalyan. It was 2 January 1933. The train would turn towards Nasik from here.

Suddenly, police whistles were heard on the platform. Subhas stuck his head out to see what the commotion was all about, when a police party from Calcutta barged into the compartment. The Bombay police who had come to arrest them, surrounded the station. As if they were in pursuit of a notorious criminal. Crowds of Congress workers and party members from Kalyan rushed to the station on hearing the news of Subhas's arrest. The police thrust him into another train. 'Where are you taking me?' Subhas asked. 'Don't know,' the police officer replied.

Where he was being taken, where he would be kept, no one knew. Every now and then, orders were received from the seniors. The journey continued. Subhas was very angry. The train was passing through the prickly scrub-covered plains of Madhya Pradesh. After crossing several hills, they entered a vast barren plain. Suddenly Shivani Prison loomed large ahead of them. Built for solitary confinement, this prison had neither electricity nor a regular water supply. It looked like it belonged to the middle ages.

Two days went by. The jailor stopped by Subhas's cell to tell him that Gandhiji and his followers throughout the country had been taken in. 'The Congress party has been declared an illegal organisation. All its offices have been sealed, documents and funds confiscated. Thousands of Congressmen are being taken into custody.'

The British had seized the opportunity. By sweet-talking their way into getting the signatures on the Delhi Pact, they had taken the wind out of the movement's sails and now were turning the screws of oppression, slowly but surely.

Shivani Prison was a terrible place. Subhas Chandra had been in jail six times before, but nothing quite compared to this one. The building had no doors, no windows. The floor had been flattened hard with bricks and mud. Overhead were zinc sheets, which radiated the intense summer heat. Stinging hot winds blew throughout the day. Absolute silence – disrupted only by the boots of the guards patrolling the prison – along with sooty, dented and misshapen utensils and prickly coir charpais gave the prison an infernal aura. How was he going to spend his days in this hellhole.

Every day, Subhas watched the sun rise and set on this wilderness. On blazing hot afternoons in the distance, a mirage would appear; while on a clear night, one could count the stars. From its place in the predawn sky, the morning star, Venus, looked down at Subhas Chandra with her twinkling eye, as if his mother were watching over her dear son.

Cramps twisted through his stomach, leaving him weak and exhausted. The same illness, the same pain, that he had suffered in the prison in Burma had reared its head. Subhas began to lose weight. His bright blooming countenance looked pale and withered.

One day Subhas sat staring at the mirage in front of him when the figure of Mej-da appeared before him. Was he hallucinating? Mej-da actually picked up Subhas's bony hand and held it tight. How had Mej-da arrived, unannounced like this? Subhas looked around and saw the guards accompanying him. They had arrested Sarat Bose and brought him there.

The brothers looked at each other with tear-filled eyes. Subhas's voice shook as he spoke, 'Mej-da, how is it that you are here?'

'Regulation Act, 1818, Section 3.'

'Mej-da, they put you in the dock?'

'There is no provision for that in the law.'

'Reason for arrest?'

'The government is not obliged to tell you that. They only know how to put you down.'

'But for how long?'

'Indefinitely.' Sarat Bose sighed.

Subhas felt much better now that he had the company of his beloved elder brother. The loneliness of the Burmese prison had been horrific.

Since the barracks had no doors, the brothers were seated in the veranda, talking.

Sarat Bose had gone to Zahira in Bihar in connection with his work. He had been arrested there and dispatched directly to Shivani. The joy of seeing Mej-da did not last very long. At the thought of Mej-da being in jail, Subhas broke out in a cold sweat. Besides serving the country, Mej-da, the head of such a large family, with a fleet of cars and a retinue of servants, worked very hard as a lawyer, earned money by the sackful only to spend it on Subhas and others. Now who would provide sustenance to the families of those political prisoners. Who would pay the fees of the numerous poor students whose education he supported. The cockatoo in the cage by the front door along with the whole household must be waiting, waiting for Subhas's Mej-da to return.

The Bose brothers were political prisoners, but they got none of the privileges permitted to them. Sarat Bose had written several letters to everyone, from the home secretary to the viceroy, demanding to be told what their offence was, what proof they had against them, why they weren't being tried in a court of law. For how long would they languish like this? But the letters were not even acknowledged.

Unexpectedly one morning, Bibha boudi turned up at Shivani. Seeing her dejected and shrunken face, both brothers felt a tight knot of fear inside. Her charming smile had long left her face. Her eyes were still deep, eloquent, but with dark rings round them. In a tremulous voice, Subhas asked her, 'How is everybody at home, boudi?'

'Chhor-da, look after yourself. Stop worrying about us.' She paused for a long while and then began to speak. 'After your brother was arrested, the police sealed the house. They went through all the papers and documents. Even now, their spies wander around the house.' Bibha boudi, who had never stepped out of her door, had stood with her head held high and her chin up, ready to face the calamity before her. Subhas felt very proud of his sister-in-law. Sarat babu, swallowing the lump in his throat, asked, 'Bibha, what about all our students?'

'They were troubled at first. But now I have made some arrangements for them.'

'Are the funds enough?'

'Some students are taking only half the scholarships' amount. Others have taken up part-time jobs. But all of them are praying for your quick release.'

There was so much to tell, so much to ask. But the guard harshly announced that visiting time was up. Bibhabati collected herself with difficulty. Hiding the tears stealing down her cheeks, she said, 'I will go to Delhi. I will meet the viceroy. Until I get you your rights and privileges, I will not rest.'

Just as she was leaving, Sarat Bose asked, 'Bibha, what did Ma and Baba say?'

'Oh yes, they asked you not to worry about them and to look after yourselves.'

For a couple of days after the meeting with Bibha boudi, Subhas Chandra slipped into depression. Again, he started suffering from indigestion. The pain in his lower back was acute. His throat felt constricted. Sometimes, the pain was unbearable. He felt like screaming out his agony. But the thought that Mej-da would worry made him grit his teeth and bear it in silence. But none of it escaped Sarat Bose's eyes. As the summer became more severe, Subhas's health deteriorated further. He could barely eat anything. Sarat Bose pleaded with the jailor and obtained permission to go into the kitchen. He made either chicken soup or watery rice kanji for Subhas and himself. Often, Subhas would be only half conscious, and he would have to feed him.

The atmosphere in the home department of the secretariat in Delhi was quite intimidating. Hardly any Indians ever went there. But that day, a typical upper-class Bengali woman, carrying a file, was seated outside the home secretary's room, inviting curious stares from passing officials and babus. She kept glancing at the nameplate, Morris Hallet, Home Secretary. Bibhabati's brother had accompanied her. Soon the peon informed her that she could go in. Observing the dignified bearing of Bibhabati, Hallet asked politely, 'Well, what can I do for you, madam?'

'Release my ailing brother-in-law. He is a political prisoner.'

'What ailment?'

'A lung infection and stomach problems.'

'Tuberculosis? Then he should be released at once.'

'That's what I have come for.'

'What is his name?'

'Subhas Chandra Bose.'

Hallet looked startled. He called for Subhas's file and opened the note on his past record. 'Subhas Chandra Bose is a fiercely nationalist leader. Possessed by anti-British feelings. He has had a long association with terrorists' groups. Used their services in Bengal Municipal Administration. In short, he is the most fiery and dangerous leader of radical wing, the biggest threat to the British Empire in India.' Hallet quickly shut the file. His ruddy face was grim. Drumming his fingers on the table, he shook his head regretfully. 'I am sorry, madam, I cannot help you.'

'I haven't come all the way from Calcutta to hear this,' replied Bibhabati.

'There isn't another revolutionary in India as dangerous as your brother-in-law. Even so, if he is ill, we will take better care of him in future.'

'What better can you do? I have myself seen Shivani and Jabalpur jails. My ill brother-in-law lies under scorching zinc sheets. If you kept animals there, their hides would peel off. No human can survive in those conditions.'

Hallet was impressed by Bibhabati's reply. He had not encountered a spirited Indian woman like her before. He said to her, 'My sympathy is with you. But I am not in a position to help you.'

Dabbing her moist eyes with her sari, Bibhabati retorted, 'So the British government wants to see Subhas Chandra waste away like this.'

'No, not at all. We had shifted him to Madras for treatment. But the problem could not be diagnosed there. He was sent to Balrampur for further treatment, wasn't he?'

'His brother Sunil Bose is a doctor. Why don't you let him stay with him?'

'For some specific reasons,' Hallet replied and remained silent for a while.

Because of Subhas's and Sarat Bose's arrests, the edifice of the Bose family was in danger of collapsing. How hard Bibhabati had tried to hold it up, only she knew. Again she said, 'We will take care of him. We will pay all expenses. But send him to some jail in Bengal.'

Hallet said nothing. He had recently accompanied the governor of Bengal on his visit to the viceroy. 'Don't even mention sending Bose to a jail in Bengal,' he had said sternly. 'Instead of him, a hundred hardened criminals are welcome. Subhas's mere presence in Bengal stimulates violence.' Having been a witness to this discussion, Hallet could only say to Bibhabati, 'Any other province?'

'Bombay will do. My brother-in-law Sailesh Babu is there.'

Hallet opened the file once more. 'Many leaders of secret international organisations travel to Bombay. So it will be risky to send Bose there.' That was the pre-emptive statement recorded by the Bombay administration. The frown creasing Hallet's brow made Bibhabati say, 'What about Punjab? He can be treated in the nearby Dalhousie.'

'Punjab?' Hallet looked even more grim. As soon as Subhas sets foot in Punjab, extremist youths will gather round him in clusters. After Bhagat Singh's death, Punjab has become highly volatile. Sending Subhas to Lahore or any other jail in Punjab will be inviting terror, the governor of Punjab had stated emphatically. Again Hallet apologised. 'I am sorry, madam. Your brother-in-law is a dangerous enemy. None of the provincial governments are willing to accept such a notorious political prisoner.'

'The British government will not let him live, but because they don't want the guilt of his death on their heads, they are playing these games!'

'We will consider giving permission to let him go abroad for treatment,' Hallet said on a conciliatory note.

Bibhabati immediately left for Calcutta. With Sarat Bose's practice closed, the goddess of wealth had left the house. Money had to be borrowed for Subhas Chandra's medicines. Jankinath Bose, too, was not keeping well. He had to be looked after, as also Subhas's mother. Apart from that were the numerous poor students who were dependent on the Bose family. Sarat Bose's five brothers were also earning, but they had their own establishments. Now, the entire responsibility had fallen on Bibhabati's shoulders.

For the last few months, Subhas Chandra had been shunted around from jail to jail. None of the provincial governments was willing to admit him into their territory. Somehow, the Madras government relented and after a stint there, he was sent to the sanatorium at Bhawali in the Central Provinces. And now he was in Balrampur. Fortunately, his gall bladder was fine. But the lung problem would not go away. Every day, he would burn with fever. The sciatica pain was chronic.

It was decided to continue the treatment in Europe. There was no other option. He asked Khitish, 'Would it be a good idea to take letters of introduction from Gandhiji and Rabindranath?'

'Why not?'

Subhas Chandra longed to meet his parents once before going to Europe. Jankinath Babu, too, had pleaded with everyone to permit him to see his son. He and his wife could not undertake the long journey due to their failing health. In spite of all efforts, there was no guarantee they would get the permission. 'At least, let me speak to my brothers,' Subhas had requested.

The administration relented. Sarat Bose spent four days with Subhas in the jail. They were magical moments. He confessed that Subhas meant more to him than his own children, and the thought of being separated from him was unbearable.

The day of departure drew near. A number of people had arrived in Jabalpur the previous day. Sarat Bose's sons, Ashoke, Amiyo, Sisir, Bibha boudi and Basanti Devi were among them. The jailor would not allow so many people to meet Subhas Chandra. Basanti Devi was horrified by the strange structure of the jail. The heat beating down from the zinc-sheeted roof had given her a throbbing headache. She yelled at the jailor, 'All of us want a meeting.'

'I do not have orders from above.'

'Above? You don't mean the sky, do you?' she asked sarcastically and moved forward. All of them were shocked to see Subhas. His emaciated body. Sunken cheeks. Unnaturally bright eyes looking out from behind wire-rimmed glasses. Arms and legs as thin as sticks. A living skeleton. Basanti Devi's heart stopped. But then she heard a heartfelt 'Ma' from Subhas, and felt his hand on her shoulder. 'Subhas,' Basanti Devi told him, 'we are all helpless in the path of misfortune. But once we get freedom, no child will be separated from its mother.'

With heavy hearts, they bid Subhas farewell.

Subhas Chandra was on board the Calcutta Mail, heading for Bombay. On a long, arduous, uncertain journey.

The Calcutta Mail finally arrived at Bori Bunder Railway Station. Immediately, the withered body of Subhas Chandra was whisked away in a municipal ambulance to Arthur Road Jail. Two officers of the secret service from Delhi were parked in the home secretary's office. The home secretary was holding a camera copy of a document and reading out aloud, 'Passport number 72308 – Not valid for entry into Germany and the United Kingdom. Good! You have effectively muzzled the man!'

'We had no choice. He is one of the most anti-British Indians alive. As it is, students in England are strongly influenced by communist and socialist ideology. If Bose gets there, then sparks are bound to fly.'

As requested by them, the captain of the ship, SS Ganges was summoned to the home secretary's office. The Delhi officers asked him, 'What route are you following to Europe?'

'Via Scandinavia.'

The ship's papers were scrutinised. 'You are definitely not going via Hansa?'

'No, sir.'

When the captain and the naval officers left the room, the Delhi officers remarked, 'Arms can be smuggled in through Hansa. Also, the waters are infested by pirates and rogue vessels. They can give all kinds of assistance to terrorists. That's why we will not permit Bose to travel by that route.'

The secret service officers were in constant touch with the naval authorities. Until the dangerous man named Subhas Bose was safely out of Bombay, they were to stay on high alert.

The ship was to set sail that night. But the ambulance carrying Subhas arrived at the harbour early in the morning. The British could not trust Subhas. The public, too, was familiar with the deceitful ways of the British. They had assembled at the harbour long before the police. With them were senior Congress leaders like Nariman, S.K. Patil, D.D. Sathe and a host of journalists. As the stretcher was lowered from the ambulance, the Gateway of India and its environs resounded with cries of 'Vande Mataram!' and 'Subhas babu ki jai!' The police commissioner had flatly refused to let the Congress delegation meet Subhas Chandra. A crestfallen Sailesh Bose, his uncle Dutt Babu and Sailesh's family stood on one side. With his fingers, Subhas motioned the kids to his side. He stroked their faces, kissed them. He begged the police officers to let him have a word with his younger brother.

'Then speak in a language we understand,' they warned.

Subhas Chandra was annoyed. Rudely he retorted, 'I have nothing to tell him that I can say in your presence!'

As the stretcher moved towards the ship, the uncontrollable crowds surged forward. Suddenly, a worker from Gandhiji's ashram rushed to Subhas's side and whispered something. Slowly, the stretcher was carried aboard the SS Ganges. Subhas Chandra raised his tear-filled eyes and joined his hands in a namaste to all on shore. Once again, 'Subhas babu ki jai!' and 'Vande Mataram!' rent the air.

The ship weighed anchor after midnight. Subhas was told that he would be free once they were out of Indian waters. Countless stars twinkled in the cloudless sky. The salty breeze was adding to the restlessness in Subhas's heart. Just when it was time for action, when the struggle was gathering momentum, his health had betrayed him. He watched the Bombay shoreline recede, the lighthouse grow smaller and smaller, as they sailed into the deep dark waters. The letter of recommendation never came from Gandhiji. Even Rabindranath's letter of recommendation seemed to be completely drab and bereft of emotion. Gandhiji's last-minute message had hurt him. He had said, 'When you are so illustrious yourself, Subhas, why do you need a recommendation from anyone?' A sugar-coated bitter pill. Subhas Chandra was no longer so naive as not to see political claws in velvet paws. Well, so what if the Mahakavi and the Mahatma denied me letters of introduction. With the strength in my wrists, I will make myself known to the world. I will carve a path through the ocean's breast, battle with mountains, and garner all the weapons and arms in the world to heap at your feet, my motherland. And with them, I will break the shackles round your feet, set you free from the curse of slavery.

Subhas was lying in the cabin, brooding over these things. A doctor was travelling with him. Suddenly, he recalled a message he had given to the youth. They were his own words, but at this moment, they were transmuted to golden words of wisdom that lit up the darkness in front of him and showed him the way ahead – of hope and glory.

Do you want the fragrance of the full-blown rose?
If so, you must accept the thorns
Do you want the splendour of the smiling dawn?
If so, you must live through the dark hours of the night.
Do you want the joy of liberty and the solace of freedom?
If so, you must pay the price.
And the price of liberty is suffering
And sacrifice.

Six

Europe was not unfamiliar to Subhas Chandra. This time his travels began in the historical city of Venice, criss-crossed by canals on which plied gondolas. Rarely would one find the identity of a city so linked to water. It was humid and cloudy in Venice. Subhas Chandra's nephew Ashoke, who was in Europe, had received him in Venice, and now they were in a gondola taking in the sights. A lawyer named Mr Mishra, who was on the voyage from Bombay with Subhas, had insisted on accompanying him everywhere, and was now seated in one corner of the gondola.

Early the next morning, Subhas Chandra and Ashoke came down to the lobby of the hotel and found Mishraji already there, bags and all, waiting for them. When Subhas Chandra asked for a cab to go to Vienna, he wanted to accompany them, as he wanted to visit his relatives there. Subhas Chandra got really annoyed at that. 'Stop this nonsense at once, you rascal, police agent. Keep your tricks for Bombay. They will not work here!'

Properly ticked off, Mishra slunk away quietly. Ashoke was amazed by the tailing indulged in by the British police. Finally, they arrived in the Austrian capital, Vienna. Subhas's treatment began at Dr Fuerth's nursing home.

Soon, Subhas Chandra shifted from the sanatorium to Hotel de France. But wherever he went, he was followed by journalists and Indian students. Naturopathy had made him feel better. His energy was gradually returning. He had started German lessons and also begun meetings with the Vienna Municipality. His thoughts revolved around how civic life in India could be made better by following the examples of corporations in Europe.

Two months went by. News came that Barrister Vithalbhai Patel, on his way back from America, was going to stop at Vienna to convalesce. Subhas Chandra rushed to Vienna Station in the bitter cold to receive him. He was surprised to see an elderly gentleman, hunched over a cane, wearing a fur cap and a calf-length overcoat, alighting from the train. Was this really Vithalbhai? He had changed so much. Age had taken its toll. Face wizened, hair sparse, eyes sunken.

To Vithalbhai, Deshbandhu had often referred to Subhas as the most precious jewel in his treasury. A deep affection and mutual respect had marked the friendship between Deshbandhu and him. Vithalbhai was aware of Subhas Chandra's many prison sentences, his demonstrations, his singular organisational abilities as evident in Bengal. Once they reached the hotel, they got into a serious discussion. 'How are the Non-cooperation and Civil Disobedience Movements progressing?' Vithalbhai asked.

'So far very well. The latest figures I have show that a lakh and twenty thousand freedom fighters have been arrested. Among them are thousands of women.'

'Subhas, the eyes of the entire world are on our movement. God willing, Gandhiji's struggle will meet with resounding success.' After a pause, he continued, 'What is your vision for India?'

Subhas Chandra began to describe his dream, 'We need a strong union with an administration that is sensitive to the needs of peasants and workers. We must have five-year plans like Russia. The foundation for heavy industries and for the industrialisation of the country must be laid. Village industries must get a boost. Population growth must be controlled immediately. Caste and creed discrimination should be done away with. Different linguistic groups must live amicably with each other. I wish to see a new egalitarian society rise out of this very earth, which will continue to lead the world as it has done in the past.'

'Well said, Subhas!' exclaimed Vithalbhai.

Barely a couple of days later, early in the morning, there was a knock on Vithalbhai's door. He was surprised to find a visibly disturbed Subhas Chandra standing outside in his dressing gown. Obviously, something untoward had happened. He silently held out a newspaper and what

Vithalbhai saw in it shocked him too. Gandhiji had called off the Non-cooperation Movement unconditionally. Subhas stood there as if drained of all spirit. Trembling with rage, he said, 'Gandhiji should not have done this. Why did he have to withdraw the struggle? It was non-violent, wasn't it?'

'It's quite incomprehensible, all this,' replied Vithalbhai, unable to keep his voice steady. 'Our commander isn't exhausted from his many fasts, I hope. What has his thirteen-year struggle achieved. Only penance, suffering and regret for us, and minimum damage to the British. Gandhiji has failed as a statesman. To keep the faith in him in future will be self-deception.'

For two whole days, both were engaged in deep discussion. It was imperative that some action be taken. As a witness, they summoned a journalist friend called Alfred Tyrnaeur. 'Alfred,' Vithalbhai said to him, 'my young friend here and I have come to the conclusion, after much thought and debate, that today India is sitting on a simmering volcano.'

'History cannot be rewritten through negotiations and fasts, can it? They must be accompanied by concrete action,' added Subhas Chandra.

'That is why we have jointly prepared the draft declaration. Read it out, Subhas.'

Subhas Chandra began, 'Until now, Gandhiji has done some commendable work for the nation. But now, his method has outlived its usefulness. He has become an obstacle to the success of the struggle.' Subhas paused, then went on, 'In the interests of the nation, a constitutional restructuring of the Congress and an immediate change in leadership is required. We no longer believe that organisational progress is possible only under Gandhiji's leadership. If the Congress party has no intention to take some corrective measures, we will have no choice but to form another party. It is crucial to bring together all the activist groups in the country, and keep up the pressure on the British.'

Alfred was shocked at this open confrontation with Gandhiji. He said, 'Don't you think, Mr Patel, that this is taking it a bit too far?'

'Alfred, this young man wanted to launch a frontal assault on the British with the sharpest weapon possible. I have toned it down considerably.'

'But doesn't it sound brash to you?'

'There is nothing objectionable in it,' Vithalbhai said, in defence of Subhas. 'In fact, through Subhas speaks the youth of my country. To some, these words may seem like blazing coals; to others, they may appear utterly foolish. But they are the robust green shoots of a new revolution. He is all girded up for it, and I am fully behind him.'

Suddenly, Vithalbhai's old eyes dimmed. He dabbed at them with the end of his dhoti. 'What's the matter, Mr Patel?' asked Alfred.

'Until now, we have followed the conservative path in politics. But freedom, our goal, is still not in sight. It is far away, beyond the horizon. When fair means don't succeed and the gods will that blood be shed, what can anyone do.'

It was impossible for Subhas Chandra to remain a convalescent for too long. He toured Czechoslovakia and visited the heavy industries there. He travelled through Poland during the rains. He wanted to see Lenin's Russia. But before that, the passport authorities got a confidential letter from the Indian government. He was refused a visa to Moscow and had to return to Vienna. No matter where he went, British agents were there, following him.

By the beginning of July, Vithalbhai's health began to deteriorate. Around the same time, Barrister Sengupta passed away while in custody. When the news reached Vienna, Subhas Chandra was deeply aggrieved. A condolence meeting was arranged by the Indians in Austria. A feeble Vithalbhai insisted on attending the meeting in a wheelchair. His voice shook as he recited,

The trees they cry out loud,
The birds they are homeward bound,
The birds they are homeward bound.

Subhas accompanied Vithalbhai to his residence. Vithalbhai asked, 'Subhas, today you seem more worried than usual.'

'Some Muslim students in London have intensified their demand for Pakistan. You must have heard about it.'

'Shame! Those who ask for chunks to be broken off from this great subcontinent must be crazy.'

Vithalbhai sat still. Deep inside, something was eating into him. Slowly, he said, 'Barrister Jinnah and Mahatma Gandhi are both sons of Gujarat. I feel distressed that such a bitter quarrel should break out between them. Do you remember the incident at the Nagpur Congress?'

'Which one?'

'In the course of his speech there, Barrister Jinnah referred to Gandhiji as Mr Gandhi. Immediately Gandhiji's followers shouted, "Say Mahatma Gandhi". But Jinnah would not relent. There was an uproar. Jinnah left the Congress camp that day and was never seen in it again.'

At the end of their conversation, Vithalbhai asked, 'Subhas, if the issue of partition comes up, what will your stand be?'

'I will fight it till the last drop of blood in my body. I will sacrifice everything to preserve the integrity of my motherland.'

Vithalbhai looked at Subhas with pride. Both he and Subhas were plagued by illness. In view of Vithalbhai's deteriorating condition, his friends moved him from Vienna to a small town in Switzerland. Subhas Chandra too suffered from intense stomach aches. But when he heard that Vithalbhai was critical, he rushed to Glaad to be with him. He remained at Vithalbhai's bedside constantly. Vithalbhai's relatives were duly informed and Nathalal Parekh and Bhogibhai Zaveri came immediately from England. The government would not give Sardar Patel permission to travel abroad. He was stuck in Nasik Jail.

It was late in the night. Subhas made a cup of coffee for Vithalbhai and left saying he would return the next morning since Nathalal was on night duty.

Vithalbhai said, 'Nathalal, I want to make a will.'

'Where's the need for that?'

'I wish to donate some money for the service of the nation to someone outside the family.'

'To whom?'

'Subhas Bose.'

'I thought you were going to leave funds for the Gandhi Ashram.'

'Nathalal, there are enough wealthy people to take care of Gandhiji and Vallabhbhai. Subhas appears to be a loner. Look after him after my death. I see in him a fearless warrior possessed by his idealism. He will not compromise on his principles. You will see that though he appears very impatient and restless, there is an extraordinary sense of sacrifice and service in him. Do nurture him. Don't fail to bring the registrar tomorrow morning. I must make my will. There is little time left.'

The following day, the will was attested and sealed. Patel placed Subhas Chandra's hand in Nathalal's. Through his tears he said, 'Subhas, you are the symbol of my hopes, my aspirations. I entrust my wealth to you for the upliftment of my country.'

'Vithalbhai, your generosity is boundless. I am deeply grateful to you, but I cannot accept your donation.'

'Why not?'

'Neither Vallabhbhai nor Gandhiji will like it.'

'Subhas, what I do with my wealth is my call.'

22 October 1933. It had snowed all night. Vithalbhai was on a respirator. Subhas felt his courage slowly ebbing away. He believed that in serving Vithalbhai, he was serving his guru, Deshbandhu.

In the afternoon, Vithalbhai regained consciousness. He pushed aside the oxygen mask. His weak eyes spotted Subhas. He noticed his tear-stained cheeks.

He whispered, 'God did not give me a life long enough to protect you. A pity. But, my son, be radiant with your own light!'

Those were his last words. Subhas placed a copy of the Gita inside the shawl covering Vithalbhai and retreated. He stood at attention as if on parade and saluted Vithalbhai in true military style.

Subhas now wanted to quickly write a book on India's freedom struggle. When he mentioned this to Dr Mathur, he said, 'How did the thought of getting into the literary field enter your head? Is it because Jawaharlal's autobiography is all the rage in Europe just now?'

'Not at all,' replied Subhas, holding out an envelope. 'Wisehart, a publishing house in London, has commissioned me to write a book for them. They have even sent me an advance. Only my health is a hurdle. If I could get a scribe ...'

'That is not a problem. So many young men and women are wandering around without jobs. Europe hasn't recovered from the recession yet.'

Very soon Mathur recommended a young woman. She met Subhas, but the poor girl was already doing two part-time jobs, so her timings did not suit him. A couple of days later, another girl came with a letter from Dr Mathur. Subhas just kept looking at her. She came in like a breath of fresh air – with her pink cheeks, rosy lips and pleasant demeanour. On the short side, but charming and attractive at first glance. 'Please come in, sit down.'

'Thank you,' she said, and placing the files she was carrying on the table, pulled a chair back and sat down.

It was necessary to interrogate her because he was worried about spies. Subhas asked, 'What is your family business?'

'My grandfather owned a large footwear store, but because of the depression, he lost everything,' she said matter-of-factly.

'What does your father do?'

'He is a vet.'

From his conversation with her, it was evident that Emilie Schenkl had faced obstacles in completing her education. Except for a few grammatical errors, her English was both fluent and chaste. Subhas was most impressed by her German. For a long while, he stared at her expressive eyes. There was an unusual spark in them. Subhas told her that he had selected her for the job. 'Thank you, sir,' she said as she rose to leave, then closed the door gently behind her.

Just then the phone rang. 'So what did you think of the secretary?' It was Dr Mathur.

'Yes, she seems pleasant. Will make an excellent secretary. Also, the poor girl seems to need the job badly.'

'Hold it, Subhas babu, go easy on the praise. You don't intend to fall in love with her, I hope?' Dr Mathur guffawed.

'What nonsense!' retorted Subhas and put the phone down.

Work on the book, *The Indian Struggle*, began in earnest. Subhas dictated and Emilie took it down. Sometimes, when inspiration struck in the middle of the night, Subhas would write it down in long hand. He wrote so furiously that on some occasions, he could not decipher his own handwriting. Perhaps, because Emilie had grasped his feel for words, she had little difficulty typing them out. The book had to have a number of references, but Vienna could not provide him with the source material he required. Subhas had already got a large number of books from Sarat Bose. Some had been sent by Jawaharlal. Yet, for the latest references much running around was involved. Emilie managed all that.

Subhas wanted to learn German and Emilie would give him lessons.

One day, Subhas said to Emilie, 'I get so desperate to find out what is happening in my country sometimes.'

'There is a simple solution to that. There are so many German newspapers.'

'But their prices are exorbitant – a foreign tourist cannot afford them.'

'Let's go to the corner café. They have many newspapers there.'

'Are you sure?'

'Of course. Come and see for yourself.' They began going to the café for an hour every day. Subhas would look at the headlines and ask Emilie to read the other news items. She would translate them into English for him.

One day, Emilie asked him, 'When you refer to Mahatma Gandhi, why do you say Gandhiji and not Mr Gandhi? What does "ji" mean?'

'It signifies a great deal – respect, affection, admiration. That's why we say Gandhiji.'

'I too feel great respect for you. So can I call you Subhasji?'

'Of course. Why not?' Subhas said, amused.

Emilie's workload began to increase. She had to pick up books from the library, buy groceries, make sure he did not miss his meals, and if he did because he was too engrossed in his books, she would make hot toast with butter and jam for him. And of course, endless cups of tea and coffee. Subhas was addicted to both.

One day, Subhas Chandra said to her, 'You take a lot of trouble for me.'

'I don't think so.'

'I would like to get you a gift. Something nice. Tell me, what would you like?'

'I like the mighty mountains with their lofty peaks. Will you give them to me?' she asked, looking him straight in the eye.

'Oh no! They are out of my reach!' he said in mock consternation, and both burst out laughing.

Gradually, Subhas began to feel a constant pleasurable but nameless ache inside. His friends knew him as a bathroom singer. Where had that habit gone? He no longer sang Rabindra Sangeet or Nazrul Geet at the top of his voice. Emilie's hazy reflection in the bathwater distracted him. The rustling leaves spoke in her voice. Long before it was time for her to arrive, he would hear knocks on the door. His eyes kept straying to her face as she was working. What was this? He scolded himself severely one day. Love buds bloom in youth. Thirty-six was no age for them to blossom. After the ICS, God knows how many seductive eyes had pursued him. Innumerable young women pined for him. All those love letters were testimony. There was Mohini, who had declared she would gladly embrace widowhood, should he be awarded a death sentence. And then that Marathi girl Mugdha! His friends were convinced that he had taken a secret vow of celibacy. But he had decided that until the matter of India's freedom was not resolved, he would not bind himself in marital bonds. He would not indulge himself. But now this Austrian charmer called Emilie had thrown him completely off-balance.

Emilie had never said anything. Yet, Subhas felt as if her being, her essence had seeped into his flesh and bones. One day at the dining table, Emilie asked him, 'Subhasji, why don't you get married?'

Subhas Chandra choked. Swallowing a few sips of water, he shook his head and stammered, 'No, no, don't want that headache.'

'Why?'

Letting out a deep sigh, he replied, 'Just one reason. If you cannot make anyone happy, at least don't make her unhappy. That is my policy.'

'Don't say that. Anyone who is associated with you can only be happy.'

'My life is a smouldering volcano. I will not be at peace until British Imperialism is overthrown. The torture in the prisons, the whiplashes at the hands of the Pathans, the radiating heat of the zinc sheets overhead, constant discussions and debates with senior leaders regarding the future of the nation, joy at meeting new companions, sorrow at losing colleagues halfway through. Who knows what may happen, when a bullet strikes me, when British imperialists behead me. I have nothing to offer to a young woman.'

Days flew by. Subhas would dictate, Emilie would take the text down and type it out. One night, it had got quite late. Emilie's eyes fell on Subhas Chandra's jacket pocket. His fountain pen had leaked and the ink stain was spreading on it. She quickly brought a pan of water and some cotton wool and began to scrub at the stain. To get a better grip, she held on to the sleeve of the jacket.

At her warm touch, a shudder coursed through Subhas's body. Before he knew what was happening, Emilie had rested her head on his chest. The feel of her silky hair, her body close to his – the sensation was so unfamiliar and yet so dear. Subhas was about to let the pleasurable feeling wash over him when the stern voice of duty broke into his thoughts like a demon, 'Where are you going?'

Subhas Chandra disengaged himself from Emilie's embrace and moved away. She looked at him through her frightened eyes, then in a barely audible voice said, 'I had warned you, hadn't I said that I love the high mountains, the lofty peaks ... I know you are a great leader. But please don't spurn your lover away like this.'

Subhas Chandra was trembling, his breathing ragged. 'What is the meaning of this foolishness, Emilie?' he asked, his voice hardening.

'What foolishness? Does a tiny butterfly not have the right to seek shelter in a mountainside?'

Subhas had no reply. His emotions were running riot. Emilie clasped him in her arms once again. He felt sharp pinpricks all over his body, as if a hundred fountains were dancing on it. His blood was on fire. Teardrops were rolling down Emilie's cheeks. Again, Subhas Chandra pushed her away. 'Forgive me, Emilie. For the last thirty years, I have been crazed by my love for her. I have ruthlessly killed my own childhood, scattered the golden moments of spirited youth over her body, I have given up my position, my prestige, even my life to her, how can I be unfaithful to her, my beloved motherland!'

Emilie slipped out of the room. The next day, work went on as usual. The German lesson ended, and she rose to leave.

'You haven't said anything,' Subhas said.

'What is there to say?'

'Something, anything.'

'Will you listen?'

'Of course.'

The floodgates were opened. Trying to brush away her tears, Emilie said, 'Subhasji, they say, sorrow shared is sorrow halved. I never wanted you to shower me with flowers. But allow me the privilege of walking beside you, sharing your hardships, as you march towards your goal. It will give me great pleasure.'

A quiet descended on Subhas. His mind was calmed. With the fragrance of the golden champa, Emilie had come into his life.

The rainy season was over. They moved to the picturesque small town of Karlovy in Czechoslovakia and rented a coor house. Like a beautiful club, it had a conference room, a concert hall, and a swimming pool too.

Every morning, the two of them would set, off arm in arm, and walk to the hot sulphur springs nearby. Sometimes they walked for miles through vineyards heavy with bunches of plump juicy grapes. Subhas Chandra's health improved. The work on the book was progressing nicely. As winter drew near, the chirping of birds in the thickets grew louder. But these two birds were silent.

'Emilie, why did I not fall in love all this while?' Subhas Chandra said.

'All bachelors feel that way in the end.' She laughed.

Several chapters of the book had been completed and the proofs had been sent back from London by the publisher. Emilie's presence had transformed Subhas Chandra's life. He was no longer sloppy. The pots and pans gleamed in the kitchen. For the first time, the newspapers and books were arranged neatly in a pile in his bedroom. His baggy long-sleeved dressing gown was altered to fit him smartly. He was amazed. Truly, God must have given women a magic wand. It was a period of love and euphoria, of happiness and sulks, tantrums and reconciliations. A blissful life.

There was an unexpected caller one morning. It was the postman with a telegram redirected from Vienna. It was from his mother. His father was critically ill. Subhas and Emilie immediately departed for Vienna Airport. Emilie was very upset as they said goodbye. 'Let me know how Baba is by telegram,' she pleaded.

'I will. Don't worry.'

'And don't just scribble a few lines. I want long letters from you, because every moment away from you will be like solitary confinement for me.'

The security check was completed. The suitcases were checked in. Emilie stood far away, watching him. Suddenly, Subhas seemed to remember something. He asked the security officer for permission to go out for a minute and almost ran outside. Emilie was flustered. She rushed forward. 'What's the matter?'

'Look, Emilie, you are very careless. Be careful when you cross the road. There is so much traffic.'

'You came back all the way to tell me this?' she asked in surprise.

'Yes.'

Emilie burst out laughing.

The plane made its way towards Cairo through a blanket of fleecy white clouds. Memories of Baba jostled around in Subhas Chandra's mind. He kept thinking how fortunate he was to have had a father like that. Which parent would allow his son to give up the ICS and become an ascetic. His and Ma's initial opposition still sent shivers down his spine. But eventually, he had relented and accepting him as a 'guru bandhu', he had given him his blessings.

The plane made its first stopover at Cairo. They had to make four halts before getting to Calcutta. In Cairo, Subhas picked some postcards of the famous pyramids of Egypt. He sent one of those and an aerogramme to Emily. 'My beloved, I have never written such letters before this. Promise me you will keep this a secret, locked up in your heart. Don't mention it to anyone, please.'

Early the next morning, the plane took off and headed for the eastern hemisphere. The rising sun looked spectacular in the cloudless sky. Subhas had not had such a clear view of the sun in a long time. They reached Karachi at eight-thirty that night. Though it was dark, Subhas felt a sense of jubilation as he landed on home soil. He had to spend the night there as there was no flight till the next afternoon. The following morning, the mayor of Karachi, Jamshed Mehta, and a popular leader, Chaitram, called on Subhas Chandra at the hotel. Together they arrived at the airport. Subhas Chandra picked up a copy of the *Patriot*. 'Sad Demise of Subhas babu's Father', the headlines screamed at him. His world seemed to have collapsed around him. He wanted to lean against the wall and give vent to his grief. But he had to go on.

Security personnel snatched his bag from his hands and examined every single item, from razor to scraps of paper that were in it. Subhas Chandra had brought some chapters of *The Indian Struggle* to show Sarat Bose. The police confiscated them.

At about four o'clock that evening, the aircraft approached Dum Dum Airport. Just as the plane started its descent, there was hectic activity on the ground. Military personnel took position, as if enemy bombers had landed. As the propellers of the plane came to a stop and Subhas emerged from the aircraft, they stared at him, on high alert, as if he were wearing a bomb-laden jacket. Just then, two police vehicles, their sirens screeching, came speeding down the runway. Subhas was bundled into the first one and whisked away. As they passed the terminal building, Subhas saw the disappointed faces of his four nephews watching him from behind the police cordon. Both sides of the street were lined with excited crowds of party workers throwing garlands and flowers at his car and shouting, 'Vande Mataram!'

A senior police officer of the special branch was in the car with him. He handed Subhas a government notice and immediately asked for his signature. Subhas opened the notice. He saw the words 'Bengal Criminal Law Amendment Act Article 2 (1)' and asked the officer, 'So what about it?'

'You will be under house arrest. An officer from the special branch will be on duty round the clock. All communications, regardless of who they are addressed to, will be vetted. Not even a scrap of paper will fall into your hands without his permission.'

'What if the law is not obeyed?'

'A seven-year sentence at least.'

The house on Elgin Road was literally under siege. It was crawling with policemen. Subhas got out of the car and saw a grief-stricken Mej-da standing on the steps. The two brothers clung to each other, no longer holding back their tears. Sarat Bose tried to comfort him. 'Subhas, you are very late,' he said.

'What could I do, Mej-da?'

'Till his last breath, Baba was talking about you.'

'What did he say?'

'He called me to his side and said, "Tell Subhas that I am taking leave of this world gratified that I have left behind sons such as you. May God bless and keep you and our motherland safe."'

Subhas's seven brothers, four sisters, a host of relatives were all seated on the floor. His mother was sleeping in the puja room. She was shattered by her loss. How could he face her. That too, alone, without Baba by her side. How would he comfort her. Sarat Chandra Chatterjee, the eminent writer, was seated near Subhas. He offered words of courage. Almost stealthily, Subhas entered the darkened puja room. 'Ma,' he called out softly. At once she sat up. Subhas averted his eyes – he could not bring himself to see her like that – hair open, broad kumkumless forehead, stark white sari ... She clung to him like a wilted creeper. All day, Subhas sat in the puja room with her head in his lap.

Sarat Bose handed a telegram to Subhas. It was from Gandhiji. 'Received the sad news about your father's passing. I pay my respects to that noble soul. He is the proud father of such worthy sons. May God bless you.'

At the time, there were two prisoners in the Bose house. Sarat Bose had been released from jail, but kept under house arrest just a few days before Jankinath Bose's death. The police had taken surveillance to an extreme. They were not allowed to meet anyone. Not even speak to anyone from a distance. One day Subhas was standing in the balcony. On the opposite side of the road were Satyaranjan Bakshi, Hemanta and Satyen babu. They were communicating with each other through gestures and signs. When the police officer noticed Subhas, he flared up and started shouting. Subhas, red with fury, stomped down the stairs and asked Sarat Bose, 'How can you bear this, Mej-da? Such excesses don't happen even under martial law.'

'That is nothing. Take a look at this.'

Subhas read the dry official document. It was a permit allowing the brothers to attend the last rites of their father.

'Mej-da,' he asked angrily, 'this letter is backdated. Even before Baba's ... you ...'

'Yes, before his death. The police made me apply in advance. "If you don't get permission at the last moment, it would not be our fault," they said.'

According to the Hindu Bengali tradition, mourning was for three weeks. Prayers were held every afternoon. All the brothers would sleep on straw mats at night. Since anything made of wool was taboo, they shivered in the cold, with only their dhotis to cover themselves with. The police vigil continued through the night. They had to beg and plead with the government for the three-week-long permit. Subhas had to return to Europe for further treatment. His health had been neglected once again during this time.

This time, he did not have to face the same tight security on his departure from Bombay as the last. Many Congress workers and journalists surrounded him. One overzealous reporter asked him, 'We hear you are all praise for Hitler ...'

'This is news to me,' replied Subhas, surprised. 'Just think, can the Nazi coat ever be our size? As far as economics is concerned, Hitler is a puppet in the hands of big industrialists. To tell you the truth, I neither have any love for Hitler nor for Nazism. But the spirit and speed with which he has restructured Germany from the ashes of the Versailles Treaty, that effort I salute.'

ೲ

Five years had passed since Subhas's exile. The youth wanted their beloved leader back. Gandhiji found politics bland and unchallenging without Subhas. The family's favourite member was not amidst them. All the birds, arrested for participating in the Civil Disobedience Movement were now flying free. According to the 1935 Act, elections were to be held soon. The outlawed Congress wore a new garb. The worn locks on sealed offices were creaking open. A fresh optimistic wind was blowing through the land, but Subhas was not to be seen.

From Kashmir to Cape Comorin, there was but one question on every lip: 'Where is Subhas Chandra? Bring him back home.' After so many years, a Congress session was held at Lucknow. Jawaharlal was in the president's chair, and so the progressive thinkers among the youth were delighted. The young members of the newly formed Congress Socialist Party wandered through the venue in groups. Everyone wanted to know when Subhas babu would arrive.

Barrister Bhulabhai Desai stood in the opposition benches of the Central Legislative Assembly in the stance of a wrestler, and belligerently asked the Indian government, 'Where is our dear Subhas Chandra? Is it true that the government has banned his entry into India?'

'A man with a brilliant mind and tremendous popularity like him is dangerous. If he is allowed to return, he will not sit idle. He will put into practice all his revolutionary views, and push us to the edge of an abyss.'

'Shame! Shame on this repressive government. Why do you shriek these allegations like jackals? Let him come back. Then if you have the guts, try him in a court of law!' challenged Bhulabhai.

A stay resolution was tabled. Barrister Jinnah and his Muslim League remained neutral. The resolution was passed by sixty-two to fifty-nine votes. The nationalists were jubilant while the government officials were in a quandary. What if he really turned up here, in India? At the Lucknow Congress. Jawaharlal was quite downcast. In his speech, he focused on Subhas's release and turned it into a prestige issue.

ೲ

April 1936. The Italian ship docked at Bombay's Alexandra. Several supporters had gathered there. Their leader emerged on the dock amidst loud cries of 'Vande Mataram!' followed by 'Up up with the Congress flag and down down with the Union Jack!'

As Subhas Chandra set foot on Indian soil, a police officer caught hold of his hand. Not giving him time to breathe, they bundled him into a police vehicle and rushed towards the prison house. Subhas took a newspaper from the constable sitting in the police van and glanced through it. There was a full-page coverage on the Lucknow Congress. Jawaharlal had co-opted Subhas Chandra to the Congress Working Committee. He had exhorted people to work for his release.

Arthur Road Jail was not considered suitable to house such a dangerous convict for more than three-four days. So the Bombay Police drove Subhas to Pune's Yerwada Central Jail. 10 May 1936 was observed as Subhas Day. Demonstrations were held in Karachi, Delhi, Calcutta, Dacca, Lahore, Bombay and Madras, among other places. Nehru had declared that Subhas's arrest was an affront to an individual's liberty, that such acts were stifling the people of India.

Soon, the government decided to shift Subhas Chandra to Sarat Bose's house in Kurseong near Darjeeling. Everything was done in secrecy to prevent any demonstrations or protest marches on the way. Administrative officials of all provinces en route were warned not to let the public get even a whiff of the plans. Delhi had issued strict orders that under no circumstances should Subhas be allowed in the vicinity of Calcutta. On 16 May 1936, the train carrying him left Hadapsar at 4 p.m. and reached Manmad in the early hours the next day. From there, it took the Lucknow route and made the circuitous journey via Banaras and Siliguri, till finally the mountain ranges of Darjeeling became visible. Nestling among those mountains was Kurseong, and for the next one year, Subhas was more or less under house arrest in that cottage. After a while, it became necessary to admit him to the Calcutta Medical College for further treatment. Finally, on 17 March 1937, he was freed from British clutches in every sense of the word.

The letters that were sent to Vienna and received from there secretly were the mainstay of his soul. National politics was waiting for Subhas's return. After the elections, following the 1935 Act, Congress governments had been established in seven states. The Faizpur Congress came and went. Jawaharlal was the president there too. Even there, in his presidential address, he had spoken about Subhas. 'The Congress has been deprived of his zeal and expertise. I have been kept away from the company of my brave colleague. And I have missed my dear comrade whom we counted on so much.'

A new wave of enthusiasm swept over everyone with Subhas's impending return to active politics. The Congress Working Committee was to meet at Sarat Bose's house in Calcutta. Jawaharlal and his sister Vijayalakshmi had arrived at Woodburn Park several days before the meeting. Jawaharlal told Subhas, 'It is a fact that you do not mince words, to the point of being rude. But to say that Gandhiji is a piece of outdated furniture, not in private but in public ...'

When Subhas recalled the incident, he was mortified. Jawaharlal laughed and continued, 'You are really bold.' For a long time, he stared at Subhas and then exclaimed, 'Why is everything about you in the superlative, Subhas? Anger in excess, love overwhelming, and shall I tell you the truth, even your patriotism is as lofty as it is deep.'

Subhas replied in a muffled voice, 'Well, Panditji, that is my defining quality.'

'And your strength too.'

They all had dinner together that night. Vijayalakshmi stopped Jawaharlal as he was going up to his bedroom. Softly she said, 'Bhai, it was not for nothing that our Dadu was hinting to you ...'

'What about?'

'That Subhas and you would not get along for very long.'

'Don't be silly. He has been a compatriot for ten years and a very dear friend. His dedication to service, his outspokenness, patriotism, anti-British sentiment, his open nature, innocence, all ...'

'So what? Subhas will always be Subhas!' she interrupted.

The working committee meeting was scheduled for two days later at Woodburn Park. Jawaharlal was already there, Gandhiji too was expected shortly. For days, the Bose household was busy preparing a grand welcome for Gandhiji. Bibhabati sent for the cooks from Sodepur Ashram and consulted Gandhiji's followers about his preferences. A list was drawn up accordingly. The whole second floor had been cleared for Gandhiji's use. The large hall there was to be the venue of the working committee meeting and for Gandhiji's prayer meetings. If that space was not enough, then the terrace on the fourth floor was made available.

The Bose clan was out in full strength to receive him. A frail dark figure emerged from the car, supporting himself with a stick. His upper body was bare and his bones and ribs seemed like they were protruding out of his skin. His front teeth had fallen out and he was almost toothless. His eyes still twinkled from behind steel-rimmed glasses. Gandhiji joined his hands in a namaste to everyone present.

He was escorted to the inner room where he chose to sit on the carpet on the floor. First of all, Gandhiji asked after Prabhabati. Kasturba was seated right next to her. Prabhabati said, 'Bapuji, let your benevolent gaze remain on our Subhas.'

'He will have to dissociate himself from the revolutionaries for that.'

Subhas retorted, 'Gandhiji, you are the most dangerous revolutionary!' which made everyone laugh.

Gandhiji spent that evening with the children, becoming one of them. On the second floor terrace, a class in spinning yarn was in progress. Gandhiji's secretary Mahadev Desai, Pyarelal, Dr Sushila Nayar and Kanu Gandhi were checking all the arrangements. Gandhiji was so informal and happy, but the coarse white khadi-clad brigade that accompanied him looked unduly harassed. There was no end to their demands and requirements.

Mahadev Desai presented a new list of things that Gandhiji needed to Bibhabati. 'Look, Bibhabati Devi, get all these things. Papdi-beans, brinjals, cluster-beans, moong sprouts, four kilos of sweet potato, five–six dozens of bananas, two kilos of dried dates, four seers of ghee and two kilos of butter.'

'Oh my goodness! The whole market will have to be bought!' little Amiyo, Subhas's nephew and Sarat Chandra's son, blurted.

'Shut up!' scolded Bibhabati.

'He's right.' Mahadev Desai smiled, 'At least half the market you need to buy!'

'Just tell me the previous day what vegetable he will have at which meal. That's all.'

'Impossible! I have been working with Bapu for so many years, but I still can't predict what he will ask for when.'

Then he asked, 'What about fresh goat's milk? It should be milked in my presence. Unless I check out the goat carefully, Bapu will not touch a drop of the milk.'

'Very well, we'll get a goat!'

'Not a goat. Goats. At least ten–twelve of them. Then I will tell you what is to be done.'

Bibhabati almost gasped. Sarat Bose remarked, 'What our Sarojini Naidu says is true. Gandhiji's simple living is an expensive business.'

As it grew dark, the crowd about the house increased. And with it, the fervour and the volume of 'Gandhi Maharaj ki jai,' 'Vande Mataram' rose and cries of 'Bapuji come out!' 'Bapuji, we want to see you' intensified. Gandhiji announced that he would meet everyone. When the gates opened to let the crowd in, there was a mad scramble towards the terrace. People had come from all walks of life, from different faiths, varied ideologies. Gandhiji made a speech before the prayer. His voice was thin and high-pitched, but went straight to the heart. There were no great oratorical flourishes, nor dramatic declamations. Rather, he sounded homely, like a grandfather chatting with his grandchildren. After the speech, to the rhythmic beats of the mridangam and the pakhawaj, the bhajan began:

Raghupati Raghava Rajaram
Pateeta pavana Sita Ram
Ishwara Allah tero naam
Sabko sanmati de Bhagawan.

During the prayer, Sheth Ghanshyamdas Birla hastened into the bungalow. Gandhiji's son Devadas was with him. He was employed with the Birlas. Everybody knew of the great intimacy between Mahadev Desai and Birlaji. As soon as he set eyes on Mahadev Desai, Birlaji asked him in an affectionately disapproving tone, 'Arre Mahadev, why have you forsaken our magnificent palace and camped here?'

'This programme was decided four months back, Shethji.'

'So what? Did we fall short in any way in Gandhiji's service the last time?'

Mahadev Desai did not know what to say. He was well aware how close to Birla Sheth Gandhiji was. It was Birlaji's largesse that ensured Gandhiji's mouthpiece *Harijan* came out regularly.

'Mahadev, you know that I don't need to send in a card when I go to see even the viceroy. And you are our own family. How can you come to our city and stay with the Boses? I alone represented Indian industry at the Round Table Conference.'

'Yes, but ...'

'Even in London, Bapu couldn't do without me for a minute. So what is all this here?'

Ghanshyamdas Birla and Devadas went up to Gandhiji and spent almost three hours talking to him. As they were leaving, Birlaji told Mahadev Desai, 'I have registered my protest with Gandhiji. Pack up your beddings and move into our mansion in two days.'

The Bose family was up very early the next morning because of the crowds thronging their house for a glimpse of Gandhiji. The morning prayer too was attended by hundreds. The house wore a festive look. A shepherd stood outside the gate with a herd of about sixteen goats. The bungalow echoed with their bleating. Mahadev Desai examined the goats' eyes, then walked around each one. He did this repeatedly, much to the amusement of those present. At last, one goat dared to meet his eye, stare for stare, and wiggled its ear. Immediately, Mahadev Desai straightened up and ordered, 'Milk this one.'

'Bapu likes the milk of bright goats.'

The Bose family was gradually getting to know about Gandhiji's fads. He would eat rotis made only by Kanu Gandhi. Every meal should consist of five items. In the afternoon, Dr Sushila Nayar sent Ila and Meera out. They went far away from the city, to get soft smooth clay from the banks of a small river. They needed it to make a pack for Gandhiji's abdomen and head.

All the major political leaders began arriving in the city for the working committee meeting. When Sardar Patel arrived, speculation was rife about who would be the next Congress president.

The peasant leader from Andhra, N.G. Ranga went and met Gandhiji with the proposal to make Subhas Chandra the president. The Bihar peasant leader, Swami Sahajanand Bharati made a similar request. As soon as Acharya Kripalani heard this, he went to meet Gandhiji late in the night. Gandhiji looked at his troubled face. He knew what had brought him there so late. Beating about the bush, indirectly and obliquely, Acharyaji tried to bring up the subject, but Gandhiji did not pick up any of his cues. Finally, he gave up and disgusted, went off to spend the night at Birla Park.

The one person who was conspicuous in the Bose household at this time was Haricharandas, the barber. A fortnight before Gandhiji's arrival, he had pleaded with Sarat Bose to allow him the honour of shaving Gandhiji and tonsuring him. He had made a new coat with many pockets for the occasion, and was strutting around Woodburn Park like a seasoned party worker. When told that his regular clients, lawyers, doctors and judges had sent for him, he would arrogantly retort, 'Who has the time for other beards when Gandhiji and Nehru have entrusted their heads and necks to my care!' One day when he had a moment alone with Gandhiji, Haricharan whispered, 'Bapuji, you are a mahatma, lofty as a mountain peak. But our Subhas babu is also like you. Keep him in mind too.' Gandhiji knew that he was voicing the sentiments of entire Bengal.

One day when Gandhiji was having his meal, Birla Sheth arrived. Naturally, Gandhiji invited him to join in. Sarat Bose too was sitting there, talking to Mahadev Desai. When Birla saw Bibhabati who was serving them, he made a comment to Gandhiji. Bibhabati's face fell and she immediately went inside. Soon after he finished eating, Sarat Bose went into the kitchen. He found Bibhabati wiping her eyes. 'What did he say?' he asked.

'He said, "Are the vegetables fresh?" That too in front of Bapuji.'

Sarat Bose was disgusted with Birla Sheth's attempts to whisk Gandhiji away from Woodburn Park. He told Jawaharlal and Subhas, 'Such meanness does not become a millionaire.'

The next day, Devadas went to Gandhiji and told him, 'Bapu, I think you should shift to Birla Park.'

'Why?' asked a sharp voice from behind. Seeing Jawaharlal, Devadas was startled. 'Has Birla Sheth managed to get a law passed that Gandhiji must stay only at Birla Park each time?'

Hearing this, Gandhiji smiled his characteristic smile.

In the passage to the drawing room, Pandit Dwivedi sat, a frown on his brow. Watching his rotund figure, Satyaranjan Bakshi grinned to himself. Subhas Chandra had selected Panditji because he wanted to learn good Hindi and Panditji was an excellent teacher. Some months ago, Subhas Chandra had held a huge public meeting in Nagpur. For the first time, he had realised how language alone had distanced him from the Hindi-speaking masses. At that instant, he had vowed that on returning to Nagpur the following year, he would address the gathering in the national language.

With the hurly-burly of daily life, Subhas Chandra had hardly any time, but his choice of tutor was perfect. Dwivedi was past sixty. His voice was melodious and his words had the resonance of a river. He found it very difficult to teach chaste Hindi to the Bengali Subhas babu. So, he tended to treat Subhas babu as a schoolboy and pursued him relentlessly. Today, though, he looked unusually worried. Bakshi teased him, 'So, Panditji, how is the pupil?'

'Who has the time. Who cares about the lessons. Politics, politics all day, nothing else!'

'Good thing you haven't started to wield the cane yet, Dwivediji!'

'Don't make fun of a guruji!' snapped Pandit Dwivediji. 'What do you think education is? The teacher is the foundation of society. One cannot learn anything without humble teachers like me.'

Bakshi mutely accepted defeat. Just then Subhas and Jawaharlal came down the stairs to meet the public. Dwivediji's glare did not escape Subhas Chandra's eyes. Quickly he said, 'Acharyaji, forgive me. Didn't get enough time last night. But I will definitely memorise yesterday's lesson.' In his presence, Dwivediji instructed Amin the driver, 'Keep this Hindi dictionary and this notebook carefully. As soon as Subhas babu gets into the car, hand him the notebook. Yesterday's word list is not yet done. Tomorrow, if he doesn't finish his lesson, I will box your ears, understand?'

Those were happy days for Jawaharlal and Subhas. Even Jawaharlal felt that after all these years of hard work, Subhas deserved the post of the Congress president. The Rightists were in favour of joining the Constituent Assembly according to the Act of 1935. Around the same time, a group of young people – Achutrao Patwardhan, Acharya Narendra Dev, Jayaprakash Narayan, Aruna Asaf Ali, S.M. Joshi, N.G. Goray – had been fired up with the ideals of socialism. Under the leadership of Swami Sahajanand Bharati in the north and N.G. Ranga in Andhra, the Kisan Sabha and peasant movements were gathering momentum. At this juncture, having a progressive young leader like Subhas Chandra at the helm of Congress affairs would be advantageous to the Leftist group.

The Congress Working Committee meeting went on for four days at the Elgin Road house. Innumerable rumours were floating around regarding the post of the president. On the night before the meet was to end, Gandhiji called Sardar Patel alone into his room.

'Sardar, don't you think that the time has come to reward Subhas for all the hard work he has done, the sacrifices he has made for the country?'

With a broad smile, Sardar Patel replied, 'After Tilak's time, you are the one who has been deciding who the president will be, year after year. We will go with whatever you say.'

The fact was that Subhas's name was being mentioned by everyone. There was no love lost between Sardar Patel and Subhas Chandra. During the days of Bardoli and Dandi, Subhas Chandra had been in prison. But the money that Vithalbhai had left for him had created a new controversy. People like Acharya Kripalani had gone around openly saying, 'During Vithalbhai's last days, Subhas never left his side, even for a moment. When the will was signed, Vithalbhai was not himself. It has all been engineered by the Bengali Babu.' Sardar Patel had not been affected by the donation. But he had found Subhas's language in the manifesto, referring to Gandhiji as an outdated piece of furniture, quite offensive.

Sardar Patel's reply made Gandhiji uneasy. 'Shall I tell you the truth, Sardar? A valiant patriot like Subhas should have been the Congress president at least twice before this.'

'So then?'

'I had obstructed his path that time. Under the circumstances, there is nobody but he who can be the president. However ...'

'If you have decided, then why the buts and the howevers?'

'Sardar, you have no idea. I could not sleep all night. My eyes are still smarting from staying awake.' Gandhiji stretched out his folded legs. In a tone of disappointment, he said, 'He is a born rebel. I don't have a shred of faith in him. I have observed that Subhas is not at all dependable. And that is my predicament. I can neither deny him this path of glory, nor can I mould him to my liking.'

The other members of the working committee were stationed at Birla Park. Ghanshyamdas Birla was in conversation with Sardar Patel and Rajendra Prasad. Soon after they were joined by Acharya Kripalani. Although it was obvious that he was deeply agitated inside, he made a pretence of being calm and collected.

Rajendra Babu was jokingly saying, 'Whatever you say, Sardar, if Subhas becomes the president, it will be entertaining to see how Acharya will serve as general secretary under him.'

'Why? Don't I know the job? For the last four years, the administrative reins of the party have been in my hands, don't forget. Jawaharlal was the president for two years running,' said an indignant Acharya Kripalani. He picked up one of the bolsters and moved closer to ask Sardar and Prasad, 'What are you both up to? This very gentleman who cannot digest even one morsel of food without criticising Gandhiji, you are more than willing to elevate him to the party president's post? What is the meaning of all this?'

'Well, Bapu too must have given it some thought, after all,' said Rajendra Prasad.

'Thought? What thought! That man is a saint, a mahatma. If he is mesmerised by someone, he will gift him his loincloth. But we cannot sit back and watch.' Every word of Kripalani's dripped anger.

'Bapu has shown his magnanimity by giving him that post,' Sardar Patel told him.

'Sardar, how can we forget the incidents that have happened before our own eyes, not once but repeatedly? Be it the Calcutta session or the chaos at the Lahore meeting. And then the drama at Karachi. Remember all that? Anywhere he could, the man has insulted Bapu, and now he has visions of becoming the party president! Insulting Gandhiji is insulting the nation, and we will certainly not tolerate that,' Acharya Kripalani said firmly.

Sardar Patel and Rajendra Prasad realised that Acharya had made up his mind, so they kept quiet. Obviously, he had been touched to the quick. Acharya continued his tirade. 'A man with a Fascist bent of mind, who has ten meetings with Mussolini ...'

'Gandhiji also met him, don't forget,' Sardar interrupted.

'But he is not a Fascist himself! This worshipper of violence is a far cry from Babu's greatness. The British are not mad to confine Subhas for so long. They must have enough incriminating evidence against him.'

'Let it be, Acharya.' said Rajendra Babu, placatingly. 'Didn't Bapu make Jawahar the president at Lahore? Gandhiji must be thinking that once he sits on the chair, he will calm down.'

'I will give it to you in writing. You are talking about Subhas. This fire will become a blaze, it can't be extinguished.'

Later Acharya Kripalani went to see Gandhiji. Everyone was curious to know what transpired between them.

Gandhiji was not willing to talk about the subject, but he could not resist saying, 'Bapu, all kinds of contradictory statements are being made outside regarding the president's post.'

'You observe silence on the subject, the issue will resolve itself.' Gandhiji's words stung Acharya. He left the room sulking.

Acharya Kripalani was downcast when he was leaving Calcutta. Sardar Patel who was seated next to him asked, 'Really, Acharyaji, why is Bapu playing this game?'

'What game?'

'Making Subhas the president at the Haripura Congress?'

'What do you mean?'

'By offering the prestigious post of president, what has Gandhiji achieved? Has he elevated Subhas, or has he sent out a veiled warning to the British?'

'Has Subhas returned from Wardha?' Sarat Bose asked Bibhabati.

'Yes,' she replied, 'he came back early this morning.'

Sarat Bose went straight up to Subhas's room. Seeing the cheerful expression on his face, Sarat Bose was happy. He knew how difficult it would be to conduct the affairs of the Congress under the noses of Gandhiji's traditional and influential loyalists. That is why he had advised Subhas to consult Gandhiji before preparing his presidential address. Jawaharlal too had made a similar suggestion. Subhas had returned from doing just that.

'What did Gandhiji say?'

'He went through the whole draft and then laughed with pleasure.'

'Which means you have already won half the battle!' Sarat Bose said.

In the meantime, a Gujarati delegation came to meet him. Some of them had been to the Haripura region. They told Subhas, 'During Dussehra itself, Vallabhbhai had shown this site to Gandhiji. It was just four hundred acres of land, overgrown with thorny bushes and nothing else. But in the last three–four months, Sardar has worked a miracle and transformed it.'

Every day news about the progress in the preparations reached Calcutta. The president himself was impatient to get there. The night before his departure, Subhas Chandra went into Sarat Bose's room with a notepad and pen in hand.

'Mej-da, I feel I need to mention some more issues in my speech, like participation of the princely states in the freedom struggle (planning as they have in Russia), the need to set up heavy industries, and family planning,' said Subhas Chandra.

'These are all contentious issues. You can discuss them in a private meeting later,' was Sarat babu's advice.

'No, Mej-da. I have spent sleepless nights thinking about them. If my address doesn't refer to these issues, I won't be true to myself. I will have compromised on my principles. I consider it my moral duty to stand by the ideals I have held dear all my life.'

'Go ahead, then,' Sarat Bose said in assent.

'Besides, I want to recognise the socialist group within the Congress.'

'Subhas, you are too innocent,' Sarat Bose exclaimed impatiently. 'All these young members of the socialist group – Dr Ram Manohar Lohia, Jayaprakash, Narendra Dev, are always around Jawaharlal. But have you ever seen Jawahar stake his own position with Gandhiji on their behalf? Gandhiji favours the Congress and only the Congress. His continuous aim is to see that it remains united. For God's sake, don't bring down these live coals upon your own head.' Subhas listened silently.

The day of departure for the Haripura Congress dawned. The post of the Congress president was the highest and the most glorious position one could attain in India. And the honour had come Subhas Chandra's way. Subhas set off on the journey after performing his puja and taking the blessings of all the elders.

He and his entourage were to take the Bombay Mail to Haripura. An enormous crowd had gathered at Howrah Station. Several of the compartments were packed with swayamsevak and sevikas. The president's second class compartment was draped with the tricolour and decked with multicolour streamers. It was occupied by Prabhabati, Bibhabati, Sarat Bose, Basanti Devi, and several nephews and nieces and friends of Subhas's.

As the guard blew the whistle and the train steamed out of the platform, the air reverberated with cries of 'Subhas babu ki jai!' 'Mahatma Gandhi ki jai!' and 'Vande Mataram.'

The train was greeted by cheering crowds at every stop en route. Subhas Chandra smilingly accepted garlands and bouquets offered to him and made a brief exhortation, 'Get ready to join the fight for freedom.'

The organising committee had estimated that several lakhs of people would attend the session. To provide all guests with fresh milk, they had purchased five hundred cows several months earlier and brought them to Haripura to acclimatise them to the new environment. While earlier one had to trudge fifteen miles to post a letter, now they had managed to get a post office to operate from the venue.

Sardar Patel and Darbar Gopaldas were waiting on the platform at Udhan, a big garland in hand. As soon as Subhas Chandra alighted from the train, Sardar Patel embraced him warmly. Subhas Chandra had attended many sessions, but never before had he seen such magnificent arrangements and so much fervour among the simple villagefolk. It was the Congress's fifty-first session. Therefore, Nandalal Bose had put up fifty-one decorative arches. A ceremonial carriage had been requisitioned from one of the princely states for the procession. It was to be drawn by fifty-one pairs of bullocks. It was all due to the untiring efforts of seven thousand swayamsevaks and four thousand craftsmen that everything was so grand.

At dusk, the president's ceremonial procession began. Subhas Chandra, in immaculate white khadi, looked impressive that day. He was flanked by Sardar Patel and Nehru. The cries of 'Subhas babu ki jai,' 'Mahatma Gandhi ki jai' and 'Vande Mataram' carried on without a pause. The Congress Nagari that Nandalal Bose had constructed out of bamboo took on a magical hue in the golden light of the setting sun. Leading the procession were dhol players, lezim dancers, fence and shield martial artists, followed by Rajasthani jathas and group dancers from Gujarat. Subhas Chandra was overwhelmed by the honour that had been bestowed upon him. But, in the evening glow of sunset, he found himself thinking of Jatin Das who had sacrificed family and home in the service of the motherland, of Gopinath Saha, the youthful Bhagat Singh, and all those political prisoners still languishing in jails across the country. Freedom was still a long way off.

Till late at night, hordes of people from Bombay and Ahmedabad kept arriving. Although more than two lakh people had gathered there, no inconvenience of any kind was felt. In the beautiful township named after Vithalbhai Patel, three big markets with around four hundred shops had been set up. Arrangements had been made in five places for about ten thousand people to be fed at one time.

The Ford Motor Company had provided a car exclusively for the president. Other senior leaders had their own campsites and tents put up for them. Subhas Chandra had two large camps to himself. Jawaharlal's camp was opposite his. Gandhiji had requested that he be located some distance away.

After the procession, the flag hoisting ceremony was held at Jhanda Chowk. It was attended by about one and a half lakh people. Near the flag pole, on the dais, stood a large portrait of Vithalbhai Patel. Subhas looked overwhelmed as he made a floral offering to Vithalbhai. Pandit Nehru was also present on the dais to formally hand over the charge as the outgoing president. First, he garlanded Subhas. Then in spite of himself, he embraced him. Both Gandhiji and Sarat Bose were moved by the sight.

On one side of Vithal Nagar, the work of the Congress party was being carried out peacefully; on the other side, the police force stationed there was growing more and more restive. The same man whom government records had branded a criminal, a terrorist, the biggest threat to British Imperialism, was today sharing the dais with Gandhiji.

One officer from Delhi muttered, 'It is unfortunate that an advocate of non-violence should himself place a flag bearer of terrorism and violence on such a high post.'

A colleague of his instructed the team, 'No matter what post Subhas Bose occupies, make sure you note down accurately every one of his utterances. Once public memory of this celebration dims a bit, declare his speech as inflammatory, and use it as evidence to throw him into jail. That's what the home secretary has ordered.'

He handed over a secret document to the commissioner. 'What is this?'

'A letter from Rash Behari Bose, the notorious terrorist who dared to throw a bomb at the viceroy in Delhi's Chandni Chowk.'

'So what is it all about?'

'He is currently in Japan. This is his latest letter to Subhas Chandra Bose.'

As he read the letter, the commissioner's eyes widened. It said,

> Do not succumb to the insistence on non-violence. Even if our pyres are built on revolution, sparks from it will ignite the dynamite sticks and smash the chains of slavery.

And then it struck him why the British government was keeping such a close watch on Subhas's every movement.

The Congress session had got underway in earnest. He stood up to deliver his presidential address. The entire country was waiting eagerly to hear him speak. India in Gandhiji's dream was constructed in a particular way. Jawaharlal's vision of it was different. Subhas Chandra too had envisaged a strong, secular and united India. Each one of these artists was painting India in their own colours.

Holding the mike in hand, Subhas looked at Gandhiji and began his speech. 'May God grant that this country will always be blessed by Mahatma Gandhi's guidance.' Thunderous applause and deafening shouts of 'Mahatma Gandhi ki jai', 'Subhas babu ki jai!' 'Hindustan ke do lal, Subhas aur Jawaharlal!' were heard everywhere.

On one side of the main stage stood a large crew of journalists and press photographers. Journalists from all over the world, including Lord Samuel of England, a delegation from South Africa that had come specially to observe the session, and the prime minister of Ceylon, were sitting right in front, in eager anticipation.

As he stood there facing the mammoth audience, scenes from his own life flashed before Subhas's eyes. He began, 'I will not be so presumptuous as to believe that I am entirely deserving of this enormous responsibility. I consider this as a mark of your generosity and a tribute to the youth of the country. A number of distinguished sons and daughters of Mother India have graced this chair. And that is why I become so emotional when I glance in that direction.' Tears of pride glistened in his mother's and Bibhabati's eyes, while Deshbandhu's memory filled Basanti Devi's mind.

'The speed with which empires reach the pinnacle of power and glory, it is with the same rapidity that they crash into the depths of ignominy and oblivion. British Imperialism is no exception. It will also end like that. The British practised an insidious "divide and rule" policy in Ireland and Palestine. They were unrivalled in the art of creating a split in a nation without getting involved themselves, and then exerting authority over it. They have started sowing the seeds of partition in this soil too, in many subtle ways.' At these words, Gandhiji looked up at Subhas in astonishment. He did not think Subhas's warning untimely, but rather was shocked at the fearful prospect of partition that Subhas had just mentioned. Subhas then went on to declare his support to the movement of freeing the subjects of the princely states from the capricious hands of their rulers.

On the issue of the minorities, he fully endorsed the Congress policy, and stated that they should be given all opportunities for their political, economic and cultural development. He appealed for the right of citizens to form associations, protection of minority languages and culture, adult franchise, freedom of the press and equality before the law. Gandhiji listened to Subhas with new respect. Subhas called upon the Congress to shoulder the responsibility of nation building, once independence was achieved. Problems of poverty, illiteracy, public health, production and distribution should be dealt with on socialistic principles, he said.

'For India's development, we must adopt a uniform international script, and that I am suggesting the Roman script will come as a shock to many.' As Subhas Chandra expected, many eyebrows were raised and mouths fell open. Then he proceeded to explain, 'It is high time we gave up our old-fashioned prejudices regarding pure and impure languages. If we are not able to enforce a common acceptable national language, at least we shall have to develop our lingua franca, and a common script will open up the path to progress.'

When Subhas Chandra brought up the new issue of population control, many Rightist Gandhians were shocked. 'Comrades, keep the demon of growing population under control. The growth rate of our population is so high that our plans and schemes will collapse like a house of cards before we know it.' This issue was applauded by the youth leaders. Such a revolutionary idea – of the need for a separate Planning Commission to look into economic development – was brought up for the first time at a Congress session. Subhas Chandra emphasised on the importance of industrial development without neglecting cottage industry.

Subhas Chandra's progressive ideas were greeted with thunderous applause from the young Congressmen with socialist and communist leanings. Gandhiji was throwing oblique glances at Subhas. His inner turmoil was reflected on his face. He realised that there were major differences between the rough draft of the speech Subhas Chandra had shown him at Wardha and what he was actually saying here. With every Left-oriented suggestion that he was making, Gandhiji's followers were getting more and more uneasy.

About the bureaucracy, Subhas had this to say, 'With every government, new ministers come and go. But the traditional structure of the bureaucracy remains unchanged. If radical changes are not made to this structure, the ruling party and its ministers will not be able to implement any of its projects successfully. Although the Labour Party came to power in Britain in 1924 and 1929, it failed just because of this. The British have laid the foundations for a bureaucracy that would suit their purpose, whose perspective is neither Indian nor nationalistic. Unless a change is brought about in the minds and the attitudes of the civil service, it will not be possible to implement policies and plans at the national level. Therefore, bureaucracy's rusty and crumbling framework must first be welded and mended.'

As he was talking about strengthening the party with motivated young people, he remembered the political prisoners languishing in prisons. He then referred to the foreign policy, which should be practical and self-respecting, and introduced the subject of future foreign investment in the country. Subhas Chandra paused for a while and then, without bothering about anyone's opinion, declared, 'If the Kisan Sabha, the Trade Union and the new socialist group wish to remain within the ambit of the Congress party, there should be no objection from anyone.' His desire to maintain unity within the party was cheered lustily by the socialist youth groups in the audience.

Gandhiji's face had hardened. Sarat Bose too became uneasy. But Subhas, uncaring about the consequences, had thrown a spark and moved away. For three hours the speech continued, touching upon diverse subjects. The young socialists and communists were whispering among themselves that never before had a presidential address been so rich with ideas on development.

As he concluded his speech, Subhas Chandra's voice grew thick once more. 'The entire nation fervently hopes and prays that Mahatma Gandhi may be spared to us for many years to come. Ours is a struggle not only against British Imperialism but against world imperialism as well, of which the former is the cornerstone. We are, therefore, fighting not for the cause of India alone but of humanity as well. India freed means humanity saved. Vande Mataram!'

Subhas Chandra sat down amidst deafening cheers. The Rightists were displeased. The Leftists rejoiced. A malicious smile played on Acharya Kripalani's lips. Glancing from one senior leader to another, he seemed to be saying, 'Serves you right. Suffer the consequences of your actions.' Before leaving the hall, Subhas Chandra stood next to Gandhiji for a few moments. He couldn't help saying, 'Subhas, you are so close to me, and yet you seem so far away.'

'Why didn't the prime minister of Madras province attend the meeting?'

'How could he?'

'Why?'

'Subhas babu was the president, you see.'

There was much merriment and bonhomie after the meeting. Leaders from different provinces sat together chatting, exchanging views. Under the Act of 1935, elections had been held in eleven Indian provinces. The Congress returned with a majority and was now ruling in seven of them. The leader of the party in power was given the exalted title of prime minister. Most prime ministers were present at Haripura. Conspicuous by his absence was the prime minister of Madras province, Rajaji.

A huge crowd had gathered at the president's camp. Subhas Chandra's impassioned three-hour-long speech had impressed everybody. Two distinct groups had formed among the delegates. One group was in favour of acceptance of power and joining the legislative assembly. This group also wanted entry into the central assembly. The other group believed that the only way to fight imperialism was to reject the 1935 Act completely and abstain from accepting power. This group had Jawaharlal and Subhas among its leaders, in addition to the majority of the youth. Gandhiji, however, gave his blessings to both. In fact, his basic strategy was Struggle–Truce–Struggle. The Leftists were against acceptance of power. But during the working committee meeting in Bombay, Rajaji was at his eloquent best as he spoke in favour of acceptance of power. His armour consisted of persuasion and coercion, threats and pleas, sweet words and angry outbursts, and finally convinced the working committee to agree with him. And now he had become the prime minister of Madras province.

In the Rightist camp, words of warning were flying around. 'Beware, the Congress has a tough new president in Subhas babu!' They were worried because he had advocated abstaining from using power. It would mean going on satyagraha, serving prison sentences, but not enjoying the fruits of their sacrifices. And the Rightists did not like that. They kept telling each other to stay away from the Bengali Babu.

Sarojini Naidu's praise of Subhas Chandra came out as inspired verse. She recalled meeting a student in England nineteen years ago. She had no idea that the same youth would one day be the pride of the nation. She said, 'That novice soldier today wields a commander's sword. The coming year is going to be a big challenge to his intelligence, his determination, his perseverance and his penchant for struggle. Subhas is a finely chiselled image of Bengal's supreme sacrifice and valour.' All the adjectives she used to describe Subhas were superlatives. But then her last comment offended his sensitive mind. 'Subhas must learn to suppress his provincial outlook and see things from a broader, national perspective.' He stood up at once to reply. 'Until this day, I have not seen anything but the image of a flourishing, powerful motherland, as a strong, unified nation. How then can I be confined within the narrow bounds of Bengal alone. Every vein in my body throbs with the blood of my India; in every country of the world, I see a reflection of my own. How can I be parochial.'

The camps were being dismantled now. Leaders headed for their own provinces. The Haripura Congress was an unprecedented success. Subhas Chandra's camp too was in the process of packing up. In two days' time, they were to leave for Calcutta. Subhas sent for the general secretary, Acharya Kripalani. With long strides, he reached there and presented himself before the president. Jawaharlal was aware of Acharya's complaints regarding the selection of the president, so he had warned Kripalani before coming to Haripura, 'Just as you supported me, you must support Subhas, all right? Imagine it is me in his place.' He had simultaneously advised Subhas to keep a distance from Acharya. Jawaharlal also understood the prominent position Acharya occupied in Gandhiji's coterie. Moreover, for the past four years, the Allahabad Congress office had been synonymous with Acharya.

'Acharya, the Congress president should not end up being only a puppet. He must be the symbol of the nation's unity. If he so desires, he can move mountains.'

'Subhas Babu, as general secretary, I will extend whatever support you require.'

'That is expected of you. I also enjoy being immersed in my work. I have so many plans in my mind. But tell me, when are you coming to Calcutta?'

'Your office is in Allahabad. So why should I travel all that distance?'

'Good thing you reminded me, Acharya,' Subhas Chandra said. 'I stay in Calcutta, but my office is in Allahabad. How can routine day-to-day matters be conducted like that? You do one thing. Shift the office to Calcutta!'

Acharya's face fell. He almost sprang out of his seat, then sat down again. 'Impossible! Just impossible! Shift the office from Allahabad? What are you saying, Subhas babu? That is the nerve centre from where the entire nation is controlled.'

'Actually, our central office ought to be in Bombay or Delhi. How did it reach Allahabad? In the last seven–eight years, Motilalji, Jawaharlal thrice and Rajendra babu once, became the Congress president. Allahabad was convenient for all of them. But that doesn't mean the strings must be pulled from there all the time, does it?'

As Acharya Kripalani stood up to leave, Subhas Chandra said to him, 'Never mind about the office. You are the party general secretary. As such you will have to come to Calcutta periodically.' Acharya looked furious. He glared at Subhas, and then he stomped off in a huff.

The more Acharya thought about it, the clearer the picture became. Not for nothing had been those cheeky socialist youngsters walking around with their noses in the air during the Haripura conference. This wonderful man was contradicting Gandhiji at every step. Acharyaji's feet led him to Jawaharlal's base.

'Jawaharlal, what happened? Why are you agitated?'

'You know what your great friend was saying? Let me see how in future the affairs of the nation are conducted from Anand Bhavan.'

'There must be some misunderstanding.'

'Forget it, Jawaharlal,' Acharya said. 'I knew you would be all for your friend. But forgive me. I tell you, right here in Haripura, not just me, but no self-respecting devotee who has been nurtured by the patronage of Gandhiji, will be able to work with this upstart. Please free me from this Fascist's yoke.'

Seven

Malabar Hill twinkled with thousands of lights in the fading dusk. Except for the Governor House, no other building there was as impressive as Jinnah House. Political power and administrative authority originated and flowed from the former, but the world Barrister Jinnah had created here was uniquely his own. He was the sole claimant to the title of 'supreme leader' of eight to nine crore Muslims in the country.

Although such an important leader lived in that mansion, one hardly saw a crowd of supporters there. That was because Jinnah valued his solitude and did not like his privacy disrupted.

Jinnah stood before his eight-foot-long mirror, scrutinising himself from head to foot. He did this often. The reflection he saw was that of a six-foot, slim frame. He had maintained his weight at a steady sixty kilograms over the last so many years. Like a film star, he was extremely particular about the cut and fit of his clothes. His bar was well stocked with whisky and champagne, and the dining table was laden with pork and chicken. The language spoken at the table was clipped Oxford English, although he was the seniormost leader of the Muslim community.

Jinnah went into the balcony and settled down, sipping champagne and blowing smoke rings. His reverie was interrupted by the telephone ringing. He glared at the servant bearing the instrument, since they all knew that he answered no calls at this time, not even from Nawabzada Liaqat Ali. The servant, chastised by the look, stood there trembling.

Jinnah picked up the receiver and barked into it, 'Yes, Mr Bose?'

'You must have received my letter. I wish to meet you.'

'When? Now? It's past nine o'clock. This is my time for rest.'

'But I am leaving for Calcutta early tomorrow morning.'

'Very well, come after half an hour. I need that much time to get ready,' Jinnah said reluctantly.

'Thank you.' The receiver clicked into place.

In his spacious bedroom, Jinnah had a showroom for a wardrobe. He found it hard to pick one out of his 300-odd suits and a pair of shoes from another hundred or so pairs. Finally, he selected one and started to dress, muttering to himself, 'The Congress president is coming to see me.' The word 'Congress' at one time had meant so much to him. As Dadabhai Naoroji's secretary, he had attended the Calcutta Congress in style. He was on good terms with Tilak and Gokhale as well. But Gandhi appeared on India's horizon and all equations changed. What did charkha, khadi, prayer, ashram have to do with politics? Who needed all this drama? He was influenced by the *poshakhi rajkaran*, politics of the elite class of the earlier generation. With Gandhiji came the wooing of the Ali brothers, raising of the Moplah question, or sometimes the Khilafat and other such problems. As a result, Jinnah found himself moving away from the Congress and Gandhi. The chasm between Gandhi and Jinnah had widened rapidly.

What did Barrister Jinnah lack? As a lawyer, he had earned immense wealth. He was hardworking and diligent. But his personal life was none too happy. His first wife had passed away when he was in England, studying to be a barrister, and he remained single for the next fifteen years or so. However, spring blossomed in the forty-first year of his life. He had gone to Darjeeling on a holiday with a Parsi friend. And in the Mount Everest Hotel, he set eyes on a seventeen-year-old girl. When she smiled, it was as if the whole universe filled with joy; when she shut her eyes, one wanted to be a little bird sheltering under her lashes. She too was drawn towards him. Her name was Ruttie.

All the obstacles that could come in the path of true love and more stood in their way. While Jinnah was forty-one, she was seventeen. He was Muslim, she a Parsi. She could not have fallen in love with him for his money, since her father was infinitely wealthier. Besides, she was the daughter of a good friend. However, they decided to come together even if it meant betraying a friendship, going against one's religion, and surmounting the age difference. On her 18th birthday, the rebel Ruttie left her father's home and set foot into Jinnah Mansion.

Some years of marital bliss soon passed and then temperamental differences began to cast their shadows. There were frequent quarrels and one day, Rattanbai Jinnah walked out of Jinnah Mansion. Ten years of companionship came to an end. Once again, a cruel lonely phase began in Jinnah's life. Within a year, Ruttie died of opium overdose.

At her funeral, Jinnah shuddered as he threw two handfuls of earth on her coffin. He was crying inconsolably, shaking like a tree, helpless in a storm.

At the time of the Second Round Table Conference, Jinnah was undoubtedly a defeated man in his personal life. But on the national front too, Gandhi's stature was growing. Numerous Muslim leaders had jumped on to his bandwagon. The Muslim League was rife with internal dissension and provincial divides. On all fronts, Jinnah was tormented by disappointment and sorrow. At that point, the pleasant and cheerful atmosphere in Europe and the cultured environment there attracted him. He chose to become an exile from his motherland and settle in London.

In the spring of 1933, a Muslim student, Rehmat Ali, met Jinnah at the Waldorf Hotel, and spreading a map of India on the table, said, 'Look, this is Punjab, this East Bengal, this Sind. All these areas, where the majority population is Muslim, can be separated to form a new nation – Pakistan.'

'Partition India?' said Jinnah, with a mocking laugh. 'My young friend, it is an impossible dream.'

As per the 1935 Act, elections were held. In seven out of eleven provinces, the Congress party came to power. The Muslim League made no impact anywhere. One day, the leader of the United Provinces Muslim League, Nawabzada Liaqat Ali Khan arrived in London accompanied by his wife. He pleaded with Jinnah, 'What are you doing here? Come back to India.'

'For what?'

'Gandhi has managed to entice Ghaffar Khan over to his side, and taken control over the Frontier Provinces. Everywhere else the Congress has wiped out our aspirations. We have no hope, no future without an Allah-blest saviour like you. Come back, Islam awaits you.'

Jinnah's dull eyes lit up. At the Lucknow session of the Muslim League, people saw him in a fez cap and sherwani for the first time. It wasn't only his dress that had changed, even his language was different. 'The Congress is an exclusively Hindu party. It is a toy in the hands of British Imperialism. In their political schemes, a Muslim will not get justice even in a thousand years.' He had become aggressive and offensive. For the first time, he was riding the serpent-hood of communalism and savouring the applause, the popularity and adulation that it brought. His naturally sharp and piercing eyes now acquired an unnatural glitter. After being politically sidelined for the past seventeen years, it seemed the gods had given him an opportunity to resurrect himself.

As Muslim society started inching towards the Muslim League, the inner coterie of the Congress began to panic. There was a feeling among them that a dialogue with Barrister Jinnah should be started. Rajendra Prasad and Pandit Nehru did hold talks. A fortnight earlier, Gandhiji had himself called on him. And now the Congress president Subhas Chandra Bose was making his way there.

At ten o'clock sharp, the starched khadi-clad president of the Congress entered Jinnah's drawing room. A white Bengali shawl was draped across his shoulders, and on his head, was a finely creased Gandhi cap. Jinnah glanced at the cap with distaste, but warmly welcomed his guest. 'What will you drink – champagne, brandy – name your choice.'

'I'm sorry, I do not drink.'

'Oh! Under the influence of that Gandhi, you have become an aficionado of lime juice, have you?' Both laughed heartily at that.

Jinnah said, 'Subhas, I am completely different from Gandhi. These satyagraha, non-cooperation movements are for the illiterate, the ignorant. Not for a refined, sophisticated man like me. Your Gandhi's ashram, that topi, the thick and coarse khadi garments – all this is beyond me. Anyway, tell me what occasions this visit?'

'Your pet subject – Hindu–Muslim unity.'

'Good you reminded me. I do not consider your dear friend Nehru a statesman. But he would have made an excellent English professor.'

'What is the problem with him?'

'After the last election, he made some lofty boasts – now there are only two parties in the country, the Congress and the British government. But Subhas, all of you, including Gandhi and Nehru, remember well, there is a third angle to Indian politics – a sharper, keener one – and that is the Muslim League. If you step on it even inadvertently, your feet will bleed,' Jinnah warned.

'Jinnahji,' replied Subhas, 'in this country, Muslims and Hindus have lived together for centuries. To sort out the differences between the two faiths, it is very important to have talks.'

Jinnah was bitterly critical of Gandhi. In his words, there was a deep mistrust. But when Subhas spoke, Jinnah put his thoughts aside and replied, 'Very well, then. I will definitely place this suggestion before the working committee of the Muslim League. Hindu leaders will speak for you, Muslim leaders for us.'

'How can that be, Jinnahji? The Congress party is not for Hindus alone. We have several Muslim leaders of national stature among us. Only the Congress represents all religions and faiths.'

'You may believe that. As far as we are concerned, the Congress is a Hindu party. When constitutional matters are discussed, we will present the Muslim point of view. You cannot speak on our behalf,' Jinnah stated emphatically.

Subhas Chandra had to return to Calcutta to attend to some important matters. But his meeting with Jinnah had left him uneasy. The future looked dark. For Subhas, the idea of an undivided country was paramount.

The working committee had met in Wardha in July and on that occasion, too, Subhas had emphasised the matter of Hindu–Muslim unity. 'We are very eager and anxious for unity,' he had stated in a letter to Jinnah. Gandhiji read every word of the letter and congratulated Subhas. His other demand to convene a meeting of the industry ministers of the seven states, in order to work out the strategies for industrial development, was accepted by the working committee. A number of people were incensed with Subhas's growing closeness with Gandhiji, and Gandhiji's obvious respect for Subhas.

During this period, a constitutional crisis had arisen in the Central Provinces. The prime minister of this Hindi- and Marathi-dominated region was Dr N.B. Khare, and the quarrels between the Marathi-speaking Khare and his Hindi-speaking cabinet ministers had been growing for a while. To enquire into the matter, a high-level committee of Prasad, Patel and Azad had been nominated by the party. But the disreputably outspoken Khare alleged that Gandhi, Patel and the Hindi-speaking ministers were plotting a conspiracy against him. In a counter move, the Hindi-speaking ministers accused Khare of working against the Congress on the advice of the governor. Before the working committee meeting, Khare and two of his supporters had sent in their resignations, and were trying to get others to resign as well. But no one was willing to resign without the permission of the senior members.

'Doctor, bear the consequences of your actions – quietly resign,' Shreshti told Dr Khare. 'I have the letter in my pocket,' retorted Dr Khare.

'You should apologise to the working committee.'

'It's not possible for me to do that,' said Dr Khare.

Subhas Chandra had upheld the role of the working committee during this crisis and received Gandhiji's encomiums for it. That same night, Dr Khare went to Subhas Chandra's room in the ashram. He looked furious. 'Today, a grave injustice has been done to me by Gandhiji and his followers. Do you place more trust in them? You wait and see. Gandhi and his acolytes will play this same game of casting aspersions on you too.'

In the meantime, a message arrived from Barrister Jinnah. Subhas was very annoyed on reading it. He marched into Gandhiji's room. 'Gandhiji, Jinnah says the Muslim League does not recognise the nationalist Muslims in the Congress.'

'Does the Muslim League Working Committee say that?' asked Gandhi, sorrowfully. 'But then that's no committee. It is all a one-man show. What kind of a person is he? A Muslim only in name. He has no connection with the sanctity of the religion in whose name he is playing his politics. He enjoys his alcohol, eats pork and probably doesn't even know which direction a mosque faces. And yet, he incites the poor Muslims with the warning that Islam is in danger. Anyway, Subhas, this man will be a troublemaker in the future.'

24 September 1938. A bewildered Subhas Chandra stood at Calcutta's Dum Dum Airport, watching the aircraft take off for Delhi. He had returned from his tour of Assam that morning and had decided to go to his Elgin Road home, pack a few fresh clothes, and come back to take a flight to Delhi for the important Congress Working Committee meeting. But the house was quite far away and by the time he reached Dum Dum, the flight had left. His heart sank. Perhaps if he hadn't gone to Assam ... but then that visit had been as important as this one.

As he stood there, a friend rushed up to him saying a flight had been arranged for him through the good offices of a private company. Subhas Chandra sighed with relief. Soon the small, twelve-seater aircraft was readied. Sarat Bose noted the relief on Subhas's face as he said goodbye to him. Accompanying him was his dear friend Lala Shankarlal.

Jawaharlal had gone abroad some months ago and was travelling extensively in Europe. During this period, Subhas Chandra and Gandhiji seemed to have forged a special bond – at least it appeared so. Subhas cherished the pleasant memories of his stay in Wardha, and of Kasturba. Yet, every now and then, a twinge of trepidation would assail him. The old guards in the party were watching his whirlwind tours, the rousing reception he received from lakhs and lakhs of admirers across the country, his untiring efforts to establish an economic plan for the nation's development based on the Russian model. And to top it all, eminent scientists and technologists like Meghnad Saha and Prafulla Chandra Roy had begun to gravitate towards him. The youth believed that only Subhas Chandra could bring about modernisation in the true sense.

Halfway through the flight, Subhas became very ill. He had a splitting headache and fever. The pilot did not want to take any chances. He landed in Kanpur, disobeying Subhas's instructions to fly straight to Delhi. For two days, Subhas lay unconscious in a hospital in Kanpur. Only on the third day were they able to fly to Delhi. And he went straight to the venue of the meeting. Subhas expressed regret at arriving late. 'I took ill during the journey.'

'But, sir, you are our pilot, after all! We only want that the Congress aircraft reach its proper destination,' said Rajaji, smiling slyly.

Everyone laughed at his remark. But the undercurrent of tension was palpable. The Rightists and Leftists had deliberately seated themselves in separate groups. P. C. Joshi, Somnath Lahiri, Niharendu Dutt Majumdar of the communists, and the youth with socialist leanings had distanced themselves from the old guard. Rajaji's presence seemed to dominate the room. Of late, he had been the butt of much criticism. He had used his authority and the police force to arrest several radical youth. His predisposition to the British government caused an irate Nehru to ask, 'Have you been appointed the prime minister of Madras province or the police commissioner?'

The afternoon session concluded. Some important decisions were to be taken later in the evening. Between sessions, Subhas went over to the Bhangi Colony to meet Gandhiji. Turning to H.V. Kamath who was accompanying him, Subhas remarked, 'Hari, this morning's meeting went flat, didn't it?'

'Babuji, for the last four days, I have been hearing the Rightist group grumbling.'

'What about?'

'They are dissatisfied with your style of functioning.'

'But what exactly do they not like?'

'Er, if the truth must be told,' Kamath said hesitantly, 'they are saying that you have no idea how to run the Congress. Secretary Kripalani is going around saying that the Allahabad office is strewn with letters and papers, but the honourable president has no time for them.'

'Has Acharya Kripalani forgotten that Allahabad is seven hundred miles away from Calcutta?'

'So?'

'Even a simple request of mine – to shift the office or at least some of the staff – has been ignored. I am isolated there.'

Subhas had led a demonstration in Calcutta protesting the Act of 1935 and the idea of a federation. During his speech, he had repeatedly lauded the efforts of the Italian and Irish revolutionaries. Besides, he had been demanding that the British be given an ultimatum that if within a stipulated period, independence was not granted, a nationwide civil disobedience movement would be started.

The Bhangi Colony meeting between Gandhiji and Subhas took place. All Gandhiji said was, 'Subhas, tone down your language about the ultimatum. The time is not yet ripe for such strong steps.'

'On the contrary, seeing how the world is rapidly heading towards war, I believe we are at the threshold of a mass struggle.'

The furrows on Gandhiji's brow seemed to have become more pronounced. The afternoon session began with Rajaji tabling a proposal. 'If a war situation develops, then the British government should be allowed to take the appropriate decision. The nation and the Congress must have more faith in the good sense of the British.'

The socialists and the communists objected vociferously. A furious Dutt Majumdar thundered, 'We will not allow for any compromise in our struggle for freedom. We will not tolerate a repetition of the mistakes that even Gandhiji has made.'

Subhas Chandra too was displeased. Protesting the proposal for compromise, seventy-three Leftist members boycotted the proceedings.

At night, all the members gathered around Gandhiji once again. Gandhiji was furious when he heard what had happened. Rajaji told Gandhiji clearly, 'We will not allow the monocracy of the Leftists to continue.' The same Leftists who had walked out of the meeting came to see him. Dutt Majumdar spoke up sharply. 'Bapuji, for how long is this policy of compromise going to carry on? Why should we mortgage our good sense to the British?'

'Look here, Majumdar. If you do not agree with the policies and ideologies of the party, say no more. If the party must split, so be it. Instead of indulging in such disruptive activities, it is better you leave. At least, the party will remain unsullied.'

Gandhiji's words seared Subhas Chandra's heart. He could see the Congress divided down the middle.

'Why are you resigning from the ICS at such a young age?' Subhas Chandra asked the young man he had met at the Nagpur Rest House.

'Babuji, what did you give up the ICS for?'

'For the country.'

'I am doing it for you.'

The bright young man who had offered his services to Subhas Chandra and his cause was H.V. Kamath. In fact, he had been toiling alongside Subhas Chandra since even before the Haripura Congress. The industry ministers' conference was a novel idea. And Kamath, who had some experience in administration, took on the responsibility.

The conference was scheduled for 2 October 1937 – Gandhiji's birthday. Subhas had invited ministers from all seven provinces. The eminent scientist Dr Meghnad Saha had been working beside Subhas night and day to make the conference a success.

Subhas was staying at Shankarlal's home in Delhi. Shankarlal could not resist asking him, 'Subhas babu, have you taken Gandhiji's permission to hold this conference?'

'Of course. I had the proposal approved at the working committee meeting in Wardha. These formalities have acquired undue significance nowadays.'

H.V. Kamath looked restive. Subhas babu asked him, 'Visvesvaraya is coming from Bangalore as scheduled, isn't he?'

'Can't say for sure, Babuji. He is eighty, after all.'

'How wonderful it will be if he does!'

Dr Meghnad Saha and Subhas had prepared a note of all the issues which were to be highlighted in the meeting the next day. Freedom was bound to come, one day or another. Subhas's primary concern now was how to build a strong and powerful nation after that. Before going to bed, he had glanced through Dr M. Visvesvaraya's book, *Planned Economic Development for India,* published just a couple of years ago. This invaluable text was almost a blueprint for modernisation. For many years, Dr Visvesvaraya, the man who had laid the foundations for a modern water distribution system for cities like Pune, who had advocated a series of dams like the Krishnarajasagar across the Kaveri in order to create a network of irrigation canals, had served with the Tata Group of Industries. He had also contributed in a big way to the Premier Factory and Hindustan Aeronautics Ltd. Not only was he an architect of incredible foresight and vision, he had also proved himself an outstanding administrator as diwan to the Maharaja of Mysore.

After the celebrations in honour of Gandhiji's birthday, the proceedings of the meeting got underway. Some revolutionary steps had been taken for the first time after the Congress came to power. The previous year under Nehru's presidentship, the Congress had passed a resolution regarding industrialisation. But the Rightists felt that such measures would create problems for the independence and self-sufficiency of rural areas.

As the invocation ended, the audience in the back of the hall stood up. All eyes turned to a tall, slender figure, impressive in his gold-bordered Mysorean turban, entering the hall, clutching the knob of a walking stick. A cry went up, 'Visvesvaraya has arrived!' Subhas rushed forward and escorted him to the dais. Ghanshyamdas Birla and a few other right-wing office bearers present began to pay greater heed to the proceedings.

Emphasising the need for modernisation, Subhas Chandra said, 'Only America can compare with India in terms of the wealth of natural resources. But because of the non-utilisation of these resources, a gaping beast of poverty and unemployment stands before us. After World War I, Russia's predicament was not very different. However, in just sixteen years, the starved peasants have waved a magic wand and succeeded in creating an imposing, strong, modern nation. The secret of its success is planned economic development. Even if the Industrial Revolution is a monster, it will prove a blessing for the dawn of a new era for us. At the same time, we will have to deal with its ill effects like pollution.'

Someone from the audience asked, 'Babuji, how will cottage industry coexist with your modernisation?'

'Don't make the question of cottage industry versus heavy industry a prestige issue. In several countries of Europe, just because they developed heavy industries, no one turned their backs upon the cottage industry. Small-scale industries are vital to the country.' Subhas Chandra paused for a moment, then continued, 'The question is, how do we achieve modernisation? By adopting the slow and cautious path like the British or rapidly and single-mindedly like the Russians?' Again, he paused, surveyed the reaction of the audience and then closing his hand in a tight fist, said firmly, 'Speed should be the essence for this country. We can never appear on the map of the developed world by moving at an ant's pace.' His resolute words drew spontaneous applause from Visvesvaraya. The whole hall responded similarly.

'I managed to get one proposal approved in the working committee meeting in August. According to it, an expert committee of technologists and professionals for the reconstruction of the nation and social restructuring must be constituted immediately. Every province must do a detailed survey of its natural resources. Inter-provincial technical committees will have to be appointed. For flood control, to plan irrigation measures, to provide drinking water, to prevent soil erosion and for other purposes, an in-depth study of the river systems must be undertaken. To deal with the gigantic problems of unemployment and poverty, we must make optimum use of our natural resources. We cannot afford to depend solely on agriculture. The farmer must prosper. But to provide employment to our people and to ensure the prosperity of our country, we have no choice but to industrialise and spread a network of small, medium and heavy industries across the country.'

Subhas Chandra's eyes fell on a group of young students as he spoke. Pointing to them he said, 'At one time, a host of young Japanese students went abroad with the sole aim of making their country strong and modern. We too must send our students out. When they return, they will use their magic touch to bring about a transformation in our country. Let there be no administrative restrictions on such students. Let them be free to sing the song of development. To do that, we need to establish a national-level research institution.'

The meeting adopted a resolution to constitute a planning committee that would eventually be expanded into a planning commission to draw up a comprehensive plan for development. The industries ministers' meeting also approved the setting up of factories producing heavy machinery, automobiles and their parts, factories to produce chemicals and fertilizers and starting large power-generation plants, and building roads to link up factory sites.

The names proposed for membership would form the planning committee later. Subhas Chandra kept thinking of Jawaharlal. 'I cannot tell you how much I am missing you,' he had written to Jawaharlal and those words kept coming back to him. Subhas had already decided on Nehru for the post of chairman of the planning committee.

Relieved that the meeting was a success, Subhas climbed down the dais. All the tension had fled. He was stopped in his tracks by Dr Visvesvaraya. Subhas Chandra bowed down before him. He felt the eighty-year-old's trembling hand pat his back. 'Well done, Subhas. In our time, if we uttered the word "planning", we were mocked and laughed at. Today, we are not willing to see beyond the charkha. To hear that the president of Gandhiji's Congress party is setting up a planning committee is very heartening.'

'These days Subhas Bose seems to be labouring under the delusion that he knows everything and has begun to expound on all subjects,' observed Maulana Azad.

'The Congress high command has never bestowed on the Congress president the kind of power and authority he expects to wield,' added Sardar Patel.

Many progressive thinkers in the Congress were happy with the outcome of the industries ministers' meeting. But there were several who were unhappy. Subhas knew this, but he and his brother had decided they would stick to their stance and see it through. That is why they had come to Wardha. India's power centre was located in Wardha. Actually, it followed Gandhiji wherever he went, like a shadow.

In spite of knowing that Gandhiji was annoyed with them, they broached the subject. 'Bapuji, the Muslim League is growing in strength. Barrister Jinnah is organising processions through Muslim-dominated towns. They are raising an outcry everywhere that under the Congress regime, untold atrocities are being perpetrated on their brethren.'

Gandhiji looked sombre. 'How do we deal with it?' he asked.

'Let the Congress appoint an impartial enquiry committee to look into these complaints. If Jinnah's inflammatory language is not curbed in time, our Sindh province, which the nobility of Ghaffar Khan is holding up, will also begin to crumble,' warned Subhas.

'Bapuji, if we don't take adequate steps in time, the fearsome monster of a Pakistan will grab us by our throats.'

'But what steps do we take?'

'Today, three provinces which are ruled by Muslim parties other than the League are Sindh, Bengal and Punjab. The Congress should support and nurture them. Either we join hands with them and accept power, or stay outside and promise full support.'

'What will we gain from that?'

'If we make them feel they are one of us, they will gradually assimilate into the mainstream. Undoubtedly, the League's influence in those provinces is increasing and even some genuine nationalist Muslims are being drawn towards it. The call for a *jehad*, a religious war, is defeating reason and rational thought. If things remain as they are, very soon the ruling parties in these three provinces will have to meekly surrender to the League in order to protect their thrones.'

Gandhiji's face broke into a smile. Turning to Sarat Bose he said, 'One just wants to go on listening to Subhas's ideas.'

Subhas continued, unmindful of Gandhiji's remark. 'Not only that, Bapuji, if the governments of these three provinces remain with us when the time comes to discuss constitutional issues with the British, we can honestly say that we speak for the whole country.'

Gandhiji seemed to be won over. 'Sarat, Subhas, both of you take the initial steps in Bengal towards this end.'

'Maulana Azad does not like the idea of a mixed government.'

'Why?'

'According to him, it is best to stay away from religion-based governments. Let them die a natural death, he says. But, Bapuji, I am afraid they won't die themselves, rather, they will kill the nation. If we ignore them, other Muslim groups will be swept up by the League. And eventually, our tricolour could sweat blood.'

'Waah Subhas! I haven't come across anyone who has given so much thought to the unity of the country.'

Gandhiji's approval meant a great deal to Subhas Chandra. The present Congress committee was consumed by envy. Behind his back, they referred to Subhas as childish and ignorant and derided him.

'Ha! He is presumptuous enough to hold talks with the Muslim League and Jinnah on his own!'

'He is prancing around the country with his troop of scientists.'

'Does this Bengali Babu have delusions of being a superior Gandhi?'

'This gentleman is going to jeopardize Bapu's lifelong efforts by his actions.'

'Just hold it for a moment. His tenure expires in two months, doesn't it? We will get a new president at Tripuri anyway. We'll decide what needs to be done then.' These were some of the views exchanged by the Congressmen.

Subhas Chandra was at Nathalal Parekh's house in Bombay. He was about to set off on a tour to Madras when he received a letter from Gandhiji. 'Don't get into the controversy of a mixed government just yet,' it said. Somebody seemed to have talked to Gandhiji. He tried to get more information. The separatist group within the Bengal Congress had had its way. The local executive committee had had its revenge. Ghanshyamdas Birla and Nilratan Sarkar, accompanied by Maulana Azad, had gone to Wardha. A crestfallen Subhas said to Nathalal, 'Bhai, in their efforts to take revenge on me, our friends have played such a cruel game with our country.'

Members of the Congress Working Committee had assembled at Bardoli for a meeting. The mood in the ashram was cheerful. Rajendra Babu said, 'In two months, the Congress party meets at Tripuri. This year has just flown by ....'

'Subhas babu is hoping to be the president again, I hear?' said Sardar Patel.

Acharya Kripalani's face at that moment was worth seeing. 'Really? But who are the other aspirants?'

'Maulana Azad and Dr Sitaramayya are being mentioned.'

'Does that mean Subhas will withdraw from the contest?' asked Acharya Kripalani.

'Withdraw? And Subhas? What are you saying?' Sardar Patel scoffed.

Once again there was laughter. But Acharya Kripalani looked distinctly troubled. Just then Dr Sitaramayya arrived and joined in the conversation. Acharya Kripalani took out a photograph and a newspaper cutting, and showing it to Sardar Patel, said, 'Have you seen this?'

'What is it?' asked Sardar Patel, putting on his spectacles.

'A news report on our enterprising president's recent visit to Jallianwala Bagh.'

Everyone took turns scrutinizing the photograph. Subhas Chandra was paying his respects to the martyrs in proper military style. Sitaramayya said grudgingly, 'Whatever you may say, he manages to create a military atmosphere wherever he goes.'

'Since the Munich Agreement, his speeches have become more aggressive,' said Sardar Patel, expressing concern.

'Tell me, how can he start sounding the bugle call for battle without the approval and backing of the Congress and Gandhiji?' said Acharya.

'Not only that, look at all the press statements,' exclaimed Dr Sitaramayya disapprovingly. 'Already the socialists Namboodiripad, P. Ramamurthi, Sajja Zaheer have shot off letters independently, demanding that Subhas be reappointed Congress president. Also, Subhas seems to have cast a spell on Muslim leaders like Humayun Kabir, Syed Hassan and Ali Chowdhary. Why else would they issue a similar demand just this time?' asked Maulana Azad.

The aggression in Subhas, who had appeared sobre and low-key after the Haripura conference, seemed to have surfaced once again. 'The Congress should stop speaking the language of compromise on any score. The call of the times is to oppose imperialism. If the federation is to be prevented from being formed at the centre, the Congress president must be from the Leftist group.' Naturally, the Rightists in the Congress were disturbed.

'Before this Bardoli meeting concludes, we should give Gandhiji an idea of what has transpired and what the repercussions are likely to be,' Rajendra Prasad suggested.

'I am certainly going to see him,' said Kripalani.

'Look, Acharya, stay calm for a while. Bapu is aware of your opposition to Subhas. He may look upon your protests as prejudice,' said Rajendra Babu.

In the meanwhile, Bhulabhai Desai had joined them. Everyone knew he too was hostile to Subhas. Therefore, it was decided that he and Dr Sitaramayya would convey the information to Gandhiji. Since Gandhiji was always surrounded by people, they would broach the subject when he set out of the ashram for his evening walk. That day, they had the additional support of Rajaji as well.

Dr Sitaramayya was a Gandhi acolyte. He always accompanied Gandhiji on the evening walk. But seeing Bhulabhai and Rajaji with him surprised Gandhiji.

'Bapu, I suspect this fiery Bengali blood will not allow you any peace now,' began Bhulabhai.

'What are you talking about?'

'Jayaprakash and Manavendranath Roy have been singing Subhas's praises of late.'

'These emotional exhortations made by today's youngsters remind me of Hitler's manner.'

Finding Gandhiji in an expansive mood, Bhulabhai continued, 'Arrogance becomes youth. But then to what extent? Subhas shows no regard even for senior leaders like Kripalani, forget about the others.'

'Several complaints have been coming in from Bengal that corruption was rampant in the election of Congress leaders from there. Dr B.C. Roy himself has alleged that the electoral rolls made with Tripuri in mind are bogus,' said Rajaji, adding extra spice.

'Subhas must ensure that his behaviour is impeccable,' said Gandhiji.

'Well, you are the one who pampers him,' retorted Rajaji. 'Presidents come and presidents go. Why have a huge convention for him, why that twenty-one-bullock carriage?'

'You must read his book, *Indian Struggle*, to see what wisecracks he has made about you and the Congress, Bapu,' said Bhulabhai slyly. 'I'll show it to you tomorrow.'

The book had been banned by the government. Bhulabhai had recently obtained one copy from London. That night, Acharya Kripalani highlighted all the sections they thought were relevant, marking out important pages, and first thing in the morning, they took the book to Gandhiji.

'Bapuji, shall I read you some portions?' asked Bhulabhai.

'All right.'

Gandhiji fixed his gaze on Bhulabhai. 'Gandhiji's followers are not capable of thinking for themselves.'

'Is that all? Read on.'

'All Congressmen have mortgaged their wisdom to one individual.'

Gandhiji took the book out of Bhulabhai's hands to read it for himself. But he did not say much. Bhulabhai and Rajaji marched out of the cottage, fuming.

That afternoon, during a moment's respite, Gandhiji summoned Sardar Patel. Patel came in and sat down. Gandhiji's hand continued to work the charkha. 'Sardar, there have been many complaints against Subhas. What should we do about presidentship?

'What can I say, Bapu? You give the directions, we merely execute them.'

Bapuji fell silent. The shaft of the charkha moved furiously. He was deep in thought. After a while, the charkha abruptly stopped moving.

Gandhiji laughed and shaking his head, remarked, 'Understanding Subhas and keeping him in check is a very tough job. I am totally floored by his sacrifice and his patriotism, but ...'

'But what, Bapu?'

Again, he was silent. Then he said, 'Subhas seems to have become rabid after the Munich Agreement. He has no words other than issuing ultimatums.'

Gandhiji resumed working the charkha, his brow creased with worry. The remarks made by Rajaji and Bhulabhai stabbed at him. 'If you let Subhas free like this, Bapu, your life's work will be jeopardised.' Finally, the charkha stopped. The yarn was to his satisfaction. Wiping the perspiration from his bare body, Gandhiji stood up and said, 'Sardar ...'

'Yes, Bapu?'

'I want to remove Subhas from the post. But without upsetting him. He is a dynamic leader.'

Neither the Leftists nor the Rightists could gauge Gandhiji's mind. The working committee meeting went on for two days in Gandhiji's presence and under Subhas's presidentship. But no one brought up the succession issue.

The ashram was unusually quiet that night. The silence was broken by the sound of a car coming to a halt outside the ashram. Bapuji was saying his prayers before lying down on his mat, and paid no attention to it. Rising early in the morning was mandatory in the ashram, so most people had already gone to bed. There was a knock on the cottage door.

'Who is it?'

'It's me, Vallabh, Bapu.'

'Sardar? At this hour?'

'An urgent matter, Bapu.'

'All right, come in.'

Sardar Patel entered. Kanhaiyalal Munshi, the home minister of Mumbai province, was with him. He looked tired after the day-long journey. Not wishing to take up too much time, Kanhaiyalal came forward and placed a file in front of Gandhiji. Curious fingers opened it and examined the dark yellow pages. An assortment of newspaper cuttings, typewritten manuscripts, telegrams, secret messages and some photographs. Gandhiji swallowed hard. He shut the file, tied it up, and placed it under his pillow. Placing his hand on Kanhaiyalal's shoulder, he said, 'I am deeply indebted to you.'

Munshi prepared to take leave. Sardar stared silently at Gandhiji, waiting for some reaction. Gandhiji only said, 'I had some idea. The burning desire for freedom has made him blind and will make him go to any lengths for it.'

'Subhas, you are very ambitious,' Jawaharlal was saying.

'No, Badebhai. I aspire for nothing but the well-being and prosperity of my motherland. If I suggest something, will you listen to me?'

'What?'

'Why don't you become the Congress president instead of me?'

'And what will be gained by that?'

'The progressives of the country will back you. The musty old traditions in the Congress will make way for modern thoughts.'

'I don't wish to be the president,' declared Jawaharlal. 'And why should people like you seek that post? You are much taller and don't need to be elevated.'

'As of now, I am not bothered by these considerations. I am totally absorbed in the demands of the moment.'

'What demands?'

'I can see the ominous storm of war building up on the horizon. The entire world is going to be lashed and churned by their onslaught. We need a diamond-fisted helmsman for the Congress, not one inclined to compromise, if we want to retrieve the jewel of freedom.'

The working committee meeting had concluded that afternoon without any controversy, but the air was thick with tension. There were rumours that some incriminatory file had reached Gandhiji's hands.

From the tone of the Right-wingers in the party, Subhas suspected that his candidature for the post of president would not be considered. As soon as the Bose brothers entered Gandhiji's cottage to take their leave, those present disappeared. Gandhiji welcomed them in his characteristic style. With a smile, he began, 'I have read your book, Subhas.'

'What did you think of it?'

'I really liked your criticism of me,' he laughed. 'Only after reading it, I discovered what an unintelligent, blockhead I am. It was very entertaining.'

Sarat Bose tried to salvage the situation. 'Bapuji, that book was written some years ago. Perhaps the author's views were valid only at that time.'

Gandhiji was staring into space. His face turned grave. 'Sarat, your knowledge of literature is as profound as your understanding of law, that's why I am saying this to you. Is it not true that long before the Roman empire collapsed, rumblings of its imminent demise had begun to be heard? Today, disregard and corruption are rampant in the Congress. I am afraid this institution with fifty years of good work behind it is soon going to disintegrate.'

The Bose brothers remained silent. Sounding exceedingly disturbed, Gandhiji continued, 'Subhas, there's something I have been meaning to tell you for a long time. I am no longer amused by your threats regarding the federation and the ultimatum you have issued.'

'They are not threats, Bapuji! They are the signs of our times.'

'To my mind, the idea of federation is dead. The Congress has no desire to accept power at the centre,' Gandhiji said sharply.

'Bapuji,' said Subhas Chandra, in a calm voice, 'before accepting power in the provinces, all of us had said the same thing. Including Panditji. Today, the wheels of power are riding the crest of comfort. No one is bothered about serving the nation or the people. As for the members of the Council of States – they are enjoying the hospitality of the governor, feasting on his cashew nuts.'

Ignoring Subhas's rejoinder, Gandhiji continued, 'Your idea of issuing an ultimatum is also half-baked and premature. To put it bluntly, it is childish.'

'So then, Bapuji, you believe that the British will have a change of heart and leave this country gladly and of their own accord? When Britain signs a pact with Hitler, it is statesmanship, but if we even whisper his name from this distance, we become Fascists. The British have slipped the noose of slavery round our necks, but before the civilised nations of the world, they sing praises of democracy. Excuse me, Bapuji, every nation is furthering its own interests. That is why I feel we should take the help of external powers to secure our freedom.'

Sarat Bose listened to Subhas Chandra's replies with trepidation. He had tried several times to nudge him into silence, but Subhas Chandra had paid no heed. His voice rose as he continued, 'I would never be party to something as detrimental to our nation as the proposed plan of the federation, and all the attendant compromises. I would prefer to resign. Please release me.'

'Subhas, it would have been better if you had not used such harsh words,' said Gandhiji, with anger and displeasure. 'You should have shown some respect for age. I assure you in your elder brother's presence that if you think any word that I have written or uttered interferes or hinders your work, just tell me. I will not commit the sin of saying anything that contradicts you. As the president, it is your duty to give a direction to the country. Go ahead with courage. You are at liberty to take whatever decisions you think fit.'

Subhas Chandra was a little embarrassed. However, he said, calmly but firmly, 'I could easily have spent the year as a puppet president, accepting garlands and bouquets. Instead, I took decisions regarding planning and reconstruction, held talks with Barrister Jinnah to preserve the unity of the country and did some plain-speaking on several issues for which I am being chastised today. Even so, I still feel that in the context of the current world situation, India should adopt a more aggressive stance and for that, Bapuji, your blessings are essential.'

With a bitter laugh, Gandhiji replied, 'When I cannot help you Subhas, why should I be a hindrance in your path?'

The Bose brothers left immediately for Calcutta. Gandhiji sent for Jawaharlal at once. He threw the letter received from Rabindranath Tagore at him. It was a recommendation of Subhas Chandra's name for the president's post.

'If the vitiated revolutionary atmosphere of Bengal has to be cleaned up, it's better to keep the Congress president's post as far from it as possible,' Gandhiji said.

'Bapu, if Subhas's becoming the president is going to cause you so much agony, drop the idea. What can he do, after all? Hail the Irish, mouth words of revolution, all merely lip service!'

'No, Jawahar. I too had felt that way until today. I made the mistake of ignoring them as just verbal threats.' Bapu's hardened expression had become almost fierce. After a pause, Jawaharlal asked softly, 'What happened today, Bapu, for you to feel this way? Your wrath causes me concern.'

Without saying anything, Gandhiji pushed the confidential file towards Jawaharlal. Nehru turned the pages in astonishment. A German delegation had come to Bombay for an international exhibition. Two of Hitler's ministers were part of it. The Congress president, Subhas Chandra Bose, had made a clandestine visit to the Taj Mahal Hotel in Bombay that night to meet them. In the photograph, he was dressed just like a European, complete with a felt hat and all. The closed-door meeting in one of the suites of the hotel had lasted about two hours. British secret agents had managed to get hold of pictures of him entering the hotel, shaking hands with the Germans in the corridor and then leaving the building, and presented the entire evidence to Munshi who was the home minister of Bombay. He in turn had handed it over to Gandhiji.

'Why would our president want to meet Hitler's representatives, that too in secret?'

'Exactly ...'

'On the one hand, our principle of non-violence has received recognition internationally. How can I now face the world, wearing the pure white garb of ahimsa, and admit that my Congress president is secretly in touch with Hitler's agents?'

'Bapuji, instead of torturing yourself like this, why don't you just forget the matter?'

'Forget? Forget Subhas? I just don't know what to do. I don't have the slightest faith in him. And yet I can't help feeling affection for him. What spell has he cast on me, I wonder.'

All the members of the Congress Working Committee except Subhas Chandra's friend, Harekrushna Mahtab, stayed back in Bardoli as per Gandhiji's instructions. Bapuji returned to his cottage late at night. Kasturba was still awake. 'Ba,' he said, 'your Subhas causes me great pain.'

All the senior members of Calcutta's Right-wing were saying, 'What does Subhas Chandra think of himself?' For the first time in the history of the Congress, an election was going to be held. Subhas Chandra had announced his candidature. Of the Rightists, either Maulana Azad or Dr Sitaramayya were to be the candidates.

No one withdrew their nominations. So the election was to be held on 29 January 1939. Sarat Bose's eldest son, Ashokenath was due to get married on 28 January. What with the wedding preparations and the political upheaval, the house was all aflutter. Just as Subhas Chandra returned home from a hectic tour, Bibhabati handed him an envelope.

'Here, a letter from Rabindranath.'

'What are you saying, boudi! The third in a month!' said Subhas, tearing it open. 'Reading a letter from the great poet is so soothing after the turmoil of politics. It's like finding the shade of a banyan tree after a long trek in the sun.'

Dr Meghnad Saha was to take Subhas Chandra to Santiniketan with him the following day. To have received a benediction from the great man himself just before this planned visit made Subhas exceedingly happy. As they drove to Santiniketan, Subhas Chandra told Dr Saha, 'It is only because of you that I am visiting Santiniketan today.'

'Oh, it's nothing,' Dr Saha replied. 'In fact, Dr Prafulla Chandra Roy has written an article in the *Amrita Bazar Patrika*, that if a progressive and forward-looking person like you becomes the Congress president again, a wave of development will sweep through the country. In fact, all the scientists and researchers are very happy about one quality of yours.'

'And what is that?'

'The fearless way in which you speak about planning and industrialisation, your efforts to make these ideas work, your sincerity and confidence in these matters makes us believe that truly there is hope for our country.'

Soon they arrived at Santiniketan. The directors of Vishva-Bharati, Anil Chand, Kalimohan Ghosh, Sukumar Chatterji and others, welcomed him. Rabindranath, bent with age, walked with a stoop. His white beard reached down to his chest. But the eyes set in his longish face were bright, full of laughter. He was like an elderly banyan tree – the trunk was aged, but in the new leaves, there was tremendous energy. Subhas bent down for his blessings. Rabindranath placed his hand on Subhas's head and said, 'I have been waiting for you for a long time!'

'Ji, Gurudev!'

'You must have been a schoolboy at the time of the agitation against the partition of Bengal. All of Bengal had come together with such fervour then. Today, the same Bengal is so enervated and directionless.'

'We desperately need inspiration and guidance from you, Gurudev.'

As they wandered slowly through the verdant environs of Santiniketan, Rabindranath said, 'My main objective in starting Santiniketan was to free children from the stifling confines of a schoolroom and give them an education in natural surroundings.'

A short programme had been organised in honour of Subhas Chandra. In his speech, Subhas said, 'Into the empty lives of politicians like us, epic poets like Gurudev bring fresh hope and joy. And from their inspiration, men are made and nations born. Gandhiji and Kaviguru are two of our noblest symbols.'

Responding to him, Rabindranath said, 'Subhas, not today, but almost fifteen years ago, I had warned a great man like Gandhi that the charkha and village self-rule is not everything. We must progress scientifically.'

Subhas Chandra went around observing the new farming, industrial and rural development projects. Later, he chatted with the students, sitting outdoors in the balmy evening air. The discussion that night was free and frank. Rabindranath said, 'A number of prominent citizens have approached me with the request to recommend you for the post of Congress president. I also agree with them. So I have sent a letter to that effect to Mahatmaji and Jawaharlal.' Subhas felt deeply indebted.

But Meghnad couldn't help himself. He said, 'Gandhiji's followers believe that Subhas babu took advantage of your age and induced you. In addition, the fact that you are both Bengalis has made several people suspicious of your support.'

This pierced Rabindranath's heart. Morosely he said, 'I had openly praised Subhas's competence. At this stage in my life, what need have I of anyone's favours?'

'Forgive me, Gurudev, I have caused you so much pain....'

'No, Subhas,' Gurudev broke in, 'I have recommended you after much thinking. Parochialism is a vainglorious idea. No one should try to confine me within its narrow boundaries.'

After a while he said, 'In ten days' time, my students are presenting a play in Calcutta. I would like to organise a felicitation for you on that occasion. My speech for the event is ready. I will send you a copy.'

Anil Chand brought Subhas the copy of the address. Late into the night, Subhas sat, going over the contents, the words frequently blurring before his tear-filled eyes. He even read it out to Dr Meghnad several times.

'As Bengal's poet, I today acknowledge you as the honoured leader of the people of Bengal. The Gita tells us that from time to time, the eternal principle of the good arises to challenge the reign of the evil. Bengal is passing through a period of dark despair. 'At such a juncture of nationwide crises, we require the invincible faith of a natural leader, who can defy the fate that threatens our progress.

'I have witnessed the beginning of your political sadhana. In that uncertain twilight, there had been misgivings in my heart ... today you are revealed in the pure light of the midday sun, which does not admit of banishment and disease, but rather than impairing, these have helped to broaden your sympathies.... You did not regard apparent defeat as final; therefore, you have turned your trials into your allies. More than anything else, Bengal needs to imbibe the force of your self-reliant courage....

'Long ago, I sent out a call for the leader of Bengal who had yet to come. After a lapse of many years, I am addressing one who has come into the full light of recognition. My days are approaching their end. I may not join him in the fight that is to come. I can only bless him, knowing that he has made his country's burden his own, that his final reward is fast coming in the form of his country's freedom.'

Gurudev was sitting on a cane chair under a banyan tree when Subhas went to take his leave. Clasping Subhas's hand fondly in his own, he said in a thick voice, 'Today, I can proudly say that the leader of my dreams stands resplendently before me.' After a pause he said, wistfully, 'I wish I could be a part of your struggle, to walk the path of your battle, even with the aid of my walking stick, even if it's just a short distance. The thought that my frail body will not obey me, makes me very sad.'

With a heavy heart, Subhas bid Santiniketan farewell.

For the first time in its fifty-five years, the Congress was faced with an election. On the one hand, Subhas Chandra was unwilling to relent and on the other, the Rightist group was bent on challenging his candidature.

Six members of the Congress Working Committee had issued a statement from Bardoli. 'Only in exceptional circumstances will an individual seek a second term as president. The present situation does not merit such action. Subhas babu should not set an undesirable precedent. We are beginning to have grave misgivings about his motives.' Though Jawaharlal was not a signatory to the statement, it was signed by other senior Congressmen.

The release of the statement resulted in a dramatic change in the atmosphere not just in the Bose household, but across the country.

While Sarat Bose was reading Sardar Patel's statement, one thing struck him. Sitaramayya's nomination had been decided upon at Bardoli. He said to Subhas, 'You were the president at Bardoli. You should have been the first to be informed of any such decision.'

'The matter was not discussed at all. Nothing came up before the working committee either. How can the Congress Working Committee take a decision like this in the absence of the president? Under what principles of truth and non-violence, does such an action fall? Mej-da, it seems like a conspiracy hatched by the Rightist faction. Gandhiji wants a mere puppet as president. I would rather die than dance to someone else's tune.'

Sarat Bose was happy to hear the strong note of self-respect in Subhas Chandra's words. Subhas asked, 'Mej-da, do you read *Harijan*?'

'I haven't seen the recent issues.'

'Without mentioning any names, Gandhiji has been venting his ire on us. He says that the politics of the election process is becoming more and more corrupt. The Congress ship is rudderless.'

~

As the day of the election drew near, the situation worsened. So far, Gandhiji had not made any public statement. Yet, his inclinations, his displeasure and his remonstrations were public knowledge. Maulana Azad was to contest the election, and Gandhiji had supported his candidature. But Maulana could not muster up the courage to oppose Subhas Chandra. Gandhiji summoned Dr Sitaramayya to Bardoli, and compelled him to file his nomination papers. These developments were enough grist for the newspaper mills.

Sarat Bose was lost in thought, wondering how to face the next obstacle when a telegram was handed over to him. His face turned pale as he read the contents. 'Who is it from, Mej-da?' asked Subhas, who was standing nearby.

'Sardar Patel.'

'Let me see it.'

Subhas glanced over it. 'Subhas's re-election will be detrimental to the nation.' He was deeply hurt by that abrupt sentence.

'Forget it, Mej-da. That is his opinion.'

'He is not some nobody. For our country, we have not only sacrificed our personal peace and happiness, but all my earnings, our family income, everything. The scorching hot roof, the freezing floors, the rust and chill which has penetrated our bones; thanks to the long periods in jail. Today, that same country is asking us, "What have you done for me?"'

The strain was telling on Prabhabati too. Some workers came rushing to Woodburn Park with the latest issue of *Harijan*. Subhas Chandra opened it and saw Gandhiji's explosive article titled 'Internal Decay.' Although no names had been mentioned, from the point of view of the Bose faction, the article would do them enormous harm. Mentioning the Tripuri Congress, it said that the voters' lists were rigged and many bogus names included. Dissensions and disputes had hollowed out the Congress party, and rampant corruption was surely going to destroy it. At this point, it seemed like there was only chaos and ruination, nothing else. All the allegations had been directed at the Bose clan. Two days before the election, the paper had reached every voter. While Gandhiji professed neutrality, he had spewed out all the bile within him. The message had reached the voters, and it would get the desired result.

The anti-Bose lobby had the support of the elite of Calcutta society – the industrialists and businessmen. Dr B.C. Roy, a surgeon by profession, was at one time a friend of Sarat Bose. However, now he had attached himself to Gandhiji in his capacity as a doctor. His anti-Bose sentiment proved to be beneficial to him.

The surge of allegations and counter-allegations died down. On the day of counting, Sarat Bose had hosted a dinner-reception for Ashokenath, at the South Club nearby. Sarat Bose was restless all day. Subhas Chandra's growing confidence merely aggravated his unease. God forbid he is blighted by failure, he prayed. Later that evening, the guests began to gather on the spacious green lawns of the club. Of them, party workers were in the majority. The elderly Marxist worker Ghosh Babu was also present. In Sarat Bose's presence, he told Subhas Chandra, 'Your defeat is certain.'

Subhas immediately pulled out a sheet of paper and started scribbling some figures and making calculations. Then he gave a province-wise break-up of the votes he expected to poll. Ghosh Babu replied, 'All these figures are very well. But who knows what is inside the ballot boxes.'

'We will know about that too soon enough.'

Around seven that evening, the phone in Woodburn Park rang incessantly. As the results came in from different constituencies, one of the nephews would come running with it. The first couple of results were disappointing. But then the picture started to change. Subhas mingled with the guests enthusiastically, playing his role as the host. His opponents in the Calcutta Congress started appearing at the reception one by one. Then Subhas's nephew, Amiyonath, ran in saying, 'Ranga kaka, results from the United Province!' Sarat and Subhas stared at Amiyo expectantly. This was the stronghold of Jawaharlal and Kripalani. 'Dr Sitaramayya 185 and you, Ranga kaka, 269,' Amiyo gasped.

Sarat Bose's eyes glistened at once. He grabbed Subhas Chandra's hand. 'Raja, don't worry. Victory is yours.'

It was ten o'clock by the time the guests left and the party wound up. At eleven o'clock, there was a call from the Chief Election Office in Allahabad. Dr Sitaramayya had secured 1,375 votes against Subhas Chandra's 1,580. And Subhas was declared elected by a sizeable margin of 205 votes.

He had received enormous support from Karnataka, Kerala, Assam, Delhi and Madras. Only in Rajendra Babu's Bihar, Gandhiji's Gujarat and his own Andhra Pradesh, Sitaramayya had been in the lead. As for Maharashtra, they had shared the votes almost equally. But the overall results proved that a huge section of the country was firmly behind Subhas Chandra. By the time the various leaders and workers departed, it was very late. Bibhabati was exhausted and fell asleep. But Sarat Bose seemed to have spent a wakeful night. When she woke up early next morning, she asked him, 'So the elections are over. Everything turned out as you wanted, didn't it?'

'Bibha, by this unprecedented victory, Subhas has committed a grave crime.'

'What?' asked Bibhabati incredulously.

'That of pulling the tiger-skin from under the Mahatma's seat.' Sarat Bose sighed as he spoke. 'Forgiveness is the mark of a great man. But if Gandhiji does not show it and treats it as a personal defeat, then we are going to face a very hard time. I am afraid the burden of this victory will weigh him down, Bibha.'

Eight

Results of the election were splashed across the front pages of all newspapers. The air over Calcutta was still heavy with the sound and smell of firecrackers. Sweets were distributed in all of Bengal. Bose's residence, crammed with party workers, resonated with good cheer. There were queues at Bhowanipore to congratulate Subhas Chandra. Barrister Nariman, Lala Shankarlal, Kavishwar, N.G. Ranga, Swami Sahajanand and Manavendranath Roy, had sent greetings. Messages poured in from across the country. The Bose brothers, however, were waiting to see how the Gandhi loyalists would react.

Gandhiji made his feelings known the very next day through a statement. 'Subhas Chandra Bose has won a decisive victory over Dr Pattabhi Sitaramayya. I was opposed to his re-election from the beginning. Also, I was solely responsible for not letting Pattabhi withdraw his nomination. That is why I take it as my personal defeat and not Pattabhi's.'

Every word of Gandhiji's statement reeked of petulance and anger. Again, he had referred to the corruption in the party. He continued, 'With a heavy heart, I say that when all is said and done, Subhas babu is not an enemy of the country. He has suffered for its cause.' While acknowledging this, he had indicated to his followers, 'I clearly tell the workers that those who leave the Congress party today will prove to be the true leaders of the future. Those who find it difficult to remain in the Congress should quit the party and dedicate themselves to the service of the nation.'

Sarat Bose and Subhas Chandra remained silent for a long while after reading the message. 'What does he mean by this sarcastic remark, "Subhas is not an enemy of the country," Mej-da? Am I an enemy of my motherland?'

'It only means one thing – the great man finds your honest victory unsavoury. He is upset. There is going to be more rancour, wait and see. The disciples will set out to avenge their guru's humiliation.'

As expected, the situation deteriorated rapidly after the publication of the statement. Some people went so far as to say if only Gandhiji had given some indication earlier they would have taught a lesson to Bose. A victory procession was about to begin from the Congress party office in Wellington Square when some mischievous elders of the Rightist faction began expressing doubts and making accusations. 'Will there be a Congress party session at Tripuri at all?'

'Will Subhas remain in the Congress?'

'If he remains in the country, it will be enough!'

Gandhiji's disturbing statement with its provocation and disappointment, confused senior leaders and the public. Subhas Chandra too was plagued by doubts – had he indeed done something wrong? Sarat Bose told him, 'Subhas, Jawahar is in Santiniketan.'

'Since when?'

'Two days. His daughter Indira is with him. Go and meet them. See if things can be resolved after discussions with him.'

Subhas wanted to meet Jawaharlal. Jawaharlal had shown remarkable restraint in the tussle. Before the election, he had gone off to holiday in the Kumaon hills. The day after the election results were announced, he went to Santiniketan for some function.

As he shook Subhas's hand, Jawaharlal said, 'I must appreciate your courage. Such a thing has never happened in the history of the party, it never will.'

Both were silent for a while. Then Jawaharlal said, 'Subhas, several times we, that is Gandhiji and his close colleagues, Sardar, Prasad, Maulana, were brought together through imprisonment. But to your lot came the jails of Burma and other harsh places. On several occasions, there have been disagreements and differences between Gandhiji, Sardar and me. But because of our closeness and long association, disputes were settled and differences ironed out quickly. Unfortunately, you did not have such opportunities.'

Subhas agreed with Jawaharlal on that. Suddenly, Jawaharlal's voice changed. 'Subhas, during your tenure, the Congress offices suffered greatly.'

'How is that possible, Panditji?'

'Many telegrams and letters went unanswered. Work piled up. Those are the complaints of the workers.'

'Not of the workers, but of Acharya Kripalani's. He could never redirect the president's letters to Calcutta. But he was very efficient at forwarding complaints against me to you in Switzerland, even before they reached Wardha! Isn't that true?'

Panditji laughed out loud. Then he broached the subject of the Krishak Party in Bengal.

'Why were you brothers so keen to form a coalition government with a regional, casteist party? Was it not a defiance of the Congress policy?'

'No, it was foresight.'

'Joining hands with a communal party? What kind of foresight is that?'

'You are mistaken, Panditji. The Krishak Party has a profound influence on the Muslims in Bengal. That is why getting close to them would, in the long run, have made a difference. Otherwise, this same party will collaborate with the Muslim League and become a nuisance to the whole country. Then all of East Bengal will be communalised and give the partitionists an opportunity to split the province.'

'Subhas, I never doubted either your abilities or your intentions.'

After a two-and-a-half-hour discussion, nothing worthwhile emerged. Jawaharlal repeatedly advised Subhas, 'Go and meet Gandhiji. Anger only increases with distance, while affection thrives on proximity.'

'Can I expect at least some cooperation from you?' Subhas asked Jawaharlal with much hope.

'Well, let us see. Actually, Subhas, I think ... Gandhiji, you and I are unfortunately trapped in some strange triangle. And so far, I haven't been able to find a way out of this maze.'

The meeting with Jawaharlal was most unsatisfactory. Nothing was resolved. A disappointed Subhas Chandra went in to meet Rabindranath. The poet was seated under a large banyan tree. As soon as he saw Subhas, his wrinkled face lit up. Subhas Chandra bowed down in respect. 'Kalyanam!' he said, and asked Subhas to sit beside him. Before Subhas could say anything, Gurudev started, 'I have read Gandhiji's statement.'

'You have?'

'Yes. Let it go. I have now learnt that even great men are not immune to egoism. It was a free and fair election, wasn't it? Shouldn't mahatmas look beyond the web of envy and prejudice?'

'Gurudev, what should the next step be?'

'Go back to Gandhiji's feet.'

'Again?'

'Why not? He is like a father to you – in age and experience. If he has the eye to recognise your true merit, if his chisel still has the old magic, he will add new facets to your personality.'

'If you say so, Gurudev.'

'Do go. But if you have to set aside your self-respect and enter into any compromise, do not remain there even for a moment.'

A group of journalists had surrounded Subhas. A note of irony crept into his voice as he said to the journalists, 'I became the recipient of the common man's respect, but was not able to gain the confidence of a noble soul like Gandhiji. What could be more tragic than that?'

'Why do you say that, Bose Babu? Gandhiji has admitted that Pattabhi's defeat was a personal defeat for him.'

'Gandhiji was not contesting the election against me, Pattabhi was. The public voted for either him or me.'

The car was waiting at the gate. Subhas was leaving for Wardha. Bidding goodbye to the reporters, he said, 'I am going to seek Gandhiji's blessings. Be assured of one thing. Under no circumstances will there be discord in the Congress. Our fight against imperialism will be carried out as one entity.'

After a two-day train journey, Subhas Chandra finally arrived at the Shegaon Ashram near Wardha. A crowd was already waiting to meet Gandhiji. Subhas Chandra was asked to wait in a small cottage. Just then Kasturba came in. She had changed so much. Her face was lined, her cheeks shrunken as she had lost her teeth. And the scorching Wardha sun had burnt her skin. She asked, 'How is your Ma?'

'She has all the afflictions of old age for company.'

As she turned to leave, Subhas Chandra said, 'Ma, you are going so soon?'

Kasturba just smiled as if to say, what is left to talk about?

Subhas Chandra handed her two packets of Darjeeling tea. 'Where was the need for this?' said Ba. 'I still have some. It's only when you come that tea is made in this ashram. Then she left. Mahadev Desai came forward to enquire after Subhas Chandra.

'Mahadev bhai, how is Gandhiji's mood?'

Trying to hide his amusement Mahadev Desai replied, 'Subhas babu, you are being very funny today.'

'Why?'

'Since when have you started worrying about Bapu's mood?'

'But permission to meet him....'

'Why do you need permission? Does a storm seek permission before knocking at your door?'

The light-hearted banter continued. The news of Subhas Chandra's arrival reached Gandhiji almost immediately. He sent for Subhas. He asked after his family. They talked about several subjects. But the matter of the elections did not come up. Finally, Subhas Chandra said, 'Bapu, you appear to be very annoyed. The statement you issued after Pattabhi's defeat has hurt me deeply. The whole family is grieved by it.'

'Let us see. You are prepared to stay for a while, aren't you? We will talk later tonight.'

That evening Gandhiji, Pyarelal and Subhas babu set out for a walk. Gandhiji's sprightly gait belied his seventy years and put many younger people to shame. Later that night, the discussion began and went on for over three hours. Both Gandhiji and Subhas Chandra voiced their concern about the growing popularity of the Muslim League and its influence on national politics. Noticing that Gandhiji's anger seemed to have abated, Subhas Chandra spoke, 'Bapu, who do you think we should induct into the working committee? I need your advice.'

'Who do you have in mind?'

'Jayaprakash Narayan, Narendra Dev, Swami Sahajanand, Manavendranath Roy, Nariman, besides Sardar, Jawaharlal, Azad, of course.' Without hesitation, Subhas was endorsing the views of the socialist group and those involved in the peasant movement. That's when Gandhiji hinted, 'I don't think Sardar and his friends will give you much cooperation at Tripuri.'

'Bapu, it is true that our personal differences have been needlessly stretched. But with your leadership, everything should get smoothened out.'

'Are you having a working committee meeting before the annual general meeting of the party?'

'Yes, on 22 February, here in Wardha.'

'Then we will have a face-to-face discussion here on that day. We will sweep away all the cobwebs from our minds. Make sure you don't miss the meeting!' Gandhiji warned gently.

'I will definitely attend it. A brief has to be prepared on what resolutions need to be tabled at Tripuri,' he said.

The next day, Subhas woke up with a splitting headache. As soon as Gandhiji heard about it, he ground some herbs into a paste and applied it to Subhas's forehead.

'My medicine is usually most effective on all politicians across the country. But dear Subhas, you are such a difficult one, I don't know if my herbal medicine will work on you!' said Gandhiji, tongue in cheek.

Both had a good laugh. By night, the headache had gone, and when he went to take leave the next morning, he was quite cheerful. The news of his return to Calcutta by train had spread through all of Vidarbha. Most halts enroute – like Wardha, Badnera, Nagpur – saw hordes of his admirers waiting on the platforms with garlands and bouquets. Soon after the train left Nagpur, Subhas Chandra began to feel uneasy. He checked his temperature. It was 101 ^{0}F. Throughout the journey, the fever would shoot up to 105 ^{0}F and equally suddenly come down below normal. When they reached Howrah, Subhas Chandra somehow managed to get home and went straight to bed. Days passed, but he was not getting better. As the Wardha meeting drew near, he began to panic. Missing such a crucial meeting was nothing short of a calamity. Besides the resolutions to be tabled at Tripuri, it was necessary to hold talks with the Rightists and find a golden mean. Moreover, Gandhiji had repeatedly told him not to miss the Wardha meeting. How could he stay away, that too on grounds of ill health. He begged, pleaded with, even threatened the doctor. 'Do something, doctor, give me any medication, any treatment, but let me go to Wardha.'

'We aren't bothered about Wardha. We are more worried about whether you will even be able to attend the Tripuri Congress,' replied the doctor.

'What?'

Subhas's face clouded over. His friends ran around to charter a private aircraft to take him at least up to Nagpur.

Subhas implored the doctor, 'Please, please give me an injection and let me go.'

Finally, the doctor did some plain speaking. 'You may be able to take the flight to Nagpur, but we do not guarantee you will come back alive,' he said. As Subhas lay semi-conscious, he was murmuring, 'This wretched illness will be the death of me.'

In a telegram to Sardar Patel, Subhas wrote, 'It is only this terrible illness which prevents me from coming to Wardha. The meeting may please be postponed till the Congress session at Tripuri.'

Sarat Bose felt as if the heavens had fallen upon him. Subhas's illness had not yet been diagnosed. The fever would not leave him. Every day brought with it some new problem. The Bose family was constantly at Subhas's bedside. Then one day, the shocking news leaked out that twelve eminent Congress Working Committee members including Sardar Patel and Rajendra Prasad had resigned at Wardha.

Once again, news of the rift in the Congress party hit the headlines. Subhas Chandra had read the newspapers even before he received Sardar Patel's letter. With shivering, fever-racked fingers, he opened the love letter from his colleagues.

> *Dear Subhas,*
>
> *All of us were distressed to read that you have been unwell.*
>
> *We did not expect you to jeopardise your health to attend the Wardha meeting. We hope that you will recover very soon and regain your lost health.*
>
> *We have carefully considered the recent developments, but because of your absence due to indisposition, we are not able to reply to your statements in the newspapers. At this juncture, we believe that in the best interests of the party, we must hand in our resignations and leave you free to constitute a new working committee.*

The letter was signed by Sardar Patel and eleven others. The thirteenth was Jawaharlal. He had not signed it. Instead, he issued a separate statement. But it was so ambiguously worded that it was not clear whether he was opposed to Subhas Chandra, or with him.

The bundle of resignation letters arrived at Elgin Road by post one day. Sarat Bose glanced over them and handed them to Subhas Chandra. With a heavy heart, Subhas Chandra sat up in bed and looked at them, then put them under his pillow. After a while, as if he remembered something, he pulled out Acharya Kripalani's letter, signed it and told his nephew, 'Go send a telegram to Acharyaji. Tell him that his resignation was the first to be accepted.'

He was not recovering. His mother and sister-in-law did not leave his bedside. Each new day seemed to be darker than the last, as if the sky had turned inside out. Gandhiji announced his decision not to attend the Tripuri Congress session. 'What next? How long would this illness last? Will I even see the venue where the all-important meeting, for which I have earned the enmity of senior leaders, will be held?'

As she stroked his forehead, Prabhabati asked, 'Raja, had you not explained everything properly to Gandhi Baba? What did he say?'

'Ma, I went to see him so many times. But, now I realise that it was not the Mahatma I had met. The man I met was a shrewd, calculating politician.'

Gandhiji had announced his intention of going on a hunger strike in protest against the tyranny of the administration, just two or three days before the Tripuri Congress. He was all set to leave for Rajkot where his fast was to begin. Several members of the working committee were gathered at the ashram prior to their departure for Tripuri. 'Bapu, why have you chosen to go on a fast for such a small reason at the expense of attending the all-important meeting?'

'According to me, this is a very important task.'

Looking disdainfully at the working committee members seated around him, he asked, 'And why are all of you going to Tripuri?'

'We must go, Bapu. In our absence, the entire party will be taken over by that Bengali Babu. We will not have even a foothold,' declared Bhulabhai Desai.

'Arre, but how can you go to Tripuri? You have sent a bundle of resignation letters to Subhas, haven't you?' asked Gandhiji.

'Actually, we can attend the session legitimately. Our resignations haven't been accepted yet.' Sardar Patel remarked.

Gandhiji burst into laughter. 'A valid point! That means technically only Acharya cannot attend the meeting. His resignation has been accepted; by telegram too.'

There was loud laughter in the room. Acharya's face turned sour. Gandhiji's group set off for Tripuri with a completely different agenda.

This was the first time Gandhiji was starting a fast without his closest acolytes beside him. Kasturba was also supposed to join Gandhiji on this fast. As they were setting out, Kasturba asked, 'How far is Rajkot from Tripuri?'

'Not much.'

For a while, she was silent, but she looked very perturbed. Gandhiji noticed and asked, 'What is it, Ba?'

'Nothing much. You don't even step on a fallen leaf, lest you kill an insect hiding behind it.'

'So?'

'Everyone says Subhas is on his deathbed ... my heart aches....'

'Ignore all that. You will not understand the deceitfulness of that Bengali. His illness is also a fabrication.'

'How do you know?'

'Everybody from Jeevith Kripalani downwards knows it.'

'In spite of that, let us go to Tripuri for a little while. The Congress is ours and so is Subhas.' Kasturba couldn't help herself.

Gandhiji exploded. 'If your heart is there in Tripuri instead of our ashram, go there by all means. I will organise the transport for you.'

Kasturba's face fell.

The Tripuri convention was fast approaching, and instead of getting better, Subhas's health seemed to be deteriorating. Sarat Bose and Bibhabati kept up their nightly vigil. After seeing Sunil Bose out, Sarat Bose sank into an armchair in the hall downstairs. Just a few minutes later, he saw a middle-aged gentleman, who seemed like a Maharashtrian, standing in front of him. A black topi on his head, a simple cotton coat that was unbuttoned, he was clad in pants. His face was flat and broad, in which were set sharp, bright eyes. Who could this be? Seems familiar, thought Sarat Bose. And then he realised. The former chief minister of the Central Provinces, Dr N.B. Khare, who had to quit his post because of differences with Gandhiji.

'Come in, Doctor saheb, an unexpected visit this is!'

'I had come to Calcutta on work, so I thought I'd see you all. So how is Subhas babu?'

'The same, stable.'

'I want to meet him.' And then involuntarily he blurted out, 'I have some serious news for him.'

'About what? Whom?'

'That means you haven't heard anything, obviously!'

'About what?'

'Gandhiji and his followers have planned to upset the Tripuri meeting,' Khare said softly.

'Is this what you wanted to tell him?'

'Yes.'

'In that case, you certainly cannot meet Subhas,' said Sarat Bose, flatly turning down his request.

'Fine! And to think I came all this way for your benefit.'

'Look, doctor, you and Gandhiji have had bitter disagreements. Why should we needlessly get involved in your quarrel?'

'Kindly do not misunderstand me. You may think I have come here to instigate Subhas against Gandhi to get even with him. If that is so, you are making a grave mistake, Sarat babu. Don't forget, till date, the saint of Sabarmati has not suffered a single dissenter. Annie Besant, Barrister Jinnah, Deshbandhu, Motilal – tell me, which of them stands beside him today? Annie bai who advocated Home Rule, is a non-entity; Jinnah walked out of the Congress party forever; Motilal and Deshbandhu started new parties, broke them up and after making a compromise, have ended the matter once and for all. What do you think is behind all this?'

'You tell me.'

'That old man is obsessed with getting rid of all opposition, believe me. He only wants head-nodding assenters in his ashram. Anyone who has a backbone must steer clear of the road to Wardha.'

'On what basis are you saying that the meeting will be disrupted?'

'Well, the method may differ, but only when you come back from Tripuri, ragged and battered, will you recall my words.' A sharp edge had crept into Dr Khare's voice.

'Doctor saheb, I'm sorry, but I cannot let you convey such a serious matter to the party president.'

'That is entirely up to you. It was my duty to warn you.' Dr Khare left.

Sarat Bose felt numb. Nothing made sense. The elections were over, so why would anyone want to stall the meeting? What reason did they have for obstructing the functioning of the party? Sleep eluded him that night. His mind was plagued by premonitions about Subhas's future. The words of Dr Khare seemed to haunt him like the warning in Shakespeare's *Julius Caesar*, 'Beware the Ides of March!'

5 March 1939. The exhausted office-bearers of the Mahakaushal Congress Party were waiting on Jabalpur platform. Sheth Govinddas, member of the reception committee, kept glancing at his watch. 'I just can't believe this. Will this session take place at all?'

'Why do you say that, sheth?' Pandit Dubey asked. 'Today is the first day of the meeting.'

'But there's no sign of the president! How can you have a wedding without the bride?'

'You have information that the train has left Dadar, haven't you?' asked Thakur Chedilal.

'True, but how do we know that Subhas babu is on it?'

'Well, that we have to take for granted.'

'Yes, but how? Will a man with a fever of 103 ^{0}F be able to travel? And assuming he does, can he face a throng of at least two lakhs? Can he hold the reins as the Congress president?'

All the faces wore anxious expressions. In the midst of all this, Gandhiji had begun a fast unto death, protesting against the princely states. Only God knew how this meeting would be held in his absence. The band consisting of Congress volunteers had ceased playing. The enthusiasm had drained out of them. Even the welcome arches had begun to droop.

Just then, an official dashed out of the stationmaster's cabin, crying, 'Shethji, shethji, the president has left!'

'Who told you?'

'Put a call through to Nariman's residence in Bombay.... Subhas babu has boarded the mail for Jabalpur.'

At last, the train steamed into Jabalpur station. All the volunteers, waving flags, crowded around the tricolour-bedecked bogie. A short while later, Dr Sunil Bose alighted from the compartment. Immediately, Chedilal and Pandit Dubey rushed in. The sight that greeted them was in complete contrast to the colourful decorations outside. On the berth, lay a live yet motionless mound of flesh, covered with pure white khadi chadors. A shudder ran through the hearts of the organisers. The local doctor performed an on-the-spot examination. The president was running a temperature of 104 ^{0}F. A stretcher was kept at hand. Sarat Bose slid a hand under Subhas's neck and helped to place him gently on it. An exhausted Prabhabati was desperately trying to keep pace with the stretcher bearers. As the party workers saw Subhas's inert body being carried towards the ambulance, their hearts sank, their legs turned weak. No one dared to beat the drums or even shout slogans. Instead of hastening towards one of the hospitals in Bombay, why were these mad people heading towards the forest along the banks of the Narmada? Shouldn't they be trying to save his life at this moment? The band, the drummers, and volunteers carrying garlands and bouquets were shocked into silence. The ambulance sped away towards the venue of the conference.

As was customary, the president was to be escorted to the venue in a grand procession. Since early in the morning, hordes upon hordes of spectators had gathered along the route to the huge Vishnudutta Nagar erected on the banks of the Narmada. The fireworks display ended. In one voice, the massive crowd exulted, 'Mahatma Gandhi ki jai' 'Subhas Chandra Bose zindabad!' 'Vande Mataram!' A number of people who thought that Congress leaders would go straight to Rajkot and not bother about this convention, were surprised to see Pandit Nehru, Sardar Patel, Acharya Kripalani, Rajagopalachari, Maulana Azad, Rajendra Babu, among others, participating in the procession in a special carriage. Seeing all of them present made the public as well as the organisers very happy. Towards the end of the procession, people eagerly rose on tiptoe, their eyes straining to catch a glimpse of that beloved face. And then, they turned away, bewildered and uncomprehending, as their greetings went unacknowledged. The photograph which had been placed there was no compensation for Subhas's presence. How dare illness lay low the one for whom all this had been done. It was as bad as a crown prince collapsing on the day of his coronation. The people's disappointment was boundless.

Yet, several state-level leaders tried to force their way in to see Subhas, and it was becoming increasingly difficult for Sunil Bose and Sarat Bose to hold them back.

The first night at Tripuri was turning out to be ominous. On the banks of the Narmada, speculation was rife in the tents at the venue.

Would Subhas Chandra be able to conduct the proceedings in this condition? Many delegates, including some office bearers, thought Gandhiji ought to come down from Rajkot. In anticipation of his arrival, a small hut had been erected specially for him near the tranquil blue waters of the Narmada. People who had assembled from remote corners of the country were eager for a glimpse of Gandhiji. So great was their reverence for him that though he was nowhere in the vicinity, people queued up outside Gandhi Kutir to lay flowers and pay homage. A number of curious visitors strolled through the Congress township in the moonlit night.

Queues had formed outside the president's camp, too, but no one was allowed to meet the ailing leader. People became nervous seeing the grim look on Sarat Bose's face, who came out to greet them on behalf of the president. Eager to see the charming Subhas Chandra, hundreds had come, only to return disappointed.

Rajagopalachari, who had deliberately avoided the previous convention, was present at Tripuri, most enthusiastically. Acharya Kripalani, who last evening had declared, 'I am Gandhiji's shadow, I will be at Rajkot only,' was today strutting about in Tripuri. Sardar Patel and Pandit Nehru were engaged with their respective supporters. Their activities were all very discreet. That night, all the Right-wing leaders had gathered in Sardar Patel's camp. Unlike Haripura, Patel had not gone to receive Subhas Chandra. Even Panditji had not been able to see Subhas so far. But they had been told by the Mahakaushal Reception Committee that Subhas Chandra was indeed seriously ill. However, no one really believed them. In fact, some of the underlings went to the extent of saying this was an illness of expediency. 'First, he dares to throw muck at a saint like Gandhiji, and then because he doesn't have the guts to face the convention, he pretends to be ill and hides among bedclothes.'

'Panditji, Sardar, you are all fortunate fellows,' Acharya Kripalani told them. 'The president has held on to your resignations. He was very prompt to accept mine and inform me accordingly by return telegram!'

'Subhas always held you in high esteem from the beginning,' Rajaji said, guffawing loudly. The gathering too exploded with laughter. Suddenly, becoming serious, Acharya spoke. 'Violence, non-violence and other principles, shastras–puranas, how they interpret them, what they follow, how does it concern us? We have nothing to do with it. But if anyone tries to criticise Bapu, we will not stand it!'

'In this meeting, I want to prove one thing – who is greater in this country: Gandhiji or someone else? Unless that issue is resolved, I will not leave Tripuri,' declared the rotund Govind Ballabh Pant.

Jawaharlal and Sardar were annoyed with Subhas for different reasons. As for Pandit Pant and Rajagopalachari, the prime ministers of the northern and southern provinces respectively, they were irked by the scathing criticism from Subhas because they had accepted the sceptre of power. Almost all the top leaders of all seven provinces who walked in the shadow of authority and their junior associates were disgruntled. During the discussion, Dr Dubey, Dr D'silva from Jabalpur and several coordinators went to meet Nehru. They drew him aside and began to talk in hushed tones. 'The president's temperature is constant at 103 ^{0}F.'

'Really?'

'To undertake any physical or mental exertion can pose a threat to his life. Get him to a big hospital at once, or postpone the convention.'

Much advice was given, much discussion ensued. When Panditji's face began to show concern, Sardar Patel reassured him. After the team of doctors had left, he said to Panditji, 'Don't worry. We will send for the health minister of the Western Province tomorrow morning to examine him.'

A pall of gloom spread over the president's camp. Subhas's two nieces were sitting on either side of the cot and fanning him. His mother and Bibhabati were placing cold compresses on his forehead. A close associate came up to Sarat Bose and said, 'No Congress member, including Nehru and Patel, is prepared to believe that Subhas babu is truly ill.'

Sarat Bose flared up. 'Let them believe what they like, say whatever they want! Of late, we have got so used to hearing and seeing unpleasantness that nothing matters any more. We have turned to stone!'

Saying this, he came out of the camp. The sound of fireworks could still be heard. He asked some of the organisers, 'Who arranged for the elephants?'

'The reception committee.'

'A more inauspicious mount there cannot be!' he muttered under his breath. He did not know that Bibhabati Devi had followed him outside. When he saw her, he was startled. She asked him in a worried voice, 'Why did you refer to the elephants like that?'

'The elephant is unlucky for the Congress party.'

'Why do you say that?'

'Prior to this, at Guwahati, elephants were similarly decorated. And then one lunatic assassinated Swami Shraddhanand. The procession had to be cancelled.'

'A barrister like you falling prey to superstition!' she exclaimed.

'What shall I do, Bibha? My world, my life revolves around Subhas. When his sun should be rising, a dark cloud floats across his horizon.'

The next day, Dr Guilder examined Subhas and his diagnosis was disturbing. Sardar Patel and Jawaharlal looked worried. But the Rightists were still not willing to believe it. After a few moments, Sardar Patel addressed Nehru, 'Let us wait a while, Jawahar,' he suggested.

'Very well.'

An air of dejection spread over the elders' camp, but some members continued their banter. Hearing the laughter, Sharmaji, an elderly leader from Jabalpur, exclaimed, 'Jawahar, Sardar, what is this you are doing? Have senior members like you too been afflicted with the diseases of calumny and obstinacy, and become utterly insensitive?'

'Mind your tongue, Sharmaji,' Rajaji thundered.

'Shut up you lungiwalla,' Sharmaji snubbed him. 'Jawahar, Sardar, why are you letting these two, Acharya and Rajaji, influence you into inaction? I have seen with these very eyes what he has been reduced to – a mere lump of flesh! Go and see his condition for yourselves. Suppose Subhas meets with an untimely end, his body is taken away from Tripuri, what answer will you give when your biographer asks you questions? At least give yourselves the satisfaction of having seen him once before his death.'

At this, the working committee was truly shaken. Nehru took Dr Guilder aside and asked him, 'Doctor, what is the actual situation?'

'His condition is alarming. Critical.'

Nehru turned pale. He quickly slipped into his mojris and rushed out. Sardar Patel followed him.

'You have risked your life and come all this way, now at least rest for a couple of days. Then maybe you will be able to participate in the general session,' Subhas Chandra's friends had advised him. Somehow, he had agreed to spend one day in his quarters. But the next day he was determined to attend the meeting. 'At any cost,' he had insisted. That's when Nehru and Patel walked in. Subhas's bones were jutting out of his thin body. His face looked haggard and his sunken eyes were bloodshot. Nehru felt a knot in his throat. 'Subhas, why are you being so foolishly stubborn?' he asked gently.

'Panditji, I can hear rumblings of the impending world war. This is the moment when the Congress as well as the entire nation must gird itself for a vigorous protest against subjugation.'

'Arre, but your health!'

'Don't worry about that. I must send out my signal to the country for revolt.'

'Subhas, it has become imperative for you to be admitted to the Jabalpur Hospital.'

'No, I refuse to step out of Tripuri.'

'But you'll have to go to the hospital.'

'Dump me into the Narmada if you like, but I will not rest until I have made my address to the people of this country,' Subhas declared.

After a brief discussion, Jawaharlal and Patel prepared to leave. Just then, Prabhabati, running a comforting hand over Subhas's tired face, said, 'Is Gandhiji coming here from Rajkot, Jawahar?'

'No, we have no information on that yet.'

Her eyes brimmed. Jawaharlal became more uneasy.

Subhas Chandra was carried on to the dais in the meeting hall on a stretcher, where a bed had been made for him. A few soft pillows were placed under his head so that even from the prone position, he could see the delegates seated below. A blanket was spread over him. His face was dark from fever and a rough stubble covered his cheeks. But his eyes glinted with determination as he looked through the papers pertaining to the resolution. The sight was enough to stop one's heart. It was no Bhishmacharya on a bed of arrows, but a twentieth-century Arjun, fighting another epic war with the British Kauravas, trapped in a maze of misfortune. In his heart was unbounded confidence, but like the hapless Karna, at the critical moment, he found his chariot rutted and jammed deep in the battlefield. He who desired to free the country from the shackles of slavery had become a helpless victim of illness. That morning, the news of Gandhiji ending his fast had descended on Congress Nagar.

On the dais, first a resolution congratulating Gandhiji was passed and met with resounding approval. For the last two days, Subhas had sent Gandhiji telegrams upon telegrams, 'Please come and put an end to this bickering!' 'Come and resolve the differences once and for all!' Finally, as the formal meeting was to begin, from his bed, Subhas spoke into the microphone. 'Sardar Patel, do come to the stage, please.' Thunderous applause followed Sardar to the dais. Acharya Kripalani, Rajendra Prasad and other Right-wing leaders were seated in the audience. Respectfully, Subhas invited them all to join him on the dais. Close on their heels was the dusky, plump Pandit Govind Ballabh Pant. He quickly thrust a rolled sheet of paper into Subhas's hands. But before opening it, Subhas politely said, 'Come, Pandit Pant, have a seat.'

'I haven't come here to sit, only to present a resolution,' Pant replied brusquely.

Subhas unrolled the paper. The Right-wing eyes shone with joy. The Left supporters held their breath. Calmly, Subhas said, 'I have received an appeal signed by one hundred and sixty members of the All India Working Committee, and Pandit Pant wishes to move a resolution in connection with that.'

Seeing the president's condition, the secretary, Shri Narsingam, read out Pandit Pant's proposal himself. Immediately, members of the Left group began to whisper among themselves. To make his stand clear, Pant stood up and began a fiery speech, 'With this resolution, we wish to express our confidence in the previous committee. We reiterate our unconditional support to Gandhiji's supreme leadership, and I hereby request the president to accept the nominations to the new working committee that Gandhiji has recommended.'

This speech caused a commotion in the hall. Shardul Singh Kavishwar was most indignant. 'Brothers,' he shouted, 'if the working committee is going to be chosen and nominated according to Gandhiji's wish and pleasure, why does the Congress party need a president at all?'

'Brothers, this is a devious plan to cut off Subhas babu's hands! You must thwart it,' Barrister Nariman roared.

'No way! Never. The resolution must be accepted,' shouted the delegates from Gujarat and Andhra.

'We will not allow any unconstitutional resolutions to be proposed. That will be the death of democracy!' shrilled the men from Punjab and Bengal.

Pant's paper resulted in complete chaos. No one listened to anyone. The meeting was adjourned for half an hour. It was suggested that this matter be thrown to discussion in the open session rather than be decided in the working committee. After the break, the meeting proceeded as per the agenda. Pandit Pant, Acharya Kripalani and Sardar Patel were determined to have their resolution passed right then and were watchful, waiting. The Left-wingers were getting exceedingly restless for they had seen through the motive of undermining Subhas's authority. When the same matter came up for discussion again, Barrister Nariman and Bapuji Aney shouted, 'This proposal has come without proper notice. Technically, it is not sound. There is no need to take it up for discussion.'

M.N. Roy saw how an attempt was being made to push Subhas into a corner and so blatantly too. He addressed the meeting strongly, objecting to the proposal. 'There is no precedent to support the resolution,' he declared.

'Accept! Accept!' clamoured the Right. From his sickbed, Subhas raised a feeble hand and pleaded with the delegates to be quiet. For a moment, there was pin-drop silence. What was going to happen to the resolution? The decision was in his hands. Was he going to accept it? What an unfair demand that was. It made a mockery of truth and justice. Not just an ordinary noose, but the coils of a slithery poisonous serpent into which he had been called upon to offer himself. Giving up the presidential privilege of choosing a working committee to another person was like asking a lion to give up his roar. Subhas had great faith in good intentions. Suppose the resolution did come up for debate. The progressive Left-wingers and the communist and socialist youth were on his side. Besides, Gandhiji's heart would have something to say! 'It would stand for satya and ahimsa, wouldn't it? At last, Subhas spoke, in a weak but firm voice. 'Look, I must give everyone a chance.'

'Whom are you giving the chance to, Subhas? With this resolution, your grave is being dug. How can you accept such a strange proposal?' Kavishwar questioned.

'Everyone. Even if he opposes me.' It seemed as if Voltaire, whom he had encountered in his study of history, had cast a spell over Subhas. For the French philosopher had announced in the assembly, 'Even though your views are unacceptable to me, you have the right to express them. And to uphold that right, I will even risk my life.'

An agitated M.N. Roy appealed to Subhas, 'Listen to me, don't let this motion be tabled!' With both hands raised, Ellen Roy also seconded the sentiments of her husband.

Finally, Subhas allowed the motion. The faces of the youngsters in the Left block fell, while the Right-wingers were hard put to hide their delight. The meeting broke up in confusion. No conclusive discussion could be held and it became clear that the matter would have to be brought up in the open session. The swayamsevaks carried Subhas back towards his camp on the stretcher. When Kaka Gadgil saw his exhausted face, in an aggrieved voice, he said to Aney, 'He is neither of the Left nor of the Right but he is just Upright.'

In the white moonlight, the Narmada flowed placidly along. Throughout Congress Nagar only one thought prevailed: What would become of the Pant resolution? Subhas's supporters chewed their fists in frustration. 'Why didn't you reject that cruel proposal?' they asked him. 'Why have you brought this calamity upon yourself?'

With a heavy heart, Subhas replied, 'Let these devotees of ahimsa and truth know that we also have been brought up on self-reliance, tolerance and mutual respect.'

The Rightists refused to postpone the session in spite of repeated requests from the Leftist camp. If fortuitously Subhas had been trapped in their web because of the Pant resolution, why let him go?

From where he lay, like a beached fish, Subhas whispered, 'This dreadful illness did not even let me write a satisfactory speech. I thought, at the appropriate moment from the dais, I would strike at the British with red-hot branding irons. In the existing war threat, I would make an impassioned appeal to the people and for the sake of the nation's future, exhort them to rebellion. But my legs refused to carry me to the dais.'

In the fading light of day, Sarat Bose was reading out the English draft of Subhas's speech. Narendra Dev had read the Hindi version. At the start, Subhas Chandra had congratulated Gandhiji for the successful conclusion to his fast at Rajkot. Sarat Bose's voice resounded through several loudspeakers. 'Last September, England and France who professed their allegiance to democracy, lowered their crests before

Nazi Germany. They signed the Munich Pact of friendship. To expel Russia's participation in European politics, England and France allied with Germany and Italy. Let Britain prove that it was working for the cause of humanity by these actions. The developed nations of the world change colours like a chameleon to serve their own ends while we weave around us a cocoon of satya–ahimsa and naively grope our way out of the darkness of slavery.

'Today, Britain finds itself caught, its hands under a stone, as it were, and is rattled. It has adopted a soft stance towards the Arabs of Arabia and the Jews in Palestine. Britain is insecure and vulnerable just now. Let us exploit the situation. Once it rises out of this abyss, it will tighten the noose around the neck of Hindustan and gradually strangle us to death. Before that happens, let us send the British an ultimatum and lay our demand for independence at the doors of the world. We will bind them to a time frame. If they choose to ignore even that, then for the sake of our country, we will have to resort to revolution.

'Come on, turn the wheels of time. Such a wonderful opportunity comes a nation's way only once in a lifetime. Grab it, take advantage of it and fight, relentlessly.'

As he listened to the proceedings from his bed, Subhas's eyes filled with tears. His wish, that after a two-day rest, he would be able to attend the open session was dashed by the gods. Against the backdrop of the war, he had in his mind listed out the means by which the nation could be incited against injustice. Like a tiger, he was to have roared out his plans for revolution before the public. Had he been on the dais, he could easily have fended off the volley of allegations. But the civil surgeon at Jabalpur had forbidden him from leaving his bed under any circumstances. He was suffering great anguish as a result.

That afternoon, Panditji's car was driving past Gandhi Kutir on its way to the venue of the meeting. A never-ending line of people waited outside this sacred spot, to offer their homage with flowers and garlands. Panditji saw Prabhabati coming out of the kutir. Jawaharlal stopped. 'Ma, how is Subhas?'

'The fever is still there.'

Jawaharlal stood still, staring at the expanse of the Narmada. She interrupted his reverie, 'Till today I have hoped that you and Subhas will always shine together like the sun and moon.'

'Ma, don't you know how quarrelsome Subhas is?'

'Can you tell me of one single instance when he has picked a fight for a selfish, personal cause?'

'I suppose that is true,' Nehru agreed reluctantly.

'Gandhiji, such a mountain of a man ... I was sure he would come here. Especially now that the Rajkot fast has ended. But I cannot understand why he too has hardened his heart like this. Had he been present, the curtain would be drawn over the controversy.'

'Ma, I will put a call through to Rajkot. Will you speak to him?'

'No. He might think that I've become Gandhari, blinded by my son's love.' There was firmness in her voice. 'Besides, Jawahar, at the worst what will happen? My child will rise from the lap of his biological mother and enter the arms of the greater Mother, Bharatmata ... that's all.'

Jawaharlal got into the car with her and set off towards the camp. She seemed to have withered. He said to her, 'Ma, Subhas and Bapu are two extremes. I get exhausted trying to make them reconcile their differences. Subhas is like a brother to me, but Bapu is a father!'

As they entered the gates, she looked at Jawaharlal, her eyes hard, penetrating, as if they were saying, 'To steady the canopy over the paternal head, don't take the crime of a brother's death upon your own.' Jawaharlal was confused. Dr Guilder and Col. Dr Mukund had accompanied him in the car. They examined Subhas Chandra. Checking his pulse, Dr Guilder said, 'Don't take any more chances, shift him to the Jabalpur Hospital at once.'

'Doctor, what exactly is this illness?' Jawaharlal wanted to know.

'Pneumonia. His right lung is seriously affected. Don't delay.'

'Did you hear that, Subhas? Why are you being so stubborn? Life is more precious than politics,' Jawaharlal pleaded.

Turning his head on the pillow, Subhas whispered, 'But more precious is the future of our country.'

Jawaharlal knew well that this crisis would not be resolved unless Gandhiji came. He had sent Gandhiji a couple of telegrams. Tripuri was not all that far from Rajkot. But there had been no communication from Bapuji.

He rushed off to the post office set up in the Congress camp. He was getting impatient to speak to Gandhiji and sort this problem out once and for all. With Subhas's condition so serious, anything could happen. Seeing Jawaharlal in person, the postal authorities dropped whatever they were doing and put through his call to Rajkot. Mahadev Desai was on the line at the other end. 'Subhas's condition is causing concern. I need to seek Bapuji's advice. The Pant resolution has precipitated a crisis too. I must speak to him about that as well. Please give him the phone.' Mahadev Desai put the receiver on hold. Jawaharlal could hear Gandhiji's voice, but the words were indistinct. Then Mahadev Desai interrupted, 'Gandhiji is not available just now.'

Jawaharlal sat there, dumbstruck. Then he rose, muttering, 'His eardrums seem to have hardened totally.' He sent Dr Guilder back to Subhas's side and headed for the open session. He read out before the gathering the latest medical bulletin on Subhas's health. Maulana Azad was conducting the proceedings in Subhas's place. Like a malevolent sea, the Pant resolution kept lashing against the Congress from different directions. Hurt by Gandhiji's recent defeat, the Rightists were not prepared to consider a compromise. But the Pant resolution had upset the youth in the Left camp. Maulana Azad announced loudly, 'A vote will be taken on this issue in the governing committee room tomorrow.'

'Why? Let it be discussed in the open session here, why behind the screen of the governing body?' demanded Nariman.

'It will be discussed only by the governing body,' Maulana declared firmly, his hand raised to silence the gathering.

'This is gross injustice,' the leaders from Punjab and Bengal thundered.

The gathering broke up. Confusion spread. N.G. Ranga remarked sarcastically to Nariman, 'Look at these Gandhians! See how they are constructing an edifice of injustice. Why are they afraid to hold an open debate?'

'They are afraid that Subhas babu may again emerge victorious! They are seeking an escape route via the governing body,' Nariman replied.

'Our Subhas babu is being led into a cruel trap laid by Gandhians.' Kavishwar was deeply moved as he spoke.

The Left group was incensed at the repeated injustice meted out to them. Unruly behaviour marked the meeting. Jawaharlal stood up amidst the uproar to make his announcement. Immediately, cries of 'Sit down! Sit down!' 'Inquilab zindabad, inquilab zindabad!' rose from a substantial section of the crowd. Many among them were convinced that Subhas was deliberately being humiliated; in his absence, his authority was being crippled and he was being emasculated. So they were unwilling to let anyone speak. That he was not allowed to speak at a Congress session came as a rude shock to Jawaharlal. He turned red with rage. His hands trembled. Out of his mouth tumbled 'Oh, you goondas, you Fascists' and other such choice adjectives.

At that, an annoyed M.N. Roy retaliated, 'Oh Pandit, you country goonda, sit down!' No one heard anyone out. After attempting to speak for about fifteen minutes, Jawaharlal gave up. In a temper, he sat down. As he was wiping the sweat off his face, Rajaji sidled up to him and whispered, 'Did you see that, the gift from the friendly parties? Why, why are you eating your heart out for this?'

Then Sarat Bose went up to the mike and repeated his request, 'Please sit down! Be quiet, please, quiet.' But the crowd would not quieten. Chaos reigned for nearly an hour. When they had calmed down a little, again Sarat Bose stood in front of the mike and joined his palms together before everyone. Relations between everyone were strained. Jawaharlal could not forget M.N. Roy's words. Similarly, Bhulabhai's loving offering, "The Bose brothers are scoundrels', was deeply etched in Sarat Bose's heart. By half past eight that night, somehow some semblance of order was restored to the meeting. Panditji in his speech confirmed Gandhiji's views on the disunity, corruption and internal dissension in the Congress, and added, 'I have been marking my attendance at Congress party meetings for the last twenty-six years, but I have never seen such behaviour in my entire life.'

A debate on the Pant resolution had become inevitable. The meeting ended around midnight.

As the last day of the Tripuri session progressed and night fell, conclaves, secret meetings, even venues took on a strange colour. Many who were already disturbed, felt their heads were ready to burst.

Rajaji was saying to his colleagues, 'What a difference there is between Jawahar's and Bapu's ideological stance. They often disagree on issues, but Jawahar never crosses Gandhiji. Whereas Subhas, he's a schemer. Bapu has numerous files against him in his cupboard. They are so horrifying, Bapu has not let anyone get even a whiff of them.'

'If some fool is plotting to dig a ditch for Gandhiji, we will prepare a trench for him!' Kripalani retorted.

Late at night, Patel and Nehru went from camp to camp, visiting all the provincial leaders. Whatever feelings of sympathy or compassion Nehru had had for the young Leftists evaporated that afternoon. That he was not allowed to speak at a Congress gathering had badly bruised his ego. Finally, he decided to do exactly as Sardar Patel told him to. On the banks of the Narmada, *Julius Caesar* was being played out in earnest. Brutus who had loved Caesar more than his own life, had drawn his dagger.

The prime ministers of seven provinces and other members of their cabinets set out on the same mission: 'Protect Gandhiji's reputation! Save the party!' Since the control of the party rested with Sardar Patel and Prasad and because the line of fortune, from party ticket to election as a member of the council originated here, both sitting members and aspiring ones threw themselves into the activities hoping their contribution would be rewarded.

Much later that night, Patel and Jawaharlal sat down with the socialists' group. True to their nature, the socialists could come to no decision. They too were divided into two factions. Seeing their vacillation, Sardar Patel said, 'If Pant resolution is not passed, several senior leaders, including Gandhiji, will break away from the Congress.'

'And if Gandhiji leaves, there will be no breath in the party,' added Jawaharlal plaintively.

'That's why I say, in Subhas's victory lies the defeat of the nation. Do you want to uphold sainthood or wish to be part of Fascist deception? Think about it, then decide,' Patel urged them.

The mere suggestion that Gandhiji might leave the party caused several spirits to sag. Besides, young leaders like Jayaprakash were on intimate terms with Gandhiji. The naive socialists did not subscribe to Gandhism, but were sure they wanted Gandhiji. By the early hours of the morning, a reverse wind began to sweep through the socialist camp. Jawaharlal's statement had raised questions in the minds of some. Unable to resist the desire, they voiced their doubts. 'Why, Panditji, till yesterday, your heart was breaking for Subhas babu. You desperately tried to intercede with Gandhiji on his behalf. All yesterday afternoon, you were on the phone. And now you are speaking against him? How can you do that?'

'Where it's a matter of Gandhiji's prestige, I have no doubts in my mind. He is a man greater than the nation and the time. If he is well, Congress is well,' Nehru asserted.

The communists too could not come to any agreement. Three times in the last two days, they had changed their stand. P.C. Joshi and his group were willing to either stay away when the resolution was presented or to abstain from voting. But the Bengali communists were infuriated. They would not accept this unconstitutional injustice heaped on Subhas. Finally, out of exasperation, P.C. Joshi yelled at them, 'You have slit our throats with a hair, you rubbish Bengalis!'

'Why? Because your masters in the Communist Party of Great Britain will be offended? Well, at least the neck of Hindustan will be spared!' the Bengalis snapped back.

All night long, till daybreak, meetings, alliances and negotiations continued. When at dawn, Jayaprakash Narayan switched sides, the Leftists were shaken up. H.V. Kamath rushed to Sarat Bose. 'Sarat babu, the Tripuri mandap is aflame!'

'What's happened?'

'All night Nehru and Patel went from tent to tent denouncing Subhas.'

Sarat Bose came out of the campsite accompanied by Kamath. It was a bright day. The tents lay silent in the cool morning air. Those, who had no tents, were asleep on blankets spread out on bales of straw, near the entrance of the camp, under trees, on bullock carts. Unaffected by politics, envy, jealousy. They had struggled to get here from far-flung corners of the country because it was a meeting of the Congress, the party that was locked in battle for the country's freedom, and with the hope that they would catch a glimpse of their revered leaders. In the still morning, the only sound to be heard was of the Narmada flowing.

Sarat Bose, who had held himself in check all this while could not control the tears. Softly he said, 'Subhas, my boy, why are all the stars and planets aligned against you at this critical juncture? Whether it was the meeting at Wardha or the session at Tripuri, why have the gods played such a devious trick on you, robbing you of the strength to present your case properly?'

Kamath replied, 'To add to it all, our colleagues needlessly hurt Nehru with their inflammatory words.'

'What difference would it have made otherwise? He was as good as absent. The world does not run on lip sympathy.'

It was the last day of the conference. Deliberately, all leaders were seated in the small subject committee hall. No one except the party leaders was allowed inside. Provincial groups were broken up and members were made to sit in blocks. Under tight security and with a shrewdly planned strategy, the in-camera proceedings began at exactly 8.50 a m. Presenting his proposal once more, Pandit Pant said, 'In the future, it is only Gandhiji's guidance that will prove beneficial to the nation.'

'But we have no objection to that!' exclaimed Kavishwar.

Ignoring him, Pandit Pant boomed, 'Take any country, it has only one leader. Just as Germany placed its trust in Hitler, Italy in Mussolini and Russia in Lenin. The above-mentioned nations prospered and progressed under the leadership of these individuals. It is our good fortune that we have Gandhiji. Why shouldn't we derive maximum benefit from that?' Carried away by his emotions, the rather odious comparison Pandit Pant had drawn did not go down well with many.

The Rightists had raised the issue of the Pant resolution. After Kaka Gadgil seconded the proposal, Barrister Nariman stood up to suggest an amendment. He said, 'To show compassion and kindness to anyone who is lying helpless, no matter if he is one's sworn enemy, is considered honourable on our Hindustani soil. But here, the president of the Congress has to beg his colleagues for magnanimity!' His voice quivered as he continued, 'Where's the need to hurry with this? Has the president hidden his face and fled? On the contrary, disregarding doctor's orders, hasn't he come to face the challenge all the way from Calcutta?'

'Nariman,' Rajaji rose to his feet and thundered, 'you can say what you like. We have no desire to risk our lives, trying to traverse the Narmada in a sinking boat. What do you say, my fellow men?'

Loud laughter broke out in the hall. The Left group looked demoralised. Rajaji's remark had a telling impact on the meeting. 'Mahatma Gandhi ki jai!' reverberated through the hall.

Shardul Singh came up with another amendment. 'Don't hide behind Gandhiji's name and strangle another. Don't invoke the "Vote of censure" on the president.'

A modified proposal was made to the effect that the new working committee be nominated, not 'according to Gandhiji's wishes', but 'on Gandhiji's advice'. But Pandit Pant objected to it violently. 'I will not allow even a comma to be altered in my proposal.' Finally, Bapuji Aney stood up and said, 'The Constitution does not bestow the power on the party to hold the president in a scissors' grip like this. No matter what Sardar Patel says, the authority to appoint a working committee rests only with the president. Instead of taking this devious path via the Pant resolution, couldn't you have brought a 'no confidence' motion against the president?'

The acting president, Abul Kalam Azad, was bent on striking down with impunity every suggestion made by Shardul Singh, Bhardwaj, Nariman, Nuruddin Bihari and others. The balance of justice was being tilted to one side by unfair means. Finally, what had to happen, happened. The Pant resolution was passed by a huge majority. Gandhiji's honour was preserved. The Rightists celebrated since their positions were intact. The socialists who had remained neutral watched eagerly what appeared to be a dress rehearsal of the impending democracy.

The gong was struck on the Tripuri session. As people prepared to return to their respective cities, their hearts were heavy. They were all wondering, 'Now what?' Will the Pant resolution be binding on Subhas babu? Will Subhas babu resign quietly and pay obeisance at Gandhiji's feet, or will he rebel? All said and done, the Tripuri Congress was held under a strange mahurat.

Tents were being pulled down, the camp was being wound up. The president's entourage also started packing up. Sarat Bose decided that in view of his health, Subhas would not be taken to Calcutta. Instead, he would go to his other brother to convalesce.

In the drama of Caesar's life, the courtyard in the Senate in Rome was splattered with blood. Here in the jungles of Tripuri, the devotees of ahimsa had preyed upon another Caesar, but only for a short while. Ahimsa had claimed its sacrifice. The wounds it inflicted were deep, but no one saw the blood.

Nine

Calcutta, 29 April 1939.

'Jawahar, at least tell me what my crime was. Just that I opposed Gandhiji's candidate, isn't it? And for that so much anger and outrage?'

'Well, Subhas, no matter what happens, the three of us must come together – Bapu, you and me,' Jawaharlal replied.

Woodburn Park had long snuggled in night's embrace. Discussions between Subhas and Jawaharlal had gone on for a long while after dinner. Sarat Bose came to Jawaharlal's room several times. The strained expressions on their faces told him that matters were nowhere near being resolved. By resigning from the party president's post, Subhas had tried to bring the curtain down on the issue. But the matter was too complicated. His decision had cast a pall of gloom over Wellington Square and its neighbourhood. There was no explosion, just simmering embers.

Even the walls of Woodburn Park were weighed down by the tension. Prbhavati lay awake for a long time. Bibhabati too could not sleep. Barrister Sarat babu sought the counsel of many advisers. All eyes and ears were trained on Jawaharlal's room. No resolution was in sight. Then Subhas Chandra and Jawaharlal came down to the porch and Amin, the driver, was woken up.

It was midnight when the car reached Chowringhee. Within minutes, a crowd gathered at Biharilal's paan shop where they stopped for special mitha paan. Quickly, the two moved away. For a long while, the car wandered aimlessly through the deserted streets.

Finally, Jawaharlal broke the silence. 'Subhas, tread carefully.'

'And how do I do that?'

'With Bapu's advice.' Jawaharlal sighed.

'Are his esteemed followers willing to concede that I came to the Congress president's post, not through the back door, but honourably, through the main entrance, brother?'

'Forget them, Subhas. It will be impossible for you to drive the Congress chariot after incurring Bapu's wrath,' Jawaharlal told him.

Eventually, the car returned home and stopped in the porch. Sarat Bose had just lain down. Heaving his tired body out of bed, he went out. They had to pick Calcutta to destroy Subhas's political career, he muttered. Couldn't they find any other place to do it?

'Don't worry,' said Bibhabati soothingly. 'Will a diamond stop shining if it is thrown into the mud?'

When Subhas Chandra bid Jawaharlal goodnight, he was overcome by sadness. Jawaharlal said, 'Subhas, our relations are taking the shape of a Shakespearean tragedy.'

Gandhiji was staying at the Sodepur Ashram on the outskirts of Calcutta. Jawaharlal and Subhas had set out to hold consultations with him for the third time. As they were about to enter, Subhas Chandra asked the driver to stop. 'Jawahar, you can go ahead if you like. I don't feel like going any further.'

'Why are you stumbling at the threshold, Subhas? Stay outside if you wish. Today, I am going to demand an answer from Bapuji.' Jawaharlal's sharp tone indicated his determination.

Bapuji was busy writing letters. Jawaharlal greeted him with folded hands. 'Today is the last day of the working committee. Bapuji, be magnanimous. Enough of this ill-will towards Subhas. Throwing someone out of the party will be an extreme step.'

'Who am I to dismiss anyone? You just said that he has voluntarily resigned, didn't you?' Gandhiji's tone was acerbic.

Jawaharlal tried to reason with Gandhiji, but not one line on his face moved. He summoned Subhas Chandra inside. 'Subhas, it is my wish that you choose your working committee yourself.' Such simple, innocent words, said with a pleasant smile. But he was adamant on his stand. His temper which had hit the ceiling since Tripuri had not yet come down, even by a degree.

'What about the noose of the Pant resolution that your distinguished followers have slipped round my neck? On the one hand, they bind me to this and on the other, they insist that I nominate the members to the working committee. Instead of being so devious, why don't they say straight out that even if the whole country likes Subhas Bose, he is not acceptable to them?'

Gandhiji showed no reaction to Subhas Chandra's outburst. Subhas could not bear to remain at the ashram for a moment longer. In a huff, he strode off towards the car. Jawaharlal followed him. Subhas's fury was turned on him. 'Why do we keep coming to the ashram? We have been hearing the same thing for three days. If he really wanted to find a way out of this crisis, instead of adopting a sanyasi's garb and staying far away from the action, he should have come to the Congress pandal during the conference. In a few minutes, the matter would have been sorted out. I know it – these are all ploys to isolate me.'

The work of the high command began. The Bengal members were demoralized. Would the resignation be accepted? What would be Subhas Chandra's political future? Sarojini Devi once again made a formal request to Subhas Chandra to withdraw his resignation. A khadi-clad Subhas Chandra stood up to reply. An expectant hush fell over the audience as the hopeful eyes of all Calcuttans were turned on him. Their leader, who inspired adulation among the young and rejuvenated the spiritless, today looked disheartened. It was barely four months since he had won the presidential election. His exultant supporters had not yet recovered from their jubilation when this calamity struck. Except for the few who were under Gandhiji's spell, every Bengali man and woman took this as a personal affront.

When Subhas Chandra took the microphone, the tension in the air was palpable. Rajaji took off his dark glasses and polished them with one end of his dhoti. The good-looking Acharya Kripalani's face was distorted with bitterness. Kavishwar, Barrister Nariman and other young Leftists waited with bated breath and perplexed minds. With a heavy heart, Subhas Chandra took out a sheet of paper from his pocket and began, 'I want Bengal to know that I came to this most hallowed post through fair and democratic means. But I must be an obstruction in the path of our very senior leaders. If the Congress high command is to nominate the new working committee, then I am superfluous.'

The anger behind the pained statement was evident to everyone. Immediately, the gathering erupted with cries of 'Subhas babu, do not resign,' 'Inquilab zindabad!' 'Vande Mataram!' The ensuing commotion was uncontrollable. Only when Jawaharlal stood up, did the crowds settle down somewhat. Placing his hand on Subhas Chandra's shoulder, he said, 'That is also my earnest wish. Subhas, don't resign.'

Subhas returned to the microphone. In a heavy voice, he said, 'If an elected president does not have the freedom to function independently, if he is constrained by the conditions of the Pant proposal, if like Gandhiji's monkeys he is to see nothing, hear nothing, say nothing, would any intelligent person accept such tyrannical terms? They can have their power and glory; for me, the flags and banners of the people's movement are enough.'

A tremor ran through the audience at the finality of this statement. Within minutes, Rajendra Prasad was declared the new president of the Congress party. Events unfolded in an almost pre-planned sequence. The crowd started to get agitated. Cries of 'Shame!' 'Shame!' interspersed with 'Why Rajendra Babu? Where's your Sitaramayya now?' rang through the pandal. The devotees of truth and non-violence had in a sense killed a democratically elected leadership. 'Injustice!' 'Unfair!' echoed the thousands gathered outside obstructing the exit as the senior leaders stepped out. Rajendra Prasad, Acharya Kripalani and Jawaharlal could not move. Jawaharlal's temper rose. 'Whose path are you blocking?' he thundered.

'All those who have treated the son of Bengal so unfairly.'

Hearing this exchange, Subhas Chandra and Sarat Bose rushed forward and tried to pacify the crowd. Some zealous workers tried to push and shove Rajendra Prasad and Jawaharlal. Others grabbed Acharya's coat. Seeing that, Subhas Chandra roared, 'Control yourselves. Don't you dare take one more step forward!' He got the swayamsevaks to form a cordon around the senior leaders and managed to escort them outside.

Jawaharlal was still fuming when he returned to Woodburn Park. Angrily, he told Subhas Chandra, 'Are we criminals that we had to be escorted out by the swayamsevaks?'

That night Subhas's niece Geeta came into the drawing room with a tray of coffee. Seeing Jawaharlal's face, her eyes filled with tears and her hands began to tremble. Sarat Bose noticed and took the tray out of her hands. He tried to comfort her. 'My child, you must treat Jawaharlal with the same warmth as usual. Why let political differences cast a shadow on our bonds of affection?' Hearing this remark, both Jawaharlal and Subhas looked at each other, embarrassed.

Subhas Chandra took Jawaharlal's hand into his own and said, 'Bhaiyya, listen to just this one thing. What I am saying is not for publicity. It is a fact based upon the views and opinions of our friends abroad. I am convinced that the Second World War is about to break out. You take up the leadership of the party. I will gladly be your flagbearer. Don't allow this golden opportunity to pass.'

Jawaharlal calmly replied, 'You are quite right, Subhas. But Gandhiji must agree.'

'Why must he approve of everything? Recall our days in the Youth League ... the zeal of the Calcutta session. If we come together once more with the same enthusiasm, we can carry the whole country with us.'

'No, Subhas. It is not going to be possible for me to take any step without Gandhiji's permission.'

'Why?' asked Subhas almost shrilly. 'Is it that you are afraid of the simmering heat of the battlefield? Or that advancing age has put out the fires of youth?'

'Take it as you please. But you will have to accept one thing – there can be no politics in India without Gandhiji.'

'So you want a protective shelter, then ...?'

'Say what you like. Gandhiji is India.'

'For me, not even God – forget a mere mahatma – is above the nation. Jawahar, educated, cultured persons like you should not succumb to the pressure of his personality,' Subhas pleaded.

With a dry sob, Jawaharlal replied, 'Subhas, my mind is with you. But my heart lies at Gandhiji's feet. I do not have your courage, Subhas, to challenge him, and that is the truth!'

Hours passed. No consensus was possible. One lion roared again and again, calling to the other. But the ringmaster had managed to mesmerise it into acquiescence. The ringmaster also knew that war was nigh. At a time of crisis, a rebellious cub's claws had to be trimmed. The cub, for its part, was surveying the hazards in the jungle and trying to find a path among the bushes and trees.

Subhas lay awake all night. When Sarat Bose knocked on the door, Subhas Chandra struggled out of bed and quickly got ready. Jawaharlal was to leave for Allahabad. As he stood in front of the mirror adjusting the shawl on his shoulder, Jawaharlal entered. Taking Subhas's hand in his, he said, 'If you think I have betrayed you, Subhas, I cannot help it. I want to be with you, but cannot snap the ties of affection which bind me to Gandhiji, either.'

'So what is your advice for me?'

'What more can I say? You have dared to mount the leopard, now how to get off ... you will have to decide.'

The car was waiting at the door. The luggage was stowed away in the boot of the car. Subhas and Jawaharlal embraced each other. As Jawaharlal was getting into the car, young Geeta ran up with a long-stemmed red rose. She knew how fond Chacha Nehru was of the flower. Subhas broke off the stem and was tucking it into Jawaharlal's buttonhole when he exclaimed, 'Wait, Subhas! Blood!' Quickly, he pulled out his handkerchief to dab at Subhas's finger. Subhas drew his hand back and smiled. 'Never mind, Jawahar. God has willed roses for you and thorns for me!'

The Japanese Consul stood in the shadows, enjoying the cool morning breeze at the Calcutta Maidan. The meeting had deliberately been fixed for this hour, so it would appear like a casual morning stroll.

'Did Sahay saheb meet your government in Tokyo?' Subhas asked him.

'Yes. He and Rash Behari Bose have made some representations.'

The Counsellor was an old acquaintance of Subhas's, but what course their friendship would take was not yet clear.

'I am hoping for support from your land,' said Subhas.

'The Japanese government welcomes your efforts to free yourselves from slavery,' said the Counsellor reassuringly.

The meeting ended. In the car, Subhas asked Satyaranjan Bakshi, 'Why has Rajendra Babu chosen both Dr B.C. Roy and Ashok Ghosh from Bengal? Only because they are opposed to the Bose brothers, isn't it? The world is changing rapidly, Satyaranjan, that is sure. How can you explain Kiran Shankar, who till just the other day stuck to us like a shadow, going over to the other side?' A tremor crept into Subhas Chandra's voice as he spoke.

Barely had they arrived at Woodburn Park when Sarat Bose thrust an envelope into Subhas's hands. It was a letter from Rabindranath Tagore. Subhas opened it with eager fingers. 'You have faced this extremely adverse situation with great courage. Well done. This present defeat will prove to be a victory in the long run. Don't ever forget that.'

Subhas had recently announced the formation of a progressive Left party – the Forward Bloc. With him were several of his young friends from across the country and colleagues with communist–socialist leanings. Senapati Bapat and Barrister Nariman had worked very hard to organise a conference of the party in Bombay on 21st June. Not just the British authorities and the police but also the Rightist faction within the Congress were astounded by the number of delegates from the provinces who thronged the conference. A select band of leaders met that night at Nariman's residence to review the situation. Subhas observed that the pot of British atrocities was full, and it would be folly to wait any longer to react.

'So what is the next step?' asked one of the members.

'The British will drag India into their imperialist war. The war is for their cause, but the resources will come from us. The blood will be ours, but victory will be theirs. And after all that, will we become free? No. So my brothers, get ready.'

The work of building up the Forward Bloc began and gathered momentum rapidly. The path ahead was also getting clearer. H.V. Kamath held a newspaper up to Subhas. 'Have you read this, Mr Bose? The working committee has declared that in future, no group or individual can indulge in a satyagraha or a movement without prior permission from the provincial Congress authorities. Only the state ministries will be outside the control of the provincial Congress.'

'It also means that I will have to take prior permission if I wish to travel in another province, not just participate in an agitation or struggle.'

'But your name is not mentioned anywhere.' said Kamath.

'So what? I am not so stupid as not to see who it is aimed at. Kamath, we are left with no choice but to throw ourselves into the struggle openly and everywhere.'

All the members of the working committee had arrived. Only Gandhiji was yet to come. The party secretary, Acharya Kripalani, was looking very uneasy. All the newspapers had carried glowing accounts of the Forward Bloc. The recent conference at Bombay had been an unqualified success, and the Forward Bloc was becoming popular throughout the country. Subhas Chandra had held demonstrations in Bombay without permission. In a sense, it could be viewed as a defiance of the Congress party's generosity, and a challenge to Gandhiji's magnanimity.

While Kripalani, Patel and Jawaharlal were arguing about Gandhiji vis-à-vis the Bengali Babu, Bapuji walked briskly into the hall. Without mentioning Subhas Chandra's name, Gandhiji spoke. 'The atmosphere has been vitiated by sounds of violence. I am fed up of all these terms – parallel government, ultimatums and memorandums, demonstrations, protests. The Congress needs to be rescued before it breaks up.'

Shuffling the pages of the pad in his hand, Acharya looked at Gandhiji very hopefully and said, 'Just tell me what to write down, Bapu ...'

'Give me that pad,' said Gandhiji, and grabbed it from Acharya's hands. He sat as usual with one leg folded under him, then peered at Acharya through his glasses. 'Jeevith, today's resolution I will note down myself.'

'You?'

It was difficult to predict what Gandhiji would write. Acharya watched the pen move across paper until finally Gandhiji stopped, looked up, smiled charmingly and returned the pad to Acharya. Hastily, Acharya strung the words together like a pearl necklace. 'The All India Congress Working Committee has unanimously decided to dismiss Shri Subhas Chandra Bose from the post of the president of the Bengal province Congress party. For three years, Shri Bose will be debarred from contesting any elected post of the Congress.'

'Waah-waah!' exclaimed Acharya Kripalani with delight. 'Bapu, I was proud of my dexterity with words, but with this one stroke, you have destroyed my arrogance! In spite of having framed hundreds of resolutions over the last five years, I have never managed such a succinct one!'

Unprecedented crowds had gathered on that day – 3 September 1939. Subhas Chandra's voice reverberated along the length of Marina Beach, Madras, as he addressed them. 'Brothers, the second great war can erupt at any moment. The British demon is going to be dragged into it, head first. This is our golden chance – to take advantage of the enemy's predicament and press further our own demands for freedom. I am determined not to let the opportunity go.

'The saintly Gandhiji is welcome to feed the milk of ahimsa to the British serpent, but for me a serpent is always a serpent. Dismiss me from the Congress party, not once but many times over. But until I free my motherland from the jaws of this serpent, I will not rest.'

His words were greeted with thunderous applause and continuous cries of 'Vande Mataram!'. Subhas Chandra was overwhelmed. One party worker was trying to slip an issue of some newspaper into Subhas's hand, but it was a while before he noticed it. When he did see the bold headlines, he was dazed for a minute. His fast and heavy breathing carried over the public address system for all to hear. They wondered what the matter was and curious, moved forward. The news was sensational. On 1 September, Hitler's army had started hammering at Poland's walls. Within a few hours, India, which had nothing to do with either Germany or Poland, was sucked into the vortex of the war when the viceroy, Lord Linlithgow, scribbled his orders on a scrap of paper.

'Look, my brothers and sisters, what I had been warning you of minutes ago has come to pass. We have been drawn into the war, for no rhyme or reason.'

Though several more meetings were scheduled in the Madras province over the next few days, a telegram arrived and upset all plans. 'An urgent meeting of the Congress Working Committee has been fixed for 8 September. You must attend. Bapu.'

Subhas Chandra left for Wardha via Nagpur. The whole international scenario was going to change in the context of the war. Lord Linlithgow, showing scant regard for the feelings of the people, had pushed thirty-eight crore Indians over the brink, and was standing back complacently. Under these circumstances, what decision were Gandhiji and the working committee going to take, wondered Subhas Chandra. Gandhiji welcomed him with the same warm smile and cordial manner.

'Why have you summoned me here, Bapu?'

'For consultations.'

'Mahatmaji, have you forgotten that you have removed me from the Congress party. It's not even been a month. Never mind, at least I get to see for myself how a noble soul can rub salt into a wound.'

Gandhiji laughed. 'Actually, Subhas, your punishment was mild.'

'Expelling someone who was the party president for two terms and the present president of the Bengal Congress, debarring him from any kind of electoral party work for three years – you call this mild punishment? Bapuji, if it falls within the principles of your truth and non-violence and if your followers get pleasure out of dishonouring me, tell them to go ahead and finish everything off once and for all.'

'Subhas, how can you be so heartless?'

'Oh, so I am heartless?'

With a tremor in his voice, Gandhiji spoke. 'Subhas, it was easy for me to throw you out of the party, but I could not dismiss you from my heart.' A tear stole out of Gandhiji's eye.

When Gandhiji entered the hall with his arm round Subhas's shoulders, all eyebrows shot up. There was a competition among the speakers to extol Gandhiji's humanitarianism. Subhas Chandra was only physically present at that meeting. He was extremely unhappy that a valuable opportunity for putting the British into a vise was being wasted. When Gandhiji asked for his opinion, Subhas Chandra once again advocated that an ultimatum be issued and a more aggressive approach be adopted. He knew that the Rightists would not be affected by what he said, but he gave expression, nevertheless, to all that had been going through his mind.

The long rays of the evening sun filtered through the neem tree as sparrows chattered. Kasturba told Subhas, 'See how emotional Gandhiji gets when he meets you.'

'Meeting him affects me too,' Subhas Chandra confessed, choking on his words. 'But, Ba, how real is this emotion, this connection between us?'

'Why do you say that, Subhas?'

'Because he will not budge from his principles nor will I veer from my goal.'

After Gandhiji's evening prayer, Subhas Chandra went for a stroll with H.V. Kamath. Suddenly, he stopped. 'My heart is not here, Kamath,' he said in despair. 'My battleground lies elsewhere.'

The Second World War had awakened the aspirations of many. Crushed the sentiments of many more. Manufacturers of war goods reaped a rich harvest, while millions of poor were squashed under the weight of armaments.

Lord Linlithgow was under tremendous pressure to ensure an uninterrupted supply of recruits and rations to the army. India's callow youth, lured by the money, were falling into the trap. Shiploads of them were sailing to the distant shores of Africa and Europe to spill their blood for some unknown British imperialist cause.

Sir Herbert, the governor of Bengal province, held a high-level meeting with the inspector general of police, the chief secretary and the home secretary. It had been a long and harrowing day. Sir Herbert was reading out a letter. In red ink was written a rather scathing criticism of the viceroy. 'The war is gathering momentum. So be alert to the enemy of our empire, Subhas Chandra Bose. Even if he is snoring, do not believe he is asleep. It can only be a ploy to fool you.'

Puffing at his cheroot, Sir Herbert looked at the home secretary who at once responded, 'We have already prepared a note requesting permission to take him into custody under the Defence of India Act, and sent it to the chief minister of Bengal, Fazl-ul-Haq.'

'So?'

'He is not willing to even touch the issue. He says that Bose has a huge following among the Muslims of East and West Bengal. If we arrest him, the Muslim student community will turn violent and take to the streets.'

'Let us wait and see for a few days. In the meantime, keep a close watch on all his activities.'

The war hung like a burden round Subhas Chandra's neck. Every passing moment was increasing his anguish. Red-eyed secret police maintained a twenty-four-hour vigil on Woodburn Park and Elgin Road.

It was past nine at night. Sarat Bose was at work in his office. The two Punjabi lawyers disguised as clients, who had been with him all this while, suddenly went into the study where Subhas Chandra was waiting for them.

Niranjan Talib, the editor of *Desh Darpan*, a popular magazine among the Sikhs and Punjabis of Calcutta, shook hands with him. He introduced his companion, the younger-looking Achhar Singh Cheena.

'He is an official of our Kirti Kisan Party in Punjab. He makes frequent trips to the Afghan border.'

'Excellent! Talib Saheb, German victory seems certain at this point. In addition, Russia and Germany are allies. We must act immediately, and take full advantage of their friendship,' declared Subhas Chandra.

'Just give us the go-ahead!' replied Talib.

Subhas Chandra was fully prepared. From the drawer, he pulled out a map showing the Afghan, Russian and Indian borders. Pointing to a small blue line, he said, 'This is the Oxus river. I wish to cross it and enter Russia. I am confident that in the land of Lenin, we will find help.'

'Taking you across is my responsibility,' assured Achhar Singh. 'That is familiar territory for us.'

'So then, get to work!'

'In the next few days, one of our smart young workers, Bhagatram Talwar, will come and meet you,' said Achhar Singh.

Sarat Bose escorted his two clients to the gate.

It was decided by the Congress not to exploit the British government's predicament on humanitarian grounds. 'But then, why are the people of India being dragged into the war against their wishes? What was the objective of the war? Please clarify,' was what Gandhiji and the working committee were asking the government repeatedly. No one from the viceroy downwards paid them any heed.

'Bapuji, Subhas was expelled from the party, but he still hasn't resigned from the post. Why?' Acharya Kripalani asked.

'What post?'

'President of the Bengal Province Congress.'

'The Bengal Province is firmly behind him. Two confidence motions have been passed in his favour, once in August and the second time in October.'

'Which means that in spite of his high-handedness, he remains the president there. We have nothing to lose. But it's you and the party that will lose face.' Rajaji poured oil into the fire.

It was decided that Subhas Chandra must be removed from the post at any cost. The whip of party discipline was invoked and cracked. A precedent had been set. The entire Bengal Province Congress Committee was sacked and a new ad hoc Provincial Congress was nominated. All those who wanted to see the undoing of the Bose brothers were brought together. So in Bengal, two Congress Committees started working parallely.

Subhas Chandra managed to get a Japanese passport for his close friend Lala Shankarlal and sent him away. Appeals were being made all round. Help for the freedom struggle from any quarter was welcome.

Efforts were on to strengthen the Forward Bloc. A special meeting was convened at Lucknow. But the young socialists, who turned up in the first flush, lost courage midway and gradually drifted away. The communists were no different.

'Over the last two days, hundreds of our Forward Bloc workers have been arrested under different sections of the law. Besides, the Gandhians have issued an injunction to boycott this meeting,' stated Professor Ranga.

The meeting was unsuccessful. With a heavy heart, Subhas Chandra stood all by himself on the platform of Lucknow station. With him was Niharendu Dutt Mazumdar. Suddenly, Subhas said to him, 'Niharendu, will you go underground?'

'Actually, Subhas babu, you should go underground rather than me!'

'I should?'

'Yes, why not? Didn't China's Dr Sun Yat Sen abscond for his motherland? Italy's Mazzini went into exile. Today, Subhas babu, only you have the calibre for a deed like that.'

'Shshsh! Niharendu, don't breathe a word of this to anyone,' whispered Subhas Chandra.

The war's rapid progress forced Subhas Chandra's footsteps towards the Governor House. He applied for a passport to visit China. Herbert's calm eyes shone with unexpected delight. Without medication, the disease would be cured. A favoured pawn had moved on the chessboard. His application was forwarded to the central government with a special recommendation. The next night itself, Governor Herbert's phone rang. It was Viceroy Linlithgow. 'It seems your knowledge of the present situation in Bengal is very poor,' he said sarcastically. Herbert was being reprimanded but did not know why.

'On what grounds did you recommend Subhas Chandra Bose's visit to China?'

'Sir, you had recently permitted Jawaharlal Nehru to go there.'

'We may give Nehru a passport again. But Bose is a blaze that we need not bring upon ourselves. The Russian border is not far from China. This troublemaker could go there and start an international band of revolutionaries and make our lives hell.'

The World War had made the Gandhians very uneasy. The British government was not willing to disclose their strategy. In protest, several provincial ministries had resigned. In March 1940, a Congress session was held at Ramgarh in Bihar. Simultaneously, a few miles away, the Forward Bloc's 'Anti-compromise Conference' was being held to strongly oppose the wishy-washy Congress policy. Oaths were taken to fight an all-out war against British Imperialism. War supplies to the British were openly objected to. The British government was stung by the challenge from Subhas Chandra's followers. Immediately, nine Forward Bloc leaders including H.V. Kamath, Shardul Singh, Professor Ranga, were put behind bars. The oppressive wind had acquired teeth of vengeance now. 'Take him! Capture Subhas Chandra Bose too!'

Subhas Chandra's eyes were scanning the horizon for that little chink through which he could escape. He was being shadowed all the time. He used his nephew Amiyo to carry a letter to the Russian government. Germany had swallowed up Poland. The Russian army too was rushing in to hive off chunks of it. Subhas held a dialogue with Comrade B.T. Ranadive. 'Go to Moscow if you like. Establish contacts there.' There was only one remedy. A military uprising.

'You know, Ba, right from Barrister Jinnah, once I turn my back on someone, I never look at them again. But this Subhas of yours, even now he plagues my conscience. His charisma does not diminish even now.'

Seeing Bapu in a good mood, Ba ventured, 'If only you had picked up the phone when Jawahar called from Tripuri to tell you about Subhas's serious illness.'

'Tripuri! Tripuri and Rajkot, both were unfortunate, Ba! Even at death's door, Subhas remained adamant, and pride had blinded me. My heart breaks at the bitter memories of Tripuri. What a proposal that Pant resolution was! Why should I deny Subhas's nobility? Not once in his disciplined, self-sacrificing life did Rabindranath Tagore even contemplate interceding on anyone's behalf, but he kept sending me just one message, "Don't be unfair to Subhas."'

'What did you tell Gurudev?' Kasturba asked.

'I told him, "Subhas is the spoilt son gone astray. It is necessary to open his eyes with some stinging collyrium to bring him back on track."'

'Why are thoughts of Subhas troubling you today?'

'He's coming here to Sevagram tonight. I've given him an appointment at eight o'clock. Mahadev too will stay on. Make sure he gets everything he needs. Welcome him with the same warmth.'

With that, Gandhiji walked off. Mahadev Desai and Ba exchanged knowing smiles.

Around four in the afternoon, a dust-covered car braked to a halt outside the ashram. From it emerged Subhas and Nathalal Parikh. Subhas looked extremely pleased to see Kasturba. His first question to her was, 'How is Bapuji?'

Kasturba replied, 'Behind each other's backs, you speak so fondly. But come face to face and you growl and roar. Why? Sometimes I think ...'

'What, Ma?'

'If such dedicated reformers like you two could control your temper and your pride, so many of the world's troubles would end. And the lives of ordinary people like us would be much more tolerable.'

Subhas was delighted by Kasturba's criticism.

Gandhiji returned a little late that night. Immediately, he sent for Subhas. He was taken aback when he saw him. In place of the usual vivacity, he saw a deep-rooted restlessness. Gandhiji felt he had never seen this Subhas before.

'Bapuji, twenty years ago, I had come to Mani Bhavan to meet you. At that time, this same Mahadev bhai had warned me, "Go carefully. The staircase is uneven and slippery".'

Gandhiji laughed heartily. Suddenly Subhas became serious. In a tremulous voice, he said, 'Bapu, in my quest for freedom, I roamed hither and thither. Finally, I was convinced that this staircase was the only sound path. I have decided to work only under your guidance.'

Mahadev Desai and Nathalal exchanged shocked glances at this declaration. Gandhiji, however, was not so naive as to be taken in by Subhas's docile manner. He smiled. 'To tell you the truth, Subhas, you might be happy to be a student of mine, but how difficult it is to be a guru to you, I know only too well.'

'Bapu, why this misgiving?' Subhas asked indignantly.

'You may not have committed any specific act of violence. But it is my firm belief that you will not hesitate. Where was the need for you to meet Hitler's representatives in Bombay?'

'It was purely a goodwill meeting with a view to trade relations. I had clarified it to you even earlier, Bapuji!'

'But I say, why should the president of our congress venture out to test poison,' Gandhiji averred. 'Vallabhbhai, Rajendra Babu, Kripalani, these colleagues of mine are assets I have acquired over a lifetime. In spite of their own lofty stature, these great men have, for the last twenty-five years and more, been around me like novitiates following their guru. But you could not show them due regard.'

'Bapuji, let us talk of respect and regard later. Let us grab the opportunity, one that comes rarely in the life of a nation. While the British are locked in the grip of the war, let us intensify our struggle for freedom. You just give the call for action, Bapuji. As the first satyagrahi, this Subhas will always walk like your shadow.'

For a long time, Gandhiji merely looked at Subhas's flushed face. How could he steady Subhas's impetuosity? What should he say to him? Subhas Chandra's impassioned appeal had filled the room, but Gandhiji did not let its impact show on his face. 'Subhas, it's quite late. Go and rest. We will talk at leisure tomorrow,' he said, ending the meeting. Then he too went inside. It was going to be a sleepless night. Wrapping a long muffler around his neck, he sat down to write a letter. But he could not concentrate. Kasturba entered the room, on the pretext of massaging his feet. Her hands had barely touched his feet when Gandhiji moved away and folded his legs. He asked her to move closer. His brow was creased, his voice distressed. Sighing deeply, Gandhiji said to her, 'Ba, did you see Subhas today? Did you notice anything?'

'What?'

The tension on Bapuji's face was frightening. Kasturba said nothing, only stared at him. Despairingly, he continued, 'Ba, all this while I thought, Subhas had gone out of our hands. It seems he is now going out of the country.'

Discussion continued the next afternoon. At first, Subhas Chandra was in a genial mood. 'Every time I begin to think of our freedom struggle, the mighty Himalayan mountain ranges float before my eyes, their lofty peaks sparkling. Gandhi, Nehru, Prasad, Patel, Naidu, so many towering personalities, too many to count. Rarely will one find such an array of luminaries on the firmament of a country at the same time. Like the garland of stars around the full moon. All that has been done under your guidance is invaluable, but …'

'But what?' Gandhiji let out a long breath.

'It is time now for a fatal blow, the final strike. The British are embroiled in the war … Just one word from you, one command to attack. Give it!'

'Under the current circumstances, that is not possible,' said Gandhiji, shaking his head.

'Such a golden opportunity won't present itself again, Bapuji!' pleaded Subhas.

'Opportunities will come and pass. But I consider it my primary duty to protect my more-precious-than-gold jewels like you,' replied Gandhiji. After a pause, he continued, 'Subhas, I have always given you unconditional love. I know about your courage and your perseverance. You are extremely emotional and impulsive, but you are also capable and brilliant. I want to use these sterling qualities of yours at the appropriate time. Don't be in a hurry. Have patience.'

'Bapu, all you need to do is call for an agitation. As one of your obedient soldiers, I am ready to serve you.'

'I must consider several other factors, Subhas. The volcano is about to erupt. There is too much violence in the atmosphere. This is not the proper time for an agitation.'

Subhas was distressed by this categorical rejection. Dabbing his eyes, he said, 'I consider it my misfortune that you do not heed my plea. But I will not be able to sit quietly any longer. If I cannot fight from within this cloistered country, I will have to go to a foreign land and ignite the fire of revolution.'

'Subhas, I am not so ungrateful as to not appreciate the selfless service that you and your family have rendered for this nation. There isn't another young man on this soil who is as passionate about freedom, who loves his motherland so unreservedly as you.'

'Bapu, if you actually believe what you are saying, give me one chance! Just say the word, Bapu, and the whole country will rise to your call,' urged Subhas. His voice had an unmistakable urgency.

'Perhaps the country is prepared, but I am not.' Once again Gandhiji was quite emphatic.

Subhas Chandra stood up. He looked as if his whole body was on fire. He moved forward and was about to bend down to touch Gandhiji's feet when Gandhiji hastily stepped back.

'Why, Bapuji? Has your heart turned so hard that you will not give me your blessings?'

'You don't need my blessings! You are a self-made leader.'

'I do need your blessings.'

'I cannot give you that. How can I bless something I don't approve of?'

'Bapuji, one day, your faith in the ability of the British to discriminate between right and wrong, is going to shatter. And you will stand at ahimsa's door and call for action,' Subhas declared.

There was nothing more to be said. Words from Gandhiji's earlier letter echoed in Subhas's ears: 'We must sail in different boats.'

A disappointed and annoyed Subhas and Nathalal turned towards the car. Gandhiji and Ba walked some distance with them. Ba looked very upset. As they approached the car, Gandhiji remembered something. 'Subhas, listen to me. I am as old as your father. I have seen twenty-eight more winters than you. This bald head, these wrinkles, the garb of age, they don't come easily. You have to soak in several rainfalls, you must decay in the process. Age robs one of everything. But it also leaves one staggering under a load of experience.'

Gandhiji's voice became shrill. 'Subhas, don't be rash. Wait. Don't talk about leaving the country!'

In the slanting rays of the setting sun, Subhas's cheeks glistened with tears streaming down. 'Bapu! The exhortations of youth are as intense as the urgings of age. They teach you to wave the flags of revolt. With your blessings or without, I am going!'

Subhas touched Gandhiji's feet. He got into the car and, like a whirlwind, drove off. Gandhiji's tremulous lips formed the auspicious words of benediction, but Subhas didn't hear them.

It had been ten months since the start of the war. And many months since Lala Shankar Seth was sent to Japan. With constant surveillance, regular arrests and harassment, the British government was trying to clip the wings of the fledgling Forward Bloc. And the feathers that remained, the Congress party plucked them out, inhumanly. Aspiring to circle the skies on the back of a wounded young bird was an impossible dream. The need of the hour was the soaring flight of the eagle, that was not to be found. The charmed mystical doors of East Asia were shut. From the West, too, there was no approach. Subhas Chandra's mind was in a turmoil.

Sarat Bose and Subhas were at the dining table together that day, after a very long time. Sarat Bose whispered, 'Subhas, we have guests from Kabul–Kandahar.'

Subhas Chandra hurried through his meal and left the table. Just then, Kali Bagchi arrived on his usual visit. Subhas Chandra told him, 'Abad Khan, Bhagatram Talwar and Ram Kishan have arrived from Afghanistan in the guise of merchants.'

'Where are they staying?'

'In a hotel in Burra Bazaar.'

Sarat Bose had recently met the Japanese Consul at a dinner hosted by a lawyer friend of his. The counsellor's message was, 'Right now, no links can be established. Don't raise your hopes.' So the eastern door was closed. In any case, the war had not reached that front yet. A flight into the burning west seemed like the only option. Take advantage of Russo-German friendship, raise an army there and approach the Indian border. The frozen plains of Russia were beckoning Subhas Chandra.

The members of the Kirti Kisan Party, who had come from Afghanistan, were experts at negotiating the mountainous terrain, the swift-flowing rivers and the dense jungles. At last, a golden opportunity had come knocking on his door. Subhas Chandra was thrilled.

A couple of days later, the chief engineer of the Calcutta Corporation, Dr Dey, came to see Subhas Chandra with his nephew Dwijendranath. 'Well, doctor, what brings you here?'

'Before you go abroad, Subhas babu, put this unworthy into the chief executive officer's chair. It will be a great favour.'

'What are you saying, doctor? Why would I go abroad?'

'Aren't you going to Russia?' The doctor's innocuous words sounded ominous.

'Who told you that?'

'Dr Balder Singh mentioned it last night.'

Laughing loudly, Subhas said, 'Doctor, how many pegs did you and Dr Balder Singh guzzle last night?'

Subhas Chandra's mood changed drastically. Sarat Bose could understand the cause of his anger. Message after message kept coming from his friends in Burra Bazaar. Subhas Chandra made the Halwell Memorial an excuse. He revived his agitation to have the imperialist monument removed. It gave the British government the chance to put him behind bars. He was sent to Presidency Jail. As expected, the Afghanis were disappointed by this news and left Calcutta.

One by one, protesters were being arrested for demonstrating against the government. Hemanta Kumar Sarkar, Anil Roy, Phani Majumdar, Narendra Narayan, Kali Bagchi. When they saw Subhas Chandra in the barracks, they would hail him with 'Vande Mataram!' or 'Inquilab zindabad!'

One day, Narendra asked him, 'Subhas babu, why did you bring this upon yourself? Think where you would have been by now.'

'In a prison on the Afghan border, most likely.'

'What?'

Subhas Chandra laughed. 'What I heard, thanks to Dey's request for promotion, made me wonder. When I checked, I discovered that my flight to Russia was an open secret. What was discussed in Burra Bazaar would have reached the police, surely.'

'So?'

'Now I have hung them by their own rope!' Subhas Chandra smiled.

One day Narendra Narayan said, 'Subhas babu, the students of Islamia College have launched a violent agitation for your release. The police opened fire in the college campus the other day. Some Pathans beat up the Muslim students. That was unfortunate.'

Grief eclipsed Subhas's face.

To prevent the Halwell Memorial from becoming a contentious issue again, the government decided to relocate it. All the political prisoners were released. But the lock to Subhas's cell would not open.

In fact, it was getting more rusty and stiff by the day. Outside, the war continued to blaze on newer fronts. Subhas babu languished in his cell like a helpless bird that had fallen into a deep crevice.

He saw no signs of his own release. 'At least Narendra Narayan must get out,' he thought. It was a year since the war had started. Gandhiji launched his individual satyagraha campaign. Vinoba Bhave was the first satyagrahi. Impatient with these developments, Subhas asked, 'What is he going to achieve? What is needed now is a gigantic blow.' But what could he do? This was the Mahatmaji's old trick – preserve your stick and keep the snake alive too. As a result of which, the imperialist monster was thriving.

The conditions in the prison were unbearable. Subhas Chandra would think of Emilie. He would imagine the footfalls of her delicate feet and then his own iron fetters would feel like a garland of flowers. Emilie wrote occasionally to a friend's address. Every sentence of her letters brought a wave of happiness. 'Stop staying awake all night. Rest. Take care of your health.' She was both the nurturing, caring mother as well as the beloved who enfolded him in the warmth of her memories. The pangs of separation were painfully sweet. Bachelors must be the most unfortunate and emotionless of all men. They don't know the secrets of the universe. Only when the earth embraces the sky can they both flourish.

Subhas Chandra began to read one of the old letters: 'Your nightgown-like full-sleeved shirt looks very strange. Please get it properly measured.' Those passionate letters filled his heart with starlight. Then the dormant poet inside the fiery revolutionary would surface. Subhas Chandra would struggle out of bed in the middle of the night and compose a reply. 'You may be far away from me physically, but actually you are always and forever hovering by my side like a shadow. A shadow goes to rest when it is dark, but your delicate presence softens the rough surroundings of the prison cell. You too suffer from acidity. I worry so much about your health ...'

Subhas Chandra had to get to Russia as soon as possible, at any cost. Form an army with his comrades and return to attain India's freedom. The long dark prison nights were getting intolerable. The chief jailor, Major Putney, was a decent soul. One day Subhas Chandra asked Narendra if he knew the story of Shivaji's escape from the clutches of Aurangzeb. Narendra had read an account of it in Jadunath Sarkar's biography of Shivaji. 'I have a great desire to read that book again,' said Subhas Chandra. Along with their lunchbox came a copy of the book. A thorough reading of the chapter, 'Escape from Agra Fort' was undertaken. Aurangzeb's harsh regulations, the tight security around the fort, the boxes of sweetmeats, and then one day the great escape of Shivaji Maharaj and his son Sambhaji – the stories thrilled Subhas Chandra to the core.

He kept recalling the letters Rash Behari had written from Japan around the time of the Tripuri session. His mind was flitting around the Afghan border. It was not just this jail that was unbearable, the whole country had become a great prison house. There was no choice but to go away. On one of his tours to Bombay, he had met the great revolutionary Vinayak Damodar Savarkar, who had also been recognised for his heroic dive into the sea at Marseille in a daring attempt to flee from the British noose. Savarkar had told him, 'I don't think your dreams will be fulfilled here. The Congress High Command will not let you rise. You will have to build your own road.'

Narendra Narayan's case came up for hearing before his. As the day of judgement drew near, Subhas Chandra began to sprout wings. If not him, at least Narendra could be sent overseas. Subhas Chandra was awake all night, writing and rewriting something.

'What are you writing, Subhas babu?' Narendra asked him.

'Letters. One to Hitler and the other to Stalin.'

He hollowed out a cake of soap. Then he wrapped the letter in fine butter paper and slipped it into the soap. The letter addressed to Stalin was concealed in the sole of Narendra's shoe. But their prayers went unanswered. Narendra was not released. On the contrary, his jail term was extended. The darkness of the prison grew teeth and began to bite.

Subhas Chandra became desperate. The stress caused his old ailment to flare up once again. His brother Dr Sunil Bose's visits to the prison became frequent. A battery of tests was conducted.

Subhas Chandra made up his mind. All methods of protest had failed. He announced that he would go on a fast unto death from 30 October 1940, on the auspicious occasion of Kali Puja. 'My decision to fast unto death may not be viewed as a threat. It is my way of protesting against my unlawful arrest,' he wrote to the governor and the chief minister of Bengal.

His health deteriorated once the fast began, news of which spread throughout the province. Sunil Bose was worried. Sarat Bose came hurrying in. 'I have just returned from the legislative assembly,' he said. 'Everybody is shedding tears for you.' Narendra was reading to him from the Mahabharata. It was the chapter dealing with the time the Pandavas had to spend incognito in the wilderness. Subhas Chandra began to look shrunken as the days went by. His stomach seemed to touch his back. Dark circles ringed his eyes. The government tried very hard to make him give up the fast, but he was stubborn in his resolve. He was inspired by the great Irish leader, Terence MacSwiney and the supreme sacrifice of Jatin Das. Gradually, his voice grew fainter. He wrote letter after letter to the governor: 'Don't try to stop me with your diabolical methods. In this temporal world, everything is mortal. But even death cannot lay a finger on true and eternal hopes, shining dreams and noble intentions. Counter-revolutions move in this manner. The individual dies, but his dreams, his aspirations, his goals are immortal.

Subhas's body crumbled due to lack of nourishment. His mind too became feeble. Gradually, he became conscious that his shackles had fallen away. Then he allowed some lime juice to pass his lips. The glare of the morning sun hurt his eyes. They began to water. He could see a blur of smiling faces – Narendra and Major Putney.

The free breeze whispered to him, 'You mad soul, you have been released from one prison. But what about the confining walls of this enslaved nation? When are you going to breach them and fly away?'

'Will someone please tell Subhas that the mayor of Calcutta, Mr Abdul Siddiqui, has been waiting for an hour to see him?' the mayor's personal assistant hollered.

Subhas Chandra's PA vanished inside. Mr Siddiqui, seated in the general waiting room, looked most offended. He kept glancing at his watch and fidgeted. A delegation of Forward Bloc members from Andhra Pradesh had also arrived and was pressing for a meeting. Subhas Chandra's nephew Kalyan came out and told them, 'He is not well. He will not see anybody for some time now.'

The mayor went off in a huff. The secret agents were surprised. Something must be seriously wrong with him, they thought. Soon, the reception area was vacated. The gates were shut and a loud announcement was made, 'Subhas babu will not see anyone for a fortnight.' The popular people's leader had placed himself under virtual house arrest. The brick-coloured house on Elgin Road wore a deserted look.

Later in the evening, a car drove up to the gate and a tall, white-sari-clad lady stepped out. 'Basanti Ma,' the word went around and immediately the doors were thrown open. She went straight to Subhas's bedside. Because of the long term in jail, he had become skin and bones. The thick stubble made his face look coarse. 'Ma, after so long!'

'I've come to invite you to my granddaughter Minu's marriage. You must come, Subhas.'

'I will try.'

Through the polite conversation, his depression was evident. Basanti Devi left. Subhas Chandra went down the wooden staircase, stared at the front door, then turned towards the spacious backyard. The trees were still. Discreetly, he studied the gate behind him. The sleuths were watching him, puzzled. The parrot in the beautifully carved brass cage screeched. He looked at the bird for one long moment, then on an impulse, opened the cage and watched as it flew away, beyond the trees, into the blue sky. Suddenly, he felt a deep sense of relief.

His attention turned towards the street. His young nephew Sisir had taken his German-manufactured Wanderer car to Dhanbad and had not yet returned.

The radio gave regular updates from the war. Only one thought plagued his mind. How to give his family and the watchful secret agents the slip and take off. Even if he got away in the middle of the night, his family would set up a clamour and then the police would hound him.

One day, Subhas called Sisir into his room. Accompanying him was a large Pathan with a ruddy complexion and the most amazing grey eyes. Introducing the guest, Subhas said, 'This is our Mian Akbar Shah. He has to leave for Peshawar today, but he wants to pick up some things on the way. So take him wherever he needs to go and then drop him at Howrah Station.' Akbar Shah enquired where Wachell Molla – the famous Muslim departmental store – was. Sisir took him to the store in Dharamtola where he bought a black fez cap, long and loose pyjamas and some pairs of socks. He left the packages in the back seat of the car.

As the car dropped Akbar Shah and turned towards Chowringhee, the driver unexpectedly turned around and exclaimed, 'Saheb, Mian has left his stuff in the car!'

'That's all right. We'll send the parcel later by post,' Sisir replied, smiling to himself.

Sisir was caught up in getting together a whole lot of things. He got visiting cards printed in the name of Muhammad Ziauddin, Travelling Inspector, Empire of India, Life Insurance Company; address: Civil Lines, Jubbalpore. Next, a bedroll, an attaché case marked with the initials M.Z., Pathani style pillow covers and chadors were procured. In addition, two brown close-collared jackets, two oldish copies of the Koran, bottles of some Ayurvedic medicines, Kabuli footwear, etc. were some of the things Ziauddin would need.

One day, Prabhabati went into Subhas's room and asked him pointedly, 'What is going on, Subhas? You have become so quiet ... and why are you growing this beard? You look so scruffy, like a goonda.'

'Ma, my interest in politics is waning. I am drawn to God and worship, religion and ritual once again.'

'Looks like the demon from your college days is back to haunt you! So are you proposing to go to the Himalayas? And yes, have you really sacked your three secretaries, Parimal Roy, Mukherjee and Vishnu Das?'

'Yes. Now, are you convinced, Ma, that I mean it? No more service to the country for me.'

One day, Subhas Chandra handed Sisir a sheaf of letters, stamped and addressed to his friends N.G. Ranga, Kamath, Swami Sahajanand Saraswati, Dr Dharam Vir, among others. 'Here is a list,' he told Sisir. 'Post the letters according to the date against each name.'

The family gathered around him so that they could spend some time with him before he began his meditation and study. His mother, sisters-in-law, Sarat Bose, nephews and nieces – all sat down for a special traditional meal. That day, Subhas, in his flowing silk kurta and dhoti, the overgrown beard, saffron mark on his forehead, looked like a sage. Will this be my last meal with my family, he wondered. The thought made him shudder. The sweetmeat his mother fed him stuck in his throat. Subhas Chandra stilled his grieving heart with great difficulty. He told them, 'I have fixed a curtain outside my room. My food and washed clothes may be kept near it. If there is a problem, inform Ila or Dwijendra. They will know what to do.'

Subhas Chandra locked himself in his room. He went into deep penance and meditation. Even the watchful police were surprised by the rigid discipline he enforced on himself. The only sounds that came out of the room were of his bathing in the morning and gargling at night. No visitors were entertained. Yet the police kept a strict vigil. Around nine every night, Sisir would take his car out and make several trips in and out of the house till midnight. Every little thing had to be carefully planned and executed.

Finally, 16 January 1941 dawned. Sarat Bose went into Subhas Chandra's room in the afternoon. He gazed at his beloved brother for a long time. Who knew better than he, the great stress Subhas had been through since Tripuri and now, the war. Waves of sorrow washed over his eyes, but he held the tears back. Tears at such a moment would be inauspicious. Fear and anxiety would not stay out of his voice as he asked, 'When will I see you again, my brother?'

'The shackles on my motherland's ankles are rusty. They have to be broken. Who knows how long it will take … maybe twenty years.'

Seeing Sarat Bose's overwrought face, Subhas Chandra's heart darkened like the monsoon sky. 'This separation is for the sake of the divine fruit of freedom. I feel very sorry that I have caused you so much unhappiness and trouble. You sacrificed your career, pushed me on to the stage and chose to remain in the wings. What have you not done for your mad Subhas?'

The yellow streetlights glowed brightly. The Elgin Road house and Woodburn Park, within shouting distance of each other, were watchful, alert. As Bibhabati stood in Woodburn Park, dabbing at her streaming eyes, her son Aurobindo asked, 'Ma, would you like to meet Ranga kaka?'

'No, son, don't ask me to stand there and watch him go away. My heart is not ready for that.'

Only a few members of the household were aware of the dramatic events that were about to take place. Subhas Chandra's room was under constant watch. Inside, Dwijendra, Aurobindo and Ila were helping Subhas get ready, when, to their consternation, Sisir walked in. Aurobindo trimmed Subhas's beard, Ila handed him the baggy pyjamas and the chocolate brown sherwani, and when he had worn them, she pulled a black fez cap down on his broad forehead. Maulvi saheb was almost ready. Suddenly, it occurred to them that his spectacles were a dead giveaway. Hurriedly, they fished out an old gold-rimmed oval-framed pair that he used to wear ten years ago. As Subhas buttoned the sherwani, he glanced at himself in the mirror and asked, 'Where's the watch that Baba gave me before he passed away?'

'Kalyan is using it.'

'I cannot leave that watch behind.'

Kalyan was woken up from his sleep and the watch was taken from him. Subhas touched the precious heirloom to both his eyes and then put it on. A host of memories swept over him, bringing a lump to his throat.

He was all set. The alsatian, who would have barked inopportunely, had been sent to Woodburn Park a couple of days earlier. The moon was slowly emerging from behind the neem tree in the backyard. Dwijendra, who was looking out of the upstairs window saw the policemen huddled round a fire, dozing off. It was a very chilly night. Subhas's suitcase and bedroll were ready. Dwijendra cleared his throat loudly to signal the 'all clear'. Subhas Chandra offered his pranams to goddess Kali's and Baba's pictures and moved towards the door. But his feet would not go ahead. He quickly turned back and stood in front of the connecting door to his mother's room. He took out pen and paper hastily. But what could one say at a time like this? Finally, he poured all the feelings of his heart into just one word: 'MA!', folded the sheet and gave it to Aurobindo.

Stealthily, Aurobindo stepped out, bedroll in hand. Subhas Chandra went behind him, followed by Sisir carrying the suitcase. They crossed the long back veranda and came to the staircase, carrying their chappals in their hands. Subhas had decided to wear his usual footwear since the new Kabuli chappals did not fit him. A slight breeze made the neem leaves rustle. As Aurobindo placed the bedroll under the front seat, Subhas took a long tearful look at his beloved home, then slipped into the back seat. The policemen outside the gate had also fallen asleep. Slowly, the car moved away. When they were a safe distance away, Subhas Chandra opened the car door and banged it shut. His eyes kept straying back to the house and the city. They passed Howrah Station, a line of taxis, and a couple of handcarts selling tea. Finally, Sisir hit the Grand Trunk Road.

Back home, the routine continued. Every morning, the dhobi placed a silk dhoti and fresh chador outside the curtained door. From inside, the sound of flowing water was heard. In the afternoon, the cook left a glass of lemon juice and some food near the curtain, and after an hour or so, took away the empty plate and glass.

Every few days, letters in Subhas Chandra's handwriting addressed to Hari Vishnu Kamath or Nariman or Kavishwar were dropped into the postbox at Elgin Road. The police would note them down in their diary and send reports to headquarters. Every night, Prabhabati would pray for Subhas Chandra's well-being. From the adjoining room, she would hear sounds of gargling and nose-blowing. The police watch would find all quiet at the house and surrender to sleep.

On 18 January, Minu's wedding day, she received a gift and a beautiful letter in Subhas Chandra's handwriting. At the same time, an alert notice was received from the central ministry: 'There is a strong possibility of the war erupting in the Eastern sector in the next six months. Increase surveillance on Subhas Chandra Bose.' Patrolling was intensified. The watch began to record how many times Subhas Chandra Bose gargled and cleared his throat at night.

On 27 January, John Green ordered the servants of the Bose household, 'Fetch him at once. He must appear in court today.' Just then Aurobindo came running down the stairs looking panic-stricken. He was shouting, 'Where's Ranga kaka? Where's Ranga kaka?' Prabhabati heard the commotion outside. She rushed to his empty bed, grabbed his chador, his books, anything she could find, and hugging them to her bosom, cried, 'Where is my child? Where is Subhas? Who has taken him away?' The house was enveloped in shrill police whistles and screeching sirens. Sarat Bose and Bibhabati came gasping from the next house.

19 January 1941. The dim lights of Peshawar's cantonment station flickered bravely in the dark. To avoid attracting undue attention, Mian Akbar Shah and his two young colleagues waited there, rather than at the main station. One was Mohammad Shah and the other was Bhagatram. 'Subhas babu had mentioned the 16th clearly, hadn't he?' asked Mohammad Shah.

'Yes, we've been waiting here for the last three nights. Subhas babu had better come today!' added Bhagatram.

Mohammad Shah seemed to have some doubts. 'Akbar Mian, if he was to leave there on 16th, then ...'

Akbar Shah ignored the question. After a long wait, the Frontier Mail finally heaved into the station belching black smoke. The three of them huddled together at a vantage spot. Groups of Pathans and Sikhs alighted from the train. Suddenly, Akbar Mian caught sight of a tall maulvi leaving the station. A close-collared sherwani, a fez cap, trimmed beard. It did not take long for the trained eyes of Akbar Mian to recognise that the Muslim gentleman was none other than Subhas Chandra.

A tonga was waiting outside. Subhas got into it on a signal from Akbar Shah. Mohammad Shah and Bhagatram followed in another tonga making sure they were not being trailed. At first, Maulvi saheb was booked into Deen Hotel. But the secret police usually kept a watch on these small places. That was not likely in a large hotel like the Taj Mahal. The Taj Mahal was full up, but the manager was kind enough to find one room for him.

The Peshawar cold had Subhas Chandra in its grip, so Akbar Shah immediately arranged for a heater. Akbar Shah asked, 'Any problems on the journey?'

'No, none at all. Once we slipped out of the house, we did not stop till the next day, which we spent at my nephew Ashoke's house near Dhanbad. That night, Sisir, Ashoke, Ashoke's wife and I drove to an out-of-the-way station called Gomoh in Bihar. Fortunately, it was deserted. When I crossed the railway tracks and looked back, I saw the three of them in the distance, frozen. I had told them that I may go to Moscow or Berlin and may not see them again. Their faces just crumpled.' Subhas Chandra fell silent for a while. Then he continued, 'When the police go to my house on the 27th to escort me to the court, all hell will break loose. I must cross the Indian border before that.'

'What can I say, Babuji. You were supposed to get out from here six months back. We had sent Ram Kishen and Achhar Singh to Moscow then. They crossed the mountainous terrain and reached the Aamu river. Achhar Singh somehow braved the torrent and got to the other side, but poor Ram Kishen....'

'What happened to him?'

'Another young life martyred.' Akbar Shah's voice shook.

The next morning, Subhas was shifted to a friend, Abad Shah's house. Akbar Shah, Mohammad Shah, Bhagatram and Abad Shah began to plan the next move. Mohammad Shah gave Subhas lessons on the customs and traditions of the Pathani tribe – how to conduct himself, speak to other guests, eat out of a common thali, drink water from a shallow earthen vessel called kandoli, etc. A wardrobe consisting of loose pyjamas, a special kind of footwear and knee length kurtas was prepared for him overnight.

Akbar Mian was more than ready to accompany Subhas Chandra on his journey to Kabul. But there were several tribesmen in that region who recognised him. Till the last moment, there was a contest between Bhagatram and Mohammad Shah to go with Subhas Chandra. 'Who shall I go with?' asked Subhas Chandra.

'Both of them are fine, but I suggest you take Bhagatram. He is courageous and enterprising. Don't be misled by his stature and appearance.'

'Is he trustworthy?'

'Trustworthy?' repeated Akbar Shah, rolling his eyes. 'He comes from a family of patriots. His father was the well-known Lala Gurdasmal Taiwan, his elder brother, Harkishen shot holes into Sir Geoffrey Montmorency – the governor of Punjab – for which he was hanged.'

Subhas Chandra looked at Bhagatram with pride. Small in size but big on achievement, that's what he personified. He told Bhagatram, 'My heartfelt salaams to your family for their great sacrifice.' The young Bhagatram zealously prepared for the journey. When he disguised himself as a Muslim, Akbar Shah rechristened him Rehmat Khan, companion of Ziauddin Khan alias Subhas Bose. 'But I cannot speak Pashtu!' Subhas Chandra said, almost in alarm.

'Pretend you are a deaf and mute on a pilgrimage to Ada Sharif.'

'Waah! Deaf and mute?' Subhas Chandra laughed. 'A leader cannot be only a leader, he needs to be a convincing actor as well!'

On 21 January, they bid Akbar Shah a fond farewell and Subhas Chandra and Bhagatram set out early in the morning. They had to walk a considerable distance before the car that was hired for them could pick them up.

They were stopped at the Jamrod checkpost. Abad Khan had entered all the names in the registration book, but the sentry was curious about the good-looking Pathan in the back seat. 'Who are you? Where are you going?'

Pointing to his ears at first and then raising his hands to the heavens, the deaf-mute uttered, 'Yava-yava-yava.'

'He is my deaf-mute brother, saheb,' Rehmat Khan alias Bhagatram explained.

'Aav-aaav,' said the brother, bowing low, seeking blessings.

The car stopped near the dargah of Afridi Shinwari. All of them went inside and paid obeisance to the pir baba. The journey ahead was hazardous. Abad Khan returned in the car, leaving the two men with an Afridi guide. Although it was winter, it was very hot as they tramped through a dry, barren tract. It was like a desert of rocks and pebbles. They passed a cluster of mud and thatch huts after they had walked a great distance. Subhas Chandra's feet picked up pace. Ahead, was a range of hills. Steep climbs and sharp descents. Exhausting even for a sturdy young man.

They spent the night in a small village enroute, called Pishkan Maina. There, they spent the night in a fifty-foot-by-sixteen-foot hall with twenty-five other people. It was bitterly cold. Someone had lit a fire inside, and a few men were warming their scrawny feet by it. There was a thick straw bed to sleep on, which protected one from the cold hard floor. Bhagatram managed to procure some salted maize cakes and insipid but hot tea. The tired Bhagatram fell asleep instantly. But Subhas Chandra felt suffocated in the crowded, smoke-filled room.

The next day, Bhagatram persuaded a Sikh trader to give him a mule for Subhas, and they set off very early in the morning. The mule was a great boon in the hilly parts. By afternoon, they were again confronted by a series of mountain ranges near the territory of the Pathan. Night fell as they began to climb the narrow and winding trail, Subhas astride the mule, led by its master. As they climbed, the darkness thickened. After a while, they began the descent. On either side were dense forests and deep valleys. Soon, the forest was left behind and the ice-covered terrain began. A cold wind started to blow, and their hot and tired bodies were rejuvenated by its touch. The mule's hooves began to slip on the ice. Suddenly it stumbled and Subhas was thrown off its back. Luckily, neither he nor the mule were hurt. But it did not seem like a clever idea to ride it any further. Subhas trudged through the ice. His shoes got soaked and became heavy. By one o'clock that night, they came by a small hamlet.

The guide knocked on an acquaintance's door. The man of the house took his time to open it. They entered the one-room hut. Goats were tethered on one side. A kerosene lamp blazed in the corner. The master of the house had been married the previous day, and his new bride was still in her wedding finery. Without a word, she proceeded to cook a meal for them. By the time they had eaten, dawn was breaking. Cocks began to crow. The man of the house eyed his guests with suspicion. He wondered if they were opium smugglers who had come to trade across the border. He told them, 'Now you can go on. There's no need to stay here.'

By three in the afternoon, they reached a village called Basol. They were famished. However, it was dangerous to enter the village at that time. Better to get to Jalalabad, they thought. As they walked along the road, Bhagatram tried to stop passing trucks to hitch a ride. Finally, one did. It was overloaded with tea chests. Somehow, they climbed in with their luggage and were perched precariously among the wooden crates. They clung to the ropes that bound the chests together and crouched to avoid the overhanging branches as the truck rolled past. They had covered a fair distance by the time the sun set. Snow began to fall and a wind began to blow. When they reached Ada Sharif, it was midnight.

The next afternoon, Bhagatram and Subhas headed for Jalalabad. Not finding even a tonga, they dragged their feet to the main road. Once again, they boarded a lorry. As they neared Kabul, they cheered up. At four in the morning, they reached the last police checkpost at Buthkhak. The policemen who had been on watch all night were tired. Some of them had sought shelter nearby and stretched out. Others muffled themselves up in their quilts. Subhas Chandra and Bhagatram took advantage of the situation and remained seated inside the truck. After asking the driver some routine questions, a fatigued constable directed the driver to move on. Thus, this last checkpost was left behind.

Kabul looked lovely in the falling snow. Without stopping to rest, Subhas Chandra surveyed the city. It seemed like a widely spread out village, and except for about fifteen to twenty cement dwellings, a few permanent structures that housed the various embassies and the palace, there were only mud walls everywhere. All the buildings, temples and mosques, shops, offices and residences appeared to be wearing white caps. Heaps of pure white snow lay piled up in the streets too.

Fed up of being confined to the sarai all day, Ziauddin and Rehmat Khan set out to do some shopping. Kabul was a tourist city, where traders and travelling salesmen often had to stay overnight. The sarai served their purpose very well. Though the inner rooms were small and stuffy, the sarai provided dormitory accommodation at reasonable rates. There was a large courtyard where one could tether one's camels, horses or mules. Subhas Chandra had found the stench of horse and mule dung overpowering, so he was happy to be out in the fresh air. The Kabul River flowed through the city, dividing it into two halves. Along both banks were small and big shops and the marketplace. As the snowfall stopped and bright sunlight broke through, the mountain ranges that encircled Kabul on three sides and a ruined fort became visible.

The piles of snow on the streets started to melt. In the cool pure air, the mind too was cleansed, thought Subhas Chandra. He and Bhagatram went into a store to buy some woollens when their ears pricked up. The radio was broadcasting the news and one report was from India: 'Leader of the Forward Bloc and former president of the Congress party, Subhas Chandra Bose, today disappeared mysteriously from his Calcutta home. The Indian government has put the entire country on high alert, and a close watch has been ordered at all airports, ports and railway stations. Sources close to him reveal that he had become deeply religious of late and was in continuous meditation. It was likely that he had renounced the world and taken sanyas.' Subhas could hardly control his laughter. He just winked at Bhagatram.

Bhagatram brought food from a nearby eating place, but Subhas Chandra was not interested in the dinner. He was worried about the onslaught to be launched by the British. He was desperately hoping for Russian help. Bhagatram was dejected. His comrades of the Kirti Kisan Party had established contact with Moscow, but before anything concrete could be discussed, they were all put behind bars. Now, they could not find any link with the Russian Ambassador. 'Babuji, this is wartime. How will we even get to the gates of the embassy?'

'Man's destiny walks alongside his feet, Bhagatram. Let us see what fate has in store for us. We will make a direct approach and see what happens.'

They trudged along the Kabul–Babar Road towards the embassies. Very soon, they spotted an impressive two-storeyed building with the

Russian flag atop it. The embassy was surrounded by a high wall with sharp spikes on the top. Bayonet-toting sentries patrolled the entire area. Both Bhagatram and Subhas gazed at the Russian Embassy like a lovelorn youth staring at the palace of his beautiful princess. The previous night, Subhas Chandra had written a long letter explaining his intention, to the Russian Ambassador.

Bhagatram sighed. 'I feel like just barging in and handing over the letter,' he said.

As they were talking, they saw two tall young women in knee-length fur coats emerge from the embassy building. They followed the ladies right up to the bazaar. Quickly, Bhagatram overtook them. 'Madam, just a minute. Can you please do us a favour?' Before they could react, Bhagatram spoke, 'We need to meet the Ambassador saheb urgently. Will you be so kind as to give him this letter?'

The women threw a contemptuous look at Bhagatram and walked off haughtily. For three days, they waited to get entry into the embassy.

Again, they went to the marketplace, located some Russian merchants, and pleaded with them to help them enter the embassy. They were told that no employee of the embassy would carry their letter, and that according to their laws, it was an offence for a civilian to try and establish any kind of contact with the embassy. Their efforts were proving futile. Subhas still managed to smile 'Rehmat Khan ...'

'Ji, Ziauddin mian.'

'Are we ever going to find Mecca? Well, never mind. If not Russia, then Italy, Germany ... they too are Britain's sworn enemies. We will knock at those doors tomorrow. But we will not give up.'

The next day also drew a blank. As they were walking along in search of the German Embassy, Bhagatram spotted a big European car stuck in snow. Delighted, he shouted, 'Babuji, it's the Russian Ambassador's car! I recognise the flag on the bonnet.' They ran towards the car, but as they approached, the driver managed to free the wheels out of the snow and was about to move off. The two men threw themselves across the road signalling frantically for the driver to stop. Luckily, he did. Bhagatram went to the back of the car and peered through the window. 'Forgive us, sir. It is very important. I am an Indian. I must speak to you.' The ambassador looked at Bhagatram questioningly. Grabbing the opportunity, Bhagatram blurted, 'Sir, you must have read about Subhas Chandra Bose's escape from India....'

The ambassador nodded. Pointing out to Subhas Chandra standing a little distance away, he continued, 'That is Mr Bose.' The ambassador noticed the urgency in Bhagatram's words. But even so, he asked, 'Why should I believe it is Bose?'

'I have many photographs. I can prove it to you. Just give me an opportunity, please,' he pleaded.

The ambassador glanced at Subhas Chandra momentarily. It looked like him, but he tapped the driver, and within a second, the car shot forward and sped away.

The two of them stood there and watched it fade into the distance. The fire in their bellies would not let them rest. After two more days of wandering around, Subhas Chandra gathered all his courage and walked straight into the German Embassy. Fortunately, the Afghan sentry did not ask too many questions. At first, no one really noticed him. But once he put on his spectacles, many people stared. A young official asked him some questions, and then rushed off to the ambassador's chamber. He came out and told Subhas Chandra, 'You may go in.'

Subhas wasted not a minute. 'Your Excellency, I am …'

'Subhas Chandra Bose!' Putting down the newspaper, Hans Pilger, the German Ambassador, smiled. 'I was just reading about you. Your sudden disappearance from India has become the sole topic of discussion in all Asia.'

'Thank God!' Subhas Chandra felt relieved.

'But, Mr Bose, how did you dare to come here?' Pilger asked him nervously. 'Kabul is infested with spies and secret agents. For a small bribe, they will happily slit your throat.'

Subhas felt gratified that someone was concerned about him after all. Pilger continued, 'Tell me, Mr Bose, what can I do for you?'

'If you can arrange to send me to Germany, I will be truly grateful.'

'I will send a telegram to Berlin with your request,' he replied. Then, very formally, Pilger said, 'Do not come here after this. All communication will be routed through Herr Thomas of Siemens. I will send him a message as soon as I receive a reply from Berlin. You can check with Herr Thomas after four days.'

Immediately, Hans Pilger sent a message to Berlin: 'Today the Indian patriot Subhas Bose walked into the embassy, unexpected and uninvited. He says he would require Germany's assistance to get to his ultimate goal.' Pilger was trying to figure out how this issue of political asylum and onward journey could be resolved. He telephoned his fellow Italian diplomat, Quaroni, who was also familiar with the name Subhas Chandra Bose. He gladly offered help. In order to travel to Berlin or anywhere else, a passport would be required, the route and mode of travel worked out. And for all this, cooperation from the Russian Embassy was crucial. Of course, Russia and Germany were allies, and the Russian Ambassador, Count von der Schulenburg, was also a friend of Pilger's. He called up the Count and asked, 'Have you heard the name Subhas Chandra Bose?'

'Oh yes, that Indian. Just a couple of days ago, he stopped my car in the middle of the road. But under the current circumstances, I do not think I can be of much help.'

'Why?'

'Please, off the record, but who knows, this could be a British plot … they may have let him off intentionally.'

'I don't think so,' Pilger retorted.

'So what have you decided to do?'

Pilger got quite carried away. 'I am overwhelmed by the courage with which this lone soldier is battling the forces of British Imperialism. I will render whatever assistance is possible within my means.'

Subhas Chandra was still a little worried. He kept feeling that he had been recognised, that someone was on his trail. One stout, white-clad Afghan was watching all as Bhagatram's and Subhas's movements. Many more pairs of eyes were following them. They had just returned to the sarai and were lying on the charpoys when the haughty Afghan entered their room. 'Who are you?' he asked, twirling his moustache.

'Travellers,' Bhagatram said.

'Where have you come from? Where are you headed? How long are you staying? Why have you come here? You don't recognise an officer? Get up, roll your bedding, we will go to the police station.'

'Forgive us, Havaldar saheb, we are poor travellers. We are on a pilgrimage to Saqi Saheb. We were delayed because of the snowstorm on the way, huzoor,' Bhagatram explained in subdued, respectful tones.

'But who is this other man? Why doesn't he speak?'

'He is my uncle, huzoor. A paralytic stroke took away his tongue. That is why we are going to offer prayers at the shrine of Saqi Saheb.'

Once more Subhas Chandra got into the act. Raising his hands to the sky, he bent low and uttered, 'Ay ay yaa yaa.'

The havaldar felt somewhat reassured. Then he whispered, 'How about arranging some tea for me?'

Bhagatram realised that this pest would not get off their backs easily. He placed some money in the havaldar's palm. Tucking it behind his ear, the havaldar's voice assumed its authoritative tone once more. 'All right, I am going now, but I warn you to better get moving soon.'

After a four-day interval, as advised by the German Embassy, Bhagatram went to Gurmukh area to look for Herr Thomas's office. Thomas told him, 'The German government is very pleased to hear that Subhas Chandra Bose has escaped the clutches of the British. They are concerned that the rest of your journey should be safe, so they will send further instructions after three days.'

Waiting for three days was like climbing three mountains backwards. Bhagatram was dragging his feet home through the bazaar when he saw the fat Afghani policeman coming towards him. The sarai had become unsafe. By that time, Subhas Chandra's escape had become known all over the world. Suddenly, Bhagatram remembered an old comrade of his, Uttamchand. A native of Peshawar, Uttamchand had been an active member of Bhagat Singh's Naujawan Bharat Sabha, and he had been jailed during the 1930 movement. He now lived in the Labe Darya Bazaar area, where he had a glassware store and a radio repair shop. But it would be dangerous to meet him. In ten years, a man's ideas and commitments could change. By the time Bhagatram reached the sarai, the Afghani policeman appeared at their door. 'Come to the police station.'

Bhagatram put eight rupees into his palm, which the man accepted with a gleam in his eyes and departed. By now, it was obvious that he suspected something. He believed they were smugglers or dealers in stolen goods from the Pathan province. His repeated visits unnerved Subhas. Bhagatram quickly locked the room from outside and went away. After some effort, he found Uttamchand's shop. Uttamchand recognised Bhagatram, embraced him and took him into the shop. Bhagatram looked around and then spoke softly, 'Bhaisaab, I am in great trouble. I have a very big leader from India with me, and I have to help him cross the border. Guess who it is.'

'Not Subhas babu, is it?' said Uttamchand casually.

'Shhh! Softly. Yes.'

Somewhat puzzled, Uttamchand asked, 'Subhas babu, here in Kabul? Only this morning, Delhi Radio broadcast the news that he was arrested in Haridwar, roaming around in the garb of a sadhu!'

Bhagatram narrated the whole story and quickly rushed back to the sarai, where the crooked Aghani policeman was waiting for him. 'You better come with me to the police station. You are a pair of rogues,' he said accusingly.

'Why are you troubling us poor souls, saheb? You are our man. Take whatever you want.'

'Everyone takes the bits and pieces. I am not one of them,' he said, looking pointedly at the gold watch on Bhagatram's wrist. Bhagatram didn't have much choice.

Rather than take any more chances, they left the sarai and went to Uttamchand's two-storeyed house. The room was warm and spacious, furnished in the Kabuli fashion, with carpets and mattresses. Subhas Chandra took off his filthy salwar, kurta and wet socks. He loosened the headgear, easing the tension in his neck. His eyes hurt because he had not worn his glasses for so long. Just then, Uttamchand brought in a big stove called sandili. The warmth from the sandili and the steaming cup of tea ... how comforting it was.

Subhas Chandra watched snowflakes come down from the window. The room upstairs was secure and secluded. They had a kitchen and bedrooms upstairs. The ground floor was occupied by a tenant called Roshanlal.

The first night was very comfortable. The next morning, when Uttamchand shut the door from outside and was about to leave for his shop, an annoyed Ramodevi, Uttamchand's wife, could contain herself no longer. 'Who are these strange guests you have brought into the house?' she demanded.

'They are from our Laghaman.'

'Don't lie. You think I don't recognise the guests from Laghaman? Don't you have any sense? Bringing Muslims into the house like this!' Ramodevi was incensed.

Uttamchand tried to silence her by placing his hand over her mouth, but she would not listen. Uttamchand was worried. What if this foolish woman caused trouble while he was at the shop? Quickly, he took out a newspaper from the cupboard and whispered, 'You see this photograph? That's who our guest is!'

Ramodevi was stunned. Her eyes filled with tears. 'Subhas babu in our house!' she almost screamed. 'How fortunate we are!' she said. Ramodevi remembered her father. How moved he was after he had heard Subhas Chandra Bose speak at the Karachi Congress. Ramodevi prepared a cup of coffee and quietly handed it to Subhas.

One day, Uttamchand's daughter accidentally left the door to Subhas's room open. Uttamchand's tenant Roshanlal had gone up to the terrace. What he saw on the way down through the open door left him speechless. He thought he had seen the ghost of Subhas Chandra, and out of fear, he developed a high fever. He suffered all night. Panic-stricken, the next morning, he hastily packed his belongings and moved out to a friend's place. Uttamchand was alarmed. If word got out that he was harbouring undesirable guests, he would have to face grave consequences. He stopped Roshanlal as he was leaving the house. 'We have ghosts and demons in our house or what?'

'Those secret guests upstairs ... forget it ... I do not wish to say anything about that.' Without further ado, he went off.

Fortunately, Roshanlal did not say anything incriminatory. Even so, there was a risk. After a discussion, it was decided that Subhas and Bhagatram should shift to a sarai that same night.

Bhagatram made innumerable visits to Herr Thomas's office, but came back empty-handed every time. Alarm bells started ringing. One day, Thomas told Bhagatram, 'Ask your leader to meet the Italian diplomat, Mr Quaroni. Rome is more eager to welcome him than Berlin. The next move will come from there.'

Subhas Chandra met Mr Quaroni at his residence. In the first meeting itself, he felt that Mr Quaroni could understand him and was inclined to help. Quaroni told Subhas Chandra clearly, 'We also realise that time is passing very fast. But be patient. Do you know what some of us think, Mr Bose?'

'What?'

'Your activities for achieving the freedom of India are reminiscent of Lenin's arrival in a foreign land to lead the Russian Revolution.'

Pietro Quaroni saw a valiant revolutionary before him. At the end of their discussion, he promised every assistance and added, 'Mr Bose, give us your friend's shop's address. My wife will arrange to leave messages for you there.' He introduced Subhas Chandra to his wife, a charming Italian lady.

Subhas could no longer stomach the rich and spicy sarai food – the greasy parathas, fried eggs, oily mutton curries. He suffered from indigestion and dysentery. He and Bhagatram moved back into Uttamchand's house.

Days passed. It was almost March. Fifty days had passed since their arrival in Kabul. Subhas Chandra was getting extremely restive. If, despite regular communication between Pilger and Quaroni, the seated horse would not stand up, how could one gallop ahead on it? One night Subhas said to Uttamchand and Bhagatram, 'My friends, we must find a way out. If the sun of freedom does not rise from the womb of this war, for the next fifty years we will continue to wear the stamp of slavery on our foreheads. If the British get me, they will throw me into jail to rot till the war is over. I feel that after all these years of fighting, struggling, going in and out of jail, if I die, I may as well die with a war cry on my lips, in the open battlefield, than waste away in a prison. Ramkishen became a martyr by drowning at the border. This will be another. What do you say, Bhagatram?'

Uttamchand was very upset to hear these words. 'Babuji, just give me twenty-four hours. I will do my best to find a way out.'

The next day Uttamchand announced, 'Babuji, we have found a man who is willing to take the risk of escorting you to the Russian border.'

'That's what I want. If I am arrested at the Russian border, though it will be the same as being confined here, yet, I know how to find my way into Moscow.'

Uttamchand hesitated a bit.

'Why, is there a problem?' asked Subhas.

'The escort is an escaped convict married into a family of dacoits. He has made several trips to the town of Pat Kesar on the banks of the Hango River. He is the only one bold enough to take you there.'

'Daku or murderer, he couldn't be as wicked as the British who have sucked our blood for two hundred years!' Subhas Chandra paused, before adding, 'Shall I tell you the truth, Uttamchand ...? For the sake of my motherland, if I have to bow down before a mangy dog, I will accept it as God.'

Uttamchand told Subhas Chandra all about Muhammad Yakub. Every day, he would send for Yakub on some pretext or the other. 'I know every stone in that region,' Yakub told him. 'Gold is smuggled from there, and from here, they take out the expensive hide of karkali goats.'

'There must be a bridge across the Hango River?'

'Yes, but it is heavily guarded. However, most smugglers use large leather bags filled with air, and swim across with them further upstream. That's what we will have to do. I know some locals there,' Yakub said.

'But how dangerous is all this?'

'Well, risky it is, but it is the only way out, isn't it?' said Yakub, stroking his beard and smiling.

One day, Signora Quaroni herself drove to Uttamchand's shop. She seemed very excited as she handed him a large sealed envelope. When Subhas Chandra opened it, he was just inches away from heaven. 'Mr Bose, our agents have left Rome to escort you. They should be here in five or six days. On 3rd March, the Russians finally agreed to grant you a visa. Keep your photographs ready for the passport. Our car will pick you up. Congratulations.'

Compared to the perilous journey through mountain paths and valleys, this was smooth. By taking this road, he would be able to enter the foreign offices of Italy and Germany through the front door. The Italian agents arrived. The pictures of an Italian official, Orlando Mazzotta, were replaced by the photographs of Subhas Chandra Bose in the passport. Now for another disguise, an expensive Italian suit was pulled on. The beard too acquired a sharp Italian cut.

On 16 March, a car came to Uttamchand's store and took away his luggage.

On 17 March, Mr Quaroni hosted a special banquet in honour of Subhas Chandra to which a select few guests including Uttamchand were invited. Subhas spent the night there.

18 March dawned bright and cold. A fancy car stood in Quaroni's yard. Inside it were Subhas Chandra, a German official, Mr Wagner, an Italian diplomat, and the driver. The diminutive, nondescript-looking

Bhagatram had proved to be a giant figure. Subhas Chandra had no words to thank him. Uttamchand, Ramodevi, Quaroni and his wife, and Pilger – all seemed to be God's own men to him. He offered a heartfelt pranam to all of them. Then his car sped away to the Russian border.

Subhas Chandra looked at his photograph in the passport. The bow-tie at his neck, the pointed beard, all looked very distinguished. He read the details:

Name: Orlando Mazzotta.
Nationality: Italian
Passport number: 64932.

Ten

'India is the cornerstone of the British Empire. Once that is shaken, the edifice will come crashing down in no time. The rays of freedom will light up the lives of thirty-eight crore people,' Subhas was speaking, as he sat in the plane with the German attaché.

'We are going to land at Berlin airport shortly,' said the Italian envoy. Subhas Chandra went into the washroom. He smiled as he looked into the mirror. The face that looked back sported a short, trimmed beard, hair neatly parted, oval-framed spectacles, above which shone the wide forehead. He would easily pass off for an Italian count.

When the plane landed in Berlin that afternoon, Dr Dhawan and Dr Melcharus were present to receive Subhas Chandra. He had met Dr Dhawan, a German citizen, several times in Berlin and Vienna. He had learnt that Dhawan was working as a secret service agent for the German government. Dhawan kept staring at Subhas Chandra, wondering who the Italian gentleman was, until Subhas addressed him, 'So, doctor?' Delighted, he exclaimed, 'Subhas!', and rushed forward to embrace him.

The car sped towards Berlin city. Taking advantage of the fact that Dr Melcharus did not know Hindi, Subhas Chandra and Dr Dhawan had a frank chat. Since he had lived abroad for so long, Dr Dhawan's speech and dress were distinctly German. Also, his loyalties were meshed with Berlin's soil. And yet, deep down in some corner, the memories of his native land were still alive. In a slightly tentative voice, Dr Dhawan asked, 'Subhas, you are a radical, it's true, but you should not have let your sympathies lie with the Nazis. Is this act – of entering into a dictator's lair – blind patriotism, bravado or sheer desperation?'

'No, it isn't a leap into the dark cavern. It is like riding a whirlwind. Today, German bombers are punching holes in Britain's body. The French have fled from Paris. Russia and Germany have signed a Non-aggression Pact. Very soon, Britain will be reduced to ashes.'

'You are certain of that?'

'That, after all, is history. A whirlwind can hardly predict its path. But one thing is for sure. This war will see the downfall of British Imperialism. When the victorious nations meet to share the spoils, an Indian leader's presence in Europe will be vital to protect India's interests. And I will fulfil that need,' Subhas Chandra said.

As they drove along, Subhas looked at Berlin city, wide-eyed. Sometime ago, Berlin, crippled by the depression, had almost disappeared. But today, it was bustling with activity. There seemed to be a sense of urgency in people as they went about their business. His eyes were drawn to the enormous cutouts of Hitler at every intersection and crossroad. More impressive than the array of medals on his chest was the arrogance on his face. He had given ethics and principles the go-by in his pursuit of power.

'Can you name one other leader who in such a brief time has built so powerful a nation and so mighty an army, Mr Bose?' said Dr Dhawan.

'No, no one at all.'

Dr Dhawan recalled Hitler's public meetings in the early years. 'Thumping his fist with rage, the Führer used to say, "chop off the hands of those who signed the humiliating Versailles Treaty." Twenty years ago, when the First World War ended, the victorious nations had declared Germany guilty of aggression and warmongering, and had penalised her for it under the Versailles Treaty. The fertile Rhineland, which was the heart of Germany, was split and distributed between France and Britain. Hitler was then mobilising people, determined to avenge this insult.'

Bestowing lavish praise on Hitler, Dr Dhawan was saying, 'Today, the Führer equates himself with Frederick the Great, and Joseph Goebbels agrees with him. And what's wrong with that? He has built Germany up from the ashes.'

Their conversation was interrupted by the shrill sound of whistles followed by the sharp screech of sirens. Subhas Chandra asked, 'Is it an air raid?'

'No, it must be Hitler going to attend some meeting.'

Just then, like a herd of wild elephants, a convoy of motor vehicles approached them. The driver quickly pulled up by the roadside, and almost cowered like a frightened rabbit till the motorcade sped past.

Arrangements for Subhas's stay were made in the Esplanade Hotel. At the entrance stood a troop of sentries. Subhas insisted that Dr Dhawan join him for dinner. After four pegs of whisky, Dr Dhawan's tongue loosened. In the quiet of the night, he began to whisper confidentially, 'Do you think, Subhas babu, our very shrewd Hitler is either happy or safe? Oh no! Several people here in Berlin are waiting to assassinate him.'

Subhas Chandra was taken aback. The doctor moved closer. 'The assassins are not outsiders, they are locals. There is a secret revolutionary group here called the Kreisau Circle. Its members are in the army as well as the government. They could bump off our Führer any time.'

After yet another drink Dr Dhawan continued, 'They say one of their agents is entrenched in the government incognito. He even went to America with some delegation and spoke against Hitler to President Roosevelt, they believe. He was so cautious in his dealings and his manner that it made Roosevelt think he was actually a neo-Nazi. What do you say to that?'

Subhas Chandra was left with many unanswered questions. Challenging Hitler was not easy, was it? He was no longer the callow youth who hung around the theatres at Linz or Vienna. The man who shovelled snow, who was a porter on the West Railroad platforms, who hauled brick and mortar at construction sites, had long disappeared behind the screen of time. Even the artist who captured nature's beauty in water colours had thrown away his brushes. By the power of his exhortative speeches, he had managed to rally around himself men like Goebbels, Himmler, Rudolf Hess, Goering, Hindenberg, and secure the support of millions of common people who were drawn to his jingoistic nationalism. His desire for vengeance and professed anti-Semitism had shaken the western world to the roots.

The hotel staff, the officials who came to visit Subhas Chandra, all greeted each other with 'Hail Hitler!'. Subhas Chandra asked, 'For how long are you going to sound the trumpet of Herr Hitler and His Excellency?'

He unpacked his suitcase, and from under the cardboard lining, he drew out the carefully concealed photograph of Emilie. He stared at her face, sighing deeply. When am I going to meet you, my beloved? When will I see your sweet smile again?

The lights in the hotel had begun to fade away. Subhas put his belongings and important papers and documents into the wardrobe, and drew the thick curtains across the glass windows. Berlin lay still after the hectic activity of the war.

Suddenly, in the middle of the afternoon, warning sirens began to shriek. The people of Vienna froze. Buildings shook, rooftops started to vibrate. Emilie clutched the railing of the balcony and sank to her knees, her gown stretched across her body. As the sirens wailed louder, Emilie let out an anguished cry and began to weep inconsolably. The whole family looked on helplessly. Her younger sister rushed out to comfort her. If there was an air raid during the daytime, where would they seek refuge? Emilie looked up at the pictures of Jesus Christ and Kali Mata on the wall, seeking reassurance. Soon, the sirens fell silent. Mercifully, nothing happened. Vienna could still hear the thunderous sounds of a recent German air raid and taste the acrid smoke in their throats. Emilie's listless eyes swept the room. The cracks in the wall from an older attack still gaped at her. But she was devastated by another kind of bomb. An acquaintance of hers had accosted her in the marketplace and told her, 'Haven't you heard the news? Your Indian friend – Bose or something – was killed in an air crash', and walked away. Emilie had dragged herself home on leaden feet.

Tears flowed incessantly. There, an idealistic young revolutionary from a foreign land had single-handedly taken on the British Empire. Here, a war which promised untold horrors. The family's finances had been badly affected by recession, and it was a daily struggle to make ends meet. When she decided to marry Subhas Chandra, her defeated, impoverished father had told her, 'My daughter, before you step into fire, think carefully about your decision.'

'I have,' she asserted.

Her father's eyes had filled with tears. He had kissed her on the forehead and the matter was sealed. Now the news of the plane crash had struck like a lightning bolt. Her father's frail body stood erect, though inside he was shattered.

Emilie's younger sister quickly went in and brought her a bowl of hot soup and some dry bread – part of the wartime ration. The soup made her feel better. Turning to her sister, she sobbed, 'Tell me, what was my fault?'

'That you threw in your lot with a whirlwind.' 'He who makes the mistake of worshipping the sun must be prepared to get burnt by its rays.'

They were interrupted by the sound of a car. Must be a military vehicle, they thought. At once, the doors and windows of the neighbouring buildings snapped shut. Someone was shouting 'Nazi! Nazi!'. That's the kind of terror the Gestapo inspired. They had no qualms about shooting people in public squares, herding them towards the concentration camps, stripping them, torturing them on the way, even killing them off. But why would they come here? Emilie's sister rushed to the door and stood rooted to the spot. The devil's messengers were at their threshold. Emilie made her way to the door. One of them held out an envelope bearing the foreign ministry seal. With a thudding heart and trembling fingers, Emilie opened it. Incredulous, she kept reading it again and again. A strange sensation overcame her; her heart hammered in her chest, but the precious words on the paper brought strength back to her legs. Her demeanour changed. Puzzled, her sister snatched the letter from Berlin out of her hands and danced around the room, reading the coded message with delight. The whole family was overjoyed. The anxiety of the past week vanished. Emilie began to make plans to go to Berlin as soon as possible.

Like a wind-drunk deer, the train thundered towards Berlin. Emilie's mind swayed with her dreams. The blue sky, the fleecy white clouds, the mountains, the tranquil lake at their foot, the valleys, the swiftly running streams – they all seemed to share in her happiness. Her joy seemed to have melted the heart of the glacier, and it flowed down to meet the lake, just as she was rushing to meet her beloved.

She had often asked him, 'What did you see in me?', and Subhas Chandra would puff out his plump cheeks and say, 'If some questions are left unanswered, their fragrance increases.' She would sulk. Would refuse to talk to him. 'Your innocence, your simplicity is more attractive than your physical beauty. That's why I love you more than anything else in the world,' he would say.

The train stopped at a station on the way. A group of youngsters, hair just about sprouting on their chins, were gathered on the platform, Nazi gun barrels were digging into their stomachs or backs. German war fronts were expanding. Manpower was needed to serve in the army and to work in the factories. Young men were being rounded up. Some of them were barely out of school. Raw, green behind the ears. But the demon of war demanded blood. They would do for cannon fodder.

At last, Emilie arrived at the hotel in Berlin. The reunion after such a long and cruel separation was emotional. Hot breaths, trembling, eager limbs. Tears of happiness, tears over the memory of loneliness. It was a golden night, as if illuminated by the brilliant rays of the sun shining through a drizzle.

'Every time I look at a mountain peak, I see you in my mind's eye. But during today's journey, the sight of the mountain ranges tore my heart.'

'Why, dear?'

'I was worried that some imperialist power would blast my dearly beloved mountain peak.'

While he was talking to Emilie, Subhas Chandra lit a cigarette. It was something she had not seen before. She snatched it out of his hand. 'You call yourself a disciple of Vivekananda, and what is this you are doing?' she demanded.

'Who are you talking to, Emilie?'

She was confused. 'What do you mean?'

'I am Orlando Mazzotta. An Italian nobleman. I have to play out that role from Germany to Russia, and smoking and drinking are all part of the act.'

He described in detail his strange and incredible journey. When they were crossing a frozen river near Samarkand, he had fallen through a crack in the ice. That was the first time he had touched a cigarette. He had his first taste of alcohol in Moscow, in the company of ambassadors of several countries.

'Mr Mazzotta, what was the first brand you had?' Emilie teased.

'Vodka. And please don't ask me what it tasted like. It burnt my throat. Was as painful as the separation from you. But shall I tell you the truth, I do not need any liquor. I am so completely intoxicated by hatred of the British, I have to become a soldier to find an antidote to it.'

Emilie, already stifled by the ravages of the war, was under tremendous stress. Subhas Chandra's path was fraught with hazards.

He took a deep breath and said, 'If Gandhi and Nehru had not backed out of our struggle at the crucial moment, there would have been no reason for me to risk my life and come here.'

'Germany is a dictatorship.'

'England wants a democracy for itself, but for its colonies, slavery. These double standards won't do.'

'But then ...'

'I can imagine how dangerous it is to see visions of freedom while living in a dictator's den. It's either the summit or the abyss.'

'You should have stayed back in India.'

'Never! Till the war ended, I would have languished in a closed room. When the wheels of history are turning so rapidly, I could not afford to be confined to a prison cell. History would have never forgiven me. One must be able to seize the moment. Remember the First World War? The Russian Czar and the German Kaiser were enemies. At that time, a man like Lenin had to turn to the Kaiser for help against Russia. British Imperialism is as heinous as German Nazism. But my enemy's enemy is my friend. There is no alternative to that principle.'

'You are a follower of Vivekananda. Rabindranath Tagore has showered his blessings on you. How can a person from the land of Vivekananda and Tagore even think of receiving aid from Hitler? Subhas, posterity is going to demand an answer to this question.'

'Emilie, a country, a culture that produces a wizard of words like Shakespeare – how can the same country and culture keep thirty-eight crore people enslaved for two hundred years? The same posterity you are talking about will have to explain this too. Today, there is no difference between the warmongering Germany and the imperialist Britain. All their dealings are governed by the same principle. There is no difference between them.'

'But in case ...'

'No, Emilie. India will find the precious jewel of freedom in the ashes of the World War. If we don't grab this opportunity, for another fifty years, the noose of subjugation will strangle us.

It was difficult to convince Emilie. He had, after all, trained her. As he struck a match to light another cigarette, Subhas Chandra remembered an incident from his childhood. He told Emilie, 'On the banks of the Mahanadi, there were several huge anthills. There used to be a long-haired, flinty-eyed sage, a great black magician. He would crawl into the anthills quite fearlessly and extract venom from the snakes that lived inside, for medicinal purposes. There are equally poisonous serpents in the anthills that are Germany and Italy. But Emilie, my poor motherland that is dying under the burden of slavery desperately needs this medicine. I have to be the snake charmer in whatever way I can. I will not get bruised, but at the appropriate time, I will escape to the East.'

Subhas wanted to go to the foreign affairs ministry. He had made extensive notes that Emilie was going to type for him. The foreign ministry car took Subhas and Dr Melcharus to the ministry office.

'This is the Wilhelmstrasse,' Dr Melcharus told him. 'Our foreign ministry has opened a special India cell here.'

They were greeted by a tall, lean, sharp-featured gentleman who introduced himself as Dr Alexander Werth. He escorted them into his room and offered them tea. Care was taken to observe protocol at every step. Then Subhas Chandra was taken to meet Ernst Woermann. After the initial formalities were completed, talks began. Dr Woermann wanted to find out the real motive behind this meeting. Subhas Chandra gladly filled him in on the background. 'I need military support from you. Not only the people of India, even the soldiers of the British Indian Army will heed my call and join forces with me.'

Lighting up a cigarette, Dr Woermann said, 'With one rebellious platoon, you can't have a national revolution, Mr Bose.'

'Not a mere platoon, sir, entire divisions will revolt. Actually, the army that the British government in India has is just a scarecrow. The total strength is three lakhs of which only about seventy thousand are whites. I need only fifty thousand soldiers armed with modern weapons to effortlessly demolish the hollow forces of the British Empire.'

'Very good.'

'To put it plainly, I do not want anyone's charity. Give it to me as a loan. Whatever is spent on my army today will be returned to the last rupee after independence. That is a promise.'

Subhas presented his request to the German government to allow him to set up an Azad Hind government-in-exile during the war. Woermann smiled. It was only a preliminary meeting, so nothing conclusive came out of it, except the decision that until the future course of action became clear, Subhas Chandra would remain disguised as Orlando Mazzotta.

The foreign affairs department sanctioned a generous fund for him. Subhas was engaged in hectic negotiations to get a commitment from Germany. To dream of building up an army in a country with a handful of Indians was impractical, but his conviction goaded him on. He prepared the draft of a treaty between Germany, Italy and India. A blitz of anti-British propaganda should be carried out outside Germany. Kabul should become the centre to facilitate undercover movement. Printing presses must be set up in the mountainous regions of Afghanistan to print propaganda material, and underground radio stations should be started. Soon, Subhas Chandra finalised a memorandum with these and other similar demands, and presented it to the foreign ministry.

Germany was fighting the war on several fronts including England and Africa. It was in a flurry of activities like recruitment drives for the armed forces, production of weapons and ammunition, communication networks, among other things. Though France was taken, the tenacious British would not give up. General Erwin Rommel's army was rapidly advancing into Africa. Not just Hitler, but Foreign Minister Ribbentrop, Göring and senior Nazi leaders were all in the thick of the action.

Every day brought new twists and turns on the battlefield. Every time he heard the bugle calls, the sharp army commands and the ominous roar of bomber aircraft, Subhas Chandra would get excited. His mind would race towards the eastern and western gateways to India. Somehow, from either of these directions, on the wings of the whining bombers or by the grating roll of the tanks, Delhi had to be reached. He slept only fitfully. Every now and then, he would sit up with a start and say, 'Something must happen soon, Emilie. I have not come all the way here to loll around in this mansion.' One day, Emilie told him, 'Why don't you go and see Hitler himself?'

Subhas smiled. 'You come up with such simple solutions, Emilie!' he said. 'He has built around himself an armour of bodyguards and taken refuge in a steel-strong chamber. To bring about a change of heart in him, all I need is one meeting. Just one. But that is not happening. It is so difficult to enter his sanctum.'

The foreign affairs department had instructed Dr Adam Trott to prepare a secret document regarding Subhas Chandra's activities. So Subhas wondered whether it might be a clever idea to meet Trott and explain his position directly to him. He asked Dr Alexandar Werth to get an appointment with Trott. But Trott avoided him on the pretext of being busy. Subhas Chandra felt even more frustrated. Dr Trott's chamber was at one end of the Wilhelmstrasse. Subhas Chandra had often passed by it, but it always appeared to be shrouded in mystery.

One day, ignoring all protocol and propriety, he went and stood outside Trott's door. The door opened as soon as he sent his card in. Some faces are naturally enigmatic, and Trott's was one such face. Just about thirty years old, Trott was a handsome man with sharp features. His blue eyes were dark and deep. Behind Adam von Trott hung a beautiful map of Asia.

He did not express any displeasure at Subhas Chandra having arrived without an appointment. Smiling, he said, 'So! With just thirty-nine people, you are going to establish a parallel government, I believe? You Indians are most unpredictable. When Gandhiji started the Dandi March, he had only seventy-eight people with him, but the dimensions of that movement changed in no time at all.'

Adam Trott became serious as he spoke. Looking around him, he asked, 'How did you, one of the seniormost leaders of the country, even attempt this crazy act of entering the city of a dictator like Hitler? Your country has a host of young people inspired by the twin goals of freedom and socialism. You have been the president of the national party twice. Didn't you think you were taking a great risk and jeopardising your reputation by knocking on the doors of a despot?'

'Under the circumstances, yes, I am sure I will be somewhat disgraced. But that doesn't bother me because I know that the blood that courses through my veins boils only for my motherland. And that is enough for me.'

Both of them were sizing each other up. Their conversation was only about the British people and their empire. Adam Trott said, 'I have many friends in England. I look upon Sir Stafford Cripps as my mentor.'

'I have as much contempt for British Imperialism as I have affection for some of its subjects,' replied Subhas Chandra.

Trott seemed to have been transported to a time past, to those halcyon days at Oxford. He recalled how Gandhiji had gone there once and was mobbed by students from all countries. He even remembered the exact questions they had asked him. Any reference to India and Trott's eyes would light up.

Suddenly, his tone changed. He asked, 'Mr Bose, will you tell me the truth about yourself?'

'Sure, why not?'

'I have uncovered one secret about you.'

'Which one?'

'Your love for the Nazis is superficial. Not only that, there is not a jot of loyalty to Germany in you.'

Every word of Dr Trott's was incisive, and accurate. It would have been impossible for Subhas Chandra to deny it outright. He was shaken. His plans were falling apart already. However, getting a hold on himself, he replied, 'How do you make such conjectures?'

'It may be my misfortune, but I am an expert at reading people's faces. That is why I can confidently say that you will never be a friend of Hitler's. I respect your selfish interests. To realise your dreams, you did not baulk at stepping into the dictator's den.'

'That's not selfishness, Mr Trott. To save their mighty country, the British today are going door to door with their begging bowls. If they who claimed sovereignty over half the world, are not ashamed of abasing themselves before anyone, why should we, bonded in slavery, have any qualms about seeking help from outsiders? He who saves us is our saviour.'

Finally, Adam von Trott dismissed Subhas with a non-committal statement, 'We will do what we can.'

When he came out of the chamber, Subhas felt as if he had emerged from a maze. His thoughts kept going back to Trott. He asked himself and Emilie, too, numerous questions. Who was this man? Why does he have such love for India? His disgust for the Nazi regime was so obvious in his words, and yet he was a part of its rotten system. Why was there so much concern for Germany's future in him? While he condemned British Imperialism, he extolled the virtues of its liberal culture. What uncommon clay was this man made of?

Four days later, Dr Werth told Subhas that Dr Trott had sent his memorandum to the higher authorities. He had not expected that a man who was enamoured of Gandhiji would entertain him.

A year and a half had elapsed since the start of the great war. Hitler's bombers continued their air raids on England. The people of England, taking refuge in cellars, kept faith only in Churchill's reassuring words. Many wondered why Hitler, who seemed invincible, had not yet vanquished England. Subhas had heard such questions floating in the air of Berlin as well. In the last fortnight, Subhas and Adam Trott had met four times. One afternoon Subhas went across to meet him, unannounced. 'Doctor, are you aware of this secret?'

'What secret?'

'An extremely dangerous group called the Kreisau Circle is planning to assassinate Hitler.'

Blinking conspiratorially, Trott replied, 'I remember vaguely hearing something like that. But, tell me, Mr Bose, why would anyone want to take the Führer's life?'

'Suppose Germany is defeated in the war, then, as after the First World War, the country will once again be reduced to ashes. This group's mission is to prevent the complete annihilation of Germany. They have entered into a secret pact with Britain as well.'

'What are you saying?' Trott exclaimed.

'Not only that, one of the members of this group even went to America on the pretext of attending a conference. He also joined hands with President Roosevelt.'

'Well, Mr Bose, you had better be wary of such dangerous people,' Trott advised.

'It is not only in the government, Kreisau agents have infiltrated even this Foreign Office and are wandering around undetected.'

'This is frightening information, Mr Bose,' said Dr Trott.

'In fact, one of their eminent leaders is in this very chamber.'

'Don't talk rubbish, Mr Bose,' shouted Dr Trott. He immediately ordered the door to be shut and wiped the sweat from his brow. Subhas Chandra started laughing at his discomfiture. Pointing a finger at him, he said, 'It was you, Dr Trott, who shook hands with the American president, who sought Britain's help against Hitler.'

'Enough, Mr Bose, that's enough!' hissed Dr Trott. 'Our Gestapo agents have been wearing out their boots to get this information all these years, and you come out of India and in no time at all manage to unearth it!' Trott looked troubled. Angrily he ordered, 'You will never meet me again.'

'Why?'

'We will meet, but not openly like this. It is dangerous for me as well as for you. Where will you be tonight?'

'At home.'

'At exactly ten o'clock, my friend's car will come to you. We will meet secretly, outside Berlin.'

They met at a farmhouse. Puffing on a cigar, Trott confessed, 'Yes, Mr Bose. I too am possessed by a crazy idealism. I may be able to understand Hitler's overweening ambition. But, by his racism, his persecution of the Jews, the reign of terror of the Gestapo, Hitler is leading Germany towards anarchy and destruction. To save Germany, there is only one option – get rid of Hitler.'

The story that was unfolding between the two men would put the most romantic of fiction to shame. To Subhas Chandra, Trott became a symbol of purity and honour. After some light-hearted banter and several cigars, he said, 'Right now, I need Hitler's help.'

'And I, his end.'

'No, you need British support.'

'But you want their end.'

They were delighted by their own wit. Both of them were committed to their own countries. Liberty, equality and fraternity. No slavery, no dictatorship. Respect for man as man. Shaking hands with Subhas Chandra, Adam Trott said, 'Really, my friend, at what a critical juncture the two of us have met!'

The Esplanade Hotel had long surrendered to the arms of the night. The security agents had just dozed off. Exhausted after a hectic day, Subhas Chandra had barely rested his back on the bed when the doorbell rang. Reluctantly, he opened the door. Standing there, in a knee-length overcoat and hat was Dr Adam von Trott. His unexpected arrival got Subhas worried. Trott said, 'I have heard your English is very good, my friend. You had scored the highest marks in English Composition at the ICS exam, isn't that so?'

'Yes,' Subhas smiled.

'I need the draft of a letter from you. And today, I cannot see anyone else in Germany, who can impress a wordsmith like Churchill.'

'Oh, so you want to obtain from Churchill what Roosevelt failed to give you, am I right?'

'What can I do? I have learnt it from you. If you want to save the country, you have to live life dangerously.'

Trott explained all the points he wanted to make. Subhas read the basic matter in German and then quickly translated it into a four-page draft in the King's English. Trott was very pleased with the result.

Then in a persuasive tone, Subhas Chandra said, 'Dr Trott, please announce a policy on India's freedom. Force the German government to act quickly. Otherwise, I will not be able to walk among my countrymen with my head held high. Something has to happen fast. Inaction is a crime. Death is preferable.'

Trott said, 'I feel very sorry for you, my friend. With such great hope, you came all the way to Germany, but unfortunately, Hitler has no sympathy for your country. He sees India through the eyes of the British.'

'Are you making this statement on the basis of the derogatory remarks Hitler has made about India in *Mein Kampf*?'

'He actually does refer to Indian freedom fighters as Asian jugglers. But besides that, do you remember the incident at Dunkirk a couple of months ago? Three lakh British soldiers were stranded in the French coastal town of Dunkirk. Had the German army so wished, not a single British soldier would have returned home. But they were all allowed to go back without as much as a scratch.'

'To whom do they owe this kindness?'

'To the Führer, Hitler himself. What can I say to you, Subhas. Just a canal had to be crossed. Ten miles away, the demoralised British Army lay, waiting to perish. They stared dumbfounded, gnashing their teeth, chewing their nails, at the German tanks mired in the slush. Do you know for how long?'

'No.'

'For three whole days. Several wireless messages had been sent to the headquarters. Repeatedly permission was sought to attack, but the permission was not forthcoming. The man who rejoiced as he drank the blood of a vanquished enemy, who remained wide awake night after night at the prospect of victory, who overruled the advice of his generals and pushed forward instead of retreating, why was this same man, the Führer, now turned into a lump of ice? You will have to seek answers to these questions in the convoluted processes of his very complex mind.'

'What an invaluable opportunity it was to raze the British Empire to the ground!' uttered Subhas regretfully.

'Actually, in his heart of hearts, he wanted to preserve the British Empire, don't you see? Otherwise, all three lakh soldiers would have been our prisoners of war. The result of the Second World War would have been decided on the beaches of Dunkirk. The Führer has an intense loathing for British Imperialism, but he also has an intense affection for the British race,' Trott explained.

How many layers and skeins make up the fabric of politics? Subhas Chandra was baffled by the rapidly changing scenario. When Trott finally got up to leave, he told Subhas Chandra, 'Our General Rommel has taken forty thousand British troops prisoners in North Africa. Of them, fifteen thousand are Indian soldiers. This could be the most likely pathway to making your dream a reality.'

There were many circles even within the Nazi administration. The hostility between Ribbentrop's Foreign Office and the propaganda ministry under Goebbels was well known. Diplomats who had served during the First World War were absorbed into the foreign ministry. They were superior in intellect and experience. But Goebbels' team was drawn from the ranks of the Nazi Party, men who had risen to these positions when the party came into power. The party and the government were both riddled with internal conflicts, intrigue and suspicion. Even the big fish behaved as if they were stifled. Everyone was wary of saying too much, and they were constantly on their guard. Everyone was being watched. Subhas had noticed this several times. Mistrust everywhere.

It was around nine o'clock in the night. Subhas Chandra was immersed in a book when the phone rang. When Emilie picked up the receiver, she heard a distinct German voice say, 'Give him up. Forget him.'

'Hello? Who is that? Wrong number.' Emilie was confused.

'How can it be a wrong number?' the voice became stern. 'You, an Aryan woman, are marrying an Indian? You are polluting our pure blood. You will have to pay for it.'

'Who is it? Who are you? Identify yourself,' Emilie said.

'Why do you want my name? You will not see the dawn tomorrow.'

Emilie's hand was trembling as she put the phone down. Subhas held the frightened Emilie close. 'Emilie, I realise I have put your life in grave danger,' he said.

'I don't care about myself, but I will not be able to live if something were to happen to you!'

Three nights later, at exactly twelve o'clock, the phone rang again. Cautiously, Subhas Chandra lifted the receiver. From the other end came the voice, 'I am sorry to trouble you in the middle of the night, Mr Bose. I am Alexander Werth.'

'Dr Werth? At this hour?'

'My congratulations. The day after tomorrow, that is 29 April, you have an appointment with the German foreign minister.'

'Where? At what time?'

'Not here. You will have to go to Vienna. He is there at present.'

The day Subhas was leaving for Vienna, Emilie had packed his suitcase and was taking down notes about the war from the Delhi Radio, at the Esplanade Hotel suite, as usual. While she was tuning in to another radio station, she heard a voice announce, 'I am Iqbal Schedai speaking from the Himalaya Radio Station. Our goal is India's independence. The British government has been spreading rumours about the prince of patriots and our beloved leader, Subhas Chandra Bose. They announce his death in a plane crash or they declare that he is in Berlin negotiating with Hitler. Is it possible that the cruel imperialists have done him some harm? Brother Subhas, where are you? Reveal yourself. The eyes of all Indian freedom fighters are waiting for one glimpse of your inspiring face. Please come forward.'

The German army officials who were to escort Subhas were getting impatient. Though they were intrigued by the words of this Iqbal, they could not afford to miss the first train from Berlin. They reached the

Anhalter Station as the train was about to leave. Dr Werth and Adam von Trott were waiting on the platform.

During the journey, Subhas asked, 'Who is Iqbal Schedai?'

'One of your brothers – an Indian revolutionary.'

'With his own radio station?' asked Subhas, in wonderment.

'Not his own. But you can say that he has penetrated Mussolini's lair. The Italian government has provided him with a private radio station for spreading the message of India's freedom struggle.'

The meeting on 29 April 1941, at the Monarch Hotel in Vienna, was a historic event. The foreign minister of the Reich, Ribbentrop, was a very important man, a senior and the most trusted colleague of Hitler's. It was on his advice that Hitler had made all the contradictory moves regarding European foreign affairs. It had been only twenty-six days since Subhas Chandra had arrived in Berlin. Therefore, getting this far in such a short time was no small achievement for a lone leader like him.

The meeting was to be completely confidential, so only Subhas Chandra was allowed entry into the conference room. Soon, the heavy footfall of army boots was heard outside and a tall, good-looking man with an authoritarian bearing entered the room. It was Ribbentrop. He shook hands with Subhas Chandra. Subhas Chandra presented his memorandum of demands. As Ribbentrop ran his eyes over it, Subhas spoke.'The Indian mind is packed with anti-British sentiment. If a country like Germany is committed to stand by us, in no time at all, we can finish off the British Army.'

Looking up, Ribbentrop asked, searchingly,'And what is Mr Gandhi's perspective on the war?'

'To speak candidly, his inclination towards compromise is tiresome. All his life, he has struggled against the British, even if through non-violence. But since the war broke out, he has softened. By adopting this suicidal attitude – of not wanting to warm our hands at the fire raging through Britain – he has demoralised the freedom movement.'

'Why did you choose Germany over all other foreign nations, to seek aid?'

'The Indian public is happy that Germany and Russia have signed a treaty. Staunch nationalists like me believe that this is the opportune moment to break Britain.'

'What exactly are you expecting from Germany?'

'We want you to provide us with a special radio station for propaganda work. We need Germany to support our government-in-exile. Besides, I need to marshal together a well-equipped army to enter the battlefield as soon as possible. But before all this, please give consent to one urgent demand.'

'And what is that, Mr Bose?'

'Let Germany announce immediately that India will be free when Germany ultimately triumphs in the war.'

'Mr Bose, Germany is right now in the midst of major upheavals. But I will certainly consider your requests.'

Breakfast was eaten, coffee served and drunk. Caution tinged Ribbentrop's voice. 'Mr Bose,' he said, 'suppose something untoward should happen. Suppose the British set Gandhi up against you and Gandhi himself pleads their cause, then what will be your stand?'

Subhas Chandra was flustered momentarily.

'Speak up, Mr Bose,' said Ribbentrop sternly.

'We may have our differences, but I cannot even imagine a situation when Gandhiji will support the British against me.'

'Why? Because such a faith is convenient for your purpose?'

'No, sir! No matter how divergent our paths are, I can say with complete confidence that Gandhiji has understood the essence of both Subhas and the deceitful British.' Calling his attention to an important issue, Subhas Chandra continued, 'I have heard that General Rommel has taken thousands of Indian soldiers prisoners in North Africa. Hand those prisoners of war over to me. I will bring about a change of heart in them and convert them into an army of freedom fighters.'

Ribbentrop was very preoccupied since the war was being waged simultaneously on several fronts. He was flooded with messages, telegrams and reports. His ADC and secretary were rushing about. Referring to some technical matters, he said, 'We will provide you with a secret radio station. You may wander about for as long as you care to, as the Italian, Orlando Mazzotta. But remember always that the British will not surrender until they are completely routed.'

'We cannot sit still until the final moment of victory, sir.' replied Subhas Chandra. 'But I would appreciate an early meeting with His Excellency, Herr Hitler.'

'We'll see. Right now, the Führer is under tremendous pressure. He will meet you at the appropriate time.'

To celebrate this singular success, Subhas Chandra hosted a dinner for his friends Trott and Dr Werth in Vienna. Adam Trott said, 'India been dear to me since my Oxford days. I have met many revolutionaries, freedom fighters, patriots from across the world. Some I got to know rather well. But none of them can equal your unbounded love for your motherland!'

'Thanks, Trott. Do whatever you can, my friend, but get Germany to declare its stand on India's freedom. Then I can rid myself of this stifling Italian disguise.'

One day, Subhas Chandra had an unexpected visitor. A Mrs Tendulkar. She was a German lady married to a Maharashtrian doctor, who had befriended Indian students in Germany and looked after all their needs. Fondly they addressed her as Taiji – meaning aunt. Taiji told Subhas and Emilie that most Indian students had left for India when the war broke out, but there was one person who might be of use to Subhas. A young man called Nambiar. 'Who, A.C.N. Nambiar? But I heard he no longer lives in Berlin.' He was in Paris at that time, and it would be very difficult to persuade him to return to Berlin since the Gestapo were suspicious of him.

They chatted for a while, Taiji telling them about her role in the Red Cross, her friendship with Rudolf Hess, and her own life with Dr Tendulkar. As she was leaving, she said, 'My husband would have stood by you, unflinchingly. I would like to fill his place. If you ever need anything, if there is any problem, don't hesitate to call me.'

'Definitely!'

'And remember one thing,' she added, shutting the door of the suite, 'though if you have left your mother behind in Calcutta, you have another mother here in Berlin.'

Around midnight, there was a knock on Dr Trott's back door. When he opened it, he found Subhas Chandra standing there, looking grim. His voice too was tremulous. Dr Trott asked, 'What is it, my friend?'

'You are aware of Barbarossa, aren't you?'

'Barbarossa – you mean our plan of invading Russia? Forget it, my dear man. It's just one more of the Führer's eccentricities. I am sure he will not be so foolish as to attack Russia. In a land where a warrior like Napoleon also had to bite the dust, what can this clown of ours do?'

'Adam, the date for the invasion has been fixed. Just a month and a half to go,' said Subhas, sounding worried.

'What date?'

'21 June 1941.'

Trott's breath was caught in his throat. 'Where did you get this information from?'

'From the Japanese Embassy. I have always been on very good terms with Japanese diplomats. A Russian secret agent called Sergei brought this news.'

'How does this affect you?'

'Adam, don't sound so heartless.' Subhas sounded even more hoarse as he whispered, 'If Germany actually tries to invade Russia, my dream will shatter into bits. In fact, it was the pact of friendship between the two that raised hopes in me. I even contemplated taking advantage of the proximity of Russia's borders with India to launch an attack on the British from there. Besides, if Germany and Russia go to war, Germany will become the enemy for our young Marxist intelligentsia, and they who supported me fully so far, will not hesitate to brand me an enemy agent.'

'So what's the solution?'

'Germany must immediately acknowledge India's independence.'

'The Führer is fully intoxicated with the fumes of victory.'

'Yes. He seems to have forgotten Bismarck's fundamental principle – "Never take on two enemies at the same time".'

∾

As the days went by, Subhas Chandra's frustration grew. Every passing moment was precious. Indian independence had to be recognised at any cost before the Russian campaign began. He prepared a supplementary memorandum of demands. The frequency of his trips to the foreign office increased.

13 May dawned. Emilie was tidying up the apartment when the daily newspaper was slipped in under the door. She glanced at the headlines and almost screamed, 'Subhas! Subhas!'

Subhas picked up the papers and froze. He could not believe his eyes. He was baffled.

'Emilie, there must be some vested interest at work here.'

'What vested interest? It's a done deed.'

'Who would doubt Rudolf Hess's loyalty to Germany and his affection for the Führer? Why would he flee his motherland in the thick of war and land in Scotland?'

He kept looking at the photograph of Hess in the newspaper. Although it was a blurred picture, his strong features and magnetic personality came through clearly. The British soldiers around him looked so menacing. Subhas Chandra was reminded of a goat used as a bait by a hunter. 'I wonder what really happened to Hess. Did he go to Scotland of his own accord, or did the Führer send him there on some pretext? Now, will England welcome him? Will Hitler abandon him? Puzzling. Very puzzling.'

'I have been hearing praises of Hess for so many years. Hitler will do anything for his dear friend. He may even intensify the attacks on Britain and destroy it completely. But one thing is sure, he will not forsake him.' Emilie sounded confident.

Subhas did not have any business at his office in Wilhelmstrasse that day, but the recent developments dragged him there. The place was abuzz.

Trott said, 'The matter is not as simple as it seems. This incident happened three days ago.'

'So why did the British cabinet suppress the news all this while? Tell me, Trott, what is the truth? Hitler hasn't made Hess the sacrificial lamb, has he?' asked Subhas.

'Impossible,' replied Adam Trott grimly. 'No matter how great a dictator one is, or how cruel, one always has a vulnerable spot. Hitler would not forget Hess's past and betray him. They used to be very close to each other.'

'But then how did he get to Scotland?'

'Definitely the Führer. But the poor man's stars turned against him, I think. Churchill must have seen through the offer of compromise of Hitler's as a swindler's invitation for a big party, and exposed the matter to rattle the whole world.'

As Trott stepped out, he heard the Führer's voice on the radio. Subhas turned up the volume. Hitler was announcing to the world,

'Yes, Rudolf Hess was a very dear friend. A fervent patriot and a brave warrior. But the increasing tension of the war seems to have affected his mind. In a fit of insanity, he took off for Scotland, and foolishly fell into the enemy's snare. It is very sad.'

Trott and Subhas looked at each other, dumbstruck. Banging his fist on the table, Subhas exclaimed with great indignation, 'See that, Trott! As soon as the British rejected his compromise offer, Hitler declared his most trusted comrade insane, and washed his hands off the matter. Besides his own selfish interests, he cares for nothing, no one.'

It was a big blow to Trott too. He said, 'I do not understand why Hitler is again making overtures to the country that was not enamoured of him even though he granted three lakh British soldiers their lives at Dunkirk. Why did he sacrifice his most loyal colleague at the altar of the British?'

'I am slowly beginning to see the logic behind it. There is only one answer.'

'What?'

'Barbarossa ... the Russian campaign.'

'But what does that have to do with Hess?'

'The Russian business is not going to be child's play. The Führer knows that. It seems his intention is to come to an understanding with England, before launching the attack on Russia.'

Adam Trott was most impressed by Subhas's analysis.

The sweet invocatory voice that floated over the airwaves from Himalaya Radio Station had charmed Subhas Chandra and Emilie. 'Beloved Subhas babu, which corner of the world are you hiding in? Bhai Subhas ... this is our heartfelt appeal to you. Brother, please don't test our patience any longer ... don't remain underground. Please appear before us. Come out on to the open battlefield and fight as a prince among patriots ...'

It was past ten at night. Iqbal Schedai's appeals were boring holes into Subhas Chandra's heart. 'Emilie,' he said, 'there are so many Iqbals all over the world who are desperate for freedom. That is why the dawn of independence, I believe, is near.'

Subhas had managed to find out about Iqbal Schedai's background with the help of German secret agents. A man of Irani descent,

Iqbal was endowed with large bright eyes, thick dark hair, a radiant complexion and a charismatic personality. Like his looks, his past was also very dramatic. Born in Sialkot, Iqbal left the country when as a college student, he joined the revolutionary wing of the Gadar Party. After the First World War, he returned to his homeland for a while. But when he got wind that British secret agents were after him, he headed for Kabul. Then he accompanied the ruler Amanullah Khan to Italy, and was instrumental in getting him political asylum there. About eight years ago, Mussolini had given Schedai and Ajit Singh permission to settle in Rome.

Several days had passed since the meeting with Ribbentrop. Subhas Chandra's growing impatience was taking its toll. Then one night, a messenger from the foreign affairs department arrived at his door. 'You have been asked to come to Wilhelmstrasse at once. Dr Werth and Trott have asked for you,' he said.

'Now? All right. I will come.'

When he reached Wilhelmstrasse, he saw the India Department brightly lit. 'Yes, Dr Trott, what is the matter?'

'We are preparing a draft regarding the declaration of India's independence. The Führer wishes to make an announcement soon.'

Adam Trott had studied the constitutions of many countries and written a memorandum. Subhas read it carefully. 'Germany and Italy recognise India's legitimate right to freedom, unequivocally. India should be one single united nation. Every individual citizen should be given the right to grow and develop without discrimination on the grounds of religion, caste, creed or any other factor. Also, the people of India should be allowed to decide what form of government would be suitable in the best interests of the nation, for its all-round development.'

'Doctor, when is the Führer going to make this announcement?'

'On 24 May.'

Subhas Chandra returned to the hotel just before dawn. He felt as if he had suddenly sprouted wings and was flying high in the sky. Emilie rushed to answer the doorbell.

'Our winter is over, Emilie!' Throwing off his overcoat, he began to dictate to Emilie a message for Bhagatram Talwar, Kavishwar and his friends at the Afghan border. 'Gather all Pathans together at the frontier. Get detailed information about the strength of British soldiers deployed at every post. Did you manage to locate a site for a secret airfield in the mountainous region of Kabul–Kandahar? What about the roads? Get everything ready as soon as possible. Within a fortnight, our freedom is going to be recognised by the Axis powers. Be prepared.'

24 May came and went. Subhas sent messages and even called Trott several times to ask when the Führer would put his signature on the statement. But his queries went unanswered. One night Trott paid Subhas a visit. Subhas's heart sank when he saw the defeated expression on Trott's face.

'Sorry, Subhas, nothing could be done,' Trott said.

'Tell me what happened. What did the Führer say?'

'The statement is fine, but what's the hurry, maybe later.'

Subhas shouted at Trott, 'Adam, I am not one to take political asylum in a foreign country just to lie back on cushions. Thousands of my followers are waiting for me to show them the way. Freedom is the only thing on our minds. Something must happen!'

Subhas's German friends who believed his fight was their fight were angry too. They tried to get another appointment with Ribbentrop, but he was due to leave for Belgium, so he told them that Subhas could meet an official called Furtwangler, a cog in the crude Nazi administration. 'Why do you have such lofty visions? You want to serve your motherland, right? Then do all the propaganda you want, over the radio. That will be arranged soon,' he told Subhas coldly.

Furtwangler's words kept echoing in Subhas's head all night. He finally woke Emilie up. 'That man's words were like boiling oil poured into my ears. What does he think – Subhas Bose is a mouthpiece, a publicity agent, who pastes posters on walls? No, Emilie. I cannot bear this setback. I have to attack the British core. I must pounce on Delhi with roaring tanks and smoking bombers. My eyes yearn to see again the fort stained red with the blood of the martyrs of 1857. Lal Qila, the Red Fort, beckons me!'

Subhas was received warmly by Italian officials in Rome and taken to the luxurious Excelsior Hotel. A couple of times, the German Ambassador in Rome also called on him.

Subhas had sought a meeting with Mussolini soon after he arrived in Rome, but since Italy too was caught up in the war, getting an appointment was proving to be difficult. He continued to stay in touch with the Japanese Ambassador as well. Subhas was well looked after in Rome, but his inability to meet the head of state was making him very unhappy. He even sent an ultimatum to Mussolini's special secretary. Then one day, he got a call from the foreign ministry, 'Mr Bose, please meet with Il Duce's son-in-law, Count Ciano.'

'But I want to meet Il Duce himself.'

'Count Ciano is Italy's foreign minister. He looks after everything these days.'

'But is he here?' asked Subhas, shrilly.

'He is in Venice just now, but is due back in the capital tonight.'

As he put down the receiver, he said to Emilie, 'Something strange is going on. Before I left Germany, my friend Lothar Frank had played mediator between Mussolini and me.'

'So what's happened now?'

'I don't know. He had told my friend that he knew me, and that I would get an appointment immediately.'

The young Ciano appeared quite immature when Subhas first met him. He was looking at him rather skeptically when Ciano asked, 'Have you met Iqbal Schedai?'

'I have been waiting to meet him,' Subhas exclaimed eagerly.

'He seems to have gone out of town to rest. Once he returns, you can meet him, and only then we can decide what the next steps will be,' Ciano told him.

A few days later, Schedai returned to Rome. The foreign ministry was hosting a banquet in his honour, and Subhas and Emilie were invited to it. When the two of them arrived, they found Ciano surrounded by sycophants. Ciano greeted Subhas with a warm 'Welcome, Indian tiger!', and shook hands with him.

The following day, Subhas met Iqbal Schedai. He was exactly as he sounded on the radio – firm, persuasive, deep. Subhas congratulated him for having lived in exile for so long and carrying on the struggle single-handed. Throughout their conversation, Schedai kept glancing at Emilie curiously. Finally, he dared to say, 'Excuse me, madam, but would you mind stepping into the anteroom for a couple of minutes?'

'Yes, of course,' said Emilie and went out.

Before Subhas could say anything, Schedai began, 'You are discussing issues of national importance in the presence of this European woman ... Who is she?'

'Don't worry, Schedai, she is a very dear friend.'

'But a German woman ...?'

'She is not just another woman for me, Iqbal. She too loves India as much as you or I do. It is her husband's motherland.'

'Husband? Which husband?' Iqbal looked at Subhas suspiciously.

'I don't wish to say more at this juncture. All I can say is, she is absolutely trustworthy.'

As Subhas Chandra summoned Emilie back into the room, Schedai looked thoroughly disapproving. Lightly stroking his thick black moustache, Schedai remarked, 'Division is inevitable.'

'What division?' Subhas was puzzled.

'I am a Muslim. You a Hindu. Pakistan for me, India for you.'

Subhas's face fell. 'What are you saying, Schedai?' he asked incredulously. 'I didn't expect this from you even in my wildest dreams. A unified India has been my most cherished dream. You may meet me again or not, I don't know, but remember one thing, Mr Schedai, don't ever mention the word Pakistan in my presence.'

'So you turned out to be a follower of Gandhi, then ...?'

'I am no one's follower nor leader. For the sake of my motherland, I am carrying out both roles myself.'

Schedai's face flushed, but he said equally resolutely, 'In that case, you and I have nothing in common. I am going to fight for Jinnah's Pakistan.'

'And I for a unified, undivided India.'

Involuntarily, Subhas clenched his fists and declared, 'I am prepared to fight a civil war for twenty years, if necessary, for it. My country will not be divided as long as I am alive.'

The discussion fell through. Iqbal Schedai and his secretary Farukh Khan went away.

As soon as they got home, Iqbal Schedai started dictating a report for Ciano. 'As directed by the honourable minister, I had a long meeting with Subhas Bose. And I was quite disillusioned. I would describe him as a very ordinary person. The gentleman talks of an agreement with Germany and Italy. He wants to meet Il Duce. His only motive seems to be to meet the Duce here, then on the strength of it, to pressurise the Führer to give him an appointment. The Führer has refused to meet him until now; make of that what you will. Frankly, I do not think he is a capable, courageous person. He is just an unsuccessful leader who has been expelled from India by Gandhi and his Congress. He is just an ordinary man with unrealistic dreams. That is my opinion.'

After he had finished, Schedai asked his secretary, 'So, Farukh, what do you think of this report?'

'Good, very good.' Farukh smiled and added, 'You snubbed him properly for opposing the idea of Pakistan.'

'It wasn't just the matter of Pakistan, Farukh. At a pinch, I may have conceded him his demand for a unified India, but ...'

'But what, sir?'

'Do you remember at the banquet last night,' narrowing his eyes, Iqbal continued, 'Ciano got carried away while welcoming him and offered my chair to Subhas. So subtly was it done that no one noticed it. But its implications are very serious. What did I spend the last twenty years in Italy for? To snap off my horns and use them to trumpet a welcome for that upstart? Never!'

There was no charm left in Rome any longer. The days dragged. Adam Trott and other friends sent messages from Berlin that a special department for the Free India Centre had been opened and the foreign ministry had sanctioned additional funds for it. These were only salves for the conscience. The wounded heart continued to bleed. Subhas and Emilie returned to Berlin, to the same disappointment, a fate that would not relent. Lothar Frank came to visit them one day. 'After all that effort, I could not meet Il Duce', Subhas said.

Frank smiled. 'What can the poor man do?' he said.

'Poor man? Mussolini?'

'Bose, Ribbentrop's telegram had reached the Duce's court even before you set foot in Italy. Berlin had warned Rome. There is just too much intrigue. We will take a decision on India's situation, in good time, calmly.'

Too stunned to react, Subhas merely listened as Lothar continued, 'I have learnt from some of my friends in Rome's foreign ministry that personally, Mussolini was eager to meet you. But that meant giving you undue importance, which another Indian was dead against, so he made sure ...'

'Iqbal Schedai ...,' muttered Subhas.

'Yes. He has bored his way into the foreign office. Besides, he and Mussolini's son-in-law Ciano are good friends. They are often seen together, in the company of dancing girls, having a good time, fishing and enjoying life.'

Subhas was seething with anger at Germany's deceit. The Russian campaign had poured cold water on all his hopes, making him reckless. He dashed off a letter to Ribbentrop rebuking Germany for its unreliability. He went to Woermann to protest vociferously. Not wishing to bear the brunt of his anger, Woermann directed him to Keppler, the foreign secretary. A letter from Ribbentrop had landed on Keppler's desk even before Subhas's arrival. In red ink, it carried the message, 'Set this persistent Indian straight'.

Keppler's English was very shaky and Subhas's German was only slightly better. Adam Trott was the interpreter. The atmosphere was charged.

Clenching his fists, Subhas said, 'By attacking Russia, you have been discredited as a warmonger. And this is Hitler's biggest blunder.'

'Stop it!' thundered Keppler. 'How dare you stand here in his capital city and find fault with him? We have never seen anyone so audacious.'

'Please do me just one favour. Declare your recognition of India's independence. Otherwise, I will be forever branded as an accomplice of a dictator.'

Subhas's raised voice shook the whole department. Keppler shot daggers at him. Trott kicked Subhas under the table, warning him to calm down.

'Bose, do you consider yourself a member of the Axis powers like Japan and Italy?' Keppler demanded. 'You stand here alone, with the arrogance of someone who has a continent behind him.'

'Mr Keppler, this is the cry of thirty-eight crore chained people.'

'You should be pleased with the Russian campaign, in fact. You can easily reach Delhi from the Kremlin.'

'But on whose feet?' Subhas was trembling with rage. 'I am aware that your actions are those of a dictatorship. Have you no scruples? It is here, with your assault on Russia, that your downfall begins.'

'That's enough.' Keppler stood up.

Picking up his file, Subhas walked out like a wounded lion. Keppler banged his fist on the table. 'He dares to say that the Führer's decision was foolish! Instruct the Gestapo to arrest the impertinent man at once!'

'But ...'

'Alexander, you foolish man, you side with someone who finds fault with the Führer?'

'Sorry, sir, but we have instructions from the Führer himself to accord Bose the status of a state guest. In fact, those papers bear your signature. I would go so far as to say, why stop at arresting him? Send him to a concentration camp! Only, to reverse the earlier order, we will have to go to the Führer himself.'

'Yes, I suppose he is right,' conceded Keppler.

Eleven

One day, Taiji came to the Esplanade Hotel. 'I have come straight from Wilhelmstrasse,' she said. 'You can move out of this hotel.'

'Really?'

'Yes, to an independent bungalow in Sophienstrasse.'

'Is it a nice place?'

'Very nice. The American Ambassador used to live there.'

Subhas, Emilie and Taiji drove out to see the place. Among the several embassies located in that area was a large red-brick building. It was a big house with thirty rooms, a beautiful garden and a large backyard.

The bungalow had been vacant, but the staff employed by the foreign ministry had been retained. An elderly, sixty-something woman came out to greet them with a hastily gathered bunch of flowers. She tucked a lovely rosebud into Subhas's lapel and smiled. Subhas thanked her and asked her name. 'Anna,' she replied. 'Mr Bose, you will be coming to live here soon?'

'Very soon.'

'We are eagerly waiting for you,' said Anna, her wrinkled face breaking into a charming smile.

When they returned to the hotel, Taiji was looking grave, as if she was hiding something. 'Subhas,' she said, 'I have news of our Dr Tendulkar.'

'Where is he?'

'He was returning to Berlin when ...'

'What happened?'

'He was arrested by the British police on suspicion that he was a German spy.'

Subhas tried to console her. 'Taiji, don't worry. This too shall pass.'

'Oh, I have no doubt about that, Subhas,' she replied bravely. 'When you set India free, I will go and live with my doctor in Tilakwadi in Belgaum. Now my personal fortunes are entwined with your struggle.'

The Free India Centre was opened in Lichtensteinallee in the Tiergarten area of Berlin. Subhas had agreed to accept funds from Germany as a national loan. During this period, strict rationing was in force. Even senior and influential Nazi officials had to survive on meagre supplies of food. But since Subhas enjoyed the status of an ambassador, he had sufficient quantities of bread, butter and vegetables. One afternoon, while they were having lunch, Emilie suddenly left the table, sobbing. Subhas quickly followed her into their bedroom, took her into his arms and asked, 'What's the matter, dear?'

'Only a few close friends know about our marriage, isn't it?'

'Yes, what about it?'

'What will the others think? They must be saying all kinds of things about this woman who is living in so openly with an Indian leader. How does one face them?'

'Your Lord knows the truth, doesn't he? Why bother about the others?'

Subhas remembered the incident in Rome when Schedai had looked suspiciously at Emilie. Then the threatening calls she had received from some Nazi zealot reminding her of her Aryan descent. Should some untoward incident occur, what would Emilie say? It was easier to survive ten bomb attacks than face insulting stares. But while the war was being waged, it was necessary to keep their marriage a secret. 'Emilie,' said Subhas, 'these dark days will end. Light will flood our lives. And then I will take my little angel from Howrah Station all the way to Bhowanipore in a grand procession. You will be welcomed with smiling faces and gaily fluttering tirangas – independent India's tricolour.'

'But what about that erstwhile wife of yours?'

'My wife?' Subhas almost choked.

'That woman who kept following you around railway stations and airports, the Maharashtrian girl who called you "My dear husband"?'

'You mean Mugdha? I had gone to Nathalal's house before coming here. She was present there too. I gave her a piece of my mind. "Do something for your country instead of pursuing me like this. A body without principles is like a hollow log of wood," I told her.'

'What did she do?'

'She looked stunned. Started crying. Then walked away. Who knows what happened to her after that.'

To cheer Emilie up, Subhas came up with all sorts of ploys that evening. He tickled her bare feet with a peacock feather, stroked her hair and cracked jokes. Suddenly Emilie, huddled up inside a thick blanket, began to shake with mirth.

'Now what? Why are you getting hysterical?' he asked, puzzled.

'Shall I tell you something?'

'Please do.'

'An intelligent and dynamic leader doesn't usually fall in love and all that.'

'And if he does?'

'Then there is no lover as mad as him in the world.'

'Who is this Orlando Mazzotta?'

'Looks like some Italian gentleman.'

'So what is the connection between him and India's freedom?'

The hall was packed with Indian students, professionals and industrial workers. They were curious about Mazzotta who had invited them there. Narahari Ganpule, a Maharashtrian youth, was greatly excited. He used to be a Congress worker, but now lived in Berlin as a businessman. Habib-ur-Rahman, mechanical engineer; Shri N.G. Swami, a chemistry graduate; Balkrishna Sharma and Abid Hasan of the Hyderabad Nawab's family, who were studying electrical engineering in Berlin – all were impatient to see this mystery man.

'As soon as the war broke out, we wanted to rush back to India,' said one young man.

'We tried too. But all voyages were cancelled.'

Just then Frau Jay von Harubau arrived and was greeted enthusiastically by the Indian students gathered there. Taiji had arranged this meeting. M.R. Vyas, a Gujarati student who had been working as Subhas's secretary, entered the hall followed by a young man with a pointed goatee beard, wearing oval-framed glasses. 'This is Orlando Mazzotta,' Vyas announced. Ganpule, Abid Hasan and the others were stunned – the beguiling smile, the expressive eyes, the face was so familiar, but ... And then a chorus erupted, 'Subhas babu! Subhas babu!' The crowd was electrified. The students crowded around him as if they had encountered a messiah. Abid Hasan rushed up to shake hands with him.

'Abid, what are you doing here?'

'Studying here, Subhas babu!'

'You used to be such an ardent follower of Bapuji in the Sabarmati Ashram ... you had even given up college to be with him.'

'I thought Gandhiji would keep up the momentum of his agitation. But that did not happen. When he conceded to Irwin, I walked out of prison, vowing to abandon politics and resumed my studies. I am studying electrical engineering here.'

Emilie and Taiji served everyone coffee. Subhas addressed the thirty-four students present. They were more than willing to be baptised in the ideas of revolution. 'Even as I languished behind bars, I dreamt of building an Azad Hind Army,' Subhas told them. 'This is going to prove a decisive battle. I need the army not only to fight for the freedom of India, but when our country becomes free, I want it to be among the great civilised nations of the world, and for that we require a band of fearless and dedicated workers. So, my brothers, let your faith in our freedom be unshakeable and your resolve to achieve it, strong.'

The German government had released the frequency of its airwaves for the Azad Hind Radio broadcasts. Subhas had his own legitimate broadcasting station now. News bulletins were prepared in fourteen Indian languages. His young colleagues slogged day and night to get everything ready. Balkrishna Sharma's voice became the signature tune of the Azad Hind Radio. His announcement 'Azad Hind calling! Azad Hind calling!' was followed by 'This is Subhas Chandra Bose speaking. I have thrown dust into the eyes of the British authorities and fled from India. But have a little patience, my brothers. At the appropriate time, I will appear as a whirlwind at the frontiers of India. Have faith in our national flag.' This was a short address over the radio. Hectic propaganda activity for India's freedom was in progress, but the British secret agents did not know exactly where the broadcasts were being aired from. News bulletins from foreign correspondents which were broadcast over the Azad Hind Radio were accurate and relevant.

One day Emilie said to Subhas, 'Your man in London gives very good news reports.'

'Yes, he is paid the highest,' Subhas replied.

'Even the Paris bulletins are interesting.'

'You know, he is highly educated!'

One day, there was a message that because of some problem with the railways, the students were unable to reach the radio station. Immediately, Subhas drove to the station with Emilie. Even the stenographer had not arrived. Time for the broadcast was drawing near. Subhas and Emilie tuned in to the Delhi and BBC stations. He shut his eyes. Then imagining what the British reactions to events in India were likely to be, he began to report the news to Emilie. When he started the next item with, 'Our correspondent in London reports that ...' Emilie could not contain her laughter. 'Oh, I see. The London reporter, the Paris correspondent, all are one and the same person, then?'

'You think it's a lie?'

He went to the cupboard and brought out an issue of *The Guardian*. Pointing an article out to her, he asked, 'Have you read this?'

'What?'

'The British police arrested two Indians believing them to be correspondents for the Azad Hind Radio.'

'Where?'

'In London.'

Emilie giggled like a schoolgirl.

Once, Subhas saw four prisoners arrive at the radio station to prepare a presentation in Hindi. They had been brought there from one of the concentration camps. All they were asking for was two square meals a day. Subhas's curiosity was aroused on seeing those four Indian soldiers. He got the truth out of them. Thanks to Field Marshal Rommel's daring assault in North Africa, the 3rd Motor Brigade of the Indo-British Army and many other soldiers had been captured by Germany. About twenty-five of them had been brought to Berlin from Tripoli by Dr Dhawan and Alexander Werth. About fifteen thousand Indian soldiers were in a POW camp at Annaburg. Subhas made repeated visits to the Foreign Affairs Office to request them to hand over the POWs to him.

Soon, the news that Subhas was in Germany leaked. The *Daily Mail* and the *Empire News* carried the headlines in bold type: 'Indian Quisling Seeks Asylum in Hitler's Court'. One night Subhas sent for Adam Trott.

While Britain's venomous propaganda was on, Italy and Germany were delaying the announcement of their stand on India's legitimate demand for freedom. Subhas was livid at their procrastination. Showing him the newspaper clippings, he told Trott, 'This should stop now, Adam. You must do something, my friend.'

'Subhas, you will have to wait a little longer.'

'How much longer? Just let me meet the Führer once, only once, Adam. I will not rest till I bring about a change of heart in him.'

Subhas's young colleagues had begun to address him affectionately as Netaji. A daily newspaper, *Azad Hind*, started coming out. Not only that, a planning committee was formed to chalk out a strategy for development plans in independent India. At last, the German government had granted permission for the Indian Legion to be formed. Now, Subhas would get as many POWs as he wanted to set up a freedom brigade, a Mukti Sena. Subhas learnt that there was a small POW camp with about thirty Indians at Schlieffen-Upher, so he decided to pay a visit. Emilie, Abid Hasan and N.G. Swami accompanied him.

The camp was like regular barracks. Subhas stood before the prisoners to make his speech, but after a few sentences, he sat down abruptly. The carefully prepared speech stuck in his throat. Instead, he addressed the men in simple words. Gurbachan Singh Magnet from Jalandhar stood up and raised the slogan of revolution. Other soldiers asked numerous questions. Finally, only three of them joined Subhas.

He next set his sights on the Annaburg POW camp. Some soldiers from Schlieffen started coming to his house. They composed patriotic songs. Subhas sent Abid Hasan, Swami and Gurbachan to make the preliminary arrangements at Annaburg. In two days, he received a message summoning him to Annaburg at once. He told Emilie, 'I must go to bed early tonight. I want to win over Annaburg tomorrow.'

An obsessive lover may be able to get some sleep occasionally, but a man inflamed by thoughts of revolution can find no rest. In the middle of the night, he woke Emilie up and said, 'Come out into the garden with your guitar. I want to sing.' Emilie looked at him nonplussed. 'At this time?'

'I will not be able to sleep until I sing the most beautiful lyrics composed by my Schlieffen soldiers.'

Berlin had surrendered to the night. Emilie strummed the guitar and the night breeze accompanied her. Subhas began to sing:

Mazaa aayega jab hamara raj dekhenge
Ki apni hi zameen hogi, apna asmaan hoga,
Shahidon ki chitaaon par lagenge har baras mele,
Watan par marne walon ka yahi naam-o-nishan hoga

Annaburg, December 1941.

Two hundred and fifty miles away from Berlin, Annaburg Cantonment shivered. Winter had just set in, and fine powdery snow was coming down in drifts. Some unusual news – that two of Subhas's aides were coming to meet the Indian soldiers – sparked off rumours and speculations. Most did not believe it. Others dismissed it saying, 'This is Germany, not the bank of the Hooghly for Subhas to send his emissaries here. It must be some trick of the perverse German authorities. They must have found a Subhas babu lookalike and planted him here.'

Abid Hasan and N.G. Swami went to Annaburg with great expectations. But the reception they received was far from cordial. As they walked through the barracks, escorted by armed Nazi soldiers, some prisoners banged their metal plates and cups against the cell bars shouting, 'Spies! German spies!' They spat at the two men. 'Go away from here, you bastards,' they yelled. But Hasan and Swami would not get discouraged. They continued to walk through the camp. Some Indian soldiers shoved and pushed them. To prevent any untoward incident, the camp commandant sent a couple more armed guards. This only made matters worse. 'We knew it. Bloody Nazi agents! They need Nazi escorts to protect them, the cowards!'

Hasan and Swami immediately sent away the guards. For two days, they lived with the taunts, the abuses, the dirty looks and the suspicion. The next night, they sent a message to Netaji that unless he made an appearance himself, not much would be achieved. But they were worried. Hopefully, Netaji would not be abused or boycotted. A story was circulated in the camp that night. 'That impersonator is arriving tomorrow. Be careful. Don't fall for his sweet words.' The British NCOs who were also POWs in the same camp, walked around issuing threats and warnings. 'We have powerful instruments like the radio in our pockets. Be loyal to the salt you have eaten. If you try to betray us, you will be hanged at the gallows.'

It snowed all night. Wondering what the next day would bring, the buildings and towers of Annaburg remained wakeful.

11 December, the Annaburg camp was enveloped in dense fog. To prevent any trouble during Netaji's speech, it was decided to hold it in a small theatre. But the number of curious Indian soldiers was large. Kurt Krappe received Subhas at the gate with about a dozen guards. Netaji stepped out of his car, dressed in a black jacket and a black peak cap. Instantly, he was mobbed by the soldiers. Somehow, the guards managed to get him to the theatre. Subhas was delighted to see so many of his Indian brethren inside the hall. Many of them were reluctant to listen to the impersonator. So someone in the first row began to cough. Soon, the coughing spread throughout the hall. Subhas raised his voice and continued, undaunted. Then someone began stamping on the wooden floor. The clatter was deafening. But Subhas, did not heed the noise. 'Listen, my countrymen,' he thundered. 'Listen to me. I was forced to remain in Germany incognito all these days. But from now on, there will be no screen between us. Let us all become united. Let us build a new army for the freedom of India. Together, we will destroy the enemy.'

Netaji's voice reached a crescendo. Unmindful of the disturbance, he went on, 'Brothers, freedom is obtained through struggle. It does not come without a price, nor from someone's benevolence. Pay that price. Pay with your blood. The blood of brave warriors!' Netaji's eloquence had subdued some of the protest. They were looking at him differently now. When he concluded his speech, Netaji looked at the men in front of him with great expectation. Only six men came forward. This would not do. He decided not to turn back until Annaburg had been conquered. That night, he stayed with Major Kurt Krappe. Hasan, Swami and Gurbachan were ashamed of their inability to handle the situation and apologised to Netaji. Consoling them, he said, 'Look, it's not what you think. Generations of their families have wasted away in slavery. For the first time, we are teaching them the language of revolution. Obviously, it will not be easy. But when the war-cry is sounded, their weapons will dazzle.'

That afternoon, Manjit Singh of the 11th Cavalry developed a high fever. Almost delirious, he ran out of the barracks, abusing his colleagues. 'You fools, the man you accused of being Hitler's agent is not the enemy agent! He is our Subhas babu!'

'How do you know?' they yelled back.

'I swear on the Guru Granth Sahib; I was present at the Haripura Congress and heard him speak for three whole hours.'

'What if he isn't Subhas babu?'

'Cut off my head and throw it outside the camp.'

After a brief silence, a Bengali captain, Bhupen Das, came forward to corroborate Manjit's statement. 'Arre, do you think the tears he shed this afternoon were false? If he were an impostor, he would have run away after all the commotion we created. This man stayed back.'

A restless Subhas was standing by the window and lighting another cigarette when someone came up to him and said softly, 'There is a whole Maratha Regiment at Annaburg.' Netaji's eyes brightened. He woke up Hasan and Swami and told them that he had to meet the Maratha Regiment at once. Their barracks were some distance away. When the soldiers heard that Netaji was going to address them, they rushed outside. Looking at them with great hope, Netaji began his speech. 'There is nothing new one can tell Shivaji's trusted Mavla warriors about sacrificing themselves for the motherland. Do you know who inspired me to escape from the British without a scratch? It was Shivaji Maharaj. Whether it was the valiant Laxmibai of Jhansi who challenged the British in the 1857 Revolution, or Nanasaheb Peshwa or the noble Tatya Tope, who hoisted his body at the gallows as a symbol of India's freedom, you Marathas have been our role models. Now, we have to strike at the foundation of the foreign power that has enslaved more than half the world. Rise, Maratha warriors, and join the Azad Hind Fauj!'

Not one Maratha responded to his impassioned pleas of Netaji. He returned to his quarters.

In the morning, Subhas bathed, performed his puja and was getting dressed when Abid Hasan rushed into his room. 'The commander of the Maratha Regiment wishes to meet you urgently,' he said. When Netaji stepped out, he was amazed to see the entire regiment lined up outside, in full military regalia. As if on cue, they sang in chorus, 'Chhatrapati Shivaji Maharaj ki jai! Netaji Subhas Chandra Bose ki jai! Hara Hara Mahadev!'

Patting Commander Subhanji Ghorpade's back, Netaji said to him, 'Today you are here to greet me, your chests swelling with pride, but why didn't a single "yes" come from your lips last night?'

Subhanji smiled from behind his luxuriant moustache. 'Netaji, our motto is "Live together, die together". That is why we were waiting till all the minds were made up.'

Netaji decided to meet the inmates of every barrack separately. He was warned that he would meet with violent opposition from one of the barracks. Abid Hasan hinted that it was dangerous for them to go around unescorted. They could even be assaulted.

'Let us take the German guards with us,' Gurbachan suggested.

'I don't need German crutches to walk to my own countrymen,' Netaji declared and crossed the barbed wire fence. As soon as he stepped inside, roars filled the air, 'You agents of Hitler, enter at your own peril!'

But Netaji did not falter. There was a war of slogans at the gate. Cries of 'Down with … Murdabad! Murdabad …!' charged the air. This was a plot of some pro-British officers. As he went some yards ahead, conflicting slogans were heard – 'Zindabad, zindabad! Subhas babu zindabad!' 'Mahatma Gandhiji ki jai!'

The black spirit of resistance vanished. The inner barracks were eagerly awaiting Netaji. They were the same men who had disrupted the meeting in the cinema hall the previous night. Today, they awaited him with a garland of leaves since flowers were not available. The incidents of the past few hours had transformed the atmosphere at the Annaburg POW camp. Netaji continued to walk through every barrack and talked to the soldiers. He drank the tea they offered him.

Though the German sentries ordered them not to break ranks, they ignored the orders and crowded around Netaji as devotees would throng a deity's palanquin. 'Netaji, set us free!' 'Take us back to our motherland, Netaji!' they begged. After three hours and eighteen mugs of tea, Netaji finished his round of the barracks.

Again, a crowd gathered in front of the gate. An emotional Netaji addressed them once more, 'Do not worry. Once India becomes free, the land shall be ours, the country our very own. Brothers, you have wasted a lifetime in bondage. But let the coming generations breathe the free air of freedom and dignity.'

'Netaji, we have eaten the Queen of England's salt. How can we betray those who feed us?' one group wanted to know.

'Whose salt, my dear men?'

'The Britishers', Netaji!'

Netaji laughed heartily. 'That was not what I meant! Where does the salt you ate come from? England or India? Our people have been making salt for centuries.'

The Annaburg camp looked like it had seen an explosion. Indian soldiers swore by freedom. Taking them all into the revolutionary fold, Hasan and Swami began to sing,

Humein sub sukhon ko bhool jaana padega
Watan ke liye dukh uthana padega,
Ay azad Hindi, utho, kamar bandho.
Watan lut raha hai, bachana padega,
Hukum Netaji ka bajana padega.

'I must extract the golden nugget of freedom from the furnace of the war,' Netaji was saying to his colleagues when the telephone rang. 'Adam?' he said.

'Congratulations, my friend. The people of East Asia are pleading with the Japanese government to take you there.'

That night, State Secretary Keppler sent a message. 'Mr Bose, the Japanese Ambassador, Hiroshi Oshima would like to meet you immediately.'

Subhas arrived at the Japanese Embassy the next day. Oshima was sprightly and eager. Seated beside him was military attaché, Gen. Isoroku Yamamoto.

'Namaste.'

To Netaji's surprise, Yamamoto replied in chaste Hindi, 'Namaskar.'

After exchanging pleasantries, Oshima came straight to the point. 'There is a Bose living in the Nakamura region of Tokyo.'

'Rash Behari Bose, I suppose?'

'That is right. Any relative of yours?'

'We are brothers in revolution. Closer than blood relations, isn't it?' Netaji said with a smile.

Hiroshi Oshima and Yamamoto laughed. They talked about many things, Gurudev Rabindranath Tagore's visit to Japan, the many Indians serving in Japan since the First World War like Raja Mahendra Pratap and other revolutionaries like Rash Behari. Gen. Yamamoto briefed him on how concern for India's freedom was getting stronger in East Asia, and how the Hindi Swatantra Sangha had opened their offices in Kobe and Nagasaki in Japan, Ipoh in Malaysia, Penang, Singapore and Bangkok. Then Oshima asked Netaji, 'Suppose, Mr Bose, the German government invites Rash Behari here, will you have a problem working under his leadership?'

'No, not at all! Rash Behari Bose is a veteran revolutionary. He will receive due respect.'

It was a common Japanese convention not to reveal much in the first meeting. Even after two hours, neither Yamamoto nor Oshima let on why exactly Netaji had been summoned. That is why when he stood up to leave, Netaji threw the bait. 'What if instead of getting Rash Behari here, you sent me there?'

'Oh yes, of course,' Oshima stuttered. 'In fact, that's what we wanted to ask you.'

'So then ask.' Netaji laughed. 'I would consider myself fortunate to work under the guidance of such a stalwart.'

8 December 1941. Alor Setar Railway Station in Malaysia. The 15th Battalion of the British Army had been waiting for instructions from the headquarters for the last thirty hours. The ruddy complexioned Lt. Col. Fitzpatrick was pacing up and down the platform, pulling on his cheroot. He had received secret information that Japanese troops were soon to enter Thailand. But most people did not believe that Japan was capable of such aggression. Col. Fitzpatrick was telling Major Mohan Singh that they would require less effort to crush the Japanese than to swat a fly. From the Alor Setar Station, one could see the aerodrome at the foot of the hill opposite, where several bomb-laden aircraft were lined up. In the blazing noonday sun, their wings gleamed like sword blades.

Suddenly, with an ear-splitting whining-hissing sound, a squadron of Japanese Zero category aircraft swooped down, scattered bombs left and right, and in the blink of an eye, swerved away. In no time at all, the fuel tanks of the planes on the ground caught fire, and the entire aerodrome was engulfed in flames. There was complete chaos. The Punjab Regiment stared disbelievingly. The Japanese had come, the Japanese had come! War was here.

Col. Fitzpatrick and Major Mohan Singh sounded the alert. The entire division scrambled to safety in the rubber plantation nearby. Shortly thereafter, some aircraft returned, targeted the railway station and poured their fire on it. In minutes, the busy platform was turned into a cremation ground. Huge craters appeared in the platform; iron rails were uprooted and flung far away, twisted and mangled. Col. Fitzpatrick was on the wireless, hearing news about the conflagration around him. Japanese bombers had started attacking Malayan ports like Jitra, Penang, Singapore and Shingora. Early that morning, Japanese troops had been dropped in the Philippines, Siam, Hong Kong and other islands in the Pacific Ocean.

Major Mohan Singh had his ear glued to the transistor radio when he heard the earth-shattering news. 'Sir, sir,' he screamed, the radio falling from his hands, 'Pearl Harbor too!'

'What!' Fitzpatrick almost blacked out with the shock. He grabbed the rubber tree for support. Attack on Pearl Harbor? Unbelievable. Japan's daring act had confounded the British troops in East Asia. Nature too changed colours. The unpredictable Malay downpour began. The troops shivered not only from the cold but also from the unforeseen attack.

Colonel Fitzpatrick, blinded by the smoke, stumbled along the forest path. Suddenly, some bullets grazed his back, searing his skin, exposing bloodied flesh. Mohan Singh leapt like a cheetah to grab him. He dragged the colonel into a clump of bushes nearby. Just then, several armoured vehicles roared past, trampling everything in their path. Col. Fitzpatrick groaned as he hovered between wakefulness and unconsciousness. Well, that was it for him. He reached for his revolver and handed it to Mohan Singh. 'Shoot, son,' he said, 'and relieve me of this agony.'

Mohan Singh looked at him in horror. He could not obey him this time. 'Come on, do it!' screamed Fitzpatrick. But courage fled and compassion took its place. He pulled some clothes out of his backpack and began to bandage the wounds. Gently, he lay him down under a tree.

Mohan Singh had done whatever he could. The terrible night would not end. The radio kept reporting a string of bad news. Around midnight, Captain Akram Khan woke up, screaming. 'Our two prime warships, Prince of Wales and Ripples, have been sunk by the Japanese!'

Fitzpatrick slowly put his water bottle to his lips. Sorrowfully, he remarked, 'Britain ruled over half the world by riding the waves. The ocean had never let us down as it has done this time.'

After a two-day halt, the regiment resumed its march on what appeared like a never-ending journey. Drenched by continuous rain, the soldiers tramped with heavy mud-caked boots, alert for enemy aircraft. Mohan Singh unexpectedly caught sight of some old newspapers lying in a ditch on the way. He picked up the whole bunch and glanced through the headlines. 'Asia for the Asians,' 'Drive the whites out of the East,' 'India for Indians'. His heart stopped when he read those golden words and his grimy face broke into a smile. But how had these messages landed in this remote jungle? Was it divine providence sending a message?

The dense jungle seemed to have befriended the Japanese. It provided the small-built clay-coloured soldiers a perfect camouflage as they marched through with large cooking utensils on their heads or nicely roasted carcasses of wild pig on their shoulders. Whenever they were hungry, they broke off chunks of meat and ate it. Sometimes they had salted fish, drank water from the streams and marched on with renewed vigour. Some carried planks of wood, which they held on their heads, to make temporary bridges over streams and fords.

After a harrowing three days and nights, some Indian soldiers of the disbanded regiment regrouped. They gave the news that two platoons accompanying them had perished. The weary Mohan Singh and Akram Khan were resting under the shade of a large pipal tree.

'You heard that, Akram? Do we have a British aircraft to provide cover for us overhead? For how long must we march through this valley of death?' Mohan Singh was furious.

'What can we do, Mohan? Our white officers merely issue orders from the headquarters, and we are left to die as we carry them out. And once the bugle sounds the victory, it is they who will rush forward with chests out to sign the pact.'

'Yaar, Akram, enough is enough. I don't think I can fight for the British any longer.'

'Then what? Are you going to revolt?'

'Revolt is bound to happen. Who knows, I might even become the liberator of the enslaved!' Mohan Singh muttered, as if in a trance.

Mohan Singh looked out at the hillock rising in front of him. At the foot of the hill, he could see a narrow path, partly covered by the overhang of large trees. Although no movement was visible in the open stretches, the trees all seemed watchful. The jungle had its ears pricked up. There must be a Japanese post nearby. The Indians had neither rations nor ammunition left. It might be worthwhile to somehow get past the post, rather than die of hunger in the jungle, Mohan Singh thought.

Akram wanted to accompany him, but was dissuaded by Mohan Singh, saying why sacrifice two men instead of one. He bid his companions goodbye, and taking one cautious step at a time, managed to reach the narrow path. He had almost got to the end of it when suddenly he heard gunfire. He turned fast, raised the gun he was carrying and looked around him, bristling. Before he could blink, seven or eight Japanese soldiers surrounded him, like a pack of lions attacking a straying prey.

Four of them dragged him to a nearby rubber tree and tied him to it. One of them shoved a gun barrel into his chest. After a moment, he said, 'Austrorian?' Mohan Singh had no clue what he was saying. What was the point in small talk when death was staring you in the face, he thought. The barrel dug into his chest again. Mohan Singh gasped. Every nerve, every sinew tautened. His entire being was concentrated on that one moment. But the moment passed. One soldier picked up Mohan Singh's gun and advanced towards him cautiously. He felt Mohan Singh's hair curiously, then asked, 'You Indo ...? Indo ...?'

The moment Mohan Singh confirmed his identity, their attitude changed completely. The Japanese soldier embraced him, leaving him absolutely confused. But guessing their intention, he began to call out loudly to the men in his regiment. They all gathered around Mohan Singh. The Japanese soldiers placed their black caps on the heads of the Indian soldiers. And with much bonhomie, the Japanese and Indians feasted on salted fish. Col. Fitzpatrick, who was sitting on one side, watched this celebration with much amusement.

A couple of the Japanese soldiers knew a few Hindi words, and Mohan Singh understood the reason for this unexpected cordiality. He learnt that in East Asia, an organisation called F. Kikkan, whose objective was to build an army for India's liberation, was started with support from the Japanese government. The news gladdened Mohan Singh's heart. A Japanese soldier, Major Fujiwara, had been actively associated with the organisation. Several patriotic Indians from Thailand and Malaya had rushed to support him. The Japanese soldiers proposed that Major Mohan Singh should also join Major Fujiwara.

A meeting was planned for the next day in the middle of the jungle. Two armed guards would accompany Fujiwara. The following afternoon, a fair, round-faced man with black beady eyes appeared. He had an interpreter with him. Mohan Singh loaded his gun. He stood on guard with Fujiwara in sight. For a moment, Fujiwara hesitated. But then he strode ahead, exuding confidence. He had dared to come alone into a war-ravaged territory. His samurai blood stood him in good stead. From his conversation, it was clear how many obstacles he had had to overcome for the F. Kikkan. Hearing Fujiwara speak with such passion about the Indian freedom struggle, Mohan Singh's chest swelled with pride.

Later, the plantation owners hosted a dinner. On all the surrounding huts fluttered the rising sun of the Japanese flag and the Indian tricolour. Col. Fitzpatrick's pain doubled as he watched all this from afar.

Presenting his side, Major Fujiwara said, 'Mohan, both of us have a common enemy. I have read and heard much about your country. It is the birthplace of our great Buddha. A culture that once showed the light to not just Asia but the whole world. Let us join together. Major Singh, you lead the revolt. Let one army stand directly under your command.'

'I cannot do that,' Mohan Singh said. 'There is only one individual who can give shape to the aspirations of the Indian people in East Asia. The one who, for his principles, took on a great man like Gandhiji. The one who broke British security and sought the shores of Germany ...'

'You refer to Subhas Chandra Bose, don't you?' Fujiwara asked. 'We have been waiting for him for so long. Our ambassador has been nagging Hitler to send him to Japan.'

'Bear in mind, Singapore's fortifications are the invincible symbols of our power in the Eastern Hemisphere,' Prime Minister Churchill admonished General Wavell.

'Yes, sir.'

'What had you said a fortnight ago? Please repeat your words.'

'To take over Singapore from the British, the greatest power in the world, will need at least six months,' General Wavell stammered.

Singapore had put both Churchill and Wavell in a spot. Wavell was extremely worried. Important stations like Alor Setar and Kota Baru were falling, and the British troops had been thrown into disarray. Churchill was bombarded with queries in Parliament. The same night he warned Wavell, verbally and on paper, 'Fight for every inch of Singapore at all costs. Not just the soil of Singapore, even its spirit must do the death dance.' Having more or less lost Malaya, Wavell had retreated to Singapore. The Japanese attack had unnerved him. His eyes kept straying to the map on the wall. Ever since the Japanese had circled the island of Singapore with a fleet of warships, the residents of Singapore had lived in constant fear of air raids. The worst affected were the Chinese, the Indians and the Burmese. The war made little impact on the pleasure-loving Europeans. Dancing girls were freely available after dark, most of whom were Chinese. They used to be called taxi-girls. The same white men who by day held the Asians in contempt, enjoyed their company at night.

Mohan and Akram spent that night with the Japanese infantry. Just before daybreak, the war suddenly escalated. Like demented fire spirits, the Japanese rushed into the city. Cannons thundered. European soldiers tried to scramble into boats and escape. But they either drowned or fell to cannon fire. Fighting went on throughout the day in every street of Singapore. Forty Japanese aircraft hovered in the sky causing unbelievable destruction. Senior British officers tried to reassure each other, 'Two hundred American planes will come to our rescue today … tomorrow …' But nothing happened. The British lost Singapore for want of an air squadron.

No service was held in the churches that Sunday of 15 February 1942. The British who were engaged with Hitler and Mussolini in Europe could not send timely assistance to Singapore. All day Singapore burned, its skies blackened with smoke, its people dying like insects. If there was no truce, it would be total annihilation. The commander of the British troops, Percival, and his soldiers were totally routed.

From eight o'clock in the morning, groups of Indian prisoners of war were gathering in Singapore's Farrer Park. Captain Gurbaksh Singh Dhillon and Captain Shah Nawaz Khan of the Punjab Regiment trudged along to the park. What the next steps would be was not clear. By the time everyone assembled there, it was after noon. There were no signs of a parade. If they were to remain POWs, why not leave them in the cantonment, why bring them here?

Some of the senior officers began to fidget. They were watching the self-assured figure of Mohan Singh approaching them, flanked by Indian and Japanese soldiers on either side. He stopped to chat with everyone as he moved forward. A big 'F' was appliqued on his left sleeve. Suddenly, someone shouted, 'Mohan has joined the enemy.' Shah Nawaz actually spat out when he saw him and said angrily, 'Ruined our reputation, the bastard!'

The yellow, two-storeyed viewing gallery of the race course in the middle of the park was the scene of hectic activity. The dais was decorated with Japanese flags and, surprisingly, the Indian tricolour, too. Soldiers flaunting the 'F' mark on their shirts were strutting about officiously.

Towards the middle of the afternoon with the blaring of horns and screeching of brakes, several military vehicles arrived at the ground. Japanese soldiers got out and scampered towards the dais and occupied the seats. The British Colonel Hunt sat beside them. Forty thousand Indian soldiers wondered what was going on.

Colonel Hunt stood up and handed over a list to Major Fujiwara. Then he addressed the soldiers. 'On behalf of the British Monarch, I am handing over all you Indian soldiers to the Japanese government.' Immediately, there was an uproar in the audience. Urging them to remain calm, Colonel Hunt continued, 'Just as you have obeyed our orders faithfully, I trust you would show the same respect to the Japanese authorities.' All the POWs cried out in one voice, 'What do you mean handed over to the Japanese? What is our future? How can the British shake off their responsibility like this?'

The leader of F. Kikkan, Major Fujiwara came to the mike. In a shrill, high-pitched voice, he began to speak in Japanese. Since he knew neither English nor Hindi, Kunizuka interpreted for him in English, and Colonel Gill translated his words into Hindi. Making an emotional speech, Major Fujiwara said, 'My dear Indian brothers, we have not accepted you as war prisoners but as our brothers. The bars of slavery are not for you. The open sky is yours. You are Asian, you are our brothers.'

The Indian soldiers were struck dumb by these words. They were mentally prepared for imprisonment and torture. What else could the Japanese do for them? So these words came as a shower of rose petals. Major Fujiwara handed over the papers officially to Major Mohan Singh, and declared that in future, complete responsibility for them would lie with General Officer in Command, Mohan Singh. His expressive face, despite his beard, was clearly radiant. His broad smile won most of the audience over. His naturally pleasant and persuasive voice was firmer that day. With supreme self-confidence, he said, 'Brothers, we fought bravely on Malayan soil, shed blood, sacrificed many of our companions, and then were disgraced with defeat. For whom? Had the British given us timely aerial support, this would not have come to pass. In future, we will give up our lives only for our motherland. Why can we not build our own country? Why are we slaves? All because we have no army of our own. Today, a powerful nation like Japan has stepped in to help us. Let us take advantage of the opportunity to constitute an army for the liberation of India.'

Mohan Singh's patriotism brought tears to the eyes of the soldiers. He had cast a spell on most of them.

Shah Nawaz was born into a family with a tradition of serving in the British Army. So Mohan Singh's words did not make much of an impact. In fact, he suspected that this was just a crafty ploy of the Japanese. But the sensitive Gurbaksh Singh was definitely affected. Having joined as a soldier ten years ago, he had risen to the rank of lieutenant through his own merit. At this moment, he was reminded of the golden words he had read in Chetwode Hall of the Dehra Dun Military Academy. A commander's priorities were clearly defined: 'First the motherland, next the soldiers under you, and finally yourself.'

That Gurbaksh Singh, who dreamed of getting Gandhiji and Jinnah to sit down and sort out their differences so that the integrity of India could be preserved, was moved by Mohan Singh's words was not surprising.

All the officers were invited to the stage for discussions. Gurbaksh drew Shah Nawaz aside and whispered, 'What do you think, Shanno?'

'What kind of Azad Hind Fauj is this? It is only a puppet in Japanese hands. Should we join them and attack our own people?'

'But, Shanno, think for a minute about the changed circumstances. Mohan Singh is from our unit. We have known him for ten years. He is very capable.'

'But he is not extraordinary. Who is he to take matters of our life and death into his hands?'

'Shanno, often circumstances lift an individual from man to superman.'

'With due respect to your flights of fancy, Bakshi, do you really think Mohan will be able to command forty-five thousand people?'

'Maybe we have our differences, Shanno, but one thing is sure, the Azad Hind Fauj must be formed.'

The POWs began to leave Farrer Park for their barracks, breathing the air of liberation. Soon, only Mohan Singh and Fujiwara were left. Mohan Singh said to Fujiwara, 'You have not forced me into the saddle, have you? After all, I am young and inexperienced. You think I will be able to carry the weight of forty-five thousand men?'

Fujiwara squeezed his hand and said, 'Look at world history – all those who became great revolutionaries were not born with fame stamped on them. They were also ordinary flesh-and-blood human beings. But they became icons by dint of their unshakeable faith, their unswerving loyalty to their country, and their single-minded dedication. I am certain you will create history.'

That night, a number of Muslim officers gathered around Shah Nawaz's camp. He was the commander of the Nissun camp with twenty thousand soldiers. Zaman Kiani asked him, 'Shah Nawaz, how far should we trust the Japanese?'

'Four generations of my family have served the British loyally. Personally, I have decided to keep a safe distance from them.'

'But what should *we* do?'

'The Japanese who tell you to betray the salt you have eaten, train your barrels on them. Shoot them down. Let us see how the Indian

National Army, puppets of the Japanese, stand up to the challenge!' said Shah Nawaz, clenching his fists.

The British were aware that their Eastern empire was in dire straits. And they were rattled. The Japanese onslaught was relentless. The British did not know exactly where Subhas Chandra Bose was. But they did know that if he landed in India with the Japanese behind him, they would face their biggest challenge ever. So they pursued the minor and insignificant leaders of the Forward Bloc. Netaji received daily updates of events in India. The British secret service was following his family doggedly. Sarat Bose had been arrested and put in a jail in south India. Shardul Kavishwar had been held in a prison in Punjab.

Netaji was awake all night the day Singapore fell. He said to Emilie, a shade wistfully, 'If only I had been in the East now, how wonderful it would have been!'

To prevent the people of India from welcoming the Japanese attack and to create a feeling of contempt for them, the British invited the Chinese prime minister, Chiang Kai Shek to visit India.

As things were getting hotter in the East, Netaji was becoming more and more impatient to leave Germany and get to the scene of action. One day, in a dejected mood, he said to his colleagues, 'Enough of this masquerade as Orlando Mazzotta. There cannot be a more auspicious moment than this to come clean before the world – the fall of Singapore.' That same evening, he went to the Berlin centre of the Azad Hind Radio and addressed his countrymen. 'My dear brothers and sisters. In this war, you have only one thing to lose – the fetters of slavery. Considering the world scenario today, it is clear that our motherland will not remain shackled to an alien power. India will become independent, that too, very soon.'

It was not clear where the proverbial paper horse had gone to graze. No further message was received from Tokyo. Netaji's unease was mounting. The meeting with Hitler had not taken place. But all the demands that Subhas had made to the government were complied with. Germany had opened a special India cell with the status of an embassy. The house allotted to Subhas would put many a royal palace to shame.

He had an aircraft at his beck and call, whenever he wanted to travel to Baad Gastein, Paris or Rome. Of course, all these demands could not have been met without the consent of the Führer. In spite of it all, Subhas was unhappy in Germany. Ever since the war had reached the Eastern sector, his heart was there. So many times, he had taken Emilie into his arms and said in despair, 'Emilie, if I do not get to my land soon, I will go mad.'

The British Parliament decided to send a delegation under Cripps to India. Even before the news was heard on the Azad Hind Radio, M.R. Vyas read about it and went to see Subhas. 'Do you believe that the British are really considering giving us our independence?' he asked.

'If that is the case, then where's the need to rush to Delhi? The decision can be made on the floor of the British Parliament itself. The Cripps Mission is nothing but a clever deceit against the innocent people and political leaders of the country. Japanese troops are marching towards Rangoon. They must have decided on this in a panic, to divert attention from the Japanese action.'

Subhas stopped suddenly, then after a pause, picked up pen and paper to write a message for the Azad Hind Radio. 'In order to maintain his prestige with the western world, my dear friend Jawahar may agree to a compromise formula at the final moment. Gandhiji's gentle spirit that believes in ahimsa will consider thwarting the British a sin. That is why it is imperative to tell Cripps, like Simon was told, to go back. Do not allow Cripps to cross your threshold.'

It was well past two on the night of 25 March 1942. The driver Spierka, had gone to drop M.R. Vyas at his residence. The cook, Rudolf had washed up the last cup of coffee and left. Emilie had gone to bed a long time back. Netaji who had been working all this while was exhausted. His eyes were burning. But before going to sleep, he thought he would listen to the latest news, and switched on the radio. When he heard the BBC correspondent mention his name, he sat up with a start. The man was saying, 'The revolutionary Indian leader who had taken asylum under a dictatorship, Mr Subhas Chandra Bose was killed in a plane crash this afternoon. He was on his way from Bangkok to Tokyo.' The news was most unnerving. Netaji's breath became ragged. He started to shiver. Emilie woke up. 'What is it? What happened?'

'BBC has just announced my demise.'

'Never mind. Besides spreading rumours like this, what other business do your enemies have these days?'

'I am afraid of only one thing, Emilie.' said Netaji, swallowing the lump in his throat. 'What will happen to my mother if she hears this terrible news? She is so old; how will she bear the shock?'

Netaji's thoughts kept returning to his mother. That terrible midnight of 16–17 January ... How could I commit such a blunder? Why had I left the house without touching Ma's feet and getting her blessings? How hurt she must have been. Ma, when will I be able to seek your forgiveness?

Netaji sent for Vyas. Within a short time, a stunned Vyas arrived at Sophienstrasse. Immediately, he contacted BND Radio of Germany and the news agency Dōmei Tsushin in Tokyo. And by 6.30 a.m., radios around the world heard the announcement: 'The well-known Indian leader Subhas Chandra Bose is very much alive and well in Germany. Right now, he is busy organising an army to fight for the freedom of his country. The enemy is making false announcements about his demise, which the Indian people should ignore. At the appropriate time, he will lead his army into India. This statement has been issued in Germany at midnight by his colleague, Mr Nambiar.'

Only after he heard this clarification was Subhas able to rest. Emilie had, in the meantime, been listening to the other bulletins. India had been shaken by the news. Gandhiji had sent a condolence message to his mother. But soon after, the denial was also broadcast. One news agency even did a short interview with his mother. Just as Emilie heard her voice, she increased the volume. Her last words, 'My Subhas!' sent a chill through Subhas's body.

This incident rejuvenated him. British politicians and statesmen hoped that Subhas would meet with his end, and the thorn in the side of the British Empire would be removed once and for all. That night, Netaji went by himself to the radio station and stood in front of the mike. 'This is Subhas Chandra Bose, very much alive and speaking to you over the Azad Hind Radio. British news agencies have reported that I died in an air crash on my way to Tokyo, to attend an important conference there. Ever since I left India last year, British propaganda agencies have from time to time given contradictory reports of my whereabouts, while newspapers in England have not hesitated to use uncomplimentary language for me. The latest report about my death is perhaps an instance of wishful thinking. I can imagine that the British government would, at this critical hour in India's history, like to see me dead.

'I would like to remind Cripps that India was unified under the empire of Asoka the Great, several centuries before the Christian era – more than a thousand years before England was born.

'Britain has, in other parts of her empire, for instance in Ireland and Palestine, used religion to divide people. Britain has been using it in India for that same purpose. Not only this, but other imperial weapons like the Indian princes, depressed classes, etc.

'Now Cripps is in India to use the same instruments for imperialistic ends. It is no less striking that he is applying the old imperialist policy of working for a compromise with one section of the people while simultaneously suppressing the other. That is why on the one side, Sir Stafford is conferring with one set of politicians, while on the other, the fearless and uncompromising fighters for independence are safely lodged behind prison bars.

'My people are aware of this vile policy of British politicians. I have no doubt that the spirit of our freedom fighters will inspire the people of India to understand that this is an insult to India's self-respect and honour.'

20 March 1942. Tokyo city was lashed by incessant rain. The sky had become dark. Thunder rumbled continuously. Indian nationalists from Penang, Bangkok, Singapore and Ipoh had already arrived. An impatient Mohan Singh kept glancing at his watch. He went up to the receptionist and told him to call the airport once more. 'Sir, I have been calling them every fifteen minutes. But no aircraft has landed there today,' the operator replied, fed up.

The thunderstorm showed no signs of abating. Till midnight, there was no news of the plane at all. They concluded that the pilot must have diverted the aircraft to some other destination because of the inclement weather, and praying for the safety of their colleagues, they retired for the night.

The Tokyo conference was formally inaugurated the following day. It was attended by about fifteen hundred people, including select nationalists like Barrister Nedyam Raghvan, K.P.K. Menon, S.C. Goho, and it was presided over by Rash Behari Bose. With him were prominent Indians of Tokyo, like Anand Mohan Sahai, A.M. Nair, Mohan Singh and Lt. Col. Niranjan Gill.

Mohan Singh had been waiting for his friends Akram Khan and Pritam Singh. But later in the morning, the news came that the plane carrying them had crashed into the ocean near Honshu Island.

Rash Behari could not contain his grief. How many more martyrs was the Goddess of Freedom going to claim? The conference went on for nine days, but a pall of gloom hung over the proceedings.

A proposal to ask for Netaji to be brought to Tokyo was put forward by Mohan Singh and Rash Behari. It was greeted with spontaneous applause. Both of them were dedicated to the cause of India's freedom. Rash Behari's energy would put any youth to shame. Mohan Singh, a former captain in the British Army, had been given the rank of general, and a special bungalow at the northern end of Singapore, called Mount Pleasant. Everybody including Fujiwara addressed him as Supreme Commander General Mohan Singh.

At the next meeting which was held in Bangkok, Mohan Singh impressed everyone with his remarkable oratory skills and untiring efforts. Everywhere in East Asia, British troops had been routed. Although the Japanese strength in Rangoon was limited, they met with no opposition when they marched into the city. British soldiers and civilians fled the city and crossed the Chindwin River. They had reserved all the transport and rations for only the Europeans and left the Indians to fend for themselves. Mohan Singh had worked really hard to protect the lives and assets of the Indians. Flush with his success, he had said to Prem Sehgal, 'Prem, my aspirations are soaring. The Japanese have been generous, they have given us forty-five thousand POWs.'

'What are your plans?'

'We will increase our strength first. We must have an army with at least three divisions. Then we will attack the eastern borders of our motherland to finish off the British.'

So obsessed was Mohan Singh that he forgot all about living, happiness, rest and peace. One night, he was at his desk going through some papers, his eyes red from the strain, when his dear friend Gurbaksh Singh walked in. He saw about seventy unopened envelopes lying on Mohan Singh's table. They were from Mohan Singh's wife

Jaswant. But he was determined not to be distracted by any personal concerns. 'Mohan, why are you ignoring your wife like this?'

'I cannot afford to think of family just now, Bakshi. My family now are my colleagues, my soldiers and my army.'

Bakshi opened a couple of the letters. He turned pale and exclaimed to Mohan Singh, 'Mohan, are you a human being at all? Do you know what's written in this letter? Your Jaswant has given birth to a beautiful baby. But you, unfortunate fellow, you will never be able to see its face again!'

For a moment, all of Mohan's ambitions, aspirations, ideals were forgotten. He felt a pang of guilt and grief.

Seeing Mohan Singh's distraught face, Gurbaksh burst into tears. 'Who am I to scold you, Mohan. What happened in your family happened in my home too, fifteen days ago.'

After a long time, the two of them got drunk, and in a valiant attempt to drown their grief, they became boisterous and said to each other, 'Let us congratulate each other ... all bonds are broken, all illusions destroyed.'

On the terrace of his Mount Pleasant house, General Mohan Singh sat with his friend, the big burly Major General Jagannath Rao Bhosale, drinking. Below them, the lights of Singapore harbour twinkled in the cool night air. Mohan Singh was visibly upset.

'Mohan, you are very young compared to us all, your experience is limited, if you go a little slow, it won't do you any harm.'

'No, General saab, I have no faith left in these Japanese people. Do you remember the plane crash in which three of our brothers died before the Tokyo conference? It was no accident; it was sabotage, murder! One more game played by the Japanese.'

'What are you saying, Mohan?'

'I swear, it's true.'

Mohan Singh broke down. He began to sob like a child. General Bhosale tried to comfort him, but Mohan Singh pushed his hand away. 'Bhosaleji, what didn't this Mohan Singh do to build the Azad Hind Fauj? Even though I heard that my own child had died, I did not look that way. But what is the use? An Indian gets no justice from the

Japanese. Thousands of Indian labourers are toiling to construct a bridge on the Kwai River. Such grave injustice you will not find anywhere else.'

'Really, Mohan, you must take this calmly. I will ask Rash Behari Bose to come here immediately and then ...'

'Don't mention the name of that hypocrite,' Mohan Singh interjected.

'Mohan, are you all right?'

'Till yesterday I wasn't, but today I am fully in control.'

Bhosale was at a loss for words. Fumbling, he went on, 'But Mohan, Rash Behari Babu is such a great revolutionary, from before your birth he ...'

'Enough, Bhosale saab, enough!' Mohan Singh said bitterly. 'I have heard a great deal about him. He had thrown a bomb at the viceroy and all that, right? That's all old news now. The man who has made Japan his home for the last thirty years, who has accepted Japanese citizenship, now starts talking about our freedom. How can you expect us to listen to him? He must be removed from the post of the president of the Hindi Swatantra Sangha.'

General Bhosale told him, 'Mohan, you are like a jaundiced man.'

'After the Bangkok conference, I sent so many representations to the Japanese government. I have been asking them to help raise a new battalion, build a three-division strong force. But why do all my demands get thrown into the dustbin? On 22 June, I wrote a letter stating that I expected a reply in one week. But nothing has come from them for the last eight months. What do these fellows think of themselves?'

General Bhosale heard him out patiently. Then he asked, 'What has made you so angry?'

'Some of our young men were undergoing commando training at the Penang Institute, and Barrister Raghavan was looking after the project. One day, some stout Japanese entered the premises, kidnapped the best cadets and took them away.'

'Where to?'

'Their war fronts. That's why I say I don't trust them at all. If it comes to that, I will disband the Azad Hind Fauj with no hesitation.'

'Don't make the mistake of taking a rash decision like that, Mohan. We too make mistakes sometimes.'

'What mistakes?'

'How do you explain the fact that one band led by Mahavir Singh Dhillon, which was under the command of Niranjan Singh Gill, entered

Burma to spy on the British, and eventually landed up in India with the British? That Mahavir turned out to be a traitor.' Mohan Singh cooled down a little.

'That's what I'm saying. Some members of the Azad Hind Fauj still have British leanings, that's what the Japanese believe and I agree with them. But for the moment, do not get into any controversy. Remain quiet for a while.'

'Quiet? For how long?'

'Till Subhas babu comes to East Asia from Germany.'

Colonel Niranjan Gill and Mohan Singh spent that night in discussion. The next morning, both of them were still in bed when there was a loud knocking on the door. 'What is it?'

'Sir, look outside, the Japanese Kempeitai police.'

'Have they come to arrest me or what?'

'Not you, but Gill saheb, sir!'

Mohan Singh came out into the garden. They took Col. Gill into custody, the Japanese General Iwakuro was personally supervising the operation.

'What you have done is not a good thing, Iwakuro,' Mohan Singh said. 'What is he guilty of?'

'Eleven British paratroopers landed near Pegu in Burma. We have learnt Mahavir Singh Dhillon provided the maps and charts they had with them. Gill is responsible for sending Mahavir there,' Iwakuro replied.

The tall and handsome Gill suddenly looked weak and infirm. What could Mohan Singh do? He cursed. 'This is going to cost you dearly.' He rushed into his office, sent for his steno and began to dictate: 'I, General Mohan Singh, Commander-in-Chief of the Azad Hind Fauj, invoke the power bestowed on me and announce the disbanding of the Azad Hind Fauj.'

Like huge marine birds, Japanese bombers were heading towards Singapore, their shadows on the ocean below following them. The decision to disband the Azad Hind Fauj had shaken Rash Behari. 'Who gave Mohan the right to declare the dissolution?' he asked angrily. 'I am the president of the Hindi Swatantra Sangha. He only looks after military affairs.'

'Never mind, it's just childishness.'

For thirty years, Rash Behari had been tormented by visions of his motherland's pitiable condition as an enslaved country and had thought of nothing else but to break her shackles.

How dejected he had been on 5 June 1915 when he had landed at the Japanese port of Kobe. A plot – much bigger than the 1857 action – had failed because of a betrayal. Many of his associates had been sent to the gallows. A message from one of his companions, 'Rash Bhai, keep the flag of revolution flying', was his only asset. And a letter of introduction that he was Rabindranath's secretary. To live alone in Tokyo, a strange land, with an unfamiliar language, was like being told not to breathe. But fortune favoured him and he encountered the famous Chinese revolutionary, Dr Sun Yat Sen.

Dr Sun Yat Sen took the young Rash Behari to Tōyama Mitsuru. The president of the secret society Black Dragon, Mitsuru was the guru of revolutionaries worldwide.

Even from this distance, the desire for revenge against the British did not leave Rash Babu. Since the Japanese government and British politicians were on good terms with each other, efforts to arrest him began to be made from the British Embassy in Tokyo. Pressure was put on the Japanese administration. The issue of Rash Behari's exile was discussed in newspapers and public places. Finally, Rash Behari Bose had to take refuge in Tōyama's palatial residence. Neither the Japanese police nor the army dared to enter his premises. He had earned for himself such a powerful position in Japanese society that no prime minister was appointed without his approval.

One afternoon, a woman called Kakoh Soma came to Tōyama and asked, 'Where is that Indian revolutionary? Hand him over to me.'

'Lady, why are you so agitated?'

Kakoh replied, 'To hand him over to the British would be like pushing him into the jaws of death. Such an act will be unbecoming of Japanese culture.'

At her insistence, Rash Behari went and stayed at her Nakamura house. The lady had a bakery business. For four months, Rash Behari lived in her basement with the smell of fresh baked bread. Secret agents went around the bakery several times. But Madam Kakoh treated them with disdain. She took care of Rash Behari with as much devotion as if he was her own. Although she gave the impression of being fearless, the responsibility did put a strain on her. It began to affect her health. She was not able to nurse her baby any longer. The baby died. Rash Behari went to her bedside and holding her hand, he cried, 'Mother, to protect me you sacrificed the life of your own child. How can I ever repay your debt?'

Gradually, police surveillance eased. Kakoh's young daughter began to look after Rash Behari and he felt secure there. One day Tōyama said to him, 'You take care of thousands of your countrymen. You need someone to take care of you.' Rash Behari understood the import of those words much later. Without asking him, Tōyama asked Kakoh for her daughter's hand in marriage to Rash Behari. She was flabbergasted. After all, she had treated him like a son. Also, his future was uncertain, the threat of deportation still hung over him and above all, there was a huge difference in age between Toshiko and him. She did not know what to say to Tōyama. She asked Toshiko, 'That traveller from a distant land is engaged in noble work. Will you marry him?' At this unexpected question, Toshiko became thoughtful. After a fortnight, she told her mother, softly, 'Mother, let me become one with this idealistic man. Let me serve him.'

That was in 1919. A Japanese marrying a foreign national was unheard of. So Kakoh Soma's decision was considered defiant and an affront to their culture. Marriage was the last thing on Rash Behari's mind. Everything was still so uncertain. He was still constantly under police watch. How could he take on the responsibility of a young girl like Toshiko? He tried hard to dissuade her, but then he did not have the heart to break off ties with Kakoh Soma, nor the courage to disobey Tōyama. Meanwhile, Kakoh fell ill. With her blessings, Toshiko and Rash Behari were married in secret.

In eight years, Rash Behari had changed seventeen addresses. Two children were born to them – a son, Masahide, and a daughter, Tetiko. Looking after the kids, taking care of her mother in hospital, facing up to the police, teaching her husband Japanese – Toshiko had to cope with many things at a time. And they all affected her young mind. On 4 March 1925, Rash Behari was hit by something bigger than an earthquake. Toshiko passed away. Kakoh began to coax Rash Behari to remarry. He said to Kakoh, 'Mother, please don't bring this up again. Divine providence has itself broken my flute. I am forever alienated from those beautiful notes. I see Toshiko everywhere.'

Rash Behari had no doubts that the British stranglehold on India could be broken only through military strength, and in all his letters to Gandhiji, he had tried to convince him of this. In the meantime, war clouds were gathering over the world. When it finally broke out, Rash Behari managed to get together the Japanese who were sympathetic to India's cause. The eighty-eight-year-old Tōyama said to him, 'Rash, I am an old man. Before I shut my eyes forever, I wish to see India free.' Tōyama contacted Prime Minister Tojo and senior military officials. Finally, on 8 December 1941, Japan entered the war. The very next day, armoured military vehicles stood outside Rash Behari's gate. He was escorted by Major Azuki to the Japanese Imperial General headquarters. The imposing edifice of the military headquarters seemed to tell him that his thirty-year-long penance was going to bear fruit.

Rash Behari told the Japanese authorities that he would try and change Mohan Singh's mind, but he did not want them to precipitate matters in the meantime. He arrived in Singapore to persuade Mohan Singh to reverse his decision of disbanding the Azad Hind Fauj. But to no avail. Eventually he gave up and decided to speak to General Bhosale, 'Bhosale saheb, I ask you as a senior military commander – what right does Mohan Singh have to disband the Azad Hind Fauj? No revolutionary army is put together by a single individual's efforts. So how can he dissolve it on his own?'

'It probably reflects his disappointment in the Japanese government,' General Bhosale said.

'But, General, when two countries decide on any policy, it is not always unanimous. Politics is a tricky business. So many factors like time, place, individual attitude, affect the framing of a policy and its implementation.'

Rash Behari was physically exhausted from his exile. And yet he toured all the cantonments of Singapore, meeting officers and appealing to them. General Bhosale was of great help. Gurbaksh Dhillon, Sehgal and Shah Nawaz were quick to follow. Rash Behari managed to persuade them to pledge their support for the cause of India's freedom.

On 29 December, Mohan Singh was called to Iwakuro's bungalow. 'Mohan Singh, your efforts to build the Azad Hind Fauj were commandable. But he who builds a temple would be foolish to break the spire. You will have to take back your decision to disband the Azad Hind Fauj,' Rash Behari told him.

'Impossible!' Mohan Singh declared. 'What kind of treatment did your government give my colleagues? Why did they arrest Col. Gill?'

'I know Mahavir Dhillon and Gill and the stuff they are made of. At least till Subhas Chandra Bose comes to East Asia, we will have to jointly hold the Azad Hind Fauj together.'

'I will maintain my stand.'

'If that is the case, then we cannot hope for even the slightest assistance from Japan. That's why I am asking you to think it over and withdraw your order. It takes years to build something, but only minutes to destroy it, Mohan,' said Rash Behari.

'You are simply a Japanese agent,' Mohan Singh said angrily.

Another meeting between Rash Behari, General Bhosale, the Japanese Iwakuro and Senda was held in the adjoining hall. Rash Behari decided that Mohan Singh should be removed from the post of commander and General Bhosale would take the position. The Japanese arrested Mohan Singh right there. Rash Behari was grieved to see Mohan Singh being led away. He said to Iwakuro, 'Please treat Mohan with respect in jail. He might be impetuous today, but he is a true patriot.' A crucial decision had been taken, but Rash Behari was unhappy.'

Mohan Singh was a simple, straightforward soldier. To command a revolutionary army, one must have a politically astute mind. That was beyond him. Mohan Singh could not lead the Azad Hind Fauj, Rash Behari was too old to handle it. The leadership of a revolutionary like Subhas Chandra was direly needed to realise the aspirations of forty-thousand POWs and thirty lakh Indians in East Asia.'

Subhas and Emilie received Yamamoto in the spacious porch of their bungalow. Yamamoto was delighted by the Indian decor of the living room. Anna helped Emilie in laying out the meal. Yamamoto, impressed by her quiet efficiency, said to Subhas Chandra, 'You are really lucky. You seem to have good servants too.'

'True. People who overcome great sorrow look more cheerful and devote themselves to others,' said Subhas.

'What's so special about this old woman?'

'Her husband was with Rommel's army in Africa. The army has declared him missing in action. She does not know whether he is alive, a POW or dead.'

'Very sad,' exclaimed Yamamoto.

'That's not all. Her older son fell prey to enemy cannons on the Russian front at the very start of his career.'

Anna knew they were talking about her, though the conversation was in English. Her face did not change a bit.

Netaji expressed his concern that the Führer's dreams of vanquishing the Kremlin by October seemed to have frozen in the Moscow winter. It was almost the end of December and there were no signs of victory.

'So when do you expect to find your pathway to freedom, Bose?' asked Yamamoto.

'That's why we are pursuing you. Sir, keep aside your diplomat's role for a while and tell me as a friend, how keen is your government to help us?'

'More than you think. For the last six months, we have been following your movements and reporting back to the government. I have informed them clearly that Subhas Chandra Bose is the torch bearer for Indian independence.

'From the secret information I have, General Tojo, our prime minister, is keen to see your arrival in East Asia. Rash Behari Bose has been after Tojo to get you there at any cost.'

'When will that happen?'

'Soon.'

'May your words come true,' exclaimed Emilie.

After Yamamoto left, Netaji left for the Indian Legion office. It was cold and oppressive. Dark clouds added gloom to his restlessness. Barely had he reached his office when ear-splitting air raid sirens sounded. Several planes of the Royal Air Force dropped their load of bombs over Berlin and disappeared. Göring and other Nazis were convinced that Berlin would never be attacked. Now they found that despite being surrounded by anti-aircraft guns and thousands of searchlights, air raids could not be prevented.

Alexander Werth came into Netaji's room. Both of them were saying the war had reached Berlin's threshold when the door flew open and Emilie barged in. Seeing her ashen face, Netaji felt the ground shake beneath his feet.

'Terrible news. Disaster for Anna.'

'The air raid?'

'No, no. In the building where Anna lives, is a local Nazi office. The chief of that place had issued instructions that the Nazi flag be flown from her balcony window every morning. Today Anna's eleven-year-old son woke up late, so the Swastika was not fluttering outside the window. The members of the party entered Anna's apartment, beat up the little boy mercilessly and threw him on the street.'

'Oh God!'

'Anna and her neighbours somehow managed to take the child to a hospital. He may not survive. I am on my way to the hospital.'

'Wait. You cannot go alone. I will come with you.' Netaji stood up. Alexander Werth stopped him. 'Mr Bose, a VIP like you cannot go there. Protocol.'

'Human life is more important than protocol.'

'It's only a matter of getting the child medical aid, isn't it? I will accompany Emilie. You don't worry.'

Emilie and Dr Werth left for the hospital. Netaji called up Taiji at once. That day's air raid had shaken Wilhelmstrasse. Adam Trott came to see Netaji. Looking at him with scorn, Netaji said, 'Adam, it seems your country has lost all sense of humanity. What more does a poor old woman like Anna have to give to this land? Her entire family has perished for the nation, and now her only surviving child was brutalised because he was slightly late in hoisting the Nazi flag. What kind of nationalism is this?'

Snow continued to fall. The dark clouds seemed to be hanging low. A dispirited Trott told Subhas, 'Hitler must have seen a few antisocial Jews in his youth. Some Jewish young men may have even committed rape. But for their sins, millions of Jews are being punished today.'

'By fanning the flames of hatred, Hitler can never be successful. Adam, I am fed up. Who does he think he is, this arrogant dictator? I have no desire now to meet such an egotistical beast. Try and speak to the Japanese Embassy, and find a way for me to leave.'

'That is not possible, Subhas. The British and American navies patrol the seas. Only with the help of the air force or the navy of an advanced country like Germany will you reach Japan. At present, there is no other way out.'

'That means, whether I like it or not, I have to meet Hitler.'

'Until then, the doors to the East will not open for you.'

Netaji returned to Sophienstrasse late at night. German Radio continued to broadcast Hitler's crude ranting against England and France. Netaji was worried about Anna's son. After a while, Emilie and Taiji returned home. Netaji's heart sank when he saw their pale faces. 'What happened to the child?'

'It would have been better if he had died.'

'What do you mean?'

'His spine is broken. He has been crippled for life.'

All of Germany had become a concentration camp. Netaji was feeling suffocated. He could not understand why Hitler would commit such atrocities on his own people and cause damage to himself in the process. He could not help saying to Emilie, 'I tell you, Hitler will not die from a British bomb. He will die from the grief and suffering of millions of innocent people.'

Twelve

In the picturesque surroundings of Bad Gastein in Austria, Netaji and Emilie were enjoying a vacation. One morning, Adam Trott arrived unexpectedly at their house. That day his grey eyes seemed more eloquent than usual, as if they had something of great significance to convey. The two friends had not been able to meet so openly in Berlin. But here, there were no restrictions on their movements, or their conversations.

'The remains of Hitler's dreams will, like Napoleon's, be scattered along the road to Moscow. I am sure of that. If Germany is defeated while you are here, Subhas, even your life will be in danger.'

'Why?'

'You know, vultures that gather around a dead animal are preferable to victors in a battle. When an international commission is set up to settle matters of compensation and reparation, they will not hesitate to use you as a pawn in their games.'

'How?'

'Suppose Germany is defeated and England is declared victorious, the British will ask the Nazi leaders for Netaji Subhas as soon as they reach Berlin. Do you think a vanquished nation will dare to refuse?'

Anxiety creased Netaji's brow. Trott continued, 'I am telling you this because I don't want to see a dear friend like you being used in such a shameful manner.'

Emilie was listening to their conversation. 'Whatever you do, get out of here.'

'Just as a faint rumbling is heard before an earthquake, so the bastions of Berlin tremble. Hitler is wasting his resources in Moscow's direction in the foolish hope of friendship with Britain. Before Germany is routed, Subhas, please take the giant leap across to East Asia.'

Trott had finalised a meeting with Mussolini. Netaji, Emilie and he waited at a military airport near Berlin for the plane to take them to Rome. Emilie had been under the weather all morning. She was constantly thirsty. The tension in the air made her break out in sweat. Just then, a bomber aircraft thundered down the runway. Emilie began to retch. Netaji quickly held her and led her into the VIP lounge. The officers left the room at once. Seating her down, Netaji began to fan her with his kerchief. Why had she taken ill so suddenly, he wondered. The nausea, the vomiting, the discomfort … and then, in that condition, Emilie began to laugh mischievously. 'Don't look so worried,' she said.

'But your health …'

'These are happy times.'

'I don't understand.'

'It's the patter of tiny feet!'

Netaji held Emilie close, but immediately, his arms slackened. A tiny life was taking shape between them, one had to be careful not to smother it. What a place to hear this – on a rough alien airstrip. Subhas's eyes sparkled. 'Emilie,' he said, with great tenderness, 'Ma should have been here with you now.'

The sentry's voice came through, urgent and loud, 'Sir, the aircraft is ready and waiting, do hurry.'

'I can't leave you alone in this condition, Emilie. I won't.'

'You must.'

'How can I?'

'Because you, my teacher, taught me that duty comes before emotion.'

Emilie held the door open for him and Netaji boarded the plane for Rome.

Once in Rome, Netaji was able to immediately get an appointment with Il Duce, but he learnt that Mussolini had asked Ciano and Iqbal Schedai to wait in the administrative office. Ciano was furious at the importance given to Bose, but he was helpless. A cordial reception was accorded to Netaji by Il Duce.

Netaji told Mussolini, 'We and Schedai can work together. But on one matter, we will never be in agreement.'

'What is that?'

'The question of India's unity,' Netaji retorted sharply. 'I may cut off my head, if need be, but I will never allow any power on earth to cut a chunk off my nation. There can be no consensus on this. No, Duce, forgive me, I speak frankly. I doubt there is a more contemptible word in the dictionary than the word compromise. Once this dreaded disease of division infects one, it stops at nothing short of taking one's life.'

Mussolini took Netaji to the anteroom and seated him there, before allowing Ciano and Schedai to enter. As soon as Bose's name was mentioned, Schedai burst out, 'Duce, why are you entertaining someone as inconsequential as him? After all, the Congress rejected him, the communists suspended him, and Gandhiji even barred him from the party! This trouble-maker has for the past eleven months been treading on Hitler's toes, but Germany did not let his pot boil!'

Mussolini had in the meantime signalled his bodyguard to fetch Subhas from the anteroom. When Netaji turned to Schedai and asked him pointedly, 'Mr Iqbal Schedai, will you answer one question? Tell me, has a Muslim monarch ever sat on the throne at Delhi or not?'

Schedai lowered his eyes.

'Duce, you are a student of history,' Netaji spoke. 'You know well that till this day, not just noble souls like Akbar, Sher Shah and Jehangir, but even tyrants like Aurangzeb have ruled the country. And those were bigoted times where religion was concerned. And yet Hindu–Muslim subjects swore allegiance to their emperors, not to their Muslim identities, but to their identity as their sovereigns, didn't they? Before I left India, I had proposed to Barrister Jinnah that he take over as the first prime minister of free India, only because I wanted the country to remain undivided. Mr Schedai, for the sake of your own selfish interests, don't forget the glorious history and magnificent culture of our country. Do not sow the seeds of communalism.'

Halfway through the meeting, Schedai walked out. Mussolini turned to Netaji.

'Tell me, Mr Bose, what else can I do for you?'

'My future beckons me. Help me to get to East Asia.'

Mussolini said, 'It is a long journey through a war-torn region. You should obtain the cooperation of both Italy and Germany. Then you will get to Japan as a representative of two major Axis powers.'

Netaji agreed. Germany had been a friend. Why create barriers prior to departure? Be a sycophant, flatter the Führer if it serves your purpose.

He said, 'But getting to the Führer is very difficult. There is an impregnable armour around him.'

'Don't worry about that. I will take care of it,' Mussolini gave his word.

Netaji rose to leave. Shaking hands with Netaji, Mussolini said, 'See what the outcome of the meeting with the Führer is.' After a pause, he continued, 'I have some fearless pilots who can fly you straight from Rome to Rangoon. Of course, such a flight is fraught with danger.'

'Let there be no blemish on my moon,' said Emilie, punning on his name, Subhas *Chandra*.

'What did you say?'

'You are going to meet Hitler, after all, that's why,' replied Emilie.

Subhas laughed. He was touched by her concern that his flawless image should remain so. But right now, Netaji was a little perplexed. International diplomatic protocol required that when meeting a head of state, a suitable gift must be offered. But Hitler was such a complex, multifaceted personality – what would be a suitable gift for him, he wondered. Finally, he consulted Emilie.

'Take a rare book or a nice oil painting. They say Hitler was a painter earlier.'

'Those colours have long since fled. Let me see. I'll think of something.'

Ribbentrop had gone to a great deal of trouble to arrange the meeting with Hitler. After changing the dates twice, 29 May 1942 was fixed. It was to be a meeting of people with conflicting views and at cross purposes. The Führer was camping at his military base, Kalfas Chez Nez, in Rastenburg in distant Prussia. On 28 May, Netaji flew to Prussia from Berlin by a special aircraft. Keppler and Adam Trott went with him. Since Netaji was absolutely certain of his mission, he was not in the least apprehensive on his way to the lion's lair.

Ribbentrop waited on a remote airstrip to receive Netaji. He was accompanied by several officers from Hitler's inner circle, all of them eager to meet this leader from India. Netaji was first introduced to Professor Weist by the foreign minister himself. Martin Borman, Hitler's special envoy, was also present.

'Mr Bose, do you happen to have the latest edition of Tilak's *Gita Rahasya?*

Netaji stopped short and stared at him. 'Mr Bose, even today I work as an academic adviser at the University of Munich,' he said, smiling at Netaji's surprised expression. 'Great men from your country like Kalidas and Bhavabhuti have occupied prized positions in my home. Lokmanya Tilak is one of my favourites.'

'How is it you are here?'

'Himmler is a dear friend. Because of him, I got an opportunity to spend some time with the Führer.'

'I am honoured that such an eminent scholar is so close to the Führer!' Netaji exclaimed.

Hitler's close aides, Himmler and Boehring, had been invited to the meeting. Ribbentrop had arranged a banquet that night. It was obvious that Hitler had instructed his officials to extend utmost courtesy to the visiting dignitary.

The momentous meeting took place in Hitler's study at four the following evening. The study was exquisitely furnished, but could seat only a few. Foreign Minister Ribbentrop, Ambassador Havell and Hitler's personal interpreter, Schmidt, were already seated in their respective places. On the wall in front were two large maps – one of Europe and Asia and the other, a similar one that marked out Germany's war fronts. As Netaji stepped into the room with Adam Trott, Hitler welcomed him with a flourish, 'The leader of the Azad Hind!' and shook hands with him. They took their designated seats.

Netaji rose and held out a gift-wrapped box to Hitler. Hitler beamed and excitedly opened it. Inside was a copper-coloured statue. Hitler stared at the bare-bodied figurine. Trott was surprised and amused. There was a Buddha seated in padmasana, the lotus pose, in Hitler's hands. It was an unexpected choice of gift. Hitler kept looking at the statue for several minutes, unable to identify it. Then, flaring his nostrils, he demanded, 'Who is this wrestler?'

'Lord Buddha, the founder of the Buddhist faith. He taught peace, ahimsa, that is, non-violence and compassion.'

'Peace? Ahimsa? Then is this gentleman senior or junior to Mr Gandhi?' Hitler asked, still examining the figure in his hands.

'Your Excellency, he is more senior than us all,' Netaji replied.

In such august company, laughter was unthinkable. Otherwise, Netaji would have held his sides in mirth. Trott could barely conceal the guffaw that threatened to break out of him. Somehow, he managed to keep a straight face. He was rather sorry for the Führer and his ignorance.

At first no one spoke. An expectant hush fell over the room. Who would break the silence? Eyes blinked rapidly. Then Hitler started to speak in German. Trott played the role of interpreter. Schmidt scribbled furiously, taking notes. Hitler's face seemed to be glowing with a strange joy, his sharp eyes gave his personality an incredible magnetism.

With a smile, he asked, 'How was your stay in Berlin? And the work of the Free India Centre, the Indian Legion, is it progressing satisfactorily?'

Subhas had at the very outset expressed his gratitude for the assistance rendered by Germany. Now he explained his role. 'Your Excellency, my desperate desire for a free India dragged me here. That we Indians will have to fight bitterly for our freedom was clear from the start. We are prepared to shed our blood, but we also need the support of friends like the three powers, Germany, Italy and Japan. Only then can we teach the British a lesson.'

Hitler laughed. 'You appear to have won over Italy and Japan already! Of course, that pleases me.'

Like two wrestlers sizing each other up before a bout by throwing a fistful of earth at each other, or a couple of veteran thespians exchanging witty quip onstage, these two men engaged each other in repartee and retort. While even God withdraws in the face of overweening flattery, it was only natural that a mere mortal, a vainglorious dictator would succumb to its charms. Netaji used words like 'old revolutionary,' to praise him. And Hitler, fully aware that it was only hollow praise, still felt a thrill rush through him. 'This meeting marks a most momentous event in my life,' Netaji told him. His sugar-coated words brought a glow to Hitler's fair face, smoothing every wrinkle, and his dark eyes glittered bright.

Again, an ominous silence fell over the study. Then clenching his fists, Hitler spoke in a somewhat harsh tone. 'I get the feeling that the Indian spirit is emasculated.'

'Your Excellency,' Subhas interjected sharply.

'What else?' Hitler spat. 'A huge country of thirty-eight crore people and you allow a couple of thousand outsiders from England to invade your country, bind you, muzzle you for two hundred years? If I had your enormous wealth of human resources, I would have become a world conqueror like Alexander the Great.'

Netaji was infuriated. Everybody watched him in apprehension. But Netaji stayed calm. 'Your Excellency, soon the darkness of slavery will be dispelled. I am completely confident that India will be free soon.'

Hitler's face betrayed no emotion. Subhas reiterated his statement, 'The British have converted my country into an iron-barred prison. Breaking through those bars, a young upstart leader from the same slave nation soars away. With no resources at his command, except an innate faith in his cause, he stands before one of the greatest commanders in the world, shakes his hand and prepares the ground for negotiations. Sir, with this live example before you, how can you accuse India of having lost its manhood?'

Hitler laughed. Then in a provocative tone, he said, 'Be that as it may, I am convinced that I am right. India will not throw off the yoke of slavery for another two hundred and fifty years!'

'That is not true, sir! British Imperialism is going to collapse under the onslaught of this war. We haven't mortgaged our spirit and put bangles on our wrists yet.'

Hitler was somewhat impressed. For a brief moment, he wondered whether a mere Asian youth leader had got the better of him. Picking up the slender cane lying on the table, he rose to his feet, pointed to the map on the wall, and traced the outline of India.

'You see that? How far your country is from Germany? We will not be able to send our armoured troops on a campaign all that way. It will be most impractical. We can only cover that distance by air. However, conditions on the western front are not conducive to such a move.'

'But I think …'

'Just wait till Moscow is demolished,' Hitler butted in. 'Once Russia lies under my feet, it will be easy for me to embark on a rescue mission to India.'

'What does the Führer feel about Japan's entry into the war?' Netaji asked.

'I am not quite clear about their intentions yet. Once Japan is victorious in East Asia, it will not be long before the British Empire starts crumbling. And then the pressure on us is bound to ease.'

'When will Germany directly assist India?'

'Even if we decide to advance towards India's borders, it will take us at least two years to get there. Instead of waiting, we must exploit the situation that has arisen in East Asia due to Japan's offensive. Your

Gandhi and Nehru cry themselves hoarse against Fascism and Nazism, but I don't think anything can be gained by pursuing some eccentric path of non-cooperation or fasting.'

The cane in Hitler's hand flitted around before coming to a halt on the Eastern sector of India, alongside Burma and Imphal. He said, 'We must choose one critical location close to your border from where we can put military pressure on the British.'

Then Netaji debated with himself whether to mention something that had been on his mind for years. In his autobiography, Hitler had made a derogatory reference to India and Subhas had wanted it to be expunged. Mentioning it could have an adverse effect on the negotiations. But not doing so would mean that the slur on the country's image remained. And Netaji's proud spirit could not endure that. The words slipped out of his mouth unwittingly, 'Sir, if in your *Mein Kampf* you could erase that one reference ... otherwise the British will use it to whip up anti-German sentiments among the Indians.'

Hitler, considered this remark impertinent. Although he maintained a veneer of politeness, his fury could not be concealed. 'I have deliberately emphasised that statement in my book as a lesson to my people, so that the slavish mentality of your country does not ever take root in Germany.'

Then swifty, he changed his tone and proceeded to elaborate on Germany's role. 'We have no intentions of reaching your frontiers in the near future. One should show one's strength only over the area covered by the tip of one's sword. If you are headed eastwards, we are prepared to assist you. I accept the request made by Il Duce in this regard.'

A load was off Netaji's mind. Trott threw a stealthy glance of relief in his direction. However, Hitler continued, 'Don't take Italy's counsel as final.'

'How do you mean?'

'Italian pilots may be very brave, but don't attempt to fly to Japan. Your life is too precious,' Hitler advised.

'But hasn't the risk reduced somewhat now?'

'On the contrary, it has increased. If you fly over territories under British domination, they can force you to land. And then anything can happen.'

Picking up a letter lying on the table, Hitler said, 'The Japanese Ambassador Oshima has requested a meeting with me. I will mention this matter to him. It would be more sensible to go to the East by either a Japanese or a German submarine.'

As he was talking, Hitler again swivelled around in the chair and once more faced the map on the wall. With the cane, he traced the likely route the submarine would take, via the Cape of Good Hope, Natal and other ports on the way, explaining that the voyage would take between seven to eight weeks. 'Along the coast of West Africa, the British have erected barricades, laid mines. Bear in mind these dangers too,' he warned. Netaji suspected that the Führer would not be able to offer any military assistance in view of Russia's manoeuvres.

Hitler pressed Netaji's hand and wished him a safe journey.

Once he reached Berlin, Netaji threw a banquet for the Japanese Ambassador Oshima, Gen. Yamamoto and Trott. When Trott told Oshima that the Führer had mentioned him, the ambassador laughed out loudly. 'I wanted to meet him only to discuss the matter of an escort for your friend here, but the poor man doesn't know it!'

Glasses were raised in toast after toast, cigarette-ends glowed. Trott addressed Netaji, 'Subhas, your retorts to Hitler's provocative statements were very clever. I felt proud of you.'

12 February 1942. When Singapore, the invincible bastion of the British, finally fell, Netaji was announcing over the Azad Hind Radio in Berlin, 'The fall of Singapore signals that the sun has begun to set on the British Empire. The dawn of India's good fortune is about to break.'

Once the Japanese troops that had marched into Singapore entered Burma, the road leading into China would be permanently closed. China knew that to avoid being pulverised under the Japanese onslaught, it had to stop their advance at any cost.

That's why Chiang Kai Shek visited India with his wife in February.

He pleaded with Gandhiji, 'Please support the British in this war. Save us from Japan's clutches.'

The flames of war not only made China's mouth go dry, it caused alarm bells to ring in the American Roosevelt's ears too. Rangoon fell on 7 March. Japanese troops began to wander through Burma's pagodas. President Roosevelt warned Churchill, 'If you do not make some drastic changes in your India policy, India will join the Fascist camp. Make haste. Do something.'

Chittagong and Calcutta were not too far away from Rangoon. Fearing a likely Japanese attack, Churchill had to make some moves, even if they were merely token gestures to appease the Indians. It was decided to send a delegation to India under Sir Stafford Cripps.

While the viceroy, his officials and his army spent sleepless nights fearing a Japanese attack, the people of India were listening to Subhas Chandra Bose's speeches being broadcast over the Azad Hind Radio from Berlin. A twin-pronged propaganda campaign was on – from Germany and Japan. The Allies – England and America – could not be victorious now, whispered the walls of the Wardha Ashram to each other.

Within a fortnight, Sir Cripps arrived for talks in Delhi. Discussions with Nehru, Azad and other Indian leaders were held. Meetings with Barrister Jinnah and Dr Babasaheb Ambedkar took place.

One day Cripps, an able individual with socialist leanings, was talking to Gandhiji. The shrewd Churchill had sent him to India because he knew Cripps was a friend of several Indian leaders. Cripps said to Gandhiji, jokingly, 'I hear you are an avid listener of Berlin's Azad Hind Radio these days.'

'You hear right.'

Cripps was stunned by Gandhiji's admission. 'Mr Gandhi, the world looks upon you as a saint, a great godly being. You should have come out strongly against Nazis and Fascists.'

'Before the war started, who had made a pact of friendship with Hitler? England, isn't it?' Gandhiji smiled as he spoke.

Cripps' plan brought some relief to the princely states and the advocates of a separate Pakistan. In that context, Gandhiji told Cripps, 'To accept your proposals would mean cutting India into pieces. If you can offer nothing more than a bankrupt treasury and empty promises for the future, take the next flight out and go home.'

Cripps made no bones about the fact that the talks had failed because of Gandhiji. Immediately, on Berlin Radio, Subhas Chandra Bose was congratulating Indian leaders on the failure of the Cripps Mission.

How should the Congress address the changing scenario? A meeting of the Congress Working Committee was held at Allahabad at Anand Bhavan on 27 April. The atmosphere was tense because a few days earlier Rajaji had acknowledged the idea of Pakistan. Gandhiji sent his message through Miraben. 'The British must leave India. We have no quarrel with any other country. If the Japanese attack us, we will oppose them also with ahimsa.' That was the gist of his message. It came as a bombshell to Nehru and Azad. For the first time, there was a difference of opinion among his favourite pupils. Dr Sitaramayya, Rajendra Prasad, Kripalani and Sardar Patel were prepared to march to Gandhiji's tune.

But Maulana Azad said to Nehru, 'He went off to Berlin so long ago, but still creates confusion in the Congress.'

'Who are you referring to? Subhas?'

'Of course. Why Gandhiji has been heaping praise on him, I don't understand. Even a socialist like Cripps expressed his disapproval of it to me.'

This world-encompassing whirlwind had begun to gnaw away at Gandhiji. He wrote in the *Harijan*, 'For how long do we wait for our freedom? Till the end of the world?' When Gandhiji was in the grip of this turmoil, the famous American writer and journalist Louis Fischer came to the ashram. He was surprised at the pro-Subhas atmosphere there. 'How can you feel so kindly towards someone who has gone over to the Fascists?' he asked Gandhiji rebukingly.

'Because I regard Subhas as a patriot of patriots. He may have taken the wrong path. In fact, he is mistaken. I have opposed him many times. Otherwise, he would have been the Congress president at least twice more.'

At the Congress session in Wardha on 6 July, Gandhiji told Maulana Azad, 'I am going to advise the British to quit India.' He was determined to call for a mass struggle, a peoples' movement. All the Congress members were amazed to see this aggressive side of Gandhiji. Nehru and Azad showed their overt disapproval of the idea. Gandhiji stayed firm. 'I am not going to waver.'

'But the Congress Committee is not ready for such a movement.'

'The Congress Committee is not India,' Gandhiji retorted sharply. 'If you are not prepared, I will go directly to the people. I will give them the slogan, "Quit India".'

Later that night, as Kasturba was massaging his feet, Gandhiji told her, 'Ba, Subhas stood at this door two years ago, begging me to call for a mass movement. Today, when I'm ready for it, he is not there to hear it.'

Gandhiji's mind was made up. 'Anyone who does not like my views may leave the Congress Working Committee,' he declared.

Rajaji, who had already got out, was telling everybody sarcastically, 'Thank God, Bapuji has not donned a uniform and joined Subhas's army.' Sardar Patel accosted Gandhiji privately. Reminding him of the Tripuri days, he said, 'Bapuji, you compelled me to get the twelve working committee members to resign in protest against Subhas.'

Gandhiji laughed out loud. Patel continued, 'Bapuji, do you still feel for Subhas?'

Gandhiji was flustered for a moment. Then he replied, 'How can I say I agree with all that Subhas says? But how can I say that I do not agree with him at all? I too have witnessed the ugly face of the British Empire. I have realised that while slavery is a great curse, British Imperialism is a greater sin. I cannot bear it any more.'

Louis Fischer asked Gandhiji, 'Why are you so impatient to launch the Quit India Movement right now?'

'Why should I answer that question? Go, go and ask Subhas!'

8 August 1942. Gandhiji was addressing lakhs of his countrymen at Bombay's Gowalia Tank. Many incidents from the past twenty years of his political career came to his mind. He had not forgotten his precious dream of Hindu–Muslim unity. In an emotionally charged voice, he said, 'God has reposed the powerful tool of ahimsa in my hands. But sadly, today both I and ahimsa have been put to test. All I will say to the British is, "You go away and leave us to God and our fate. Do not worry that our country will slide into anarchy." We may survive or we may perish. I am giving you just one mantra. Let it come to you with every breath. Do or die.' Never before had anyone heard such inflammatory words from Gandhiji.

Netaji was thrilled to hear Gandhiji's proclamation, 'Quit India'. Over the Azad Hind Radio, he placed before the people a twelve-point non-violent guerrilla warfare programme to complement the August Revolution. He exhorted his countrymen, 'Brothers, our actual national struggle has just begun. Every Indian within and without the country must leap into the struggle. Our companions in the Azad Hind Fauj in Germany are going to be the pioneers on the hallowed path to freedom.'

The August Revolution was much more vigorous than the 1857 one. Sparks were being ignited all over the country. Three hundred and eighteen police stations were burnt down, nine hundred forty-five post offices were attacked, fifty-nine trains were derailed. Jails across the country were overflowing with political detenues. More than sixty thousand people had courted arrest. The oppression continued unabated.

Netaji felt helpless as he sat in Europe, longing to do something drastic, to keep up the pressure of the August Revolution. He told Adam Trott and Alexander Werth, 'Hurry, make haste. Help me leap across into East Asia. Let me embrace my battlefield.'

It was over a month since the meeting with Hitler. No doubt Germany had administrative and ideological problems. In the thick of war, the path between Germany and Japan was fraught with danger. Also, the means of transport were inadequate.

Emilie was pregnant. Her mother had been asking her to go to Vienna, but since Netaji was to leave for East Asia at any time, she was reluctant to leave him.

Three and a half thousand soldiers of the Azad Hind Fauj were prepared to sacrifice themselves on one call from Netaji. A band of Japanese and German friends were accompanying them. But for himself, he needed only Emilie's shoulder to rest his exhausted head on, to soothe the turbulence of his mind, calm the desperation in his heart; and he needed her presence to take down his speeches. She was the one he could trust. That is why she did not want to be far from him.

One day, a message arrived from Rome. On 15 October, an aircraft was due to take off for Rangoon from Rome. Two Italian pilots had volunteered to fly this hazardous mission. Since they had very little notice, packing went on through the night. One of Netaji's bags was full of his travel kit. Emilie began to empty her suitcase for him. She took out a box from it and put it aside. Netaji, curious about its contents, opened it. A pair of embroidered mojris lay in it. 'You had sent me these when you became the Congress president.'

'But why don't you wear them?'

'They will wear out.'

'Footwear is meant to be worn. How long will you preserve them?'

'All my life. Sweet memories of you.'

Netaji's mind went back to that Congress president's procession through the streets of Kalbadevi in Bombay. He had stepped out of the decorated car to buy those mojris. Emilie looked at her delicate white feet and giggled. Netaji shook his head at her innocent joy. The next day, both of them left for Rome.

They had breakfast at Mussolini's official residence. Then they proceeded to Rome's military airfield. A cold wind was blowing from the nearby valley. With great effort, Emilie controlled herself while saying goodbye. Netaji embraced Trott. When he disappeared into the aircraft after waving his hand in farewell, Trott moved back and was talking to some military officials when suddenly someone Trott knew came dashing up to him, waving a copy of the *Daily Sketch* published from London. Emilie saw the headlines, 'Indian Quisling Bose is headed for East Asia aboard an Italian aircraft'. Her knees buckled under her. She clutched her stomach and wanted to scream, 'Stop! Wait!' But no words came out. Trott, stunned for a second, charged after the taxing aircraft, shouting himself hoarse, 'Stop! Stop the plane!' The officer who was going to give the final signal for take-off saw Adam Trott's agitated face and indicated to the pilot to stop.

That night in Rome, Emilie clung to Subhas. For a long time, tears fell, like raindrops dripping from a tender creeper.

'You're going off in such haste!'

'I must, Emilie.'

'Leaving me in this condition?'

'What condition?'

Emilie stared at her feet. Taking her little hand in his, Netaji tried to comfort her. 'What is it? Why don't you say something?'

'Never mind. That was an outburst of the mother-to-be.'

'And this?'

'A dutiful husband's dutiful wife. Practical, sensible. The mother in her, emotional!'

'But tell me, tell me truly, what does the mother-to-be say?'

'What can she say, poor thing! You are going so far away – at least wait till you see your little one's dear face. Its tiny little eyes, its red, pomegranate lips ... that's all she asks.'

Netaji laughed softly. 'You're absolutely right. I will go only after I see my baby's face.'

Emilie looked up in surprise. Gripping Netaji's shoulders hard, she said, 'Please don't even entertain such thoughts. There are enough obstacles in your path as it is. You have a monstrous enemy to grapple with, how can you let your resolve weaken? You said yourself that the opportunity to make history is transient and could easily slip out of your hands.'

A wave of anguish washed over Emilie. She looked like a young sapling drenched in the first monsoon showers. Netaji gently flicked off her tears with his forefinger. 'Emilie,' he said gruffly, 'compared to a baby's innocent smile, the world's deadliest weapons and armouries appear so ineffectual, its dimples make ambitions and aspirations so meaningless. Tell a brave man to resist a hurricane and he will not demur. He will quell a volcano with his power. But where does all his bravado go when confronted with a mother's tears? A mother's love?'

'You are so overwhelmed by my condition!' Emilie exclaimed. 'Please, don't fret about this mother-to-be. I will warn her, "Woman, this is not only about your child – your man is going away to set free thirty-eight crore enslaved Indians, to dispel the darkness that shrouds their future; don't pin down his wings for selfish reasons."'

Four days later, another secret meeting with the Japanese officials took place at Netaji's residence. Gen. Yamamoto had some new information to share. 'The Russian province of Ukraine is under German occupation today. Some aircraft fly to East Asia from there. Right now, that route seems the only option to me.'

'You could take a Lufthansa or a Russian Air flight from Ukraine,' said Oshima, 'but this journey will have to be undertaken at night. Also, it will be quite risky.'

Almost helplessly, Netaji said to Yamamoto, 'So what if it's risky? "Live life dangerously" is my motto. So tell me, when are you scheduling the onward journey?'

Yamamoto and Oshima looked at each other uncertainly. Oshima mumbled, 'I'm not very sure if our department of foreign affairs will give permission to take this route.'

'Why?'

'If Japan approves of this plan, it will be a betrayal of Russia. It does not fit in with our scheme of things.'

'Tell me once and for all what your scheme of things is!' Netaji growled impatiently. 'You come up with ten problems at one time – either a plane is not available, or you can't locate a submarine. Above all this, there are restrictions imposed on your naval forces. Really, why don't you state clearly whether you want to get me across or not, and be done with it?'

This meeting too ended inconclusively. That night Netaji tossed about like a beached fish. In the outer room, M.R. Vyas was busily typing an urgent message. Just then the phone rang. Picking up the receiver, Vyas shouted, 'Netaji, phone from Tokyo. From Rash Behari.' Hearing those words, Netaji scrambled out. Hope, impatience, anticipation flashed their vivid colours across his face.

'How are you, Subhas?' Rash Behari's voice came from afar.

'This exile is intolerable, Rash Babu! I am desperate to come to East Asia to gather INA and leap towards the borders of India.'

'Come, Subhas, come to the East quickly. Thirty thousand prisoners of war have been watching the streets at Farrer Park for your arrival. The ocean is heaving, the vessel is ready, it only needs a fearless captain like you.'

The line went dead, abruptly ending the conversation. But the important news had been exchanged. Subhas threw aside the receiver. With a passion, he embraced Emilie. She shrugged off his arms and stepped back, exclaiming, 'Careful! You forget there's a baby inside me.' Chastised, he gently stroked her belly, then laid his ear against it.

'What do you think it will be, a boy or a girl?' asked Emilie.

'A girl.'

'Why do you say that?'

'Instinct,' Subhas replied. 'I have always been fascinated by womanhood and its manifestations – like the goddess Kali Mata, Mother Earth, the Rani of Jhansi. Not for nothing is woman called Adishakti, the primal power.'

After a short pause, he continued, 'Emilie, what name shall we give our little one?'

Emilie couldn't help laughing. 'So soon you want to decide?'

'Yes! What about Anita?'

'Why? Why that particular name?'

'What's the point in revealing all the secrets at once? Will tell you some other time.'

Till late into the night, they talked, about their baby, their future. Finally, Netaji managed a couple of hours' fitful sleep. Even as he woke, he muttered, 'I'll have to find the way myself.' And the search for a new direction began.

It had snowed through the night. Outside the bedroom window, the ledge was piled with snow. The wind whistled and trembled to its own rhythm. But inside, a fire raged.

Emilie, who had fallen asleep, woke with a start to see Subhas leaning against the wall, staring outside, as if in a trance. All round him was a scatter of cigarette butts. Emilie got up and held Netaji close. Suddenly, some recollections of the past prompted him to speak. 'Before departing from India, I had gone to Nathalal in Bombay. At two o'clock in the night, we were strolling along Marine Drive, listening to the sounds of the ocean. Some strange thought ran through my mind then. I asked Nathalal, "What kind of death is that, if it is death at all, that comes to one laid up with an illness?" What do you think, Emilie?'

'True, it's a very ordinary way to die – to die of a disease.'

'Compared to that, if one should die in the service of one's motherland, while flying high in the sky, how sudden, brave and beautiful a death it would be, no?'

Emilie screamed and slapped him across his mouth. Just then wave after wave of pain shot through her. Her face turned white and her whole body was drenched in perspiration. Gently, Netaji gathered her in his arms. He felt awfully guilty for speaking of such unseemly things when she was in a delicate condition. Taking a big gulp of water, Emilie said, 'Don't ever say such things again. I will cross heaven's threshold long before you. Your Azad Hind Fauj has yet to march to Delhi, you have to be united with the star of your dreams, Lal Qila, and Gandhi and Nehru, and the lakhs of people who love you dearly ... You have said so often that gaining independence is only the first step. The second and more important one is the reconstruction of the free nation. Who will permit you to retire before your cherished vision of India, not only as a free country, but also as a culturally, socially and politically powerful nation, is realised?'

Netaji, Trott and Dr Werth went to Paris to meet Prime Minister Pierre Laval. Emilie was now in her seventh month. Taiji often came over to help, but since she was an important member of the Red Cross, her responsibilities had increased. Netaji had to shuttle between the Indian Legion office, the Annaburg POW camp and the Japanese Embassy. As a result, it had become unsafe to keep Emilie with him. With the help of some friends, Netaji managed to send Emilie by a special military carriage to Vienna.

The idea of taking the aerial route to East Asia had to be abandoned. Travel by submarine was decided. But the Japanese Navy kept raising all kinds of objections to this plan. To sort out the matter once and for all, Netaji and Trott presented themselves at the Japanese Embassy. There they learnt that Gen. Yamamoto had already departed for East Asia via Russia to prepare a welcome for Netaji. Yet the administrative hurdles could not be overcome. Netaji flared up at Ambassador Oshima.

'Once the Prime Minister of Japan has given the green signal, what is the delay about?'

'We have not received the consent of our navy.'

'And why not?'

'You can find out for yourself on the wireless radio if you like.'

Netaji got into an argument with senior naval officers in Tokyo. From across the oceans, one of them said, 'You will not be able to travel by submarine.'

'Why?'

'It is a naval vessel. No civilian is allowed to board it.'

In sheer frustration, Netaji handed the receiver over to Trott. Again, the same arguments, the same exchanges. The Japanese officer was stating unequivocally, 'Subhas Bose may be a very great man, but according to the rules, no civilian can go on board a military submarine. Even if the prime minister himself orders it, it cannot be done.'

'He is not simply a civilian, gentleman!' Trott thundered. 'He is commander-in-chief of the INA.'

Those three words changed everything. Immediate consent was obtained from the other side. Once more, the wheels were set in motion.

On 29 November, a baby girl was born to Emilie. Subhas was still in Berlin when he received the joyous tidings. When Emilie first set eyes on the fair little bundle, she was overjoyed. All these days, she had been so preoccupied with being a prop for Netaji's life's mission, she had not given much thought to her child. But now, this angel from heaven would become a precious part of herself. Since Netaji's plans to set off for East Asia were progressing rapidly, everyone believed that this time, things would go according to schedule.

One night, Subhas turned up, unexpectedly, from Berlin. His joy knew no bounds as he stared at his ten-day-old baby with her crinkled eyes, her tiny hands and feet. Leaning forward, he kissed the little face, over and over again.'

The hours just evaporated like a camphor flame. It was time to return. Grimly, he turned to Emilie. 'In the next fortnight or so, I may have to leave for East Asia.'

'I'll be there to bid you goodbye!'

'Don't be silly! Don't even think of doing something so foolhardy,' Netaji warned.

It was bitterly cold outside. But the cold in Netaji's heart was much greater – it was the cold of separation from his daughter and his beloved. As he got ready to leave, he cradled the infant gently in his arms, and like a cloudburst, his emotions gushed out of him. The little one, wakened by his arrival, was now fast asleep. As he removed his finger from her tiny fist, Netaji felt as if an avalanche of sorrow swept over him. On the one hand the silken bond of a father's love held him back, but on the other, the harsh reality of filial duty beckoned him.

Netaji was startled out of his sleep by the persistent ringing of the doorbell. Someone was tapping on the glass pane of the outer door.

A gust of cold air rushed in. What he saw turned his blood to ice. A woman stood on the doorstep. He could not see her clearly in the pale-yellow light of the street lamp. Her overcoat was sprinkled with snow, as were her boots. The chill had crept into her and she was shivering uncontrollably. From the way she breathed, Netaji guessed it was Emilie. And he was stunned. Barely out of childbirth, what was she doing here?

'Emilie, you? Here?' said Netaji harshly.

'Yes. The train was late.'

'But alone? Where's my little darling?' An edge crept into his voice.

'In Vienna, snug in my mother's arms.'

'What a heartless, cruel woman you are! How could you leave that six-week-old infant and come away?'

'I heard that you were leaving for Asia in the next few days. Like a bird, you would have flown away. Who knows how long it will be before we are together again.' Emilie sounded like a stricken sparrow, every word wrenched out of her.

Quickly Netaji lit the fire in the living room. He threw in a couple more logs to make it blaze. Emilie ran a brush through her damp hair and scattered droplets of water around her. She stood by the fireplace, gathering the warmth inside her as she dried her hair. From the corner of her eye, she watched Netaji.

Emilie had no home – all of Europe was ravaged by the war. There was no telling where the next bomb would drop. Some bold British planes had dared to make several sorties over Berlin. They had screamed their warnings. Berlin had become truly unsafe. Netaji had been preparing for flight. But he could not, rather, did not want to, tell anyone where he was going, how and for what. Though one day he did say to Nambiar, 'Nambiar, from now on you will have to look after the affairs of the Indian Legion.'

'As you wish, Subhas babu.'

On 23 January, Netaji's birthday, several visitors, all uninvited, came to Sophienstrasse – P.B. Sharma, Narhari Ganpule, Balkrishna Sharma, N.G. Swamy, Abid Hasan, Gurbachan Magnet and Taiji. A flag hoisting ceremony was conducted in their presence. This simple ceremony had now acquired a special significance. In his address, Netaji said, 'Perhaps I may have to go to Paris or Tripoli for some time. The war front needs to be reviewed. It is likely that we will not meet for a long while.' As he spoke, his voice thickened with emotion. Soon after, Taiji went inside. She could see an unusual expression in Netaji's eyes. Uncertainty about the future had caste its pall. The experienced Taiji was not to be fooled so easily. She took off all the gold ornaments she had on, almost half a kilo, and handed them over to Netaji. Tremulously she whispered, 'May our Dr Tendulkar's Mother India become free soon.'

Sleep eluded Emilie. The last three days had been so depressing. They had slept for barely a couple of hours each night. Preparations had to be made for departure. Through the night, two pairs of desperate eyes were locked with each other. On the last night, their hearts seemed benumbed. 'Emilie, how do I take leave and of whom? Do I say goodbye to my very breath, with whom I exchange my deepest thoughts every day? Or to those eyes which, with silken threads, weave beautiful dreams to bind me? My heart wishes that this ethereal night never ends. But what can be done? The dawn must break, a new day must come, and for that, through the womb of night, this journey must be undertaken.'

As Netaji picked up his bags, his warm breath came in sharp, short gasps. His heavy feet were reluctant to move. He held Emilie in his warm embrace once more. Their imminent separation seemed to have affected everything around them. The only sounds were of passionate breathing, silent sobbing. Words sulked on the edge of lips and refused to be voiced. Emilie rested her chin on Netaji's arm. It remained buried there for a long moment. Then suddenly, she screwed her eyes tight, gave herself a hard shake, and broke away. 'Come along,' she whispered, 'I'll go with you.'

'It's all right, some people are accompanying me to Kiel port.'

'I didn't mean till the German port, till Japan.'

'What? Of course not, you silly girl!'

'Yes, I'm coming with you, I am,' Emilie exclaimed desperately. 'I will be your shadow.'

'Take a hold of yourself, dear. Our little bud has yet to grow and blossom.'

Netaji seemed to have stumbled over something. 'The Russian expedition is going to prove disastrous for Hitler. Germany may have to face defeat. If that happens ...'

What if Germany were vanquished? What would happen to Emilie? To whom would she turn? What if something happened during the voyage and he were to be captured? Who would take care of her? The anxiety was killing him. Even the lamp in a storm has the breeze for company, but in the whirlwind of war, what am I doing, leaving her to her own devices? Netaji took Emilie's cold hands in his and said, 'Very few are aware of our secret marriage.'

'Yes, I know,' said Emilie, as a sob escaped her.

'I have many enemies like the all-powerful and mighty British Empire. I don't want you to suffer at the hands of anyone. That's why I've tried so hard to keep our marriage a secret. But at this critical juncture, I wonder, was my decision of concealing our marriage a mistake?'

Emilie was silent. She had suffered derisive laughter and swallowed snide remarks about young women associating with some foreign revolutionary, without protest. But now she snapped. Her hackles rose. Some deep wound surfaced, stinging her. Her shoulders shook in huge racking sobs. Netaji was startled by this unexpected outburst. And bewildered. 'What is it, my love, tell me the truth. Upon my life, you must speak the truth ...'

Emilie slipped away and returned with a carefully preserved piece of paper which was given to her by Dr Werth. She thrust it into Netaji's hands. Netaji read through the missive of the British Intelligence officers. There were several references to his sojourn in Berlin, but one sentence caught his eye. 'Mr Bose stays in the area of Sophienstrasse in Berlin. His Austrian mistress Miss Emilie Schenkl lives with him.'

Netaji was stricken. Gradually, the sparks of rage burnt out and were replaced by angry tears. Somehow, he managed to stem the tide of emotion. 'Emilie, in nurturing my life's dream, I have wronged you gravely. For so long you have held this burning ember close to your heart, concealed it, why? Why did you put up with it all, the censure of Nazi friends, enduring the depression, the war-ravaged times, caring little or nothing for the enemy, only to be insulted with crude words like mistress and concubine?'

He restlessly paced the living room. Then stopping in his tracks, he said to Emilie, 'Some day, people in India too must understand the true nature of our relationship. Otherwise, with the passage of time, needless misunderstandings may arise.' He went to his desk, hastily scribbled a few lines on a sheet of paper, and gave it to Emilie.

It was addressed to Sarat Bose, Subhas's favourite older brother.

> *Dear Mej-da,*
>
> *Once more I have put my life's boat in jeopardy. I am setting out on a hazardous journey. Should I not return or should something untoward happen, you must know what the situation is. This letter is to put you in the picture.*
>
> *I have got married here in Europe. We also have a jewel of a baby daughter. Just as you gave me your boundless love and care,*

and nurtured me, protected me from harm these many years, I beg you to shower the same on my wife and my child should anything happen to me.

Subhas

Wiping her tears, Emilie folded the sheet of paper as Netaji instructed her. 'Don't lose it, keep it safe, even if you have to guard it with your life.'

Before daybreak, Netaji completed his puja and chanted some hymns from the Bhagavad Gita. He was ready to leave. But his feet were reluctant to cross the threshold. As if he had remembered something, he went into the bedroom and from the wardrobe, brought out a box. He opened it gingerly as if it were a treasure chest. And what a treasure it held! A red-beaked, emerald green talking parrot, a little red-faced monkey that clambered up and down a tree, a scarlet uniformed trumpet major and a toy princess blissfully asleep on a bed of down. 'Give this to my princess when she grows up. She is sure to lisp, where's my Papa. At that time, make sure you tell her I have gone out on an important mission. But the moment it is done, I will rush like the wind to gather her in my arms and shower her with a million kisses.'

Emilie cried. 'When will I see you again?'

'In Delhi, at Lal Qila!' How confident his every word was.

The train for Kiel was due to leave Berlin Station in a short while. Most of the bogies were loaded with war supplies. In the VIP lounge, Netaji waited, smoking cigarette after cigarette. The previous night, Adam Trott had said he would not be able to come to see him off. Netaji had had no time to ask him why, so now he was wondering if Trott was annoyed about something.

Just then, like a character from a mystery movie, a gentleman in a large felt hat and long overcoat entered the lounge. He looked like he had something urgent to say. Netaji recognised him.

'Subhas, you don't know what a big risk I have taken by coming here,' Trott said. 'Why, what happened?'

'All these days I successfully ran the underground resistance movement against the Führer. But I am afraid this secret might be out soon.'

'What?'

'The Gestapo has put me under surveillance.' Trott's eyes glinted with vengeance. 'Subhas, God should be with us a little longer. Once Hitler is finished, I don't care if I am sentenced to death a hundred times,' he said, gripping Subhas's hand tightly.

Netaji told Adam to take care. Then suddenly he remembered that Adam had asked him to write a draft proposal for Churchill. He said, 'Adam, what happened to that draft?'

Adam laughed heartily. 'What can I say, my friend. You sealed my fate.'

'How is that?'

'My guru Sir Stafford Cripps was most impressed by your English. He showed the draft to Churchill who also praised it and then said, "I cannot believe that a German can write such excellent English." This draft will become a historic document some day.'

'Nothing wrong with that,' said Netaji.

'The best part is yet to follow,' laughed Adam. 'Was this draft written by a revolutionary or was it a trap laid by the German enemy, Churchill wondered, and entrusted the task of finding out to the foreign minister, Anthony Eden.'

'And then?'

'British secret agents in Berlin informed Eden that Adam Trott and the Indian leader Subhas are very good friends. That draft has been written by none other than Subhas himself.'

'Oh my God!'

'The words that he had praised immediately assumed the threat of a spearhead. The hand that was raised to help me, stopped midair. Instructions were issued to that effect. It is said that he told his officials that any friend of Subhas's can never be a friend of the British Empire. Adam Trott must be a Nazi.'

Just then the train's whistle was heard. Netaji and Adam embraced each other. Adam said, 'I will continue to fight so that my German brethren can breathe freely. May your country also be free soon.'

On 8 February 1943, a fleet of submarines was anchored in Kiel Harbour. Netaji took leave of Alexander Werth and Keppler there. When he turned towards the submarine, the young Abid Hasan was stunned. His beloved leader had sent for him from the military camp one day and asked him if he was prepared to undertake a dangerous mission.

For ten days after that, nothing happened. Once earlier, it was planned, to send Abid on Haj to persuade Indian Muslims to join the movement. Others whispered that he was going to Greece to start a branch of the Indian Legion in Athens. That's why the sight of a submarine surprized him.

As soon as they stepped into the submarine, all the charms of this shimmering fish-like object vanished. The interior was damp and reeked of diesel fumes. Fortunately, there was an independent cabin for officers, but without a door or any comforts. The blankets and sheets were damp and smelt of diesel, as did the breakfast the cook served them. Netaji laughed and said, 'Anyway, we are observing a fast today!'

Cutting through the water, the submarine sped along.

Netaji took out a small portable typewriter and told Abid that he intended to utilise the journey to rewrite his book, *The Indian Struggle*. As Netaji dictated, Abid began to type.

It soon became obvious that the submarine carrying Netaji was a part of a convoy of seven or eight other subs. After a while, the captain of the submarine, Werner Mussenberg, came to see Netaji. Abid asked him, 'Will the other submarines accompany us all the way?'

'No, they are an escort only for a few days.'

Captain Werner enquired if Netaji was comfortable. The clock showed that it was dusk. From the portholes of the submarine, all one could see was ink-black darkness. Suddenly, the submarine shot upwards. Abid's heart missed a beat and his typing came to a halt. Seeing his alarmed face, Werner explained, 'Nothing to fear. Every night we will be riding on the surface.'

'Is that mandatory?'

'It is, so that the batteries of the submarine can be recharged. It is dangerous, but necessary, since the batteries do not last more than forty-eight hours.'

Two bombers flew overhead as they were speaking. This was a risk they had to take. Wishing Netaji goodnight, Werner went away.

They crossed the shores of Christianshab as they sailed towards the north of Scotland. That entire region was a high-risk zone. Every so often, they could hear the muffled blasts of bombs exploding in the water. Captain Werner was steering the submarine with great caution.

As the days went by, lethargy spread through their bodies from lack of exercise. Intensive patrolling of the seas continued. As they sailed near the Atlantic, they saw ice floes in the water. It was a beautiful sight. The fleet finally reached Cherbourg in France for refuelling.

On the next leg of their voyage to Africa, something strange happened. One evening they sighted a British cargo vessel. Immediately, the captain brought the submarine to the surface. Scared of an attack from it, the submarine launched an offensive. The oil tank burst, the oil spilled and caught fire. The leaping flames thrashed through the water like an angry serpent.

They encountered another enemy cargo ship off the coast of South Africa. Capt. Werner asked, 'Shall we blow her up?'

'Why not?' said the crew members.

The submarine shot to the surface. But the cargo vessel proved to be more powerful. The submarine was a little chick compared to its elephantine proportions. While Werner was making up his mind, the cargo ship spun around and charged at the submarine. The terrified crew felt as if they had entered the jaws of death.

'Dive! Go under!' Everyone was shouting. But it was not so easy once the submarine was on the surface. Somehow, it managed to slide out of reach of the cargo ship.

At last, they crossed the Atlantic. Henceforth, enemy threat would be considerably less. It was no longer necessary to remain submerged during the day. Also, the speed of the submarine had gone up, so their destination seemed to be approaching more rapidly.

By this time, they had got used to the smell of diesel, though the two-foot-by-five-foot space was very stifling. Netaji continued with his reading and writing. His mind was active all the time. He was constantly thinking about the future course of action once they reached Japan. Abid had to, on several occasions, play the role of Prime Minister Tojo. Netaji would hold discussions with him, read maps, pinpoint important locations on the Burma, India and China borders, plan the deployment of troops and trace their route to the India front. The dress rehearsal was as serious as the real event.

On 26 April 1943, the Japanese I-29 quietly slipped into Mozambique harbour. Captain Mesao Teraoka stared at the turbulent ocean grimly. The Portuguese had their base nearby, but no one had a clue of the I-29's presence. They had left Penang six days ago on the pretext that enemy ships had entered those waters and had to be destroyed. Captain Teraoka said to his colleague, Negishi, 'The responsibility of taking Bose back safely is weighing me down.'

'When naval officers started buying cinnamon, pepper and pickles in the Penang market, some people became curious, some even got suspicious,' Negishi replied.

Captain Teraoka had just put his eye to the periscope when in the distance, he sighted the German submarine. They too found the I-29's location. Both the vessels began signalling each other.

When Captain Teraoka was convinced of its identity, he began to move forward slowly and up. Suddenly they surfaced. As did the German U-boat. Both were measuring each other up. It was late. The ocean heaved and swelled. The heavy clouds had touched the water and darkness tightened its grip. It was not at all wise to disembark in these conditions. Deciding to wait until the seas calmed down, the two subs headed north-east.

The dawn of 25 April was frightening. The sea was still very rough, bubbling and seething like a cauldron of boiling oil. The red-eyed sun seemed to glare at the world. They had no choice but to wait. The two subs began to circle each other.

This must have been the longest day of Netaji's life. Fortunately, no enemy aircraft came within sight that day. Night too was almost over. The crew of both vessels began to feel that the God of the ocean was testing them out.

'We may run out of fuel,' said the captain, swallowing hard. Netaji's eyebrows rose. 'Two days more like this and we could face a crisis,' Capt. Teraoka added.

After midnight, the waves began to fall, almost miraculously. Faces brightened. Breath came easier. They waited for sunrise. Negishi alerted Capt. Teraoka. 'Captain, look ahead!'

'What?'

'Two men from the German U-boat have dived into the water and are swimming towards us.'

Japanese ropes hauled the two swimmers on to the deck. The captain and crew welcomed them aboard. 'Brave soldiers, we salute you,' Capt. Teraoka said to them.

'We have some information that enemy planes are on a race mission. It is important to turn back as soon as possible.'

The two submarines came as close to each other as possible. A rope was thrown across and fastened. Between them, two huge inflatable floats were suspended. The sea was not fully still yet. Waves lashed at the float. But the mission had to be completed as quickly as possible.

Netaji said goodbye to the German captain and climbed into the float. Abid Hasan followed. The submarines kept rocking back and forth to prevent the floats from colliding. Holding on to the rope and pushing the float, Netaji and Hasan inched their way to the I-29.

A long hour later, the dripping wet, red-eyed Netaji and Hasan clambered on to the Japanese submarine. They were greeted by enthusiastic applause. Netaji wrote a brief note – 'Mission accomplished'. The German sub rushed back with the message.

The Japanese submarine was much larger and more spacious. After almost two and a half months, Netaji got some hot rice, vegetables and pickles. It tasted heavenly. The next day, 29 April, was a joyous occasion – the Japanese emperor's birthday. Everyone celebrated with glasses of sake.

Somehow, the map and the compass were at variance with each other. Netaji was startled. He told Negishi, 'According to me, we are definitely not heading for Penang.'

'You are right. We are going to Sabang. It is further away, but we have no choice. The news of our landing at Penang has already broken there. Naval Headquarters have warned us to be on full alert.'

'We have been instructed by the prime minister himself not to forget that the visiting dignitary is accorded the status of a head of state. It is our job to escort him safely to his destination.' Captain Teraoka told Netaji.

Thirteen

Like a caged lion, Netaji paced up and down. He told Lt. Gen. Arisue, 'For how long do I have to stay confined in this hotel? Did you bring me here from Berlin to place me under house arrest?'

Lt. Gen. Arisue had no answer. It was a fortnight since Netaji had come to Tokyo. Across the road from his suite was the Habia Park, and beyond that, the wide expanse of Shaan Hill. The magnificent buildings that housed the office of the Japanese prime minister, the emperor's palace and the army headquarters were all located there. The centre where all important policy decisions on military matters were taken was also in the same area. And yet, nothing seemed to be happening.

Gen. Yamamoto and Lt. Gen. Arisue sat there dejected since they had no answer.

Netaji, making Gen. Yamamoto the object of his displeasure, said, 'You have forgotten all the promises made in Germany, it seems.'

'Sir, you misunderstand ...'

'Oh no, I understand very well. I had heard that the Japanese are cold, but you are colder than ice. Do you think I came here because time hung heavy on my hands?'

'Prime Minister Tojo is too engrossed in his work to meet anyone.'

'In that case, arrange for my return immediately.'

Netaji was impatient to take the struggle into its next phase. He had to meet Tojo. To organise the battle troops. To set eyes on Delhi. How long was it all going to take? The ramparts of the Red Fort, with the tricolour fluttering proudly above it, his brave companions standing before it, their chests swelling with pride, singing the song of freedom – that's all he could think of.

Was this going to be a repeat performance of his stay in Germany where Hitler had made him wait endlessly? His patience had worn thin, and Gen. Yamamoto bore the brunt of his ire. A nervous Yamamoto informed the foreign affairs ministry. Immediately, the foreign minister, Shigemitsu, and his chief of staff, General Sugiyama, arrived at the Imperial Hotel to meet Netaji.

One day, Abid Hasan rushed into his room. 'Netaji, Rash Behari Bose has come,' he said. A shudder seemed to shoot through Netaji. He had arrived that morning from Singapore to meet Subhas. Though age had caused Rash Behari to stoop and his skin to wrinkle, it had not dimmed the glint in his sixty-three-year-old eyes. Rash Behari embraced Subhas.

'Subhas, thirty lakh Indians in East Asia have been waiting for your arrival. Finally, you are in the Land of the Rising Sun. I welcome you.'

'Rash Babu, since boyhood, I have been hearing the bugle of rebellion that you have been blowing.'

'That fire is now ashes. Age.'

'What you call ash, we consider it sacred angara. We want to smear ourselves with it and ignite the fire of revolution.'

Rash Behari then explained to Netaji the achievements of the INA, and told him about the irregular and convoluted ways of Japanese politics. 'If you had come to East Asia just one year ago, things would have been so different!' Rash Behari said regretfully.

'Why?'

'Your arrival is a little delayed. The Axis powers, Germany, Italy and Japan, are not in as commanding a position as before. German and Italian forces are entrenched in the deserts of Africa. German troops have abandoned the Russian campaign midway, and retreated ignominiously after being beaten at Stalingrad. Prime Minister Tojo too is under great stress.'

'Perhaps he is annoyed about the Mohan Singh episode? Babuji, what do you think of Mohan Singh?' Netaji asked.

'Considering his age and lack of experience, the task he was entrusted with was impossible for him. And then he was let down by his friends like Mahavir Singh and Gill.'

Along with Rash Behari, Anand Mohan Sahai, Manibhai Doshi, A.M. Nair, Murthy, Narayan, Vinayak Supanekar and several other leaders and workers got drawn into Netaji's movement in Tokyo. Rash Behari also took Netaji to meet the elderly Tōyama Mitsuri, who blessed him, 'Before I die, may your country become free.' When Netaji finally went to Rash Behari's house, it was as if the festivals of Dussehra and Diwali were being celebrated together. Rash Behari's daughter, Tetiko, welcomed him in the traditional manner and his thirty-year-old son, Masahide, was all dressed like a prince, so much so that Netaji nicknamed him 'Bharat Bhushan'. He had just become a commissioned officer in the Japanese Navy. Netaji said, 'Son, how handsome you will look when your uniform is decorated with the Indian colours!'

'I am eagerly waiting for that moment, uncle,' he replied.

'That day is not far away. But for now, do well in your job with the Japanese Navy. The training will be invaluable for India in the future.'

Toshiko's photograph had been placed in a basket of roses, and when Rash Behari looked at his departed wife, his heart felt heavy. He told Netaji how she and her mother, Kakoh Soma, had looked after him. Many Japanese women had made such sacrifices for India, he said, and that is why he was able to lay the foundation for the Azad Hind Fauj. His words transported Netaji to the distant shores of Vienna, where his daughter and wife were.

Twenty days went by. Prime Minister Tojo invited Netaji to his office. Although he knew that Subhas Chandra Bose was a top-level leader, he had been putting off meeting him. In view of the conflict within the Indian community, especially the rivalry between Mohan Singh and Rash Behari, he thought the Azad Hind Fauj would be another unnecessary headache. He also felt that Indians did not have either the resources or the mental strength to undertake a powerful movement.

Prime Minister Tojo's personality did the military uniform proud. His longish face with a razor thin moustache gave him a stern appearance, but he was quite talkative. He was a leader of that faction of the armed forces that was totally devoted to the Japanese monarch. For the last three years, he had been leading the Japanese military operations as prime minister and war minister. Tojo had signed a pact with Germany and Italy, but had never set eyes on either Hitler or Mussolini.

'Japan must have thought of attacking India before this?' Netaji said, a small smirk on his face.

'No, never!'

'Something like that was definitely brewing in army circles a couple of years ago.'

Tojo's laugh was an admission of the fact. Netaji said, 'No Indian would have consented to exchange one bond of slavery for another. Besides, considering our ancient cultural and ideological ties, it would have been most unbecoming of you.'

'What do you think of our plans to set up military bases on the borders of Burma?' Tojo asked pointedly.

'Definitely praiseworthy. That way you can control the aid America is receiving from China.'

Tojo's suspicious gaze was trying to size Netaji up. Had this man, recently arrived in his capital, been reading top-secret military files, he wondered. Seeing a civilian's knowledge of military strategy and geography, everyone was surprised.

When the subject of British Imperialism came up, Netaji became emotional. He said, 'The British Empire must be shattered. Only then the poor countries of Africa and Asia will breathe freely. British politicians including Churchill extol the virtues of humanism and then trample over our freedom.'

'Does accepting military assistance from foreign nations fit in with Gandhiji's philosophy of non-violence?' Tojo asked.

'I am not concerned about that. My primary duty is to free the thirty-eight crore brethren from the shackles of slavery.'

'But you have turned to dictators like Hitler and Mussolini for help …'

'Why only dictators! I will not hesitate to make a pact even with the devil for the freedom of my country. Because my conscience tells me that even the devil cannot be as deceitful and treacherous as the British.'

Tojo, who had been reluctant to meet him, invited him for another discussion in four days' time.

16 June 1943 was a momentous day in Netaji's life. Japan's parliament, the Diet, was holding its 82nd session, presided over by Emperor Hirohito himself, and Netaji had been given a seat of honour in the distinguished guests' gallery. Finally, he had abandoned his disguise as Masuda and

assumed his true identity – as Subhas Chandra Bose. Welcoming him, Prime Minister Tojo began, 'That India is still being crushed under Britain's imperialist feet, is disturbing. We not only sympathise with Indian people's desire for freedom, we wish to see India prosper and flourish. To enable them to achieve their goal, I as the prime minister, pledge to assist Subhas Chandra Bose in every way possible.'

Once the Japanese policy on India was announced, the business of the special session was over. Most Tokyo newspapers carried headlines about his arrival and traced his career through the past several years. That night when over Tokyo Radio, thirty lakh Indians in East Asia heard the booming voice declare 'This is Subhas Chandra Bose speaking' and the slogan, 'Inquilab zindabad!' once again, they almost became hysterical. The next day onwards, the precincts of the Imperial Hotel were crowded with Indians waiting to meet Netaji.

At receptions and over the radio, Netaji carried out his exhortations. 'I am not very far from India's borders now. Come, let us all prepare for the final assault. So many of my revolutionary brothers, languishing in jails across the country, are eagerly awaiting my arrival in India.'

Subhas expressed his ideas, and the Japanese carried them out. He had been in Tokyo for forty days and the congratulatory telegrams were still coming from Singapore. Now he was waiting to get to Malaya. The night before he left for Singapore, his speech was broadcast over Tokyo Radio. 'Let us launch one lethal assault on our common enemy, match sword for sword, dagger for dagger. Only if the people of India go through a baptism of revolution will they obtain the sweet fruit of freedom.'

Netaji, Rash Behari Bose, Abid Hasan and Gen. Yamamoto came to the Japanese military airstrip, their every word, action and bearing reflected a renewed fervour. Not only in Tokyo, but throughout East Asia, he had received such immeasurable acclaim that Subhas seemed to have become the leader of leaders, the mahanayak of the new era. At the airport, journalists accosted him; the European ones were persistent with their pointed questions. 'What kind of political system do you intend to introduce in the India of tomorrow – democracy or dictatorship?'

'Disciplined democracy,' Subhas retorted.

'How can you sit in a dictator's den and talk about democracy?'

The barb hurt him deeply. He stopped in his tracks, turned around and replied sharply, 'What right have they, whom you all refer to as the custodians of equality, to make tall claims about democracy with their feet resting firmly on the heads of twenty per cent of the world's population, that is, the Indian people? How does Stalin, who lavished fulsome praise on Hitler till yesterday, raise his voice today in favour of a people's war? Why does Churchill, who could not bear the odour of communism, today joins hands with Stalin? It is pure expediency. Besides, had not England, the advocate of humanism, signed a pact of friendship with Hitler just four years ago? Where was your democracy then?'

Netaji's reply silenced the reporters. But one of them still asked, 'Have you forgotten the atrocities committed by the Japanese in China, Mr Bose?'

'I still condemn those acts. But today, if Prime Minister Tojo and his country offer assistance, I will have no compunctions about accepting it.'

During the flight to Singapore, Netaji said to Prime Minister Tojo, 'I want to set up an interim government in India as soon as possible.'

Rash Behari Bose and Subhas were having a conversation in Bengali. As if recalling something, Subhas asked, 'Is it true that Japan had planned an Imphal campaign?'

'Yes, it was called Operation 21 and planned by Col. Hayashi.' Rash Behari laughed.

'Why was it abandoned?'

'Gen. Mutaguchi, an able and brave officer, felt it was impractical. He was the stumbling block.' Rash Behari continued, 'Before your arrival in Japan, an important meeting was called to discuss the Imphal campaign. Since I have some close friends in the army headquarters, I got this confidential information.'

'If it is so, I will discuss it with Prime Minister Tojo.'

'Do not be hasty. There is a big anti-Imphal group among the senior officers. So it is better to be cautious.'

During the flight, Rash Behari filled Netaji in about Gen. Renya Mutaguchi, Lt. Gen. Masakazu Kawabe and Count Hisaichi Terauchi. A little while later, Rash Behari Bose suddenly took ill. Subhas gave him some medicine he was carrying. He sweated profusely. He said to Subhas, 'I have had no rest since the explosion in Chandni Chowk. Now I am tired. You take charge of everything.'

'Don't talk like this again.'

'Truly, Subhas, I am exhausted.'

'Rash Babu, what can I say to you? A true revolutionary never gives up. We still have much to learn at your feet.'

All the eminent Indians living in Singapore had gathered at Kallang Airport to welcome Netaji. Among them was the only lady doctor in Singapore, the young, attractive Lakshmi, from Madras. Also present were a group of Hikari Kikan officials and several officers of the Azad Hind Fauj with their commander Col. Jagannathrao Bhosale and Capt. Shah Nawaz Khan. Shah Nawaz kept glancing at his wristwatch and the clear blue sky alternately. Unable to contain himself, he said to Col. Bhosale, 'For three days now, we have been hearing that Netaji is arriving ... how can we trust them?'

Gradually, everyone was gripped with uncertainty and mistrust. Subhas had better come today, they thought. The white clouds began to darken. Suddenly, through the clouds, came the shrill whine of a bomber aircraft followed by the silver plane. The airport sprang alive. Everyone stood still, tricolours fluttering in anticipation. The plane taxied to a halt and pulses began to race. All eyes were fixed on Subhas. Dressed in a milky white suit, carrying a dark brown felt hat in his left hand, Netaji alighted on Singapore soil to take his first salute. To the bugles and drums, he marched forward with measured steps. He accepted garlands and bouquets, shook hands with Col. Bhosale, Dr Lakshmi and Barrister Yellappa. When he began his address with the Hindi words, 'Saathiyon aur doston,' ears pricked up. 'I will not make a long speech. All I want to say to my fellow Indians is that I am delighted to be among you. Let us together endeavour to set free our motherland.'

The next day, thousands had thronged the Cathay Cinema Hall to see their favourite leader. The hall was packed and the crowds spilt over into the streets. At 10:30, a convoy of motor cars arrived with much fanfare, and from the cars alighted Subhas, Rash Behari and Col. Bhosale. The sky was filled with cries of 'Mahatma Gandhiji ki jai!' and 'Subhas babu ki jai!'.

The theatre broke into thunderous applause as soon as Netaji entered. Behind the dais were pinned the Japanese flag and the tricolour.

The Azad Hind officers waited expectantly for Netaji's instructions. Yellappa had left no stone unturned to make this meeting a tremendous success. The idea of an interim government had been buzzing around in Netaji's head ever since he had left the country. Using Burma and Singapore as a springboard, he wanted to take a mighty leap and vanquish the British Empire. Jamadar Ram Singh's mellifluous violin accompanied the sweet voice of Saraswati who sang:

Subhasji, Subhasji,
Jan-e-Hind aa gaye,
Hai naaz jinko Hind pe
Woh maan-e-Hind aa gaye

Once more the audience was stirred. As Prime Minister Tojo's message was being read out, all eyes were scrutinising the two Boses on the dais. While one was a veteran of the First World War, the second was burning to shape the course of the Second World War on the Eastern front. If Rash Behari appeared like an old edifice, Netaji stood out like the sharp peak of a tall mountain. As he stood up, it was obvious that age had taken its toll on the exhausted Rash Behari. He stood up and taking the audience into confidence, he reminded them that he had promised to bring them a precious gift when he next came that way. 'You will ask me where is that gift?' Pointing at Netaji, he smiled and said, 'There's your gift.' His words evoked spontaneous applause. He looked around the hall again, then narrowing his eyes he said, 'In the last fifty years of exile, my body has become tired. It is the good fortune of our struggle that I have found the most capable pair of hands to take over the reins and fly the flag of rebellion. Today, I hand over the presidentship of the Hindi Swatantra Sangha to a younger, more efficient revolutionary, who will be your leader, your guide, who will take you to victory and glory. Inquilab zindabad! Azad Hind zindabad!'

Immediately after Rash Behari Bose, Col. Bhosale took the stage and publicly pledged the support of the entire Indian Army to Netaji. An overwhelmed Netaji took the mike into his hands and paid a tribute to Rash Behari Bose. 'The younger generation may not know it, but ever since we were children, we had heard of the daring exploits of Rash Babu. Doubting your love for your country would be equivalent to a son abusing his mother. You may say you are tired, but we aren't going to let you off so easily.'

Addressing the three thousand representatives from East Asia, Netaji said, 'Friends and compatriots, for the past two years, I have wandered through the remote and distant corners of the world. I have had close encounters with the war. I am convinced that however drawn out this war is, it will end in the breaking up of the French and the British Empires, and the triumph of India's freedom struggle. The British Empire is already in the death throes. The British are running around with a begging bowl. Their propagandists are plagued by fear about the amount of help India's allies like Germany and Japan would give us. But I have faith in the new declaration on Asia that the Japanese have recently announced.' Netaji's impressive voice, affected the audience deeply.

When the prophet meets the lord, divinity radiates out of his every pore ... That's how Netaji felt at that moment. What he had studied for, striven for, sacrificed for, throughout his life, had bloomed and blossomed. Sketching the demonic rule of the British, he told his countrymen, 'Today, we are in the final phase of our journey to freedom. A hard struggle lies before us. Our enemy is as deceitful, cruel and ruthless as he is strong. You will have to face hunger, thirst, arduous travel, all kinds of atrocities. But once you get over this hurdle, it will not be long before the vistas of liberty and freedom open up before you. So are you ready to join me on this mission?'

An official of the Hikari Kikan was taking down Netaji's speech. He was worried that Netaji's remarks would be detrimental to Japan's policy. Netaji, obsessed by the idea of freedom, continued in his intrepid fashion, 'It has become our primary duty to establish an interim government in order to take our nationwide struggle to its logical and successful end.' The Hikari Kikan official turned pale at this utterance.

At dinner that night, he whispered to Netaji, 'Your Excellency, your remarks about the interim government were rather inopportune this morning.'

'Why?'

'Because the Japanese government has not accepted this idea on principle.'

Shah Nawaz and Col. Bhosale were watching Netaji at the table. Many choked on their food. Netaji picked up his glass and had a sip of water. Then looking directly at Gen. Yamamoto, he said, 'Do you expect me to seek your government's permission before I take each breath?

Enough is enough. Gen. Yamamoto, your only job is to look after protocol and liaison. Since you brought it up, let me make it very clear, I had mentioned this matter to Prime Minister Tojo before boarding the aircraft to come here.'

Netaji ticked off Gen. Yamamoto keeping in mind the fact that he was a friend from his Germany days. But Yamamoto left in a huff soon after dinner. Shah Nawaz was delighted by Netaji's unequivocal speak. He told Prem and Dhillon, 'Put all doubts to rest now. Let the British plant hazards in our path, or the Japanese their cunning. We have finally found the man who will take us towards our cherished goal – we have found our mahanayak!'

Netaji was to be felicitated at the Padang Ground in Singapore, and the mayor's bungalow was abuzz with the preparations. Orderly Devi Singh answered the insistent phone and handed it to Netaji.

'Saheb, Japanese headquarters.'

'Subhas Chandra Bose? This is Staff Officer India from Japanese Command.'

'Yes?'

'Our Prime Minister Tojo is likely to visit Singapore either today or tomorrow.'

Netaji was surprised. He had met Tojo hardly ten days back. Why would he want to follow him to Singapore?

Netaji's car drove through Singapore's streets. Rash Behari and Col. Bhosale were with him. The tricolour fluttered proudly on the bonnet. An escort of fifteen army personnel on motorcycles flanked the car. Following them was a convoy of army vehicles carrying important officers of the Azad Hind Fauj. Singapore had not yet recovered from the effects of the war.

Standing on the stone platform of the Town Hall with tall majestic pillars and graceful arches were several members of the Indian Independence League. In front of them was the spacious courtyard. A black tar road separated Padang from the blue sea beyond. The setting was perfect. On the green lawns sat thousands of Indian soldiers, their weapons beside them. On the dais were a huge picture of Bharatmata and a life-size oil painting of Mahatma Gandhi. Netaji alighted from his car, accompanied by Col. Bhosale, Rash Behari Bose and the Japanese official, Kunizuka. The audience was impressed by Netaji's military uniform. He stood up to speak.

'Tell me, how many of you are prepared to embrace death in the service of our motherland?' Netaji's question received instantaneous response. Rifles were raised and cries of 'Chalo Dilli!' 'Onward to Delhi!' reverberated through the Padang Ground.

Netaji carried no notes, no papers, he spoke from the heart. 'George Washington fought for American independence and won it because of his military strength. Garibaldi could fight for the unification of Italy only because he had the support of his brave army. Ours is a great and glorious nation. But we are weak and crippled because we do not have our army with us. Now you have kicked aside the last obstacle in our path!'

For almost two hours Netaji spoke. Rash Behari Bose was so moved by his oratory, he was seen surreptitiously dabbing his eyes with his handkerchief. Netaji continued his impassioned speech. 'Brothers, what can I give you in the present circumstances? Only hunger, thirst, privation and death. But trust me, friends, in the darkest hour of defeat or the brightest moments of victory, I will stand alongside you.'

There was not a dry eye in the audience. Many were so carried away that they felt they were already in the precincts of the Red Fort. Gradually the troops began to move forward to the army band, saluting Netaji as they marched past – first the tanks, then the armoured vehicles, gun carriages and then, the armed battalions.

After the parade, Netaji remained there. About a hundred and fifty officers of the Indian National Army drew up chairs and sat around him. Netaji spoke to each one of them individually – where they came from, what batch they belonged to, their home and family, what they wanted to do. And then he told his colleagues, 'In a couple of days, the Japanese prime minister is coming to Singapore. We must hold another parade in his honour. Show him that the Azad Hind Fauj soldiers are not to be trifled with.'

Bidadari camp was abuzz. Lunch was being cooked for the soldiers in separate kitchens, and the soldiers waited at their respective messes with their plates and bowls, tired and hungry after the morning's exercise. As they were about to be served, the guards began to sound the alert. Everyone was perplexed, but soon after, Netaji's car drove up to the mess, and Col. Bhosale and Col. Zaman Kiani followed him. He responded to the greeting, 'Jai Hind!'. Then he sent for the quartermaster to discuss the menu, the quality of food and the conditions in which it was prepared. In the meantime, the soldiers had taken their places in their respective messes – Sikhs, Muslims, Madrasis, etc. None of them paid much attention to what was being served. They were waiting to hear what Netaji had to say. In a voice that was audible across the hall, Netaji said, 'I would really like to sit beside you and share your food.'

'Come here, Netaji,' 'Sit with us, Netaji,' the different groups cried out. 'How can I? Look how you are divided ... When I challenge the British, my strongest argument is about the unity of India and its people. But here, in our dining hall, look what has happened. If we cannot eat together, how can we go into the jaws of death together? What do you say, Kiani? And you, Pritam Singh? Shah Nawaz? How can we fight the common enemy?'

'What do you want us to do, Netaji?' Pritam Singh asked.

'Just give the command and it will be obeyed,' Zaman Kiani spoke up.

'Do you think I should fight for a unified India?'

'Yes, of course!'

'Then break these boundaries. Let all food be cooked in the same vessels and all soldiers eat in the same mess. We must be careful about how we tread. If we aren't, the British will pick up any slip we make and twist it to their advantage.'

'Netaji zindabad!'

'Inquilab zindabad!'

That one gesture, and all distinctions of caste and creed were wiped out from the INA. A contented Netaji declared that food hadn't tasted so good in a long time.

Later, he visited the military hospital and spoke to each patient, offering solace and reassurance. Then he went to the office of the Indian Independence League. Barrister Yellappa and Dinanath who were there asked Netaji, 'Why did Japan decide to offer help to us so hastily?'

'As long as the British have us under their heels, their empire in the East will continue to flourish. But if they are cornered in our country, then Japan's influence in the eastern hemisphere will increase. Even if not philanthropy, pure selfish interests have made Japan rush to our aid. When an Asian brother extends a hand of support, should we scorn it?'

'Netaji, I must apologise to you,' said Shah Nawaz.

'What for?'

'I have sinned. I have been insidiously trying to split the Indian National Army from within.'

'And now ...?'

'Not only in the Azad Hind Fauj, but even later, I will fight to uphold India's integrity till I die.'

Netaji smiled. Even the strongest opponent to the idea of the INA was gradually coming under the spell of Netaji's persuasion. All dissenters, fence-sitters, some from Rash Behari's group, others from Mohan Singh's, now shared a new enthusiasm.

6 July 1943. The *Shonan Times* had announced the public meeting Netaji was to address at the Padang Ground, and people from as far away as Ipoh, Penang, Alor Setar had congregated at the venue, many seeking vantage points atop buildings, trees, wherever they could catch a glimpse of Netaji. The venue was packed with journalists, photographers and visitors from many countries. Many Indian women came with their little ones in their arms. It was the first time such a crowd had gathered for an individual's address.

After some patriotic songs were sung, Netaji stood up to speak. 'To take our gigantic struggle to its logical conclusion, we must set up an interim government. All the Indians in South Asia must come forward. We need manpower. We need money. We need sufficient supplies of rations.'

For an hour, Netaji spoke. As darkness fell, it began to pour. A mild stirring was seen, but no one really moved. Netaji's speech was reaching a climax. The rain became heavy. A volunteer went forward with an umbrella and held it over Netaji's head. But Netaji brushed it aside and continued to speak. Warning the audience, he said, 'Friends, four days ago, my brave soldiers took the oath that they will continue to fight until they successfully tie the garlands of victory on the ramparts of Red Fort. "Chalo Dilli" is their motto. Let the thirty lakh Indians of South Asia cry out in unison, "*Karo sab nichhavar, bano sab fakir*".'

Breaking into Hindi, he asked the gathering, 'Tell me, for the sake of freedom, will you sacrifice everything?'

'Yes! Yes! Netaji, we will give our lives!'

After an hour and a half, the meeting ended. Inside the hall, Netaji and members of the Indian Independence League sat around, drenched, marvelling at the response to Netaji's call. The lines before him were growing longer. Women came forward with the gold jewellery they were wearing. Netaji gratefully accepted it and thanked them with folded hands.

A frail old woman in a simple sari came up to Netaji, with three crumpled rupee notes in her hands. Shah Nawaz and Bhosale wondered what Netaji would do. Obviously, she had very little besides that money. Netaji ought not to accept it, they felt. The woman held out the money and said, 'Here, take it. It's all I have.' Tears trickled down Netaji's cheeks. He accepted her offering with folded hands.

Later that night, Shah Nawaz asked Netaji why he had taken the old woman's money, though he had been moved by her plight. He said, 'I agree, it was a dilemma. While I was aware of her financial condition, I could not ignore her sentiments. Had I refused her money, she would have believed that only the rich and the important have the right to contribute to India's freedom. To tell you the truth, those three rupees are much more precious to me than the lakhs that come from an overflowing treasury. The India of my dreams is enmeshed in the sweat and toil of people like her.'

Padang, 9 July 1943. Preparations were in full swing to receive the Japanese prime minister. Once again, the tricolour and the Japanese flag adorned the stage. The INA had rehearsed the parade to perfection. The ceremonies opened with the sweet strains of Ram Singh's violin. Then the tall, handsome Major B.S.J. Bhurewal took the stage to enthusiastic applause from soldiers. He had been an instructor at the Swaraj Institute in Penang which Barrister Raghavan had started. He sang in his distinctively Punjabi accent.

Sar par tiranga jhanda
Jalwa dikha raha hai

Ho teri sar bulandi
Jo chand asma hai …!

Prime Minister Tojo did not understand the lyrics, but the sincerity with which Major Bhurewal expressed his love for the country touched his heart.

'Who is this officer, Your Excellency?' he asked Subhas.

Netaji looked at Zaman Kiani, who replied, 'Major Bhurewal. From the Punjab Regiment.'

The march past was impressive. Soon the armoured vehicles rolled past, the tricolour fluttering proudly. Netaji's face had a beaming smile. But before they knew what was happening, the flag got entangled in some electric wires and was yanked out. It fell under the tanks that were following. Netaji turned red with fury, his whole body trembled. Prime Minister Tojo noticed, took his hand in his and reassured him, 'Don't worry, Bose. It is a small thing. Japan is behind you at every step, don't forget.'

That night, Prime Minister Tojo hosted a banquet for Netaji. Before proceeding to the dining room, he invited Netaji into his private quarters. The conversation was informal and cordial. Then the subject of atrocities during war came up. Netaji told Tojo that Japanese reputation had been sullied because of what their troops had done in Manchuria and China.

'Atrocities during a war are an inevitable evil. Do you mean to say that our troops are inhuman and British-American soldiers are holy padres?' Tojo retorted.

'How do you mean …?'

'The atrocities committed by British and American troops in Manchuria, the Philippines and other islands in East Asia are neither few nor far between. I can give you innumerable examples of repeated rapes of innocent young girls. The "taxi girl" racket is perpetrated by British soldiers here in Singapore. The morbid eyes of the children born out of such liaisons tell their own story.'

'But they claim you are a cruel dictator …'

'Forgive me, Bose,' Tojo interrupted. 'At least as a friend, do not count me in the league of Hitler and Mussolini. Their struggle is driven by personal ambition and greed for power. All my efforts are for the Emperor. Nothing is more precious to a Japanese than his Emperor.'

A pile of letters in Tojo's beautiful handwriting lay on the table. Seeing Netaji's glance falling on them, Tojo explained, 'They are letters to my dear wife, Katsuoka. No matter how busy I am, I always think of her and my little grandchildren, and however late it is, I write to her. Helps me pass the long lonely nights.'

Netaji stared speechless at Tojo. Like a Japanese wrestler, Tojo had a smooth-shaven head, bright, piercing eyes behind his spectacles, sharply pointed moustache and a tall, slim build. The strain of the position he held was evident on his face. He had been trying to set up a Japanese sphere of influence to unite all the eastern nations. Netaji was surprised to see this sentimental side of Tojo, who was known to the world as a ruthless military leader. Dinner was announced. Smoothening down his tunic, Tojo asked, 'Where is Bodh Gaya?'

'In the state of Bihar. Why?'

'I have been wanting to visit that holy place with my family. Maybe someday, when the war is over ...'

There were many important Japanese military officers at the banquet. Lt. Gen. Kawabe of the Burma area army stood out because of his versatile nature and impressive moustache. Tojo introduced him to Netaji. Next, he met the stocky, much decorated Gen. Mutaguchi. Netaji was taken aback for a moment and then he was angry. He was responsible for Japan withdrawing the Imphal campaign. Netaji was keen to talk to him. When he came face to face with him again later that evening, Netaji asked him, 'General, was the Imphal campaign – Operation 21 – abandoned because of you?'

Sipping his drink, Mutaguchi replied, 'Circumstances were such, Your Excellency. Imphal, Chindwin, Kohima ... they are marshy, densely forested, impossible terrains – frightening to even look at, forget about waging a war there!'

'Even so, we should have braved the odds.'

'Had there been proper tracks or even footpaths, I would not have hesitated.' Netaji's unconvinced expression made him continue, 'Mr Bose, have you heard of Brigadier Wingate?'

'The young British officer of the Chindit fame?'

'Yes, the same. Daring fellow, airdrops troops and animals into Burma's jungles, builds temporary airstrips, troubles our army personnel endlessly.'

A drunk Mutaguchi flung his empty glass down, startling all the guests. He turned to Netaji and invited him to the tent in the neighbourhood. Netaji asked Col. Kiani and Major General A.C. Chatterji to wait outside. Mutaguchi seemed more relaxed in the privacy of the tent. 'The plans are ready, Mr Bose!' he announced. 'We will give the Allied forces a blow-for-blow reply. Finish off the American and British strongholds on the Indo-Burma border. We will destroy the air-base and cut them off from all communication and transport. That is my Imparu, I mean Imphal Campaign Objective.'

Amazed, Netaji asked, 'That means Operation 21, which you had opposed, has been revised and redrafted?'

'Yes, absolutely. It will give me an opportunity to get even with Wingate and Churchill.'

'When did you plan it? When will it be executed?'

'Go and ask that drunken Field Marshal Terauchi. He is the commander-in-chief of the Southern Army, and a close relative of the Emperor's.'

'He opposes it?'

'Well, he neither supports nor opposes it. Like him, our military headquarters at Sudan Hill in Tokyo are sucking on a lump of salt. One group in the army thinks my plan is unrealistic. I honestly believe that the reins of this campaign should be handed over to me. I am confident that I will ride my horse through the town of Imphal in triumph.'

Netaji took Mutaguchi's hand proudly in his own.

During the dinner, Rash Behari took ill. Netaji took him to the bungalow. He was due to leave for Tokyo the next morning. Thanking him, Netaji said, 'Rash Babu, your information was accurate. Operation 21 is ready on paper.'

'Don't worry. I will not remain inactive in Tokyo. I have been a frequent visitor to Sudan Hill and the emperor's palace all these years. I will continue to pester them. You keep up the pace of your work. Not just Imphal, now even Delhi is not far away.'

Netaji was very happy after meeting Mutaguchi. He sat on the terrace of his house, watching, listening to the waves, late into the night. He was thinking of the maps of India and Burma. Along their borders, six hundred miles long and two hundred miles wide, was a belt of thick forest, high mountain peaks and deep gorges. Mighty rivers like the Chindwin, Salwin and Irrawaddy flowed through it. It was infested with leeches, and mosquitoes carrying the germ of malaria. To top it all, its annual rainfall was between seven hundred and eight hundred inches. The only paths were animal tracks. The animals and the terrain were completely hostile to human beings. Japanese and Azad Hind Fauj troops had no choice but to traverse this land to reach their destination. The ramparts of the Red Fort were beckoning Netaji. Turning to Zaman Kiani, Netaji said, 'Speed up the training. We must have a fit and able force ready.'

Good fortune was smiling on the mayoral bungalow on Singapore's Malcolm Road. The vacant bungalow had acquired a new personality since Netaji had moved in. The murmur of the ocean beyond the backyard and the fresh sea breeze kept him company all day.

It was an imposing building. On the ground floor was a large and spacious drawing room with a high ceiling. A circular staircase led to the upper floor where there were several rooms occupied by important officials like Netaji's publicity secretary S.A. Ayyar, personal physician Dr D.S. Raju, secretary Abid Hasan and stenographer E. Bhaskaran.

This estate, spread over five to six acres of coconut and other palm trees, looked cheerful now. The narrow stretch of golden sand shone like a necklace around the house. Copper and yellow oleander blossoms were in full bloom, adding glow to the garden. The iron gate was guarded by five sentries in shifts, round the clock. In the front courtyard stood a fleet of three cars and six motorcycle escorts. Netaji had been accorded the status of a head of state by the Japanese government. And one band of Hikari Kikan officials was deputed to ensure that there were no slip-ups.

An important meeting was in progress on the upper floor that day. E. Bhaskaran and the Japanese bilingual interpreter, Kakitsubo, were making notes. That day's meeting was attended by the head of the women's wing of the Indian Independence League, Mrs Chidambaram, Barrister Yellappa and John Thivy. Also present were the famous Gandhian writer and journalist from Kerala, Kesava Menon, and Swami Balasubramanyam of the Ramakrishna Math of Singapore.

The subject under discussion was the controversial Mahila Sena or the women's army. Kesava Menon said, 'Netaji, it was all right for you to have referred to the women's army at the last meeting. But to put it into practice is not advisable.'

'Mrs Chidambaram, do you not think that women, too, should carry guns?'

'Of course, I think they should,' said Mrs Chidambaram, hesitantly. 'But in practice, Netaji, men dominate this field. They will be flustered by the idea of a women's regiment.'

'Not "they will be", we already are! Hands which should make embroidery, paint rangoli patterns, put guns and pistols in them!' Kesava Menon exclaimed.

'Why not, Menonji?' Netaji asked him.

'Forget our country, can you show me any other nation in the world that has entertained the crazy notion of establishing a women's army, Netaji?' Kesava Menon's voice rose with indignation.

'Hadn't our mothers and sisters participated in Gandhiji's salt satyagraha, promoting khadi, picketing?'

'Subhas babu, why are you trying to equate yourself with Gandhiji? He never stood at Japan's threshold.'

'Menonji, I crossed over to the devil's door because of the inhumanity of the British. Even the devil cannot be as treacherous as them. And I have explained my actions innumerable times,' Netaji replied sharply.

'Then this discussion is pointless.'

Kesava Menon departed in a huff. Everyone wondered if it would affect Netaji's mood. Netaji addressed them all. 'No, there is no such army anywhere in the world. But does that mean we should not move ahead? Ahilyabai Holkar, Chandbibi, Raziya, Jhansiwali were born in this soil. Here, Yashoda brought up Krishna and Jijabai raised her Shivaji. If this glorious land will not support a women's army, where else will it happen? Call it eccentricity, but I am determined to realise this dream, whatever the cost.'

Mrs Chidambaram had tears of joy at these words. Others too were overwhelmed. Now, Netaji was only awaiting a message from the Japanese camp.

While the meeting was in progress, Gen. Yamamoto rushed in and handed an envelope to Netaji. 'Bose,' he said, 'our leaders found the idea of women marching with rifles on their shoulders strange and ridiculous.'

'Naturally!' Netaji retorted. 'Had Japan produced one Jhansi ki Rani, the idea would not have seemed so bizarre.'

The waves were high that night. Their continuous crashing and heaving made Netaji restless, yet he was resolute. The sails would not rip, no matter how strong the wind. The ship would sail forward. Yellappa said, 'We will start with four women. Eventually they will become four hundred.'

'Why four, Yellappa saheb? Just one bright spark is enough to start a blaze,' Netaji told him confidently.

'Fortunately, there is one such – Lakshmi.'

'Who, Dr Lakshmi Swaminathan?'

'Yes, our Ammu Swaminathan's daughter.'

There was hardly anyone in Singapore – Chinese, Malayan or Indian – who did not know the name Lakshmi. Lakshmi, the only lady doctor in Singapore, was much loved and highly respected, as much for serving the poor and the needy, of all communities and races, as for her vivacity and her striking good looks. She had inherited her sense of service from her aristocratic family.

Years ago, a young man named S. Swaminathan went to Madras to seek his fortune. Fighting adverse circumstances, he became a barrister. And a very successful one of his time. Ammu, a simple village girl, came into his life as his bride. She was twenty-three years younger than him. Barrister Swaminathan achieved the feat of having the unlettered Ammu tutored in English first and then sending her to study further in England. Ammu was the first Indian woman in Madras to ride a horse and drive a motor car. Her two daughters were Lakshmi and Mrinalini. The first found her calling in medicine, the second, in dance. Lakshmi was married to a pilot with Tata Airlines. However, within six months, her marriage crash-landed and a heartbroken Lakshmi accompanied one of her classmates, K, to Singapore where she settled. Her patients came from all parts of India and were poor labourers, wealthy traders and affluent business families. She had joined the Indian Independence League through her association with Barrister Yellappa and Kesava Menon. K disapproved of her social work, but she was fully involved with the people for whom she worked.

Yellappa returned with Lakshmi. However, all day and much of the evening, Netaji was engaged in meetings and discussions. It was midnight when he finally looked up from his desk. He looked into Lakshmi's expressive eyes and asked, 'Lakshmi, will you accept a challenge?'

'Just say the word, Netaji.'

'The very religion that does not wish even the sun's gaze to fall upon the faces of its women and advocates the use of a burkha, produced the rebel daughter Raziya Sultan. You know of her?'

'Raziya Sultan ... the first woman to occupy the throne of Delhi.'

'She called for a jehad against male domination. There was unity among the Hindu and Muslim brethren. In our country, we have at least nineteen crore women. If this enormous resource is awakened, British Imperialism will be struck at its roots. Tomorrow's world will rest not on the Sesha's hood, but on power of women. For the sake of our country, let Raziya's spirit flow through your body. Pick up boldly the sword that fell from Jhansiwali Rani's hands. Blow into the smouldering volcano just once and infuse life into it.'

Lakshmi stood up and bowed to the paternal figure of Netaji. Netaji invited her and Yellappa to dine with him. At the table, the emboldened Lakshmi asked Netaji, 'How is it you have so much respect and regard for women?'

'My guru Deshbandhu took his wife, our Basanti Ma, to the streets on a satyagraha. All of Bengal was simmering with the idea of revolution that time. Besides, it was also Vivekananda's teachings.' Netaji was all fired up. 'Let our army be formed, then see how divine providence will bless it and grant it success.'

Barrister Yellappa assured Netaji that Lakshmi would be up to the task.

'Will you be able to recruit at least a hundred young women for a start?' Netaji wanted to know.

'If I really try hard, I could gather five thousand women,' Lakshmi told him confidently.

'So when will you begin?'

'Tomorrow.'

Dawn was about to break. Barrister Yellappa got into the car to escort Lakshmi home. She seemed to be totally under Netaji's spell. 'What a great man he must be to carry these magnificent dreams in his heart. And yet, he is so simple. He never imposes his will on anyone. Every step he takes is so carefully thought out.'

'Yes, his personality is like that – captivating. Our practice, mine and Barrister Goho's, is worth at least two–three lakhs a month. But since Netaji stepped into Singapore, we have not entered the courts. The briefs are gathering dust.'

'Then what happens to your clients?'

'They too are following Netaji like us.'

'I feel so confident that this man's feet will not falter on life's slippery slope. I hereby commit my life to Netaji's call,' Lakshmi declared.

Barrister Yellappa, Dr Lakshmi and Mrs Chidambaram were all in a tizzy. Netaji was due to visit the women's wing of the INA in four days. They wanted him to have a unique reception. Yellappa suggested that they offer him a purse as a token of their support for his cause.

'That we will, but we must also give him a welcome befitting a military regiment of women,' Lakshmi said, with an unusual gleam in her eyes.

Everyone admired her zeal. But how was she going to muster such a big women's group? Even today, girls did not go to school. The burkha was very much in use. How would those women who did not even step out of their kitchens, march on the battlefield, weapons in hand? Yet, Lakshmi was undaunted. Netaji's colleague N.G. Swami had recently returned from Germany. She had sought his as well as Abid Hasan's support to get her army together.

What uniform should the women wear? They went to Netaji for advice since they could not decide. N.G. Swami said, 'The charm of the traditional sari is quite extraordinary.'

'But you cannot wear a sari and perform the military drill, nor can you move nimbly,' Lakshmi said.

A solution was slow in coming. Netaji was thoughtful. Then turning to Lakshmi, he asked, 'Is your decision firm?'

'Yes, why?'

'Then I will give you just one example. When the Rani of Jhansi fell fighting a bitter battle with the British, her blood-soaked clothes were those of a man soldier.'

Getting women to enroll was not easy. While they readily gave up their jewellery in response to Netaji's call, the very idea of stepping out of their homes or sending their girls out to the battlefield bearing guns, participating in army manoeuvres, wearing men's uniform and armour, was unthinkable. By virtue of her medical background, Lakshmi had access to the inner courtyards of most homes. Somehow, she was able to persuade fifteen women to join her. But getting five more was proving to be an almost impossible task. Of her fifteen volunteers, some were labourers, others were nursing mothers who tucked their saris and joined the drill. Maj. Gen. Chatterji had recruited special trainers to instruct them in Hindi commands.

When Mrs Chidambaram and Capt. Lakshmi went to the Japanese camp to ask for arms, the officers there burst out laughing. 'See this – Bose desires to put guns in these women's hands and make a spectacle of them! They could have run cookery classes better!'

'Oh, never mind! They want a few guns for practice, let them have them. Won't make any difference to anyone.'

The women were sent away with some ordinary weapons and old uniforms.

The army began to take shape in Singapore. Common English commands were replaced by basic Hindi terms and the grounds echoed with '*Asthey kadam*,' '*Dayen mud, bayen mud ...*,' etc. Drill went on for four–five hours every day. The girls were exhausted. Singaporeans passing by were entertained by the sight. The day of Netaji's visit was near. Lakshmi went to Kesava Menon's house to get his blessings. Both of them came from the same state, but Menon refused to give her his blessings. Instead, he scolded her, 'Subhas babu does not know what he is doing. Only when the British rulers leave and the Japanese sit on our heads, will the fog clear from his eyes.'

A tearful Lakshmi left Menon's house. She was very upset by the veteran Gandhian's criticism of Netaji. As soon as Yellappa heard what had happened, he consoled her. 'Most of Gandhiji's blind followers feel that anything Subhas does is against him. The fools have failed to understand either of them.'

Dr Lakshmi, Mrs Chidambaram and Yellappa were awake through the night before Netaji's arrival. Swami Balasubramanyam had come to help them with several of his students. The function was to be held at the reception hall on Waterloo Road. Women from all over had begun to arrive early that morning, some having walked as much as ten miles. When Netaji arrived, he was greeted with bugles and drums. But his feet stopped midair as he was getting out of the car. The sight in front of him was unbelievable. About twenty women soldiers stood at attention in a row. They were dressed in men's trousers and tunics; their hair neatly tied back, their bearing, proud. At the head of the line was a smartly turned out officer who saluted Netaji sharply. Netaji was surprised by Lakshmi's transformation. In a long khaki woollen coat, breeches, knee-high leather boots and a round beret, her slender figure gave her the appearance of a young prince. She had even cut off her long hair.

Netaji's chest swelled with pride as he took the salute and inspected the parade. He addressed the Rani Jhansi Regiment, 'It is not important how many guns you can carry or how many rounds you can fire. But this effort of yours will give birth to a tremendous power. Your sleeping brothers will awaken and rush to the battlefield. You will become the harbingers of a new era. Of that there is no doubt.'

Photographers were jostling around him to record this moment for posterity. The Japanese photographers clicked away. Even for the European journalists, this was a rare moment.

Dr Lakshmi was truly amazing, Netaji thought. Her marriage had broken; she was supported by a friend who had asked her to choose between personal happiness and service of the motherland. Wiping her eyes, she had told Yellappa, 'Maybe once in a century, you get a noble soul like Netaji. In response to his call, I have broken all bonds of love, family and attachment.' Yellappa told Netaji all this that night.

'Give me your blood and I will get you freedom! Chalo Dilli! Until the tricolour is fluttering atop the viceroy's residence and the historic Red Fort witnesses the victory parade of the Azad Hind soldiers, we cannot rest!'

Netaji had begun a whirlwind tour of Malaysia. East Asia had witnessed the visits of several dignitaries, but the rousing reception Netaji had received was incomparable. As he drove through Kuala Lumpur, he was escorted by machine-gun-wielding guards, a couple of Japanese military trucks, ADCs, interpreters, spokespersons, all travelling in a convoy of seven to eight cars. Also with him were senior Japanese officers and some office bearers of the Indian Independence League. The sky over Kuala Lumpur reverberated with cries of 'Jai Hind' and 'Chalo Dilli!'.

Unlike Abid Hasan and Prem Sehgal, Netaji was quite unmoved by the celebrations and the clamour. His attention was divided between the daily developments on the battlefields in Europe and the eastern borders of India. Hitler's arrogant army had nearly frozen in the chilly Russian winter. Allied forces had captured most of Italy and were rapidly advancing towards Rome. Mussolini's supremacy was in its death throes. Air raids by American and British aircraft had completely destroyed the western sector. Netaji was banking on the easing of pressure on the Eastern sector, to push his way through.

At the Azad Hind Training Centre, formerly a British camp, seven hundred men were being given military training. Most of them were students and small traders who would not have had anything to do with the army, but the thought of accompanying Netaji to India had enthused them.

His call met with spontaneous and generous response. People stood in queues to donate whatever they could – money, jewellery, valuables. Among them was Janaki, her eyes aglitter with a mad zeal. Without a moment's hesitation, she took off her earrings and dropped them into Netaji's palm. Netaji called the photographers. Giving her his blessings, Netaji said, 'Child, what is your name?'

'Janaki Davar.'

'What does your father do?'

'He is a businessman.'

'Child, what else are you prepared to do for our sad and broken Hindustan?'

Janaki was confused. She looked at Lakshmi alongside. The meeting ended. Janaki picked up her bicycle and started walking it towards home, getting nervous as she neared the house. Her father was understanding, but her mother was a strict disciplinarian. How would she explain the loss of both her earrings? She sneaked in through the back door, took a plateful of food from the cook, and hid in her bedroom. All night Lakshmi's striking figure remained with her, as did Netaji's words, 'What else are you prepared to do?' The next morning as she walked into the living room rubbing her sleepy eyes, she was shocked to see her photograph – handing over the earrings to Netaji – on the front page of the *Shonan Times* that her father was reading. Her father folded the newspaper and put it away without a word, but her older sister Papathi screamed, 'Mother, look! See what Janaki has done!'

Her mother was furious, and was about to raise her hand to slap Janaki when her husband intervened. 'You cannot undo what has happened,' he said calmly.

He knew several members of the Indian Independence League. Janaki decided to take advantage of the fact. She invited Capt. Lakshmi home for tea. Everyone was fascinated that such a highly educated doctor had sacrificed everything for her country. In the presence of her father, Janaki asked Lakshmi how she could enlist in the women's regiment. It's true that her father did not object, but he could not sleep that night. He called Janaki into the veranda. His heart was heavy. How could he send her to Singapore, that too all alone. He tried to reason with her. Hoarsely he said, 'You are still very young. You have no idea of politics, of agitation ... you haven't even seen our Hindustan.'

'Papa, while listening to Netaji, I saw the jungles of Imphal and Kohima, the swollen Brahmaputra, and the Red Fort of Delhi ... I saw them all.'

'Silly girl! But how will you go? Your mother will be heartbroken.'

'You comfort her then, Papa,' she said, clinging to him.

Her mother created a huge scene. How could the little child, who still went around saying Ma! Ma! all day, go away so far, all by herself? Who would take care of her? She began to think it was a plot hatched by father and daughter. She asked, 'And when will you come back?'

No one knew.

'What about your marriage? Your future?'

No answer to that either.

'When is this battle for freedom going to end?'

The most complicated question.

With a loud sob, she hugged Janaki. 'Don't leave me and go away, my little one!' she wept.

'Ma, don't stop me. Hasn't Netaji left his home and family for the sake of his country? Lakshmi didi gave up her practice. Now my heart is fully committed to Netaji's call.'

Janaki's mother turned to her husband as the last resort. 'I beg of you, stop her! Make her see reason ...'

'Krishna has come all this way to lift up the Govardhan Parbat. Should we not help him? Isn't it selfish to think only of oneself at such a moment? Now I too intend to go to the IIL office every day.'

Janaki's decision influenced a few more girls to join. On the last day, Janaki's sister Papathi also packed her bag.

When he dropped them off at Netaji's place, their father said tearfully, 'Netaji, I am confident that both my girls will be safe under your wing.

Sending a boy away is painful, yes, but letting go of a daughter … you probably will never understand how heartbreaking that is.'

Netaji's face suddenly flushed. Tears streamed down his cheeks. He could not say a word. But his heart cried out, Anita, dear, how are you? Not for me the gurgle of your laughter, the lisping words that you utter. I only saw a delicate baby all of fifteen days. My daughter, please forgive me.

Those present could not understand Netaji's grief.

Fourteen

Netaji and Col. Bhosale were in Penang for a special reason. The Japanese military school had been set up in the scenic natural harbour long ago. Netaji had requested Field Marshal Terauchi to revive it. Major Swami who had recently returned from Germany, Mr Koyama and Mr Yomonami, who had been instructors there earlier, had taken charge of it. Secret agents who could roam the world in disguise and launch terrorist attacks at the appropriate time had been trained here. As Netaji stood gazing at the blue ocean, Maj. Swami told him, 'This will be the most convenient port for our secret troops to board the submarines for Madras and Calcutta.'

'Batches of at least a hundred secret agents should be sent to India every two months, Mr Koyama,' said Netaji.

'We will do that.'

'We expect these brave comrades to spread out across the country and start their acts of terrorism to harass the British government by the time the Japanese and the Azad Hind soldiers enter India together via Imphal and Chittagong.'

Netaji was on a three-day visit to the Sandicraft School and Swaraj Institute. He inspected the surrounding areas thoroughly the first day.

The following day, Netaji wanted to observe the training programme in Penang. He had just finished his bath and was reciting the Gita when he heard sounds of marching.

The cadets were already on parade. After that, for a couple of hours, they learnt how to use the radio. Then they had a light breakfast. After that they assembled in a large hall where they were shown enlarged pictures of enemy ships, submarines and fighter planes of different types. Netaji was also present in the hall. They were taught how to become human bombs to hit the target, decode enemy messages, read maps as well as to create their own codes to send messages.

Capt. Konako gave Netaji a piece of paper. 'You want to read a secret message?'

'What does it contain? Something the British have written?'

'Throw it into water and see,' Maj. Swami told him.

Between the printed words began to appear a secret message.

Next, they were taught how to make powerful explosive devices with minimum raw materials.

Before leaving for Singapore, Netaji addressed the students. He told them that some of them would have to enter India by submarines or take the overland route through the jungles into Chittagong. There his Forward Bloc colleagues would help them. By the time the Japanese and INA crossed into Manipur, they should have taken control of airports, harbours, railways and other important centres.

Shah Nawaz, Prem Sehgal and Barrister Attavar Yellappa were with Netaji, studying a detailed map of the eastern hemisphere. The rivers, mountains, valleys and the sea occupied a small space on the map, but unless one walked till one's soles were blistered and one's lungs were about to burst, one would not get an idea either of the distance or the difficulties that were present en route. Across the sea of Singapore was Malaya, then Thailand, the narrow strip of Burma and beyond, the vast expanse of India. One could reach Burma in a few days via the sea from Malaya. Or one could travel through the dense forests with the attendant hazards. Through Burma flowed the huge rivers, Chindwin, Salwin and Irrawaddy, then there was the vast Kabaw Valley before one caught a glimpse of Manipur.

'Prem, how far is Singapore from Imphal?' Netaji asked.

'Two thousand eight hundred and twenty-three miles.'

'So our troops have to travel all that distance.' Netaji said, almost to himself.

He stared at the map as if trying to etch it on his mind. 'Staying in Singapore won't do. We must maintain good relations with Thailand, Malaya and Burma too.'

He decided to tour Burma soon. The Burma headquarters of the Japanese were in Rangoon. The commander, Lt. Gen. Kawabe, was a tough man. It would be good to meet him as well, thought Netaji as he boarded his bomber aircraft for Burma.

When he landed at Rangoon's Mingaladon Airport, he was greeted by at least twenty thousand Indians waving the tricolour and shouting, 'Netaji zindabad!' 'Mahatma Gandhi zindabad!' Then the Burmese military band struck up, drowning all other sounds as the Burmese prime minister Dr Ba Maw, received Netaji with an enormous bouquet of flowers. His entire cabinet was with him. A young man of about twenty-five rushed forward to shake hands with Netaji. Introducing him, Dr Maw said, 'This is our defence minister, Gen. Aung San.'

'Delighted to meet you,' Netaji said.

Aung San was one of the younger Burmese officers, specially trained by the Japanese to fight for Burma's independence. Dr Maw had led a rebellion to free Burma from the grip of the British, but was caught and put in Mandalay jail. He escaped and joined forces with Japan. After Rangoon fell, he set up his government in Burma. An expert in legal matters, Dr Maw was familiar with and sympathetic to India's freedom struggle. He decided to extend all possible support to Netaji. Hardly had the reception ended when members of the Burma Hindi Swatantra Sangha crowded around Netaji. Among them were Bhai Dina Nath, Bhai Paramanand, Debnath Das, Dr Pranjivan Mehta and other citizens from the Indian community in Rangoon. Later, at Dr Mehta's house, he asked Bhai Paramanand, 'How many Indians live in Rangoon?'

'About five to six lakhs. But don't be content with Rangoon alone, Netaji. Come with me to Ziyawaddy,' Bhai Paramanand told him.

'Why there?'

'Because relatives of our Rajendra Babu, the Prasad family from Bihar, set up a sugar factory there and brought in thousands of Indian labourers. The Arya Samaj has already sowed the seeds of nationalism in the sixty-four small colonies around Ziyawaddy. Your visit can trigger a mass movement.'

On 30 July 1943, Netaji addressed a crowd of about two and a half lakh Indians living in Rangoon.

'Brothers and sisters, be prepared for the coming struggle. I am not a preacher. Rather, just a foot soldier of the freedom brigade. All my life I have tried to figure out how a handful of Englishmen could subjugate thirty-eight crore Indians. Where is our valorous spirit? Our national pride? Even if our young people come together with bricks and stones, the British will find it hard to escape. Our war must continue till the enemy has been crushed. Brothers, rise!'

The Town Hall reverberated with cries of 'Chalo Dilli! Chalo Dilli!.'

The dais was laden with offerings of flowers, garlands and sweets. Suddenly, Netaji went up to the mike again and said, 'Whatever you have with you – money, jewellery, valuables – donate it for your motherland. I am going to hold a symbolic auction of all the flowers you have offered me. Be generous with your bids. All the money will go towards breaking the shackles around Bharatmata's feet, I promise you.'

An expectant hush fell over the gathering. John Thivy stood up and began to invite bids. 'Come, speak up, who will be the proud owner of this precious garland that lies around our beloved Netaji's neck?'

The spirit of competition gripped everyone. The figures kept rising. When a gentleman called out 'Twenty-one lakh,' it seemed the bid would stop there. Curiously, Netaji asked John Thivy who the bidder was. 'He is Noor Singh. Owns a big export–import business here, and has opened several warehouses.'

Then Netaji chipped in, 'Can you buy freedom for only this amount?'

This taunt incited a Madrasi gentleman into raising his bid to thirty-one lakh. Gradually, the figure reached fifty lakh. Suddenly, Noor Singh rushed up to the dais like a possessed man, whipped out his chequebook and declared, 'This is my final bid. I dare anyone to match it. That garland will be mine alone. I offer everything that belongs to me to the cause of my motherland.'

The audience was most eager to know the figure on the cheque. When Netaji announced that it was one crore fourteen lakh, cries of 'Netaji zindabad! Bharatmata ki jai!' echoed through the hall.

As Noor Singh accepted the garland from Netaji, he said, 'I feel I have won the Second World War, Babuji.'

The next day, Netaji set off for Tamu. Along the way, he stopped at the shrine of the Sleeping Buddha at Pegu. Across the ancient bridge was the old highway heading north to Mandalay, Michina and Assam. Outside Pegu, it branched off towards Bangkok via Moulmein. Running parallel to the highway was a railway track built by the British.

After a three-hour drive, Netaji's car, with Col. Jehangir, Debnath Das and Bhai Paramanand, arrived at the Ziyawaddy Sugar Factory. The plantation labour and the factory workers dropped whatever they were doing and gathered to meet their beloved Subhas babu. He told them, 'Brothers, this road which passes through your village will take us to Delhi one day. Be prepared for a fight. Soon the torch will be lit. Join the INA. Sacrifice, give up everything!'

Burmese Independence Day was celebrated while Netaji was in Rangoon. Dr Ba Maw accorded him the status of the guest of honour. During the banquet that night, Dr Maw asked Netaji, 'Are you confident that Japan will stand by Burma and India?'

'Definitely. But if anyone betrays us, it will be my duty to draw my sword against the enemy.'

The next day, Maj. Gen. Chatterji informed Netaji that Lt. Gen. Kawabe Masakazu had invited him to dinner.

'Who gave the message?'

'His ADC called.'

'If the general speaks to me personally, I may consider accepting it,' Netaji replied.

Finally, at 9 p.m., the general called and Netaji went across to the Japanese camp. Lt. Gen. Kawabe was known for his arrogance because of his samurai lineage. He greeted Netaji with a low bow. Even by Japanese standards, he was a diminutive man and tried to compensate for it by his military regalia, upturned moustache and affected manner. Aware of the imminent developments, he said to Netaji, 'Your dream campaign is not too far away.'

'Well, we have asked Japan for at least five divisions.'

Kawabe was puzzled. 'You are talking about divisions? We were considering taking a few of your battalions with our troops.'

'Which is about two hundred soldiers?' Netaji's voice rose.

'That is several battalions.'

'I will never accept such a proposal. How can our battered troops face the superior British forces? I have promised my divisions that they will fight alongside the Japanese as equals. I am committed to that.'

August 1943. Prime Minister Churchill, Dickie Mountbatten and Brigadier Wingate were on board the luxury liner, The Queen Mary, heading towards Quebec in Canada to attend the summit of the Allies.

It was late evening, and as the heavy-jowled, large-framed Winston Churchill reclined against the cushions in his cabin, puffing at his cigar, he said to Mountbatten, 'We have discussed the Eastern sector in considerable detail, I think? Do you still have any questions?'

'JIFC – I am worried about the Japanese Inspired Fifth Columnist,' explained Dickie.

'You mean Subhas Chandra Bose and rebels like him? It makes me mad to even mention those names. In fact, I am more concerned about them than you are.'

Mountbatten handed over a file to Churchill. He examined the coded messages and the flagged maps carefully. A particular photograph caught his attention. Near the municipal building in Singapore, attired in full military uniform, stood Netaji, ready to take the salute of the twenty-five thousand troops in front of him. Churchill sneered contemptuously. 'Look at the man's style. India's future dictator.'

'Whose strings are pulled in Tokyo.'

'And this obedient puppet will dance in India. Wonderful!' Pulling on his cigar, Churchill continued, 'Dickie, I will not spare anyone who dares to shake even a stone in the fortress that is our beloved empire. Call me arrogant, egotistical or selfish, I don't care. But no one can accuse me of not holding the British Empire close to my heart.'

Churchill, in the seventieth year of his life, was struggling to prevent the German python from swallowing up his nation, while the forty-four-year-old Mountbatten was standing firm to defend England's colonies, especially India. Dickie Mountbatten, christened Prince Louis, was the grandson of Queen Victoria. While he served in the Royal Navy alongside his cousin, the Prince of Wales, the empire and its affairs were close to his heart.

With an air of supreme confidence, Wingate said to Dickie, 'If I have your support, I will break the Japanese resistance.'

'Remember, Wingate, to win a battle in the jungles, you must first conquer the heavens. For that you need solid air cover. Unfortunately, our air force is woefully inadequate.'

When the talks began in Quebec, the situation on the Russian front, the battles in Europe, and the campaigns in the African desert were discussed. But when the matter of East Asia came up, the reactions of the other members made Churchill cautious. Roosevelt began by saying, 'The China problem is more important from America's point of view. Let us resolve that first.'

Churchill interrupted politely, 'Mr President, let us first clear the Singapore and Rangoon path.'

'No, no, China is of primary concern to us.'

'No, sir. The Japs have handed the torch of revolt to the rebels. To the shouts of "Chalo Dilli" they are assembling on the eastern borders of India. We have barely managed to extinguish the flames of the "Quit India" conflagration, and now this new fire threatens to break out. If the Japanese and the INA chaps reach the border, we will have a greater mutiny than the 1857 one on our hands.'

'That's strange.'

'Indeed, Mr President, my viceroy is literally sitting on a volcano. I desperately need your help on the Burma front,' pleaded Churchill.

Unable to resist the temptation, Roosevelt taunted, 'Why create such a hue and cry about that, Mr Prime Minister? Sooner than later, you will have to let go of India.'

'Not while there is breath in my body!' fumed Churchill. 'I have not become the prime minister of England to chop up the British Empire, Mr President. I have reiterated this often enough.'

Soon after the morning session ended, Churchill presented Brigadier Wingate to Roosevelt. 'I'd like you to take a look at this short film made by Wingate.'

'So, you are a filmmaker as well, are you?'

'He is one of our best military officers. He has devised a long penetration strategy for guerrilla warfare in the jungles. Once you see the film, you will understand what it is about.'

The film opened with shots of the Burmese campaign that Wingate had carried out. Dense forests, deep ravines and valleys appeared on the screen. And into their dark depths, aircraft began to drop paratroopers – British, African and Gurkha. Some soldiers took off from the tops of the cliffs in gliders and entered enemy territory. Wingate, along with his troops and supplies, reached the interiors of Burma. In the interiors, secret airstrips were being constructed. Troops based there would intercept Japanese supply convoys. The film told a story of rare courage and enterprise. There was spontaneous applause as the lights came on. Everyone congratulated Wingate.

When Roosevelt left in his wheelchair, he was accompanied by Churchill, who continued to appeal to him for air cover in the Burma sector, in order to quell the Burmese and stop the advancing Japanese. He snatched the secret files out of Mountbatten's hands and showed some of the pictures to Roosevelt. Pointing to the photograph of an imposing young man standing in full military regalia, the president asked, 'Who is this?'

'Subhas Chandra Bose.'

'Who is he?'

'An extremist Indian leader.'

'And where are all those troops in front of him from?'

Regretfully Churchill had to concede, 'Japan had taken forty-five thousand of our British and Indian troops prisoner in Singapore. About twenty-five thousand of them rebelled and went over to Subhas Chandra's side. He has raised an army of rebels and deserters, and declared that his objective is to take over Delhi with the help of this raggle-taggle brigade. The pity is that the Japanese fully support this.'

'Even so, what can this one man do? What are his credentials?' Roosevelt asked.

'A completely untrustworthy person. He was selected for the ICS, but did not take up the service. The youth of India are with him. He defeated Mr Gandhi's candidate during the Congress party's presidential election.'

'Gandhi's?'

'Yes. Eleven times he was incarcerated. Left to languish in jail. But the unbelievably ambitious and idealistic character that he is, he slipped out of our hands and escaped to Germany. Mussolini was all in favour of supporting him, but then when no concrete support was forthcoming, he took a ninety-day voyage in a submarine and landed in the Japanese military headquarters.'

'What assistance has Japan promised them?'

'Assistance? Mr President, the prime minister and field marshal declared in the Japanese Parliament that they would extend every support.'

'Winston, this is a big story!' exclaimed Roosevelt. 'We seem to have ignored East Asia what with tackling the German and Italian fronts and the campaigns in Africa and Russia. Who would believe that an insignificant individual from a backward country like India would take centre stage in the international arena!'

'But what are you going to do about it?'

'Winston, you seem to be quite perturbed.'

'Perturbed?' Churchill retorted, his eyes flashing. 'Mr President, I give it to you in writing ... if you don't come to our aid at once, with the backing of the Japanese, Bose and his army will reach the Indo-Burma border, and once they step into Bengal, it will be the end of the British Empire.'

Churchill laid out the map of the eastern end of the Himalayas, the Hump Route, and a secret document from military intelligence. 'To foster friendship between Japan and China, Mr Bose has sent in some revolutionaries from Singapore and Rangoon to China. It is important to check his diabolical manoeuvres immediately. If China does not get timely help from America, it is likely to form an alliance with Japan – who has crushed them ruthlessly in the past – merely to save themselves.' Roosevelt was confused after reading the message. But before he could ask any questions, Churchill reminded him about Pearl Harbor. 'Sir, if Burma and India fall, do you think the victorious Japs will sit still? They will use the same bloodstained weapons to turn on the American troops in the Pacific, don't forget.'

Roosevelt was furious. Without a word, he left for his living quarters.

At dinner that night, Roosevelt whispered to Churchill, 'I am willing to give you whatever support you ask for in Burma. Only, Winston, I demand nothing short of victory.'

Churchill beamed. That same night, the decision to form the South-East Asia Command under the guidance of Dickie Mountbatten was taken. And Wingate's Chindit Campaign was approved to deal with the INA and the Japanese.

'Having done such good work for the country, for you to sit on the sidelines now is not correct,' Netaji told Barrister Raghavan.

'But Subhas babu, we know from experience what Japanese jails are like, so how can we believe what you tell us?'

'Well, if we harbour prejudices and mistrust about people, we will never achieve anything.'

Raghavan was not easy to convince. Finally, Netaji promised him, 'If ever the situation should arise, Barrister saheb, when I have to choose between you and the Japanese, I will be on your side.'

This reassured Raghavan, but before he could respond, Netaji's bodyguard, Sher Singh, rushed in. 'Netaji, Gen. Yamamoto is here to see you.'

'Send him in.'

Recently, Yamamoto had taken charge of the Hikari Kikan for Netaji's convenience, but their friendship which went back to his days in Berlin, had slightly frayed.

'Well, Colonel?'

'All of us, including Terauchi, in the Japanese military believe that if you set up your interim government, all sorts of complications in terms of military, political and international relations will arise. Japan is engaged in a critical battle – it would be best not to add to our troubles.' Yamamoto got it all off his chest in one breath.

Raghavan realised that the conversation was taking a grim turn and got up to leave. Netaji stopped him. 'Stay, Barrister Raghavan, there is nothing to hide from you. You should be informed about my decision that our Azad Hind government is going to take the oath of office within four days, on 21 October. But the idea seems more distasteful to this local representative of the Japanese government than to the government itself.'

'Are you taking the Japanese government for granted, Mr Bose?'

'I had made it very clear to your prime minister when he came to Singapore.'

'How can a private conversation be accorded legal status?'

'Let me take care of that. You will not face any repercussions. And if questions are asked, I will answer them in your emperor's court.'

Since nothing more was to be said, Gen. Yamamoto departed. Raghavan's eyes shone at the prospect of having one's own government – even if it was an interim one? 'In exile', it would attain the status of statehood with its own emblem, currency and international identity.

'The news is music to my ears, Subhas babu,' he said.

'Yes, Raghavanji, very soon I will announce the formation of the sovereign Indian National Government. I am really impatient to get on to the battlefield. If you recall, in 1928, during the Calcutta Congress, I had suggested that a government on the lines of the one in Ireland be set up, and Gandhiji had become worried. I had advocated that with a definite objective in mind.'

'The idea is quite daring and dramatic and a bit too hasty, perhaps?'

'That it has to be. The word "daring" loses its meaning without the element of haste. Once one has an identity, the enemy too takes one seriously. It gives one's compatriots self-confidence.'

'You have already started preparing for war, then?'

'Absolutely. Very soon it will be sparked off on India's eastern borders. After losing Burma, the British are bound to retaliate. But we will not wait for them to make the first move. The INA will approach India from Assam.'

'In that case, preparations for the war must get underway,' said Raghavan. 'Why waste time over unnecessary formalities like setting up a government?'

'You are wrong there, Barrister,' Netaji intervened. 'This is an essential ritual, not a mere formality. When the war does break out, there must be a definite power centre. In what capacity will we go forth with the Japanese troops? If we do not have our own government, the soldiers I have gathered together will be no better than a flock of sheep in the eyes of the world.'

'Setting up a government has many advantages. Once Tokyo accords us recognition, according to International Law, our troops will be seen as their allies.'

Barrister Raghavan was speechless. Pressing Netaji's hand, he stammered, 'Netaji ...'

'If you want to say Subhas babu ...!'

'No. In future, I will address you only as Netaji. You deserve it. No more convincing required. I am back at work from this moment on.'

The news that Barrister Raghavan was to assist Yellappa spread rapidly in Singapore and was received with much joy. The excitement among civilians and army personnel increased when it was confirmed that the Indian National Government was to be formed. Netaji only had to write a proclamation for the interim government. The chief of the news agency Reuters (East), S.A. Ayyar, had joined Netaji and shared his home. Together with another senior journalist, Shivaram, he kept Netaji posted about the latest international developments.

For the last two nights, Netaji and Ayyar had been wanting to put down the proclamation, but they had not found the time. Finally, that night, as they sat on the terrace after 11 p.m., Ayyar asked, 'Netaji, people are very curious about your cabinet.'

'Why? Do you have any suggestions?'

'Don't include anyone. Keep the prime minister's and war minister's portfolio with yourself.'

'A one-member cabinet, then?'

'Yes, Netaji. No one else has the calibre.'

'Ayyar, you are totally wrong. A true leader is one who has immense self-confidence, no doubt, but in whose heart, springs the sense of team spirit. And through the vicissitudes of circumstances emerge giants. It will be a sin for me to ignore your dedication and contribution, the sacrifices all of you have made.'

Ayyar's typewriter was waiting for some action. It was well past midnight. The heaving ocean waves seemed to find an echo in Netaji's mind. A sheaf of clean white sheets and a cigarette case lay before Netaji. He began to write. The words just flowed from his pen. Sheet after sheet was filled and promptly taken to Ayyar's room for typing. Netaji needed neither reference books nor notes, nor clippings. Centuries of history had been assimilated into his being. Glorious moments and extraordinary individuals, victories and despairing defeats, shrewd alleyways of European statesmanship, sufferings of revolutionaries, the hazardous paths of idealism, perseverance and dedication, were all carved out like a sculpture in his heart. Aspiration was holding him by the hand and drawing him towards the distant shore where flowed the majestic Jamuna, and on her banks lay the Lal Qila, stained by the subjugation of crores, the symbol of British Imperialism, the viceroy's residence and the Union Jack atop it. Breaking the shackles, destroying the power-drunk British, marched the Indian National Army.

Netaji's proclamation invoked all the heroes of 1857 – Rani Lakshmibai, Tatya Tope, Kunwar Singh, among others. Words dripped from his pen, 'By a tragic twist of fate and some flawed leadership, the first war of independence ended in humiliating failure for us. But those noble fighters will always guide us with their steadfastness, their sacrifice and their valour.' He also acknowledged Mahatma Gandhi's contribution in infusing new life into the freedom struggle, so that every single Indian, from the remotest village, the deepest valley, the highest mountain and the modern city, became part of the struggle for independence.

The ocean reflected the state of Netaji's mind – at once turbulent, thundering and lashing at the shore and silent, reflective, like the soundless meditation of a sage in a Himalayan cave.

As dawn broke, Ayyar handed over the typescript to Netaji.

An ecstatic Prabhabati, joyous Sarat Bose and Bibhabati stood at the door of the bungalow. They had gone to Singapore especially to celebrate the setting up of the Azad Hind Government. Tripping along, flowers woven into her silken hair was little Anita. When did you grow up so, you naughty little girl? Anita ran to her father standing at the top of the stairs, but as he reached out to take her hands, like magic, the staircase vanished into thin air. Netaji woke up from the dream.

21 October 1943. Cathay Cinema in Singapore was bedecked like a bride. The place was abuzz with journalists, photographers and Indians, thronging to hear Netaji make the formal proclamation.

At 3.45 p.m., Netaji arrived to the deafening cries of 'Azad Hind zindabad!' 'Netaji ki jai!' 'Vande Mataram!'. But the person who had cast the mantle on his shoulders, four years ago in the same place, was not present. Rash Behari Bose was too ill to attend. Today, the chief of the Hikari Kikan represented the Japanese government. At four o'clock sharp, Netaji stood on the dais. He read out the names of his ministers. While he kept the portfolios of War and International Affairs to himself, Capt. Lakshmi was given women's affairs, while finance went to Maj. Gen. Chatterji. In addition, Netaji had included civilians and military officials like Col. Bhosale, Lt. Col. Bhagat, Gulzar Singh and Anand Mohan Sahay. Among the advisers were Rash Behari Bose, Barrister John Thivy and Yellappa.

That night, the first meeting of the Azad Hind cabinet was held at Netaji's house. 'I declare war on England and America.' That was the first announcement Netaji made. It struck terror in most hearts. Finance Minister A.C. Chatterji could not resist asking, 'Declaring war on England is our birthright. But why America? Why tread on the tail of such a powerful nation?'

'Because England rides on America's back.'

Prime Minister Subhas Chandra Bose's resolution was accepted and passed by the cabinet.

Later at dinner, Netaji said, 'On this very special occasion, we should all remember Mohan Singh. Let me ask you, no matter what faith, what sect, what ideology you believe in, I need everyone to lend me their hands for the greater glory and honour of the tricolour. How can we fulfil the dream of a strong and stable India without the unity and cooperation of every one of her warriors? I will make a presentation to the Japanese authorities about Mohan Singh and do my best to get him an honourable release.'

Just then Gen. Terauchi's ADC arrived with a basket of flowers. 'The general has requested that you set some time aside tomorrow evening.'

'Why?'

'He is hosting a banquet in your honour at the Boat Club. All members of your cabinet, senior military officers and civilians are invited.'

Amid twinkling lights, the party, attended by many senior Japanese officials, was in full swing. Gen. Yamamoto alone looked anxious. During the dinner, Gen. Terauchi's secretary handed him an urgent wireless message. Gen. Terauchi held Netaji's hand, congratulating him. But before he could say what it was, Japanese radio made the announcement. 'The Japanese government today decided to grant recognition to the interim government. Emperor Hirohito and Prime Minister Tojo send their congratulations to the prime minister of the Indian National Government, Subhas Chandra Bose.'

As Netaji, accompanied by Cabinet colleague, Maj. Shah Nawaz, was on his way home, Gen. Terauchi stopped him. 'Another piece of good news. Next week, there is going to be a meeting of the Asian region and all heads of state will be present. As Prime Minister of the Azad Hind Government, you are also invited.'

Since there was no direct flight to Tokyo, Netaji had to fly via the Philippines. His first halt was at Manila, where he stayed at the Macmillan Palace as the guest of the president, Dr Jose Laurel. After two fuelling stops, they reached Taipei and spent the night there.

Bhosale, Chatterji, Dr Raju, Abid Hasan, Shamsher Singh and Sahay were part of Netaji's entourage. At the Tokyo airport, Netaji was greeted with a low bow by the smiling, smooth-skinned foreign minister, Shigemitsu. Netaji embraced him. 'Bose banzai!' and 'Long live Bose!' rent the sky as little tricolours and Japanese flags danced joyously in the air.

In the car, Shigemitsu told Netaji, 'All newspapers carry detailed reports and photographs of your government, your immensely popular public meetings in Malaya, the army you raised from among the POWs, your women's brigade, on the front page.'

'Do you like the idea of a women's brigade?'

'It is praiseworthy. It will be a long time before Japanese women join the army and carry guns in their hands.'

Netaji was in high spirits. Japan, Germany, Italy, Manchuria, Burma and the Philippines had formally accorded recognition to his government. He was invited to the All Asia Summit to resolve the issues raised by the Hikari Kikan, discuss financial matters and most importantly, the last battle of Imphal, with Prime Minister Tojo.

When Netaji met the prime minister, he said, 'Sir, October has almost gone. It would be criminal to waste more time.'

'I know. The campaign must end before the rains begin in Assam.'

Prime Minister Tojo frowned as he absently spun the globe on the table in front of him. 'We believe the Allies plan to set up a South-East Asia Command and deploy a huge force on the Indian border.'

'Well, let our Azad Hind and Japanese armies reach the borders, then see the country explode.' Netaji said confidently.

'The Imphal campaign will start soon, but be a little patient. We have sent Col. Kinoshita and Maj. Takashahi to survey the Julpi Mountain region. Maj. Fujiwara, Staff Officer, 15th Army, is checking both banks of the Chindwin River for possible military manoeuvres. Let us wait for their reports,' Tojo informed Netaji.

'I have news that the American Air Force is going to give Britain large-scale support. There is no telling what Churchill and Mountbatten will stoop to, sir.'

'You are in touch with Field Marshal Terauchi and Kawabe, aren't you?'

Netaji nodded. 'There seems to be a proposal that when our troops reach Imphal, my men will be broken up into small groups and given messengers' or ration providers' jobs. Please don't give your approval to such an idea. Let us fight honourably, like men. No matter if we die fighting.'

'What exactly do you wish for?'

"Three proper divisions, thirty thousand men.'

'You believe your soldiers will fight bravely?'

'Mr Prime Minister, don't look at our army through the narrow eyeglass of the military. They are not the run-of-the-mill soldiers. They are revolutionaries. Just think, twenty-five thousand prisoners of war, who had fought for a master, now join forces against him, for some abstract notion of freedom ... is that a mean consideration? History has no similar example to offer.'

'Bose, there is no cause for worry. I will organise at least one division for you that you can fight with, shoulder to shoulder. Field Marshal Terauchi will be informed accordingly, tonight.'

Netaji had to make one more request. 'Your Excellency, the British bards refer to me mockingly as a king without a kingdom. If you give back the territory that belongs to us, your love for India will be publicly acknowledged, and my detractors will be silenced.'

'What territory are you talking about?'

'The Andaman and Nicobar Islands.'

The prime minister did not say anything to that. The Japanese had important naval bases on the islands. Madras City was just two hours away from there. A little further, in Ceylon, Mountbatten was likely to set up the Allied Army headquarters. Both were very important posts from the military point of view.

Netaji showed Tojo a few new currency notes. Tojo remarked, 'Bose, your preparedness and perseverance are astounding.'

'To administer a conquered land, one must have currency, isn't it?'

Tojo smiled. 'Japan has not helped any other Asian country as much during this great war. Don't worry. Your government will rule over the vanquished land.'

The All Asia Summit was organised by Prime Minister Tojo on the lines of the Allies summits in Casablanca and Tehran, on 5 and 6 November 1943. It was attended by the Chinese President, Wang Jinwei; Prince Wan Waithayakon of Thailand; Zhang Jinghui, prime minister of Manchuria; Dr Jose P. Laurel, the Philippines president, and the Burmese president Dr Ba Maw. Netaji was invited as an observer, but he practically ended up conducting the meet.

The proceedings began with Dr Ba Maw tabling a resolution to congratulate Netaji. 'For those who know the story of this extraordinary man, Subhas Chandra Bose, nothing needs to be said. Unless India becomes free, there is no hope for Asia.' In his reply, Netaji said that there must be a joint effort for the progress of all Asia. Thanking Japan, he said, 'If we miss out this opportunity of the Second World War, we will have to wait another hundred years for our country's freedom. Today, it seems time and fate are on our side. My government has given the slogan, "Chalo Dilli". The Azad Hind Government and the Azad Hind Army are committed to driving the alien powers out of our country and creating a powerful united India.'

Dr Ba Maw whispered to Netaji, 'No matter what you say, the Japanese government is not going to hand over the strategic bases of the Andaman and Nicobar Islands. The other countries also think the same.' While concluding the summit, Prime Minister Tojo said, 'Today, the Indian people have put aside their differences and united under Subhas Chandra Bose's flag. There is no question of our withdrawing the support we have extended to him. We have information that a British military headquarters is being set up in Ceylon. But we respect Bose's request and are pleased to announce the handing over of the islands of Andaman and Nicobar to the Azad Hind Government.' Dr Ba Maw hugged Netaji with excitement.

Emperor Hirohito received Netaji in the famed Phoenix Hall on 10 November 1943. Netaji briefly outlined his plans for the movement.

Netaji could not possibly leave Tokyo without meeting Rash Behari Bose. Accompanied by Sahay and Zaman Kiani, Netaji went to his house and was shocked to see him lying on a cot, frail and emaciated. Netaji laid some flowers at the photograph of the lovely Toshiko. Rash Babu asked him how the Japanese visit had gone.

'We have permission to fight as equals. We have Andaman and Nicobar.'

'But when will you get Dilli?' Rash Babu asked impatiently. 'I have packed my bags for the final journey. All I am waiting for is the victorious bugle call to send me on my way. Hurry up.'

Netaji took his bony hand in his own, reassuringly.

During lunch one afternoon, Netaji asked Dr Raju, 'What is happening about Mohan Singh?'

Dr Raju almost choked. 'I went to see him last week. He is suffering from malaria.'

'Where have they kept him?'

'On a tiny, sparsely populated island near Singapore called Pulao Ubin. Only a few fishermen live there. The islanders all suffer from malaria. It's as bad as Kala Pani.'

'Mohan Singh is an exceptionally patriotic individual.'

Yamamoto said, 'Perhaps he is, Netaji. We don't doubt it at all. But the men who he had around him like Niranjan Gill, Mahavir Singh and others, and the bitter experience we had with them is not easy to forget. Mahavir Singh entered India and supplied some vital information to the British.'

'Anyway, let us try.'

'We did release all the men from the Mahavir Singh–Gill group before you arrived in the East, as per your wish. Take the example of Major Bhurewal. We were against taking him, but you were adament. How is he faring?'

'He has transformed. No other officer takes so much interest in training soldiers.'

Finally, the Mohan Singh matter went up to Kawabe.

Dr Raju went personally to fetch Mohan Singh.

Around 4 p.m., a motorboat stopped near the bungalow and a thin bearded man with a stoop got out. What a contrast from the photographs they had seen of him. His smile was the same, but some terrible burden seemed to weigh him down.

Netaji went up and embraced him warmly. 'Jai Hind', they said and sat down. 'I am thrilled to meet a comrade.'

Mohan Singh just laughed.

'It's not right that the Azad Hind Government is being celebrated while Mohan Singh languishes in a Japanese jail. I am going to get you back with honour, Mohan Singh,' Netaji promised him.

'How many months is it since you came here, Subhas babu? You didn't meet your comrade before. Did the Japanese not permit you?'

Nobody liked Mohan Singh's mocking tone. Netaji replied calmly, 'Mohan, we must all come together. If you are prepared, we can sort out our disagreements. I will even speak to Prime Minister Tojo.'

'Tell me to jump off a cliff, and I will obey you, Subhas babu. But I don't wish to see the treacherous Japanese again. I'd rather not get my freedom from them.'

'The tussle between you and Rash Behari Bose should not have gone to such extremes,' said Netaji.

'Don't even mention the name of that sinner in my presence. It's a shame that he was born an Indian.'

Netaji tried to change the subject. Then Mohan Singh on his own began to enumerate the pros and cons of the Azad Hind. 'You came to the East too late, Subhas babu,' he said.

'Yes, travel plans were complicated. But if we plan it well, I am very confident of hoisting the tricolour on Lal Qila.'

'Subhas babu, those who betrayed me can do the same to you.'

'I don't think so. Once the Japanese emperor and prime minister give an assurance that they will support us fully, what more do we need?'

'What about personal experience?'

'The local authorities do bring up some minor technicalities and obstruct the process, but that happens everywhere. The seniors make the policies and the juniors sabotage them.'

'What did a man like you gain from befriending the Japanese, Subhas babu?'

'Because of the war, I could show the world how crucial the question of India's independence is to world affairs.'

The discussion turned to Indian politics. Mohan Singh said, 'Pandit Nehru is my idol. I have read every one of his works, treasured every scrap of paper that speaks of him. I cannot accept anyone else's leadership.'

'Mohan Singh,' he said, 'how would you know how deep and close the relationship between me and Jawaharlal is? But this struggle is not against Gandhiji or Nehru, it is against the British Imperialists who claim that the sun will never set on their empire. Today, all national leaders including Panditji are behind bars. Someone must hold up the flag of rebellion. This British arrogance disgusts me. They have reached the dregs in the war, but will not even consider the issue of India's independence.'

'You don't think Churchill will have a change of heart?' Mohan Singh asked.

'Never. He is no indecisive Hamlet. Rather, a Shylock who will demand his pound of flesh from the region closest to the heart. The enslavement of thirty-eight crore Indians is a blot on the twentieth century. My entire being screams to rip the curtain off the face of British hypocrisy.'

'But with whose help? The dastardly Japanese? What if they let you down in the midst of the action?'

'Mohan Singh, in the fight for worldly power, there are no saints nor sinners. Exploiting the resources that are available under the circumstances is important. There is nothing wrong in taking foreign help for the freedom of our country. Lenin too wandered around the world like this. The French warrior Lafayette's sword, too, was bloody in the American war of independence.'

Gen. Bhosale and Dr Raju were shocked by Mohan Singh's intense distrust of the Japanese. Netaji turned towards the ocean, and after a few moments of quiet contemplation, looked at Mohan Singh again. 'Don't worry, Mohan. If the Japanese harbour even the faintest intention of betraying us, my soldiers will not hesitate to make sieves of their bodies. But I am certain no such thing will happen. I feel myself breathing much more freely here than I ever did in Germany. It must be the result of our bonds of culture and understanding.'

Dusk was spreading its dark wings across the ocean. Birds twittered as they made their way home. Again, Netaji said, 'Mohan, to reinstate you in the INA honourably, I will spare no efforts.'

The gentle pressure of Maj. Gen. Bhosale's hand and Dr Raju's mute appeal did not move Mohan Singh. 'Subhas babu, it is beyond me to be on the side of the Japanese again. The yellow serpent will sting you one day, be warned.'

'If you are not ready to change your mind, my arguments have been in vain. How can I plead your case now?'

Mohan Singh bade Netaji an emotional farewell. Obviously, the differences were too deep for reconciliation. As the Japanese guards led him to the motorboat, Netaji called out, 'Take care of yourself, Mohan. I will soon have you moved to a better place ...'

'The first act of this drama has ended. We threw down our arms and fled from Singapore and Rangoon. The Japanese must have thought heaven was within their grasp. But they have no idea what preparations we have made before the second act opens, the fools!' said Mountbatten.

He was like the director with a powerful script – planning entries and exits, cues and props. Ever since he had taken over the South-East Asia Command, his face had acquired a new glow. Under his command were great soldiers like the American Stilwell and the Britishers Slim and Scoones, as also a large number of Indian and Chinese leaders. The meeting under his leadership at New Delhi promised to be a stormy one.

Mountbatten indicated that Act II was about to unfold. 'It is time to decide what we want to do. Do we recapture Burma and march in triumph to England, or sink our historic empire in the eastern seas and slink away to Europe?'

The proceedings began with an appraisal of the situation in Burma. Mountbatten said, 'Our four divisions will launch surprise attacks on the unsuspecting Japanese and put them at sixes and sevens.'

Stilwell wanted to open up the main highway in Burma and quickly ensure justice for China. 'I will make a thrust from the Lido side,' he declared.

'Our air force will strike about two hundred miles behind the tail of the Japanese supply lines, spring upon the unsuspecting soldiers and finish them off,' announced Wingate.

The plan was slowly taking shape. Maps were consulted; circles and semicircles appeared at important locations; stenographers, staff officers ran hither and thither. Gen. Scoones, commander of the Imphal Sector, said, 'My troops are spread out in a semicircle for two hundred miles east of Imphal. If I don't get timely assistance, I will be in permanent disgrace.'

Dickie did not like Scoones's whining. 'Don't forget, General, India is the jewel in the crown, and if we lose it, we would never live down the shame on our military prowess.'

At the end of the discussion, one thing was clear – that this war, which was going to be played out in the eastern regions of Imphal, Kohima, Dimapur and Lido, would be a life-and-death one. It had to be won at any cost. Then a curious announcement was made: 'Sandhurst alumni, remain behind. The rest may leave.' Indian officers were effectively segregated.

As night fell, the deepening darkness seemed to hold more terrors. Mountbatten began in his sonorous voice, 'The loyalty of the British-Indian soldier is a glorious aspect of human history. Even today, some two lakh Indian soldiers are laying down their lives for us in Europe. Unfortunately, of late, attempts have been made to breach the strong walls of trust. And this has made our Prime Minister Churchill very unhappy.'

'INA is a blot on the shining record of the Indo-British forces,' Scoones said.

'But ignoring them would be foolish. During the Quebec meeting, Mr Churchill had hinted at this. The Japan-controlled rebel Subhas Chandra Bose has launched a propaganda war. Make sure his poisonous words don't affect the rest of our soldiers. Explain to them that Japanese culture is totally different from the Indian culture. They are cruel people, as is seen in the torture they inflicted on Formosa, Korea and China.'

'I don't understand one thing,' Field Marshal Sir Claude Auchinleck said. 'Why are the stupid Japanese bending over backwards to please Subhas Chandra Bose? Why have they recognised the baseless Azad Hind Government? Why parade him at the All Asia Summit?'

The INA was being hotly discussed when Gen. Slim placed a confidential piece of information before them. 'Sir, this is the latest. Four of Subhas Bose's JIFCs were attempting to enter India through Chittagong. Fortunately, they were intercepted by our patrol.'

'Have they been interrogated?'

'Yes.'

'What did they reveal?'

'Bose has sent in numerous secret agents by different routes into India.'

'With what intent?'

'When Bose and his Japanese colluders launch an attack on Imphal, these agents will spark off revolts within the country. Blow up airports, remove tracks, disrupt ports. For this, they have opened two training schools in Penang in Malaysia.'

'Dreadful!' the others chorused.

It was decided to send an alert to all governors, with a special message for the Governor General. 'Maintain a strict vigil on all borders. Prevent all Azad Hind intruders from entering. If caught, dump them in jails instantly.'

Mountbatten told his colleagues, 'You must have guessed why I sent all the Indian officers away. Bose can be extremely dangerous. If his words reach our soldiers, you can be sure our unity will develop cracks. The country will erupt in flames. If the man who got elected as the Congress president despite being opposed to Mr Gandhi steps into the country in a military uniform, on whose side do you think the forces will line up? To keep him out of our rank and file, strict censorship will have to be enforced. Forewarned is forearmed.'

'Dickie, we have already taken pre-emptive measures,' Auchinleck said. 'We have a new group among the troops called the "Josh Group". We have planted very bright agents in every unit. Through their network, the latest news should reach the commander in no time at all. Special investigation cells have been opened in Dimapur, Chittagong and Silchar. We will keep every JIFC out, you see.'

'Keep the headquarters in Calcutta,' Mountbatten suggested. 'It's a crisis situation. Amend the Press Act if necessary. Keep all papers confidential.'

That night, when Auchinleck and Mountbatten were sitting together, the conversation turned once more to the JIFCs. Sipping his drink, Mountbatten said, 'Bose has revolution on his breath. We believe that the government he has set up is a gathering of crooks, porters and traitors. Yet if we look at it from the objective standpoint of International Law, nine countries have accorded it recognition. Let us not forget that.'

'But, Dickie, if this man becomes India's prime minister in the future, will India remain in the Commonwealth? Will we be able to hold him in check?'

'Don't even dream of it. When that sad moment comes, if it does, when India has to be given her independence, how it will be done, what lines will have to be drawn – leave it all to us.'

'But what about Bose, now?'

'He should be killed. If not physically, then morally.'

The Subhas Regiment was standing at attention on Taiping Railway Station in Malaya. They had been instructed to move to Rangoon immediately, and were about to board the goods train under the command of Shah Nawaz and Capt. Ransingh. It was going to be a long and arduous journey of four hundred miles through three countries – Malaysia, Thailand and Burma, by road, by rail, through dense forests on foot, and even ferry where necessary.

The endlessly long train snaked its way in, panting and gasping. The soldiers rushed into the open wagons, squeezing themselves into the spaces they could find. Some wagons had come loaded from Singapore. All of them were afraid of enemy air attacks, which were imminent. But their hearts also thudded in anticipation of action. The guards were frantically blowing their whistles when all ears were drawn to the plaintive sounds of a song:

Deheli mein jaane wale
Mera salaam le jaao
Gana azadi ka
Dil se bhai gaao
O Deheli mein jaane wale.

An old blind musician played the harmonium and sang along with a little girl. Their rendition was so sweet that people involuntarily reached for their pockets. Soon, all the soldiers were packed into the train. Shah Nawaz went and sat in the bogie right in front. Green flags were waved, whistles were blown, cheers of 'Netaji zindabad!' 'Azad Hind zindabad' echoed through the station, but the train would not move. Impatient, Shah Nawaz got down to find out the cause of delay, and to his surprise, he found the tracks blocked by a crowd of crippled, lame and wounded soldiers. 'Unless you take us with you, we will not let the train pass,' they insisted. No amount of persuasion and cajoling would get them off the tracks. They were promised that another special train for the injured and the maimed would be sent, and then they cleared the tracks. The train began to huff and puff its way out. Soon, the strains of the song, soaked in nationalist fervour, were lost in the breeze.

Shah Nawaz was eager to get into the thick of battle. But when he looked at the plight of his soldiers, his heart sank. They had no heavy artillery with them. Little wireless equipment, some of it non-functional. Machine guns but limited bandoliers, not enough ammunition, three thousand soldiers with only four doctors, inadequate medical supplies, and the soldiers themselves in tattered khaki uniforms of the British Army.

The train sped past desolate villages, ravaged by both Japanese and British armies. American bombers carried out their sorties regularly and sank Japanese ships that had set out from Tokyo, in the Pacific

Ocean. Only among the Indian people was there a surge of hope, of courage, because they had heard Netaji's message. Members of the vast network of the Indian Independence League turned up at every station to greet the train, gaily waving little tricolours. Along the tracks were several labour camps. For many years now, the Japanese had employed poor Indian labourers to build the railway tracks in Thailand. Most of them were of Tamil descent. They toiled for twelve hours a day and then to get over their fatigue, drank themselves into a stupor with cheap country liquor. The Japanese had managed to lay a railway track through the dense jungles between Bangkok and Moulmein for which about eighty thousand Indians had laboured. When Netaji heard of their plight, he appointed a committee under Brahmachari Kailasam. It was learnt that the oppression of labourers had decreased considerably. But the last four years had reduced them to skin and bone.

The route march started from Champun. Almost three hundred miles had to be traversed on foot. Every soldier carried a rucksack with belongings, a pistol and thirty-six rounds of ammunition. They sang as they marched,

'*Kadam kadam badhaye jaa …*'

The soldiers would cover about twenty-five miles a day. Healthy competition sometimes spurred them on to do even thirty-five miles, like Capt. Amrik Singh's and Capt. Sota Singh's men.

Soon, the Japanese columns came into view, like endless lines of marching ants. They came up to Shah Nawaz. 'Whose army?'

'15th Division. Leader Lt. Gen. Yamayuchi.'

'Why are you on foot?'

'Transport problems. Railway tracks blown up, not enough wagons.'

'Where are you coming from?'

'Bangkok. Delayed start. Gen. Mutaguchi waits for us on the border,' the captain said anxiously.

The Japanese slept for barely four hours. Yamayuchi's jeep had broken down, so he marched with the men. When tired, he rode an elephant. Heavy artillery guns were loaded on to the elephant's back, while the bigger guns were dismantled and packed in wooden crates, which were carried on heads. The two armies marched side by side.

Even the common soldier had heard of Netaji, so every now and then they would shout, 'Bose banzai! Bose banzai! Long live Bose.'

The Indians were shocked to see thousands of Japanese soldiers bathe in the rivers, completely naked. Shah Nawaz asked a major, 'Why do you bathe in the nude? We feel embarrassed.'

The major laughed and said, 'You do not know? Our Goddess of Justice is also nude. She says, hide nothing. That is why we have decided to hide nothing from your Bose.'

The war situation kept changing rapidly. News came that Chinese, American and British troops were being amassed on the northern borders of Burma. Japan had deployed its air force in the direction of Australia and the Pacific Ocean. The clear skies were an invitation to the American bombers who sneaked into the interiors of Burma, sprayed the poor Burmese farmers working in their fields with bullets and departed. People fled their villages and took refuge in remote areas. Once called the paddy granary of the East, most of Burma lay barren, like an arid infertile desert. They passed the battle-scarred Moulmein. As the Azad braves marched along the banks of the Mergui and the Tovhoy, all the heavy machine guns and other equipment were transported by boats; their journey continued by boats, called 'maru' in Japanese. The threat of air attacks would now increase. Finally, they reached the shores of the Sittang and crossed over into Meiban town. When they saw the numerous pagodas dotting the landscape, the Azad Hind soldiers felt they were close to their home soil.

From here, a train would take them to Rangoon. The exhausted soldiers considered it a luxury to rest their boots on the floor of the train as it made its slow and cautious journey. The following morning at around eleven, the train belched its way to the Wav River. Once they crossed Pegu, how far could Rangoon be? The three-week long life-sapping journey from Singapore was coming to an end. Every face brightened in anticipation. Suddenly, the sky rumbled ominously. An American bomber dived and dipped crazily around the train, spitting fire in its wake. Pandemonium broke out. The driver checked the motion of the train. Japanese and Indian soldiers leapt out of the open wagons. Some took refuge in the narrow gap between the wheels and the tracks. Others sheltered under the trees on the side.

The aircraft returned and hit its target. A couple of wagons caught fire. The sudden outburst took eight Japanese soldiers, and six lay wounded. Jeet Singh of Garhwal was the first martyr of this campaign.

The train halted there for a while, partly hidden by the trees. There was not much point in continuing the journey by day. Once darkness enveloped the Wav, the train with a mighty clatter and roar started off on its way. Shah Nawaz looked grimly at Ransingh. 'What a difference the last two and a half years have made! Japan ruled the skies then. Now, you barely see a single Japanese plane. British and American air power is gaining strength. Things are getting tough. We must launch the attack on Imphal quickly.'

Netaji, quartered in a bungalow at 11 Jamal Avenue, Rangoon, belonging to the Ziyawaddy Sugar Estate, was busy organising supplies.

A jeep screeched to a halt and the six-foot-tall Shaukat Malik got out. His eyes looked red, and even if he had sworn that he had not been drinking, Netaji would not have believed him.

'So, Malik?'

'Sir, look at this jamadar ...'

The man stood there, ragged, as if he had been in a fight.

'Have you started taking jamadars also to the booze shops now, Shaukat?'

'Allah kasam, sir, nothing like that.'

'Recruits from Bahawalpur state are only mercenaries. Who's to trust them.'

The jamadar spoke up. 'Netaji, so what if they are Japanese? We are not their slaves, why should we salute them?'

'What's the problem?'

'This donkey has fought with a Japanese captain.'

'Why?'

'It was like this, Netaji. I was walking across the parade ground when a Japanese jamadar accosted me. "Salute me," he said. "Why should I? You are not my boss," I retorted. So then, he abused me and said, "You live on our mercy, remember that." Just then a Japanese captain strolled along and threatened me, "If you don't salute him, I will hang you upside down."'

'And then?'

'There was a scuffle. I refused to salute even if they killed me.'

'Well, Shaukat, what's wrong with that?' Netaji asked.

Later Netaji told Yellappa and Bhai Paramanand that the matter was more serious than it seemed. Inside the office were seated office bearers of the Hindi Swatantra Sangha and some leading businessmen. Netaji had a long discussion with them regarding the establishment of the Azad Hind Bank.

By the time the discussions and preparations for Imphal were sorted out, it was past midnight. A tired Netaji turned towards his bedroom when Abid Hasan handed him a sheaf of letters, saying, 'Read them tomorrow, at leisure.'

'What are they?'

'Nothing much. Kesava Menon has sent a clipping from the *Hindustan Times* of a year ago. Pandit Nehru's criticism of you. It is funny from one angle, but worrisome from another. Anyway, rest now. Read it later.'

Netaji longed to sleep. But his restless mind denied him that luxury. As he tossed and turned, his mind flew back to the early days in the Congress, his pleasant association with Jawaharlal ... He switched on the bedside lamp and began to read the news clipping:

'I have no doubt at all about Subhas Chandra Bose's patriotism. He was a dear friend and a valued colleague. But many years ago, we drifted apart. That old friendship will not come in the way of my opposing his present actions and ideology. He is a lost traveller. I do not approve of the path he has chosen. If his role derives its identity from that path, then I cannot be a silent spectator. I too believe that Hitler and Mussolini must suffer in hell. That is why, no matter how pure Subhas's heart, intent and objective might be, if he attempts to enter India with the Japanese Army, I will not hesitate to draw the sword to prevent him.'

Netaji put the paper down. It lay there for a long time. He was beset with doubts. Was he really misguided? Had he deceived his country? Was all this debate, argument, conflict with so many people futile? Was estrangement from dear friends like Jawahar worth it? I lost the company of my precious family – those who loved me – Mej-da, Bibha boudi, Ma, Basanti Ma – and that unfortunate girl in a distant land to whom I could offer nothing but long years of loneliness, my dear Emilie. I have caused so much suffering, so much grief to so many.

The sentries fell asleep at their watch. Silence reigned supreme. Suddenly, a strong wind whipped the curtains in the room into ropes. From nowhere appeared before his eyes a sword – drawn from its scabbard – glinting, challenging, bold. What were the implications? He had to think them through. He addressed it:

'What is my fault? A tiny island squeezes the life out of thirty-eight crore of my countrymen, so I draw my sword against them. Is that wrong? England today wages a war for democracy, for humanity, doesn't it? If their intentions are so noble, then let them grant India her freedom and my struggle will end. What more do I want?'

'But your struggle is hard and bitter,' the sword warned.

'I am aware of that. I will have to fight till the empire crumbles and the portals of freedom are thrown open.'

'It is more than that. It will test your endurance.'

'How?'

'You have taken birth in the land of Gandhi who has drawn the attention of the entire world with this new weapon of non-violence and acquired the halo of sainthood, of Mahatma during his lifetime. You will have to outshine that glow.'

'Has anyone got freedom without a fight? If the despotic British rule were to be overthrown by mere ahimsa, why would the jails be packed for the last twenty years? Why would young men like Bhagat Singh have worn the noose like a garland? I am convinced, only when the British rule is hollowed from within, when they are held at gunpoint and cannot afford to run the economy of my country, only then they will leave India. They didn't conquer my country to spread the sacred word of Jesus Christ or to safeguard humanity. Instead, an ordinary company, that had come to trade, used deceit to loot my golden land. They will be paid in their own coin. Only then will they leave my country. This will be a last-ditch battle, and I must sharpen my sword for that.'

Netaji flung aside the quilt and went to his table. He began to make notes for his discussions with the Japanese. No one else in the world drove such hard bargains as the Japanese. By the time he had finished, it was daylight. Throwing a shawl across his shoulders, Netaji walked down the stairs. In the adjoining room, Prem Sehgal threw on his clothes and rushed out behind Netaji.

Accompanied by an escort of twenty-one armed 'jaanbaaz' crack guards, Netaji walked towards Royal Lake. Rangoon was surrounded on three sides by water so the morning air was very cool. To the east was the Irrawaddy Delta, beyond it the Gulf of Martaban. Between the railway track and the water was the narrow city of Rangoon.

When Netaji visited the Shwedagon Pagoda, he stood outside it for a while. The tension created by Nehru's statement had eased slightly. In fact, his resolve had strengthened. Buddhism was born in India and was acknowledged in all of East Asia. Rabindranath's *Gitanjali* had become an international possession. To bring truth, beauty and prosperity to earth, the blood that dripped from Jesus Christ's wounds became a symbol of inspiration for all martyrs. How much difference was there between the thoughts of peace and prosperity as preached in the sanctum of the stupa and the bugle call for revolt?

Prem Sehgal remarked, 'You seem under tremendous strain, Netaji ...'

'What strain, Prem? What right do British scoundrels have to place me alongside Hitler and Mussolini? And Jawaharlal has joined their chorus. To tell the truth, Prem, I would never use unfair or unethical means. If I even faintly suspect that my deeds would besmirch my motherland, I will jump into the fire. Let Nehru look after his politics. I prefer to work for the people.'

While discussions about the setting up of the Azad Hind Bank were on, Netaji was preoccupied with the meeting that was to take place later that night with the Japanese. He had no other resources except those that the Indian community in East Asia had offered, and they were minuscule as compared to the scale of the war. So how could he bargain as an equal with the Japanese?

The first topic to come up was about conquered territory. 'I have set up the Azad Hind Government. I have trained my officials. We must administer the acquired territory,' Netaji declared.

'Agreed. When our prime minister has agreed to these terms, who are we to question them? By handing over the Andaman and Nicobar Islands to you, we have already put this decision into practice,' said Kawabe.

Next was the issue of the Azad Hind Bank. The members of the intelligence mission of Japan, Iwakuro Kikan came up with a long list of objections, which Yamamoto handed over to Kawabe. Glancing over them cursorily, Kawabe replied, 'What do you hope to accomplish by opening a bank in a foreign land during wartime, Mr Bose? If it runs into a loss, no one will be able to stop its closure. The investors will be in trouble. Why take a risk?'

'I don't see our bank as a rival to any other financial institution. On the contrary, I consider this bank as the inspiring store of blood and tears that my Indian compatriots have offered for their motherland in a time of crisis.'

Netaji's sentiments touched the Japanese, and Kawabe gave his silent approval. Immediately, Netaji looked at Yellappa, who began his calculations.

Finally, the vital question of whether Azad Hind soldiers came under the purview of Japanese military law came up. Twirling his moustache, Lt. Gen. Kawabe declared, 'When the war is knocking at your door, why insist on discussing trivial issues like this? Just accept our law and be done with it.'

'Now that we have codified our own military law, General sir, how can we obey yours?'

'What's wrong in that?'

'Are we slaves of Japan?' Netaji's voice rose several octaves.

'Many other armies are fighting with us in this war, for example the Nanking Army, the Burmese National Army or the Thai Army. If all of them obey our law, why won't you?'

'No matter what difficulties this might lead to, we will never bow before the Japanese law.' Netaji was infuriated. So was Kawabe. Netaji knew the Japanese law was harsh, tyrannical. He was certain that his soldiers survived on the idea of freedom would never agree to be bound by either the despotic German Gestapo or the cruel Japanese Kampeitai. There was a breach in the talks. Tensions ran high. Both sides were unwilling to yield. Once again, they gathered around the table. Slightly softening his stance, Kawabe began, 'Mr Bose, you make every trivial matter a prestige issue. We are bound to other countries also by treaties and pacts. If we grant you exemption from our military law, other countries?'

'That is your internal problem, General,' Netaji said. 'I have only one concern. Your government had granted recognition to our government. I don't wish anyone of our thirty-eight crore brothers to think that Japanese assistance given to us is a sham. If you have any reservations, please call your chief of army staff, Sugiyama. Or the foreign minister, Shigemitsu. Or speak to Prime Minister Tojo. Let us resolve the matter once and for all.'

Kawabe was a bit taken aback by Netaji's aggressive attitude. He also knew the extent of the influence Netaji had on the emperor and his subjects. 'Let us leave this issue to Tokyo,' he said in a reconciliatory fashion. He was sure Tokyo would decide in Bose's favour, but he was indignant that he should be led by the little finger of this upstart.

Netaji managed to get a written agreement that the INA should not be broken into units smaller than a battalion; they should fight shoulder to shoulder with the Japanese troops, and that they would control all captured land.

Addressing Kawabe, he said, 'Sir, I am fully aware of all the assistance Japan is giving my country. Once my country becomes free, I will most humbly return every paisa that we have borrowed from you. In case another government is formed, I will go from door to door and ask for money to pay back your loan.'

Finally, they adjourned for dinner. There again Netaji brought up the question of salute. Kawabe burst out laughing. 'You make an issue of this as well, Mr Bose? What is the harm in greeting each other? There must be friendship among soldiers. We have outfitted you, equipped you. If your men show us some respect, it will be good.'

'Must find some solution for fights among the soldiers!'

'Like what?'

'Any soldier who is junior in rank will salute his senior, whether Japanese or Indian.'

'That is natural. But if both are of the same rank?'

'Let both salute each other simultaneously!' advised Netaji.

After dinner, Shah Nawaz took Prem Sehgal to his quarters. Shah Nawaz, who once tried to split the INA, was now a complete loyalist. He said, 'Shall I tell you something, Prem? The future of our people is secure in the hands of this great man!' Tears rolled down as he continued, 'Prem, our noble leader, who will not compromise on the matter of who salutes whom, when he has no platform to stand on, will he ever compromise the integrity of our country? He is a nayak, a true mahanayak for whose sake, I will sacrifice my life not once but a thousand times!'

Fifteen

Capt. Shamsher Singh, Netaji's ADC, rushed into Netaji's office in 11, Jamaal Avenue. 'Netaji, the American B-29 bombers are making sneak sorties, dropping bombs randomly and running away,' he said agitatedly.

'Let them do their job. We will do our duty by freedom,' Netaji told him with a smile.

Several divisions of the INA were preparing to set out from Rangoon and report to Gen. Mutaguchi at Maymyo, about 450 miles away. Since Col. Lakshmi was away in Singapore on work, Netaji had entrusted his Yellappa the responsibility of leading the Rani Jhansi Brigade to Maymyo. With so many parents sending their daughters to join Netaji, Yellappa was in a tizzy. One of the first to arrive was Manavati Arya, the Rangoon-born daughter of an artist. While her father had drawn a picture of India for her with his brush, Netaji's words had painted in the colours. Her mother was unhappy about her decision, but her father warned her, 'Remember, beti, don't commit the sin of turning back on the battlefield and fleeing.' Some fathers told Netaji, 'We have only daughters. If we had sons, they too would have fought for freedom alongside their sisters.'

Then came the shy Lavanyavati, newly married to Abhay Chatterji who worked for a firm in Rangoon. Just listening to one speech of Netaji's had driven them both to join the INA. Abhay was on his way to the front with Gen. Kiani's troops. The fair, almond-eyed Lavanyavati, or Labo as she was affectionately called, was eager to go to battle.

Netaji asked Manavati, 'Have you asked after each girl?'

'They are all there, Netaji, right in front of us.'

'You are wrong, beti. They have just left the security of their nests and come to us. It is our primary responsibility to take care of every one individually.'

Manavati obeyed. All night, girls kept arriving at Netaji's residence since they were to leave early the next day. In the courtyard, Netaji's car, the big Lincoln, was being painted green. All the trucks were being covered with green twigs and branches. Several ministers of the INA, military officials, secretaries and doctors were to accompany Netaji. He had decided to shift his headquarters to Maymyo so he could be closer to the scene of action. The prospect of INA soldiers setting foot on Indian soil made him particularly happy. He told Shah Nawaz, 'Gen. Mutaguchi is waiting at Maymyo. You will have to step into the battle immediately.'

The next day when Netaji went to the Mingaladon airfield, Shah Nawaz's regiment was waiting for him. As he stepped out of the car, his eyes fell on a tall, slender officer with a large, bushy moustache, crooked, uneven teeth and a smooth-shaven head. He was wearing a colonel's uniform. As soon as he saw Netaji, he puffed out his chest even further and smartly stood at attention. While the air of basic honesty was evident, the reek of alcohol could not be concealed. Looking at him scornfully, Netaji asked Gen. Kiani, 'Are all Bahawalpur recruits like this, Zaman?'

'Yes, Netaji. These useless people were recruited by the princely states for their own protection. The British needed more men so they picked them up and brought them here.'

'This Shaukat is a strange man and so is Mohammad Durrani. Both are from Bahawalpur.'

Although Shaukat was very capable, Netaji disdained him because of his alcoholism. Bugles sounded, drums rolled, boots clacked in unison as Netaji took the salute. This was the select force that was going to battle and make his dreams come true. As shouts of 'Chalo Dilli' resounded, Netaji's heart filled with pride.

Just then the air-raid siren sounded. Panic struck. Within minutes, two huge American aircraft darkened the sky. Sounds of gunfire followed. And as suddenly as they had appeared, they vanished.

This unexpected raid threw everyone into confusion. Burmese and Japanese soldiers leapt into the bamboo thickets. Shah Nawaz was yelling, 'Netaji, get down! Get down!' But he continued to stand arrogantly erect, as if defying the enemy. Shah Nawaz was for a moment amazed at this display of courage, but then military prudence asserted itself and he yelled, 'Netaji, you have no right to endanger us and put your own life at peril.' Just then another plane roared overhead, emptied its bombs below and disappeared. One bomb fell in front of Netaji. The sulphur inside it was smouldering and could explode any moment, swallowing the dais. Within a split second, Yellappa rushed forward as Major Bhurewal leapt like a cheetah from behind. He managed to grab the explosive and fling it away. Barely had it hit the ground when an ear-shattering explosion was heard.

The medical corps personnel quickly rushed him towards the ambulance for first aid. But Netaji remained steadfast at the spot until he was certain everyone was safe. Then he calmly climbed down from the dais. He too sought refuge in the bamboo forest. Soon after, a squadron of twenty-odd aircraft eclipsed the sky and dropped their load of destruction across the entire parade ground. Immediately, anti-aircraft guns from the airfield nearby began their counteroffensive. The planes scurried away.

Again, everyone assembled on the ground. Every pore of Netaji's body exuded a new determination, his every word struck a challenge. Pointing to the Indian border he thundered, 'There, across the river, beyond the dense jungle and behind the mountain ranges, lies our motherland. We are all born from her hallowed womb. Let us return to that great and noble soil. Listen. Can you hear her calling? Blood cries out to blood, breath summons breath. Arise. Prepare yourselves. Chalo Dilli! We will split the enemy's defences and forge a path within. God willing, with our sacrifice, we will make our victory towers immortal. In our final sleep, we will kiss the road which will bring our army to Delhi.'

Everyone was full of praise for Bhurewal. Patting him on the back, Netaji told him, 'Bhurewal, I am proud of you.'

When the regiment arrived at Thongyan Railway Station for the next leg of its journey, Netaji was already there. He was accompanied by his ADC, his secretary and other military officials, but he stood quietly in a corner, watching everything. Every now and then, he would ask about the arms they were carrying, or even about their personal baggage. The station was a scene of hectic last-minute bustle. He touched Shah Nawaz's shoulder and said softly, 'You are the first soldier of the INA to carry the fluttering tricolour to the Indian border. May God bless you.' Shah Nawaz, worried by the earlier bombing incident, said to Netaji, 'Take care of yourself.'

'Don't worry, Shanno.' Netaji laughed. 'No bomb has yet been made with Subhas Chandra Bose's name on it!'

The train began to move. Netaji raised his hand to his temple and saluted the troops. As each bogie moved forward, every soldier was moved. Their weapons were old. Their clothes, foreign. Footwear, worn out. Discards from the Japanese Army. Yet, their courage was unbounded, their resolve unflinching. Netaji stood to attention until the whole train had passed. Tears of pride and joy were trickling down his cheeks. They were all set to go to Delhi, the dense Burmese jungles, the unfamiliar terrain, enormous rivers like the Irrawaddy, notwithstanding.

The Azad Hind Government's Advance Headquarters was shifting from Rangoon to Maymyo, closer to the battlefront. On the occasion, the Burmese Prime Minister, Dr Ba Maw, hosted a dinner in honour of Netaji.

Netaji was in a relaxed mood, laughing and joking with the gathering. Among the invitees were several prominent families of Rangoon. Pretty young girls with beautiful black eyes and slim figures, wearing traditional colourful longyis, were offering flowers and garlands to Netaji. Everyone was in high spirits, talking about Netaji's imminent departure for the front. Suddenly, his gaze fell on Col. Shaukat. It was clear that the colonel was very drunk. His inebriated state was causing some mirth among the guests. Netaji was embarrassed to see one of his officers behave inappropriately with the host Dr Ba Maw. He signalled his men to take Shaukat away.

The following day, Shaukat begged Netaji to forgive him. Netaji handed him a wad of currency notes and told him to take off – to go and have a good time in Bangkok. 'And leave us to fight our own battle for freedom.'

Shaukat grovelled and whined. Netaji ignored him for a few days. Finally, he summoned Zaman and said, 'Take Shaukat with you.'

'Where to?' asked Zaman puzzled.

'To Imphal.'

'But Netaji ...'

'Follow my orders.'

And Shaukat wept and swore he would never touch alcohol again, as he saluted Netaji, crying, 'Jai Hind!'

At Gen. Slim's headquarters in Barrackpore, there was a commotion. A bomber aircraft stood waiting on the airstrip. The c-in-c, South-East Asia Command, Lord Mountbatten and a team of high-ranking officers had arrived to carry out an inspection of the forward area.

Gen. Slim, a tough man with a prominent jaw and hawkish, penetrating eyes, was the commander of the newly raised 14th Army. On that day, he was in conference with Lord Mountbatten. The 14th Army had been raised specifically to fight in the Burma campaign. Though Dickie Mountbatten would be in charge of the new South-East Asia Command headquartered in Kandy, the responsibility for the forthcoming campaign was entirely with Gen. Slim. Next to Slim sat Gen. Scoones who, as the head of the Fourth Corps that was responsible for the defence of Imphal, was in an unenviable position. He hadn't slept properly for days. There was no saying when the Japanese would attack.

Forty-three-year-old Mountbatten, excited about his new command, asked Slim, 'General, don't you think it would be to our advantage if we attacked the Japanese before they attack us?'

'Even if we advance right up to the Chindwin River in Kabaw Valley, it would still be a hundred miles from Imphal. How can we hold such a long line of defence? At any rate, we still don't have a clear idea of the strength of the advancing Japanese Army and the traitorous INA accompanying it.'

'In that case, as soon as the Japanese begin to cross the Chindwin, we should attack them ...'

'That would be dangerous.'

'Then the only option we have is to call back our units spread across the plateau and hold Imphal. We should strengthen our defence by building a strong wall around the headquarters and wait for the enemy to attack,' Scoones suggested.

'There's one problem with this plan – all the territories we have taken so far will revert to the enemy. This plan is audacious and risky,' Mountbatten pointed out.

'That is what makes it beautiful. If we stick to it, we will be closer to victory,' Gen. Slim said.

A message was received that the aircraft was ready for take-off. Everyone converged on the airstrip. Within minutes, the bomber was airborne. It flew over Calcutta, leaving behind the Hooghly River, Howrah Bridge, the dockyard, and climbing higher, headed towards Assam. Next to Mountbatten was seated Air Marshal John Baldwin of the 3rd Air Force.

'I keep telling everyone that the only way to triumph over the dense jungles of Assam and Burma is from the air. For which we need these strong wings, which only you can provide,' Mountbatten said to Baldwin. Lt. Gen. Geoffrey Scoones was still mulling over the defence of Imphal. Expressing his concern to Mountbatten, he said, 'Sir, the area under the 14th Army is immense. It extends from the China border in the north to the Bay of Bengal, seven hundred miles away. It is covered with forests so dense and dangerous that they strike terror in the hearts of men even in broad daylight. There are high peaks to be crossed and deep valleys. There are no paths or tracks in the region. Our reconnaissance parties have got lost without a trace.'

'No trace at all?'

'That's right,' Slim corroborated. 'All we have by way of paths are dry beds of streams and rivers and here and there, a few tracks made by wild animals.'

Mountbatten peered out of the window at the vast expanse below. The fields and open vistas of Bengal were gone. The hills and valleys of Assam were coming closer. Wherever he looked, he saw a thick forest cover. At the Quebec meeting, Churchill had advised him, 'You have a twofold responsibility, Dickie. To harass the Japanese in Assam, to maximise your air attacks and force the Japanese aircraft in the Pacific to head towards India.' Now, he would also have the task of crossing the Chindwin River and subduing the Andamans. In order to keep a close watch on the Japanese, he had to establish headquarters in Ceylon. If needed, it would be easy to attack Singapore and Rangoon from there.

While in command of the British navy's battleships Kile and Daring, Dickie had ridden through many storms and dangers. He was related to Britain's royal family and considered it his duty to safeguard its heritage from the Japanese.

Baldwin ordered the pilots to turn the aircraft towards the China border in the north. There, in Lido, General Stilwell had established a base. Below, the vast bed of the Brahmaputra that traversed through Assam disappeared from sight. Only forests and tea gardens came into view. Running through them like a parting in the hair of a beautiful girl was a railway line.

'Calcutta is eight hundred miles away from this end,' Slim said. 'This railway track was built with the assistance of American engineers over the last two to three years.'

'And the labourers?'

'For the stretch from Lido and Dimapur to Tamu, seventy thousand Indian labourers were employed. They were lured away from the tea gardens or threatened by the use of force to work day and night.'

'Excellent. It will be as useful to us as it has been for the Americans.'

The aircraft flew over the jungles towards Dibrugarh. The neighbouring airfields of Chabua and Margarita came into view. Soon, the American base of Lido was visible with its narrow landing strip. Next to it were a few bomber aircraft camouflaged with leaves and dense branches. Clearly, Stilwell too was expecting a Japanese attack any time. On one side of the airfield was a mountain range in the shape of a bull's hump.

'Sir, do you see that hump-shaped mountain? That is the Hump Route.'

'Oh!'

'Stilwell's aircraft will cross this Hump Route and descend into China.'

The aircraft now turned back. Soon the town of Dimapur nestling in the hills was visible with its long rows of godowns. Forty miles beyond Dimapur, past a deep valley, there were several high peaks. On one of the lower hills lay sprawled a large outpost. This was Kohima.

A line of peaks stretching from Kohima to Imphal came into view. Recently the British Army had constructed a road beyond the range. It was the only route that connected India to the Manipur plateau. The ninety miles between Kohima and Imphal were covered in minutes. The forty-mile-long and twenty-mile-broad plateau began to move out of sight. It was the only plain between Burma and the eastern end of the Himalayan range. The aircraft began to circle over Imphal. The pilots pointed out the Palel airfield, twenty-five miles away. Besides Palel and Imphal, which were all-weather airstrips, the British had built three more airfields in the region. In case of a sudden, enemy attack they would be extremely useful as forward bases. A ring of gentle, rounded hills surrounded the Imphal plateau. To the east was Jhobu Peak and in the south stood Chini Peak. Mountbatten stared at it worriedly.

'If the enemy manages to get his guns on that peak, the Imphal airfield will be at risk, won't it, Geoffrey?'

'Sir, we have prepared for that eventuality.'

The aircraft landed at Imphal airfield. Ignoring the reception committee waiting for him, Mountbatten got into an open jeep with Slim and drove off to the Fourth Corps' headquarters. The sun was blazing hot. The earth was already parched. Imphal was crowded. Two years ago, when the Japanese had attacked Rangoon and Mandalay, some sixty to seventy thousand refugees had fled to Imphal. In recent times, the Japanese air patrols had grown bold and often entered the airspace over Imphal. Their bombs had destroyed several houses and uprooted huge trees.

The Imphal Valley looked as if it was a massive factory opened by the British in preparation for an impending war. Roads were under construction, airfields were being built. Thousands of labourers and coolies toiled away. The landscape was dotted with the thatched huts in which they lived, depots of explosives and godowns full of grains. The local Nagas watched the hectic activity in amazement. They were starving, impoverished. They had no idea why this war was being fought.

Scoones's headquarters was far from the township. Bamboo, available in plenty, had been used to construct hutments called bashas. Everything – offices, hospital, godowns for supplies and explosives – was housed in these bashas. The entire camp was like a mini-city. Batteries of anti-aircraft guns were positioned around the perimeter. In preparation for air attacks, trenches had been dug. A particularly large basha served as a canteen for the officers. That afternoon, a lunch for the c-in-c was organised in the canteen.

In the course of the meal, Mountbatten said to Lt. Gen. Scoones, 'Two years ago, your army suffered a humiliating defeat at the hands of Japan's 33rd Division.'

'I wasn't the commander then, sir.'

'The 33rd Division is likely to approach via Tamu and attack Imphal. The enemy is an old one and so are the wounds he inflicted. This is a providential opportunity for you to settle scores.'

A map of the Manipur region was spread on the table. The 17th Indian Division was positioned on the right of the map, on Chini Hill close to Tidim, while the 20th Division was on the left in the Palel–Tamu sector. Pointing out the distance between the two positions – all of eighty miles – Mountbatten said, 'This entire distance is covered with thick jungles and that could be dangerous.'

'I have a division in reserve,' Scoones said. 'Whenever the Japs choose to attack, we will be prepared.'

On this inspection of the forward area, one of the c-in-c's tasks was to boost the morale of the men who would soon face an enemy who had inflicted a terrible defeat on them two years ago. Not only that, apprehensions about the dreaded jungle warfare loomed large in the minds of the men. There were other problems – monsoon, malaria – which they needed to be well-equipped to handle. Mountbatten visited the hospital; he drove around the entire camp in an open jeep. Every now and then, he would stop and address the men.

'Till yesterday, these men of the INA were in the Congress, and wore the thick and rough khadi of nationalists; today they are being supported by the Japanese Army and talk of revolution. Don't fall for their lies. Who says that the Japanese are invincible? There's no one as stupid and cowardly as a Jap. We will fight in every weather; in the monsoon as well. We will fight with all our might. If necessary we will airlift entire divisions. Why would a navy officer like me leave the high seas and come to this hilly region? At any cost, I must win this war.'

'Netaji, when will Japan take its next step?'

'Even as we speak, consultations are on at Kawabe's headquarters in Rangoon. Prime Minister Tojo has sent two of his staff officers as observers.'

'Meaning, very soon there'll be a war?' Prem Sehgal asked eagerly.

'Can't say. Japan is four thousand miles away from Burma. The distance is a big obstacle. Their headquarters are in Tokyo. The Southern Army which falls under their command is based in Manila in the Philippines. The commander is Field Marshal Terauchi. Next to him is Lt. Gen. Kawabe who is in charge of the army in Burma. He is in Rangoon. Below him is Gen. Mutaguchi who is stationed in Maymyo in the hills of north

Burma. The distance from Maymyo to Rangoon is five hundred miles. The entire army is spread over a vast region. Communication is a big problem. And there's simply no solution. If someone has to be sent by air from Rangoon to Tokyo, the journey will take at least four days.'

Despite outlining these hurdles to Prem, Netaji could not help but let his imagination take flight over the valleys and mountains, right across the sky to Delhi.

'Prem, according to my information, Mutaguchi has come to meet Kawabe in connection with this matter. He is going to be our steersman through this journey. We should meet him.'

'Right now?' Prem's eyes widened. It was 1:30 in the morning.

'Why not? There's no difference between day and night for me any more.

Shamsher Singh was just waking up. He roused the driver. Netaji and his secretaries left for the Boat Club where Mutaguchi was staying in a large bungalow. The sentries recognised Subhas Chandra and immediately let him in. The light was burning in Mutaguchi's chamber. He was surprised to see Netaji. 'Come in! Come in! Looks like you too are spending sleepless nights. That's good, very good!'

Maps and plans relating to the campaign were spread across Mutaguchi's desk. Pointing to them, he said, 'Imparu! Imparu! Your Excellency Chandra Bose, apart from you and me, there's no one in this entire world who gives a damn about Imparu.'

'And why is that?'

'My staff officers have been up all night putting together this plan, but all of them have only this to say – Imparu is going to be Mutaguchi's biggest headache. A real nightmare. Mutaguchi is mad.'

'Why?'

'Because they are dead scared of the Kabaw Valley. In Burmese, it means the valley of death. A name it gets from those intractable China mountains, from the great rivers, Chindwin, Irrawaddy and Salwin, that play out their dance of death every monsoon. But all this does not frighten me. I have to create history – with my strength, my passion.'

'All the same, what is the Japanese plan?'

'To maintain a defensive posture on the Burmese border, to stop the American assistance to China by closing down the Burma road, and as a fellow Asian, a friend, to put you on the road to Delhi. Bose, that day is not far. Soon, I will take you to Imphal.'

Netaji said, 'General, just wait till I reach Imphal, the entire nation will erupt in a revolt. My supporters, who number in thousands, are just waiting for that day.'

'According to our plan for "Operation U", we will reach Imphal. I had requested that we be allowed to mop up Lido and Dimapur too, but the others couldn't swallow that. Let's see. Whatever happens, will be for the best,' Mutaguchi said.

'You are geared up for the enterprise then?'

'Absolutely. Two of my divisions, forty thousand men, are on full alert at Maymyo. There's only one hitch.'

'What's that?'

'15th Division has not yet arrived.'

'Why?'

'It will, eventually. It is coming on foot from Bangkok.'

Dawn was breaking when Netaji left Mutaguchi's house. Among the Japanese Army, the general opinion was that this whole Imphal mission was fraught with danger.

On 23 December 1943, in the presence of Ayabi and Lt. Gen. Eitaro Naka, Kawabe signed the plan for the Imphal campaign. Three days later, Ayabi was in Manila. Field Marshal Terauchi viewed Operation U with a great deal of scepticism. He read every word of the plan carefully. Then, with trembling hands, he signed it and said to Ayabi, 'If those brave men who are in the field are confident of victory, why should I be an obstacle in their way?'

The atmosphere in Prime Minister Tojo's official residence in Tokyo was grim. Tojo stared at the maps of East Asia spread across his table. He had given orders not to be disturbed. The flags on the map indicated how many fronts the battle was being fought on. After Dunkirk, everyone in Japan believed that Germany would eye the East Asian colonies of Britain and France. America was deeply embroiled in China, and Japan would not accept its supremacy in the Pacific. Despite efforts to make peace, it became clear on 8 December 1941 that war was inevitable. That night, President Roosevelt sent out his final message for compromise. But it was too late. Japanese destroyers had already set out to finish Pearl Harbor. They had to avenge the blow to their tradition of bravery, their samurai pride.

After the victory at Pearl Harbor, the morale of the Japanese navy was sky-high. They had established supremacy over the Pacific and were waiting to take Hawaii. The victory was, however, short-lived. American destroyers had begun to sink the Japanese warships. Prime Minister Tojo was under immense stress. Pale and hollow-eyed from lack of sleep, he looked ten years older.

An ADC tried to wake him, but it was several minutes before he finally responded.

'Someone from Rangoon?' Tojo asked 'No, sir. Rash Behari Bose.'

As Rash Behari Bose was leaving, Tojo remarked, 'I don't want to hear anything else. My eyes are fixed on the borders of India. In the present situation, there's no hope of victory in the Pacific. To preserve our honour, we need one resounding success. Apart from Imphal, I don't see any hope of it.

It was past nine in the night. Prime Minister Tojo entered his bath. He'd had a tiring day. Slipping off his kimono, he entered the tub filled with hot water. The steam helped him relax. If only he could hang all his cares and responsibilities on the peg like the kimono and soak in the soothing warmth of the tub, he thought. Through the thick plate glass of the shower cubicle, he could hear a voice, faintly. 'Who is it?' Tojo shouted, annoyed.

'Col. Nishiruva from the Emperor's office.'

'What's the problem?'

'A team of officials from Rangoon has arrived in connection with Imphal.'

'Wait.' Tojo called Col. Nishiruva into the dressing room and fired off questions through the small glass window.

'Has an adequate supply of rations been arranged?'

'Is there any inconsistency in Mutaguchi's battle plan?'

'Our air force in Burma is weak. Have we made any plans to equip them to counteract the enemy's effort to gain territory?'

'Once the Imphal plateau is breached, will we need additional forces?'

'If most of our army is on the Indo-Burma border, have we taken steps to ensure that there is no slackening in the defence of Burma?'

'If the Allies were to attack us from the sea, what arrangements have we made to counteract that?'

Seeing Col. Nishiruva taken aback by the sudden barrage of questions, Prime Minister Tojo ordered, 'Get on the phone and find all the answers. Then come and talk to me.'

A short while later, the colonel returned. Raising his voice over the sound of the flushing toilet, he said, 'I've spoken to headquarters. Everything's clear. There's no reason to worry.'

Tojo smiled and stepped out of the tub. He read the notification for the Imphal campaign, number 1776. He signed it with a flourish and put down the date – 31 December 1943.

As he lay on his bed, perspiring from the hot bath, his wife watched him, her eyes anxious. Tojo smiled and sighing deeply, said to her, 'Who knows what lies in store. The end of me? My throne? The Japanese Army? Or the way to freedom? Mine and Bose's too. Whatever it is, I have prepared to commit suicide along with Bose. It cannot be helped.'

Gen. Mutaguchi had hosted a special dinner for Netaji at his headquarters in Maymyo. The commanders of the three Japanese divisions were also invited. Through this dinner, Gen. Mutaguchi wanted to convey several key messages to his associates and carry out a last-minute review of the entire operation. Netaji and Gen. Mutaguchi were sitting in the general's office. To fight the cold wind, some soldiers were lighting fires. Just as Shimla was the summer capital of the British in India, in Burma it was Maymyo, a hill station established by an Englishman, May, from whom it got its name. Situated thirty miles from Mandalay, it went on to become the summer capital of the governor of Burma and the Government House was a symbol of the autocratic power of earlier days. Now, it housed Gen. Mutaguchi.

In front of the Government House was Kandawgyi Lake, built by the British with the help of Turkish POWs during the First World War. Beside the lake, two hundred acres of land had been allotted to the Azad Hind Government to set up their base. This region was closer to India than Rangoon, and Netaji had moved here along with the Rani of Jhansi Regiment.

In the moonlight, Maymyo looked beautiful. The landscape was dotted with bonfires. Imphal dominated the thoughts of both Netaji and Mutaguchi. Mutaguchi kept studying the maps of the region.

Using a coloured pencil, he highlighted something on the map every now and then.

'Three of my divisions – each twenty thousand-strong – have left for Imphal. Their courage will determine our destiny – yours and mine.'

'Your plan to attack Imphal and Kohima simultaneously is amazing,' Netaji said in admiration.

'Certainly. Look at Kohima's position. My colleague Gen. Sato's 21st Division will climb those mountains and seize Kohima. For Imphal, I have reserved two divisions. Capturing the territory up to Ukhrul, my 15th Division will head towards Imphal. My old and experienced officer, Gen. Yamayuchi, commands it. The 33rd Division under Gen. Yanagida will clear Tiddim Road, the traditional route from Burma to Imphal. Using that route, the other two divisions will attack Imphal. By then, Gen. Sato would have won Kohima, and he will turn around towards Imphal and attack from the other side.'

Netaji studied the map thoughtfully.

'Your Excellency, have I missed out something?' Mutaguchi asked.

'I have just one request that our Gen. Kiani's 1st Division of the INA be given the opportunity to fight.'

'Certainly. We are sending Zaman towards Moray–Bishenpur in any case. Your Shah Nawaz will fight in Haka Falam, and down below, in the Arakan, Col. S.N. Mishra will engage the enemy. In keeping with its promise, Japan will implement its policy.'

'General, that is not enough. In Malaysia, at Ipoh, Penang and Singapore, our centres are recruiting even now. I have to raise two more divisions.'

'Why? In three weeks, we would have captured Imphal,' Mutaguchi said.

'One can't be too sure. If more blood is needed to fight for the motherland, it will be readily available.'

So eager was Mutaguchi to win Imphal that he had started an Animal Training Centre to ensure there was no shortage of transportation. Netaji asked him, 'Is the training of animals over?'

'Oh yes!' Sipping his drink, Mutaguchi said, 'Everyone said, there's no way one can travel through these jungles. So I said we'll use animals to transport war supplies. 'I've given them such excellent training that you will see these animals fly across the peaks to Kohima.'

So confident was Mutaguchi of winning Imphal in three weeks, that in a large gathering, he admitted, 'There are only two reasons why I am attracted to Imphal. One, I can't wait to cock a snook at Wingate. And, two, Bose's patriotism has mesmerised me.'

Netaji and Mutaguchi were welcomed with a great show of respect and honour. Several members of the staff and senior officers gathered around them. To inspire them, Mutaguchi said, 'Friends, speed. Speed is our best weapon in this war. Within a month, all three of my divisions will have pinned down the enemy in Imphal. Therefore, move ahead with the swiftness and force of a wildfire and burn up the enemy's territory. Attack with light weaponry and win the campaign within three weeks – that is what binds my plan together.'

In the earlier Sino-Japanese war, Mutaguchi had been a commander. He had witnessed the fall of Singapore. With every fibre of his being, he hoped to witness this third attack which would make history. 'From the belly of this campaign will emerge the dawn of India's independence and Japan's good fortune,' he would say to everyone.

'General, you strongly opposed the Imphal campaign at one time, didn't you?' Netaji asked.

'To tell you the truth, I was mad then,' Mutaguchi said. 'When the British fled from Singapore and Rangoon, we should have followed through with Hayashi's plan and taken Imphal. The reason I objected was the extremely hostile terrain – thick jungles, malaria, torrential rainfall, slush, swamps and blood-sucking leeches. That is why even today Imphal seems a distant dream.'

'General, if you want to reach the moon, you must stretch on your toes, isn't it? Neither you nor I have any choice.' Netaji said.

'The enemy is not asleep. He is constantly alert. On the one hand, Stilwell is growling about clearing the road to China; on the other, Slim is desperate to achieve the impossible by recapturing Burma. And that Mountbatten is roaring like a wounded lion and pacing about in ten different directions at once.' Mutaguchi was trying to size up the situation, adding loudly, 'Friends, that Nippon's victorious flag of the rising sun should not sink in the Pacific is the biggest concern of our Emperor, the Japanese people and Prime Minister Tojo. At this juncture, whatever the cost, show the world that you can win Imparu and protect the honour of the Japanese flag.'

Mutaguchi seemed lost in his own dream. Everyone clapped at Mutaguchi's emotional speech. At another table were Sato and Yanagida. Looking at Mutaguchi, Sato muttered, 'Wishful thinking, that's all it is.'

'Sato, honestly, what's going to happen?'

'A pipe dream! We are going to sink.'

'Sir, how can we possibly attack with just three weeks' ration?' Lt. Gen. Eitaro asked.

'There's no better alternative speed. If every soldier charges ahead forcefully, everything will be fine,' Mutaguchi replied.

Sato scowled at Mutaguchi. The enmity between him and Mutaguchi was an old one. About fourteen years ago, in 1930, the Japanese Army became divided into two groups. One faction, Kodo-Ha, comprising the young radical loyalists who looked upon the Emperor as god, had Prime Minister Tojo and Mutaguchi among its oldest members. The second faction, Toje Hi-Ha, was supported by the Japanese capitalists and had leanings towards Russia. Sato, Yamayuchi and several other commanders were firm supporters of this faction. Eight years ago, they had rebelled openly and had got several officials executed. The Emperor had had a hard time winning them over and now this same extremist group had political power in its hands. Sato knew very well that at one time Mutaguchi had been told to keep an eye on him.

Sato, strong and well built, looked like a Chinaman although he was of Japanese descent. He watched the assembly with an inscrutable expression in his heavy-lidded eyes. A senior officer in the Nippon army, he had practical knowledge and experience of war. He had commanded the 23rd Division in Manchuria and at fifty-two had seen most of the world. Sato did not enjoy the rapport that Tojo and Mutaguchi shared. He belonged to another camp. Standing in one corner with his friends, Sato chewed on a piece of fried meat and said, 'Yamayuchi, Imphal is a child's whim. If Mutaguchi is willing to sink our entire army just to satisfy a personal ambition, then I am not prepared to risk my life in this exercise.'

'But will the victory over Imphal not be a victory for Japan?'

'Huh!' Sato's scowl deepened.

Mutaguchi's staff officer was a part of the group around Sato. The laughter emanating from that corner attracted Mutaguchi's attention. Seeing him approach, everyone fell silent. Addressing Yamayuchi,

Mutaguchi said, 'Don't forget one thing. Before the end of summer and the onset of the monsoon, this campaign must be over. 29 April is the birthday of our Royal Highness. On that day, let us fly our pennant on the eastern boundaries of India and present him with the victory in Imphal as a birthday gift. And therefore, just three weeks' ration is adequate.'

As the night progressed, liquor flowed and the guests grew increasingly drunk. Staff Officer Oben, under the influence of alcohol, said, 'To date, no one has ever attacked India from the east and succeeded. Ask Bose if you like.'

'That's why my audacious plan will ...'

'It reeks of folly,' Oben said harshly.

That sent a chill through the gathering.

Netaji was stunned at the turn the conversation had taken. He looked at Mutaguchi, who was trying hard to control his temper. His presence made the situation all the more intolerable. Oben continued undaunted, 'I'm only stating the truth, Commander Mutaguchi.'

'Oben, don't talk nonsense. I have confirmed news. Imphal's godowns are packed with foodgrain,' Mutaguchi tried to say calmly. 'They could feed our army for six months. Go and enjoy Churchill's hospitality.'

'General, sir, first worry about your own burning house rather than dreaming of the comforts of your neighbour's home.'

The bonhomie had dissolved. The general had been humiliated before the gathering and that too by a junior officer. The liquor began to hit Mutaguchi. Whose staff officer was he? His or the enemy's ... In a voice shaking with anger, he said. 'I don't mind losing my life, but I will not tolerate such indiscipline in my army. Oben, rather than nurturing a snake like you, I would prefer to be crushed by the enemy's tanks.'

'General, be calm,' Netaji tried to intervene. But Mutaguchi ignored him and ordered for the steno to be called in. Glaring at the entire gathering, he dictated, slowly and clearly, 'By virtue of the authority invested in me by the great Emperor of Japan, I, General Mutaguchi, order that Staff Officer Oben be dismissed from service immediately.'

Pin-drop silence greeted this proclamation. Netaji did not consider it advisable to remain in the gathering any longer. Gen. Mutaguchi was mortified at having lost face in his presence. For the first time, he became aware that though everything seemed well with his army, it was not quite true. If this kind of dissension had risen before the campaign had begun, how would it all end? Yanagida and Sato were visibly shaken. Oben slunk away. An uneasy hush fell on the gathering. The dishes were cleared away and maps were spread out. Imphal and Kohima. Mutaguchi marked the two spots with coloured pins. He stared at them with the intense concentration of a chess player.

Staring at the mountains, valleys and rivers marked on the map, Mutaguchi muttered, as if to himself, 'What should one do? Attack Imphal first or attack Kohima? No, friends, we will grab both these rabbits in one go.'

'A brilliant idea,' Naka agreed.

Then, placing his finger on Kohima, Mutaguchi said to Sato, 'General, if Kohima is conquered quickly and you have the opportunity, you must move ahead and attack Dimapur.'

'Dimapur? Where's Dimapur?'

Sato's cool indifference made Mutaguchi boil. 'I wouldn't like to say that such a valiant general has not even bothered to study the map. Here ... look here. Thirty to forty miles away from Kohima, that is Dimapur. The last station on the Britishers' Eastern Railway. It is possible that there are godowns of food supplies there.'

'Has it not been confirmed?'

'General, a bold man should explore the waters as he swims in them. He has nothing to lose, everything to gain.'

The rival group was considerably chastened by Oben's dismissal. It was past midnight and all three commanders had to set out at dawn. Bidding farewell to Sato, Mutaguchi said, 'Good luck, General Sato. We will meet in Imphal and celebrate your victory over Kohima and the Emperor's birthday together.' He tried to grasp his hand, but Sato's curt response to this display of warmth sobered him. He said, 'General, is it necessary to remind you that death in pursuit of a noble goal an honour? Not just that, it even pleasurable.'

'But to die needlessly – what purpose does that serve?' Sato countered. The coldness in his eyes, the crease on his forehead, everything about him suggested that the matter had better be dropped. While Mutaguchi was open-faced, Sato's expression suggested reserve and aloofness.

Mutaguchi returned to his tent, furious. Oben's behaviour had wounded him and Sato's ridicule had sprinkled salt on those wounds. Despite drinking heavily, the oblivion of being drunk was denied to him. Irritated, he called Naka, 'Get my staff officer. I'm going to sack Sato from my army forever.'

'This is not the time to act rashly, General. By now, our army would be on the banks of the Chindwin.'

'So what's the worst that can happen?'

'Sato is the leader of the Toje Hi-Ha group. There will be a furore in the Imperial Army. Will you ignite the fire towards Imphal or will you try and control the fire caused by dissension in Tokyo?'

Mutaguchi was embarrassed by his own outburst. Naka went away to rest. A few geishas were invariably a part of Mutaguchi's entourage. His favourite, Noon, had been waiting for him, bright with anticipation. He pulled off his uniform and embraced Noon, but tonight her charms did not arouse him. Instead, in a corner of his brain, a warning bell of rebellion jangled. Noon's beautiful body left him cold. Instead, the peaks around Imphal and a white horse dancing on the road to Delhi was all he saw. 'Stupid fool,' he suddenly shouted at Noon and slapped her so hard that she fell off the bed. Hastily, he dressed and strode out of the tent.

There were only two bodyguards with him as he walked briskly over the cold, dew-covered grass. The chilly wind soughing through the trees made the branches creak. He had gone quite far when he saw two to three horsemen warming themselves around a bonfire. They were talking about the campaign. One said, 'Mutaguchi is riding the chariot, but the three horses pulling it are murmuring complaints. How will this chariot run? How will they mount the Imphal campaign?'

Mutaguchi stopped. Motioning to the bodyguards to remain silent, he ordered them to move some distance away. Covered as he was in a fur-lined cap and a coarse woollen overcoat, it was hard to recognise him. He joined the gathering near the bonfire. 'How long have you served in the Emperor's army?' he asked one of the horsemen.

'Thirty years. Half my life.'

'Do you remember any occasion in your army life when the Emperor's orders were disobeyed?'

The old man was petrified by the question. 'Don't even say that,' he said. 'Our great Emperor is a descendant of God. One cannot even dream of disobeying him.'

As dawn broke, Mutaguchi returned to his tent, at peace with himself.

The news from the front was encouraging. Accompanied by Prem Sehgal, Netaji went to meet Mutaguchi. Major Fujiwara had recently been appointed the staff officer of the 15th Army. 'Jai Hind,' he greeted Netaji who shook his hand. Fujiwara said with obvious pleasure, 'Your wait is over. In ten to fifteen days, we will be in Imphal.'

In the one and a half years that he had spent in Maymyo, Mutaguchi had taken up gardening. He had planted many varieties of roses in his front garden. Right then, he was busy tending to the large-blossomed Chinese rose. Seeing Netaji appear unexpectedly, he handed the watering can to an orderly and welcomed the visitor with a formal bow.

'Jai Hind,' Netaji responded. 'General, there's heavy fighting on the front and here you are ...'

'The responsibility for the war rests with my officers. I only take care of my roses,' was Mutaguchi's confident reply. The assurance of impending victory was reflected in the brightness of the general's eyes. His confidence was contagious. It pleased Netaji. These days, the two were in constant touch. Mutaguchi's three divisions had been committed to the battlefield. There, in the Arakan sector, Major Mishra of the INA was in the front line, while in the Tamu sector, Gen. Zaman Kiani was leading the attack at the head of the Gandhi Division. The second and third battalions of the Subhas Brigade under Shah Nawaz had crossed the Chindwin near Kalewa.

'Shah Nawaz is a bit unhappy that they have not been given a chance to be where the real action is.'

'Please don't think that way,' Mutaguchi said. The fighting on the Arakan coast is an important part of the whole campaign. The plan is to engage the enemy there and draw him in while simultaneously attacking Manipur. If it works, the British forces will be annihilated.'

The two went into the general's office. 'Shah Nawaz's task is a very dangerous one. He has to maintain the Japanese supply lines. His two battalions are braving the bitter cold of the Kabaw Valley with nothing more than the clothes they are wearing and an additional sheet. That is not any ordinary valley; it is the valley of death. But my Japanese soldiers are very impressed with the tenacity of your men.'

'General, Shah Nawaz writes, "Netaji, just a few miles away from us, the enemy's Dakotas airdrop fresh food and biscuit tins. But we don't feel sorry for ourselves on account of this. We survive on dry rotis, damp mud and wild grass, because we have just one dream in our eyes – that of freedom." I was deeply moved by his words.'

'Mr Bose, the difficult phase of your life is coming to an end,' Mutaguchi said. 'I have some good news for you. The army headquarters in Tokyo sent a message – "Inform Bose to be prepared to enter India."'

Netaji placed the tip of his stick on the map lying on the table and stared at the region marked Manipur and Assam. The waters of the Brahmaputra seemed to have reached his eyes and his voice was fraught with emotion. 'Just let Imphal fall and my feet touch that soil. Thousands of my supporters have entered India secretly via submarines. Members of the Forward Bloc, teams of underground rebels are just waiting for a signal from me. The India–Nippon army on the border and a mighty revolution within. Between the two, the British will be finished, once and for all.'

The poet within Netaji was soaring high on the wings of imagination, but his revolutionary spirit was trying to find a way out of the tumult of emotions. 'I have no desire for high positions or honours. All I want is a free motherland. Its youth invited Gandhiji's wrath and supported me in Tripuri. After my escape from the British prison, this will be my first chance to set foot in my motherland, and I wait for that day impatiently.'

'You are confident that the entire nation will welcome you back, then ...' Mutaguchi said.

'Just as all of France stood up to support Napoleon on his escape from Alba, so too will my country welcome me and my supporters. My beloved Bengal will turn out in millions to march with me to Delhi.'

Netaji's optimism affected Mutaguchi. A ceremonial photograph of the two men was taken. Netaji laughed. 'The next one will be in Delhi,' he said.

'I'll make your wish come true within fifteen–twenty days,' Mutaguchi promised.

Studying the map carefully, Netaji said, 'General, please don't close the road between Imphal and Kohima.'

'But that's the idea,' Mutaguchi replied. 'If we block that road, we will cut off Imphal from Kohima. My plan to bag these two rabbits in one go is foolproof. Why do you doubt it?'

'All the same that route should be kept open.'

'Why?'

'To allow the British to escape. As soon as Imphal is attacked, they will flee to Kohima exactly as they did when Malaysia and Rangoon were attacked.'

'No, Bose. I find the army base at Imphal strangely attractive. There is a big, naughty fish there. He swallows his prey and slips away. But my net is just as strong. I'm going to cast it cleverly. Believe me that he will be caught.'

'What will your next step be?'

'29 April! Tenchosetsu, our Emperor's birthday. We will celebrate it together in Imphal.'

Netaji returned to his camp that night accompanied by Fujiwara. Netaji discussed several issues with him, with one ear to the radio, which was broadcasting news of the war from different fronts.

Netaji had a busy routine in Maymyo. He would go to the neighbouring villages and give speeches exhorting the local populace to be prepared. He had to ensure that the forces in the frontline were being supplied with the necessities. The headquarters at Singapore were in Maj. Gen. Bhosale's charge. Netaji was in constant touch with him. Zaman Kiani's division was fighting in Tamu–Palel, but the 2nd Division under Gulzar Singh was making its way out of Burma. The 3rd Division was undergoing its final training in Singapore. It included several Tamilian and Keralite labourers as well as some enthusiastic local citizens. Netaji was after Kawabe to arm and equip the division.

Across the sea from Chittagong, close to Indian borders, were the thick forests of the Arakan. The INA had displayed unusual courage while fighting in this region. Lt. Col. Mishra had launched a fierce attack on the British South African force and compelled it to leave Buthiyadang and retreat by a hundred miles. For this bold action, Netaji awarded the title of Sardar-e-Jang to Lt. Col. Mishra. His colleague, Col. Pyare Singh, lost a leg in battle, and was sent to the hospital at Maymyo to recover. Netaji had organised a function to honour him. Mutaguchi was the chief guest. In the introductory speech, Col. Lakshmi reproached Netaji, saying, 'You did not keep your word. Please give the women of the Rani Jhansi Regiment permission to fight. The news from Imphal has got us all charged up.'

Netaji smiled and said to Mutaguchi, 'Did you see our girls' enthusiasm? We don't want to stay in Maymyo any longer.'

'Just wait a bit longer. As soon as your 2nd Division crosses the Indian border, you can prepare to leave.'

'Will we get a chance to fight?' Lakshmi asked

'Certainly,' Mutaguchi said. 'Imphal will be captured in a few days. In any case, I have to move on. When Netaji enters Imphal with his 3rd Division, shouldn't I be there to welcome him?'

The statement was greeted with loud cheers. Cries of 'Netaji zindabad', 'Vande Mataram', and slogans of 'Hindi–Japani bhai-bhai' were raised.

Mutaguchi took the megaphone and said, 'All you brave men and women of Hindustan, I cannot keep it to myself any more. I have some good news. Should I tell it now or save it for the end?'

'Now, please tell us now.'

'Yesterday, our Prime Minister Tojo announced in the Japanese Parliament, that as we keep winning the Indian territories, we will hand them over to the Azad Hind Government.'

Once again, there was a loud burst of clapping. Col. Pyare Singh who had displayed outstanding valour in the battle in Arakan was brought forward in a wheelchair. His leg had been amputated at the thigh and the stump was still wrapped in bandages. Netaji stepped forward and pinned the medal, saying, 'Pyare Singh, this honour is not yours alone; it belongs to us all.'

Pyare Singh said, 'I am only returning what belonged to my land in the first place. I've lost just one leg. There is the other leg, too, these arms, this head. At the most crucial moment in the battle, you had me brought away on a stretcher. Why did you do that, Netaji? You are the one who taught us that a man's bed is in the front and not the rear of the battlefield.'

Netaji spoke, 'Brothers, the charmed and blessed feet of the Azad Hind Fauj have finally stepped on our holy soil. Fighting its way through, the army is on its way to Delhi. Our most important goal is to throw out the British–American forces, and establish a stable government that is chosen by the people. Wherever my Azad Hind Government is formed, please welcome it. Please work with our officials in the glorious task of nation-building. The Japanese Army aims to defeat the Anglo-American forces and free the road to India's independence. Breaking through this dreadful dark hour, the radiant light of independence is going to shine.'

After the refreshments were served, Netaji said quietly to Mutaguchi, 'At the dinner, day before yesterday, I found General Sato's notes slightly out of tune.'

'Let it go. There are always some internal differences.'

'How far is Maymyo from Imphal?'

'About two hundred miles.'

'Wouldn't it be to your advantage to shift your headquarters a bit closer to the army?'

'Now, how would you understand what Japanese planning is all about? Don't worry, Bose. I told you, didn't I, that I'll take care of my roses, my officers are quite capable of taking care of the war.'

The freezing cold of the riverbank, the wide expanse of the Chindwin River, the deep jungles clad in the dark, mysterious garb of night. Even the Japanese Army, experienced in jungle warfare, found the surroundings terrifying. For the past four days, the 31st Division had been trying to cross the river. Twenty thousand soldiers, three thousand mules and five thousand bullocks. The bullocks were laden with explosives and rations. Apart from these, the mobile hospital, motor vehicles, heavy equipment, spare parts for guns, tents – so many things had to be ferried across.

Thousands of soldiers had been busy making rafts out of bamboo, light jungle wood, creepers and vines. Finally, the crossing began. The soldiers guided the bullocks into the water. Frightened by the darkness and the swift current, the animals were swept away. Getting the elephants on to the rafts and tying them down was like wrestling with death. The panic-stricken animals trumpeted crazily. Several soldiers and animals drowned in their attempts to cross, yet the rest persisted. It was imperative to ferry the army across under the cover of darkness. In the daytime, the activity would attract the attention of the British–American fighters.

On the first night, despite the loss of human and animal lives, a sizeable quantity of supplies was moved. Gen. Sato stayed up all night, supervising and drinking. As dawn broke, his irritation grew. Speaking to Staff Officer Naka, he said, 'Are we going to eat this stupid plan for the campaign? What about food and water? Is anyone bothered about my stomach?'

'Prime Minister Tojo must have thought of all this, isn't it?'

'I've not seen a bigger fool than Mutaguchi in my entire life.'

'But Prime Minister Tojo ...'

'He is a buffoon. His grandfather and great-grandfather were good dancers. Why did he have to give up his family profession and play at fighting a war?'

Naka laughed. 'General, don't you think you are saying all this simply because you are fed up?'

'Take it that way. But if this Tojo–Mutaguchi duo win the war tomorrow, do you really think they will allow me to walk freely on the streets of Tokyo?' the general rasped out.

The shouts of men, the bellowing of bullocks, the elephants trumpeting – the cacophony and chaos of the crossing went on all through the night. Despite the current, the elephants made progress, the bullocks raised their heads and swam. Every single creature – man and beast – was in a hurry to reach Kohima. The deep rumble of the river echoed through the forest. And the night added its own dark cry.

The Dakota carrying Mountbatten landed on the airstrip in Lido. He was on an inspection visit to the US Army's base near Kamain. The American general, Stilwell, was waiting to welcome him. A military band was playing; a guard of honour comprising American soldiers stood at attention. As Stilwell and Mountbatten had begun to inspect the parade, an officer came running towards them. He saluted and handed over an envelope to Stilwell.

Stilwell opened it and read the message. He turned pale.

'What's it, General?' Mountbatten asked.

'The Japanese are hunting wild pigs, goats and other animals on the banks of the Chindwin.'

'Oh!' Mountbatten looked thoughtful. 'The Japanese invasion is not far off,' he said.

'On what basis do you say that?'

'They'll skin those animals, rub the flesh with spices and smoke it in preparation for the attack.'

The bandmaster was waiting with baton in hand. The bugles and drums had stopped playing. Seeing this, Stilwell and Mountbatten gave indications for the parade to start. The guard of honour gave its salute. Climbing into an open jeep with Stilwell, Mountbatten reviewed the parade. When the review was over, in an unexpected gesture, he asked the driver of the jeep to get off and took hold of the steering wheel with boyish enthusiasm. 'Come, General, let's go for a drive,' he said to Stilwell.

The lush greenery, the neighbouring peaks – the entire scenery seemed to have enchanted him. He was in high spirits, laughing and joking with his host as he drove past a dense cluster of bamboo. Suddenly, he braked very hard at a turning. He was trying to reverse the jeep when a bamboo hit the windscreen and shattered it. A splinter of glass entered Mountbatten's eye. Somehow, he managed to stop the jeep. The pain in his eye was unbearable; there was blood all over his uniform. He was given first aid and put into his favourite Dakota Mercury and shifted to the base hospital which was close to the airstrip. Specialists immediately attended to him. To relieve the pressure on his good eye, they bandaged it. He felt as if the whole world was doomed. It was an ominous start. That night, while Mountbatten was resting after dinner, there was a commotion in the corridor. His ADC came into the ward shouting, and began to bang on Mountbatten's door.

'What is it, Robert?' Mountbatten asked sleepily.

'Sir, they are here! The Japanese are here!'

For a second, it looked as if Mountbatten was going to jump off the bed. But his eyes? Damn them, why did he have to lose his sight at such a critical time? Scoones's 17th Division had gone ahead. There wasn't sufficient time to recall it. And now Japan's 15th Division had surrounded Imphal.

There were daily bulletins about the progress of the Japanese Army. In fact, it was even being said that 17th Division was in Mutaguchi's hold the way a frog is in a snake's jaw. Mountbatten was like a wounded bird in a well. A couple of days went by like this. One day, he flared up at the doctor, Capt. Shea. 'Enough, that's enough! You cannot keep me tied down like this!'

'Sir, please be calm. Impatience will cost you your eyes.'

'All right, but at least take the bandage off the other eye.'

'That's not possible,' the doctor said firmly.

Five days passed in this state of intense, almost unbearable pain. Mountbatten got panicky to know that a couple of divisions of the

Japanese Army along with a division of the INA were coming towards Kohima and Imphal.

One day he woke early and questioned, 'Why is it still so dark?'

'Sir, it's only 5:30 in the morning.'

He was not bothered about his eyes or the darkness. A cunning enemy had thrown a challenge. Without caring for the doctor's warning, he tore away the bandage over his good eye. At least that was working fine. The nurse was agitated, she called the doctors. They came at once, but who could say anything to the supreme commander of South-East Asia?

The Mercury took off from Lido. Mountbatten flew towards the battle zone.

Why were the jungles still so dark? Why was everything so blurred, wondered the pilot as he flew at full speed towards the 14th Division. Gen. Slim was in his office. Compared to Barrackpore, Comilla was closer to the front and the headquarters had been shifted there.

On 13 March 1944, Mountbatten's plane landed at Comilla at 10 a.m. Baldwin, Slim and other familiar faces were waiting to greet him, but it was clear from their expressions that the recent news had shaken them. Immediately, they began discussing the recent developments, reviewing the situation and the future course of action.

Back in Delhi, Mountbatten phoned Churchill. Claude Auchinleck was present at the time. After listening to Mountbatten with a sinking heart, he said, 'Dickie, our nation's honour is in your hands.'

'Sir, it is very difficult to save our skin.'

'What's the problem?'

'The 5th Division has to be transported from Arakan to Imphal immediately. It's the only solution.'

'So bring them in.'

'We don't have enough aircraft, sir.'

'Dickie, our air force has been swallowed by Germany. You know how much of it is left to fight. Think, think, there must be a way out. By rail?'

'That will take up to four weeks. It will give ample time to the Japs and that army of traitors to cross the Brahmaputra and forge ahead.'

'Any other solution?'

'If the Americans send their aircraft to our aid immediately then we stand a chance.'

'Use the Americans, then, you are the Commander of South-East Asia. Tell Stilwell.'

'It's not in his hands. The air force headquarters is in Washington.'

'All right, if need be, I'll rub my nose in the ground before Roosevelt, but you'll get your aircraft. As long as I am the prime minister of England, India's dream of independence will remain a dream.'

April 1944. Jorhat. The Mercury had just landed and Mountbatten was getting off on to the tarmac. In the distance lay the dry bed of the Brahmaputra. There was a dejected air about the place. With the war on, the tea gardens were closed. There was dust everywhere. To top it all, the April sun was blazing. The American officials waiting to welcome him looked tense. Apart from Scoones, every other senior commander from the Burma front was present at this important conference. As soon as Mountbatten entered the conference hall in the company of Slim, he was surrounded by journalists and photographers.

'Sir, sir, did you expect the Japanese to attack so soon?'

'No, I didn't. But this is what war is all about.'

'How will your South-East Asia Command emerge out of this storm?'

'The fight is on.'

The Japanese attack was like a knife wound in the stomach. Gen. Slim had decided to take Burma, but before he could do that, the Nippon army and the forces of Azad Hind had attacked him. The shadow of Gen. Wingate's recent death in a plane crash in the Kabaw Valley hung over the gathering. As a mark of respect for the dead man, everyone observed a two-minute silence at the start of the meeting. Wreaths were placed before his photograph.

Before the next issue was discussed, Stilwell asked, 'Dickie, how is your eye?'

'Painful.'

Gen. Stilwell looked grim. He resented being a junior to a man younger than him by ten years. He explained the difficulties his men were facing in keeping the supply lines open through the Burma–China road. Their airfields in Chabua, Lekhapani, Ledo, Jorhat were in grave danger, and Imphal was definitely threatened.

'Even Kohima is not safe any longer.'

Dickie stared at Stilwell in surprise. The presence of the Japanese Army near Kohima was a closely guarded secret. How had the Americans come to hear of it?

Stilwell's tone and words annoyed Mountbatten considerably.

In an overly respectful but puzzled tone, the American Army commander said, 'If they get their hands on Dimapur and cut the rail route to Lido, it'll be all over. To flee to China will be the only option before us.'

'I won't allow that situation to arise.'

'Dickie, today, good intentions and good wishes don't keep marriages going; this is war,' Stilwell pointed out.

America had given a squadron of aircraft at a crucial time. The 5th Division was being flown out of the Arakan. Mountbatten did not delude himself: if America hadn't helped out, then by now, the withdrawal all the way to Delhi would have begun.

Stilwell said, 'The danger that may arise for our naval bases in the Pacific cannot be discounted.'

'If Japan had wanted, it could have taken Assam when it conquered Rangoon. From where has it got the resolve to do it now?' Slim asked.

'General, at that time, they had not met that traitor, Subhas Bose. Today Mutaguchi and Tojo are dancing around with him,' Stilwell growled.

The Manipur plateau held everybody's attention. To his subordinates, Mountbatten said firmly, 'Do whatever you consider necessary to stop the Japanese. Break the back of Mutaguchi's 15th Division. Those stupid Japs have no idea of how far behind their supply lines are. Keep them engaged till the monsoon. The slush and mud will rot their feet, the floods will drown them. Even if they search for it desperately, they would have lost the way back home.'

'But their plan is to capture Imphal before the monsoon. Once that is in their hands, Calcutta won't be too far off,' Slim said.

'Thank God, Manipur is thinly populated. A handful of tribals are spread over a large area. They don't know much about the workings of the Congress. About Gandhi, Nehru, Bose they know next to nothing. Forget Calcutta, if even a city the size of Jabalpur had been in this region, the people would have been incited to rebel and we would probably have reached Oxford Street by then.'

'That danger is still there,' Stilwell warned.

Mountbatten said, 'General, the disorder in the Arakan is not settled yet. Chittagong too is in danger. Our Gen. Christian has not been able to control the Japanese general, Hanya. Imphal is in the crocodile's mouth. Kohima is smouldering. What help can we expect from London? Our prime minister gives long speeches, but the German bombers set London afire every night. When I accepted this command, I was very confident of myself, but, General, when I look for victory through these hurting, streaming eyes of mine, it seems obscure.'

Nobody had ever heard Mountbatten speak with such dejection. Even Stilwell was moved. The resentment he had felt towards Mountbatten disappeared.

Before the conference ended, Stilwell asked once again, 'Who will guarantee that my communication lines from Lido will not be disrupted?'

'Assuming the Japanese are successful in destroying the rail route, within four to five days, we will win back that territory and repair it. Don't worry about it,' Mountbatten assured him.

The conference ended and Mountbatten left immediately for Imphal. Before the Mercury became airborne, he asked for wireless contact with the India command based in Delhi and spoke for a while.

'Why was Gen. Scoones not present at this meeting?' he growled as the aircraft headed for Imphal.

'Sir, Imphal is in dire straits. How could he leave?'

'Oh yes!'

'Sir, even at this difficult time, we should congratulate one another,' Slim said.

'Why?'

'While returning to Imphal, our 17th Division was surrounded by the Japanese. But their commander, Yanagida had the wrong impression, or perhaps his spies had misinformed him, who knows –'

'Why?'

'Because that stupid man suddenly let them go – he let eighteen thousand men go just like that. In short, God protected us.'

As soon as dawn broke, the Mercury was circling the air above Imphal. Through the front window, the hilltops around the town were visible. The sight of them raised several questions. In the distance was the Tiddim–Bishenpur road and the road to Silchar. On either side were thick jungles, apparently without any sign of life. Imphal too had been devastated by the Japanese bombers. During the day, there was a semblance of calm and one could even hear the birds sing. Come night and the Japanese attacks would begin. Their air force being limited, during the day the aeroplanes would remain hidden in the forest. They preferred to come out after dark. As soon as dusk fell, the guns would start booming. On one side the Japanese were seven to eight miles away; on the other, they were emerging out of the jungles in small groups, barely fifteen miles away. The morale of the Japanese Army was high. Hearing the enemy guns fire from such close quarters, Mountbatten was seething like molten steel.

The supreme commander had organised a post-dinner discussion. When the officers assembled, they saw Mountbatten studying a secret message. 'There is a possibility that a few soldiers from the Indian regiments may desert and join the INA.'

'Mr Scoones,' Mountbatten's tone was like a whiplash, 'are you taking precautions to contain these traitors?' Banging his fist on the table, he shouted, 'How does one miserable man have the audacity to challenge such a vast and strong empire?'

Then controlling his temper, he stood up to leave. 'Before I leave Imphal, I want to see action taken against the treacherous JIFCs. Or you'll see me here again,' he warned.

That night, sleep eluded him. His had been an illustrious career. Tonight, it seemed to mock him. As a naval officer, as the captain of the destroyer HMS Kelley, he had guided his ship safely through an enemy attack in a rainstorm. Despite fifty-one enemy shells having landed on the ship, it had fought on for ninety-one hours before heading for the port. Where had that bold commander gone? In the Mediterranean, near Crete, the enemy had sunk his ship and all his men drowned. Somehow, he had managed to evade the bullets and swim his way to the shore. Where was that brave man hiding now?

On the ceiling of his drawing room, someone had painted a beautiful peacock. The eyes reminded him of another pair of large, beautiful eyes. When he was leaving for India to take over his new command, Edwina had come to the airport to say goodbye. As she put her arms around him, there was a strange brightness in his eyes. 'Darling, this is the first time in history that a naval officer has been given charge of the army and the air force. As always, I am going to be successful in this mission too.'

The bombing had intensified. The sounds of the guns, Wingate's coffin, the sea of invasion unleashed by Japan and an ordinary Indian dressed up as a soldier. An army of India! A nation that had accepted servitude quietly for three centuries, that considered a foreign invasion as the will of God, spineless people who, for the sake of meaningless titles like Raisaheb, were ready to be spat upon by foreign rulers, where hundreds of rajas and maharajas would address him as 'Your Excellency' and stand in a queue to bow till they touched the ground, where science was a slave to religion, where even the children were taught to sing 'God Save the King' – in that dead soil, an insignificant human was born who reached the Land of the Rising Sun and now swore to overthrow the British Empire. Today, India's eastern boundaries were trembling under his attack. There was a knock on the door. It was Gen. Scoones.

'Sir, we have caught four JIFCs who were hiding in the jungles, four spies of the INA.'

Mountbatten glared at the four men: a Muslim, a Hindu and two Sikhs. Scoones said, 'They made contact with three of our Indian battalions. Bose's propaganda material – pamphlets and newsletters – were found on them. Those three battalions were planning a mutiny and were going to join the enemy in Bishenpur tomorrow.'

'How did you discover them?'

'Two loyal Indian soldiers informed us in time.'

'Good. Now, remove those three battalions from the frontline and keep an eye on them. The rest of the army should not get even a whiff of their seditious intentions.'

'Along with the four of them, six of our soldiers who had turned dangerous were also caught.'

'Where are those scoundrels?'

'Outside, in handcuffs.'

Mountbatten turned his attention to the four in front of him. Glaring at a Sikh, he asked, 'What's your name?'

'Santa Singh.'

'Occupation?'

'A teacher of English, in Penang.'

'Where did you get commando training?'

'Swaraj Institute, Penang.'

'How many others have entered India with you?'

'Don't know.'

'Or won't say?'

'Yes, yes, I won't say. In the INA, we don't betray our comrades.'

'What form of death would you like?'

'What a treacherous enemy would give the revolutionaries fighting for their motherland.'

All four of them faced him without a trace of fear. Not one showed any sign of guilt or hope of mercy. Their cool unconcern infuriated Mountbatten even further. He ordered that all four men and the six standing outside be executed by a firing squad. No trial, no judgement, no justice. The accepted norms of the army and the international laws were completely defied. A few minutes later, the sound of gunfire was heard in the courtyard outside.

Mountbatten came out. Ten bodies lay on the ground. They were still warm. Before Stilwell could ask the question, Mountbatten said, 'Wrap these bodies in the Union Jack and send them via Calcutta to their homes.'

Scoones looked shocked.

'Scoones, I am not that stupid. By wrapping these traitors in the Union Jack, we will give the message that they died in the service of the British flag. Though the INA is a reality, we should not acknowledge its existence. We may be fighting against it here, but to the world at large, we will deny its presence and portray it as a farce concocted by a few traitors. And remember, in future, this is going to be the stand we take in all matters concerning the INA.'

Sixteen

The shadows of the tall peaks played on the level ground below. Sato's army, chilled to the bone by the freezing wind, huddled around bonfires trying to keep warm. The maps indicated that they would soon be seeing the mountain peaks around Kohima.

Capt. Nishida said, 'At last, our five-thousand-mile-long march is nearly over. We've reached the Indian border. Now, we have to fight together for the glory of Japan.'

'Mutaguchi has ordered that we move with speed and agility. We must seize the peaks of Kohima in one stroke and then move straight towards Imphal,' Miyazaki said.

Sato's animosity towards Mutaguchi could not be hidden. His darting eyes seemed to say only a miracle would ensure that we reached our homes alive. The Kohima–Imphal road would be lined with the graves of Japanese soldiers. Sato's defeatism on the eve of an important battle angered Nishida, Koboyashi and other officers. Nishida said, 'General, we will receive our daily rations as decided by the commander, won't we?'

'The amount of valour we display will depend upon the quantity of rations we receive,' Sato replied.

These tactless and bitter comments were not appreciated by anyone and they said what they wanted to say while pretending to be mild and respectful.

The next two nights proved to be really black for the Japanese Army. The mountain before them was so tall that when one looked up at it, one's hat slipped off. The British assumed that it would be impossible for the Japanese Army to move its heavy artillery up that slope full of thick sal forests, hairpin bends, slippery paths and elephantine boulders and attack Kohima. But the Japanese soldiers felt the blood rush to their heads at the prospect of battling with the jungles, of a confrontation with the forests. Even Sato could not remain unaffected as he measured that peak with his eyes and the challenge it presented. The stocky Japanese attacked the slope energetically. The animals, superbly trained in the jungles of Maymyo, were up to the task. Bullocks carrying the bags of rations on their backs bent low as they climbed. The horses were foaming at the mouth trying to find footholds as they made their way up the narrow curving paths. The elephants carrying heavy loads of dismantled cannons and guns were so charged despite the tough climb that it seemed they were drunk on mahua liquor as they trampled through the undergrowth.

At last, the two terrible nights were over. At the end of the second night, when dawn broke and the breeze from the valley began to caress them they had reached the brow of the mountain. Through his binoculars, Sato stared hungrily at the Kohima valley spread before him.

Situated in the eastern ranges of the Himalayas, Kohima, at the end of a steep climb, was like a precious stone mounted in a ring. It sat, like a saddle, astride the two mountains. The mountains in the west went up to 10,000 feet, in the east they were not less than 7000–8,000 feet. As the breeze blew through the valley, it seemed to echo with unusual sobbing sounds. A long, curving road panted its way down from the crest of these mountains towards Imphal, then with a sharp bend headed for the Burma plateau.

As Gen. Sato watched, the mist rose and slowly stirred the town awake. On a hill slope across the valley, the red-roofed bungalows of the British officials added a certain charm to the town. The collector's bungalow, small but impressive, stood on a western slope. Some distance below was a public road. The main part of Kohima was sprawled on either side of this road.

For the past few days, Col. Richards, with the help of a contingent of British troops, had been guarding Kohima. The news that the Japanese Army was on the outskirts of Imphal had just reached Richards. Though the secret agents were saying that the Japanese would probably attack Kohima soon, he did not believe it would be so easy.

By the end of March, pressure from the Japanese increased. The Nippon flag fluttered gaily on many of the surrounding peaks. The first to move ahead was Major Miyazaki with his regiment. He ordered the artillery to commence firing at the British cantonment on the western slopes. The British troops and a unit of the Assam Regiment stationed there returned the fire. In the first two days, the Japanese tried to assess the strength of the British garrison but did not succeed. The British too were trying to ascertain the strength of the Japanese. Col. Richards kept scanning the skies in the hope that someone – Scoones, Slim or Mountbatten – would come to his aid. He looked around, hoping to see the infantry marching to his aid from Dimapur. But in vain.

On 5 April, the Japanese soldiers started moving down the slopes behind the Naga villages. Col. Richards had pitched camp in the collector's bungalow. As the news of the heavy fighting around Imphal came to him, his heart was in his mouth. He felt utterly helpless as two whole Japanese divisions approached them like hungry hyenas. He picked up the phone and dialled Gen. Scoones's number. Scoones told him, 'The situation is still the same. My neck is in the noose. These Japanese are determined fighters. I've set defensive positions all round Imphal and somehow managed to protect it so far. What's the news from that side?'

'Kohima is still peaceful, but these past two days, some itinerant Nagas have reported seeing the Japanese advancing furtively down the slopes in small groups.'

Gen. Scoones's voice turned hoarse. The protection of Kohima was his responsibility as well. At how many places had the Japanese infiltrated simultaneously? Below, along the Bay of Bengal, there was fighting on in the Arakan. The Japanese commander Haana had almost overcome Col. Christian. In North Burma, Gen. Stilwell's forces were up against an entire division. The perimeter of Imphal was already in flames. Two British divisions were seriously threatened. And now, Kohima too was under fire. How was one to tackle this conflagration?

'Richards, why don't you capture the peaks? Position your guns on them?'

'Sir, I don't have sufficient men to protect Kohima alone. The fastest we can haul the guns up on to the peaks is fifteen days.'

There were only fifteen hundred soldiers in the Kohima garrison. In addition, there was a battalion of the Assam Regiment and about a thousand non-combatants. On hearing that Japanese soldiers had been seen in the vicinity of Jesami, Kharasom and Lyashi outposts on the opposite hill, Richards was panic-stricken. When he noticed shadows moving along the not-so-distant peaks, he was almost paralysed with fear. Like ants crawling out of a huge anthill, Japanese soldiers were swarming down the slopes.

'Sir, sir,' a staff officer shouted as he ran up to Richards. 'All hell's broken loose in the bazaar down in Kohima.'

'What? What has happened?'

'The Japs are coming! There's utter chaos.'

The bazaar was clearly visible from the bungalow. Everyone was running helter-skelter, screaming, 'They are here! They are here! The Japanese are here!' Richards couldn't believe his eyes. One regiment might somehow have made it across those peaks, but here was a deluge of them! How many divisions were there? One? Two? More?

When he was faced with this crisis, Richards found his nerve. He ordered the guns to open fire. Since the garrison was at an altitude, they had an advantage. The Japanese soldiers had reached the public thoroughfare below and were beginning to climb the hill when the artillery fire began to knock them off, one by one. The forested slopes around Kohima watched the two human races battle out their lives. How insignificant those creatures were compared to their own immensity! Whether they were twenty thousand in number or thirty, what difference did it make – they were, after all, mere ants.

The two armies had fought in countries all over the globe, but this battle was quite different. The narrow Imphal–Dimapur road running through the valley was the only battle line between the two sides. This initial exchange of fire was stopped rather quickly. Miyazaki conjectured that though the British garrison was cornered, they would not surrender so easily. Besides, a reserve brigade was positioned on the hill behind the garrison. Seeing the possibility of a long-drawn conflict the Japanese, like foxes and jackals, began to make holes and dig trenches.

Sato took a sudden decision to block the road to Imphal. So total was the blockade that not a bird nor an insect could get into Imphal. Except for the hilltop on which the garrison was, the collector's bungalow and a part of the western range, three-quarters of Kohima was in Japanese hands. They positioned their guns in strategic spots and set up wireless sets at regular intervals. Unlike the Japanese, the British were not able to position their unwieldy guns on the heights. Caught in a terrible bind, Richards scanned the skies ceaselessly. Even if he were to order the guns to fire, the Japanese were out of range. It was not feasible to enter their territory under cover of darkness, because their engineers had laid mines along all the approaches.

'Sir, what should I do now?' a nervous Richards asked Gen. Slim.

'Inform us when the situation becomes critical. We will send one squadron to assist you,' Gen. Slim tried to reassure him.

There, Maj. Gen. Miyazaki stood before Gen. Sato. 'General, we could wipe out the British garrison in just one assault,' he pleaded.

'The orders were – block the road to Imphal and capture three-quarters of Kohima. We've accomplished that. What more is there left to do?' Sato questioned.

'We'll fling the entire division at them and the fate of Kohima will be settled with just one blow,' said Miyazaki.

'I have no objection. You speak to Mutaguchi if you like. Try and get in touch with the air force. As soon as air support is provided to me, see how I roast the British garrison.'

'Sir, don't take this cynical view. You know very well that our air force is weak and there is no hope of air support.'

'So what is the big rush? We'll take Kohima in our own time.'

Miyazaki was furious, but the Japanese military tradition did not permit him to raise his voice before a senior officer. He was a prisoner of that tradition.

Having crossed Tiddim, Maj. Gen. Yamamoto's division was heading for Bishenpur. The Japanese and Indian armies were confident that Moirang, which was slightly further ahead, would be in their hands by the next day. About fifteen to twenty miles away, lights flickered in the dark. Col. Shaukat Malik looked at those lights and drew a long sigh. He mumbled to Abhay Chatterji, 'Those lights belong to Imphal.'

'Imphal!' Everyone was surprised.

'Instead of pitching camp on the way like this, why don't we rush across to Imphal?' Abhay Chatterji asked.

'You're off your head, boy. To defend that post, Gen. Slim has three divisions standing on full alert. There are four airfields around Imphal alone.'

'If only these stupid Japanese had not let the 17th Division slip through their fingers, our fortunes would have changed completely,' Abhay Chatterji said.

The commander of the Japanese 33rd Division was also awake. It was past midnight but he was unable to sleep. His tent was pitched under a mango tree. Suddenly, there was a crunching of dry leaves. It was a staff officer with a message.

Yamamoto read it in the faint glow of the lamp: 'Increase your pace. There should not be any more mistakes like Maj. Gen. Yanagida's. Our emperor Tenchōsetsu's birthday is just a fortnight away. Whatever the price, pay it. I want to present Imphal to His Majesty.'

Together with Zaman Kiani's division of the Azad Hind Fauj, Yamamoto had struck at Manipur. Zaman was fighting in the Tamu valley. A wheel may have many spokes, but the central pivot is the same for each one. Similarly, there were many roads but only one destination – Imphal.

'General sir, we are desperate to get to Delhi,' Shaukat Malik said.

'Well, attack Moirang tomorrow and capture it.'

'What do we have to do, Sir?'

'A few miles ahead, there is a post called Bishenpur. If we get our hands on it, the enemy will be alarmed and we will be closer to Imphal.'

'How do we get there?'

'On the other side, there is a road that goes to Bishenpur via Silchar. One of the bridges on that road is of immense strategic importance. We must get control of that bridge.'

'Why don't we attack?

'We cannot afford to be rash. The bridge is heavily guarded.'

Col. Shaukat had a map of Moirang under his pillow. He took it out and studied it several times during that night. Half a mile away, there was a lake called Lohtak. Moirang was a small Naga settlement on its edge. There was a fair chance that British troops would be patrolling that area. In the dim light of dawn, suddenly a cry rang out from the settlement,

'Netaji zindabad! Azad Hind zindabad! Vande Mataram!'

Col. Malik was stunned. What was going on? As it became louder, a horde of Naga braves came rushing at them. After confirming that they were indeed loyal to the INA, Malik let them come close. Prominent men of the village like! Kuriyan Singh and Sanba Singh were leading the crowd. Shouting 'Jai Hind!' Kuriyan Singh saluted Malik. He handed over a letter of introduction given by Netaji. 'I am Kuriyan Singh, sir!' he said.

'This is my village. On getting a message from Netaji, I crossed the jungles and secretly entered Singapore. Like me, several other Naga youth have met Netaji. We are workers of the Azad Hind Dal. When Netaji comes here with his government, we will assist him in the administration. Malik saheb, what can we do to help you?'

'Thank you. Ration supplies are a major concern.'

Kuriyan Singh's face became grave. 'Colonel saheb, it is just misfortune! Because of the threat of war, there was no harvest this year. Our Naga brethren live in jungles, caves and on trees. They are terrified of the shelling. Eight days ago, the British Army passed this way and destroyed all the villages so that we would not be in a position to help you. Moirang too is looking like a graveyard.'

Col. Shaukat was annoyed to hear this. Kuriyan Singh consoled him, 'Don't worry. Most of the villagers believe that Netaji's army is the army of Swaraj. Whatever we have, roots, flowers, fruits, we will share with you. But we must continue to fight. How else will we get freedom?'

14 April 1944. It was dusk. The Nagas started to beat their traditional drums. The youth formed a huge circle and danced in honour of their new king and his government. Since the 'king' himself was not present, they hung a picture of Netaji on a bamboo pole and placed a garland of flowers around it. Young Naga girls joined in the dancing. Completely oblivious to the destruction caused by the British attack, they participated in the celebrations.

Next to the village square, the house of Hemaru Thambulya Singh was one of the few that was undamaged. Col. Shaukat Malik announced that it would be used as the forward headquarters of the INA. In the distance, from Bishenpur came the sound of cannon fire. As the tricolour fluttered in the setting sun, the braves of the local Bahadur group of the INA were overjoyed. Some of them were so happy that they rolled in the mud and even ate some of it. 'Why are you eating mud?' asked someone.

'We are made from this mud, aren't we? Here, eat some, see for yourself how good it tastes.'

Col. Malik gave a brief speech. 'Imphal is not far and from there, Delhi is not far either.'

This was greeted by cries of 'Netaji zindabad!' and 'Vande Mataram!' An elderly Naga stood up and asked, 'You people have come ahead, but why have you left that lad behind?'

'Lad?'

'Yes, that Subhas. Why have you left him behind?'

'Baba, that lad of yours has very heavy responsibilities. The INA is fighting on seven–eight different fronts. He has to arrange for weapons and clothing, he has to organise the movement of the fauj-army – he has a million tasks. You people keep helping us in this way. Soon, Netaji will appear like a flash of lightning in a dark sky and strike at the British Empire. That day is not far.'

'Before I die, you boys must take this flag to Delhi,' the old man said.

That night, Col. Malik called a meeting with a few selected Naga villagers. Under the leadership of Kuriyan Singh, they were given the task of gathering the information. That night, the villagers brought whatever little rice they had stored in their homes and cooked it in a big pot. As the Japanese captain, Isoda and Col. Malik were enjoying their dinner, two Naga youth came forward with a pot of homemade liquor.

'Sahib, do have some,' they requested.

'I've stopped drinking,' Malik said.

'Why?'

'However potent liquor is, the high that one gets from it is temporary. I have tasted the nectar of love for the motherland; that kick is so strong that till I see the tricolour flying on the Red Fort, I will be on a high.'

The night wind was chilly. Gen. Yamamoto was fast asleep on his camp cot. His ADC was not prepared to wake him up. But the four soldiers of the INA were firm. 'It is important that we meet Yamamoto,' they said.

'He cannot be disturbed.'

'Tell him it's an important message from Netaji Bose.'

'Chandra Bose?'

'Yes.'

Yamamoto woke up reluctantly. Looking at the four men sleepily, he asked, 'Why have you come? What's the problem, now?'

'Sir, why should we lie? We can't get to sleep.'

'Idiots, is there anything new about that?'

'The sight of Imphal nestling there in the distance is like a knife twisting in the stomach. The agony doesn't let us sleep.'

'But what can you do about it so late in the night?'

'The bridge on the Silchar road is the biggest obstacle in our path, isn't it? Give us a couple of powerful bombs. We'll tie them to our stomachs and blow the bridge into oblivion. The road will then be open to you.'

Yamamoto was stunned. He stared at the four young men. Fujiwara too was speechless. Yamamoto sent two strong soldiers to accompany the four men.

The bridge, spanning an eighty-foot-deep gully on the Silchar road, was guarded by British Tommies. The cold was intense and they had lit a bonfire. Behind them was the bridge, vast and silent, shrouded in darkness. The six men crossed the stream and moved silently through the gully. They found a strategic spot under the bridge and quickly went to work. Simultaneously, each one pulled the pin. With a deafening roar, the entire bridge crashed.

In the distance, Yamamoto and Malik watched the flames rise. Above Moirang, the tricolour fluttered proudly.

~

Netaji's aircraft, 'Azad Hind', landed on the Maymyo airstrip. Bhai Parmanand, Yellappa, Barrister Raghavan and other ministers were waiting to welcome him. Col. Lakshmi placed a huge garland around his neck. Netaji was smiling but he seemed rather tense. His eyes searched for someone. A Japanese Army vehicle drove up. Gen. Mutaguchi got off and greeted Netaji. The two men went into a makeshift lounge to confer.

'First, I must go with you to the Government House,' Netaji said.

'Is something wrong?'

'How can I tell you here in the open? It's a serious matter.'

On reaching Mutaguchi's office, Netaji explained, 'General, today is 22 April. Your Emperor's birthday is just seven days away. What about Imphal? When will we enter Hindustan?'

Mutaguchi's face fell. The row of medals on his breast also shrank with embarrassment as his breathing became heavy. The next seven days would fly. Though there was news of progress from the other fronts, from Kohima, Ukhrul and Bishenpur, there were no bugles blowing victoriously. How was this delicious fish from Imphal going to be hooked?

'There is a problem somewhere,' Mutaguchi said.

'General, the future of your fifty-thousand-strong force and my two divisions hangs in the balance. Tomorrow, my countrymen will say, Subhas, you went halfway around the world, but what did you achieve? And what reply will I give them?'

Never had Mutaguchi looked as depressed as now. 'I have been cursed with a bad second-in-command. Right in the beginning, we had the opportunity to take the 17th Division, but Yanagida let the chance go. From the point of view of strategy, nothing can be more serious than this,' he said.

'Mutaguchi, do whatever needs to be done, but get yourself and me out of this dark valley. As soon as Imphal falls, the entire country will be ignited. Thousands of my compatriots are just waiting for that moment,' Netaji retorted.

'Chandra Bose, at my indication alone, China and Japan went to war. The man who took Malaya with almost surgical skill now assures you that he is confident of achieving his goal. There may be a few hitches, but believe me, Chandra Bose, time is still in my favour. In this world, wherever Mutaguchi goes, history is created, be it China, Malaya or India. Netaji, when you hoist the tricolour on the Red Fort, I will be there to have my photograph taken with you for posterity. That is my ambition.'

Grasping Netaji's hand firmly, he added, 'I repeat what Tojo has said to you. India gave Japan the teachings of Lord Buddha; it gave Japan a new culture. By giving you Imphal we will try to repay that long-standing debt.'

Netaji stood up. 'If one odd rose garden dies, it does not matter. Tomorrow, you can make a thousand rose gardens bloom. But hurry and move out of this place,' he warned.

These words made Mutaguchi wonder about the wisdom of depending too much on his subordinates. The roses of Maymyo had sharp thorns! He said, 'Chandra Bose, by this afternoon I'll move lock, stock and barrel to the front.'

On 22 April, Netaji saw a Zero-type Japanese aircraft leave Maymyo.

Netaji spent the entire day overseeing the work in his office. Food supplies were running low, so with the help of the Indian Independence

League in Maymyo he had ensured that several lorry-loads of supplies were dispatched from Rangoon to the front.

The Japanese air force's presence on the Burma front was almost nonexistent. As a result, American and British bombers would regularly swoop down on the jungles in north and central Burma and wreak havoc. Nights in Maymyo were terrifying. At dusk, a blackout would be imposed. Work in the INA's hospitals and camps went on in the light of candles and tiny oil lamps.

Accompanied by Dr Bawa and Col. Lakshmi, Netaji went on an inspection of the army hospital. The wounded soldiers spoke with pride and gratitude about Col. Lakshmi who had so selflessly taken care of them. They were aware that there was a shortage of medicines. But no one mentioned it to Netaji. One soldier told Netaji with a smile on his pain-wracked face, 'This nurse hasn't slept a wink for the last two nights.' Netaji turned around. He saw Lavanyavati. Her face was drawn, there were dark shadows under her eyes. Where was that shy new bride of just a few months ago? The golden glow of turmeric had left her skin, the mehndi had faded away. Months of holding a rifle had calloused her palms. Her hair was short. She was dressed in the rough khaki-coloured uniform, common to men and women alike.

'Jai Hind,' she said and saluted Netaji. Then, 'Netaji, where is my Abhay?' she asked.

'In the battlefield! With the army under Col. Shaukat at Moirang.'

Netaji spent the next two days in his office. One afternoon, he was interrupted by a distraught Lavanyavati and her friend Manavati Arya.

'Netaji, I've had an awful dream!'

'What dream, beti?'

'He was covered with blood! Netaji, tell me the truth – has something happened to my Abhay?'

'Don't be afraid, child. A bad dream can also be a good omen.' Netaji tried to console her.

'Then why did my watch fall into the ditch?'

'So what if it did? There's nothing to it.'

'But why? All these seem like a series of bad omens.'

Col. Lakshmi joined them. They were all worried about Labo. She looked like a terrified doe standing at the edge of a precipice. Netaji called her near, comforted her, then took off his wristwatch. 'You've lost your watch, haven't you? Here, take mine.'

'But what about my Abhay?'

'He'll come back! He will return safe and sound. He is fighting for his motherland at this very moment.'

Netaji's words seemed to give Labo some strength. A feeble smile appeared on her lips. Netaji asked Lakshmi, 'Your girls have prepared a play, haven't they?'

'That's right. It'll be staged on 30 April. You are hosting a dinner for the soldiers that day, aren't you, Netaji?'

'What play is it?'

'Parivartan' – 'the transformation,' Manavati replied. 'I've written it.'

'Have you given Lavanyavati a role or not?'

'Of course. She plays the hero,' Manavati said.

'If the hero is so nervous before the play, what will happen on stage?' Netaji joked.

Manavati, Shakuntala Gandhi and the Ganguli sisters, Aruna and Karuna, were working very hard towards the show. The play was about a girl who loves her country dearly. She joins the INA. But her beloved is a materialist. He values money above all else. Annoyed by his greedy nature, the heroine flings his ring away, telling him that if he does not join the INA she will have nothing to do with him. He becomes an alcoholic. Ultimately, he repents and begs his beloved's forgiveness. Labo was playing the man's role. Rehearsals kept her busy so she had no time to brood. A day prior to the performance, Netaji called Lakshmi and Yellappa. Looking rather grave, he said, 'Lakshmi, shift tomorrow's programme to this evening.'

'But we aren't ready ...'

'What difference will one day make?'

Everyone assumed that Netaji wanted this because some urgent matter had come up. Lakshmi and Yellappa were leaving the office, when Netaji said in a whisper to Yellappa, 'All is not well, my Kuber.'

That night the sky was cloudless. A bitter wind blew down from the hills of Maymyo. The programme started with the singing of patriotic songs. Amongst the singers was Prem Sehgal. His robust singing reflected his army background. Everyone knew of the romance between Lakshmi and Prem, but their personal life was on hold at this point. The play held the audience's attention from the start. Manavati came alive in the role of the heroine who loved her country above all. Labo, too, infused the character of the money-grubbing hero with life.

Lakshmi, Netaji and the others were engrossed in the performance when Dr Bawa quietly approached Lakshmi and whispered, 'Lakshmi, please come away for a moment.'

'Doctor, don't be a spoilsport … the play is so absorbing …'

'Lakshmi, didn't you hear? Come away for a minute. Please!'

The tense note in his voice alerted Lakshmi. She got up immediately and moved away from the audience.

'Lakshmi, I've got some terrible news,' the doctor said. 'Abhay and a few of his comrades were crossing a river in a boat near Moirang. Their intention was to blow up the British gun carriages with grenades, but the enemy spotted them and turned their cannon on them. A shell blew their boat into smithereens. Lakshmi, it's all over.'

Lakshmi was stunned. How was this dreadful news to be broken to Lavanyavati? Who would tell her and in what words? Who would console her? Soon the play was over. Lakshmi took Manavati with her to Labo's room. Labo was rubbing oil on her face to remove the makeup. Lakshmi and Manavati couldn't find the words to broach the subject.

'Labo, have you read the play *Jhansi ki Rani* written by P.N. Oke?' Lakshmi asked.

'Yes.'

'She fought so bravely for her kingdom, didn't she?'

'Yes.'

'Even before their husbands start out for the battlefield, Rajput women begin their preparations for sati,' Manavati said.

'Why are you telling me all this? What is it that you want to say?'

Seeing their faces turn pale, Labo's heart stopped beating. Grabbing Lakshmi's arm, she said fearfully, 'Didi, you are our guide. Please don't hide anything. Tell me the truth.'

There were tears in her eyes. Holding her close between them, Lakshmi and Manavati told her everything. Labo began to tremble violently. Like a flash, she was out of the room. Lakshmi and Manavati ran after her. Locking herself in a room, Labo wept inconsolably. 'Let me cry my heart out for my Abhay. Don't stop me,' she pleaded with those who tried to comfort her. Finally, Netaji himself came to console her.

The night of 30 April. The waters of the Kandawgyi Lake reflected the moon's pale glow. Lily, a woman soldier, was ill with a high fever. Dr Lakshmi had tended to her and was now going to look in on Labo, when an ear-splitting roar shattered the silent sky. Squadrons of enemy bombers were heading straight for Maymyo. Dropping everything, the girls dived into the trenches just as the first bomb hit the earth. The camp and the hospital seemed to be their targets.

Lakshmi suddenly remembered Lily. She scrambled out of the trench, ran back to the camp and somehow managed to pull Lily out just in time.

When it was daylight, the extent of damage was visible. There were huge craters everywhere. The enemy obviously knew the precise location and layout of the camp.

Temporary shelters were pitched in the forest. New barracks began to be constructed out of tall bamboo grass. Labo was babbling to everyone she met, 'If Netaji hadn't rescheduled the programme, what major catastrophe would have occurred?' Netaji looked very grim. Though he tried not to let anguish get the better of him, he railed at Yellappa, 'How did the enemy get to know about our programme?'

Lakshmi and Yellappa looked at each other. Netaji said, 'Yellappa saheb, that day I had said to you, all was not well. It's certain that there are some wolves in the flock. Find them and finish them. Soon.'

Labo's grief had distressed Netaji greatly. He had no words to comfort her. Later, when he was talking to Lakshmi, he suddenly said, 'Separation is such a hard punishment! The iron prison bars did not make me weak, but being far away from loved ones is heart-rending. Seeing Labo's grief reminded me of Emilie.'

'Who is that?'

Netaji realised what he had unwittingly said, but then after a pause, he continued, 'Keep this to yourself, Lakshmi. Emilie is my wife. I have not spoken of it to anyone because of the war. How the fortunes of war-torn Europe will go, who can tell? I don't want Emilie and my darling daughter Anita to suffer because of me.'

Lakshmi did not know what to say. She just stared as Netaji's eyes grew moist. 'When I left Germany, Anita was just eight weeks old. I was not fortunate enough to see her take the first steps, to hear her first words …'

'Netaji, you accepted this separation for the sake of a great cause, didn't you?'

'Like me, those who chase an ideal believe that they will create a paradise for humanity at large, but for their near and dear ones, they can offer only an arid wasteland.'

'But your goal is so noble, Netaji.'

'Yes, it is an obsession – it has no feelings, no limit, no horizon. Break the silken threads that bind you to your loved ones and run after the illusory golden deer called an ideal. Madness. That's what it is!'

After the news of the victory at Moirang, the Gandhi Regiment was restless. Their headquarters was in Tamu Valley. Several soldiers had gathered outside the bunker of Gen. Kiani, their division commander.

Maj. Gen. Yamamoto was sitting with Zaman Kiani and Dr Akbar Ali, chief of the medical corps. 'General, our blood is boiling. Allow us to show what we can do. Netaji too must be waiting to see us in action,' said Dr Ali.

Just then, four enemy planes zoomed across the sky. Yamamoto paused for a moment, then snapped, 'The enemy's strength is its air force. Fine. We will strike right there. I permit you to blow up an enemy air-base.'

'Which one?' Inayat asked.

'Palel. It is a few miles away and very well guarded,' Yamamoto said. 'An attempt to get near it is a sure invitation to death.'

'We'll do it. We will destroy the airfield,' chorused the soldiers of the Gandhi Regiment.

Impressed by their grit, Fujiwara told Kiani, 'If the INA rather than the Japanese Army manages to destroy that airfield, I will feel very proud.'

Kiani replied, 'True courage lies in taking danger head-on. We will prove ourselves by reducing the Palel airfield to rubble.'

'One of my regiments will rush to your side at the crucial moment,' Yamamoto promised.

'Tell me, who will lead our team for this task?' Kiani asked loudly.

'I will!' Col. Pritam Singh, the fiery Punjabi, roared. Dr Akbar Ali volunteered to go along. Three hundred warriors set out, with just a day's ration, confident that the mission would be accomplished in twenty-four hours.

Though Palel was only twelve miles away, the path was full of hazards – thick jungle, hilly terrain, wild animals and sporadic bursts of enemy gunfire. After a seemingly endless journey they reached Pooram Chepung village close to the airfield and lay in wait there.

2 May 1944. The night, dark, silent, fearful. Standing on the outcrop of a hillock, Pritam Singh studied the airfield carefully. Imphal was so near and yet so far. Netaji's exhortations and the call of the distant peaks to free them from slavery had Pritam Singh all fired up. If Palel fell, Imphal would be within reach. But the airfield was so well guarded, anti-aircraft guns all round, sentries maintaining a strict round the clock watch. These posts had to be destroyed before they went inside. Pritam Singh decided to take one post and sent one of his comrades to take the other.

Like a bat, he charged into the sentry post and took the sentries unawares. Two of them were Gurkhas. They were trembling as they begged, 'Comrade, don't kill us! We're Indians.'

'Don't listen to them, Pritam,' shouted Lal Singh said. 'Shoot them!'

Pritam Singh hesitated. 'Don't fire on Indian soldiers,' Netaji often said, 'Explain our cause to them.'

'Will you join us?'

'Yes, we will and bring our other comrades with us.'

Two British sentries were huddled in a dark corner. Two shots rang out and the British soldiers fell over. Trusting the two Gurkhas, Pritam Singh moved ahead, when suddenly they whipped out their concealed weapons and fired at the Azad Hind soldiers. By the time Pritam Singh turned around and shot them dead, it was too late. Several of his men, including Lal Singh, had fallen to their bullets.

Meanwhile, the second team had attacked the airfield. There were seven assaults on the airfield and the battle continued all night. As dawn broke, the INA soldiers gained control of the airfield. They entered it and began to destroy the five to six aircraft standing there.

'Where are Yamamoto's men?' Pritam Singh asked angrily. 'They should have been here by now. Who will guard this airfield for us?'

'We'll do it,' Sadhu Singh said.

'Are you mad? Imphal is barely twenty-four miles away. The British have a huge squadron there. How will a hundred soldiers guard the airfield?' All the British traffic controllers at Palel had been shot dead. But one among them, though mortally wounded, dragged himself towards the wireless set and fixing the broken wires managed to send a message before dying. 'Hello, hello, headquarters? Palel airfield taken … Jai Hind people are here … help! Save us!'

The news of the Palel massacre had reached Gen. Scoones. 'If those traitors have captured Palel, how long will it take them to reach Imphal,' he shouted.

On Baldwin's orders, a squadron of Dakotas was airborne within minutes and was over Palel in no time at all.

The air-raid warnings went off. Hearing them, the INA soldiers dived into the jungle. Armed with ordinary rifles and Bren guns, they had no chance against the air attack. From the air, the soldiers looked like ants and the low-flying Dakotas began to rain bullets to crush the ants. How they fell, these brave men, with 'Jai Netaji' on their lips! Some were on fire. Others had their limbs torn off. An incensed Dr Akbar Ali dragged or carried the wounded to the shelter of the trees and started his surgical operations on them right there in the open. He had no instruments, except an ordinary pair of scissors and a sharp cut-throat razor blade. Through the hail of bullets, without a thought to his own safety, Dr Ali attended to every soldier, cleaning wounds, administering first aid. He performed his operations without anaesthetic drugs or sedatives. The brave men tried their best to bear the excruciating pain and agony, but their moans and cries echoed through the jungle. That day, two hundred soldiers of the INA gave up their lives with 'Chalo Dilli' on their lips.

After thrashing the enemy at Palel, the Gandhi Regiment had pitched camp in the Kumaon hills. On the other side, in the distant forests of Sittang Changi, platoons of British soldiers of the 33rd Division could be seen.

Through his binoculars Inayat Kiani saw some activity next to the enemy outpost. Then he turned his gaze skywards and was dismayed to see the approaching rain clouds. The enemy was well entrenched in Imphal. Both from Rangoon and Tokyo came impatient queries, 'Have you seized Imphal? Were you victorious?'

In the forests, along the Burma border, the Azad Hind forces were encamped at different spots from Maymyo to Moray. Everyone was impatient to capture Imphal and proceed on to Delhi.

But now, they had to contend with depleted rations and the impending monsoon. The sudden thundershowers were terrifying. Two days ago, some soldiers of Scottish Highlanders had attacked them but Netaji's warriors had responded viciously like bees from a disturbed beehive and forced the white-skinned enemies to retreat. These skirmishes and minor victories were meaningless now. Unless Imphal was captured in a decisive battle, Netaji's dream would not be fulfilled.

Col. Inayat Kiani had called an important meeting that day. Dr Akbar Ali of the Gandhi Regiment had come all the way to attend it. His exploits at Palel were still fresh in everybody's minds. With his tall Pathan frame, he stood out in the gathering. Maj. Bhurewal had returned from the hospital. The scars from the bomb explosion in Rangoon were still visible on his hands.

It was decided that the enemy would not be allowed to enter the neighbourhood of Tamu and at the first opportunity the Japanese force would mow down the British resistance and capture Imphal.

Dr Akbar Ali said to him, 'I would never have joined the INA if I had not heard you sing that song:

> *Sar par tiranga jhanda jalwa dikha raha hai.*
> *Ho teri sar bulandi jo chand asaman hai ...*

They evoked for me visions of a full-flowing Jamuna and the magnificent Lal Qila on her banks,' Dr Ali said.

'Yes, but the army is hungry. How long can we suck in our stomachs?' Bhurewal asked.

'What can we do? We had started out from Maymyo with just three weeks' rations, a rifle and a blanket apiece. The route back is closed. We must move towards Delhi,' Inayat said.

'Our supply depots are thirty-five miles behind us. It would take a man eight days to bring one sackful of rice on his head. The damp grain will germinate during that time!'

A few soldiers came and whispered, 'Sir, near the stream there, the starving Japanese soldiers have slaughtered one of our transport elephants!'

'Ya, Allah! Show us a way out of this difficulty,' Zaman Kiani prayed aloud.

Everyone agreed that the local people's help should be taken to obtain supplies of rations. The Naga and Kuki tribes were at first afraid of the INA, but slowly, because they used to sell eggs and chickens to the soldiers, they came close to the camp and began addressing the army as the new government. They were hostile towards the British and did not care too much about the Japanese either. Unfortunately, they were few in number and their food stock too was very limited.

The Japanese soldiers had fallen ill after eating elephant flesh. There were just about a thousand soldiers in Kiani's regiment. Many had fallen victim to malaria or diarrhoea. Manpower was being wasted in carrying the sacks of grains. The monsoon was upon them. It would rain for hours at a stretch. Cherrapunji, the wettest spot on earth, was not far away.

The soldiers were inadequately equipped. All they had were plastic sheets to protect them. In the cold wet weather, they were reminded of Netaji's words, 'I don't know how many of us are going to come out alive in time to see the dawn of independence. My brave comrades, only those who are ready to suffer the travails ahead should go into this battle. In the present situation, I can give you nothing except thirst, hunger, labour and forced marches. Only those who have the courage to embrace death should go on. The rest should step back.'

Lt. Mansukhlal was extremely worried. The enemy had captured the hill opposite. One night, he went to Kiani's tent.

'Sir, I have to conquer that hill tonight,' he said.

'Mansukh! We only have about seven hundred men. The enemy has placed an entire brigade there. In addition, the 33rd Division is lurking in the caves beyond the hill.'

'Sir, I need just one platoon.'

'One? What will you achieve with just thirty-five men?'

'I feel terribly frustrated that we cannot get Imphal. I must do something!'

'You are mad!' Col. Kiani laughed it off.

Early next morning Col. Kiani was awakened by the sentries on duty outside his tent. When he looked out at the hill before him, he couldn't believe his eyes. The tricolour was fluttering proudly on the hilltop. News of victory had come in but there was no mention of Mansukhlal. Inayat Kiani and Maj. Bhurewal set out to investigate. As they climbed the slushy hill path they saw what had happened. Mansukhlal and his thirty-five men had attacked a company of a hundred and eight British soldiers and defeated them. Just then seven hundred soldiers of a British regiment rushed to the assistance of the company. Though heavily outnumbered, Mansukhlal and his men had fought bravely. They found Mansukh lying on the path, mortally wounded, his khaki tunic soaked in blood. The twenty-five-year-old youth had taken thirteen bullets. Yet, the satisfaction of wresting the hill from the enemy was reflected on his face. Seeing the tears in his eyes, Kiani said, 'Mansukh, why these tears?'

'The shadow of death is terrifying,' Bhurewal said.

'Death! Who's afraid of death?' Mansukh laughed. 'My only regret is that even now we have not been able to take Imphal. If our tricolour had been flying there and I could catch just one glimpse of Netaji's smiling face, my life would be vindicated.'

'Mansukh, have courage. We'll get you to the Tamu hospital. You'll live to see that day too.'

'No, Colonel saheb. Don't worry about me. You go and fight. Jai Hind!' In the rainy weather, there was not a single dry stick to be found. They buried him on the banks of some unknown river.

At Kohima, the two armies were so close to one another that the mud from one trench as it was being dug would land on the other's shovel. At first, the British forces seemed to be in the grip of the Japanese, but after the initial success, General Sato appeared to have slackened. His army, however, was still determined to present their Emperor with a victory on his birthday.

One day, disaster struck the British – the Japanese captured Kohima's water supply. A couple of staff officers came running to Richards. 'Sir, the garrison is without water.'

'So am I,' said Richards, scratching his unshaved cheek. 'Go on, blast the rocks, if you like and get us some water. Drink whatever you find suitable but keep up the fight.'

Col. Richards was at the end of his tether. Japanese incursions were getting bolder. Their grip was tightening. On Jorasoma Hill, a Japanese brigade lay in wait, debating whether the British should be chewed slowly or swallowed in one gulp. The helpless colonel kept scanning the skies with his binoculars. They had enough food, weapons and explosives, but not a drop of water. Risking their lives, the men began to hunt for a water source. They found a narrow stream half a furlong away. Every now and then, a man would crawl to this thin trickle, fill up a single pan and return to the garrison.

Soon Miyazaki's force captured the hill-top right in front. They entered the settlement and burnt down the simple bamboo and grass huts. To stop them, the West Kent Force began to fire on them. The Japanese continued to move ahead. On the way, there were five or six bakeries that catered to the needs of the Christian officials. Seeing this, the British began to throw flaming torches to set the bakeries on fire. Both sides had taken prisoners of war. In the chaos of the fight, the prisoners began to escape in every direction. Fighting intensified to the point that the two forces were in hand-to-hand combat. The heap of dead bodies grew but no one had time to remove them.

The Japanese Army was highly motivated but the rations had finished. A rumour went around that Sato had received a secret message from Maymyo. Miyazaki, Nishida, Koboyashi and others went to see Sato. Koboyashi said, 'General, the daily ration supply has not come for a week.'

'Is it my fault?' Sato retorted.

'The rations are finished …' said Miyazaki.

'It's not my responsibility. Tell your commander.'

No one dared argue with such a senior officer. In a mild tone, Miyazaki said, 'Our army expects efficiency and foresightedness from us.'

'Watch your tongue! What efficiency? What foresight? What do you want to say?' Sato asked harshly.

'Mutaguchi's message – Dimapur is only forty miles away. There may be a large stock of rations.'

'*May be?* It doesn't mean there is, does it?' Sato said. 'What was the order given to me? To seize Kohima. Fine. Why should I act on mere conjectures? I am not your Mutaguchi, lolling about in the company of geishas, understand?'

Supply lines to Kohima had not improved. Only if they took Dimapur would they have access to food, ammunition, transport. However, Sato was reluctant to obey Mutaguchi's orders to advance towards Dimapur. 'Unless you come here you will not understand how difficult it is to venture out when the enemy aircraft are constantly hovering overhead,' he told Mutaguchi.

'I will instruct Kawabe to provide you with increased air cover. Meanwhile, you prepare for an assault on Dimapur,' Mutaguchi replied.

Kawabe was in Rangoon. He promised to do what he could. 'I will speak to Tazo's 5th Air Division,' he told Mutaguchi.

Meanwhile, Netaji was getting extremely restless.

Even the calm Kawabe had begun to understand Chandra Bose's impatience. By now, practically all of Japan's air force had been deployed in the Pacific. The remaining aircraft deployed on the Burma front were desperately in need of repair. They were lined up along the tarmac like a flock of diseased birds. Mutaguchi again roared over the wireless at Sato, 'Dimapur! Dimapur!'

'Dimapur was never in the plan for the 15th Division,' Sato mumbled. The mountains were riddled with trenches and bunkers. The Japanese troops were stuck in these burrows like sick foxes. If the British received reinforcements, what then? For almost twenty-five days they waited. When would the siege of Kohima end? Who would defeat whom?

Neither army had slept for days. Apart from cannon fire, no other sound was heard. No one bathed, nor changed uniforms. Kohima was becoming uglier day by day. Many buildings were reduced to rubble, roofs had been blown off, walls were left with gaping holes. Giant trees had been uprooted. War-torn Kohima was reduced to a smoke-filled graveyard. On top of all this, there was an acute water shortage.

Continuous shelling forced the soldiers to remain in the trenches. The wounded were in agony because of infected wounds. The odour of decaying bodies was everywhere. Richards hadn't slept for nights. Early one morning he heard, 'Sir! Sir! Wake up!'

'What's the matter?'

'We've been tricked, Sir. On the other side of the hill, two Japanese platoons have climbed down the slope and are headed for Dimapur.'

'Oh my god!' Richards cried. 'Dimapur! The last stop on the eastern railway. Rows and rows of godowns full of rations and explosives – supplies meant for the entire British Army in Assam, Manipur, Burma and China! Send a wireless message ... where is Slim? Where is Mountbatten?' The weather was bad. Lines were not clear. 'Go! Come back in two hours and confirm reports!' Richards told two of his men.

Richards spoke to one of his brigadiers, 'If Dimapur is taken by the Japanese, they can fight on the Burma front for another year.'

The officer lowered his head. Richards went on in a despairing tone, 'Our four-armed force has been broken. There won't be enough place in these jungles to bury the dead.' He gazed at the church below the tennis court. A bomb had destroyed its roof.

The afternoon slid past. The spies returned. They were smiling. 'The Japanese came down the slope all right, but it was not to go to Dimapur. They were searching for water.'

Richards began to breathe normally again. He ran down the slope to the church to pray for mercy. The padre was sitting there. Unkempt, unwashed, pale and skeletal. 'Colonel, don't worry. Perhaps our fortunes are reversed but our God has not abandoned us yet.

∾

As Sato stepped out of his tent he noticed a plume of smoke rising from the far side of the hill behind him. He asked his staff officer, 'Where is that smoke coming from?'

'Probably a kitchen, Sir.'

'Why another one? We already have one mess,' he said and went out to investigate. On the other side of the hill, he saw many fires burning, with huge pots and pans over them. Groups of soldiers were sitting around waiting for the cooking to be over. Sato was mystified. Just then his eyes fell on a lump of red meat. Looking further he found the freshly cut head of a mule. The sight came as a terrible shock. God knows how many mules had been slaughtered. It looked as if some horses too had been killed.

A deep revulsion churned Sato's insides. He retched again and again. A few of the soldiers gathered around him, their attitude brash and insolent. Choking on his tears, Sato, deeply agitated, stammered, 'How could you do this? These dumb creatures carried you on their backs; they carried your guns and explosives all the way up to Kohima. How could you cut their throats?'

'We cannot live on grass, Sir!' replied one soldier insolently.

Sato turned back. It was all Mutaguchi's fault, he thought. If he spent more time organising supplies for the army than with his geishas, the situation would have been different. When he expressed his anger to Gen. Miyazaki, the general informed him that Mutaguchi had made all the arrangements as promised. However, while crossing the Chindwin river near Homalin, twenty of their vehicles were destroyed by the last few of Wingate's men.

'But isn't Wingate dead?'

'Yes, but his ghost continues to harass us.'

The heat of battle was unbearable. Waiting it out was worse. A month had passed and Kohima was all but destroyed. Men were being reduced to monkeys. During the day, Dakota aircraft provided protection to the British infantry, but at night the Japanese bombarded them heavily. There were no rations left in the British garrison. Morale was low. It finally hit rock bottom around 17 April. Richards called Scoones. 'Sir, we are on the verge of giving up.'

'Be patient,' Scoones advised. 'Just a little longer.'

Despite occupying three-quarters of Kohima, General Sato had remained inactive. He thought his boldness was established by sending tough messages to Mutaguchi and being generally intractable. All it needed was one determined assault to bring the British to their knees. Unfortunately, Sato did not realise how close he was to victory.

On 18 April, the unbelievable happened. The deserted route to Dimapur showed signs of much feverish activity. Succour was coming to the British forces. A Punjabi battalion and a tank regiment were leading. Right behind them was the 5th Brigade. Taking cover of the forest on the western slope, they managed to reach the besieged garrison. Richards' spirits began to rise. The new force was fresh and energetic. All night long, they went on with the task of demolishing the tunnels the Japanese had dug into the hillside. Soon, the 7th Division too rushed to reinforce them.

Sato stood at the entrance to his tent and surveyed the battlefield. The night was pitch dark, lighting up only when a shell was fired. Where it was absolutely necessary a few torches had been lit. It was 29 April – Tenchosetsu! The Emperor's birthday. On the other hand, the sense of impending doom had never been stronger. Sato frowned in extreme annoyance as he reviewed the state of affairs.

The army preferred mule and horse flesh to grass. The number of animals was depleting. What next? Ailments like malaria and stomach infections were afflicting the men and the animals. How long were they expected to stay in these terrible conditions? The British garrison was still vulnerable, fearing defeat. Just one command was needed to finish them off. Sato was confronted by his officers and men, resolute, with the pride of the samurai glowing on their faces.

'Have you come to tell me that Mutaguchi's rations have arrived?' Sato's voice grated.

'We'd prefer to die fighting than starve to death,' Miyazaki said.

'What's your intention?'

'Order us to attack tonight itself. We'll march across hills and valleys and attack Dimapur. We may die in the fire but Dimapur too will burn with us.'

'I am bound by rules. I will follow only those orders that are given in writing. Henceforth, please don't take the trouble of teaching your commander his job.'

'But, General, Mutaguchi himself has advanced to Kalemav. He has ordered us to win the war at any cost. Why, then, are you hesitating?' Miyazaki asked, enraged.

'I am not a fool and neither am I a coward. However, I will not sacrifice my division to satisfy some stupid man's whim.'

May came bringing with it the season of storms. Strong gales and incessant downpours created havoc. The torrential rain showed no signs of stopping. The entire terrain became slushy. The soldiers believed that death was better than living in this hell. Most of the trees had been destroyed by the shelling. Vehicles stuck in the mud had been abandoned to the rats. Faces dark, eyes red, the soldiers would peer out of their trenches and holes. Their uniforms hung on their emaciated bodies like shrouds. No more elephants and horses arrived from Chindwin. The miasma of death hung over the whole valley. Sato began to look more and more harried. He continued to dash off angry letters to Kawabe, Mutaguchi and Field Marshal Terauchi.

In the burning heat of May, hand-to-hand fights broke out frequently. In mid-May, the intrepid Japanese gained control of the road and began to advance. The doughty tommies resisted them fiercely. Both sides fought to take control of the collector's bungalow. The two-hundred-year-old building was in a shambles, blackened by the smoke. Its broken-down chimney with the tattered Union Jack on it was the only evidence of its former identity. For fifty days, the battle for Kohima continued, with the fortunes of both sides swinging. Soon, the Japanese response weakened and they were driven back. British forces hoisted their flag.

One day, taking advantage of the thick fog, the British forces advanced into the territory held by the Japanese. They started climbing the hill with the help of ropes. It was raining heavily and the Japanese bunkers and trenches were flooded. As they came out into the open, British bombers would take aim at the soldiers. One such bomber kept hovering over Sato's headquarters like an angry hornet. The aircrew signalled to the gunner. He loaded the cannon but before he could fire, the captain yelled out, 'You fool, what are you doing?'

'Sir, that's Sato's headquarters. I'll roast him right away.'

'Stop it!' the captain roared. The bomber circled around and flew away. A golden opportunity had been lost. The aircrew could not hide their dismay. The captain laughed and said, 'Have you forgotten Slim's message? Don't bomb Sato. Let him carry on seeing dreams of taking Kohima. A bomb might wake him up and set him on the road to Dimapur or Imphal. Here, he spends his hours measuring the peaks ... why disturb him?'

Lt. Gen. Scoones's condition was like that of a fox that had fallen into a crevice. Every time he got a foothold and tried to inch upwards, he would slip and land on his nose. If he did manage to escape into the thickets, a tiger lay in wait. The Japanese had blocked the road to Kohima. Two Nippon divisions had him by the throat. The Americans were demanding back the aircraft they had loaned for a month. It was imperative to resolve the situation at the earliest as the Japanese Army's python-like grip was tightening.

Scoones was in his headquarters when there was a call from Ceylon. It was Mountbatten.

'Yes, Sir?'

'Any progress?'

'None. The Japanese refuse to withdraw.'

'Do whatever you think fit, but you must break the siege. Stop the Japanese advance.'

'Sir, they are starving and yet neither the Japanese nor the INA are showing any sign of surrender.'

'Spread disaffection, offer bribes, promise promotions – do whatever you like. I must have Imphal at any cost,' Mountbatten said firmly.

'The Subhas Regiment must leave at once. Go via Tamu towards Kohima and join in the last battle.' The order thrilled Shah Nawaz. Once Kohima was in their hands, next would be Assam, then Bengal ... Bihar. And Delhi!

'Chalo Dilli! Onward to Delhi!' the cry echoed in all directions. Everyone gathered around Shah Nawaz. Major Mehboob and Major Ramswarup were part of the near festive crowd. They were preparing to leave immediately. The wounded soldiers were helped on to bullock carts. Crossing the hilly forests, they reached Kaleva camp. The wounded were admitted in the hospital.

Ahead were the eight-thousand-feet-high mountain ranges. Beyond them the impassable Chinese peaks. Dense forests. Wide, swift-flowing streams. Unfamiliar terrain. Somehow, the Subhas Regiment reached Moray. This was where the Indian border began. To protect themselves from air attacks, they dug trenches. At three o'clock in the morning, Shah Nawaz had a meeting with Major Fujiwara. The two men embraced each other. Fujiwara eyed the two grenades in Shah Nawaz's belt with some apprehension. Shah Nawaz did not bother to hide his impatience. 'Why are you Japanese not giving us a chance to fight on the battlefield?'

'What can I say, Shah Nawaz? Whatever has come to pass has never happened in our century-old army's history. Disaffection is rife. Mutaguchi and his divisional commander cannot see eye to eye.'

The regiment was to move in a day or two. The enemy was fully aware of its whereabouts. Aircraft would regularly drop propaganda leaflets and signed notes from the British commander promising a secure life if they surrendered. Every now and then a voice would be heard on a loudspeaker, 'Indian comrades, don't fall into the company of the Japanese and ruin yourselves. Your families are worried about you. With tears in their eyes, they are asking, "When are you coming home?" Don't worry about anything. Cross over to this side. The British government will put you on a flight that will take you safely home. You will also be given three months' paid leave.'

Tempting though the offer was, no one took it up as each soldier was firmly committed to Netaji and his cause. They were looking forward to marching into Kohima.

Shah Nawaz was fast asleep when he felt someone trying to shake him awake. It was Maj. Mehboob Ahmad.

'What is the matter, Mehboob?'

'General saheb, your brother Noora has been captured by our patrol,' Mehboob whispered.

'Noora? My younger brother? Captured?' Shah Nawaz stood up.

'He wants to leave the British forces and join us.'

'Would they have sent him here in order to trick us?' Shah Nawaz voiced his suspicion.

'No reason to worry. He is in our territory.'

'All right, let's meet him.'

'He has set conditions,' Mehboob said.

'What?'

'He wants to speak with you alone. If things don't work out he wants a firm promise that he will be allowed to return unhindered.'

Shah Nawaz thought for a moment, then nodded. After all, this was his own brother! He was meeting him after five long years.

When Noora embraced him in a tent, Shah Nawaz was overwhelmed. After their parents' death, he had brought up Noora like his own son. He offered some biscuits to Noora. Seeing his elder brother looking so thin in a dirty, patched uniform, his body covered with scratches, his hair long, made Noora want to cry. 'Brother, I can't bear to see you like this. How many days is it since you last had a full meal?'

'Days? Who has the time to count? In this jungle one is only aware of darkness and light,' Shah Nawaz said, patting Noora on his back. 'Truly, Noora, apart from you, who else do I have in this world? Now that you've come, I won't let you go back. We will fight for freedom together. Netaji is our commander-in-chief.'

'Bhai, look at your condition. By starving yourself and roaming in the wild, will you get freedom?'

'So what should I do?'

'Bhai, you were the award winner in Dehra Dun. The King of England is merciful. Just a nod. You will be made a major general and given a special command.'

'What do I have to do for that?' Shah Nawaz asked carefully.

'You have to admit that you were misled by Subhas Bose – that's all.'

'I had a suspicion of this when you displayed such concern for my present state. Noora, just go back the way you came.' Shah Nawaz was boiling mad.

'Bhai, just think it over once,' Noora pleaded. 'Mountbatten himself is hopping on one foot to welcome you back. You won't get another opportunity like this.'

'You foolish boy, if life itself flies away from this prison of a body, then what is left behind? No matter how much you earn and spend, in the end, this body has to die and decay. A tree of gold will not grow from it. Rather, a magician who can breathe life into ash and create a new form out of it is born only once. Only out of respect for his promise, we have suffered these travails and deprivations. The soles of our feet have cracked, let them crack, the leeches suck our blood, let them drink as much as they want. We will continue to advance towards Delhi as long as there is life in us!'

'But what about your career, your future?'

'We have gone beyond all that a long time ago. Netaji began this yagna for a strong, united and secular India. I am only the kindling for it. I have to die tomorrow, might just as well die today.'

'But Mountbatten himself is waiting to give you a command.'

'That means nothing to me. Who is that Mountbatten to you, anyway? An ordinary servant to the King of England! While Netaji is the uncrowned emperor of our hearts. What will I do with a command? Brother, to serve the British crown, men like Mountbatten and Wavell are a dime a dozen, but to save India, a poor enslaved nation, it is only after centuries that leaders like Gandhiji and Netaji are born.'

Noora had nothing more to say. He left quietly. Just then there was a movement outside the door. Mehboob had secretly listened in on the entire conversation. Seeing the sten gun in his hand, Shah Nawaz asked, 'What were you about to do?'

'What else could I do?'

'You overheard our conversation?'

'That's right.'

'Assuming for a moment that I had left with Noora, what would you have done?'

'I? I would have done nothing. But this sten gun of mine would have riddled the two of you with bullets.'

Shah Nawaz burst out laughing. Placing an arm around Mehboob's shoulders, he said, 'You lunatic, you had better believe this. For thirty-eight crore Indians, Netaji has thrown his life into the fire. Not even the old gods and goddesses would have endured the hardships he has faced. Forget my brother, if my God had tried to separate me from Netaji I would salaam him from afar and tell him to return the way he came. I will never leave Netaji as long as I live.'

Seventeen

Lt. Gen. Geoffrey Scoones, bleary-eyed, dishevelled and gaunt, was in bad shape. Not even in his worst nightmares had he imagined such a plight for himself. Recklessly, he kept driving around Imphal in his open jeep. His hopeful eyes turned towards Lido, expecting American reinforcements. He had spoken to Kohima that morning, but for the last fifty-sixty days, Kohima too was in the python-like grip of the enemy.

'Richards, has the siege of Kohima been lifted?' he had asked.

'Sir, the Japs are sticking on like iguanas,' Richards grunted.

'Has the road between Imphal and Kohima at least been opened up?'

'If it had, wouldn't I have rushed to your aid?' Then more gently, he said, 'Sir, what next? What will become of us in this rain? Our soldiers cannot live on patriotism alone—they need food.'

'What can I say? Our seniors are hiding in their cosy offices and leaving me to face the music ...'

Though there was discontent even among the Japanese, they kept the pressure up on the British with a stranglehold on Imphal and Kohima. Even Air Marshal Baldwin was worried. Between the Japanese anti-aircraft guns and Maj. Wingate's obstinacy, they had lost many Dakotas. Scoones turned to Baldwin in despair. 'Aren't the Americans coming to help us?'

'Gen. Slim has been trying desperately, but the Americans are subjected to immense pressure by the Japanese Air Force on the Chinese border and in Australia.'

'Had our planes not been diverted to the Pacific campaign from the Burma border, what would have happened?'

'Our graves would have been dug here by now.'

Pointing to the hill in front of them, Gen. Scoones said, 'The Japanese 5th Division is trying to break into Imphal from that side. They have installed heavy artillery on those hills. If they advance a little further, consider this airfield finished.'

'Oh my God!'

'Exactly! They have us in a scissor-like grip.'

'Is it true that a few nights ago, the Japanese had reached the foot of the hills?' Baldwin asked fearfully.

'Yes, twice. Somehow, we managed to fend them off. But I cannot do it again.'

'Why?'

'Ammunition is running out. What do I feed into the cannons?' Plucking at his beard in frustration, Scoones continued, 'The food stock is depleting. What do I feed our soldiers? What about those refugees from Rangoon who are looking to us for succour?'

'And there's no way of escaping into Kohima.'

'The road to Tamu on the other side is with the enemy. They have taken Bishenpur twice. And they have Bose's INA a few miles away. I believe they stick a photograph of Bose on to a stick and march through every little hamlet. Col. Malik addresses rallies. Cannot say when the Manipuris from this part will turn into traitors.'

'Why should that happen? I have personally strafed Moirang village several times. Those Azad Hind fellows are still there?'

'Why will they leave? The local Manipuris have pressed them to their bosoms. Baldwin, we are done for, I tell you.'

'What about Mountbatten?'

'He only talks. All our army commanders are basking in the reflected glory of America. Had it not been for American support, the Japs and Bose's INA would have sunk us all in the Brahmaputra by now.'

The 14th Division of the British was demoralised. Imphal would rot in the rain. The eastern front could not be defended without American support. From malaria-infested Comilla, Gen. Slim was trying to get through to Kandy.

'Dickie, we have not received any more Dakotas. Consider the battle lost. Imphal cannot throw off the enemy noose.'

'Forget about the planes.'

'Why?'

'America wants us to return the hundred aircraft loaned to us. Where will the new ones come from?'

'Still, please speak to Churchill.'

'Both of us have been ignoring Roosevelt and trying to hold on to the aircraft we have.'

Mountbatten was receiving blow after blow in the last two days. Gen. Mutaguchi's advance into Manipur was alarming. But worse was Prime Minister Churchill ignoring his calls.

Then he received a call from Lt. Gen. Scoones. 'If the situation remains as it is, we suspect that many units of our army will join Bose's force. Something is brewing.'

Scoones was desperate. The nights were sleepless, the days without hope. News of Japanese infiltration into every hut and dwelling of Bishenpur had shaken him to the core. Everyone is willing to share the glory, but no one wants a hand in the responsibility. As a commander on the battlefield, I will have to bear the entire burden of ignominy, he felt. Just then, he was called to the phone. It was Gen. Slim. 'Tell him I was grievously injured by a cannon ball,' he said to his staff officer.

'But, sir, he seems very cheerful.'

Surprised, Scoones picked up the receiver. 'Geoffrey, are you truly helpless? Like me?'

'If one is strangled, the whole body will turn cold, won't it?'

'Thank you for all your service and loyalty ...'

'What is that supposed to mean?'

'I cannot say more now. The message will be sent by wireless. Decode it and read it calmly.'

Scoones translated the message himself. Every word of it was like an earthquake tremor.

'Wait for four days only. Otherwise, on 4 June 1944, at 12 noon, surrender to Gen. Mutaguchi.'

'A wise man should never plan a mighty audacious campaign, but if he does, he should not sign his own death warrant by leaving its execution to his subordinates.' Every word of Gen. Renya Mutaguchi's was like a whiplash as he addressed his officers. Sparing no one, he ranted, 'The minute I realised that if Imphal was to be taken I would have to take charge, I rushed to the front. It has been a month since our deadline and we still don't have Imphal. What have my efficient officers been doing?'

Mutaguchi's venom was directed especially at Lt. Gen. Motoso Yanagida and Lt. Gen. Kotoku Sato. 'With such pride I told Bose that I only take care of my roses, my officers take care of the battle. And you let me down! What do you have to say, Yanagida?'

Yanagida did not speak. 'My plan was a hundred per cent foolproof. Before getting out of Maymyo, I had told you to tackle the British 17th Division spread across the plain. Had I not, Yanagida?'

'Yes, sir.'

'It is true that you had the 17th Division in your grip, right?'

'Yes, sir.'

'Then why did you let them go?'

His voice shaky, Yanagida said, 'Sir, it was a problem of communication. The coded message from Col. Sasakar was, "Military-code set on fire, tackling every individual in the enemy camp".' Mutaguchi, weighing the emerging equations of authority, ignored Yanagida completely and addressed Col. Ryūkichi Tanaka. It was obvious Tanaka was going to take over the 33rd Division. Tanaka was a competent officer.

'I want to tighten the noose on Imphal once and for all. But where is Toshio Miyazaki?'

'Sato says he cannot be spared.'

Mutaguchi was speechless with rage.

May was slipping by. Both sides were fighting hard for control over Imphal and Kohima.

One night, Subhas Chandra Bose called from Rangoon. 'General, I am arriving there tomorrow.'

'Where?'

'On the Imphal plain.'

'Please don't do something so foolish.'

'General, a fish may be able to live without water. An infant may survive without its mother. But I cannot exist outside Hindustan.'

'Please do not commit this huge blunder,' Mutaguchi pleaded. 'Hundreds of American planes are patrolling the skies, something untoward may happen.'

'Like what? The plane may catch fire. And I may perish. But new fires will be kindled. Subhas must die so Mother India can be saved!'

'Don't get carried away. Think calmly. It's too dangerous for you to fly there.'

'Then I will walk in through Maymyo.'

'That will take fifteen days, too risky ...'

'Never mind.'

'Why are you being so stubborn, Bose? Don't you trust me, the Japanese Army?'

'Of course I do.'

'Even if there is a revolt in my ranks, the institution of the army hasn't broken down. But even if it does, Mutaguchi is still alive. Be assured, my friend.'

'You are my primary hope. Every pore of my body cries out for Imphal.'

'Then here's some good news, Bose. We may be in trouble, yes, but the enemy isn't doing very well either. The defence of Imphal is crumbling. They will either surrender in four days or flee. The rain obstructs me. But I will overcome the deluge and get across. Once the Japanese and Azad Hind armies enter Imphal, we will send you a message ... then you can take off—', The line went dead. Only a harsh grating sound was heard.

Mutaguchi had entered the battlefield unmindful of the inclement weather or the tenacious enemy that clung to Imphal. He was exhorting his troops, 'I don't accept irresponsible answers that we had no weapons, so we could not fight. Fight, men, fight. Don't let the empty ammunition store stop you. You have gleaming bayonets. If they break, use your hands. Your legs. Your teeth. Fight till there is breath in your body. Don't ever forget the Japanese motto, Yamato Damashii!'

Calcutta
18 April 1944

Beloved Netaji,

Greetings.

Netaji, when is Imphal going to fall? When will you appear on the eastern front? We are all waiting eagerly for you. Preparations have been made for an internal revolution.

The revolutionaries you sent from Penang, Singapore and Rangoon have arrived and dispersed to important centres like Bombay, Madras, Calcutta, Karachi and Delhi. Our secret centres are seething like ammunition dumps. We await your command to go into battle.

As soon as you begin your march to Delhi, thousands of our brethren will join you, crying 'Chalo Dilli!'.

British authorities are harassing us continuously. Many of our companions have been hanged. Many more are imprisoned. The old disease of mutiny still gnaws at our bones, and some anti-nationals are trying to hinder our activities. Even so, we assure you that we have prepared the entire nation for a fight.

Come back, Netaji. Come back soon. Dispel the centuries'-old darkness. Revive the hopes of thirty-eight crore enslaved Indians. May God be with you always.

Your companions and old colleagues
from Anushilan and Yugantar

The letter was a month old. Sato had almost swallowed Kohima. Yamamoto Force was breathing down Imphal's neck. Brave men like Shah Nawaz, Shaukat, Mehboob, Pritam Singh, Kiani, had reached the Manipur plateau. But nothing had happened. Revolutionaries had infiltrated into India, submarines had entered Indian waters. So why had the spark not triggered off the revolution yet? Netaji had summoned N.G. Swami and Lt. Col. Mahmood Khan Durrani from Penang. 'Swami, Imphal is burning as planned, but when will the fire be kindled in the rest of India?'

'Everything is perfectly planned.'

'But why is there no action yet?'

'Sir, one unit has already penetrated the fields of Gujarat. We even have a unit near the Konark Sun Temple. We have received messages from Lala Shankarlal and Sheelabhadra Yaji that Delhi is ready.'

'But then why hasn't the effect been felt?'

All this while Durrani was quiet. Now, as he spoke, his nostrils flared. 'In the army, our Bahawalpur Battalion is tauntingly called the Labour Battalion. But the fact is that we are carrying out the real labour.'

'Durrani, one Bahawalpuri, Shaukat Malik, has become our Sher-e-Hind. He hoisted the tricolour at Moirang and earned fame and glory for seven generations. But what do you do except empty talk.'

'Sir, all of India has become a simmering cauldron ...'

'Come to the point.'

'Sir, Chopra, Dubey and Amrik Singh's groups have long since departed for ...'

He was interrupted by Ayyar. 'There's some important news on the radio,' he said. Everyone listened.

'Some Japanese agents have successfully landed on Indian shores. Some of them have managed to mingle with the local people. The central home ministry has warned the public to be careful of any strangers. The names of some leading agents are Chopra, Dubey ... a reward of Rs 10,000 is offered for the capture of these agents. If any suspicious movements are noticed, please inform the police immediately.'

Netaji switched off the radio. 'Swami, Durrani, what is this?' he roared.

'Sir, the radio referred to Japanese agents. They did not say Azad Hindwale,' explained Durrani.

'Why would the British authorities be so foolish? They know that any reference to Subhas Chandra Bose can only vitiate the atmosphere and intensify terrorist activities, Durrani.'

Just then, Netaji's personal security guard Kundan Singh came forward. 'Netaji, someone in our INA is playing a dirty game, he is doing propaganda for Pakistan.'

'How do you know?'

'See these notices.'

Kundan Singh showed Netaji the copy of a letter. 'The Muslim leaders of the INA, in the sinful hope of attaining name and fame, you have forgotten your religion and race. For how long will you follow a Bengali? Why are you being more slavish to Bose than even the Hindu officers? Both that pretender Gandhi and this Bose are opportunists and true-blooded Hindus. They want a Hindu nation. Don't become slaves of the Hindus. Make a pledge to Pakistan. Give up your lives for Jinnah saheb ...'

'Stop, Netaji, stop. I am not prepared to hear one more venomous word,' Mahmood Durrani shot up. 'It's better to die than utter the word Pakistan. Who dares to make such allegations about the INA? I will not rest until I drag that beast before you!'

Durrani stormed out of the room. Netaji told Swami, 'Bahawalpuris are robust but innocent. Keep an eye on disruptive forces.'

Later that night, as he lay in bed, Netaji's attention was drawn to a news item on the radio. 'The enemy is becoming more active in Bombay, Karachi and other ports on the western coast. Japanese agents have recently exploded an ammunition-laden ship in Karachi port. A female human bomb is supposed to have boarded the boat to set off the explosion. The Karachi police have found evidence to suggest that the woman was a Maharashtrian girl from Bombay called Mugdha Sahasrabuddhe ...'

Immediately Netaji's mind raced to the past. He could see the shy Mugdha who had been infatuated with him. He had forgotten about her all these years. Today, she had covered herself in glory before fading forever into the ocean at Karachi.

At Rangoon's Mingaladon Airport, Netaji strode towards the row of aircraft. His gaze rested on the nose of an eleven-seater plane which had Azad Hind written across its body. The eyes of the leaping tiger beside the words seemed to be saying something to Netaji. He turned to his ADC.

'Capt. Rawat, fuel?'

'Sufficient. Enough in reserve also.'

'And the pilot?'

'He sleeps here in the lounge itself. He is keener than you to get to Imphal.'

Netaji stared at the plane. The colours of the rainbow reflected in the dewdrops on the wing captured the many beautiful moments in his own life. He remembered his dear ones – Mej-da, Ma, Basanti Ma, Deshbandhu, Vithalbhai, Emily and Anita. He also felt two pairs of eyes staring back at him, quizzically. Gandhiji's and Jawaharlal's.

Mentally, Netaji was already airborne. His breath, his goal and his aspirations had given the aircraft wings. Swiftly, his mind flew – hovered above Imphal and Kohima, then over the Brahmaputra. Beyond its banks was the vast expanse of Bengal. Thousands of voices in chorus, shouting 'Chalo Dilli!'.

It wasn't only his dear ones who accompanied him to Delhi. Even the tiny inanimate objects had joined in the fray. In a flashback, he saw the gently swaying palanquin that brought him to the dais in Tripuri, the bloodstained batons of British soldiers as they were swung around in the streets of Calcutta, Ziauddin's loose-fitting shirt that was left behind in Kabul, Mazzotta's expensive clothes in Berlin, a tin of Darjeeling tea on the shelf in Kasturba's kitchen, and the gallows where the valiant Bhagat Singh and others became martyrs. All of them had only this on their lips – 'Chalo Dilli!'.

In a trance, Netaji entered Lt. Gen. Kawabe's office. Kawabe was engrossed in a map. Netaji's eyes fell on a painting on the wall behind him. A dark sky, snow-clad mountains, rows of frozen horsemen, and leading them was Napoleon on that fateful Russian campaign. The fur-lined cap and the tattered overcoat, the drooping shoulders and the hopeless faces conveyed a feeling of bleakness. But in that grim picture, Netaji spotted two glowing spots that instantly touched a chord in him. They were Napoleon's eyes. Bright with unshakeable resolve and soaring ambition. They became his inspiration, setting his blood on fire.

Mutaguchi was rattled to hear Sato had begun to dig his grave. He sent his staff officer, Hashimoto, to verify the news. The man braved the inclement weather, the hazardous path, and when he reached an outcrop overlooking the Kohima camp, he saw the camp being dismantled. Tents and other paraphernalia were being loaded on to the backs of animals that had escaped human hunger.

When Sato saw Mutaguchi's emissary, he turned away. Hashimoto begged Sato to wait. 'I have no time,' Sato replied.

'I have a message from Mutaguchi for you.'

'I have no desire to read it.' Sato stamped his foot into the slush as he spoke, splattering Hashimoto's uniform.

Hashimoto had samurai blood flowing in his veins. He would not give up so easily. He began to read the message out. 'Sato, my friend, I can well imagine the trying conditions under which you have been fighting all this while. Put the evil thought of retreat away. A mother may commit the sin of putting a knife to her infant's throat, a bird might peck at its own fledglings, but a commander would never let his soldiers perish while he seeks salvation in suicide. I am working hard to restore your supplies, believe me. Such crises are a challenge to our Bushido tradition. The rays of a rising sun are putting us to the test ...'

'Lecherous poet!' spat Sato.

'It's all right. Don't fight. Just stay here!' pleaded Hashimoto.

'Impossible.'

'Once Imphal falls, these hardships will seem worthwhile.'

'Such high expectations of a gamble!' Sato's temper was high.

'God guides the determined.'

'Shut up and get out!' Sato screamed, snatched the message out of Hashimoto's hand and tore it up.

Miyazaki and other officers also pleaded with Sato. 'Just a little longer, patience ...'

'Your leaving Kohima will be disastrous.'

'I don't think so.'

'The road to Imphal will open up for the enemy. The British will rush to Imphal's aid. It will be a great blow, sir!'

Sato paid no heed. He wrote a note. 'For the last two months, we defended Kohima to the best of our ability, despite all hardships. But we cannot bear it any more. Now our swords are broken, our bows have become stiff. With a heavy and despairing heart, I bid Kohima farewell.'

The officers present were stunned. Sato was so emotional. Who was he taking revenge on? Himself? Mutaguchi? The Royal Army and therefore his own motherland? Sato sealed the envelope himself and handed it over to Hashimoto.

In the incessant rain, the trenches and dugouts lay empty. A pall of silence had descended over Kohima after three months of simmering and seething. Soon, its northern boundaries would be open to the enemy.

Sato was worried that his men would revolt. He yelled at his juniors, 'Go on, destroy all the communication systems of the 15th Division. I don't wish to hear or see Mutaguchi again.' Lines came down, instruments were smashed.

The retreat from Kohima began.

On the way back to the Kabaw Valley, the paths were obliterated. To prevent pursuit, the Japanese were blowing up bridges once they crossed them. None of the soldiers could stomach the retreat. It was against their proud warrior tradition. Many were moved to commit harakiri on the way. Some emaciated soldiers could not brave the lashing rains. Others were washed away by the wild rivers. The trail of corpses would show the enemy the path the retreating men had taken.

It was a dreary wet night. The Japanese had set up camp six miles south of Ukhrul village. The division headquarters somehow withstood the heavy rain. Sato had just dozed off when he was rudely awakened by his guard. 'Sir, wake up, the chief commander has come to see you.'

Sato could not believe his ears. Mutaguchi here? Before he could scramble out of bed and put on his kimono, Mutaguchi walked in and stood before him. For a moment, Sato was confused. A gamut of emotions played on his face. But, he quickly got a hold on himself and stood still.

Mutaguchi reached out and placed his hand on Sato's shoulder. Confidently he said, 'Friend, we can still turn the tide of the war. Together we will launch a final assault on Imphal.'

'It is too late for that.'

'Please don't speak like that. The 15th Division needs to be backed up. If they get no support, it will be disastrous.'

'Help we will, but what with?'

'I guarantee you supplies.'

'Can you give it in writing?'

'Kawabe's instructions are very clear.'

'But many things have been left vague in it,' Sato muttered.

'You don't need a royal proclamation for every breath. You must read between the lines,' Mutaguchi said. 'General, don't fail in your duty because of your hatred for me. Don't play with Japan's future.'

'Ration first,' Sato said calmly.

Mutaguchi was at the end of his patience. He growled, 'General, are you aware of the consequences of disobedience? I can court-martial you. Send you to the gallows.'

'You may do as you like. You were not able to fulfil my simple request – for food to be air-dropped for my soldiers. We had guns but no ammunition, hands to fight and lots of courage, but our stomachs were empty. How could we proceed? We did the best we could in Kohima,' Sato retorted.

'It was a tough journey. I did not get air cover either. From where would I get it for you? It is your duty to fight for the nation. Unless you give it everything, success will not be fully yours. During a war, there is no guarantee that instructions on paper will be executed. War is not child's play.'

'But the army marches on its stomach ...'

'But not only for the stomach! Sato, if only you had obeyed my one order and attacked Dimapur, the course of Japan's, no, the entire region's history would have taken a different course.'

'Yes, but my troops would have been wiped out.'

'Dying for a cause gives a unique pleasure.'

'What joy can spilling blood unnecessarily bring?' Sato asked. 'I was disgusted by the mindless loss of lives.'

'If one gets disgusted by mud, one should not become a farmer.' The two men hurled allegations at each other – Sato blamed Mutaguchi for making absurd and impractical plans, and Mutaguchi accused Sato of cowardice resulting in Japan's loss of face. For a while, Mutaguchi paced up and down. The officers present quaked. Once again, Mutaguchi tried to persuade Sato to join him in the assault on Imphal. But Sato was adamant. 'Put me before any military court and I will prove to Field Marshal Terauchi and Army Headquarters that yours was a foolish plan. I am blinded by blood now and cannot see beyond it anymore.'

'And my eyes are dimmed by tears of shame. I do not see any life for myself without Japan's pride and our beloved Emperor's glory. You may have a desire to live, but I am driven by the insane wish to die for my country.'

Imphal had swallowed thousands of men and was not satiated yet. Malaria, dysentery and leeches had claimed a share of human lives too. Col. Inayat Kiani's foot had got infected from a leech bite. Dr Akbar Ali tried to do a minor surgery, but the wound became septic and would not heal.

Col. Inayat lay on a small sheet of cloth, under a makeshift canopy. He could hear the distant boom of gunfire, but his eyes wouldn't open. He knew that Maj. Gen. Zaman Kiani was seated by his side. Kiani was looking haggard from hunger and exhaustion. Inayat tried to get up, but his leg refused to move. Slowly he propped himself up and said weakly, 'Leeches ate up my leg, bhaiyya.'

'Don't worry, Imphal will bite the dust in a couple of days.'

'How is that possible?'

'They are in a much worse situation than us. Imphal is cut off from the rest of the world. Air-dropping of supplies has become infrequent. We are definitely better off.'

'Really?'

'Besides, we have succeeded in planting explosives inside their territory. We are on the threshold of victory.'

Inayat felt his hair stand on end. Forgetting his throbbing leg, he asked eagerly, 'Tell me what happened!'

Kiani spoke softly. 'Col. Malik had captured about sixty to seventy men in Moirang. We brainwashed them and sent them back to the British Army. Many Hindi battalions are now anxious to join the INA.'

Inayat closed his eyes and thanked Allah. 'When will that golden dawn break?' he asked Kiani.

'In two or three days. That's why I am heading for Bishenpur now. As soon as we receive the message, we launch our assault on Imphal,' Kiani said. Yet he was worried.

Starving Azad Hind soldiers had their eyes on Imphal. Inayat was ashamed of his injury. Who would lead his brigade? Kiani seemed to have read his thoughts. 'We will have to make that magical Garuda leap very soon. The British are demoralised. Their stockpile of ammunition appears to be running low. Their empty trucks are turning back from Palel. They might surrender before there is a revolt.'

Zaman Kiani continued, 'Whom should we give your command to?'

'Major Bhurewal.'

'Exactly what I was thinking. We need reliable people at this juncture.'

Maj. Bhurewal was summoned. 'It is imperative for us to cut through the mountains and cross into Imphal. I am entrusting the charge of Col. Inayat's unit to you.'

Maj. Bhurewal saluted smartly. Inayat took Bhurewal's hands into his own and said, 'I cannot even stand up, that's why we are entrusting this charge to you.'

'Don't worry.'

'Of course we won't. We are proud to hand over the reins to a man who risked burning his hands to save Netaji.'

'Sir, Netaji freed me from the rusty shackles of the Japanese. If it weren't for our beloved leader, I too would have been languishing in jail like Mohan Singh and Gill.'

It was unusually silent that night. Except for the swiftly flowing water, no other sounds were heard. Maj. Bhurewal went to the brigade headquarters with his orderly Shyam Kant. He opened up the map indicating the location of his troops. His staff officer was watching him, bleary-eyed. 'You don't seem to have got enough sleep,' Bhurewal said to him. 'Go, rest tonight. Don't worry about me.'

'But, sir ...'

'What have I to fear? Our men are all round. If Shyam Kant is with me, that's enough.'

Bhurewal picked up some maps and went out to continue his inspection of the patrol parties and the night watches with Shyam Kant in tow. Shyam Kant had joined the INA in Singapore and leaving his family behind, had come to the front. He too was impatient to break the enemy's back and cross the Brahmaputra.

Suddenly Bhurewal began to vomit. Handing him the water bottle, Shyam Kant asked, 'What did you eat, sir?'

'Half-cooked yam and raw banana ... so hard to digest.'

Bhurewal rested under a tree for a while. Gazing across the river, Shyam Kant said, 'Sir, enemy troops must be close by.'

'Of course they are. They have surrounded us, that is why we are stuck.'

Bhurewal examined the flow of the river. Was it as strong at night as during the day, he wondered. He stepped into the water, rifle in one hand and a loaded pistol tucked into his belt. Shyam Kant was stunned. 'Sir!' he shouted! 'What are you doing? It's dangerous!' Bhurewal went in a few feet.

'Shhh. You want to come with me?'

'Where to?'

'Our Hindustan.'

'Of course I want to, but, sir, alone, like this? All together … with Netaji …'

'You fool! Your Netaji's Chalo Dilli bubble burst long ago. Even if ten generations die, the British Empire will not crumble. We were never worthy of independence. Slavery, servility, these are our traits …'

'Sir, this is betrayal …'

'Betrayal, patriotism, all just words, my boy. The rats that first flee a burning ship are the wisest. Come on, come with me!'

Shyam Kant was confused. 'Why such a cruel joke, sir?'

'Well, goodbye, my boy!'

'Sir, don't do this when we are about to win.'

'No chance. It's all over.'

'Netaji will lead us all into Delhi.'

'Forget it. Freedom will not come even if Netaji breaks his head against a rock. Save your own life. Follow me. For the sake of your family.'

Shyam Kant picked up his rifle. The song Bhurewal had taught them, which had made him swell with pride, rang in his ears. '*Sar par tiranga jhanda jalwa dikha raha hai …*'

He cried out in anguish, 'Sir, come back. Otherwise I will fire. You taught me to shoot. I will not miss.'

Bhurewal's trembling finger reached for the rifle trigger. But then he realised that the gunshot might alert the patrol. He carried the moment with a laugh. Shyam Kant's innocent mind believed that Bhurewal was just teasing him. He relaxed as Bhurewal said, 'Wait, let me think,' and bent down, pretending to drink water. He whipped out his dagger and flung it at Shyam Kant's chest. Shyam Kant fell. Bhurewal splashed his way to the other side.

Early next morning, the patrol party found the dying Shyam Kant. His breath fading, he warned them, 'Bhurewal sir had turned traitor … took maps … plans … take care of Netaji … Jai Hind!'

A pall of goom fell over the Gandhi Regiment. Betrayal at this juncture. The dark water, the silent birds, the still forest were all overcome with shame.

The fire in Imphal was dying down. The British authorities had tried hard to keep their surrender a secret, but the troops had suspected it all along. Empty trucks hovering around, signs of pack-up were visible everywhere. It was eight o'clock in the morning, but the sun had not come out. It was a hazy day.

One patrol jeep was speeding along to the headquarters when suddenly the driver spied a man in uniform frantically waving his arms and crying 'Stop! Stop!'. The driver screeched to a halt and in a second, bayonet-tips pressed into the man's chest and back. 'Who are you?'

'Major Bhurewal. I have risked my life and escaped from the Japanese. Don't waste even a moment. Take me to your commander. I have valuable information for him.'

From his bearing, the soldiers could tell he was a senior military officer. Bhurewal quietly surrendered his weapons and showed them his INA badge and the rolls of maps he had. Convinced of his credentials, the jeep rushed with its very special cargo towards Gen. Scoones's office.

Scoones pushed away his half-eaten breakfast and stared at the words on a yellow sheet of paper. The words smote his heart. His crestfallen expression, the dark circles under his eyes, the drooping shoulders, revealed a defeated man. Surrender. It was all over. Gen. Slim's signed instructions lay before him. Just then the phone rang. How like a death knell it sounded.

He picked up the receiver. 'Yes?'

'Geoffrey, this is Slim.'

'Yes, sir.'

'Has Jayant Sen from our Army Medical Corps reached there?'

'Yes, sir.'

'Did you see the surrender orders?'

'Yes, sir.'

'Any contact with the Japanese Army?'

'I have been trying to contact Gen. Yamamoto. There should be no trouble if we are surrendering.'

'This is final, Geoffrey. Don't entertain any hopes at all of a change.'

The conversation ended.

The white flag was ready. In just two hours it would be over. Fortunately, the job of taking the white flag was given to Dr Sen by the authorities in Comilla. It was intentional. But then if Yamamoto insisted, then Geoffrey Scoones had to be prepared to meet him.

Wingate's death had marked the beginning of the down slide for Britain. The road to Kohima had not yet opened up. American aid was not forthcoming. There was no let-up in the rains. Many Indian troops were on the verge of joining the INA. If the lives of sixty thousand men were to be saved, there was only one option – surrender.

Outside, Maj. Bhurewal was pleading with the officers. 'Let me see him for just half a minute, please.'

'It's all over for us. What difference can you make now?'

'No, it's not over yet. That's what I want to tell him. I have very important news.'

Reluctantly, the security officer sent a message inside. As expected, permission was refused. Bhurewal was desperate. How could he convince these people? Was suicide a better option? Suddenly, he remembered some code words that had been used by British agents during Gill's and Mahavir Singh's time. He pleaded with the security guards once again, literally debasing himself until he got an audience with Gen. Scoones. The code words had done the trick. Scoones and his staff officer almost dragged Bhurewal into the room.

An air of defeat pervaded the room. Soon, the 'Forgotten Army' would be sent to oblivion, a blot on the British Military. Gen. Scoones eyed Bhurewal with hope. He was the straw the drowning man would clutch at. 'I beg of you, sir, just endure it a little longer. Do not surrender.'

'What alternative is there? No rations, no ammunition, no future. To save the remaining troops, this is our only option.'

'But they have nothing either, sir. Those beggars will give up in a couple of days' time. Take my word ...'

'How do you say that? According to our information, Subhas Chandra Bose's army is sixty to seventy-thousand-strong. Only the vanguard has reached the Imphal plateau. The rest is to follow.'

'Don't be misled, sir. Including the reserves, they are not more than fifteen thousand. The stupid Japanese have given them undue importance.'

'But two of their divisions ...'

'One of them is still on the way. It is nowhere near Imphal.'

Bhurewal showed them the maps he was carrying. 'Believe me, sir, a little patience, and everything will be all right.'

Scoones and Baldwin were stunned. The maps showed every detail – troop locations, position of heavy artillery, every inch of the route. Immediately, Scoones established contact with the troops at the front.

'Stop the jeep heading for Bishenpur with the white flag,' he ordered. But soon he realised that he had unilaterally taken such a momentous decision. Should something go wrong he would have to face the consequences. However, a message from Richards that evening set his mind at rest. 'Congratulate me, sir!' exulted Richards.

'Why?'

'The Japanese troops are leaving Kohima.'

Tears rolled down Scoones's bristly, unshaven cheeks. 'How unfortunate the Japs are, how unlucky the traitors. They never realised how close they were to victory, else they would have dared to take those last few steps forward. In which case, our base in Imphal would have been destroyed.'

On the other side of the river, a grave was dug. With heavy hearts, the soldiers had just about buried Shyam Kant's body in the damp pit when there was a huge roar, and before they knew what it was, enemy bombers began raining fire on the camp below. Kissing the tops of the trees, they dropped their bombs and shot upwards. Sounds of gunfire were all that was heard.

Inayat tied up his wounded leg and with a roar, stood up, ready for action. Abid Hasan asked, 'How is it that the enemy is attacking specific targets?'

'Bhurewal did not go empty-handed. It is obvious that our maps and charts are with the enemy,' growled Inayat. Then after a pause, 'On the one hand, you have Mansukh's great act of courage and on the other, Bhurewal's betrayal. Under these circumstances, I appoint you second-in-command of the Gandhi Regiment.'

'Yes, sir.'

The shelling continued. A meeting was held and instructions given to change the location of troops and to move trenches. But it was dangerous because of constant firing from the enemy's side. Incensed by their guru's betrayal, all ranks were determined to take revenge. A bitter battle was waged with some losses and some gains.

The next day, an enemy bomber flew low over the Azad Hind camp and dropped several sheets of cyclostyled paper.

> *Stop siding with the Japs. The British Government is compassionate. Move over to this side. Enjoy three months' paid leave and a permanent job. Go back to your families. Forget the traitors. You will be greeted with honour as I was. Position, pay, pension are all yours – hard times will end. I remain one of you,*
>
> *Yours,*
> *Maj. B.S.J. Bhurewal*

Those innocent words were like salt on a wound. The Gandhi Regiment became even firmer in their resolve to put up a fight. The battle raged on. Abid Hasan's courage and his army's tenacity gave the enemy a hard fight.

That night, Yamamoto met Zaman Kiani. 'That traitor has shamed Bose,' he said.

'The Japanese haven't exactly covered themselves with glory, sir. If Yanagida had not let the 17th Division of the British slip out of his hands, the bugle of our victory over Imphal would have sounded in the first month itself.'

Yamamoto nodded, embarrassed. Kiani continued, 'Maybe one man has turned traitor, but there are still hundreds who will make human bombs of themselves for their beloved Netaji. Mr Yamamoto, we have only just begun our campaign.'

The command headquarters in Kandy wore a joyous air. Mountbatten was on the phone with Geoffrey Scoones. 'Destroy every single piece of paper, Geoffrey. No one must ever find out how close we had come to putting our weapons down. They must not find out that a common Indian traitor had seen the invincible British Army on the verge of surrender. Destroy INA and its arrogant leader totally, obliterate them from the face of the earth and the annals of history.'

'Where have they gone, my rabbits? Find them! Find my two rabbits.' Mutaguchi's staff was confused. What rabbits was the general talking about, in the middle of this forest, in the pouring rain?

Timidly his staff officer asked, 'Rabbits, sir?'

'You fool! Imphal and Kohima – they were in my grip ...'

Everyone was convinced Mutaguchi had lost his mind. He used to talk to himself very often, lamenting the loss of his rose garden, his rabbits. He whimpered that his staff had stabbed him in the back. It was folly to be dependent on one's subordinates. Worse to trust them implicitly. He was full of regret. He had placed four short decorated bamboo poles outside his bedroom. Every day, he looked at them and prayed to the eight hundred Japanese deities.

He began to believe that an evil spell had been cast on him because of which he, his army and his country were being destroyed. He castigated himself for keeping his headquarters at Maymyo, for being a coward, for destroying himself by laying his trust in unworthy colleagues. His men were very upset to see their chief in this state.

Mutaguchi still dreamt that he would win the day. However, the incessant Manipur rains would wash away all his hopes. Even tigers did not venture out of their caves in that weather, so what could a mere human do.

On 22 June, the Imphal–Kohima road was opened, and British supplies reached Imphal via Dimapur. At once the troops were rejuvenated. Under the command of Stopford and Richards, they launched an assault on Imphal.

Mutaguchi had never heard, let alone uttered the word 'retreat' until that moment. No one was prepared to accept responsibility for the decision. He finally consulted Kawabe in Rangoon. Unwilling to stick his neck out, Kawabe forwarded his query to Terauchi of the South Command. And from there, it was sent on its five-thousand-mile journey to the military headquarters at Tokyo. The soldiers eagerly awaited orders. But flights were delayed due to the weather. The staff officer sat in the airport lounge, freezing. Even the act of surrender was marked by misfortune.

One night, in pouring rain, Col. Shah Nawaz and about eight hundred of his soldiers appeared before Mutaguchi. Mutaguchi was nonplussed. He had been so matter of fact in his confrontation with

Sato. But here, in the case of Netaji and his INA, the situation was always emotionally charged.

'Colonel, where have you come from?'

'Please don't ask. We have seen such suffering and misery we wouldn't wish them on our enemies. I set out from Haka-Phalam with three thousand men. I have eight hundred left. General, why did you not let us fight in a way that we could have reached our destination? Why did you insult Netaji thus? Why did you play with the feelings of our poor soldiers?'

'It was never our intention to deceive you.'

'How can you say that?' Shah Nawaz spat out. 'Hadn't you and Netaji decided that I would lead my troops to Kohima and meet General Sato there? Sir, we rushed across rivers, climbed mountains in the hope that we would see our motherland. We had braved malaria, dysentery, the unsparing weather, just to see the tricolour flying on the ramparts of Kohima. We lost so many companions on the way. But before we could get there, your soldiers betrayed us and abandoned Kohima. And we were ordered to head for Ukhrul. Where do you want us to run? We met your Gen. Sato near the village of Sunjahak. Do you want to know what he said?'

'What?'

'I cannot bring myself to repeat those shameful words. "Why are you seeing futile dreams of battle," he said, "save your lives … come with me to Chindwin."'

Mutaguchi lowered his head in shame. Shah Nawaz continued, 'With your false promises, you have slit Netaji's throat with a hair.'

'Don't talk like that, Colonel. This is the first time there has been a revolt in the Japanese Army. Unfortunate that eminent leaders like Sato have dug my grave on the way to Imphal.'

'What about the promise you made to Netaji?'

'If my word was not important, I wouldn't be standing here, bearing the entire responsibility on my shoulders. Let me tell you, Shah Nawaz, defeat, victory, they are all games of providence. Let me also tell you that if we did not respect Netaji so much, the Imphal campaign, which had been abandoned on file, would never have appened.'

With great difficulty Mutaguchi was able to pacify Shah Nawaz. Just then, the royal decree withdrawing the Imphal–Kohima campaign was received. The humiliation of a failed campaign was too much for him to take.

Even nature had turned against them. Why else should the monsoon have arrived much before its time? Food supplies had long run out. Some had eaten poisonous roots and were suffering the consequences. At first, the Indian soldiers scrabbled for tender bamboo shoots, but soon those too became rare. Then any moving animal became a target. Half-cooked meat was unpalatable. Most Hindus baulked at it. But hunger is a merciless adversary. Add to that dysentery and malaria. The dejected Gandhi Regiment was beset with one disaster after another. Their struggles were ennobled briefly by the immortal sacrifice of Mansukh, but some still hung their heads at the thought of Bhurewal's betrayal.

There was no news at all from the Japanese Army. Small groups of the INA were scattered across two hundred miles from Bishenpur to Palel and Kohima, all of them suffering the same fate. For a couple of days, Dr Akbar had not been seen. When Gen. Kiani heard that he had been unwell, he went to visit him in his trench. Seeing the strapping Pathan reduced to a shadow of himself, Kiani was shocked. Dr Akbar tried to stand up. 'You are very ill. Please take care,' Gen. Kiani said to him.

'How can I lie in bed posted on the battle front? What will Netaji say?'

'Doctor, he is aware of the tremendous job you did at Palel during the air raids.'

Orderly Babu Singh held a spoonful of sugar to Dr Akbar's lips. There were no drops of milk to be had. Fearful of the air raids, entire villages had been abandoned for safer locations. Gen. Kiani was distressed.

Before dawn, Fujiwara arrived at the Indian camp. Kiani could tell from his expression that the news he had brought was bad.

'Forgive me, my brave colleagues. Japan has withdrawn. Mutaguchi has been instructed accordingly.'

This was a bolt from the blue. Infinitely worse than the bombs that fell out of the sky regularly. The word was more horrifying than death. What did we endure death and acute hunger pangs for?

'Fujiwara, whose orders are these?' Gen. Kiani demanded.

'Mutaguchi's.'

Retreat, surrender, withdrawal were not words Netaji had taught them. How could the man who had ignited the fires of revolution speak the language of defeat?

'Sir, Netaji had called for a forward march to Delhi. After all, that is our motherland. Where do we withdraw and go to? No. We will march forward, come what may!' Gen. Kiani was ready for the fight.

Fujiwara was overcome with grief. 'I had myself planted the sapling of the INA at Farrer Park. I too had exhorted you to jump into the fire. But what can one do? When the whole fabric is in shreds, where will you start patching it up?

Kiani was unwilling to hear Fujiwara out. 'You can go back to Japan, sir, but we will not leave our land. Netaji and retreat? Never. Even if we are killed, our dead bodies will grow feet and march to Delhi. There is only one direction in which we can move – Delhi.'

'Please listen to me.'

'If you have the guts, get us written orders from Netaji. Then I will decide whether we will don the red of sacrifice or the black of shame.'

Netaji had an unexpected visitor that day. Col. Lakshmi had come all the way from Maymyo to see him. Netaji was surprised. 'What brings you here, Lakshmi?'

'My girls have sent a message.'

Netaji opened the blackish-red stained paper. They had written in blood: 'We have not joined the army to be mere nurses and attendants, Netaji. Please let us go to the battlefield.'

'I will be marching towards Imphal in the next few days. Then all of us together will have to fight the last battle for freedom,' Netaji promised her.

Lakshmi had barely left when a terribly disturbed Kawabe arrived. His face was drawn and gaunt. 'Bose, sir, forgive me. I have bad news.'

Netaji's eyebrows shot up. Kawabe continued thickly, 'Our 14th Division has almost entirely perished in the jungles of Imphal.'

Netaji was shocked.

'Who knows whether it was Mutaguchi's overconfidence, carelessness, or the deceit of his subordinates. The weather did not help either.'

'What are you getting at?'

'Nothing is left,' said Kawabe, collapsing into a chair, wracked with sobs. 'Mr Bose, the Japanese Emperor has conceded defeat and withdrawn his troops from Imphal.'

Netaji let out a choked sob. Kawabe continued, 'Sir, Japan has known nothing but success till today. Hundreds of our soldiers are committing harakiri rather than surrender. A man like Terauchi has taken to his bed because of the shock of defeat. This retreat has been disastrous for us.'

'Why should you speak the words defeat and surrender? What has happened to warrant them?'

'Our depleted air force, irregular supplies of food and ammunition ...'

'These are all lame excuses. Kawabe, you may have withdrawn, but not we. There are several roads leading to Delhi and we will take them. God himself will not be able to stop us. And no matter if our army is reduced to ghosts and spirits on the way. Goddess Kali will take the fierce role of the Destroyer and assist us. We will fight, we will die, but we will not give up.' Netaji was flushed with rage and frustration. Kawabe sat there quietly in the face of such fury. He had no words left. An hour passed. Both had been silent. Finally, Netaji spoke. 'Tell me, Kawabe, what do you want now?'

'Send a message to Gen. Kiani. He refuses to hear the word retreat. We will march ahead on our own, he says. So does Col. Malik in the Moirang sector.'

'General, I will support of them both. I will join them on the front.'

The indomitable spirit of the INA shook Kawabe. Netaji pointed to the map and said, 'Kawabe, your path returns to Tokyo, ours can only head towards Delhi. So why should we turn back? As long as there is blood left in our veins and breath in our bodies, we will keep walking towards Delhi.'

'Bullheadedness at a critical time like this does not suit a national leader, sir.'

'Kawabe, you will not understand what the road to Delhi means to us. It is the symbol of our hopes, our dreams, our aspirations. The cries of the Jallianwala victims echo along with it. Gandhiji's prison terms were for it. Not just our men, even our animals were sacrificed for it. Listen ... the immortal neighing of Jhansi Rani's brave steed. Look at the wilting flowers on Bahadur Shah Zafar's tomb that we have there. Hear the cries of our young revolutionaries ringing off the gallows. Here you will find the glistening blade of Tipu Sultan's lost sword. And Tatya Tope's pointed shield … the smiling faces of Bhagat Singh, Rajguru and Sukhdev …'

'But …'

'But what? To retreat at this stage would be a betrayal.'

'Bose, sir, please keep the actual status in mind.'

'Kawabe, do not try to put a fence around a whirlwind.'

'What could we do, Mr Bose? We were let down by our own comrades and the fierce weather. Now you please don't turn against Japan.'

Kawabe's quivering voice calmed Netaji somewhat. 'Lt. Gen. Kawabe, I give you my word … until the final victory, I will stand by Japan.'

Kawabe was greatly reassured by this statement. 'Bose, sir, if only our Sato and Yanagida had your spirit and your wisdom, this day wouldn't have come.' Taking Netaji's hand in his own, Kawabe said, 'What is the point of destroying our entire force? Come, let us take four steps back.'

'Temporarily …?'

'Yes, of course. Till the rains stop. We will attack once the Imphal forest dries out,' Kawabe promised.

Netaji wrote to Kiani ordering a temporary retreat. He wrote another letter to the Japanese Emperor. 'Regardless of what happens in the Eastern sector or the western, there will be no compromise on my goal and objective of fighting until India gets her freedom.'

'A temporary retreat is only taking two steps back to be able to jump ten steps forward in the future. Even in deep slumber, we will be kissing the road to Delhi.' At these words of Netaji's, a visibly moved Gen. Kiani wiped his eyes and switched off the radio. Bandmaster Captain Ram Singh was almost hysterical. His fingers grazed the strings of his violin. His feet were tapping out the rhythm to his song, '*Jayenge, jayenge, hum Dilli, Dilli jayenge, apni neev banayenge.*'

Incessant rain had ravaged the Gandhi Regiment. The night seemed to continue even after daybreak. The sky sagged under the weight of clouds. The starving soldiers were surviving on leaves of trees and bushes. The roar of enemy aircraft and the thunder of cannons were growing louder. Suddenly, a messenger appeared, panting. His voice shook with fear and fatigue. 'An entire battalion of the Seaforth Highlanders is rushing towards us.'

Gen. Kiani's division was already broken up. He had only one brigade with him now. The danger of being trapped in the enemy's net was imminent. A volley of machine-gun and sten-gun fire was opened. Cannons spewed forth burning red balls of death. The Gandhi Regiment was under siege. The exchange of gunfire went on and on. The enemy seemed to have a limitless supply of ammunition. The Azad Hind soldiers had to clutch their rifles to their chests and remain hidden. They were waiting for that moment of lull when they could run for cover into the hollows across from them.

At last, night fell. There was some respite. The remaining soldiers gathered together.

Kiani commanded his men, 'First we will go towards Moray, then head for Mandalay.'

It was decided to take only as much arms and ammunition as they could carry. With them was also the office of the Azad Hind Government. But it was impossible to transport that through the shower of fire and water. In the end, the regiment had to surrender not just the symbolic office but also the very history of the Azad Hind. All documents were consigned to flames.

By early dawn, the firing had stopped. A Sikh officer came with a message from Inayat. 'The British soldiers would be having their breakfast now. This is the time to give them the slip.' Inayat's guess turned out to be correct. All of them were able to get across the ditch and move ahead. Soon, most of them got beyond the range of artillery fire. But as the regiment crossed the Siboyan Bridge, the sound of bombardment assaulted their ears once again. Breakfast was over apparently. Soon, the whirring of airplanes grew louder.

On the way, they encountered maimed Japanese gun carriages and empty ammunition cases. The withdrawal of the Japanese 15th Division was literally a glimpse into hell. No other general on the face of the earth must have suffered the indignity of a defeat as shameful as Mutaguchi and his dejected band. Officers of a lame cavalry, behind them a wounded and ill medical corps, damaged communication equipment, and following them a straggling column of dispirited infantry – enough to break the heart of any soldier.

The starving troops marched ahead, battling heavy rains and bitter cold. An overpowering stench pervaded the Kabaw Valley and the Chindwin mountains right down to the central island in the Chindwin River. On either side of the road, bodies were strewn. Thousands of soldiers walked on unshod feet. They had neither weapons nor uniforms nor knapsacks. Only the occasional bamboo pole to support them as they tramped through the slush. No one stopped to pick up those dropping dead in their tracks or even bury them. Streams of pus flowed out of festering wounds. Medical supplies were gone. Many fell unconscious from sheer exhaustion. Many soldiers were delirious from malarial fever, others were losing blood because of dysentery. But some suffered infinitely more from the thought of defeat, the sense of shame and disgrace that they had let their Emperor down. They just drew out their swords and committed harakiri.

The rancorous British and American troops were bent on pursuit. There was a shower of bombs which competed with raindrops, giving up only when the rain became heavier. Starvation had swallowed most flesh and blood. Emaciated soldiers pleaded with their friends, 'Go ahead. Don't endanger your lives for us.' Those unable to bear the searing pain of their injuries held grenades close to their chests and pulled out the pins. In seconds, bits and pieces of flesh and bone were scattered all round.

Kiani's heart bled for the men who had sacrificed their lives to attain Delhi. From the heap of corpses, some half-dead voice would moan, 'How can we carry our wounded, malaria-ridden bodies all the way to the Chindwin River, General? Do us just one favour. Convey our Jai Hind to our beloved Netaji. Tell him we fought till our last breath.'

All along the way were strewn sightless eyes staring from skull sockets, exposed ribcages, limbs peeping out of ragged uniforms. Mutaguchi himself sat on his horse, benumbed. The enemy appeared determined not to let them reach the Chindwin River. Suddenly, two airplanes came swooping at them. But, they didn't drop any bombs. Perhaps out of respect for International Law. Instead, the British bombers sprayed those below with petrol. And then they somersaulted and like a shark dived back and out of sight. Soon, they began dropping bombs from high above. And within moments, a blaze erupted. Tongues of flame swallowed the entire road. The jungle filled with terrified screams and agonised cries. No artist, however imaginative, could have portrayed a more horrifying picture of hell. What a gruesome picture of naked cruelty, violent injustice.

And through this hapless jungle trudged the unfortunate ten thousand soldiers of the INA, looking towards Chindwin, via Haka, Phalam, Kaladan and Bishenpur. Dr Akbar's condition had deteriorated. Suddenly, the doctor's breath began to come in short rapid gasps. All hearts went out to the man who had spent his life saving thousands. Abid put down the stretcher and said to Zaman Kiani, 'Give me a small contingent and I will go to the hospital at Manewo. Maybe we'll find medicines there.'

Dr Akbar said, 'I am not going to survive. Convey my Jai Hind to Netaji. Tell Netaji,' he whispered hoarsely, 'the doctor carried on until there was life in his body. But Khuda did not give me the opportunity to serve him further. Alvida! Jai Netaji!'

His head rolled back. On the damp banks of the nallah, his frail body was laid to rest. Babu Singh lost control. Gritting and gnashing his teeth, he went for Gen. Kiani. Tears ran unchecked down his cheeks as he demanded an answer. 'Who ordered this retreat? Why did you make us give up, General? Why? In order to make us die of starvation by the roadside?' Soon Babu Singh began to falter. At once, two of his companions rushed to steady him. With their support, he dragged himself along. Kiani lifted the rifle off his shoulder and held it himself. Babu Singh was offended. 'What are you doing, General saheb? A soldier without arms is no different from a woman without clothes. Don't insult me by depriving me of my rifle, sir!'

Another day passed. Babu Singh collapsed into the wet mud. Zaman Kiani picked up his slush-covered body and rested Babu Singh's head on his lap. A brief smile crossed Babu Singh's face and then softly, he whispered, 'Your Khuda will not forgive you, General saheb.'

'Why are you so pessimistic, my brother?' Kiani said to him.

'Sir, there, on the front, the battlefield was familiar, facing us was the enemy. And we actually had weapons in our hands. What a glorious death that would have been! Instead of dying like a rat by the roadside, why didn't you feed us to the cannon?'

This accursed path had been trodden by more than forty thousand Japanese and ten thousand Indian soldiers. Even if memorials were to be erected for them, how many would one put up?

As they stood on the soil of Moirang, Lt. Gen. Tanaka and Shaukat Malik continued to look towards Imphal with bloodshot eyes. The mountains around Imphal were no longer visible, nor were the planes, the smoke or fire. From the distance, waves of rain came rushing into Moirang and lashed at it.

The overcast sky seemed menacing. Based on information supplied by traitors like Prabhu Dayal and others, the enemy spat fire at the most vital spots. They had to change their hideouts frequently. But Tanaka's battalion and Shaukat's army refused to turn back.

Leaving the defence of Moirang to Shaukat, Tanaka marched towards Bishenpur that night. Sounds of gunfire were heard from there. Once again, Japanese troops occupied Bishenpur. For two days, the town was under their control. But later, the bad news came. Tanaka's hungry army had disbanded. There was no trace of Tanaka. Was he lost or killed? No one could say.

Shaukat geared up for the defence of Moirang. The town kept receiving frightening news that British troops were marching towards them. On the tiled roof of the Azad Hind Government headquarters, the tricolour fluttered, braving biting wind and lashing rain. Only about eighty to ninety men were left to assist Shaukat. He had trained the Naga and Kuki youth and enlisted them in his army. The stock of ammunition was depleted. When they saw the despair on Shaukat's face, his Naga companions brought out their bows and arrows.

'Sir, orders to withdraw have just come over the wireless,' one soldier rushed in to tell them.

'Shut down that equipment. Don't heed anybody now. Just keep one goal in front of you. Delhi! Only Delhi. Pick up the bow and arrow, chant Netaji's name and prepare to die!' Shaukat shouted.

British spirits were high now that fresh reinforcements had reached Imphal. Heedless of the rain, Dakota aircraft roared over Bishenpur and Moirang. The few buildings that still stood were razed to the ground and the odour of smoke mingled with the smell of wet earth.

Naga women and children armed with bows and arrows gathered in Moirang. That night they took shelter in treetops and ditches. As dawn broke, a band of twenty-five planes rumbled over the town and let loose a shower of bombs. It seemed the sky was raining fire.

Shaukat Malik, Kuriyan Singh and the natives waited, alert. The murderous dance of the airplanes ended. A short while later, with a noise that made the sky shudder and the earth tremble, a column of tanks entered Moirang. Behind them were long lines of who knows how many divisions. Must be at least an entire regiment of about three thousand. Outside the boundary wall of the devastated town, the tanks halted, as if to catch a breath. Seeing no signs of retaliation, the tanks rolled forward then, scattering wet earth in all directions.

The small, tiled building that housed the Azad Hind Government looked deserted. Two loud explosions were heard. Two huge gaping holes appeared in the belly of the building. It seemed to lean towards one side. When British soldiers ran forward to take down the flag, suddenly, sharp native arrowheads whistled through the air and found their targets. British tommies crashed to the ground. Numerous white bodies lay in the mud. The army commanders were flabbergasted. They couldn't gauge what spell the Naga–Kukis had cast. Where were the arrows coming from? The trees, the wells or the debris of buildings? But they kept coming, with accuracy and speed, and bodies continued to fall.

Throughout the day, it seemed as if the game of catch-me-if-you-can was being played in Moirang. Night fell. But the British still had not laid hands on the flag. The INA and the Nagas too had lost many soldiers. Just as the tommies took a couple of steps towards the flag, thinking the resistance was over, a fresh assault would begin. Arrows would zip through the air slicing off chunks of flesh.

The earth of Moirang too had sensed that its beloved flag would be desecrated under the cover of darkness. British commanders crowded around the flagpole. But before they knew what was happening, about fifty intrepid Azad Hind soldiers and three hundred Nagas appeared as if they had sprung out of the ground and surrounded the British. There were a number of women among them. The British warned them to withdraw. But the natives continued to close in on them. Volleys of gunfire were heard. Like camphor, human bodies burned. Like moths to a flame, the soldiers were sacrificing themselves for their flag, their precious tricolour. 'Netaji's symbol is being taken away,' cried some boys and girls as they ran forward, and soon their tender young bodies were wrapped in shrouds of fire.

As soon as he realised that the flag was about to be removed, Shaukat flung a hand grenade and charged like a cheetah. The grenade claimed five to six men. A hail of bullets greeted Shaukat and his blood-soaked body crumpled.

A hush fell on Moirang. Bodies lay everywhere. Who was going to clear the hundreds of corpses? Finally, bulldozers were commissioned for the task. Even now, an occasional arrow sliced through the air. British tommies marched ahead. So did the bulldozer, collecting corpses. The Gurkhas, who had eaten the salt of the British, ran around, shoving their kukris into those who were still grappling with death. A British soldier asked a Gurkha, 'Why are you doing this? They aren't going to survive once they are buried.'

'Saheb, how will we seek a place in heaven then?' he replied.

'If we bury a living person, it would be considered a sin in our religion,' another explained.

Four days later, Shaukat regained consciousness. He peered around. Under the branches of a gnarled old tree, a straw bed had been made. With great difficulty, some Nagas had managed to rescue him. They had somehow kept him alive with medicinal herbs and leaves. Weakly, he looked at the eight dispirited companions gathered round him. The moment he opened his eyes, their spirits lifted. 'Where is Netaji?' was Shaukat's first question. No one had an answer to it. Then he said, 'Well, if only eight are left, even eight are enough.'

'For what sir?'

'To raise another regiment with the Nagas.'

'In this condition?'

'The spirit of patriotism infused by Netaji can never fade away.'

That same night, a soldier came running to Shaukat with a transistor. It was Netaji speaking over Rangoon Radio.

'Shah Nawaz, General Kiani, Pritam Singh, Shaukat, Gulzar Singh, where are you all? My brothers, in the rising sun, or the fading sunset, in the deafening darkness of death or the exuberance of life, in the warmth of joy and the despair of sorrow, I have given you my word that I am with you. I have taken birth solely to break the chains around my motherland, even if I am burned to ashes in the process. I have never cared for my own life. I too will fight with you, in the jungles of Imphal. But for the sake of the promise I made to a true friend like Japan and to prepare for an eventful tomorrow, my friends, give your seething blood a moment's respite. To be able to leap a mile ahead tomorrow, take just two small steps back today.

'Brothers, this world is perishable. Here everything that is born comes with its death tattooed on its forehead. But there is no such curse on visions and dreams of glory. There is no death for one's hopes and soaring aspirations.

'From our smouldering ashes will spring innumerable new revolutions. So what if one road to Delhi is blocked. Where there is a will, there is a way. And who will dare stop us? Even mountains will walk. Heaving, foaming oceans will split. And high dancing waves will transport us gently to Lal Qila's shores. We will hoist the proud tricolour and sing the song of victory!'

Eighteen

November 1944. Netaji was on his way to Tokyo with his colleagues and had stopped at Formosa on the way. His journey would take him via Bangkok, Saigon and Turen.

Time had flown relentlessly. And in its wake, men of extraordinary endurance had collapsed. After the debacles on the Pacific front and in Imphal, Prime Minister Tojo was persona non grata. He had been replaced by Kuniaki Koiso.

'Netaji,' asked one of his colleagues, 'what policy will the new prime minister adopt towards the Azad Hind Government?'

Netaji had no answer. This visit to Tokyo was meant to find one.

After a short halt at Taipei, they took off for Tokyo. Just as the pilot announced they were entering Japanese territory, the plane shuddered violently and dipped from left to right. Objects fell out, passengers panicked. Young Col. Habib-ur Rahman held on tightly to Netaji's hand. Was it a bomb?

'What's the matter, Captain?' Netaji asked.

'Land where you are, the air traffic control orders.'

'Where are we?'

"Above Osaka.'

Somehow, they landed at the military airstrip in Osaka. After a compulsory rest of two hours, they were given permission to resume the flight. Soon they were flying over Tokyo airport. But, there too they had to circle the city many times till they got permission to land. Doubts began to assail them. The runway lights appeared brighter in the growing darkness.

When they finally landed, the Japanese foreign minister Shigemitsu, Gen. Isoda of the Hikari Kikan and office bearers of the Indian

Independence League welcomed Netaji warmly. Netaji and his delegation were to stay at the government guest house. The defence secretary, Gen. Kiani quickly organised a dinner, which was attended by Shigemitsu. During the course of the meal, some messages were received that left Shigemitsu extremely worried. 'Mr Bose, the war has arrived at Japan's doorstep,' he said worriedly.

'How do you mean?'

'This afternoon, about one hundred B-29 bombers violated our airspace and bombed our ammunition factories in Osaka.'

'About what time did this take place?'

'Three o'clock.'

Netaji shot a glance at Kiani. Shigemitsu was muttering, 'We were confident that Japan could never be a target for the Americans. If secret agents are to be believed, the Americans have built huge bases on the islands of Saipan and Litte. Their powerful planes can easily fly into our territory and wreak havoc.'

The Japanese government had gone all out to make Netaji's visit special. He was a very popular figure and so his motorcade was stopped several times for people offering him greetings and flowers. The crowds at the famous Hibiya Park where Netaji was to address them were unprecedented. In a rousing speech, Netaji said, 'Just because Imphal fell, it does not mean we have lost the war. Our spirit can never be cowed down.' Though Netaji's popularity with the common people of Tokyo was undiminished in spite of the setbacks, he was not sure of the attitude of the new administration. One afternoon, he received a call from Shigemitsu, 'Bose! Banzai!'

'What is the matter, sir?'

'A dinner reception is being hosted in your honour by Prime Minister Koiso.'

It was a gala affair, attended by ambassadors and diplomats of many countries. Among the crowd was a man standing alone in a corner, glass in hand. That gaunt and defeated look, surely it wasn't the former prime minister Tojo! How could Netaji forget his unequivocal support when he was in power. He broke away from the crowd around him and went up to Tojo and embraced him warmly. 'Mr Prime Minister, where do you live now?

'I have a little farmhouse on the outskirts of the city.'

'I will certainly visit you before I leave Tokyo,' Netaji promised.

Later when discussions began in Prime Minister Koiso's office, it was a most significant moment for Netaji.

'Sir, it would not have taken me very long to vanquish the British and take Imphal. But nature played a cruel trick on me. In spite of that, if only the Japanese Air Force had provided us cover, we would have drowned the British in the Brahmaputra and rushed towards Delhi.'

What Koiso would say to that was crucial. The interpreter, Kakistsubo was flushed with tension. Koiso said, 'Bose, you are well aware that Japan does not normally enter into friendships with anyone.'

'Yes, sir.'

'And once the hand of friendship is extended, it is rarely withdrawn. I believe it is my duty to honour the commitment that was made to you by former prime minister Tojo. It would not be fair of Japan to let down a friend at a critical juncture.'

As a token of their deep friendship and gratitude, Netaji handed over a sum of fifty million yen to Koiso. Koiso was surprised. In a public meeting, Netaji appeared reserved and reticent. But across the negotiating table, he was a tiger. Doing away with all the formalities, Netaji said, 'There should be a direct dialogue between us. We don't need the Hikari Kikan's mediation here.'

His request was immediately accepted. Netaji announced that Hachiya was nominated the ambassador to the Azad Hind court and S.A. Ayyar would represent the INA government in Tokyo. When the discussions concluded, Koiso, looking as if he was carrying a heavy burden, grasped Netaji's hand tightly. 'Bose, Japan is firmly in the jaws of America in the Pacific. We haven't faced this throughout our twenty-six-hundred-year-old history. At this juncture, we have only one request of you,' he said.

'Please tell me what it is.'

'Thirty–forty thousand of our troops are still posted in Burma and Singapore for their defence. The Burmese consider you God. That is why I am asking – please help us save our soldiers.'

∾

It had rained the day Netaji went looking for Tojo's farmhouse. He was determined to meet his friend at all costs. When Tojo saw Netaji at his door, he could not believe his eyes. His voice was thick as he said, 'When a man loses his throne, there is no place for even his shadow in the world.'

'Mr Tojo, no Indian will ever forget someone who has done him a favour. Their faith makes them worship a stone.'

'The new prime minister may not like your visiting me.'

'It doesn't bother me. In fact, I told him I was coming to see you.'

Mrs Tojo brought Netaji fresh sweet potato and fruit from her garden. Their meeting was full of memories of earlier times. When Netaji stood up to leave, Tojo's little granddaughters brought Netaji a bunch of roses. Tojo could not restrain himself. 'Whatever I did, I did for my country,' he said passionately. Netaji comforted him.

∾

In Tokyo, Netaji met the poet laureate of Japan, Nagayuchi, and also visited the hostel where he had sent forty Indian students to get advance training in the modern air force. Netaji gave them an inspiring talk. Then he expressed a desire to see the ageing Rash Behari Bose. Kakistsubo looked embarrassed. 'Why, is there a problem?' Netaji asked him.

'How do I say this, Bose? When the unconfirmed news was received that Imphal was taken, the ailing Rash Behari got a new lease of life. He dragged himself out of bed and came to the radio station to address India. However, when the reports were proved untrue, the shock was too much for him. He has not left his bed since.'

When Netaji took the frail hand into his, Rash Behari was touched. Only two words escaped his lips, 'Imphal' and 'freedom'.

Rash Behari always had two photos by his bedside, his beloved wife's and his daughter's. That day, there was one more photograph next to them – that of his son. Netaji was shocked to see it there. Rash Behari began to narrate brokenly how his son had lost his life when his ship had been hit by enemy gunfire and how without warning, his cold body was returned to him. Netaji squeezed his hand and reassured him, 'Rash Babu, don't worry. I have not yet sheathed the sword that you had drawn against British Imperialism.

'I will carry you on elephant back from the same Chandni Chowk where you had thrown a bomb on the viceroy, and make sure you hoist the tricolour on Lal Qila, I give you my word,' Netaji told him.

The students of Tokyo University had invited Netaji to address them. His revolutionary ideas went down very well with them. 'It is not true that India became united only after the British came. If, after independence, we wish to take some revolutionary steps for reconstruction and modernisation, we will need to have a strong central government. Education, defence, agriculture, industry and such important sectors should remain with the centre so that some bold, progressive measures can be taken. The government must have the authority to take revolutionary decisions. Though it may appear to be a dictatorship, it will be closely aligned to the people's hopes and aspirations. Caste is an accident of birth and religion. It should not be allowed to interfere in public affairs ...'

After the talk, the students surrounded Netaji and questioned him again on his political ideology. Netaji explained, 'I believe that my country needs a synthesis of National Socialism and Communism. Government's primary concern should be unity of the country and the welfare of the common people. I am excited by Russia's system of economic progress through planning. As Congress president, I had first advocated planning in India. Class struggle as a concept will not work very well in India because here the problems of farmers are more urgent than those of factory workers. The Marxists give great importance to economic questions. That is why it has become so important in the eyes of the world. But it should not become the be-all and end-all of all life.'

'So, which principles of nationalism appeal to you?'

'The construction of the nation. Patriotic sentiments must make us take a bold step. But this cannot be done at the expense of a particular community, like the Jews. The chariot of common good and welfare must be drawn forward for the betterment of all faiths and denominations. A new social system must be created in Asia, based on the principles of justice and freedom,' Netaji said.

The students were greatly impressed by Netaji's words. They said they hoped that his great wisdom would be utilised for the development of the country.

Netaji left Tokyo for Nagasaki, satisfied. He had pressed for many demands and most of them had been met. Opening an embassy was agreed upon and monetary assistance from the Japanese government for the INA government, which hitherto had been on a personal surety, would now be on the same terms as a loan between any two countries. Netaji went through every agreement with a fine-toothed comb to ensure that the INA government retained its sovereignty.

After Tokyo, Netaji was to go to Shanghai via Nagasaki. The governor of Fukuoka, Japan's southernmost province, had made all arrangements for Netaji and his delegation as if they were visitors to a royal court in the days of yore. The official banquet was followed by a music and dance performance. Among the performers, was a young geisha who drew the attention of the entire audience. But she had eyes for Netaji alone. Every time he smiled or applauded, she glowed. When the distinguished guests left, the young Kumi, the most beautiful geisha in Nagasaki, accosted Netaji and offered to play the banjo specially for him. Much as he tried to dissuade her, she was persistent. So, Netaji invited his entire team to accompany him, much to her dismay. The private performance dragged on. Finally, Netaji politely told her that it was time for them to say goodnight. Even after everyone had left, Kumi stayed back. She told him how she had adored him ever since she had seen pictures of him in the newspapers, and even listened to his speech once. 'My arms cannot claim to contain a tornado,' she said, 'but I beg you, just for tonight to let me remain in your majestic presence, share in the power of your persona just for tonight ... I will be eternally blessed ...' Netaji was discomfited. Adopting a paternal tone, he said to her, 'You are like my daughter. As a father, I now order you to leave the room.' But Kumi was not prepared to listen. 'It is the privilege of a beautiful woman to ensnare a powerful man,' she said.

'Kumi, in your eyes, I do not see beauty but compassion, your lips reflect the hunger and suffering of my beloved countrymen, and in your body, I see those young lives who have sacrificed themselves in the fire of revolution. My base desires have long been sublimated in my passion for my country's cause, in my idealism and my goal. God has not intended for me the life of pleasures and gratification.'

Kumi departed, but left behind her banjo for Netaji.

Senior officers of the INA were in a meeting, six months after the disastrous Imphal campaign.

'I have promised Prime Minister Koiso that we would offer protection to the Japanese soldiers trapped in Burma,' Netaji told them. His words created a mild flutter among the assembled officers. Then Major Mahboob stood up and said, 'Is there any point holding on to a crumbling wall? What remains of the INA will also be destroyed.'

Netaji was shocked. He glared at everyone before bursting out, 'Well, my brave heroes, why did you not ask this question when fifty thousand Japanese soldiers were dying at Imphal? Why did you not say to them: Why are you fighting for us? What is your connection with Indian soil?'

Immediately, eyes were lowered.

'We must be prepared to sip from a friend's cup of troubles with as much relish as we share his plate of food. Japan has a new prime minister now. I was very worried that the new government would leave us in the lurch. But they have assured us of continued support, despite heavy losses. Don't we owe it to them to offer whatever assistance we can?'

Netaji's argument changed hearts.

'Let one more record be placed on the pages of history – that Indian soldiers stretched themselves as much to help to defend Japanese soldiers as the Japanese had done while fighting for India's cause.'

Netaji had decided to send the 2nd Division to Burma under the leadership of Gen. Shah Nawaz to counter the British forces that were approaching Mount Popa and Meiktila.

It was late night when Netaji returned to his residence. While they were having dinner, Gurbaksh Dhillon was staring at Netaji. For the past several days, he had been troubled by a nagging doubt. Finally, he said, 'Netaji, before you left India, had you spoken to anyone about your goals?'

The words brought back some fond memories. Netaji was lost in reminiscences. Then he said softly, 'There is just one heart in India where I have kept the innermost secrets of my life safely.'

'And whose heart is that?'

'Mohandas Karamchand Gandhi.'

Everyone at the table was surprised.

When the new Nehru Brigade – comprising mostly local people from Kuala Lumpur, Penang and other cities – was formed, the question of who its commander would be was widely speculated. At the last minute, some Tamil labourers were also enlisted. About eight hundred of these men had at one time even raised rebellious voices. So when Gurbaksh requested that this command be given to him, Netaji was taken aback.'Are you aware that two very senior officers have turned down the responsibility?' he asked.

'Yes, sir.'

'How soon will you be able to confront the enemy?'

'As soon as we get there.' Dhillon sounded impatient to move.

Netaji was relieved. Dhillon saluted Netaji proudly. 'Have faith in me, Netaji. I will never let you down.'

Gen. Slim was rapidly approaching the Irrawaddy River and the Nehru Brigade was supposed to stop him right there. Dhillon rushed to the Minjaon region accompanied by Capt. Izumi. 'Bless your great leader! At this crucial moment, everyone has turned their backs on Japan. The Burmese defence minister, Aung San, who supported us all this while, has switched parties,' Izumi informed him.

'What!'

'Yes, he went to Kandy and begged Mountbatten's forgiveness. We have been betrayed. But Japan will never forget how Netaji honoured his word.'

Trying to contain the victorious British Army was like trying to hold back a landslide. The brigade Dhillon led was one of the most pathetic ones he had ever seen. Many soldiers had exchanged their uniforms for the garb of local farmers, to disguise themselves. They had neither training nor discipline. Dhillon reminded them of Netaji and made wearing uniforms compulsory. He planned strategies and held drills.

During this time came the sad news that Maj. Khosla had been killed in Mandalay. Dhillon had with him Capt. Chandrabhan, Lt. Hariram and Lt. Khan Muhammad leading a battalion each – in all about twelve hundred soldiers, armed with some old rifles, no backup of heavy artillery or cover of aircraft. And they were going to take on the enemy's 7th Division and three brigades with just their spirit and courage.

Somehow Capt. Izumi managed to obtain three cannons. Dhillon had not slept a wink for five nights. The enemy's strength was phenomenal. If the Nehru Brigade succeeded, it would only be because of their guerrilla tactics. Dhillon realised that he needed the support of the local people wherever they had to engage with the enemy and was doing all he could to ensure that. He took the farmers in the neighbouring region into confidence. He came across a village headman's beautiful daughter called Mai. She seemed familiar with Sarojini Naidu, the Rani Jhansi Regiment and Netaji. As Dhillon was leaving her tiled Burmese-style home, she fastened a snake-like copper armband round his arm. Shutting her eyes tightly, she said, 'Brother, as long as you wear this amulet, you need not fear death.'

An enemy attack was imminent. In that tense atmosphere, someone started a rumour that Dhillon had been killed in a bomb attack. When Dhillon reached a pagoda near the village of Pimin, he heard a downcast Chandrabhan telling someone that their commander had been killed and the enemy had crossed the Irrawaddy River.

'Both stories are false!' Dhillon interrupted. 'Look, Chandrabhan, I am Commander Dhillon, very much alive. Nor has the enemy crossed the river.'

Everyone was relieved to see Dhillon. The Azad Hind headquarter was a palm-thatched shelter where Col. Dhillon summoned a meeting of his battalion commanders. They had only eight machine guns between them, but some of their parts were missing. So they dismantled three, used the parts and got five guns fully ready with four rounds of ammunition each. Just then a local Burmese arrived with the news that on the other side of the river, the enemy was shooting down the dogs in the village.

Col. Dhillon realised that a massive enemy attack was imminent. They spent the night in watchful anticipation, but nothing happened. Towards dawn, a squadron of bombers rent the air, followed by rapid explosions. Their target was the advance party of the INA. Fortunately, most of them were safe in the trenches on the banks of the river. After dropping tonnes of bombs, the enemy fell silent. By afternoon, it was expected that the infantry would appear. But nothing happened. Some thirty to forty Japanese soldiers prepared to swim across to find out what the enemy was planning. They had almost reached the other side when a hail of bullets began to dance off the waters. Dhillon saw the pale young faces of the swimmers, a sight he would not forget.

On 13 February 1945, several men of the South Lancashire Division began to swim across the river. In the dark waters, their heads bobbed like slashed coconuts. The INA troops around Bagan were on high alert. As the heads came within range, the Nehru Brigade started firing, picking the heads off one by one. The enemy kept coming – in boats, big and small. But Dhillon's men got their targets. Several boats caught fire, others capsized in the rapid currents. With every hit, the Azad Hind soldiers yelled, 'Chalo Dilli! Netaji zindabad!'.

Suddenly, some Indian voices carried across the water. 'These seem to be the Chalo Dilliwalas!'

Hariram's battalion opened fire. The enemy was thrown into disarray. Boats sprung leaks and went out of control. Hariram kept up the assault. The rays of the setting sun stepped into the water. The South Lancashire soldiers retreated. While the INA lost thirty to forty men, the enemy had lost four hundred.

Another day passed.

Dhillon and Capt. Izumi began to march towards the Japanese headquarters. In the distance, some covert movement was noticed. They had gone about two miles along the river when the sky darkened with planes heading in their direction like vultures. Dhillon knew that some British troops were in the vicinity. He noticed the opening of a cave in one of the hillocks, so they rushed into it. Enemy machine guns were trained in their direction. The face of the hillock was pock-marked by bullets. Dust and smoke filled the air. For a while, they remained in the cave. Staying longer would mean capture. But there was no way out, except a little opening at the other end. One Japanese soldier tried to clamber out that end, and within seconds was reduced to a bleeding lump of flesh.

However, it was safer to get out of that opening than to walk out of the cave. About a hundred and fifty yards away was a dense thicket. That was their only choice. Dhillon's and Izumi's survival depended on the accuracy of the enemy's aim and the swiftness of their own feet. Dhillon moved towards the opening, but Izumi stopped him. 'You cannot go first, sir! Let me go ahead.'

'Why?'

'If I should get killed, you lose only a captain. If something should happen to you, we lose a commander.'

'Don't be stupid. Move aside. I am the senior. I should go first.'

The two of them managed to dodge the continuous enemy firing, took zig-zag curves and reached the shelter of the thicket.

Night fell. Dhillon began to walk back towards his camp. There had been no news from Chandrabhan.

Soon, they got the news that the enemy had advanced between Thethe and Bagan, and that Chandrabhan's troops had been scattered.

At daybreak, some of Dhillon's junior officers came up to him and asked, 'Hasn't enough blood been shed already? How long are we to go on like this? Please allow those who have survived to surrender.'

'Wait. Let me think.'

Dhillon pulled out a photograph of Netaji. 'Surrender! Such a cruel word ... what shall I do, Netaji? What shall I do?'

At the same time, he began to pray to Guru Gobind Singh. And in that still silent morning, high above the trees, Guru Gobind Singh appeared before him. Radiant. Smiling. Encouraging. He told Dhillon,

'In this world, your guru is Netaji. Give up your life, but not the path he wants you to tread.' And Dhillon was transformed. Gone were the tears, the fears, the doubts. His mind was made up.

He saw the white flag all ready to be waved. He snatched it out of the officer's hands and ripped it up. His bullocks had been killed so he took two others, yoked them to a cart and began his journey to Bagan.

The bullock cart seemed to plod through centuries ... His Burmese sister Mai's village was heavily bombarded. Dhillon was lost in thought. If Mai were wearing that amulet that day ... He was shaken out of his reverie by a high-ranking Japanese officer. 'Please hurry. Netaji is waiting for you in the Meiktila jungle.' Netaji? Here? Was he dreaming?

Imphal was now fully under British supremacy. The fires that had been raging for a year now had died down. But the fire raging in the heart of the chief of the South-East Asia Command, Mountbatten, was not quenched. 'In how many days will our troops enter Rangoon?' he asked Gen. Slim.

'They ought to have got there by now. But Japanese troops are waiting in full readiness at Meiktila in central Burma. Maj. Gen. Kasuya has rebuffed our attacks all this while.'

Dickie Mountbatten had one major regret. Six Japanese divisions had fought on the Assam–China border. Because of the split among themselves and the onslaught of the weather, many of them had retreated. But not a single division had been completely destroyed. He and Gen. Slim now were dreaming of annihilating the Japanese, here in Burma.

'Dickie, one of Subhas Bose's divisions is waiting near Mandalay, ready to assist the Japanese.'

The name brought a frown to Mountbatten's face.

'You seem to dislike that man intensely?'

'Of course! No slave from the vast British Empire has dared to show such contempt for it.'

'How is that?'

'If the Japs had not been encouraged by him, they would never have ventured as far as Imphal and Kohima. If Japan had wanted to take over India, they would have made moves soon after Rangoon, in 1941.

But whatever they have done since then is all at Bose's instigation. He should be killed. Then our biggest headache will be gone.'

'Do you think he is more troublesome than Gandhi?' Slim asked.

'We have never been perturbed by Mr Gandhi's threats of fast unto death. But I am afraid of Bose's destructive strength. Don't you recall his bold, though unsuccessful attempt to build an alliance between Japan and China a year and a half ago? Can you imagine what might have happened if the American Air Force had not come to our rescue in Imphal?'

'One air squadron is hovering over Burma to get Bose, dead or alive. They have even bombed their headquarters at Rangoon. But the shrewd man he is, he changes his base frequently,' Gen. Slim remarked.

'Do whatever you can but get us out of that man's clutches,' a disturbed Mountbatten ordered.

Netaji had acted on his statement – 'If necessary, I will present myself at the front.' He had arrived at Meiktila in the third week of February 1945. From where he stood, Netaji could see the dark outline of Mount Popa and its ranges in the distance. Only the tops reflected firelight, as if the enemy had created a halo round the mountain peak. Netaji was determined to go to the Popa army camp, about two hours away from Meiktila, to give his troops a pep talk.

Meiktila was an extremely important military centre. Not only was it an important junction on the Mandalay–Rangoon route, but also a number of Japanese administrative offices and godowns were located in its close proximity. Several arterial roads went out of Meiktila to Chakpadang and Bagan in the west and also to Rangoon along the Prome Road. To the north was the highway to Mandalay, Maymyo, Michina. To the south were Ziyawaddy and Pegu from where one could get to Rangoon by a long roundabout route. There were several mountain paths through which one could enter Thailand, illegally. Two temporary Japanese airstrips were also located there.

Netaji was standing in the Meiktila jungle, in his uniform, looking into the darkness. He noticed some murmuring among his officers. 'Japanese troops let go of the unconquerable peak of Mandalay.'

'Which means that the enemy is barely a few hours away from here.' Netaji's words rang like a bell in the night air.

'Netaji, please turn back,' Shah Nawaz whispered.

'Shanno, I have to reach the top of Mount Popa.'

'We will defend the borders, Netaji, till there is breath in our bodies. But you please get back to Rangoon. Thousands of Shannos may die, but one Netaji must live.'

'Impossible, Shah Nawaz. How well will the crown of martyrdom sit on my head!'

Of late, Netaji had been clutching a book on Ireland's history, and every time he got a few moments, he would pore over the pages. The Japanese officer Takashahi was trying to persuade Netaji to pull out. 'Germany's back is broken, Japan is on the downslide. It's almost over for us. Why don't you please turn back?'

The menacing sound of the war planes did not bother Netaji anymore. Strangely, his words had lost their hardness and acquired a gentle, prayerful colour. So he turned to Takashahi and said, 'Look at that mountain range. It is beautiful. Like God's lap. I feel I should lay down my life right there, with the song of freedom on my lips.'

A knife seemed to slice through many hearts at this. Not just his bodyguard, Capt. Rawat, but also Dr Raju and Takashahi dabbed their eyes. The air strikes continued in the distance. In an effort to cheer up his cold and nervous colleagues in the INA, Netaji said, 'My friends, has anyone of you read the history of Ireland? Most of their foremost patriots were slain at the very outset. Decades went by. But one day a new generation of revolutionaries was born and quickly rose to the surface. Like them, I want to see a resurgence here.'

It was apparent that Netaji had made up his mind to sacrifice himself at the altar of revolution. Just then, a Japanese captain came galloping into the camp, and as he dismounted, he gasped, 'Pack up! Prepare to run. Enemy troops are at the village of Chawse. A tank brigade and a lorry load of infantry are heading this way.'

'They are only an hour away, then? Come on, Bose, hurry up.'

Gruffly he said, 'What if I cannot find the way to Delhi? Who will stop my path to martyrdom?'

Shah Nawaz could not hold himself back. 'Netaji, you do not have the right to your life any more. With your sacrifice and dedication, you have become the symbol of the aspirations of thirty-eight crore Indians. You have lost the right to play with your life.'

'Shanno, God himself will not be able to stop me from going up Mount Popa.'

'But all these airplanes, the bombs they drop ...'

'Stop worrying, Shanno.'

Since Netaji was adamant, his well-wishers, concerned about his safety, played out a drama. The driver was instructed to head for Popa. But the car wouldn't start. With a flashlight, he fiddled around with the engine but to no avail. Netaji wanted to send a couple of urgent messages, but Bhaskaran's typewriter would not function. Soon, it was daybreak. Netaji had lost patience by then. He shouted at Shah Nawaz, 'What's going on, Shanno? All these excuses? You take me for a fool?'

Shah Nawaz, Bhaskaran and Capt. Rawat pleaded with Netaji. Their persuasion worked. But it was impossible to stir out during the day, so they sheltered between the tall grass and dense thickets. Two nights were spent on a bed of grass. Then a message came from Gen. Kiani in Rangoon. 'Danger. Move quickly.'

It was an endless night. They could see the glow of Meiktila in flames, they heard loud explosions. An ammunition dump must have been hit. Some Japanese officers came with the terrible news that Meiktila was about to fall. The earth shuddered for a moment.

'The enemy tanks and armoured vehicles just marched in. We were prepared to stop them, but our brave soldiers did not have hand grenades to blow up the tanks,' they said. 'We only had heavy bombs to be dropped from a plane.'

There was a stunned silence all round. They continued, 'Our Nippon army and your Azad Hind force were unbelievably brave. They dug trenches in the path of the tanks. They held the bombs between their legs and when the tanks were above their heads, they pulled out the pins and threw them upwards. They ripped through the belly of the tanks and went skywards. Their courage knew no bounds.'

Netaji's chest swelled with pride. His tears paid homage to their martyrdom.

Again, the officers requested Netaji to start moving. Enemy tanks were circumventing Meiktila and coming forward. The middle road had been cut off. The road to Rangoon would soon be closed too.

'Netaji, I am not going to Popa. I will escort you to Rangoon. It is an extremely hazardous journey,' said Shah Nawaz.

Enemy aircraft had captured the sky. Secret agents had infiltrated every village. There was no telling where the next strike would be. The car was checked and readied, its boot packed with grenades. Netaji was carrying two grenades in his pockets. Across his lap lay a fully loaded tommy gun. The driver, Dr Raju and Shah Nawaz were similarly armed, but Shah Nawaz also had a bren gun. A Japanese captain stood on the footboard, keeping a lookout. The headlights were switched off and the car trundled along the rough and uneven path.

Gen. Slim had issued orders for the capture of the Japanese puppet and traitor, Subhas Chandra Bose, dead or alive. Planes scoured the jungles of Burma as did secret agents, for signs of him.

The car was moving slowly out of the danger zone. Twenty miles later, as day was breaking, they arrived in the village of Indo. Half of it had borne the fury of an air raid. Shah Nawaz went in search of the headman of the village, but Netaji called him back. 'It may not be wise to shelter here during the day,' he said. They turned back and camped in a thicket of cactus bushes. Within fifteen minutes, they heard the whirr of airplanes, and in front of their eyes, the rest of Indo went up in flames.

They had to spend all day there. Netaji spread his tunic on the ground and lay down. The *History of Ireland* was in his hands. Dr Raju made some rice, which everyone relished. Netaji only had some rice water. He had been thinking of his mother. As they were eating, a couple of Burmese itinerants stopped by, gazing curiously at them. Somehow Dr Raju felt insecure there. 'Let us move deeper into the jungle,' he suggested.

Barely had they settled down when two reconnaissance planes swooped low over the cactus clumps, their machine guns tat-tat-tat-tating feverishly. Netaji smiled and said, 'See, death comes looking for me and I for it. We are playing hide-and-seek, it seems!'

Quickly, Shah Nawaz and Dr Raju dug a trench and they squeezed into it. Shortly thereafter, the planes appeared over the jungle too. Either they had been spotted from the plane or someone had squealed on them. After circling around for some time, dropping their load, the planes flew away.

That day, the British Air Force bombed the Azad Hind Hospital in Meiktila. Almost a thousand wounded soldiers were killed or grievously burnt. When Netaji heard, he was furious. He decided to move base to Pyinmana. A messenger arrived from Kawabe with an ultimatum. 'It has become impossible for Japan to continue the defence of Burma.'

The message shocked everyone. No one could eat that night. Netaji looked like his mind was in turmoil. Around midnight, he summoned everyone and said, 'What is the point of returning to Rangoon? Sehgal and Dhillon are engaged in the battle for the Popa range. Col. Thakur Singh's regiment is nearby. We will send for them and form an X regiment of selected soldiers under his command.'

'What is to be gained by that?' asked Shah Nawaz.

'Call it the last battle for freedom if you like. But I want to fight this battle like a regular soldier.'

There was a grim silence. Finally, his will would prevail. At about half past two in the night, Capt. Shinde and a few soldiers came looking for Netaji. When he heard that they had come all the way from the Popa range, Netaji sat up to greet them. 'Captain, how are things at Popa?' There was no answer. 'Don't be afraid, Captain. Tell me the truth.'

'I wish it had not been my misfortune to convey this terrible news,' stammered Capt. Shinde. 'Netaji, four majors and one lieutenant from our forces at Popa went out on an exercise and did not return. They crossed over to the enemy!' he said and broke into sobs.

The news was earth-shattering. Netaji had not been so disturbed by the news of Japan's withdrawal from Burma but it broke his heart when he heard that Maj. Riaz, Maj. Madan, Maj. Sarwar, Maj. Dey and Lt. Muhammad Baksh had all defected. Utterly despondent, he sighed, 'I feel ashamed of these men who, for their own selfish interest, turned their backs upon the larger cause of their motherland.' He turned to Capt. Rawat and instructed him, 'Immediately send word to our troops everywhere, that if they are not willing to continue in the struggle for independence, they are welcome to turn back right now. But if they betray us, shoot them then and there.'

Shah Nawaz went away towards the Popa front. The others resumed their journey to Pyinmana. Enemy bombs were scorching the land of Burma. Not even a rat dared to stir out during the day. Netaji, in his black Lincoln, set out under the cover of darkness. He was in good spirits but physically exhausted. In spite of that, he would visit the villages along the way, and talk to the people about independence.

At Zeyawaddy, the Indian community would not let him venture out. They were aware of enemy troops in the vicinity, so they disguised

Netaji as a Burmese peasant and accompanied him in a bullock cart, having hidden some ammunition and a tommy gun under it. The Lincoln with some Japanese officers followed some distance away. Several times, they had to dodge air attacks.

Soon, they arrived at a Japanese armoured regiment base where the Azad Hind's 1st Division was also stationed. Those injured during the Kohima–Imphal campaign were being treated in the base hospital there. When Netaji saw Gen. Kiani, he embraced him warmly. Kiani had never seen Netaji so tired. After a long time, Netaji was served freshly cooked hot rice. Later, as he stood out in the open, gazing at the mountains and valleys of India beckoning him, Netaji declared to Gen. Kiani and Sgt. Maj. Kitano, 'I will gather whatever resources and manpower I can, and fight the final battle for India's freedom here. I want to die fighting.'

A shudder went through Kiani. Then Kitano spoke. 'What is this little skirmish compared to the greater battles you have to fight. You must hasten to Rangoon, so many challenges await you there.'

That same night, a message was received from Commander-in-Chief Gen. Kimura in Rangoon. 'Return immediately.'

Netaji set out.

Netaji went to visit the hospital in Kalewa which was under the supervision of Col. Lakshmi, Yellappa and others. As he came out, an agitated looking Maj. Mahboob handed him a coded message. Netaji deliberately read it aloud. He said, 'Have you heard, the supreme commander of South-East Asia, Mountbatten, has issued a fatwa to his men to capture me dead or alive. Special aircraft have been deployed to hunt me down. But I don't care. I have told you even earlier that the bomb which would blow Subhas Chandra Bose has not yet been born in the Royal Ordnance Factory.'

Netaji was pleased to see how Yellappa and his colleagues had managed to set up the hospital. He was reminded of Dr Akbar Ali of the Gandhi Regiment. They would never find the spot where the brave man had attained martyrdom.

'What about all those traders and merchants from Imphal who emptied their coffers for you, who lost their lives in the jungles – will we ever know where they perished?' Yellappa asked.

'Kuberji, the road to Imphal has been built with the blood, sweat and tears of ten thousand unsung Indian heroes. The next generation must be told about them. Plan to erect an epitaph in Singapore in their honour, and let it be a reminder and an inspiration to our youth.'

'This Kuber has never let you down, Netaji. I will come to Rangoon as soon as I get some time off from this hospital.'

As Netaji prepared to leave for Rangoon via Mandalay, he called Col. Lakshmi aside. 'Lakshmi, the situation is getting worse. You are under no pressure to remain here. Would you like to go to Rangoon and join the other ladies?'

'Netaji, I am a doctor by profession. How can I leave these injured, sick people?'

Placing his hand on her head in blessing, Netaji smiled and drove off.

Yellappa set about collecting funds for the hospital. They were running out. During his association with Netaji, Yellappa had forgotten he was one of Singapore's wealthiest men. One morning he said to Lakshmi, 'We must finish our work here quickly and go to Rangoon. Netaji needs people who understand him. There are so few of them.'

'You haven't seen your wife in six years. Do you ever think of her?'

'Used to, sometimes. But now I have forgotten that I was ever married.'

On 2 March, in broad daylight, there was an air raid on Kalewa. Lakshmi watched from the hospital as two aircraft flew low, almost touching the tiled roofs of the houses in the bazaar area, dropped their bombs, and left a trail of flames, screams and destruction. Lakshmi's heart stopped. Yellappa lived in the bazaar.

She ran towards it. Her fears were justified. Yellappa's house had caught fire. Soon, she saw an injured Yellappa stumbling out. He had a piece of shrapnel in his left leg. The injury did not look very serious. But he had burns on his other leg. Lakshmi quickly put him into an ambulance and took him to the hospital. They did not have enough medicines, nor X-ray facilities. Lakshmi managed to bandage his leg somehow. But the hospital was one of the enemy targets and it would not be wise to remain there much longer. The superintendent, Mr Banerji, and Lakshmi decided that it would be best to move with all the inmates. Quickly, two Japanese trucks and several bullock carts were organised, and they prepared to move. Yellappa's wound was festering. He was in great pain from internal injuries too. How was this journey to be accomplished? Lakshmi looked at her fellow doctors. Should they endanger the lives of the other patients by taking Yellappa along? How could she leave Netaji's dear friend Kuber alone in the middle of the jungle? The doctors were practical. 'You stay back and look after him. Then join us when you can.' Lakshmi had no choice but to agree. The distance between Kalewa and Rangoon was nine hundred miles. This was the second retreat for the INA after Maymyo. Lakshmi had a group of just ten to twelve people with her. She took shelter in the jungles near the village of Nyaungshwe. Her group stayed in the village. Soon, this peaceful hamlet also saw some firing. The Burmese villagers blamed the presence of the INA soldiers for it. It was no longer safe to remain there. So the troops moved deeper into the forest. With no radio, they had no way of knowing what was going on outside. The sole responsibility for saving the life of Netaji's right-hand man was on Lakshmi. How was she going to do it?

One night, a truck arrived at their camp and Maj. Bawa got out, a tone of urgency in his voice. 'Lakshmi, I have been sent specially to take you back to Rangoon. All of Burma is being overtaken by the British. Netaji is also planning to leave Rangoon. Also, we are terribly short of fuel.' Yellappa's feeble voice interrupted, 'What happened to all the reserve stocks I had asked Raghavan to store?'

Maj. Bawa had brought some first-aid equipment, and Yellappa's pain was eased somewhat. In two days, they reached the village of Tangai. On the way, they encountered some Japanese troops and Lakshmi joined them. The roar of the trucks drowned the sounds of Yellappa's groaning. Suddenly, the trucks stopped. A messenger came up to Lakshmi and informed her that the important town of Tangu would fall to the British very soon. 'To continue ahead would be walking into the jaws of the enemy. Don't risk it. We are going to abandon our vehicles and supplies, and head for the Salwin Valley on foot.'

Lakshmi and Maj. Bawa exchanged worried looks. She thought of Yellappa lying in the back of the truck, moaning in pain. Her mind was made up. She bid farewell to the Japanese and decided to move out on her own. Before they moved on, the Japanese set fire to their trucks and destroyed all their supplies, and scurried away into the forest.

Maj. Bawa took a small path away from the main road and camped near a village in the Karen jungle. The Karens had only one objective – shoot any Japanese in sight. Not only that, two days ago, British paratroopers had landed in the adjacent valley. This caused Lakshmi and her colleagues great anxiety.

Yellappa called Maj. Bawa aside and told him, 'Once a cannon is damaged, no matter how powerful it used to be, it has no value. Forget about me. I have little time left. Netaji needs you urgently. Go to him.'

Lakshmi promptly retorted, 'Yellappa saheb, we are Indians. We care not only about the people in our homes, but the cattle in our sheds. We are not so ungrateful as to leave you here in this condition – you who have been our guardian, our guide.'

The situation was worsening. Hungry Japanese soldiers were attacking local homes for food. Those who had come from the China border stopped at nothing in their desperation. The villagers, even the Gurkhas, began to flee their homes out of fear. In view of the rapidly depleting food stock, Lakshmi told her men to give themselves up to the British. At least pressure on the rations would ease. Yellappa was delirious and kept babbling throughout the night. 'Netaji, stop work now, come and eat something, the food is getting cold ... Netaji, today we are going to weigh you in gold – you in one pan and the jewels of our mothers and wives in the other ...'

One night, Lakshmi was awakened by the sound of boots. She found herself staring into a bayonet. Some Japanese soldiers had surrounded their hut and were ordering the five Azad Hind men to get out. The Burmese youth were trying to explain that they were not British spies, but the words Netaji, Subhas Chandra Bose and Azad Hind meant nothing to the men who had returned from fighting against Stilwell's troop at the China border. Lakshmi quickly changed into her uniform and placed her cap proudly on her head. The five of them, along with Lakshmi, were marched outside and tied firmly to trees. The Japanese soldiers were ready to rip the five into shreds. They must have been waiting for orders to shoot from some height. The captives realised there was no point shouting for help or explaining anything. Language was a barrier. Just then, a youthful-looking man strolled up with a magazine in his hand, whistling. He stopped when he saw Lakshmi. He glanced at her, then at the magazine. Then he held it out to her. It was a photograph of hers in that Japanese magazine. It had been taken when the Rani Jhansi Regiment had been founded in Singapore. The officer said, 'You, this?'

'Yes.'

He smiled and cut the ropes that bound her. All of them were freed. He offered them some biscuits he was carrying. Lakshmi asked for medicines. But he had none. He conveyed to them that he was returning from north Burma and there were many like him. This spot was too dangerous. They ought to move away. Lakshmi thanked him. He turned back from some distance and called out, 'Don't think that you will be lucky every time.'

They had to move. But where to? Lakshmi learnt that on the other side of the valley was a hamlet that was fairly safe. Lakshmi gave Yellappa another dose of morphine, stroked him to sleep and set out to find that village. After trudging for over six hours, she and her colleagues found a small habitation. But seeing her companions, doors would shut on their faces. No one would let them even stand in front of the pagoda in the village. Disheartened, they walked back till they came to an abandoned hut on the outskirts. It was damp and dirty, but unoccupied. Lakshmi was trying to clean it up somewhat when suddenly three British officers accompanied by a Gurkha soldier entered.

They started marching to the camp early in the morning. Lakshmi kept pleading with them to let them carry Yellappa on a stretcher. But the soldiers would not listen. The path was too narrow, it was a steep climb, they said, before finally agreeing to speak to their commandant to somehow get him there. They had recognised Lakshmi and were not going to let her out of their sight for even a second. By dusk, the following day, they reached the camp at the top of the mountain. Col. Peacock, the commandant, knew all about Lakshmi and treated her with courtesy. Maj. Bawa who was also there, begged Col. Peacock to send someone down for Yellappa. But he had only one answer – 'I have no troops to spare. I cannot help you.'

Lakshmi was tormented by guilt. What would she say to Netaji? What would become of Yellappa? Soon Col. Peacock received instructions to move the camp to Tangai.

As the camp was dismantled and they marched down to the base, Lakshmi could think only of Yellappa. What had become of him? By a strange coincidence, when they reached the foothill, she saw a Burmese family she recognised. They had a basha, near the hut where she had left Yellappa behind. She asked them for news.

A Burmese youth had remained with him right through. One evening, when he had lit a fire to cook the evening meal, some Karens reached there. Assuming its occupants to be Japanese soldiers, they threw a grenade at the hut. The youth ran out, shouting Yellappa's name, but it was too late, the hut was on fire. The boy dashed in and was dragging the ill Yellappa out when the burning thatch fell on both of them.

Lakshmi was sobbing as she walked. Maj. Bawa went up to her and said, 'Lakshmi, hold back your tears. You are Netaji's Jhansi ki Rani, the warrior queen of freedom. No matter what the difficulties, remember Netaji's message: We may be dead or alive, but India will be free! It is bound to be free.'

While Netaji was inspecting the Azad Hind Bank in Jamal Avenue, S.A. Ayyar said to him, 'Gen. Aung San has gone by a special plane to Kandy. He has joined Mountbatten.'

Netaji was aware of it. Things were going to get tricky now. Aung San commanded great support among the common people. The same afternoon, Maj. Gen. Kimura, chief of the Japanese troops in Burma, called up to say that it would not be possible for Japanese troops to hold out against the Allied forces much longer. They would have to clear out of Rangoon soon.

Netaji's mind was buzzing. There were so many things to be taken care of – the interim arrangements, finding another location for the Azad Hind headquarters, handling the funds collected for the campaign, the loan taken from Japan. He had hardly slept for days. Just as his eyes were closing that night, Kundan Singh knocked on his door.

'What is it, Kundan Singh?'

'Get up, Netaji, some important work.'

Kundan Singh would not dare to wake Netaji and if he did, it must be really urgent. Netaji opened the door. 'Rash Behari Babu has come to see you downstairs.'

'Rash Behari? Are you dreaming? So late at night ...' Netaji scolded.

'There's also a Japanese jeep at the gate.'

Netaji looked out of the window and saw the jeep in the pale-yellow light. Quickly, he got dressed and went down. It was indeed Rash Behari, with his stoop, thick black-rimmed glasses and pointed chin. Why should he be here at this hour? Netaji went down to receive him. Just as he said, 'Jai Hind, Rash Babu,' four shots were heard. Netaji leaped away from the steps and escaped the bullets just in time. At once, the guards rushed in, opening fire. The man collapsed. Netaji rushed to him and took off the spectacles. 'The enemy has created an impersonator! Only the eyes are grey. Anyone would be mistaken from a distance!' In the meantime, the jeep had sped away.

This dastardly attack on Netaji had shaken them all. Gen. Kimura immediately sent a team to investigate. The Azad Hind members realised how great the threat to their beloved leader was. Pointing to the corpse, Kundan Singh was repeatedly saying, 'I have seen this man somewhere!' But he could not recollect exactly where. The body was removed and everyone went away to rest. Netaji too began climbing the stairs when Kundan Singh exclaimed, 'Netaji, I know where!'

'Where?'

'Sandicraft School in Penang. He was part of Capt. Mahmood Khan Durrani's special team.'

Netaji was puzzled. He sent a wireless message to the Japanese headquarters at once. The message was sent to all the centres from Rangoon to Singapore, Penang and Ipoh: 'Catch him! Arrest the traitor Capt. Durrani.'

Gradually, all the pieces started falling into place. Someone had voiced the suspicion that it was Durrani who was causing a rift between the Muslim officers in the INA. His suspicion turned out to be right. Durrani was the one who had given away the young revolutionaries who were heading for India by sea to ignite the revolution there.

'You must be exhausted after all this battling, Bose. Rest for a while.' Gen. Aung San's voice crackled over the phone.

'What use will it be, my waiting?' asked Netaji.

'Come and join the British like me. Break all ties with the Japanese. I will personally intercede with Mountbatten on your behalf,' Aung San said.

'General, are you serious, or is it just a joke?'

'What do you mean?'

'If I meet Mountbatten, it will be on the battlefield. To decimate his beloved British Empire,' declared Netaji.

When Netaji put down the phone, Aung San's representative, sent to discuss matters personally, was still standing there. Compromise with the British? What a ridiculous idea! The very thought made Netaji's hair stand on end. Suddenly, he was overcome with emotion. Memories of his companions who had supported his Imphal campaign and lost their military regime, like Gen. Mutaguchi, Miyazaki and others, came flooding back. The bodies of thousands of Japanese soldiers that were strewn on the road to Imphal floated before his eyes. In a choked voice, he said, 'If at this juncture such traitorous thoughts of stabbing the Japanese in the back come to my mind, I will immediately cut off my hand. How can I forget the sacrifice made by a whole generation of Japanese soldiers in Kohima, Arakan, and in the jungles along the Irrawaddy? I will always carry the burden of that debt.'

Judging the overall mood there, Aung San's representative got ready to leave. Netaji addressed him calmly. 'Convey my best wishes to your general. May both our countries break free of the shackles of slavery very soon.'

No one had control over Rangoon now. Normal life was completely disrupted by thieves, dacoits and brigands. A terrible sense of insecurity prevailed over the whole city. Panic-stricken groups of citizens ran helter-skelter.

Several Indian, Chinese and Burmese citizens met Netaji and expressed their anxiety over the security arrangements in the city. Netaji did not want to leave Rangoon. He wanted to stay there. In three to four days, the British troops would surround and swallow the city. Batches of members of the Azad Hind Government met senior leaders like Maj. Gen. Jagannathrao Bhosale, Gen. Zaman Kiani and others. Pressure mounted on Netaji to hold an exhaustive meeting of all members.

The tempestuous meeting began. An annoyed Netaji addressed the gathering. 'I know exactly why you are present here as a group. But remember one thing, the city of Rangoon will be the last bastion of our struggle. It is my desire to stand here and fight to the last man.'

'Netaji, in order to execute your command, we tramped thousands of miles, barefoot. Even now, our loyalty is at your feet. We shall keep fighting here. But please, you go ahead, leave.'

Netaji's voice rose sharply as he replied to Gen. Kiani, 'Kiani saheb, are you giving me this advice as the chief of the 1st Division of the INA? My brave warriors, Sehgal, Dhillon and Shah Nawaz are still battling in the forests of Burma. Our guns are still firing at British aircraft along the banks of several rivers including the Sittaung. And you are asking me to leave my courageous companions and my dearest friends. Where will I go, all alone?'

Gen. A.D. Loganathan stood up slowly. He said, 'We are aware of the revolt of Aung San's liberation army. But now, Gen. Slim and Mountbatten have begun to drop paratroopers in the Karen sector. To prove their loyalty to the sahebs, the Burmese community of Karen has begun to decapitate their Indian and Japanese brethren. In the Burmese towns of Rangoon, Meiktila and Mandalay, looting, arson, rape and murder are rampant. If the fortunes of our Hindustan are going to be embroiled in this chaos, what have we been fighting for all this while?'

Just then Gen. Isoda of the Hikari Kikan arrived unexpectedly. He announced, 'Netaji, a grave crisis looms over us. The British have crossed Tangu. Any day now they will be knocking on our doors.'

'Yes, Netaji. Please hurry. Pegu can fall any minute now,' Kakistsubo told him.

Everyone seemed to freeze at the mention of Pegu. The town of Pegu on the banks of the river by the same name, was barely twenty miles away. It was strategically located. The road to Rangoon from northern Burma passed through Pegu. Also, one had to pass through Pegu first on one's way to Bangkok. Important links to two to three different places originated in Pegu. If Netaji did not make haste, British troops heading for Rangoon would trap him in the vicinity of Pegu.

Zaman Kiani could not hold himself back any longer. He exclaimed sharply, 'Netaji, what did I escape the pyre at Imphal for? If I am fated to see you in handcuffs and chains, I would rather put an end to myself.'

Capt. Pritam Singh leapt up like a cobra. Wiping the tears flowing from his eyes, he said, 'You gave the call and our bodies gladly turned to flaming torches.'

Finally, Netaji agreed to depart for a safer destination. Before the meeting broke up, Netaji told them, 'I owe a great debt to this Burmese soil. Until British troops come in and assume legitimate power and restore law and order, five thousand soldiers of the INA will stay in Rangoon and protect the people from arsonists, rapists and marauders. Loganathan, will you take command of them please?' Maj. Gen. Loganathan was quick to register his acceptance.

In view of the changing scenario, Netaji had sent most of the girls from the Rani Jhansi Regiment back to their homes. He entrusted the responsibility of the safe transport of the remaining fifty or so women to Gen. Isoda. 'Netaji, you carry on ahead. We will make arrangements and follow.'

Netaji cut him short. 'Isoda, ask me to embrace those fire-spitting bombers and I will listen to you, but on this issue, no arguments.'

Hikari Kikan promised Netaji that the transport would be arranged. Netaji then delegated his personal physician Dr Raju to take charge of the health department in Rangoon. The women of the Rani Jhansi Regiment were to leave by a military train that night. After midnight, Netaji was to leave the city with most of his group. Swami, Capt. Rawat, Shamsher Singh, Bhaskaran and his other associates began to pack up. Every ten minutes, Netaji would summon Ayyar and issue new instructions.

A cold breeze had started blowing. Suddenly, a bomber aircraft swung into view, its guns blazing. Netaji barely managed to escape. They all huddled around him. Netaji was calmly lighting a cigarette, a smile on his lips.

Just then Shamsher Singh and Janaki Thevar arrived there. The train which was to carry the Rani Jhansi Regiment could not move because the track had been taken over by the British.

Janaki was sitting beside Netaji with her friends. He placed an affectionate hand on her head. 'Beti, when I see the fire of revolution in the eyes of young people like you, the lava within me also rises. And then, there is no fear of any threat, human or divine.'

24 April 1945. On that extraordinary moonlit night, about one thousand soldiers and the Rani Jhansi Regiment, along with loads of gold, silver and precious stones, were ready to leave.

Netaji too was about to leave. As if the banished Ram was setting off on his exile, his subjects in Ayodhya escorted him tearfully till the limits of Rangoon.

The crowd around Netaji was becoming uncontrollable. Some climbed on to the bonnet of the car. The guard of honour presented by the Azad Hind soldiers gave him a salute. Netaji addressed them: 'Protect the city. When the British troops enter Rangoon, hold our beloved tricolour close to your chests. As prisoners of war, go forward proudly, with your heads held high, shoulders squared, march ahead like true men.'

'Netaji, what is your message?' Dr Mehta asked.

'Brothers, remember, the children of tomorrow will take birth as the offspring of an independent India. No one will ridicule them as sons of slaves. Your immortal sacrifices will not go in vain. This is only a short-lived retreat. Tell Mountbatten and Churchill that I will definitely return to fight the final battle.'

Troops of the Azad Hind Fauj were running. As if they had wheels tied to their feet. Even in the dark, enemy aircraft had not given up pursuing them. There was a shower of bombs. Soldiers jumped down from the lorries and took refuge in the fields beside the road.

They crossed Pegu by dawn. The city was an inferno. A fiery glow spread across the sky and was visible far and wide. Only the lazy refrained from adding to the conflagration their flaming torches. The Burmese had rebelled. The fire-spitting British bombers were making periodic sorties. Even as they evacuated the city, the Japanese were burning their dismantled offices. The fire was being fed with the remaining ammunition, to prevent the British from laying hands on it. All around, roofs were collapsing. Things made of iron were twisted out of shape. The walls gasped and choked in the heat.

By the time it was daylight, everybody was on the other side of the river Wav. Soon the enemy air raids would intensify. Hachiya and Kakistsubo requested Netaji to halt for a while. They took shelter under the trees and bushes.

Ahead of them lay terraced paddy fields. Netaji had a cup of tea. Just then, Ambassador Hachiya brought a young Japanese boy and introduced him to Netaji. His name was Masami Tsuruta. The twenty-five-year-old was working with the Gaimusho, the Japanese foreign affairs department. He was carrying an urgent message.

Netaji had hung a mirror on the trunk of an ancient tree in the hollow where they had stopped and had begun to shave. Suddenly three aircraft flew overhead. 'Netaji! Netaji! Hide!' Tsuruta was shrieking. Netaji ignored them. The razor steady in hand, he calmly finished shaving. Tsuruta was amazed. 'Air raids take place. Bombs fall. How is it that nothing touches you, Netaji?' Netaji merely smiled. In the meantime, some soldiers had learnt that three days earlier, a plane had crashed in the ditches nearby. They had managed to extricate several half-burnt things from the wreckage. A bundle of maps lay beside the pilot. Tsuruta showed them to Netaji. Everyone was startled to see a marked-up map of Rangoon and its vicinity. There was red circle where Netaji's bungalow had stood.

It reminded them of the air attack from three days ago.

The next morning, thousands of lorries and troops of the Japanese Army could be seen rushing along the banks of the Wav. Before the enemy caught up with them, they wanted to get to the other side of the Sittang River. The convoy began to move. Just then rain came down in torrents. The wheels of the lorries, bogged down in the mud, began to spin backwards. Quickly, the troops began to lay wooden planks along the ruts. Groaning, grunting, straining, the lorries gradually lumbered out of the furrows and inched forward.

Netaji's car also began to sputter and jerk. Netaji, wearing high leather boots, got down. The girls also alighted from the lorries. The rain had drenched them all to the skin. As they traversed the paddy fields, the ground became slushier. In between were large puddles of rainwater. Many a time they could see nothing, neither slush nor water. One particularly large ditch was hidden amidst the shadows of the moonlit trees. The soft soil found the weight of Netaji's Lincoln too much to bear. In front of their eyes they saw the car sink three to four feet deep into the water. Tsuruta was beside Netaji, helping to push the car out of the mire. Gen. Isoda and Gen. Hachiya rolled back their sleeves and began to push the car with all their might. Though he was soaking wet, Hachiya had not lost his sense of humour. Between great bursts of laughter, he remarked, 'Lucky car, Netaji! Imagine, one prime minister, several major generals, an ambassador, are all pushing it out!'

The ground was getting more uncertain now. Their feet had begun to slip and slide in the slush. As if they were all on a skating rink. Netaji stood on an elevated spot for hours guiding, signalling and instructing the troops. They abandoned several lorries and cars in the muddy flats. They were all impatient to cross the river and get to the other side before nightfall. The enemy had long destroyed the enormous bridge that spanned the river. In many places, the banks had collapsed, leaving huge gaps. Crudely made rafts were floated to transport the lorries and cars. Some soldiers clung to either end of the raft and tried to get to the far bank. The lorries that keeled over midstream remained stuck there. Gen. Isoda said to Netaji, 'You carry on ahead. We'll make the rest of the arrangements.'

'If you are in such a hurry, you can go on, go drown in the ocean,' Netaji thundered. 'Only after my girls are safe on the other side will I lift a foot from here.'

Col. Shaukat Malik and Swami were both six feet tall. Netaji suggested to them, 'Why don't you go and test the depth of the water? Then escort these girls to the other side?'

The two men and the girls, stepped into the water. It was freezing cold. Shivering, stumbling, falling into the water, the girls moved forward, holding on to each other for support. At last, they straggled up the other shore, their backpacks and their rifles balanced precariously on their heads.

Innumerable lorries crowded the riverbank. To prevent the enemy from using them, the Japanese soldiers set fire to the lorries. Within minutes, they burst into flames. Raindrops sizzled and hissed as they fell on hot metal. Netaji still remained standing on the edge of the river. The muddy waters of the river seemed to have turned to molten copper by the flames.

'Come on, Kiani, get two more rafts,' Netaji called out, 'this lorry, this car ...'

Eventually, Netaji succeeded in getting many trucks of the Azad Hind troops ferried across. Those that had to be left behind were given up. When Netaji boarded the last raft, day had broken. The next camp was at a small village called Apiya. There were no trenches or underground shelters there. So the soldiers had to make use of the dense shrubs for sanctuary. The trucks were concealed in the bushes. On the outskirts of the village was a Buddhist temple with a mandap attached to it. Most of the mandap had been burnt down during an air raid. In its shadow, Netaji spread a dirty quilt on the cold hard stone and lay down. Except for a few sips of tea, he hadn't had anything at all. He didn't even get up to eat some of the rice the girls had cooked. It was obvious that his body was exhausted.

At about three o'clock in the afternoon, like an unexpected swarm of locusts, six airplanes zoomed overhead and dropped bombs. Hachiya and the young Tsuruta tried to wake Netaji up. The women of the Rani Jhansi Regiment let out a loud wail. With great difficulty, Netaji opened his eyes. Then he shut them again, turned on his side and went back to sleep. The air raid went on for twenty more minutes. The women were furious with Netaji. Why was he inviting disaster upon himself? The bombers succeeded in reducing five of their lorries to cinders.

Midnight, 26 April. It was still raining. The few vehicles available were packed with soldiers, like fish in a basket, but their progress was slow because of the slush. Couriers brought urgent messages that the enemy was on their heels and gaining ground rapidly. The Sittang River was ten miles away. The divisions would not be free from danger until they crossed the Sittang. On that side of the river, among the mountains, was stationed an artillery division of the INA. Netaji was proud of them. As soon as the lorries stalled, the women jumped down. Netaji called Col. Chopra. 'Before daybreak, make the next destination across the Sittang,' he instructed. The women accompanied by Maj. Gen. Bhosale, Maj. Gen. Chatterji and Col. Chopra trudged through the wet mud. With them were E. Bhaskaran and Bhosale's secretary, P.N. Oak. The rain continued to play havoc.

By the time the women reached the banks of the Sittang, Netaji and his band had arrived there. Netaji was consumed with anxiety for the safety of the women. He quickly ran along the bank looking for a safe spot. The Rani Jhansi Regiment followed. They waded through knee-deep slush. The women were fearless. They forged ahead, their backpacks and rifles secure on their heads.

On the banks of the Sittang too, Japanese troops had abandoned hundreds of trucks. Just then some Japanese armymen arrived with Netaji's car. Now all the wealth Netaji was left with was that car and one lorry. Somehow, Sittang was forded. They had to decide upon the next campsite before the sun appeared on the horizon. The early morning rays were forerunners of the British Air Force.

Where the women finally caught up with Netaji, they bent down and touched Netaji's feet. What a long and arduous journey this had been. Like sleepwalkers they had marched on, oblivious of hunger and thirst. If on the way, they managed to get tender coconut, raw jackfruit, or by good fortune, some milk, that was divine nectar. By morning, their calves felt taut, cramped and leaden.

When they set up camp, two soldiers rushed towards them, their faces grim. Netaji asked, 'What is it? What happened?'

'Sir, that young Japanese boy of ours, that Tsuruta or something.'

'What happened to him?'

'Our soldiers have assaulted and injured him.'

'Why?' Netaji almost screamed, his eyes flashing fire.

'It wasn't anyone's fault, Netaji. His fair complexion confused them. Our soldiers thought that he was a British spy ...'

A lump rose in many throats. They could picture the slender young body constantly beside Netaji, like a shadow. Netaji was silent. Hachiya and Kakistsubo looked extremely displeased. Just then, an armoured car rolled up, bearing the injured Tsuruta. Netaji rushed forward. He placed a hand under his neck, and they gently lowered him on to a stained and dirt-splattered mat. A deep gash in the head. The dark black hair was plastered with blood. His body was pierced with sharp stab wounds. Gritting his teeth to suppress the pain, he was trying to speak to Netaji. Netaji's temper finally got out of hand. He shouted to Col. S.N. Mishra, 'Who is responsible for this dastardly act? How will I face the world?'

'Netaji, truly, it was a mistake. His colour made him look British. He was making enquiries about you at our artillery station ahead. Our Indian soldiers could not understand his English. Their suspicion grew. And because of that, they attacked him.'

Maj. Gen. Chatterji dressed and bandaged Tsuruta's wounds. But, there was a dearth of medicines. In the early morning sunlight, the wounded Tsuruta's face glowed. His delicate fingers had been crushed.

His shirt had got embedded in his flesh everywhere the dagger had stabbed him. As Maj. Gen. Chatterji picked out pieces of fabric from the gaping wounds, Tsuruta winced. Finally, he could bear it no more. He told them to stop. 'Netaji, don't, please don't blame anybody. Your men thought I was a spy. My death was near, that's all.'

Janaki helped him to sip a little milk. But immediately, he threw it all up. His dark eyes were fixed on Netaji. Netaji was hard put to hold his emotions in check. Tsuruta motioned to Hachiya and when he was near, told him hoarsely, 'I haven't seen my wife for a year now. If you ever meet her, tell her ... that it was her memory alone that kept me going ...'

'My valiant soldier, don't give up yet. We will make sure you get to the hospital in Moulmein.' Netaji tried hard to reassure him.

Tsuruta smiled feebly, as if to say nothing was going to matter any more. Then he took Netaji's hand in his own, pressed it once. Cruel, unfeeling death. Playfully, it tapped Tsuruta on the shoulder and called him away from a full assembly of patriots. No one knew when his soul departed. Netaji embraced his still body and held it to his heart. Sobbing uncontrollably, he kept repeating, 'I wept for my younger brother Santosh who was called to God's home in the prime of his youth. But this boy has made me weep much more.'

The last rites were performed according to the Japanese tradition. Netaji appeared inconsolable. Tsuruta had left a deep void in his heart.

Night fell. And once again, the nightly march began. Netaji changed his boots. But all that walking had made his feet unsteady and he dragged his feet diagonally, like a crab.

The morning of 29 April, shelter was sought and a halt called. Netaji sat at the foot of a tree, leaning against its trunk. He was fatigued. His face was drawn, but eyes still very alive and eloquent. Clothes crumpled. Stomach hollow with hunger. He kept bending and stretching his legs, as if he were getting cramps in them.

Janaki was watching Netaji. Was this the prime minister of independent India? The leader of an army, the saviour, the companion of millions – an older brother, great revolutionary, an exceptional wayfarer – who saw visions of a strong, stable India – was this the same man? At whose call thousands of armed Indian brothers from

East Asia had come, forsaking their families, at whose command thousands of young men and women in India would plunge into a river of fire? That beloved lord of the INA had been starving for who knows how long. Today, he was sitting on a filthy quilt in the middle of the wildest jungle between Burma and Siam. Janaki's eyes filled up. How could this man have so much compassion, so much selflessness? So much idealism. So much courage to take on the might of America and England?

She stepped forward boldly, took off Netaji's high boots, then started to tug at his socks. At that, a wave of anguish washed over Netaji's face. When Janaki saw Netaji's bare feet, she gasped. His soles and his calves were covered with angry red blisters. Like the early morning dew, Janaki's tears glistened as they fell. Silently, she applied iodine to Netaji's feet.

Once more, the march began. Netaji was walking with the soldiers. The Rani Jhansi Regiment inched forward in a rickety old truck. In spite of his sore and peeling soles, Netaji gritted his teeth and marched on. The women in the truck began to clamour: 'Netaji, don't walk. Sit in the truck.' Most of them were weeping.

Evening came. The moon was trying to tear through the layers of clouds, but the clouds were pelting it with raindrops. 'Bose, get into the lorry, please,' Isoda pleaded.

'What about my friends here?'

'Arrangements will be made for them later. You go on.'

'Who do you take me for, the Burmese Ba Maw, to desert my dearest companions?' Netaji retorted.

Isoda was taken aback by that reply. He said to the Azad Hind soldiers, 'Now we Japanese are beginning to understand how the Buddha's penance was done, in sun and rain!'

On 1st of May, the procession reached Moulmein. On the same day, the British had swallowed Pegu. The local Hindi Swatantra Sangha took excellent care of the soldiers. Most of them had lost their appetite after the long, tiresome march on half-empty stomachs. All they did was sleep, as if afflicted by a grave illness. The rest of the journey to Bangkok was to be undertaken by train.

Everybody arrived at the railway station. Netaji was relieved to see the girls had been properly looked after. He was going to send Col. Shaukat Malik with them. The train was to leave at midnight. Suddenly, Netaji could not hold back the thought that had nagged him for days and that he had been suppressing all this while. He said, 'Of late, thoughts of Ma have been haunting me. I committed a serious offence while leaving home in Calcutta.'

Netaji's voice was thick. He continued, 'Three times I went towards my mother's room, but each time I turned back. I made a mistake. I shouldn't have done that.'

The train was actually a goods train. The women were crammed into one of the bogies like cattle. It was bitterly cold. Intermittent rain sent sprays into the wagon. Somehow, they travelled for two hours. Then the train stopped in the middle of nowhere. The railway bridge had collapsed, blown up by British aircraft. The women vacated the wagon. They set out on foot once more. They waded across a jungle stream, and after trudging all night, by the next afternoon they had covered a substantial distance towards the connecting train. But the train was nowhere to be seen. At one spot, they saw massive piles of hay stacked up. It was dusk by then. Quickly, the Japanese soldiers began to dismantle the stacks. As they rummaged through the bundles of hay, they uncovered several railway carriages. The Japanese were renowned for their camouflage techniques. This was an ingenious way of protecting the train from air attacks. The bogies were coupled together one by one. Finally, the whole train was assembled. During the night, the wheels of their journey began to turn once more.

Netaji was in a car, driving on the road alongside the train track. As they travelled further, they found another bridge that had been destroyed. The journey had to be continued on foot. Netaji and his companions joined the women soldiers.

The Japanese had built that railway line through the dense jungles of Burma and Siam with the labour and sacrifice of thousands of Indians. It was said that one Indian labourer lost his life for every ten metres of track. That is why, the line was known as the Track of Death. On the way, they met an old, decrepit Japanese man. His entire body was covered with blisters. His cheeks were sunken. Yet, he was meticulously digging up the stones from the tracks and casting them aside in his desperation to ensure the safety of the trains.

The scrawny old man asked Netaji for some food. The women gave him some of the rice they had cooked.

Netaji stared at him, astonished. Most of his companions had been killed in bomb blasts. This sole survivor was still in a state of shock, and for the last four years, he had been slaving away at the tracks. Netaji said to him, 'Come, you have done enough. Come with us to Tokyo.'

Shaking his head, the old man replied, 'I have received a royal decree to protect this railway line. For my Emperor, I will spend my life on this track and die here.'

A long stretch of the journey forward was undertaken on foot. They could not find the train. The Japanese mechanical mind is a curious thing. They had taken the steel wheels off the train and replaced them with the rubber tyres of the lorries. So the carriages of the train dragged themselves on rubber boots. Netaji and the Rani Jhansi Regiment boarded one such train-truck. And finally, the three-hundred-mile journey from Rangoon, came to an end.

The Hindi Swatantra Sangha in Bangkok had made elaborate arrangements to welcome Netaji. A dinner was held at the home of a businessman, Sewakram Mehta. Netaji seemed to be in a good mood. Janaki said to him, 'Netaji, you appear to be very happy today.'

'Last night I dreamt of Ma, my mother,' said Netaji. 'As soon as I started asking for her forgiveness, she smiled and said, "Subhas, you are still the same madcap. At least you could have met me before leaving." I told her, what if you had started weeping? To that she replied, "You foolish boy, I am Subhas Chandra's mother, aren't I? How could you forget that?"'

Soon, the Rani Jhansi Regiment was safely dispatched home, all except Janaki. 'I will not return home, Netaji, now that I have broken all ties and bonds with my family for the sake of the nation,' she said.

Netaji tried to coax Janaki. 'The wheel of war is spinning in the opposite direction now. But as soon as things are better, I will send for you, my child, I promise.' Janaki was left with no choice.

Janaki was on her way to Kuala Lumpur. Somebody tuned into the Japanese radio station. One news item caught Janaki's attention: 'Last night, Prabhabati Jankinath Bose, respected mother of Subhas Chandra Bose, passed away in Calcutta.' Janaki was shaken. So after appearing in a dream, the mother went away without meeting her child. How must Netaji be feeling? Who would lend a shoulder to the mountain when the mountain itself had been rocked from its very base.

After bidding Netaji farewell, Shah Nawaz travelled twenty-five miles by jeep before he reached Mount Popa. The road leading out of Bagan and Nyaungu followed the Irrawaddy River and ran along the shoulder of Mount Popa before coming to Meiktila. This range was of great strategic importance. One of its peaks rose up into the sky like a symbol of Shiva and was crowned with three pagodas. Shah Nawaz ran into Gurbaksh Singh there. Gurbaksh's troops had scattered, and it was difficult to muster them again. But there were still a few brave men left with him, Capt. Bagri being one of them. He declared that he wanted to dance at the sight of the tricolour fluttering majestically on the Lal Qila, but if that good fortune was denied him, he wanted to be the first to reach heaven.

Under Shah Nawaz's leadership, Prem Sehgal and Dhillon together built up a force of about seven hundred men and Shah Nawaz left the defence of the stretch between Chakpadang and Meiktila to them. They were to stop the British Army advancing towards Rangoon.

As expected, in a couple of days, the enemy was seen moving along the Irrawaddy. But, instead of going towards Meiktila, that division was heading in the direction of Dhillon's territory. Prem Sehgal stopped them near the village of Legi. He had only a small unit with him. There was no backing of artillery fire nor aerial cover from the air force. And yet, they managed to engage an entire British brigade because of the tenacity of Yasin Khan, Kanwar Singh and a few others. Shah Nawaz was pleased to hear about this.

One night Prem came rushing to him. 'Betrayal! Yasin Khan has deserted us.'

'How? Why?'

'I cannot understand, sir,' said Prem. 'Why do they fight so hard at first and then give up in the end? I have lost faith in everybody, General.'

'Don't lose heart, Prem!' Shah Nawaz reassured him. 'As long as Netaji is in Rangoon, we will risk our lives and disrupt the enemy's ranks.'

That night, Shah Nawaz summoned all his troops to the temporary office at the foot of the mountain. With folded hands, he said to them, 'Friends, those who are afraid to take on the enemy, who do not believe in Netaji's cause, the return path is wide open for them. Please go. Join hands with the enemy, if you wish, or do whatever else you want. Only leave your weapons behind. And don't commit the sin of betraying our movements to the enemy.'

'General, the cowards have already left. Don't worry!' said Capt. Bagri.

The British moved as if pursued by a tiger. The Japanese held out against repeated air attacks, but were hardly any match for the enemy. Gradually, Burma was being swallowed up. Expecting the British to take Prem Sehgal's route, Shah Nawaz had detailed Lt. Gyan Singh Bisht to attack the British. Trenches were dug at the foot of the mountains. With a column of hundred soldiers, Lt. Bisht kept vigil. The night Shah Nawaz left the camp, the enemy arrived with thirteen tanks, eleven armoured vehicles and ten trucks. Gyan Singh held his breath till they came within his line of fire and then in unison, the soldiers launched an assault. The enemy was big and strong. They had sophisticated and mechanised weaponry. The Azad Hind contingent was in that sense raggedy. All they had was boundless courage. Yet, through the night, they held off the entire regiment. Hopelessly outnumbered they were, but Gyan Singh would not hear of retreat. When the trenches were bombarded, fifteen soldiers of the Azad Hind jumped out and joined in hand-to-hand combat, with cries of 'Fire!', 'Netaji ki jai!', 'Chalo Dilli!'. Many of them were blown into smithereens. Others had magazines emptied into them. Then Gyan Singh strapped some grenades to his waist and went about stealthily planting them under the armoured vehicles. That single unit destroyed a whole lot of enemy vehicles. History had been created at the foot of Mount Popa.

The winds had changed in Burma. Gen. Aung San's liberation army was secretly marking out Japanese positions. The INA continued to fight the British, but without the same support and sympathy from the Burmese.

When Shah Nawaz was barely five miles away from Prem Sehgal, he heard that the Japanese were withdrawing from Burma.

In the meantime, the rains had started in Burma. The paths through the forest became fetters on the feet of the soldiers. Like Gyan Singh, Capt. Bagri was also waiting for an opportunity to annihilate the enemy. One day as he was camping in the paddy fields with his battalion, a British motorised infantry column suddenly surrounded him. Capt. Bagri and his men shot out, with cry on their lips, 'Netaji zindabad!', 'Bharatmata ki jai!'. They tried to fend off the enemy. But they were outnumbered, in manpower and weapons. Capt. Bagri and some of his men attacked the tanks with petrol bottles. Bagri was blown up along with the tank.

The next day when Shah Nawaz was passing that way, he saw many charred bodies and iron skeletons scattered around the paddy fields. Human courage had melted the steel of machines.

Rain fell incessantly. Shah Nawaz, Dhillon and Mehardas arrived at Legi on 14 May 1945. The village chief gave them all milk to drink. The entire region was ravaged. While he was resting in his hut, Shah Nawaz had a visitor – Capt. Izumi. 'General, the British took Pegu ten days ago,' he said. That made Shah Nawaz's hair stand on end. Was Netaji stuck in Rangoon, he thought. Had he been arrested?

After crossing the swollen Pegu River, they were caught in a cruel maze because they could not enter the nearby village as it had been taken over by the British. All roads were obscured. After some thought, Shah Nawaz took off his holster belt and handed it with the pistol to Dhillon. 'Here are six bullets. Four for the enemy and two for me.'

'What! Are you going to commit suicide?'

'No. Sacrifice. I do not want to be captured by these dagger wielders.'

A meeting of the Azad Hind soldiers was held in the forests adjoining a village called Sintpinzex late that night. The cold night air alone kept them company. But everyone sensed that the enemy was just a few yards away. Shah Nawaz said, 'We have only three options. One is suicide.'

'That is for cowards!' retorted Dhillon.

'The second, destroy the enemy or be destroyed.'

'That is an honourable death,' came in a chorus.

'And the third … surrender and be taken as war prisoners. So what do you want?'

Shah Nawaz's eyes shone with a fierce determination. 'Either the first or second for me,' he murmured. 'As long as I am alive, my friends, I will not let those devils get their hands on me. We lost Gyan Singh. Our precious Kuber, Yellappa saheb is no more and Capt. Bagri …'

'That's what I am reminding you of Shanno,' Gurbaksh said to him. 'Their heroic deeds in the distant land of Burma must be told to the coming generations. They must be made aware of the great fire Netaji had ignited. Here in the jungle, who knows when our lives will end. But there, before we climb to the gallows, at least by way of a court case or court martial, we will tell the world Netaji's story.'

Gurbaksh sounded convincing, but Shah Nawaz was not prepared to be taken prisoner of war. 'I will remain here alone and fight if need be.'

Dhillon took Shanno aside and whispered to him, 'I know exactly why you want to remain here. You are worried about Netaji's safety, aren't you? Well, there is some good news for you. Netaji has long since left for Bangkok via Moulmein. So stop worrying.'

Shah Nawaz hugged Dhillon with delight.

Once they had decided that Netaji's story had to be told to the outside world, the Azad Hind soldiers decided to surrender. Some of them, along with a local peasant, went forward with a white flag. Mehar Singh gave them some bread and butter, and that was the last breakfast the Azad Hind soldiers had together.

By midday, the British sent two trucks. With heavy hearts, the Azad Hind soldiers threw their weapons into them. Prem Sehgal, Shah Nawaz and Dhillon sat in the jeep beside a British officer and an Indian. Both of them looked at the three men as if they were some rare species of wildlife. Soon, they arrived at an artillery camp. Many Indians in the British Army stared at them in amazement. Before they were formally taken in, all three hundred men were lined up. Their uniforms were filthy and tattered, their feet were bare, but the pride with which they wore the INA badge on their sleeves was unmatched. Shah Nawaz gave the command to take guard from the right. Those heroes were being taken prisoners, yet, with gusto, they were shouting, 'Azad Hind zindabad!' 'Pyare Netaji zindabad!' 'Chalo Dilli! Hamari Dilli!'.

'Bose is coming to Bangkok with his cabinet of ministers. Send out a team to welcome him,' Field Marshal Terauchi ordered his colleagues.

It had taken Netaji three weeks to traverse the mountains and valleys between Burma and Thailand, and in that time, the situation in the rest of the world had changed completely. The Germans had fought resolutely till the end. A few months ago, Hitler's army had overrun almost all of Russia and burnt down half of Moscow. But now their own capital, Berlin, was falling target to Allied air raids. Pits and craters from the bombings scarred the city. Finally, the Berlin Wall fell, Hitler committed suicide, and it was all over. There was quiet on all fronts in Europe. Only Japan refused to be cowed down by the powerful western nations.

But for how long could they fight? What new strategy was America planning? Russia and Japan had signed a Non-aggression Pact. There was no telling when the Red Bear would thrust its snout into the anthill. How was INA to carry forward? Netaji worried. Behind the closed doors of his office in Bangkok, Netaji contemplated in solitude.

The last surge of battle had erupted on the Asian front. The Americans were in hot pursuit of Japanese troops on an island in the Philippines and heading for Tokyo. At the same time, Allied B-29 bombers continued to wreak havoc in the Pacific. Netaji's condition was like the sky before a solar eclipse – the effulgence of a moment ago transformed into pitch darkness.

If Netaji's remaining companions were worried for his life, his sights were fixed on India's future. Ayyar kept providing the latest news from radio broadcasts. The deceitful British were playing a new trick on India. Viceroy Wavell had announced that he would give Hindus and Muslims equal representation on his council.

Netaji told Debnath Das, 'They have sharpened their knives.'

'How?'

'By playing their shrewd game. Of dividing our land.'

'That means you are opposed to partition?'

'Yes. And I will remain so till I die.'

Although the Bangkok radio station had been badly damaged by American attacks, Netaji insisted on going there. He convinced the technicians to get the equipment going. After several hours, they managed to make it work temporarily. Netaji addressed his motherland: 'I cannot bear to see the partition of our beloved country. To preserve its integrity and unity, I am prepared to fight an epic battle, even a civil war for twenty years. Abraham Lincoln fought for a unified America. History did not find fault with him. If I fight for the same ideal, for the same goal, how dare history label me a villain? Our country must remain united and strong. So, my brothers, treat Wavell's proposal in the same manner as you did the Cripps Mission. Reject it outright!'

Hachiya, the Japanese Ambassador to Netaji's government, arrived unexpectedly to meet him. 'Japan has decided to grant political asylum to all Asian leaders,' he said.

'What next?'

'The president of Philippines, Chen Kun Po of the Chinese government at Nanking and Dr Ba Maw have already accepted asylum. Others are about to follow.'

'Hachiya, neither I nor my government have sheathed our swords yet. We will have to fight unto death, for a breath of free air.'

Netaji summoned his colleagues. 'Things have come to such a juncture that anything can happen. It seems that one will have to spend some time in the frozen plains of Siberia. Keep the fires of your hope burning as always. We will set fire to the ocean, burn the desert, melt the glaciers. But we will re-deploy our forces with renewed energy even if the Third World War has to be fought for India's cause.'

Netaji's restless mind was exploring every avenue and every possibility. He suddenly remembered his old friend Nakoda, the Japanese naval commander. The man who had sailed around half the world would definitely have a solution. Nakoda had told Netaji, 'If something goes wrong during the Imphal campaign, do let me know.' Fortunately, he was in Saigon at that time. So he came to Bangkok as soon as Netaji summoned him. Nervously, he told Netaji, 'At least ten thousand Japanese are being killed in American bomb attacks every day. Bose, the situation can become explosive at any time.'

Sighing deeply, Netaji asked, 'Nakoda, what is the point of falling into the enemy's hands after having started such a revolution? A hero's death is preferable.'

Nakoda placed an old map on the table. Pointing to it, he said, 'This enormous land mass is Russia. Only this country can stand up to America in the future.'

'I am sure of that. Their uneasy friendship cannot last very long. The world is going to be divided into two distinct halves – America and Russia.'

'Take advantage of the Non-aggression Pact between Russia and Japan. I have all the experience. I can promise to take you safely either to Tashkent or Samarkand.' While they agreed on that course of action, Nakoda refused to move without permission from the Japanese imperial headquarters. Netaji sent the proposal to Tokyo and received an immediate reply. Permission was flatly refused. A disappointed Nakoda went away. Netaji kept muttering to himself – 'What difference is there between being enslaved by the British or by the Japanese. I spurn all shackles.'

Staying on in Bangkok was like living on top of a volcano. Netaji learnt that many Thai officials had been passing on secret information to the British. To remain idle would be risking arrest along with the Japanese, should the Americans and British capture them. If the Azad Hind Government is taken prisoner, his revolution would fail.

Netaji had sent Zaman Kiani to Singapore, Inayat Kiani to Ipoh, Maj. Gen. Chatterji to Rangoon and A.M. Sahay was trying to contact someone in Hanoi.

In the midst of all this, Netaji learnt that Field Marshal Terauchi was arriving in Bangkok to meet him. Netaji could not figure out the motive for the visit. He had been a true friend to Netaji from their first meeting at Singapore and supported Mutaguchi fully during the Imphal campaign. Had he heard about Nakoda's proposal? Was he going to persuade Netaji to change his mind?

Terauchi was looking as devastated and helpless as his country was, in the face of the American attack. Tokyo had been bombarded for more than six hours. Neither weather nor the spirited Japanese resistance deterred them.

Netaji said, 'Just suppose, purely hypothetically, if Japan has to accept defeat – then what?'

Terauchi was stung to the quick! 'Bose, the word defeat has no place in our history, so where will the bastard word "surrender" come from?'

Placating him, Netaji said, 'What brought you here despite your ill health?'

'To thank you.'

'Actually, *we* are indebted to you.'

'No, Bose. You too could have saved your skin by betraying Japan like Aung San did. When the Japanese Army was retreating from Burma, if INA had not given them protection from Meiktila to Moulmein, thousands of our men would have perished. And the British would have been successful in their effort to wipe out the Japanese Army. That is what I came to express my gratitude for.'

'So far, we have been only speaking hypothetically,' Netaji said anxiously. 'Tell me, if there is a pact like Versailles in the First World War, if the British ask you to hand over Subhas Chandra Bose to them, what will you, as an ally, do?'

Netaji's doubts about their integrity brought tears to the old warrior's eyes. 'Don't even entertain such doubts, Bose. There are many in Japan even today who are totally overwhelmed by your personality and your patriotism.'

'But when the war finally ends, anything can happen. Churchill and Mountbatten are impatient to get their hands on me.'

'This Terauchi has tested many waters, seen many countries, experienced many revolutions, known patriots and rulers. But no one comes close to you in their love for their motherland. 'Bose, you may not know it, but the day I heard that our Royal Army had been defeated at Mandalay, I had my first heart attack. But I have hidden all my pain and suffering under the uniform of my country and my love for my Emperor. Just suppose what you said did come true. If my own king commands me to hand you over to the British, he would have to go over my dead body before laying hands on you. No one will dare touch a hair on your head as long as this Terauchi is alive.'

Nineteen

July 1945. Seremban. One hundred and fifty miles from Singapore.

Netaji was due to arrive at the Japanese camp. Power supply had been disrupted so about fifteen lanterns had been lit, but they did not dispel the darkness. At the central square Mohammad Durrani, looking like a sacrificial lamb, had been tied to a stake. He had been brutally tortured by the Japanese Kampeitai, and for several days he had been wishing that, they would finish him off once and for all. He knew how the Japanese treated traitors. The previous day, as he lay on the cold floor, moaning in pain, a Japanese soldier had shouted at him, 'Stand up, you ... you are lucky you have been saved from our clutches. Now the Azad Hind Government will deal with you. Their prime minister berated us for taking action against an Indian, so we are handing you over to him.'

'Who? Subhas babu?'

'Yes, Bose.'

It was past nine o'clock. The palm fronds were swaying in the salty breeze from the Seremban. The atmosphere was grim, tense. Kunizuka, the Japanese officer, was pacing up and down. Suddenly, the glare of three to four pairs of motorcar headlights fell on Durrani. Lt. Col. Nagar calmly announced the arrival of 'His Excellency, Netaji Subhas Chandra Bose, Supreme Commander, Indian National Army and Prime Minister of Azad Hind'.

One unit of the elite corps marched up and smartly saluted to the resounding cries of 'Jai Hind!'. Netaji glanced at Durrani and he felt as if a hundred spears had been jabbed at his body. 'Capt. Durrani, we committed a grave sin by nurturing a snake, an international spy like you.'

'No, Netaji, I am innocent!' whimpered Durrani.

'That's what we believed and regret it now. You have brought it upon yourself. Not only are you guilty of treason, you also spread hatred between the Hindus and Muslims. Who informed British headquarters about the movement of our submarines?'

'Not me, Netaji ...'

'Fortunately, some of them changed course and my brave colleagues were saved. Otherwise, British machine guns would have welcomed them ashore, thanks to you.'

'Netaji, I swear by the Kali Ma.'

'Shut up, you lowly beast, don't soil your tongue further. We treated you with compassion because you were an Indian and you repaid us with treachery!'

Durrani was in a terrible state, trembling, twitching against the stake. There was a rain of blows on him, but he still would not confess to his crime. Finally, Netaji passed the verdict. 'Capt. Mohammad Durrani, you have betrayed your motherland and a valuable friend like Japan by turning into a spy for the enemy. You have slit the throat of your own people.' He consulted the findings from the other members of the court-martial committee. They were unanimous. Explaining their views to him, Netaji said, 'Capt. Durrani, your crime is so heinous that to award you any sentence other than death will be a travesty of justice.'

Durrani clutched harder at the stake when he heard the verdict. Netaji got up and went into one of the cells nearby. The notepad with the death sentence lay on his lap, duly signed by the jury. Once Netaji put his signature to it, the guns lined up outside would swing into action. For some reason, Netaji was uneasy. Col. Aziz Ahmed said to him, 'Sir, signature ...'

'Umm, yes.'

Again, he sat still. Just then his stenographer, Bhaskaran, came rushing up to him and said, 'Netaji, you must go to the rest house quickly. There's a call from Singapore. Zaman Kiani wants to urgently speak with you.'

Netaji handed the pad to Aziz and went towards the car. Aziz followed him with the pad, 'Sir, your signature ...'

'We'll see about that tomorrow. Leave it for now.'

Before departing for Seremban, Netaji had left Zaman Kiani to handle the matters in Singapore, Inayat Kiani in Kuala Lumpur and John Thivy in Ipoh, with instructions to keep their reserve troops in full readiness and inform him instantly of any developments.

The last few months had been fraught with tension. Netaji had not received any letters from Europe for a while now. He often thought about Anita – what did she look like now? He could only guess. Of late, he had been haunted by memories of his loved ones. Why did they trouble him so, he wondered.

The next day, again Aziz Ahmed came up to Netaji. Neither of them said anything, but both knew what needed to be done. After a while Netaji said in a pained voice, 'My mind will not let me sentence an Indian to death.'

'Well, if after all this you still consider him a loyal soldier, say so and I will release him at once,' Aziz Ahmed said angrily.

'Don't think I will forgive him.' Netaji lowered his voice and scribbled something on it and put his signature to the paper. 'Aziz, I have pronounced the sentence – death by hanging. Now you carry it out. But ...,' he hesitated, 'only after I have left Seremban. A dying man's cries will be too much for me to bear.'

Aziz Ahmed's stern heart too melted. Tears welled up without him noticing it. 'Netaji,' he said, 'your opponents are so foolish. They consider you a dictator, they revile you for that.' He continued, 'Dear Netaji, you can never be a dictator!'

On the night of 6 August, Netaji was at his table, working, when Bhaskaran rushed into the room, radio in hand. His face crumpled as news of the Americans dropping the atom bomb on Hiroshima broke. An area of thirteen square kilometres had been scorched. Thousands of people were feared killed. America wanted to teach the Japanese a lesson. Four days later, they repeated the attack on Nagasaki situated on Japan's western shore. Nagasaki was a beautiful port city and now it had been reduced to a graveyard. On the night of 11th August, Maj. Gen. Zaman Kiani sent an urgent message: 'Leave at once. Avoid travel at night.'

After this inhuman massacre, what would the future bring? The fallout of the American action shook the whole world. The global scenario had changed. The descendants of the sun, the Japanese military and government, came to their knees.

Russia, sitting on the fence till recently, suddenly rushed its troops to Manchuria in a show of hostility to Japan.

Once again Bhaskaran reminded Netaji that he ought to be leaving Seremban. But it was a night of major developments.

Calmly Netaji said to Bhaskaran, 'What's the hurry? We have nothing to lose if Russia enters the fray. Even if the world is turned topsy-turvy, we will find our path.'

There was no point remaining in Seremban any longer. Raghavan and Swami had invited Netaji to Penang. Thivy was to come from Ipoh. It was decided that they would all meet in Singapore to review the future course of action. Netaji arrived in Singapore two days later. Maj. Gen. Kiani and Habib-ur-Rahman had been waiting eagerly for him. Discussions began on the terrace of the Mayor Bungalow. Negishi brought a message from the Royal Army Headquarters. His face looked hard.

'Sir, Japan has surrendered.'

Negishi was weeping inconsolably. The American president, Harry S. Truman, had invoked the conditions of the Potsdam Pact on Japan, and demanded unconditional surrender. Japan had only given in because it was impossible to survive otherwise.

Controlling himself, Negishi told Netaji, 'Today, every Japanese citizen feels like committing harakiri. Our proud nation had not heard the word defeat in its twenty-six-hundred-year-old history.'

'One has to accept what happens,' Raghavan said.

'But that is the problem – the Rightist party, a large section of which are young soldiers in the army are protesting violently, almost hysterically, before the Emperor's palace, that they will not step back an inch, despite Hiroshima and Nagasaki. Secret discussions are going on in the cellars of the palace.'

Netaji could only stare at the distraught Negishi as he continued, 'Eight hundred of our aircraft are heading towards Formosa on a suicide mission. Death in action is preferable to surrender, they say.'

The cabinet ministers turned to Netaji. What could he do to help matters? Would he collapse under the shock of Japan's humiliation? Or stand up erect once more?

Clearing his throat, Netaji said, 'Japanese surrender does not mean the INA has retreated.' The fighter in him asserted himself.

He told Negishi, 'So far, your country has given the Azad Hind Government a hundred million yen of which we have only used ten.

The rest is deposited in the South Development Bank. Please withdraw it at once and give it to your Emperor, with my regards.'

In the course of their meeting, the news agency Domei confirmed reports of the surrender. Now what should the next step be? Netaji ordered disbandment of the remaining troops. The officials of the Hindi Swatantra Sangha in Singapore were entrusted with the responsibility of escorting home some of the girls from the women's army. His cabinet and loyal companions were in a quandary – what were they to do with Netaji? Just then a telegram from Gen. Isoda was received. 'Leave for Saigon immediately. Do not delay.'

A worried Col. Pritam Singh announced, 'I cannot imagine Netaji being captured by the British. If that happens, the entire 3rd Division will march to heaven.'

'Why should he go to Japan under these circumstances? The British and the Americans will not let him be,' Debnath Das added.

'Neither this nor that. I must leave this place. But I think my final journey will be through the ice fields of Russia,' Netaji said. 'Setting the glaciers of Manchuria and Russia on fire, I will march to Delhi.'

'Netaji, please hurry. Our aircraft will not fly much longer. There is no point in all of us risking capture or confinement here.'

They decided they would sacrifice themselves, but the most precious jewel of India's freedom struggle should not fall into the enemy's hands.

Netaji decided to board the first flight to Bangkok the next day. When Ayyar asked him where he was going, Netaji replied, 'Adventure into the unknown, what else.'

As he was preparing for his flight, Netaji had an unexpected visitor, Narsingh from Germany. Before Netaji could ask him about Nambiar, Narsingh handed a large packet to Netaji. It was from Nambiar. After Germany had been defeated, the Free India Centre had been shut down and Nambiar had gone to France. 'When did you take this decision to close our mission, Narsingh?' Netaji asked.

'In the beginning of April. Germany's decline and Hitler's suicide was the end of Nazi Germany.'

'What became of our friend Trott?'

'Hitler had him arrested and hanged in July, last year.' The news caused Netaji great grief. Trott had been a dear and trusted friend, who had done all he could to get Netaji out of Germany. On 20 July, Col. Stauffenberg and Lt. Woerner had plotted to assassinate Hitler at Rastenburg. Unfortunately, the bomb had exploded some distance away and Hitler escaped.

Trott had been waiting at Wilhelmstrasse all day for news from Rastenburg. He too was part of the conspiracy. The Gestapo had evidence that he had been in touch with all the anti-Hitler groups across the world. He was arrested on 25 July. 'Netaji, Himmler personally pleaded with Hitler not to send Trott to the gallows, but can a stone melt?' Narsingh reported. 'In fact, he ordered that Trott be hanged by a piano wire so that it would be a slow torturous death.'

That evening in Singapore was very depressing. Thoughts of Trott would not leave Netaji. As he sat brooding, Col. Stracey came up to him. 'Will you come to see the progress of the Martyrs' Memorial?'

'Is it finished already?'

'You had ordered that it should be completed within three weeks ...'

How appropriate a day to remember the martyrs. They hurried towards the beach with Col. Stracey. The Indian National Army had many Anglo-Indian officers like Stracey and Rodricks. He congratulated Stracey on the magnificent job they had done. As he stared at the memorial, a thousand faces, Japanese and Indians, swam before him. They had battled not just the enemy, but nature, hunger, sickness, and sacrificed themselves for the freedom of their country. Kuber Yellappa, Mansukh, Dr Akbar Ali, Yanagida. Tomorrow would be another uncertain journey ... Netaji's own words comforted him:

Everything in this world is mortal
But there is no end
For the fire of idealism,
The wings of aspiration that span the sky
Man dies, his ideals don't.
Time does not stand still.
The ancient seed of idealism
Passes on from generation to generation

And takes birth each time to erect
A glorious edifice.

With a shudder, the plane finally landed in Bangkok. The city seemed to have been affected much more by the Allied attacks than Singapore. Since Netaji and his party had arrived without warning, there was no one to receive them at the deserted airport. It was two hours before Maj. Gen. Bhosale arrived, panting. The Hikari Kikan was also intimated about Netaji's arrival. Dramatic changes were taking place all round the world. In that volatile environment, what should the Azad Hind's next step be, what was Netaji's future? These were the issues being discussed that night with the members of the Hindi Swatantra Sangha, when Gen. Isoda, chief of the Hikari Kikan and Ambassador Hachiya arrived. They too had been rattled by the fate of their country. In reply to Netaji's polite 'How are you?', Isoda said, 'We would not have given up so easily, but those two atom bombs ...'

'I know. I heard your Emperor's surrender speech.'

'What a drama that created in Tokyo!' Hachiya added. 'Although the whole of Japan was destroyed, some extremists protested against the Emperor for surrendering. They destroyed the recording of the Emperor's speech, but luckily, the administration had anticipated this and made arrangements for an extra one which was broadcast over another station.'

Netaji was full of admiration for the persistent and courageous Japanese but was surprised to hear that some five hundred pilots were preparing for suicide missions. Three lakh Japanese soldiers were still fighting on several fronts. The Emperor was worried about the formalities of their final surrender. Isoda wanted to know where Netaji would be going from there.

'I want to get to Russia via Manchuria,' Netaji told him.

'But Russia has joined the Allies, so as an enemy of Japan, what can they offer you?'

'Japan's doors are closed to me forever. If not Russia, then the depths of the ocean or the expanse of the sky will be my haven. But until I blow British Imperialism to smithereens, I will not be able to rest.'

'We are floored by your determination. We will offer you whatever help we can. But I doubt if the strapped Japanese authorities will allow you to go to Russia,' said Hachiya.

'What is the way out?'

'Only Field Marshal Terauchi may be able to help you.' Both Isoda and Hachiya offered their assistance even to go to Saigon and formally request Terauchi.

Another journey. Another flight. Saigon too wore a deserted look. After Japan's surrender, neighbouring countries like Thailand had become very unstable. Some of their army personnel had entered into secret pacts with Mountbatten and the South-East Asia Command, Netaji heard at the airport. The road ahead was blurred. Field Marshal Terauchi's headquarter was at Daret, nearby. It was decided to contact him and discuss future action.

Saigon was in the grip of the fear of an invasion by the French Army. On the roads, only the occasional vehicle was seen. Doors and windows were shut and barred. Rumours floated free and furious. The people of Thailand were terrorised by the thought of punitive action by the Allied forces.

After the entire Japanese Air Force had been taken over by America, Japan rejected outright Netaji's request to fly to Russia. Now his last resort was Terauchi who was in Daret. Everyone knew in what esteem and affection Terauchi held Netaji. After getting Netaji's permission, Isoda and Hachiya left for Daret to convince Terauchi.

The Daret Military Headquarters was in disarray. Japan's surrender had caused the nation to completely lose its bearings, and it was now lifeless, like a body with its main artery damaged. Field Marshal Terauchi had not been able to bear the humiliation of surrender and since 15 August, lay in a hospital bed, paralysed.

Many senior officers had gone mad, others had committed harakiri. The Sumidha River was overflowing with decaying bodies. Japan was one helpless, rudderless ship. Hiroshima and Nagasaki had been turned into infernos, and the moans and the cries for water of the hapless victims echoed for miles. The Japanese Emperor had sent a message of surrender through Prince Kanin who was in Formosa.

Isoda and Hachiya's army car was stopped before they reached Terauchi's tent. A major ran out, ordered the guards to bring the two men inside and went away. Both of them were shocked to see Terauchi's shrunken body. The field marshal asked about Netaji in a feeble voice. 'He is determined to go to Manchuria,' they told him.

'I had sent his request to our general headquarters long back.'

He asked his deputy to call Tokyo and check. But when the answers from the other side were not encouraging, as Terauchi could tell from the deputy's expressions, he took the phone. 'This is Field Marshal Terauchi. Bose wants our permission to go to Manchuria.'

'After all the help that Japan has given him, he wishes to seek asylum in an enemy country? It is most improper.'

'Regardless of how much we have helped him, Bose is not Japan's vassal. If you do not grant him permission, you will be reported to the Emperor. Who do you think you are? Give the prime minister my message. I have given him permission on my own authority. And I will make arrangements for his onward flight.'

Terauchi put the phone down. Obviously, he had been speaking to the foreign minister. He realised he had said too much. Picking up the receiver, he found it was not disconnected, so in a conciliatory tone he continued, 'Is it not my duty to support a dear friend whose cause is just and whose ideas are so noble? So, Major, what aircraft shall we assign him?'

'Sir, we have no bombers in Saigon. Most squadrons are headed for or already in Tokyo.'

'Wasn't our chief of the Burma Army, Lt. Gen. Tsunamasa Shidei to go to Manchuria?'

'Absolutely right, sir. He is being taken there with his staff today. He has to sign the surrender papers in front of the Russian commanders. The plane must be on the Saigon airstrip as we speak.'

Just then two officers came and informed, 'Our commander of the Formosa Army has just committed harakiri, sir.'

The news came as a shock to Terauchi. The Allies were stalking the Japanese from all sides, bent on total destruction. Despite the chaos around him, Terauchi was worried about Netaji's safe departure from Saigon. Fortunately Shidei was fluent in English, French and other languages. Terauchi decided that Netaji would accompany him to Manchuria. He instructed the Saigon Airport accordingly.

When Netaji realised that the messengers who had gone to Daret had not yet returned, he became very restless. Just then a car carrying Hachiya, Isoda and a couple of Terauchi's staff officers screeched to a halt in front of him.

'When he goes to sign the surrender statement, Terauchi says he will introduce you to some Russian officials,' Hachiya reported to Netaji, adding, 'and he has informed Shidei accordingly.'

Netaji felt a sense of relief. But it did not last long. A message was received from the airstrip, 'Only one seat is available on the bomber aircraft.'

As soon as they heard this, Ayyar, Habib-ur-Rahman, Abid Hasan, Debnath Das, Pritam Singh and all the others looked extremely troubled. Even as Japan was on its deathbed, Terauchi had managed to find a way out for Netaji. But how was one to leave behind one's dearest friends and companions who had walked with one through the thorny and tangled fields of calamities? Ayyar wore a morose expression. One couldn't bear to look at Pritam Singh's defeated face. Netaji's feet stumbled involuntarily. 'Take a decision immediately, Bose. All our airfields are rapidly passing into American hands. This is probably the last plane to take off from Saigon.' Gen. Isoda's voice shook as he spoke.

Netaji's vision blurred. 'How can I leave my companions behind, what will I do alone, where will I go? Do something, find another plane ...!'

'That is impossible. Don't give up this chance.' Isoda was almost pleading with Netaji.

Everyone was shaken. Netaji was to abandon the Azad Hind ship and go far away. When the mast is lost, what use is the oar? Without the soul, what is a body? Was there, perhaps, some devious game the Japanese were playing here and other similar doubts raised their heads in many minds. Silently, they were gritting their teeth at Hachiya and Isoda.

'My brothers, I shall be with you in darkness and in sunshine, in sorrow and in joy, in suffering and in victory. I pledged to stay by your side. I will not put one foot forward without you. Victory or defeat, death or life, we will taste it together. If the plane leaves without me, let it.'

These words fell on delighted ears. A new energy gushed through their bodies.

Isoda was annoyed. 'Even God will not doubt your devotion to Netaji. But be realistic. Think of the situation. Just as you love your country and your Netaji, the Japanese love their country and their Emperor. If only the bomb had not complicated matters. Even if America had fought for another hundred years, Japan would not have lost. In God's garden, first flowers bloomed, in the devil's rotten mind, the atom bomb took birth.'

'Well, what is the worst that can happen?' Debnath Das wanted to know.

'In a very short while, America will tie Japan's hands at its back. Our army, our administration, our law enforcement bodies will be in America's grip. Under those conditions, how are we to protect your Netaji?' Isoda said.

'The American troops will land in Japan and the first thing they will do is put handcuffs on Netaji – as a war criminal,' Hachiya told them gravely.

An agitated Pritam Singh shouted, 'Ayyar, Das, if this world should drown, it doesn't matter. But if Netaji's hands are put in handcuffs and his legs in chains, I will not be able to bear it.'

'So then, what is to be done?' Isoda was getting impatient.

'Even if there's only one seat on the plane, Netaji, don't hesitate. Board it,' Netaji's companions chorused.

'If Netaji is safe, he will establish a new order,' some others exclaimed.

'No, that won't do,' Ayyar objected. 'At least one of us should accompany Netaji.'

Isoda could not bear to see Netaji's companions wavering like this. 'Let us go to the aerodrome and make one more attempt,' he said finally.

The vehicles moved at breakneck speed. As they drove along, Isoda promised Netaji, 'I will do whatever I can and get another aircraft to transport all your companions soon after you depart.'

They knew they were near the aerodrome when they could hear the engines of the plane revving up. The captain in charge of the aerodrome shouted, 'Hurry up! The engines have been running for the past one hour.'

The staff and twelve passengers on board were getting restless waiting for Netaji. Lt. Gen. Shidei had been held up for two hours.

The chief Pilot, Lt. Col. Nonogaki followed by Lt. Gen. Shidei climbed down quickly. They bowed to greet Netaji in the Japanese manner.

Before even acknowledging the greeting, Netaji blurted, 'General, how can I leave my dearest friends behind? You must make space for at least one more person.'

Shidei looked at the pilot. Nonogaki's face fell. Very politely he said, 'Impossible. Quite impossible, sir! Only nine persons can travel in this bomber. Already twelve have been accommodated. The cargo capacity of this bomber is a maximum of one tonne. Already the weight is over two tonnes. Everybody's life is precious!'

'No, no, you will have to take one more person,' Netaji insisted.

'It will be just too much load.'

'That's an order.

'We are under orders, sir! Truly, we will be excessively overloaded,' said Taro Kono, the co-pilot, despairingly.

Finally, it was agreed that one more person would go along with Netaji. Some more time was spent waiting for the car in which the others were travelling. Nerves were taut, tempers high. The drone of the bomber's engines added to the tension. The heat inside was stifling. Two huge trunks were brought out of the car. When he saw the heavy chests, Nonogaki advised them to reduce the luggage. The trunks were opened. Clothes were discarded. They were full of the jewellery, of gold and precious stones offered by the mothers and sisters of East Asia to Netaji. This treasure was essential for their revolution. Eventually, the trunks were loaded on the plane.

Col. Habib-ur-Rahman was chosen to accompany Netaji. The others felt envious of him. The drone of the engines turned to a deafening roar. The hot vapours that emanated from the propellers seared the body. Netaji embraced Hachiya and Isoda. He hugged every one of his companions. He once again reminded Isoda, 'You will not forget to arrange another plane to transport my colleagues to Manchuria, will you?'

He ran up the short flight of stairs to the plane. Before getting in, he saluted those waiting below, 'Jai Hind!' His mind was in turmoil, his voice was choked, but he managed to shout, '*Milenge, mere bhai, jaroor milenge. Jai Hind!*'

It was half past five in the evening. The sky was thick with black clouds. A strong wind was ripping through. A smiling moon seemed to be chasing the edge of the darkening horizon. The bomber was picking up speed as it taxied down the runway. The aircraft had no windows. So Netaji's companions standing on the airstrip could not catch a final glimpse of their beloved leader. Not one eye was dry. The plane went far, far away until it became a speck in the boundless sky.

Hurry, make haste! Every particle, every atom at Saigon airport seemed to be screaming. Lt. Col. Nonogaki's pale face had a hard, set expression. His two co-pilots were barely able to control their annoyance and desist from making a scene. On the aerodrome, Japanese anti-aircraft guns were on full alert, surveying the surroundings intently. After all, Netaji was a Head of State, the revered leader from East Asia. Field Marshal Terauchi entrusted the responsibility for his safe passage to Nonogaki and his crew.

The 97-2 Sally bomber had been standing on the runway, panting, for so long. Thoughts of Hiroshima and Nagasaki were stinging the heart of every Japanese. It was imperative that Shidei and Netaji were taken to a safe place before the great war took an even more grim turn.

As the bomber was preparing for take-off from Saigon Airport, Nonogaki's eyes fell on the control panel in front of him and he shouted, 'Taro Kono, look! Look in front!'

'What is it, sir?'

Taro Kono caught sight of the rapidly increasing number of cycles of the bomber engine. He broke out in a cold sweat. He began, 'Sir, 3300 cycles mean … so much power required?'

'Yes. When taking off, the number of cycles should be 1600 to 1700.'

The droning of the straining propellers choked Nonogaki. He looked at Sergeant Major Aoyagi. He was piloting the plane. There was no other pilot as competent as him in the entire Japanese Air Force. But fear had creased his brow too. Seeing that, Nonogaki said to him in Japanese, 'Aoyagi, what's the problem?'

'We're overloaded,' Aoyagi blinked.

'We have enough fuel, don't we?'

'Yes. Those two tanks at the back of the aircraft, that's fuel. They are adding to the weight too.'

'That cannot be helped. Such a long flight, across the ocean ... this much extra fuel is essential. There won't be any problem mid-flight, will there?' Nonogaki asked.

'Doesn't seem likely,' Aoyagi replied.

Maj. Takizawa was the sub-pilot. He confirmed Aoyagi's statement. Nonogaki had faith in both his pilots. The Sally bomber was a sturdy plane. It had two powerful engines, which were manufactured by the famous company Mitsubishi. The Japanese had used it extensively in the war. And so far, it had not let anyone down. It was true that a couple of days ago when Nonogaki had flown to Singapore in the Sally bomber, one of its propellers was damaged and had come loose. It needed to be changed at once. But where was one to find such a major part in that small airport? In addition, one was being pounded by the thought of surrender. The threat of enemy air raids loomed large. Instead of waiting for a spare to be brought, the damaged propeller was repaired, tested stringently to make sure that there was no risk involved, and only then had they left Singapore airport.

Now these dangerously high revolutions threw Nonogaki into a quandary. He began to look for the control hands. In case of an emergency, it was good to know where they were. But they were not easily accessible. Suddenly, it struck him that they were to the right of the chief pilot. Not a very convenient location. At last, the aircraft was airborne and to the relief of the pilots, began to cruise along in the vast expanse of blue. Since it was not a passenger plane, there were no seats for the passengers. Lt. Gen. Shidei and Netaji were sitting on the floor.

Their departure had been delayed and they were way behind schedule. As a result, soon after they left Saigon, it became dark. Flying at night was dangerous. Besides, the bomber was crossing the territory targetted by enemy aircraft.

The tall, well-built Shidei was friendly and candid by nature. He was well travelled and knew several languages. Within a short while, he struck a rapport. He said to Netaji, 'This surrender has gagged Japan. But you have not wavered from your goal. You have set out for Manchuria looking for new avenues to continue your fight. I appreciate that.'

Netaji smiled. Then he asked Shidei, 'Have you seen that oil painting?'

'Which one?'

'The one with Jesus staggering under the heavy cross of defeat and humiliation, yet not giving up his search for salvation. I have always been inspired by it. I must carry a similar burden.'

Netaji noticed that Nonogaki kept glancing towards the back of the aircraft. His anxious eyes were on the two fuel tanks that had been secured in the rear. Suddenly, Nonogaki scrambled up and rushed towards them. He inspected them to see they were securely fastened, then returned to his seat. Trying to get through the dark, war-prone area was risky. Just one shot by an enemy missile or anti-aircraft gun was enough to destroy the bomber. No point, this blind groping in the dark. Shidei and Netaji suggested that the aircraft should halt for the night in the small town of Tourane.

Netaji felt a gentle tug on the sheet covering him. His eyes flew open instantly. There was no one in sight. On the cot beside him, Shidei was dead to the world. He glanced at his watch. 3.45 a.m.

He finished bathing and bare-bodied, sat down to his prayers. Just then, Shidei woke up with a start. He stared at Netaji, astonished. Fresh from his bath, Netaji's wide forehead was wet and glowing. Like a yogi he appeared, a tiny Bhagavad Gita in one hand, a rudraksha mala in the other. Shidei was filled with a sense of peace. The meditation over, Netaji opened his eyes.

As he was wrapping the Gita in a silken cloth, a photograph fell from Netaji's hand. Shidei bent down to pick it up. It was the picture of a European woman. Netaji explained, 'She is my wife.'

There was no time for the entire story. But Emilie had peeped out of the window of his heart. Except for his involvement with his motherland, nothing else had held Netaji in its spell. Only Emilie. With her absolute devotion, she had won him over. After a long time, memories suddenly came crowding in. The countenance of Europe had changed drastically. The Allies had crushed both Germany and Italy. 'Emilie, what must you have gone through in the turbulence of this war. Where are you now, my dear?'

'Bose, I have two sons. Do you have any children?' Shidei asked.

'I do, a baby girl. Anita.'

'Do you have a picture of her?'

Netaji turned pale. 'No.'

That unexpected question wrenched his heart. If only he'd had one photo of her. The memory of Anita when she was just a few days old floated before his mind's eye. Little one, I long to touch your sweet, soft face. 'Perhaps if I had a son, I wouldn't be so affected,' Netaji said.

'Why is that?' Shidei was quick to interrupt.

'Boys are like a wilful spring. They will leap off a cliff; they will jump and frolic anywhere. But for a father, a girl is like a stream hidden under layers of rock. They dwell in the depths of the heart. They keep pricking you with a sweet pain, an intoxicating ache.'

Soon, the others were all waking each other up, rushing to the bathroom. 'Come on, let's get moving fast,' Shidei was urging them. 'I must get to Manchuria to sign the papers of surrender on time. It's very important. It may lead to a crisis situation otherwise.'

'This meeting with you is providential. You are going to be signing the papers before Russian military officials. Which means I can travel up to there without fear,' Netaji said.

'I have many friends in the Russian Army. We'll find a way,' Shidei assured him.

Netaji checked his kit. He was taken aback. Who had packed this little bag? Toothbrush, toothpaste, shaving kit, soap. Only Emilie knew his needs so well. But she was so far away ... did he really do it himself?

'Come on, Bose, sir!'

'Come.'

Netaji closed his bag. Habib-ur-Rahman came running and took charge of the bag. Everyone hurriedly packed up and rushed to the Tourane airstrip on that wet grey morning. It was half past five.

That day, 18 August 1945, seemed strange and mysterious to Netaji. Who had woken him up? Packed his bag? Netaji and the others got out of the car on the tarmac. He took a couple of steps forward and then stood still. He turned to look back. There was no one there. But he definitely felt as if someone was walking beside him. These were hallucinations perhaps. Probably the consequence of sleepless nights, Netaji thought.

The crew was assembled on the Tourane runway. They were impatient to take off. But before that, the aircraft had to be carefully scrutinised and its airworthiness established. The technical staff was examining every part of the plane. Just then the staff officer of the air force, Taro Kono drew Lt. Col. Nonogaki aside. He pointed to one of the wheels. From that distance, Nonogaki couldn't see anything amiss. On closer inspection, however, he found that one of the wheels was slightly bent.

'Sir, it is absolutely necessary to reduce the load,' the engineer, Aoyagi, told Nonogaki.

'Sure, we can do that. Anyway, we are outside the enemy strike zone,' Taro Kono said.

Heavy cargo, such as twelve machine guns, boxes of ammunition, extra magazines was quickly offloaded. The weight was reduced by six hundred kilos. After ensuring that everything was shipshape, the bomber took off from Tourane in the soft morning light. In the next phase of their journey, they were to make halts at Heito and Taipei before proceeding to Dairen. The Sally was cruising at an altitude of 4000 metres as a result of which the temperature inside had dropped considerably. The passengers were shivering. Shidei and Netaji had their ears to the radio and were trying to catch news from the war front. Suddenly Shidei shouted, 'Did you hear that, Bose? Russian troops are advancing towards Dairen. They will be there any moment.'

Pressure was mounting on the crew. Even if they wanted to get as far as Taipei, it would mean another six hours of flying time. They still had to cover a distance of eleven hours when the disturbing news about the Allied troops approaching Dairen was received. Shidei looked extremely worried. How would the enemy who was blinded by the war tell whether the bomber was on a diplomatic mission or on any other business? Suppose an aircraft gun accidentally made them a target, what were they to do?

'Wasting even a moment will be a crime. Somehow, we must make it to Dairen,' Shidei announced.

'Mr Shidei, I am in a greater hurry than you,' Netaji said wryly.

Shidei summoned Nonogaki and asked, 'How are the engines of the bomber doing?'

'Excellent. Since the guns were offloaded, the aircraft is much lighter.'

'Can we skip the Heito halt, then?'

'Sure, why not. The weather conditions are good, we have enough fuel. We can head straight for Formosa Island and land at Taipei.'

Netaji told Shidei, 'I cannot afford to spend much time in Russia either. I have to reassemble the Indian National Army on the side of the Himalayas.'

'Bose, I have friends in high posts even in the Russian Army. I met them during a special training programme in Europe,' Shidei told Netaji once again.

'Will they help me?'

'They will also guarantee your safety.'

'Russia is under Stalin's dictatorship. Problems could crop up.'

'I don't think so.'

'How do you have so much confidence?' Netaji asked.

'Not all hearts are made of steel, even in a dictatorship. Lots of people still respect the idea of freedom and humanity, even though they might be in uniform. I will introduce you to such people in Dairen. Besides, the man who could rouse passions in reputedly the most hard-hearted people in the world, namely the Japanese, he is unlikely to leave the Russians cold!'

Netaji burst into a loud guffaw. Seeing the delight on his face, Shidei asked, 'Were you reminded of someone else?'

'There are people with hearts softer-than-wax under an armour of steel. I just remembered such a friend.'

'Who is that?'

'Adam Trott. A good man destroyed by Nazi Germany.'

The plane had been flying for six hours. It was after half past twelve in the afternoon when they caught a glimpse of the beautiful island of Formosa. Before they knew it, the aerodrome of Taipei swam into view. Taipei city was like a coconut half, guarded on all sides by high mountains and nestling in the deep hollow. Through the glass pane in front, the airstrip and the smoking chimneys of brick kilns all round became visible. Netaji had halted in the Railway Hotel there many times.

The bomber began to descend. Once they left Taipei, the next phase of the journey was going to be over the deep blue ocean. So they would rest here, give the engines time to cool before embarking on the five-hour flight. It was decided that they would reach Dairen before sunset. As the bomber taxied down the runway, the friction of the tyres increased. A grating sound filled the sky.

Matsuyama Airport, Taipei. It was a blazing hot afternoon. The recent bomb attacks had played havoc all round. This airport too was ravaged. The Japanese Infantry had set up a temporary camp. Netaji and Lt. Gen. Shidei sat in one of the tents. The orderlies placed some snacks before them. Stomachs were empty, but there was no hunger. At Shidei's insistence, Netaji ate a couple of bananas.

Pre-flight inspection began. The engineers were checking everything minutely. Shidei and Netaji were chatting away. Shidei suddenly recalled something and said, 'Oh, Bose, I forgot to mention this to you.'

'What?'

'When I spoke to Saigon last night, our officers gave me some shocking news.'

'And what was that, General?'

'Within minutes after we left Saigon, four American bombers made a sortie over the airport, rained a barrage of bombs and flew away.'

'Mountbatten and Churchill are burning their insides to get me, dead or alive. But those sinners will not even get a glimpse of my dead body. A thousand Subhases will rise from the soil of Hindustan. Sooner or later, the British will have to wend their way back home. Soon India will be free.'

Shidei began to ask Netaji all kinds of questions about India, the land of Buddha's birth. Netaji got carried away. 'One-fifth of the world's population lives in my country. Where else do you have such a large work-force? As for natural resources, only our land can boast of as much wealth as America. India is a gold mine. Unfortunately, it is not brought into use well. Barriers of discrimination, blind faith, superstition, caste conflicts – all these diseases are easily curable. But they need immediate and drastic remedies. Only then will we come out healthy. My India will certainly be free, it will also be one of the most powerful, most cultured nations of the world. That is what I aim to bring about.'

'After independence, you will have many questions before you ...'

Not waiting for Shidei to finish, Netaji replied, 'Colossal problems will have to be faced. Unemployment and poverty will have to be tackled within a specific time frame. The demon of overpopulation will have to be locked up in a bottle. The rigid administrative framework that the British have established for their own convenience will have to be remoulded to suit our needs. Divisive forces that play on religious and caste sentiments to incite hatred and mistrust have to be taught a lesson.

Incentives for cottage industry, major industrial projects, agricultural reforms, river water management, irrigation projects, complete literacy, a uniform script, planned development and progress ... will create a strong, powerful and dynamic nation.'

Inspection of the aircraft continued. Nonogaki called out to Taro Kono. In a low voice, Nonogaki asked Taro, 'Did you look carefully?'

'What?'

'The left engine is shaking slightly.'

'But I didn't notice it while landing,' Aoyagi interrupted.

It was clear that unless the repairs were satisfactorily carried out, there was no question of proceeding further.

Quickly, the engineers removed the covers of the engine. They checked the plug points. All three of them were engaged in the inspection to prevent any oversight. The hands of the clock were moving relentlessly forward. Shidei, Netaji and Habib-ur-Rahman gathered around the aircraft, flustered. The radio in Shidei's hand was giving a news bulletin. The Japanese governor general of Formosa, on hearing of the surrender, had committed harakiri. Russian troops would capture Dairen within the next few hours, the correspondent was reporting. Shidei urged Nonogaki, Aoyagi and Taro Kono to hurry.

'But, sir, why the urgency?' Taro Kono asked sharply. 'We have already sent an advance message to the enemies that our bomber is heading that way for the purpose of signing the surrender document, haven't we?'

'My good man, what you say is probably very convincing from a technical point of view. But once it gets dark, chances are the wet will burn with the dry. As it is they are crazed for vengeance.'

The repair job was almost done. Everyone's patience was growing thinner by the minute. Finally, Aoyagi gave the signal. The engines began revving up.

As soon as they entered the aircraft, Netaji said to Nonogaki, 'Colonel, will we be flying at the same altitude as we did this morning?'

'Of course!'

Netaji laughed and said, 'So you intend to make me freeze in the cold.' He asked Col. Habib to fetch his winter jacket. The deep purple turtle-necked jacket fitted snugly over his wide chest. Over that, he strapped on his leather belt. 'Habib, this is getting very tight!' He smiled softly. It was past two in the afternoon. Aoyagi prepared for take-off. He had never flown to Dairen before. That is why he wanted to get there before dark.

Finally, the aircraft began to taxi down the runway. Taro Kono and Nonogaki's eyes were fixed on the engine's cycles. A knot of fear began to form in their stomachs. The revolutions were increasing rapidly. The pilots' throats went dry. Still they reassured themselves that this was what had happened when they were taking off from Saigon. As soon as they felt the aircraft lifting off the runway, they let out a huge sigh.

The Sally bomber must have climbed about twenty to twenty-five meters when it began to rock violently, like a small boat tossed about by an enormous wave. It was accompanied by an ear-shattering explosion. Had the earth split asunder because of an earthquake? Or had a lightning bolt rent the skies? Had enemy planes attacked the aircraft? Every one of the fourteen people onboard was frozen, hair to nail. Though stationary, they were being jolted and jerked.

Nonogaki looked around, bewildered. One of the plane's propellers had detached itself and was hurtling towards the ground. At the same time, as if a demon had picked up a mountain and hurled it into the distance, one of the five-hundred-pound engines of the bomber came loose and rushed earthwards, spinning. With the sudden loss of weight on its left side, the bomber tilted to the right as if a dreaded shark had inadvertently slapped it with its tail. Habib-ur-Rahman was staring ahead helplessly. Fearing for their lives, the Japanese were screaming. Netaji's grave eyes were staring into the distance.

The bomber would crash without a doubt. But it had to be prevented from catching fire immediately thereafter. Nonogaki yelled at his fellow pilots, 'Takizawa, turn off the engines! Takizawa, the engines, switch the engines off!' He leapt out of his seat and tried to locate the controls. But the bomber tilted sharply and leaned to one side so he couldn't get up. For a moment, it seemed as if the two hemispheres were colliding with each other. Thudding, shuddering, rattling, the bomber crashed to the right of the runway. It had tucked its right wing under its belly. That's why it wasn't smashed to smithereens.

Since the plane had nosedived, its bridge was broken. The passengers were tossed around inside, somersaulting, cartwheeling, like a ball. Suitcases and other luggage tumbled on top of Netaji and Habib. They were all trapped inside. The temperature inside the bomber was rising rapidly. The skin felt as if it were being branded. There was a mad scramble to find a way out. Nonogaki struggled to his feet somehow. He saw Shidei sprawled in front. He grabbed Shidei's collar and tried to drag him to the back when he noticed a deep gash on his neck made by a piece of falling metal. Blood was gushing out from it. He must have been killed on the spot. From Aoyagi's screams it was apparent that he was alive. But his leg had been trapped under a steel bar. Nonogaki made a futile attempt to extricate him from under it. The engines were still running. The heat inside was mounting. Screams, groans, struggles to get out continued. With great difficulty, Nonogaki managed to smash the glass in front of the cockpit, and jumped out of the furnace-like plane.

Habib-ur-Rahman struggled to his feet. He stared at Netaji. Somehow, Netaji had remained erect. Blood was flowing out, bubbling and gurgling down his forehead, his neck and shoulders. Just then the plastic petrol tank behind him burst and like an enraged cobra, it began to hiss and spit. Within seconds, he was bathed in petrol. His blood mingled with the pale liquid making him look frightful, grotesque.

Heart-rending cries filled the bomber. Pilot Takizawa had been struck sharply by the handle and had died instant. Two others had their heads severed and lay in pools of blood. The fire engulfed the bomber like an evil spirit dancing to the beat of a drum, licking its lips, preparing to attack. Any minute now, the aircraft would explode into a million fragments.

Habib-ur-Rahman screamed, 'Netaji, get out! Come on!' Netaji had lost a lot of blood by then. With great effort, he ran to the back of the plane. But the passage was blocked by luggage, equipment and other paraphernalia, and the rear door was jammed. It refused to open. Despite being injured, Netaji moved back and kicked the door hard a few times. But the metal and the plastic, as if frozen in fear, were clinging fast to each other and refused to budge. Again Habib-ur-Rahman shouted, 'Netaji, from the front, out from the front!'

Netaji rushed to the front. In that instant, the jaws of the fire swallowed the front door. Now its tongues were darting inwards. The fire had smelt the petrol. The rear door wouldn't open, the front door was blocked by fire. There was no alternative but to brave the fiery stream and jump out. Gathering all his strength, Netaji propelled himself out of the nose-end of the plane like a cannonball ejected from a canon. Habib-ur-Rahman followed him. But what did he see – Netaji's clothes had caught fire in midair. That was not their Netaji, it was some resplendent Fire God who had descended on earth.

Earth, fire and wind were all fighting to gain control over Netaji's flesh and blood. Fire, so eager to rock him on the tip of her bright red tongue, kept hovering around his body. The wind was twisting, whirling and whistling as if in a trance. And the earth was desperately trying to hold on to him.

Netaji was rolling frantically in the sand where he had fallen. But fire would not leave him. Forgetting his own throbbing wounds, Habib-ur-Rahman lunged towards Netaji. He rolled over, doubled up on his stomach, trying to put out the flames. Netaji's foam winter jacket, sodden with petrol, was fodder for the greedy flames. Habib-ur-Rahman was trying desperately to pull the jacket off, but the leather belt of Netaji's uniform strapped tight across his chest would not let it go.

Habib fumbled for the buckle, but in the heat, he couldn't lay hands on it. By now, the fire was slithering across Netaji's back and dancing on his shoulders. Habib's hands were burning. At last, he was able to rip the burning jacket off. Just then he saw some soldiers from the garrison stationed at Taipei airport running to his aid. They poured buckets of sand on their bodies, threw water, wrapped them in thick blankets. Finally, they managed to release Netaji from the clutches of fire.

Habib-ur-Rahman looked at Netaji. Not one hair was left on his head. The skin was charred, flesh exposed. Jagged pieces of metal had left many gashes on his face. The skin on his stomach and back was badly burnt. Blood had clotted under the skin in many parts of the body. It dripped from open wounds elsewhere. He was straining to open his eyes.

Seeing Netaji's disfigured face, Habib-ur-Rahman's courage drained away. Sharp waves of pain rose from his scalded hands. Injuries from different parts of his body clamoured for attention. His head was reeling. His limbs stiffened. Helplessly, he collapsed on the sand next to Netaji.

About a mile away from the ravaged outskirts of Taipei town, the Nonmon Military Hospital had somehow managed to remain safe. Till recently, the four-ward, eighty-bed hospital was fully equipped with all kinds of medical facilities. However, for fear of air attacks, all the equipment had to be shifted to another location.

On the afternoon of 18 August, Dr T. Yoshimi sat in his room, listening to news of the surrender on the radio. He was feeling strangely disturbed that day. The only thought on his mind was to wind up matters in the hospital and return to Japan …

The insistent ring of the phone shattered the silence in the room. An unfamiliar, grim voice pierced his eardrum. 'Hello Doctor, I'm calling from the airport …'

'Yes, yes, speak up.'

'A bomber has crashed. Some people are seriously injured. We are bringing them to the hospital right away.'

The seasoned Dr Yoshimi rose to the occasion. Nurses, stretchers and emergency equipment, all waited by the hospital entrance. The ambulance came in ringing its siren. The stretcher bearing Netaji was lifted gently out of the ambulance. A couple of military jeeps arrived and several Japanese officers jumped out to push the stretcher. 'Doctor, hurry. He is not an ordinary officer. He is Subhas Chandra Bose of India,' one of them said.

'Oh my God!' exclaimed Dr Yoshimi.

Netaji's condition was critical. Dr Ishi and Dr Tsurata rushed to assist him. Netaji's scalp, hands, legs, back, abdomen and chest were scorched. Not one part of him had been spared by the flames. But he was still conscious. He was trying hard to suppress the agony. Dr Tsurata helped Yoshimi smear white ointment and Rivamol all over his body and cover it with bandages. Four Vitacamphor injections were administered. Netaji's heart was weak, so Yoshimi gave him two Digitalis injections as well.

'This has to be a miracle,' Yoshimi said.

'How do you mean, sir?' Tsurata whispered.

'How can Mr Bose endure such excruciating pain without a whimper?'

'Doctor, you must save him!' a Japanese officer pleaded.

The other injured officers were groaning and wailing. The searing pain would not let them rest. Though Netaji was the most badly wounded, he did not make a sound. The doctor then noticed that he was trying hard to say something. He leaned over and heard Netaji ask him in English, 'How is Gen. Shidei? Take good care of everyone.'

The Japanese soldiers were moved to a larger ward. Only the unconscious Habib-ur-Rahman was allowed to lie in the bed next to Netaji.

'Ishi, Bose needs a transfusion,' Yoshimi said.

Dr Yoshimi took Netaji's ashen hand in his own. Dr Ishi and he tried to find a vein. They couldn't find one at first. At last, Ishi managed to locate one and inserted the needle. Beads of sweat covered Netaji's brow. Yoshimi was alarmed. He and Ishi exchanged worried glances. Instead of the fresh blood going in, his dark impure blood filled the syringe.

'Sir, what shall we do?'

'Keep trying till the end. The blood is turning dark due to lack of oxygen. Not a good sign.'

Just then they heard Netaji mutter feebly, 'Mizu, mizu …' His parched body was clamouring for water. He was fed a few drops at a time. He had suffered almost 95 per cent burns. The doctors were stunned by his endurance. He complained about nothing. In comparison, the moaning and whimpering from the ward next door were frightening.

The army officers had to send for an interpreter. With his help, they asked Netaji, 'Are you trying to say something?'

'Convey my best wishes to the Japanese Emperor. And my deepest gratitude to my dear friend Terauchi.'

Netaji was finding it very difficult to open his stinging eyes. His eyelids too were blistered. His body temperature continued to rise alarmingly. He called Dr Tsurata to his side and asked, 'Have you informed the chief of staff?'

'Yes.'

Netaji needed fresh air. He was moved that close to the entrance of the room. 'Where is Gen. Shidei?' he asked.

'Oh, he is fine.' An office said, turning pale and nervous.

'Where is he?'

'In another hospital.'

'My other companions are due to follow us. Do take care of them,' Netaji was gasping for breath.

'Doctor, I lied to him. Shidei was killed on the spot in this wretched crash,' the officer told Dr Yoshimi outide the room.

It was 6 p.m. The darkness was terrifying. Netaji's condition began to deteriorate. His pulse was very fast. He called the doctor to his side and biting back the pain, he said, 'I want to sleep, a deep sleep …'

Habib-ur-Rahman woke up with a start and looked around. He could see Netaji's bandaged body. He was surrounded by doctors and medical personnel. One look at his scarred deformed face and Habib involuntarily shut his eyes tight. His hands and feet turned cold. How could he go back to Hindustan without Netaji? How would he face the nation? When members of the INA would pursue him, 'Where have you lost the jewel in our crown,' what would he say to them?

Habib's palms were bandaged, but he knelt on the cold stone floor and started to pray, begging Allah to protect Netaji.

It was eight o'clock in the night. Netaji's laboured breathing was making the doctors nervous. Every now and then, he would somehow open his eyes and look around the room. Since afternoon, he had felt as though someone was crouching in the corner of that large, dark ward. He opened his eyes wide. Head between his knees, Death himself had been cowering there all afternoon. He had not dared to hover by Netaji's bedside yet. Someday, they were bound to meet. That was why even under a barrage of bomb attacks Netaji had never paid heed to him. At this moment too, he was not prepared to acknowledge him.

The map of India floated before Netaji's eyes – the calmly flowing Ganga and in her limpid waters the image of his mother, yearning to hold her Raja close, yearning to stroke his head. In the Yamuna was the loving embrace of Basanti Ma. Mej-da, Deshbandhu, Gurudev Rabindranath Tagore, Vithalbhai, Gandhiji and Jawaharlal too – their images surrounded him. The Arabian Sea and the Bay of Bengal were washing the feet of his motherland. On every wave floated the face of his lifelong companions – Nariman, Swami Sahajanand, Khitish, Dilip Roy, Shardul Singh, and those who had shared the turbulent times of the Azad Hind with him – Stracey, Yellappa, Rash Behari, Kiani, Dhillon, Sehgal, Shah Nawaz and countless others. Responding to the call of freedom – Manavati, Labo, Janaki and Lakshmi Swaminathan – had left their homes for him and stepped on the battlefield. Adam Trott, already seated in God's court, was still seeking truth. Emilie, his beloved Emilie of the distant land. His own hapless Shakuntala.

The picture of a wounded bird fluttering about in panic swam before his eyes. Burning eyes erupted in tears. Shakuntala stood before him. In a Bengali-style sari, her fair forehead smeared with bright red vermillion.

Emilie, beloved, where are you going all dressed up?

Hindustan.

What for?

For the celebration at Lal Qila! After saluting the tricolour and your motherland, your eyes were going to look for me in the throng of thousands, remember?

Lal Qila! The Red Fort! So near … yet so far!

Why do you say that? You had taught me yourself, hadn't you, that even rocks will crumble in the face of perseverance and oceans will freeze. Determination and hope are the two wings which will take you to the height of success.

My love, I think God is concerned that man's achievements may render pale the colour of the limitless sky and the lustre of the moon and stars. That is why He has given man the curse of death along with the gift of life.

I just feel sorry that he chose to use his ultimate weapon against me so soon. Never mind … because of the good deeds of thousands of patriots and martyrs, the British Empire will collapse and fall. Hindustan will be free, that too very soon … but I will not be there … to witness that moment … But you must go.

Me? Alone?

My motherland will welcome you like a daughter.

No, don't talk like this. I will not go.

Why?

On that land where my moon, my Subhas Chandra will not rise again, my feet will never step on it ...

Who is that?

Like the moonlight tripping gaily along was a little girl.

Anita! Anita, careful!

Why, Papa?

Can your little hands carry the weight of that flower basket?

I brought them for you.

Too late, my child! Seated in Time's palanquin, I have begun my journey into timelessness …

What are you saying, Papa?

How can I explain? I must go.

Where?

To God's haven.

I won't let you go. You never played with me, we never fought nor did we ever make up ...

No, we didn't, my girl. Just give me one sweet kiss ... I must be reborn to get another kiss from you. Let me go, don't hug me so. Tie these moments to your heart and let me go.

From the corner of the room came sounds of someone sobbing. That moment was too much even for Death to bear.

Netaji came out of the delirium. He called out to Habib. Words would not come out of his charred lips. With great difficulty, he managed to utter one word at a time. 'Habib bhai, my end is near. When you return to our motherland, tell all my brothers, my mothers and sisters, tell the wind, the flowing water, that their Subhas fought till his last breath.'

He continued to speak, 'Just one request to the merciful Lord: let me be born again and again in this holy land. Let me be a storm that blows through it for its glory. Jai Hind!'

The exhausted doctors and nurses were slouched in their chairs. Seeing the look of despair in their eyes, hearing their sighs, Death did not dare move closer to the bed. His axe on his shoulder, he sat glumly in a corner. His limbs felt sapped of their strength. Suddenly, he noticed a slight chink in the guard around Netaji. He seized the opportunity and jumped in.

The bandaged body of Netaji trembled, stiffened, then relaxed. Forever. Hiding his black face, Death fled from the spot. Habib-ur-Rahman began to wail. Who were all these people – nurses, ward boys, army staff? What nationality? What race? Grief had dissolved all boundaries. The Taipei Military Hospital was deluged in tears.

How black the Nanmon Hospital in Taipei looked. The air raids had left the surrounding region desolate, bleak. Col. Habib-ur-Rahman had not yet recovered fully from the shock. Doctors had advised him to remain lying in one place. Four sentries stood guard outside his room to prevent him from getting up.

Dr Yoshimi came up to him. Habib-ur was sobbing. His body trembled. Only when he held out his hands to take the doctor's did he realise both his were bandaged. Again, his mind went to Netaji, lying in the morgue. And he began to wail even more loudly.

'Colonel, this accident was an act of betrayal of your country by God himself. Four others were killed in the crash. Gen. Shidei's death has shaken the Japanese Military machinery to its core.'

'Please, Doctor, you must let me take Netaji's body to Tokyo. There are many Indians in Tokyo. They will decide what to do next. What can I do, alone, on this unfamiliar island?'

'Col. Rahman, don't worry. Tomorrow you will be able to accompany Bose's coffin to Tokyo. I have instructions to that effect from our senior officers. I have injected formalin into the body. The coffin too is ready.'

The next day, 20 August, Col. Habib-ur-Rahman arrived at Taipei airport. Japanese officers helped carry the coffin. The sky was dark. There was a strong possibility of American troops taking control of the airport. The faces of the Japanese officers were downcast.

Just then, a group of Japanese Military personnel arrived there. One of them announced gruffly, 'The Taiwanese Army has turned against us.'

'They have been given the authority by the American High Command. The question of our life and death will now be decided by the Taiwanese Army,' another officer explained in a frightened voice.

The flight of the bomber by which Habib was to depart for Tokyo was cancelled. The news made Habib's legs buckle under him. His grief was boundless. The sight of the coffin was adding to it. He went to the seniormost Japanese officer in Taipei. Throwing himself at Gen. Andy's feet and crying bitterly, he begged, 'General, just this one favour. Let the last rites be performed in the presence of his countrymen. Do something, sir, anything, but get me to Tokyo.'

'Yes, I knew Bose,' the general said. He motioned Habib to take a seat.

Gen. Andy was trying to establish contact with the Imperial Headquarters in Japan, but he was not able to connect. Every now and then, a report would come about some senior officer or the other having committed harakiri. How close the American Army had reached. How many ministers had fled Tokyo with their women and children. Just then a young captain rushed in with a message: 'Sir, Field Marshal Terauchi.'

'What happened to him?'

'He's unconscious. Critical, they say.'

Gen. Andy looked shattered. He leapt up to try to get in touch with Tokyo. Finally, he was able to get the foreign minister, Shigemitsu on the line. The general handed the receiver to Habib. As he grabbed it, the line got cut. Habib was infuriated. 'General, I had such an important message to convey, why did he hang up on me?'

'He may not have disconnected; the lines must be bad.'

'That's a lie.'

'Perhaps the American general MacArthur has reached our foreign office. Our country has been turned into a cremation ground.'

Habib could not stop his tears. Gen. Andy immediately got in touch with the Taiwanese Military Headquarters. The Taiwanese authorities were not willing to let any flight take off. They wanted permission from their American bosses before deciding to give the Japanese on the island food and water. A disappointed Gen. Andy got up from his seat. His old face looked defeated. Placing a hand on Habib's shoulder, he said, 'Son, I am helpless. I can't even consider harakiri. If I do, I will be free, but this office will shut down. Thousands of Japanese soldiers will be massacred. For their sake, I must stay alive. Son, I share your grief. But right now, I am powerless.'

A sharp wind was slicing through the cremation ground at Taipei. Some Japanese Army personnel had gathered there. A wave of sadness washed over the military band. A group of Taiwanese soldiers had already marched into the Japanese office to arrest Gen. Andy. He could not reach the cremation ground, but he did not forget to send a basket of fruit and a cake for the departed soul, according to the Japanese custom. Habib-ur-Rahman cried continuously as he watched Netaji's burning pyre.

'Thirty-eight crore people should be freed from slavery. That was his goal. And for that, he treated life as a battlefield, fought valiantly for his motherland to the bitter end. And now, on an alien soil, he was consigned to fire. His last journey into timelessness had begun.'

Habib had informed the Japanese authorities that the aircraft was carrying all the treasure Netaji had collected. A guard had been posted at the site of the accident.

For three days, the wreckage of the ill-fated bomber lay smouldering. Fire tenders had put out the flames, but the embers still smoked.

The army men sought the help of the students of Taipei's middle school. Netaji's ashes were collected. Habib-ur-Rahman's swollen eyes peered at every piece of jewellery that could be located. His mind conjured up images of all the East Asian women who had stripped themselves of their ornaments for a motherland they had never even seen. What had they not offered to Netaji? Not just the talismans from around their necks, but also their sons, their young daughters. Their husbands, the lords of their homes. All to pave the way to Delhi. Even now the people of East Asia were willing to trade their own lives with God for Netaji's.

The school children were carefully sifting through the ashes for every bit of gold that had melted in the fire. But the Mahanayak who had wanted to gild ordinary lives, who had promised to safeguard them, had long been spirited away by a cruel twist of fate. Gold had turned to ashes.